DARK SLEEPER

DARK
SLEEPER

Jeffrey E. Barlough

ACE BOOKS, NEW YORK

DARK SLEEPER

An Ace Book / published by arrangement with
Jeffrey E. Barlough

PRINTING HISTORY
Western Lights Publishing trade edition / 1998
Ace trade edition / September 2000

The Penguin Putnam Inc. World Wide Web site address is
http://www.penguinputnam.com

Check out the ACE Science Fiction & Fantasy
newsletter and much more at Club PPI!

ISBN: 0-441-00730-9

ACE®
Ace Books are published by
The Berkley Publishing Group, a division of Penguin Putnam Inc.,
375 Hudson Street, New York, New York 10014.
ACE and the "A" design are trademarks belonging to Penguin Putnam Inc.

Printed in the United States of America

10 9 8 7 6 5 4 3 2 1

To my Brother

GARY BARLOUGH

CONTENTS

CONTENTS

CHARACTERS

MISS LUCY ANKERS, *a chambermaid at the Blue Pelican inn and public house.*

MR. EPHRAIM BADGER, *late senior partner in the legal firm of Badger and Winch; now moldering in a churchyard.*

MR. GERVAISE BALLIOL, *landlord of the Cutting Duck public house.*

MR. HARRY BANISTER, *the master of Eaton Wafers; formerly a student of Professor Titus Tiggs.*

BETTY, *a gentle mastodon cow, partner to the Kingmaker.*

MR. BENJAMIN BLIZZARD ("Blaster"), *the nephew of Mr. Hatch Hoakum.*

MR. FREDERICK BRITTLEBANK, *a facetious booking-clerk in Timson's coach-office.*

CAST-IRON BILLY, *an execution man, and associate of Mr. Icks.*

MISS MARY CLINCH, *the head chambermaid of the Blue Pelican.*

MR. NICHOLAS CRABSHAWE ("Busket"), *a friend of Mr. Icks.*

MR. GEORGE CURLE, *an old hunks.*

MISS LAURA DALE, *the young governess to Miss Littlefield.*

DR. DANIEL DAMPE, *a learned but nonetheless good-natured physician.*

MR. HENRY DUFF, *a carter.*

MR. CHARLES EARHART ("Sheephead Charley"), *a feeble-minded vagabond.*

EPSOM, *a servant in the household of the sisters Jacks.*

FALLOW, *footman and general factotum of Mr. Josiah Tusk.*

MR. GEORGE GOSLING, *the industrious pot-boy of the Blue Pelican.*

MRS. AMELIA GREENSHIELDS, *the wife of Professor Greenshields.*

PROFESSOR CHRISTOPHER GREENSHIELDS, *former professor of classics and fellow of Antrobus College, Salthead University.*

CHARACTERS

HANNA, *a ruddy young farm lass; Mrs. Minidew's helper in the kitchen.*

MR. JACK HILLTOP, *a newcomer to town with no visible occupation.*

MR. HATCH HOAKUM, *a driver of mastodons.*

HOBBES, *a servant in the employ of Professor Greenshields.*

MISS MOLL HONEYWOOD, *the starchy proprietor of the Blue Pelican.*

MR. JOHN HUNTER, *a mysterious young gentleman of independent means.*

MR. SAMSON ICKS, *agent to Mr. Winch.*

MISS MONA JACKS, *a tiny and interesting young woman.*

MISS NINA JACKS, *her elder sister.*

MR. JINKIN, *a printer.*

MR. AUSTIN KIBBLE, *personal secretary to Professor Tiggs.*

KINGMAKER, *a mighty bull mastodon belonging to Mr. Hoakum and his nephew.*

MISS BRIDGET LEEK, *a pretty charwoman.*

MISS FIONA LITTLEFIELD, *the young niece of Professor Tiggs.*

MAGGIE, *a buckskin mare belonging to Professor Tiggs.*

MRS. MINIDEW, *cook and housekeeper to Professor Tiggs.*

MITTON, *a servant at Eaton Wafers.*

THE REV. MR. SAMUEL NASH, *the rector of St. Barnacle's parish.*

NESTOR, *a black gelding belonging to Mr. Kibble.*

MR. ROBERT NIGHTINGALE, *a slippery waterside character.*

NUTMEG, *the resident feline of the Blue Pelican.*

MR. HAM PICKERING, *a boatswain's mate, late of the SWAN.*

PIGEON, *an apprentice pot-boy at the Cutting Duck.*

MR. LEW PILCHER, *an execution man, and associate of Mr. Icks.*

MR. PUMPKIN PIE, *an orange tabby cat enjoying the largesse of the Tiggs household.*

MR. JOHN RIME, *a cat's-meat man.*

CHARACTERS

MR. JOSEPH ROOKE, *an associate of Mr. Icks; a volatile young man.*

SALOP, *the servant of Mr. Hunter.*

MR. RICHARD SCRIBBLER, *a lawyer's clerk, in the employ of Badger and Winch.*

MR. TOM SPIKE, *a groom in the service of Professor Tiggs.*

MISS SALLY SPRINKLE, *an ancient lady, residing at the Blue Pelican.*

SUSANNA, *maidservant of the sisters Jacks.*

DR. SWEETMAN, *a self-satisfied physician.*

PROFESSOR TITUS VESPASIANUS TIGGS, *professor of metaphysics and fellow of Swinford College, Salthead University.*

TUCHULCHA, *a flying man.*

TURK, *a surly mastiff belonging to Mr. Tusk.*

MR. JOSIAH TUSK, *a cunning, voracious miser.*

MR. NED VICKERY, *the chief groundskeeper of Eaton Wafers.*

MR. JASPER WINCH, *a greedy attorney; surviving partner in Badger and Winch, solicitors.*

The world belongs to the rascals.

J. S. LE FANU

Evil calls to evil.

LIVY

BOOK THE FIRST

A GATHERING OF GHOULS

《☉》

CHAPTER I

Something Remarkable

Fog, everywhere.

Fog adrift in the night air above the river, creeping in through the estuary where the river glides to the sea. Fog curling and puffing about the headlands and high places, the lofty crags and wild soaring pinnacles, fog smothering the old university town in cold gray smoke. Fog squeezing itself into the steep narrow streets and byways, the roads and cart-tracks, into the gutters and shadowy back-alleys. Fog groping at the ancient timbered walls of the houses — the wondrous, secret, familiar old houses — and at their darkened doors and windows, filling the chinks and cracks in the masonry and coaxing the tightly fastened surfaces to open, open.

Not your common ordinary fog but a genuine Salthead fog, drippy and louring — the fog of my distant remembrance, of the days of childhood. How long ago those days were, precisely, there's no point in relating; suffice it to say that they were over long before most of you were born. My childhood! When such unimaginable vistas of life lay open before me, and the years stretched endlessly forward. Ah, Salthead — my dear old birthplace, the seat of my irretrievable youth! How long has it been now since you've known my footsteps?

You'll forgive a mawkish, maundering old fool if he occasionally strays, ever so slightly, from the path of his story. Life is slower now and not nearly so endless. The clocks tick and I find myself listening to them. But my story — my true story, for know you that every word of it is the literal truth — already I've lost track of my story. Oh, yes, I remember, I was telling you about the fog — the old Salthead fog — and how it was exhaling its icy vapors into the pinched faces of the passers-by, those unfortunate enough to be abroad on a frosty night. How the Salthead fog was exhaling its vapors into the pinched face of young John Rime, the cat's-meat man, one such unfortunate passer-by on his way back from an evening's ramble in the High Street.

1

Young Mr. Rime has enjoyed himself immensely this night. His clothes have an interesting, devil-may-care sort of disarray about them, and his hat, tilted forward at a rakish angle, is like the needle of some fantastic haberdasher's compass pointing the way home. It was, I venture, a not-inconsiderable achievement that his hat still clung to his head at all.

At each stop along the way Mr. Rime has drunk the health of the patrons of the worthy establishment; tendered his regards to the landlord of the worthy establishment; nuzzled the chin of the pretty daughter of the landlord of the worthy establishment; hailed and farewelled everyone with great ceremony, and hailed and farewelled everyone again for good measure — all in all, has been the greatest friend and boon companion to himself he has ever had.

So it should come as no surprise that Mr. Rime, like a foot soldier lost in a desert of night, having undertaken numerous unsuccessful forays into the maze of narrow streets, uncertain of his way, at length finds himself in an empty lane down near the docks, but down near very little else with which he is at all familiar.

The crispness of the night air, the quiet plashing of the water against the pilings, the creaks and groans of the dark-bodied ships straining at their moorings, the distant wail of a whistle-buoy — all send restless shivers through the body of Mr. Rime. He stops for a moment to listen, and glances about and behind with an uneasy, searching expression. At length he gathers his coffee-colored great-coat more closely about him and forges on, in as straight a line as it is possible for him to trace out.

Overhead a faint beacon of moon glows through the fog blanket, casting a diffused light by which the cat's-meat man guides his steps. To his right, the dim outlines of some broken buildings lining the wharf rear up out of the ground; to his left, in a deserted boat-yard, a landlocked fleet of disabled vessels sails silently into the fog. From somewhere among the craft in the yard comes a low growling, then a hoarse bark. Once again Mr. Rime stops to listen, and once again moves on.

A shaft of moonlight cutting through the gloom illuminates a turning in the lane, and as the cat's-meat man negotiates this change in course he is startled to hear a voice demand harshly in his ear —

"Are you pleased with your station in life, man?"

From out of the fog slides a tall, lean figure, clothed in nautical garb that had seen its better days. Young Mr. Rime looks blankly at this inquisitor, uncomprehending, as if the question had been posed in an unknown tongue spoken only by the inhabitants of some remote kingdom — so astonishing was its substance and so unexpectedly had it been uttered.

"Well? Speak out, man! Have you nothing to say?" demands the stranger, with sudden vehemence. "Have you no thoughts? Have you no desires? Have you no regrets? Have you no opinions, you fool? What! Nothing at all going on inside that under-stuffed brain-box of yours?"

The cat's-meat man responds by altering his vacant expression not one jot.

"What about your life, man? Are you satisfied with it? Are you happy? Are you unhappy? Damn me — you've got to be one or the other, or you're not living!" (These verbal sorties carried out without the least response on the part of their designated target). "Have you no regrets? No words unsaid, no deeds undone? Nothing you'd like to change, while you've got the chance? Nothing you'd like to have done differently? Have you no one you've left behind, man?"

In his stunned condition the cat's-meat man manages only a faint shrug in reply.

"So then we're a satisfied man, I take it. A very satisfied man. A very satisfied little squit," says the stranger, his eyes nervously darting here and there, from Mr. John Rime to the muddy tracks in the lane, to the timbered frontage of the warehouses over the way. A slight inclination of the head brings forward into the light a tangled mustache, and a gleam of gold in the lower jaw. "Oh, no, no, no. I don't think we're satisfied. I don't think we're satisfied in the least. No, no, I think we're just a liar. What do you say to that, man? Just an ordinary, common, vulgar, everyday little liar."

No reply from Mr. Rime to this gauntlet hurled at his honor, apart from a brief, spasmodic gurgle in the throat.

"Well, then, do you know how to caper, man? Young liar like you ought to know how to caper. Capered much myself in my shipping days. Caper, you see? Like so!"

Whereupon the stranger proceeds to execute a ghastly caricature of a sailor's hornpipe, an exercise that resolves itself into little more than an aimless flailing about of his ungainly limbs. The horror of this performance is accentuated by the size of the stranger's hands and feet, which are seen to dangle a trifle too stiffly for comfort from the shafts of his bones.

"So, man," says the figure, bringing this mockery of a dance to a close. "What do they call you besides Liar? Or is it *Mister* Liar? Nothing else? Nothing even remotely remarkable? No, I don't believe so. For God's sake, man, do something remarkable with your life while you can! Listen to me, listen to me, I know what I'm talking about. Why — "

At which point the figure stops, whirls about on his heels and leaps toward the cat's-meat man, with one long, bony hand thrust forward, its extended forefinger directed straight at the nose of Mr. Rime.

"Why, it's — it's *John*, ain't it?"

Upon mention of his name Mr. Rime grows conscious of an uncomfortable dryness in his throat.

The corners of the stranger's mouth lift up beneath the ends of his mustache in a ghoulish leer. "Ah, I thought so! It is John. John, John, John. Johnny. Ho, Johnny boy! Johnny, Johnny, Johnny. Now, Johnny *WHAT*, I wonder?"

Here the cat's-meat man manages to gather sufficient inner strength to disgorge the requested item.

"*Sssssst!*" The stranger pauses, swishing his extended forefinger in lazy circles round the victim's nose. "Well, Mr. Johnny Rime, I'll give you a point for that, man. You finally spoke up for yourself. You finally showed a glimmer of self-respect. Johnny Rime you are, no doubt. No lying there with a name like that! Just the common truth. Just a common fact. And facts, after all," says the stranger, coldly, "are *FACTS*."

This sudden alteration of voice causes Mr. Rime to regard the sailor with a new and wholly disquieting sense of dread.

"Well, Mis-ter John-ny Rime," continues the inquisitor, separating his syllables for emphasis. "Well, Mr. Johnny, that's all fine and good, man, but it's time to present you with something remarkable in your life. Here, Johnny, Johnny. Hey, Johnny, Johnny. Would you mind holding this for me, man?"

With no little anxiety the cat's-meat man accedes to this seemingly innocuous request, taking into his hands a generally oblong, weighted object about the size and consistency of a musk melon.

"Thank you, Johnny," replies the melon, with a satisfied chuckle. "That's most comfortable. That's most comfortable indeed."

The eyes of Mr. Rime jump from the melon to the stranger, back to the melon, then back to the stranger, and to the empty spot between the stranger's shoulders where his head used to sit — then back to the head now resting in his hands.

"No need to look surprised, man," smiles the head, contentedly, as if to say, Yes, this is a most enviable situation. "No need at all. Why so nervous? Ain't this remarkable, now? What! Ain't you never held a melon before, Johnny?"

The eyes in the head of the sailor rove this way and that, while the eyes in the head of young John blow up like balloons. With a cry the cat's-meat man flings the horrific object from his hands, and staggers through the turning in the lane as rapidly as his legs will carry him.

While in the half-darkness left behind there erupts a mocking laughter, full of a harsh and scornful arrogance, that fills the street and echoes from the building walls, growing louder and louder and soaring higher and higher until it fills the entire sky over the sleeping city, and so becomes one with the drifting fog.

CHAPTER II

Many Happy Returns of the Day

MR. Josiah Tusk was a conscientious man. Certainly no one, male or female, unfortunate enough to have run afoul of him in the course of affairs would deny that Mr. Tusk was, first and foremost, a conscientious man.

Certainly not the unhappy family man with the household of hungry mouths, not he. That man who, having lost the income upon which those mouths relied, now offers himself up in menial servitude to Mr. Tusk — which conscientious gentleman very conscientiously takes him in, and works him, and grinds him, and works him some more, and grinds him some more, and whittles him down until nothing of his dignity remains but a little pile of shavings, all of which blow away at the first whisper of a wind.

Certainly not the sorrowing young widow — her husband having so rudely forsaken her warm embrace, with creditors all unpaid — who in her destitution and her grief finds herself and her belongings in the custody of Tusk & Co., which conscientious enterprise in its turn conscientiously delivers her and her small child over to a life of drudgery in a parish workhouse.

Certainly not the high-spirited young seaman, newly discharged, who, having signed away his future in a sudden paroxysm of promissory notes, is conscientiously run aground by the warship *Josiah*, and discovers his once-bright tomorrow to be a very dismal and a lonely place now that the notes, one by one, have been called in.

Certainly not the infirm pensioner who has squandered his last morsel of savings in defense of an indefensible bill, and having engaged Mr. Josiah Tusk in the conscientious preservation of that bill, now receives all further "Bills" in the retiring atmosphere of a debtors' prison.

Certainly none of these unfortunates would deny that in all his benevolent dealings with the common chaff, Mr. Josiah Tusk had proved himself to be a most able and a most conscientious man.

And a cunning man, and a crafty man. And a grasping man and a greedy one. Surely was there ever such a cunning, crafty, calculating, clutching, squeezing, grasping, grinding, greedy old miser as this Josiah in the whole history of conscientious men?

It was the most marvelous thing in the world to Mr. Tusk, in his daily excursion along the High Street, to observe the confused mixture of wonder, apprehension, hatred, and fear with which he was regarded by the common folk of Salthead. "See them," he would tell his conscientious self, pleasantly, and with a grim little smile playing at the corners of his mouth. "See them. See their weakness, their deference, their servile fawning, their sheep-like docility. See how soft they are! Observe the translucent veil of their emotions, their longings, their secret desires, their loves — *ha!* See how transparent they are, how readily they yield to superiority."

And how could it be otherwise? In my mind's eye I still can see that bold superior figure, striding its bold superior stride down the High Street, the magnificent haughty head planted on its turret far atop the tall gaunt frame — how could it be otherwise? Striding forth in his magnificent black coat with resplendent buttons, superior red velvet waistcoat, black silk hat, and richly lacquered strap-boots — how could it be otherwise? The proud chin, the sharp falcon-eyes beneath their dark brows, the streaming white hair, the great hands with their long bony fingers clenching and releasing like breathing things — how could it be otherwise?

And those long nimble legs, with which Mr. Josiah Tusk often condescended to sport with members of the populace. On many an occasion he would amuse himself by singling out some deserving citizen — an old washerwoman, a crippled boy, a broken-down beggar, or some such easy mark — approaching from the opposite direction. Then striding that bold superior stride he would make directly for this victim, swiftly and unerringly, as if to run him down — only to veer off sharply at the very last moment, and with a final deceptive movement of the leg or ankle drive his startled opponent into the street. To observe this towering white-headed potentate, this sultan of superiority, bearing down at full flank speed on some poor innocent among the crowd — how could it, I say, be otherwise?

One chilly morning Mr. Tusk arose, attended to his toilet in silence, and descended to breakfast, whistling, in cheerful anticipation of the task at hand. A visitor was expected at the Tuskan villa, and as always a visitor was to be received with conscientious hospitality.

"Come in, Mr. Hatch Hoakum," said Josiah, when presented with the visitor by his footman. "Many happy returns of the day to you."

The small sturdy gentleman to whom this was addressed doffed his cap, which he proceeded to roll and crush into a tight little wad with his hands. "It be a tol'rable morning, Mr. Tusk."

"So you must tell me, Mr. Hatch Hoakum," pursued Josiah, "how goes it with you?"

"I b'lieve it passes pleasantly, sir."

"And your occupational activities? How go your occupational activities this morning?"

Mr. Hoakum wrung his cap a little more tightly, as though to squeeze it dry of all accumulated moisture.

"Ah — as well as can be expected, sir, considering. That's about all I can say on that point, I b'lieve."

"I see. I see. And the stock? How are the stock this morning?"

"The beasts, they're tol'rable, sir."

"Well-fed and well-watered, I trust."

"As always, sir. As you know my nephew Blaster is a fine one for the beasts. He knows their ways and they trust him, and that's very important, sir, when dealing with such creatures. The young lad knows what he's about, sir, and that's — "

"That is very good," interrupted Josiah, sweeping aside the speaker's last remarks with the wave of a bony forearm. "Let us proceed to the subject at hand. You know very well, Mr. Hatch Hoakum, that I'm a man of business. I'm not a man for chatter. Chatter is not for me. Chatter and I do not get along. That is why we must come straight to the subject. You understand why you have been called here this morning?"

Mr. Hoakum made a few smart tugs and pulls at his checked waistcoat and cleared his voice.

"Business, it's fallen off a small bit, sir, since the clearing of the roads," he said. "But all in all I b'lieve we've still got the safest and most reliable method for crossing the fells and the high mountain meadows — considering the cats. Arter all, nothing can stop the beasts, sir."

"I see. I see. Well, then, Mr. Hatch Hoakum, I must presume that your late difficulties have been resolved? I refer here to the matter," said the miser ominously, "*of the loan.*"

Mr. Hoakum coughed and looked slightly askance, as though unwilling to match the gaze of the Superior One on this issue.

"Ah — yes, sir — ah — no, sir. What I mean to say, sir, is that I'm in your debt, sir, and am attempting under the present circumstances to — ah — honor that debt. As I mentioned," continued the sturdy little man — with a shifting of his feet, and some vague stretching movements of his legs and arms designed to enhance his height and thus strengthen his position, but with no obvious result — "I b'lieve we have the best and safest means for traversing the mountains. I also b'lieve the passengers as have temp'rarily bounced over to the coaches — they being a slightly more convenient method of travel, sir, though not necessarily a safer one — they'll certainly bounce back to us, once the circumstances have been taken into account, and that's flat. The coaches can't last forever — considering the cats, arter all, sir."

Mr. Tusk received these words of bouncing and coaches without immediate comment. There was, however, no mistaking the outward signs of his inward displeasure — the rapid flow of breath, the clenching of the fists, the swollen jut of the chin, the growing sharpness of the eyes. In silence the miser paced to and fro across the floor before Mr. Hoakum, his tall gaunt frame towering over his short, sturdy little visitor. For his part Mr. Hoakum kept his eyes mostly averted, obliquely noting the passage of the creaking strap-boots from one side of the drawing-room to the other.

At length the enforced march came to an end. The boots directed themselves back towards the visitor; the great white head of the miser swiveled on its turret and tendered its conscientious reply.

"The quarter payment on the loan is due this day. Are you prepared to deliver up the sum, Mr. Hatch Hoakum?"

Mr. Hoakum plucked again at his checked waistcoat and lifted his small blue eyes slowly upward until they made contact with the icy stare of Josiah.

"I am not, sir."

"I see. I see. Then do you expect, Mr. Hoakum, to deliver the sum — before this day is out?"

"No, sir, I don't."

"Then, Mr. Hatch Hoakum," said the miser, summarily, "you leave me with no alternative. I am a man of business, Mr. Hoakum, and in my business I am known widely as a conscientious man. Monday shall find me in consultation with my attorney, Mr. Winch, whose firm will attend to all final details concerning the disposition of the case. Good day, Mr. Hatch Hoakum."

"Ah — excuse me, sir," said the small sturdy man, fumbling with his crushed cap, which in its present condition might be taken to represent the state of its owner's fortunes, "excuse me, but — might you tell me, sir, just exactly what is meant by the final details, and the disposition of the case? I b'lieve I've a right to such an explanation, arter all."

"It's very straightforward, Mr. Hoakum. Not only am I a conscientious man, but a straightforward one as well. Simply put, by forfeiture of the security provided to you, all further rights to the goods and chattels covered by that security are forfeit as well. You see? A simple case."

"By goods and chattels, then, you include the beasts, sir?"

"That is correct. I believe that's all. Good day to you," said Josiah, and turned on his heel.

"Ah — excuse me, sir," said Mr. Hoakum, waving his cap in one outstretched hand, by which small gesture he hoped to forestall the miser's departure from the room.

"Yes, what is it, Mr. Hoakum?" asked Josiah, with peevish irritation.

"Ah — I b'lieve you won't mind my saying afore I go, sir, that I don't blame you for what's happened. I'm an honest man, Mr. Tusk, and I b'lieve you are too. We're two honest men who made a fair and honest bargain. The lad and I thought we still could make a go of it — thought we could beat the coaches, sir, at their own game — in short, it was a gamble and now that gamble's lost. I just wanted you to know, sir, that I don't blame you for holding me to my end of the bargain."

The miser responded with a cynical grunt. "If you're looking for sympathy from me, Mr. Hoakum, you're looking in the wrong place."

The honest little man smiled and shook his head, resigned not to contest such a point with his charitable benefactor.

"I don't look for sympathy from you, Mr. Tusk. I just wanted to state the case, and state it plainly. Honest and straightforward, sir. That's all."

"Well, you've stated it. Good day."

"And I b'lieve you won't mind my also asking afore I go, sir," continued Mr. Hoakum, meticulously unfurling his cap in preparation for its return to his round gray head, "but I was more than a little curious — what a busy gent of your upstanding condition in the world of business means to do with a herd of mastodons?"

A cold gleam of wickedness flashed in the miser's eyes. Smiling, he bent down from his great height and whispered into Mr. Hoakum's ear —

"Not to worry — I'll think of something!"

Having then applied a confidential pat to Mr. Hoakum's shoulder, he called loudly for his footman.

Which minion proceeded to respond in a most unexpected fashion — hot in pursuit of a large brindled mastiff, which at just that moment came bursting through the rear door of the drawing-room. Slavering at the mouth the dog bounded in a single leap for the tall form of Mr. Tusk — perhaps in joy at sight of his beloved master, perhaps with some other, more sinister purpose in mind.

On sensing a stranger, however, the massive brute immediately shifted his focus of attention, raising his head and threatening the sturdy little man with a host of fearful snarls. In a moment the dog would have been upon him, had not Josiah grasped the animal by the collar and held it as it lunged.

"I'm dreadfully, terribly, profusely sorry, sir," apologized the footman, "but the dog — he ran in from the back-garden so quickly and suddenly, before I had a chance to get to the door, so that I couldn't prevent him — "

"Get out of here," said the miser, in his ugliest manner.

The mastiff howled and foamed at the lips, twisting his head round and round in his attempts to free himself from his master's grip.

"Steady, dog!" commanded Josiah, yanking furiously on the leather collar while at the same time endeavoring to avoid entrapment of his hands between the snapping jaws. "Steady! Steady, Turk!" Another great howl from the beast, and another massive lunge toward the stranger. "Turk, no! Steady, dog!"

"Why, he looks to be a good, honest, simple fellow," said Mr. Hoakum, blithely, and without the least show of fear. "Very honest, arter all, Mr. Tusk, in comparison to the cats. Why, I'm sure my nephew Blaster could teach him to — "

"If you would leave now, Mr. Hoakum, I'm sure it would improve the situation immensely. Good day to you. Steady, dog! Steady, Turk!"

In response to the dog's sudden plunges, Mr. Tusk began pulling steadily on the leather collar in an effort to drag the animal from the room — a few sharp blows to the dog's head being administered at opportune moments, whenever one of the miser's hands became free for chastisement.

"Ah, he's not a bad dog," protested Mr. Hoakum, viewing the scene with sad disapproval. "You needn't treat him that way, Mr. Tusk. Just let him be. Let him be. If you'd allow me to take him for a minute or two — "

Concern for the well-being of his visitor (which was negligible) being superseded by rage at the animal's contempt for his authority, Mr. Tusk at last resorted to the kindly tactic of planting one huge shiny strap-boot upon the dog's neck, effectively trapping him against the floor.

"That'll teach you," said Josiah, in tones that disturbingly resembled the growls of the dog. "That'll teach you!"

All the empathy welling up in Mr. Hoakum's heart for the plight of the mastiff now burst forth.

"That ain't right, Mr. Tusk. Don't treat the poor dog such. He's just an honest, simple fellow. I know, 'cause I've dealt with such creatures and others all my life. They don't mean to harm nobody. They can't help it; it's their nature. Arter all, you can't change nature, Mr. Tusk. Don't hurt the fellow — "

Nearly exhausted from his efforts but for the moment still in charge, the miser hurled his response to the mastodon man.

"Will you leave now, Mr. Hoakum!"

The small sturdy visitor placed his cap on his head, and gave a vainly defiant pull at his checked waistcoat. For the first time during the entire interview resentment against this tall cruel man rose within his breast.

"He's not such a bad fellow, Mr. Tusk — "

"Good day, Mr. Hatch Hoakum!" cried Josiah, adding as an afterthought, with the grim little smile playing at the edges of his mouth — "Many happy returns of the day to you."

Thus Mr. Josiah Tusk — a conscientious man, and a dog lover *to boot*.

CHAPTER III

Considering the Cats

IN a quiet corner of the docks, where an embayment of the Salt River drains off from the main stream, just above the harbor, stands an ancient inn. Shaded by trees and hidden from view of most of the harbor traffic, the existence of this cheery hostel is announced to the world by means of an enormous sign that hangs, very low, just above the door. A great, hulking, oaken thing, this sign — which, when the brisk wind from the sea knifes its way through the sheltering foliage, has been known to stagger an unwary customer with greater dispatch than any of the cordials served within. On either side of this latently homicidal board is the figure of a blue pelican, in heraldic profile, with a rather droopy disposition as to eyes, and with the fin of some late unfortunate protruding from its mouth.

A homely structure, with a plain plaster face framed and crosshatched by beams of oak timber, and with two twinkling eyes formed by a pair of lattice windows, this good house of the Blue Pelican has provided shelter and comfort for as long as anyone in Salthead can remember. At the time, the proprietor of this sequestered lodge was a Miss Honeywood — a tall, narrow, angular woman, who, though still in the throes of middle age, had been blessed with an early frost of starched white hair, all of it drawn together tightly behind her head and anchored in an enormous knot resembling a hornet's nest. Her skin too was white, and her eyes, of a fine, pale gray, were framed, like the pale plastered sides of her house, by beams of spectacles, in a very narrow and a very angular arrangement.

In her command of the Pelican and its adornments, Miss Honeywood reigned supreme — said adornments comprising one industrious pot-boy with large flappable ears like handles, very convenient for pulling, and a shiny head of hair anointed with suet; one greasy cook with a frizzled wig and an inflamed countenance; resident ostler and accompanying stable-hands; a coterie of female domestics, with various accessory minions; and lastly, one lounging nut-brown tabby cat (over whose will Miss Honeywood's authority held perhaps less sway).

From her customary position at the tap, behind the great oak bar in the common-room of the inn, Miss Honeywood wielded her scepter with an equanimity and firmness that had gained for her the admiration of her public for many years. Her word was venerated by all the inhabitants of the neighborhood and accounted good as law; her judgment, unimpeachable; her friendship once sworn, ever constant; so that among the patrons of the Pelican, it was only a bold and reckless courtier who dared challenge the mistress of the house on her home ground.

One late cold evening found a gibbous moon riding low in the heavens. The blustery wind driving in from the sea, having dispersed the rival fogs of the previous night, now found for itself some stiff competition in the conversation and joviality filling the common-room of the Pelican. A full complement of Honeywood regulars was attendant at court, their pipes busily smoking, their glasses and pint-pots alternately rising and falling, their voices drowning out completely the mad rushes the wind made at the walls of the house; while the esteemed lady herself, exhibiting her customary industry, could be seen at the tap drawing long draughts of bitter from the beer-engine.

"You needn't be so upset with me, Miss Moll," said a man with a spotted face, with whom the mistress of the Pelican had been speaking in low tones for some minutes. "You know I'm telling you the truth, don't you see. If there'd been any other way, I would've taken it, but there weren't. I wasn't trying to steal the blessed thing from the old lady — I just wanted a look at it, that's all. You know how close she is with it."

"I don't care how close she is with it," returned Miss Honeywood, drawing back on the handle of the beer-engine to release the dark liquor.

"But I just wanted a look inside it — a look at the pictures. It's a personal thing, don't you see." This point he emphasized by laying one outstretched palm upon his chest. "I thought she was flat out. I thought I could get a clear look at the pictures while she was dozin' away there by the fire. I didn't expect her to wake up an' all!"

"I'm telling you, it makes no difference to me, Jack. It's quite clear you're not to be trusted; there's no getting around that. Frightening a poor old woman half into her grave, thinking she was being robbed. Robbed, and in this good house! A poor old woman with nothing left in the world but her fading memory and a little trinket she'd prefer strangers" — here the mistress of the Pelican cast him a meaningful glance — "would kindly keep their hands off."

"I nearly had a good look once, when she was peekin' at the locket, the way she does, you know," pursued Spotted Face, undaunted. "I was standing behind her, over there, and I thought I recognized that fellow's face in the picture. You know I've asked her I don't know how many times, `Sally, may I have a peep at that little locket of yours, just for a moment?'  But she always tells me, `No, sir,' just as she tells everyone else, and closes it up like a clam. It's just that I might've recognized the fellow, that's all. As I've said it's a personal thing, don't you see."

"I haven't any interest in your personal things, as you call them, so don't bother me with them," said Miss Honeywood. "A man should be judged by his actions. Your action speaks for itself. So be it. End of conversation."

"But, Miss Moll, if you could see things from my point of view — "

"I don't care about your point of view, Jack — really, I don't. What's plain is plain. It's either black or white; there's no gray in it for me. I'm not one of your common gray persons who slither their way through life compromising their principles. I'm not a compromiser. I'm a black-and-white person all the way. End of — "

"But, Miss Moll — "

When particularly vexed, Miss Honeywood was known to express her displeasure by touching the extended fingers of both hands to the sides of her eyeglass frames, and leveling the lenses at the offender; thus conveying by implication the very real possibility that, at any moment, bolts of yellow flame might come shooting from her eyeballs and blast the offender into eternity.

"End," repeated Miss Moll, now vexed, and emphatically leveling lenses, "of conversation."

Having made her point without resorting to the launch of missiles, Miss Honeywood resumed her duties at the bar. The man with the spotted face, recognizing the futility of further discourse on the issue, shrugged his shoulders, tipped his drink in the general direction of his lips, and merged himself with the crowd.

To one side of the great hearth a cozy corner had been formed by placing a table between an ornamented screen and the wall, the wall being heavily wainscoted in dark oak and papered with narrow vertical stripes in red and gold. The flow of stripes was interrupted at eye-level by the framed painting of a cow in three-quarter view, standing in a meadow and captured by the artist in full mid-chew — a tender portrait, apparently meant to impart a healthy bucolic flavor to the meals, and so perhaps ease their digestion.

On this night the cozy corner was occupied by a pair of older gentlemen, one with a soft brown beard, hazel eyes, and a cherry-colored waistcoat, the other a collegiate gentleman, sprightly and clean-shaven, with gray hair clipped short and stiff like a bristle-brush. Settled comfortably in their well-cushioned chairs, with their pipes and glasses commuting regularly from hand to mouth, these two pampered fellows had whiled away the greater part of the evening absorbed in the latest newspapers, the combined glow from the fire and the wax-lights on the table providing illumination for their scholarly researches.

One candle now having burned low, the gentleman with the bristle-brush head dispatched the flame neatly between a thumb and forefinger. Producing a box of matches from his pocket he lit a fresh candle, blew out the kindled match and tossed the end into the nearby fire. His companion, unconscious of this activity, maintained his lazy perusal of the columns, now and then setting aside his pipe to dig at his teeth with a silver toothpick.

A blur of a pot-boy rushing past, the collegiate gentleman raised a hand in a bid to attract his attention, without apparent effect. A moment later a second run was made by the pot-boy, on his way back to the kitchen, and a second unsuccessful snare was recorded. A third run produced the same result — no result. Unable to bag his catch in the usual manner, the collegiate gentleman appealed to his friend across the table. But in this too he was doomed to failure, his companion remaining wholly oblivious behind his palisade of newsprint.

It so happened that Miss Honeywood had been observing this little pantomime from her place at the beer-engine. Relinquishing her duties to one of her accessory minions, she made her tall and angular way toward the cozy corner and inquired into the nature of the collegiate gentleman's request. The gentleman remarking that the busy pot-boy seemed always to be dashing about "like a house afire," Miss Honeywood replied that she hoped the gentleman didn't mean literally *this* house, but that she understood the simile.

Almost immediately a blur of white came charging from the kitchen.

"Where are you going, George Gosling?" demanded Miss Moll, hooking the pot-boy with a nimble lunge at one earlobe as he flew past. Despite his very professional apron and the very professional manner in which his shirt-sleeves were rolled up tightly onto each arm, the victim George, with his great flapping ears and intensely pained expression, resembled now nothing so much as a schoolboy enduring a reprimand from his well-starched headmistress.

"It hurts, Miss!"

"The professor asks for tea and sundries, George Gosling," intoned Miss Honeywood, crossing her arms and gathering herself to her full height, from which altitude she rained down stormy looks. "Didn't you see him calling for you? Well, what do you stand there for, George? Bring the gentlemen their tea and sundries. Double-quick!"

Motivated by this gentle reproof — and perhaps also by the late discomfort of angular fingers pinching his earlobe — the pot-boy vanished in the direction of the kitchen.

After offering a few words of apology to the professor, the mistress of the Pelican returned to her post at the bar. The professor glanced again toward his colleague across the table and found him still enveloped in newsprint, heedless apparently of the entire exchange.

Returning in a few minutes with a tea-caddy containing the requested items, the industrious Mr. Gosling was nearly brought to ground by a strange apparition that bumped and lurched across his path.

It was a gaunt figure of uncertain age, with a dingy beard, mean shabby rags for clothing, mottled skin, and small, nut-like eyes, like the eyes of a forest creature unused to the light. It had pinched cheeks and a mouth that mumbled and chattered to itself, generating rhythmic extrusions of the lips and tongue through the dingy beard. Its mouse-colored hair was naturally curled in a most fantastic manner, and so thickly distributed over the head that it resembled fleece — this effect combining with the weak eyes, mobile mouth, and a bulging nose to create a curious sheep-headed appearance. Like the lips and tongue the body too was in constant motion, the arms jerking and squirming with exaggerated movements.

"Out of the way, you! Out of the way!" shouted the boy in white, crisply side-stepping to avoid the loss of a single drop of hot water, before completing his run to the table in the corner.

"Clear off, you!" retorted the strange figure, with a spasmodic fling of his hands into the air. Chuckling quietly to himself he rolled his eyes at the ceiling, and very daintily straightened and tidied his rag of an old coat as though it were nothing less than the very *beau idéal* of finery. Then he resumed his quick eager trot toward a far corner of the room, where a sturdy little man in a checked waistcoat sat meditating over shrimps and a huge pewter-pot of grog. On the table in front of the man crouched a species of hairless rodent, which a casual observer might easily have mistaken for a crumpled cap.

The Sheephead — for this was one of several names by which the strange lurching figure was known — held forth a grimy hand with undisguised joy. The gentleman in the checked waistcoat grasped it firmly.

"Why, Charles," cried Mr. Hoakum, rising. "Why, Charles, how are you, man? How have you been? Where have you been keeping yourself these many weeks? Give me the time of day, sir!"

"Time of day," echoed the strange figure, bobbing his head at a furious pace. "Time of day. Charley has time of day." Saying which he drew forth from among his rags a great silver watch hanging from a dark ribbon, which he slyly offerred to the mastodon man for his inspection.

"You see? You see?" whispered the strange figure, confidentially, as he dangled the object before the surprised face of Mr. Hoakum. "Charley has time of day!"

Mr. Hoakum expressed astonishment at the size of the watch and its high degree of polish, remarking on its antique appearance and the ornate initials engraved on the cover. This he did with cheerful and unaffected enthusiasm, to please the Sheephead — suppressing for now his misgivings concerning the ownership of the watch, and the means by which said timepiece could have fallen into the hands of the impoverished Mr. Charles Earhart.

As slyly as it had been offered the brilliant object was withdrawn, the Sheephead putting the watch to his ear as though trying to determine if it were alive or dead. Then he threw back his head and laughed in a wild manner.

"Ah — that thing there, that watch," said Mr. Hoakum, sipping some of his grog. "That's quite some turnip, Charles, quite some turnip. An heirloom is what I conclude it to be, and I b'lieve I'm right in that."

Another wild laugh from the Sheephead; its exact meaning, however, remained open to interpretation.

"You'll want to hold onto that watch, Charles," counseled Mr. Hoakum. "Don't allow your val'ables to be taken from you. Don't trust 'em to anyone in this world, not a soul, apart from yourself. Arter all, Charles — nobody's going to take care of you in this world but yourself, and that's flat."

"Oh, Charley knows that," returned the Sheephead, dropping himself in his jerky way into the chair beside his friend.

"You're an honest fellow, Charles. I've always said that, you know. Here — have a little bit of this, sir." Suiting the action to the word, Mr. Hoakum poured a quantity of grog into a fresh mug and offered it to his companion. Without hesitation the Sheephead downed the entire draught in one swallow, grinning broadly. Then the small nut-like eyes fluttered several times as the strength of the liquor gained his attention.

Mr. Hoakum laughed very heartily, patting his companion on the back with good-natured humor.

"My nephew Blaster, he wonders what's become of you, Charles, and how you've been getting on. You know, it's been quite some time since you've been up to the camp to see us. We don't get many visitors these days, what with all the passengers bouncing over to the coaches — which they'll be bouncing back from soon enough, considering the cats, arter all — and we miss a fellow like you, sir. It's a lonely life in a way, up there on the fells, but it's a good life and a worthwhile one, that's what I've found. Now, to get on, my nephew Blaster's told me — and he swears by the memory of his dear dead mother that this is the very truth — that when he's out in the morning at first light, feeding the beasts their treats, and they hover round him in that way they have, and like they're wont to do afore pitching in — that it seems as if they're waiting for something, or for someone — that it seems as if he can hear them asking, `Where's Charles? Where's Charles? Blaster, have you seen Charles?' Can you hear 'em saying it? I can. I b'lieve Blaster, sir, because I've been around the beasts all my life, and I don't doubt for one minute that what he says is true. So to put our minds at ease — would you mind explaining your absence, sir?" These last words delivered by Mr. Hoakum with facetious severity, and a few smart tugs and pulls at his checked waistcoat.

"Charley, he's been very, very busy, Mr. Hatch," was the solemn response, delivered with a hollow, self-pitying sigh and a few feeble extrusions of the lips and tongue.

"Busy? Busy with what, Charles?"

"Very busy."

"Yes, but busy with what?"

"Very busy. Very, very busy. Very busy time for Charley. Charley can't say no more now. Don't tell Blaster about Charley. Don't tell Blaster how busy Charley's been. Charley don't want Blaster to know."

Before Mr. Hoakum could inquire further into the nature of these remarks, the voice of Miss Honeywood pierced the smoky din, quickly gaining the attention of the patrons. Said Miss Moll in her most commanding manner —

"I'll tell you again, my good friends, I don't wish to see Mr. Robert Nightingale in this house. If any of you here ever see Mr. Robert Nightingale in this house, or see him making his way toward this house, I trust you will inform him that he is not welcome at the Pelican."

19

A ripple of agitation spread through the room. A minute passed, perhaps two. At length a mustached fellow standing in the crowd grudgingly pulled off his slouch hat, thereby making his identity known to everyone present. He was a burly, hardened, brutish ruffian, of slovenly appearance and a certain carelessness of personal hygiene. His greasy hair was matted down over a declining forehead, and his eyes, which were large and protrusive and had black circles round them, were screwed into an ugly squint, creating a not necessarily false impression of chronic ill-temper.

"Mr. Robert Nightingale," announced Miss Honeywood, peering sharply at the object of her disapproval. "I see you there, Bob. Don't think you can hide for long among these good people. You're not wanted on these premises. You know that very well, don't you, Bob?"

"You're awful hard on me, Miss Moll, awful hard," growled the burly man, with feigned deference and more than a hint of sarcasm.

"You know very well why I'm hard on you, Bob. You know why you're not welcome on these premises. Every honest soul at the Pelican knows what you've done and why you're not welcome here. It's always black and white with me, Bob, you know that. I'm not one of your common gray persons. It's a black-and-white issue, and you know which side you're on. So you'd best be on your way," continued Miss Moll, folding her arms in a combative manner, as if making awful preparation for the defense of her realm — "for you're not wanted here."

"You never treats others like you treats me," said Mr. Bob Nightingale, squinting horribly. "You treats me different, Miss. You treats me *bad*. You treats me like I was one of the crim'nal element. Well, I'll tell ye, Miss Malapert," he exploded with sudden heat, "I ain't one of them. I ain't never been one of them, and I ain't never gonna be one of them." With a furtive leer Mr. Nightingale slid his eyes in and out among the crowd, endeavoring to gauge the effect this outrageous declaration had on the assembled company.

Miss Malapert, otherwise Honeywood, leveled her spectacles in her most offender-blasting manner. "Stow the gammon, Bob! I'll not take sauce from the likes of you. You've heard all I've got to say on the subject. End of conversation! The company will be pleased to note your departure from the Pelican. The wind is up tonight; mind the board on your way out."

The ruffian cast an ugly glance about the room, with a further view toward the courting of public opinion. But the icy, expressionless stares of the onlookers provided little cheer or comfort for his soul; rather, they served to assist Mr. Nightingale in deciding that in the present instance, the better part of valor might be capitulation.

"It don't mean nothin' to me," said the resilient Bob, gathering himself for his departure like some ugly frigate preparing to weigh anchor. "It don't signify nothin'. I ain't got no reason to keep me here — I ain't got no reason to stay, and I like it that way just fine. I ain't a socialite. You monkeys" — these words directed at no one in particular, but apparently intended as a general indictment of the clientele — "you monkeys can bunk in this hole for as long as you want, but I ain't gonna. I ain't gonna."

But before the ugly frigate could clear the harbor, attention was diverted by sounds of a hue and cry in the public road outside the inn. Voices calling for assistance rang in the air, to be answered by two dozen Honeywood regulars who charged from the Pelican to assess the situation and render whatever help they could. Diving through the crowd of bodies, cleaving them with a few sharp words and the passage of her tall angular frame, was the mistress of the Pelican herself, determined as always to take charge of any and all emergencies arising within her domain.

"Out of the way there, John Stinger! Move aside, George Starkie! You there! Out of the way! Let me pass!"

The murmuring of the crowd rose and fell in waves. Harness bells, cart-wheels and horses' shoes, the whistling of the wind, together with the cries of the stable-hands, could be heard above the general clamor. Shouted words filtering into the inn provided a semi-informative narration on the rush of events —

"What! Is he dead?"

"He's dead, all right, Thomas!"

"No, he ain't!"

"Sure, he is!"

"He ain't neither!"

"You're a white-livered hound!"

"I'll pound you for that, Donald Thompson!"

"Why don't you go home to your mother!"

"Blood and thunder, look at his face!"

A knotted cluster of fellows bearing a limp brown form hurried inside, trailed by a stiff blast of wind that threatened to drive them clear through the room.

"Dr. Dampe! Dr. Dampe!" cried an excited George Gosling, as the door blew shut. "Lord save us, find the doctor!"

At the table in the cozy corner the palisade of newsprint came crashing down, as the gentleman with the soft brown beard and cherry-colored waistcoat rose from his chair. In a loud authoritative tone he announced —

"All right, all right, ladies and gentlemen, step back, step back now. Clear the way! You there — don't move him. Let me see to the fellow."

The limp brown form was deposited on a cleared space before the fire. The doctor knelt beside the unconscious man and commenced his examination, administering occasional instructions of a medical nature to Miss Honeywood. Quietly the doctor plied his craft, listening intently to the sighing of the lungs, the fluttering of the heart.

The crush of onlookers formed a circle and pressed in around, eager both for a glimpse of the stranger as well as for a verdict from the attending physician. If you had searched closely among these onlookers, you might have noticed a certain callow fledgling of a youth, of scarcely fifteen winters, standing wide-eyed at the periphery of the circle. That youth was none other than myself — my shadow, my lost innocence, my early unformed forgotten self, gazing at me now across the gulf of years. For you see, I was there that night they brought the stranger in.

"He's a dead 'un, that's certain," opined Mr. Nightingale, his ugly face peering through the crowd.

"Clear off, Bob," warned Miss Honeywood, reaching for her eyeglass frames.

"I hear ye, I hear ye, Miss Malapert," replied the brutish ruffian. "I'm headed out, you monkeys don't be afeared of that. I ain't a socialite." Saying which he turned his back on the company (who mostly ignored him) and passed out into the windy night. His departure was followed immediately by a solid wooden *Thump!* heard just beyond the door, accompanied by a howl of pain.

"Ah — I b'lieve, gentlemen and ladies," said Mr. Hoakum, evaluating events as best he could from the low ground behind several towering boatsmen, "I b'lieve that, from my experience, in such a situation as this, and under such circumstances, we must, arter all, consider the cats."

A general hush attended this pronouncement, which was subsequently taken up by a tremulous murmuring and the whispered words —

"*Saber-cat!*"

Sheephead Charley, hearing this dread declaration, threw back his head and uttered a strangled cry, tearing at his hair.

"What! Cats — here in the city?" exclaimed an anonymous tar, his eyes white with fear.

"These marks on his face are either self-inflicted, or the result of his falling face-down in the street," concluded the doctor. "My inclination is toward the latter, actually. Here — here — look here. And here. His clothes are soiled but they've not been torn. It seems to me this young fellow has had a pretty lively evening — I don't think we can blame the cats for that!"

"Who found this man?" asked Miss Honeywood, of the others.

"Why, 'e did," replied Mr. Henry Duff, the carter, and pointed out a young gentleman of fashionable exterior who was standing at the back of the crowd. The gentleman wore a bottle-green coat with a black velvet collar, a buff kerseymere waistcoat, and dark trousers. A turf hat was pulled down over his brow, rendering his face imperfectly visible; a long narrow nose, a broad mustache, and a finely-hewn chin were the major features in evidence.

"It was 'e what found the poor chap lyin' in an alley, over t' the ware'ouses," explained Mr. Duff. "I 'appened along jist at the right time. When I got there, the poor chap was writhin' on the ground, holdin' 'is head an' mumblin' words as I couldn't quite make out. Then 'e went all quiet-like. So we tumbled 'im into the back o' me cart and brought 'im 'ere, which was the nearest friendly place I could think o'."

"Why, I know this man!" exclaimed the doctor's friend with the bristle-brush head, on gaining his first unobstructed view of the patient.

"Who is he?" asked Miss Moll.

"What's his name?" asked Spotted Face, but with his eyes on the gentleman in the bottle-green coat.

"Tell us!" cried the pot-boy.

The reply was lost in the doctor's sudden shouted commands. "Here — here — someone help me off with his coat — here — gently now — "

An army of well-meaning coat-removers assisted the doctor in peeling the garment of interest from the unconscious figure. Subsequently a coffee-colored great-coat could be seen snaking its way through the crowd and into the waiting arms of the pot-boy. The doctor then ordered the patient be taken immediately to a quiet room where he might be cared for, and said that he (the doctor) would be up to observe him presently.

"Didn't you hear that, Mary Clinch?" demanded Miss Honeywood of one of the female domestics, who was standing nearby in a semi-paralyzed condition with a mouthful of fingers and a stricken look on her face. "Go up

23

and see that a place is made ready for the reception of the young gentleman. Quickly, girl, quickly! And don't slobber."

The delicate maiden in her fright managed to disengage fingers from mouth, before engaging legs for swift propulsion up the stairs.

"What are the poor man's chances, do you suppose, Doctor?" asked Miss Honeywood.

"That's a difficult question, actually," the doctor replied, smoothing his beard. "A very difficult question, Miss Honeywood. We physicians, we're always having to answer difficult questions, actually. It's part of the job. I'm afraid we simply must wait and see if he rallies from this stupor he's in. The fellow looks as though he's had his hat knocked into the end of next week. And here — notice here, Miss Honeywood, how his clothes are virtually soaked in spirits. I fear," said the doctor, hunting absently in his pockets for his pipe, of course forgetting that he had left it on the cozy table, and fishing up nothing more pipe-like than the silver toothpick — which he gazed at with a vaguely baffled expression, as though wondering how *that* could possibly have gotten *there* — "I fear this gentleman has drunk very freely of strong waters, Miss Honeywood."

"Yes?"

"Very strong waters. Shocking, Miss Honeywood."

Saying which the doctor wandered off toward the bar in search of his missing pipe and a fresh glass of bitter.

"What happened to the gentleman what found the dead gentleman?" cried George Gosling, staring about, after several strong fellows had carefully raised the unconscous man from the floor and carried him to his room.

Despite a thorough search by the mistress of the Pelican and her minions, with the aid of Spotted Face, the mysterious young gentleman in the bottle-green coat refused to surface. Subsequent inquiries proved equally fruitless; no one had seen him come, no one had seen him go. No one knew even who he was. The sole finding of interest was contained in the testimony of the ostler, who had seen a dark look cross the face of the young gentleman soon after he had entered the inn.

"He's not a dead gentleman yet, George Gosling," said Miss Honeywood, belatedly acknowledging the pot-boy's unfortunate choice of words with a sharp pull on a convenient earlobe. "There's no doubt in my mind that recovery is in order, no doubt whatsoever. Look here, George — nobody pops off at the Pelican, not while Honeywood is in charge."

I have it on good authority that the patient, following a stupendous sleep, did indeed exhibit remarkable improvement by the next afternoon. The good authority came to me in the form of an upstairs chambermaid, one Miss Ankers, who confirmed that the gentleman had seized upon his luncheon of steak and kidney with a wholesome and a manly fervor. My good authority went on to relate, however, that upon being presented with dessert in the form of a musk melon, this same manly fellow let out a violent shriek and fainted dead away.

CHAPTER IV

A Tale Told by Two

THE drumming of fingers on the room-door was followed by the opening of the door. The collegiate gentleman with the bristle-brush head looked up from his desk and responded in his usual sprightly manner —

"Yes? What is it, Mr. Kibble?"

An earnest young gentleman with thick orange hair and green spectacles stepped into the room, closing the door behind him.

"There's someone here to see you, sir," he said.

"Did I have an appointment with the fellow?" inquired the professor, with a puzzled expression.

"It's a she — a young lady — and I don't believe so, sir."

The professor's glance brushed the ornamental clock on the mantel-shelf. "Why, it's gone past eight o'clock, Mr. Kibble. You needn't stay behind to this hour."

The secretary replied that he had additional work to attend to, sir, but that it shouldn't take much longer.

"Well, what does this young woman wish to see me about?"

Mr. Kibble gave utterance to the fact that he didn't know, sir, only that she wouldn't tell *him*, she'd only tell *you*, and that she thinks you're the top, sir.

"The what, did you say?"

"The top," repeated the secretary.

"The top of what?"

The door opened a crack and four thick square fingers came curling round its edge. A face with a soft brown beard and two hazel eyes in it interposed itself between the door and the jamb.

"I see you have a young lady waiting for you out there, Titus," whispered the face, which of course belonged to the doctor. "I didn't think you'd care to be disturbed, actually, so I took it upon myself to enter into a conversation with the young lady. But she wouldn't offer much more than a few commonplace remarks. Seemed rather preoccupied, really — took no notice of me at all. Extraordinary! Not the usual case with us physicians."

"Come in, Daniel. Come in, and shut the door," invited the professor.

The doctor complied, after lofting one final precautionary stare at the visitor in the outer chamber.

"Who is this young woman?" asked the professor. "Do I know her?"

"A Miss Jacks," replied Mr. Kibble, adjusting his spectacles. "A Miss Mona Jacks, resident in Boring Lane, Key Street."

The professor shook his head to indicate his unfamiliarity with the name.

"Do you know, she's got an unusual little voice," remarked the doctor, sliding comfortably into a nearby chair. "A strange little voice with a `chirpy' quality to it, like birdsong. Quite a charming effect, actually, quite merry. At least I think so."

The professor's brows narrowed and the corners of his mouth lifted slightly. His gaze drifted from the doctor to Mr. Kibble, then spread itself along the side-row of lattice windows through which the night was pressing, before returning to the face of his secretary.

"Well, we must see what it is that has brought the young lady here. Please show her in, Mr. Kibble."

The young lady being shown in, came in.

"Good evening, Miss Jacks," said the professor. "My name is Titus Tiggs, and this is my professional colleague, Dr. Dampe, whom you have already met, it seems. Also, may I present my personal secretary, Mr. Austin Kibble, whom you have met as well."

The young lady came forward. She was very thin and small, and delicately constructed. Her face was a clear oval with a pretty red mouth and slim nostrils. Her eyes, large and moon-shaped, were planted beneath widely separated brows that sagged at their farther ends, so much so that they seemed poised to drop off her face altogether. She wore a cloak with a fur tippet, appropriate for the season, and a fringed bonnet over an ocean of short dark curls.

Dr. Dampe, rising from his chair, echoed the professor's greeting and waved the young woman toward one of the comfortable armchairs distributed about the hearth-rug. "Won't you sit down, Miss Jacks?"

"Thank — you — sir," replied the young lady, hesitating, "but — I am here expressly for a confidential interview with Professor Tiggs. I was informed he was at the top of his profession."

"Why, I shall be here, too," exclaimed the professor, hastily coming round from his desk. "My colleague Dr. Dampe was simply exhibiting his usual courtesy in offering you a chair."

"I see," murmured the lady, very self-conscious and, as the doctor had observed, noticeably distracted. "I apologize, sir, for calling on you — and your colleagues — without prior notice, and at such an hour, but circumstances have progressed at a rapid pace. I had no choice, and my need is great. I trust you will not be upset with me for taking such a liberty."

As noted by Dr. Dampe the voice of the young woman was unusually chirrupy, but most engagingly so, having a soft pleasant tone that was altogether rather sweet and in no way unattractive.

"Of course not, my dear, of course not," the professor replied in his sprightly way. "But, please — won't you have a seat, Miss Jacks? We'll have the fire going in no time. The autumn is upon us and the nights are brisker now."

The young lady glanced from the professor's outstretched palm to the empty chair, then to Dr. Dampe, then to Mr. Kibble, with a questioning expression, as though she remained uncomfortable with the presence of the physician colleague and the personal secretary.

"Be assured, Miss Jacks, that our conversation will be held in the strictest confidence. With regard to Dr. Dampe, don't hesitate to speak frankly in his presence — he is one of my closest associates and his knowledge in many areas greatly surpasses mine. However, should you be ill at ease I'm sure he'll understand and graciously accede to your wishes. The same may be said for my secretary. Be assured — you are among friends, my dear."

The visitor looked again from the hand to the chair. After a moment's consideration, followed by a spate of nervous chewing on her lower lip, she nodded and took her seat. The chair was a large and very comfortable one, and her tiny figure seemed to slip away into it. She removed her gloves and bonnet and set them aside.

In preparation for the evening, which was a frosty one, the professor raked the embers in the hearth and threw on several fresh pieces of turf. A prodigious fire soon arose, filling the apartment and the faces of the company with a cheery warmth. Eerie shadows leaped and danced upon the papered walls and the old oak wainscot. Reflected images trapped in the diamond-shaped panes of the casement flickered weirdly, as the cry of a whistle-buoy came sighing through the glass.

Titus Vespasianus Tiggs, professor of metaphysics and stoker of blazes, was a short, heavy man with the stance and shoulders of a boxer. As he stood on that autumnal night before the wild blazing chimney, with his stocky frame and his bristle-brush head silhouetted against the fire — and with the cry of the

28

buoy fresh in the ears of everyone present — even wilder images of primeval ritual and invocation, nocturnal sacrifice and the awakening of ancient awful unfathomable powers, might have insinuated themselves into the mind of an impressionable observer.

The secretary having retrieved a decanter and glasses from the sideboard, the company gathered together in their chairs before the fire.

"This will help to warm you, my dear," said the professor, pouring a quantity of wine for the young lady.

"Thank you, sir."

Following some small talk and a brief discussion of the merits of the vintage, the professor folded his hands across one knee and smiled genially at the visitor to put her more at ease.

"How may we be of help to you, Miss Jacks?" he asked.

"I'd like you to know, firstly, that she's not to blame," replied the young woman, seemingly *in medias res*. "After all, there was nothing more she could have done. I realize she's very vain and spoiled, but there is nothing else she could have done to prevent it. He didn't believe her, and because of that everything has turned out the way it has."

"Yes?"

"Isn't that always the way it happens? But she isn't to blame."

"Of course not. To blame for what?"

"And now — what else could possibly happen? It's all so unexplainable. But unexplainable things do happen. Such things in fact happen all the time, as I have been given to understand. That is why I've come here to the university to see you. That is why you were recommended to me."

Professor Tiggs nervously crossed and re-crossed his legs, a frown creasing the space between his eyebrows. "I'm sure you're correct, Miss Jacks, but really — I must stop you here and confess that you've lost me somewhere. Could you try explaining things again, a bit more clearly this time, and from the beginning? For example, could you tell us first of all just who these people are you're referring to?"

"I am sorry — forgive me. You see how unsettling this business is! The subject is my sister Nina. She is a year older than I, and generally accounted something of a beauty." The faintest moderation of voice as she spoke, together with a self-effacing compression of the lips, communicated to the listeners that a similar description, in the visitor's view, little fit the visitor herself. But this minor discomposure passed quickly like a summer cloud.

"About two years ago my sister began seeing a young man — the boatswain's mate from a large merchant ship — whom she'd met through a mutual acquaintance. Our father — there is only our father, for our mother died many years ago — our old father, who's a bit old-fashioned, but a dear nevertheless — our father would hear nothing of it. He's wanted only the best for Nina, and for me, and couldn't abide the young fellow my sister had chosen. The young man flattered her immensely, and my sister, in her vanity, believed every word of it. You see, Professor Tiggs, although Nina is older than I she remains a foolish child in many ways."

The face of the professor glowed at the natural good sense evident in the young woman's character. The doctor smoked his pipe and endeavored to look very sagacious, while Mr. Kibble jotted down relevant points in the small memorandum book he carried when assisting in the professor's researches.

"My sister's young man often being absent for periods on his travels, Nina took occasion at such times to confide in me concerning the plans the two had devised for their future. She told me that her young man had grown disillusioned with his life at sea and was casting about for some other occupation. Apparently he'd had some sort of accident aboard ship, not long before, in which he'd been tumbled overboard and nearly lost. The incident had affected his mind and plagued him constantly. Nina said that he'd developed an horrific fear of drowning, of dying at sea and being swallowed up by the dark cold waters. His dreams were haunted by an image of his body drifting down into the abyss, where it was ripped apart by monstrous unseen sharks and other hideous creatures."

The young lady seemed to retreat further into the depths of her chair, as though magnetically repelled by the words she had spoken. For several moments all was quiet save for the ticking of the ornamental clock and the spit and crackle of the turf-fire. She sipped a little of her wine.

"Knowing what you do of this young fellow, would you say that in this regard he was telling your sister the truth?" asked the professor.

Miss Jacks frowned briefly while considering. "Yes, I believe so. And I can say as well that in this great fear of his he frightened my sister, and so in turn frightened me, in a way I can't readily describe. It was plain he'd grown to despise the life he led, but he'd been driven to it by necessity and circumstance. I believe he was in complete earnest in wanting what he referred to as a better life."

"I see. Please go on, Miss Jacks."

"It may be that in Nina — and thus in our father's resources — he saw his opportunity for that better life ashore. As I have said he often was away on his travels, but upon returning to Salthead lost no time in renewing his attentions, of course without our father's knowledge or consent. On such occasions, I must confess, either I or our maid Susanna — for whom Nina has ever been the favorite — acted as a go-between and confidante for them. He gave her many tokens of his affection collected on his voyages, and in this way flattered her too.

"For a long time my sister has been the object of the unreciprocated passion of our neighbor, an old hunks named George Curle. Mr. Curle is a widower and well-stricken in years. In his youth he was apparently quite a swell upon town; but in his present state of disrepair, as Nina is fond of saying, it's difficult to spot the resemblance. Mr. Curle is a substantial businessman and is known to have amassed a fortune. And so his interest in Nina — someone young enough to be his granddaughter — has actually been encouraged by our father, who has always been on the look-out for such matches for both his daughters. I say this with no disrespect; our father is, after all, a gentleman of what I should term the `old school,' and approaches such matters in a very practical and business-like fashion.

"My sister, even while encouraging the advances of Ham Pickering — her young nautical man — and seeming to discourage those of Mr. Curle, nonetheless could not muster the will to refuse certain gifts bestowed on her from time to time by our elderly neighbor, and with the full knowledge and approval of our father. Once again it was her vanity — poor Nina never can refuse any compliment to her person, no matter the source. Thus she'd come to acquire a quite astonishing collection of baubles from both her admirers, neither of whom was aware of the other's existence.

"One evening we received an unexpected visitor in the shape of Mr. Pickering. A meeting in the park had been arranged for the day next, but instead Ham appeared suddenly on our doorstep. By some stroke of good fortune Father was not home when he arrived. The young man was in an agitated state. It had lately been worded about that Nina was accepting gifts from Mr. Curle, and this rumor had been overheard by Ham. Despite her protests to the contrary (which of course were shameful lies), he didn't believe her. But you see — it wasn't her fault! It was simply her vanity. Unfortunately, several of the items given to her by Mr. Curle being about her person at the time, she was forced to confess her guilt.

"Mr. Pickering had just returned to Salthead and had been prepared to remain in town for an extended period. Now, however, all was changed. I don't know whether he truly loved Nina or not, but I am certain he thought she preferred Mr. Curle — a preposterous match! In his mind his glorious new future ashore must have disappeared before his eyes.

"Convinced that Nina had deserted him, he left in a great heat and took temporary refuge at a sailors' inn near the docks. Nina followed him there and sought to convince him of the error of his beliefs. It was fruitless. Rather than forgiving her, he entered himself aboard a ship leaving Salthead the very next morning. That ship, Professor Tiggs, was the *Swan*, bound for Nantle and the southern islands. As you may recollect the *Swan* never returned from her voyage, but went down with all hands in February's ferocious storm."

Here Miss Jacks paused, her small body shivering despite the wine and the glow of warmth from the fire.

"I'm afraid," said the professor at length, "I'm afraid, Miss Jacks, that it isn't clear to me how we can be of assistance to you in this matter."

The young lady bathed her lips with a pink tongue and looked down at her shoes. She screwed herself up in her chair and made a little preparatory cough before resuming her story.

"The night before last," she said, her lilting voice acquiring now a certain tautness, "the night before last, Nina called me to her room with a look of undisguised terror in her eyes and asked me, in a barely audible whisper, would I look out her window and tell her what I saw there? As you probably remember the fog was very thick that night. Nevertheless, the swirling banks were shot through from time to time with shafts of moonlight by which it was possible to see more clearly.

"As I looked down from my sister's window, which gives out onto a little cobbled lane leading into Key Street, I saw that the moon had temporarily returned, revealing a strange figure below. He was a tall, awkward fellow, and he wore a sailor's garments. What was unusual was that he was dancing a hornpipe, all to himself and seemingly for his own amusement. But beyond this there was something wrong with his legs and arms, the way they thrashed about this way and that in an uncontrollable fashion — all horribly awkward and stiff, like the limbs of a dead body actuated after death."

Miss Jacks inhaled a long breath before continuing. "This is why I've come to see you, Professor Tiggs. Your experience in such matters is well-known in Salthead, and your reputation among your colleagues is, I understand, of the very highest. You see — in that faint shaft of light from the moon as it broke

32

through the fog, the features of the dancing sailor became quite clear to me. I am prepared to testify, on my honor, that it was Ham Pickering dancing under my sister's window that night."

A cloud of smoke blew in from the vicinity of Dr. Dampe. The secretary looked up from his notes, his pen stilled, and peered inquiringly at his employer. The professor remained silent for a time, though his interest in the direction the young woman's narrative had taken shone out from his face.

Miss Jacks moistened her lips again with the tip of her tongue, and watched the professor with her moon-shaped eyes glistening in the firelight.

"There are no known survivors from the *Swan*," he said at length. "She was far out to sea, and the gale she went down in was as fierce a wintry blast as anyone can recall. Scarcely a vestige of her timbers or cargo ever was found, let alone a living human being. There's not one chance in a thousand any member of her crew could have survived. Nevertheless, Miss Jacks," he went on, hurriedly, noting the look of disappointment in the young lady's face, "contrary to what you are thinking, you've no need to fear our disbelieving your story. In fact, we ourselves are witness to what may be a corroboration of it.

"Last night — the night following your visitation by the sailor — a young friend of mine, Mr. John Rime, whom I have known for some years, was discovered lying unconscious in an alley near the docks. He'd been drinking heavily, and apparently had wandered about town for some time in a crazed state before collapsing. The night before last — the very same foggy night you relate — he, too, encountered a sailor who danced a ghastly hornpipe. The sailor interrogated him with all manner of wild and impertinent questions, and as well performed a certain — shall we say, physical impossibility — that drove my young friend nearly to the point of madness. It's amazing to me that the poor fellow has recovered well enough to tell his story."

"What sort of physical impossibility?" asked Miss Jacks.

As if in response, the sound of the whistle-buoy came wailing out of the night. The clock on the mantel-shelf seemed to miss a tick.

"The fellow," said Dr. Dampe, with the confident matter-of-factness of the physician, "apparently unscrewed his own head and handed it over like some bloody cabbage. Extraordinary! Must have been a most striking performance. Wish I'd seen it, actually." He swallowed some wine, and threw himself back in his chair with his glass in one hand and his pipe in the other, looking immensely comfortable.

"A melon," said the earnest Mr. Kibble, flipping through the leaves of his memorandum book. "I believe the article mentioned by Mr. Rime was a melon. I have it noted here — "

"A melon, yes, Mr. Kibble, but `bloody cabbage' is much more visually expressive, don't you agree?"

"But you must agree, Doctor, that `bloody cabbage' can in no way be considered factually accurate. As everyone knows, a cabbage is a green culinary vegetable but a melon is a fruit."

"Fruit or vegetable, vegetable or fruit, it's simply a bit of artistic license, Mr. Kibble — nothing more. We physicians, we employ artistic license every day when dealing with our patients. It's part of the job, actually; patients expect it. Surely in this case `bloody cabbage' is infinitely preferable to `plaguy pineapple,' for example, or `confounded cantaloupe' — "

"Oh, stop it, you're both being horrid!" cried Miss Jacks, clapping her hands to her ears and appealing to the professor. "I tell myself that Ham Pickering is dead, that his body disappeared with his ship. Yet there is the paradox, for I'm certain of what Nina and I saw. And then I have my doubts again, and tell myself that he can't be here, he simply *can't*. Ham Pickering can't be here any more than the *Swan* can come floating into Salthead harbor. So what was it that was dancing under my sister's window?"

"I have complete faith in my young friend John's testimony," said the professor. "I've known him since he was a lad. He's a lively young fellow and enjoys his evenings about town, but I can't imagine any reason for his inventing a story as patently wild as the one he related to us, quite openly, this afternoon."

"But what was it?" persisted Miss Jacks. "Nina is driven nearly out of her mind — it's kept her from sleeping from the moment she saw it. It wasn't her fault, at least in intention. There was nothing more she could have done to stop Ham from boarding that ship. She tried, you know, but he wouldn't listen to her. It wasn't her fault. How is it someone drowned at sea can return and be walking about the streets? How can Mr. Pickering possibly be here?"

"It may be that `return' is not quite the proper word," said the professor. "What is more likely, I should think, is that he never went."

"I don't understand. Do you mean to say he was never aboard the *Swan*?"

"No, I've no doubt at all he was. What I meant to say, Miss Jacks, was that on occasion — on very rare occasions, and I am speaking of metaphysics here — the tie to the world we know is so powerful that it cannot be severed, even by a catastrophe. Indeed, in most cases it is the very fact of its being a catastrophe that is responsible for holding the spirit here after death. The jolt of the separation is so sudden, the trauma so severe, the tragedy so harrowing, that complete dissolution is delayed for a time. Nothing less than the sheer force of personality can explain it — a defiant refusal to accept what has happened, as from outrage or indignation, overwhelming sorrow or a desire for revenge. Such a soul is condemned for a time to restlessness and anguish, while trapped in a dream-like state between one world and another. Your `rappers' and such-like mocking spirits, and your vaporous apparitions, as are occasionally reported in town and in certain isolated country houses, are good examples of this. Fortunately the condition is almost always temporary; eventually the tie to the world is broken, the spirit is freed."

"But what was the thing Nina and I saw? It certainly was no vapor. It moved, it leaped, it made horrible sounds. I can still hear the dreadful tapping of its shoes on the cobblestones in the lane."

"I don't know for certain, Miss Jacks — I can only guess at present."

"Perhaps it was a trick," suggested Mr. Kibble, impulsively running a hand through his orange hair. "A bit of skylarking, perhaps, by someone who happens to resemble your Mr. Pickering. After all it was dark, and you and your sister were looking down from the window above. Apparently he didn't speak so you couldn't hear his voice. Is there someone who might be capable of springing such an offensive joke on your sister? Or on you?"

"It was Ham Pickering," said Miss Jacks, firmly. "The more I consider it the more certain I am. I saw his mustache, and his gold tooth gleaming in the moonlight. There's no mistaking him. And what about your friend Mr. Rime? Aren't you forgetting about your melons and your culinary vegetables?"

A hushed silence fell upon the little group, as they considered the alternatives to this seemingly unassailable point. It was true; to accept John Rime's story was to accept that the corpse of Ham Pickering was walking the streets of Salthead.

All at once it seemed to get very cold in the room. The professor rose from his chair and stepped to the casement, where he unlatched one of the windows and poked his head out into the night.

Another dismal fog covered the ancient city. A few nearby lights could be seen shimmering in the mist, here and there; beyond these the town receded into darkness. A faint smoky odor, derived from the wood-fires burning in innumerable unseen chimneys, drifted on the night air. Stray footsteps and the ring of horses' shoes could be heard echoing in the street below. The fog was an unusually heavy one, even for old Salthead, leaving huge beads of moisture clinging to the glass and moldings of the window. For a moment something colder than the fog seemed to pass between the earth and the faintly glowing spot where the moon was.

The professor gathered his mulberry coat about him and with a troubled frown shut the casement. Returning to the warmth of his chair he sat for a time with his legs stretched out in front of him and his hands buried in his coat-pockets, allowing his thoughts to wander where they would. His face acquired a look of concentrated attention, as though he were striving after something that remained always just out of view.

In the end it was Dr. Dampe who broke the spell.

"Well, I for one am in complete agreement with you, Miss Jacks," he said, brushing a few stray ashes from his cherry-colored waistcoat. "I think there's little doubt your Mr. Pickering is indeed the same apparition seen by the fellow at the Blue Pelican — your cat's-meat man, Titus. By the way," he added, launching an artful circle of smoke high into the air, "I've never quite understood what use any self-respecting mouser has for a meat man. Expand on that, if you would — how is Mr. Pie getting along without his services at present?"

"Who is Mr. Pie?" asked Miss Jacks.

A sprightly radiance brightened the professor's face at mention of his favorite feline companion.

"Mr. Pie," he answered, "is ever Mr. Pie, and a very independent young man, and he will always get along exceptionally well, thank you."

CHAPTER V

Further Dealings with the Firm of Tusk & Co.

THAT conscientious philanthropist, Mr. Josiah Tusk, in advancing his little game of "feints" with the populace, had devised a scoring system, which afforded him much delight, whereby he awarded to himself a certain number of marks for certain specified accomplishments. For example, should he send some ancient barnacled pensioner, deaf and lame, tumbling into the way of a passing coach, then such-and-such number of marks would he allot to himself. Should the intended victim instead be hale and limber and of a more healthful disposition, then fewer marks (naturally) would be etched into his mental scorecard. The greatest number of marks Mr. Tusk reserved for children, which small creatures were to him abhorrent beyond all things in life. So intense were his feelings on this issue that he would rejoice in a positively festive manner whenever some unsuspecting urchin fell victim to his canny leg, after which an entire schoolyard of points would come romping in to rally the score.

Thus Mr. Tusk, on a leisurely stroll in the High Street —

A wastrel vagrant is engaged, the battle is joined, and the vanquished is driven into the gutter. ("*Four marks!*")

A waiter balancing a supper tray makes a dash from a nearby public house to a customer in adjoining chambers, only to be deceived by a sly motion of the miserly legs, which sends him flying beneath the wheels of a pony-chaise. ("*Seven marks!*")

A lazy-eyed youth, suspected by Josiah of having cast an ugly face at him, is tripped up by the subtle turn of a Tuskan ankle and catapulted head-first into a water-butt. ("*Eleven-point-five!*")

And always at the conclusion of such exercises the grim little smile would work its way across the face of Josiah and betray his satisfaction with the final score, which was duly logged in his cerebrum. ("Thirty-seven-point-five marks, total. *It's a banner day!*")

I believe the sole exception — and this a kindly one — made by Mr. Tusk in his little game was that of the patient young mother, with a clutch of unruly brats at her feet and a screeching hell-babe at her neck. Why, what need had such a long-suffering soul to fear Josiah? For surely it was to his credit, the way his heart melted at the sight of one whom nature, in Josiah's eyes, already had pitched headlong into the water-butt of life!

So never wonder at that grim little smile on the lips of the conscientious man as he surveys his field of flesh. Never wonder at the continuing prosperity of that highly prosperous species, *Tuskus voracius*, for it's all in the way of the world. Never wonder, and never fear. Wherever there are bills to be taken up, Tusk & Co. will be there. Wherever there are trusting clients to be defrauded, or tenants to be squeezed, Tusk & Co. will be there. Wherever there are the weak and infirm to be exploited, be assured — Tusk & Co. will always be there.

A cheerless morning with a brisk wind, cruel and searching, and black clouds swooping from the sky like harpies, finds a defiantly jaunty Josiah striding his bold superior stride down the High Street, into the heart of town. Buffered as usual against the world by the very superior red velvet waistcoat, richly lacquered strap-boots, black silk hat, and magnificent black traveling coat, the miser makes his usual rapid progress along the busy thoroughfare. Today, however, is not a day for feints; the sharp falcon-eyes, instead of scouting for a suitable victim, remain fixed on the road ahead. Nonetheless the grim little smile is there, evidence of the eagerness with which the morning's business is anticipated.

Down and over into Great Wood Street, past Milk Lane, through an improving neighborhood, up a dark court and along a greasy alley Mr. Tusk makes his way. All about him the morning rituals so common to the low folk of the city already are in progress. Over there are the two burly laundresses, Janet Stork and Sarah Sloper, departing with their charges of bundled linen. Across the way that's young Mr. Legge, the confidential clerk, tickling the rusty lock of an office door with an equally rusty key, hoping to be safely inside before the arrival of his employer. Over here two old apple women are tending to their wicker baskets, while over there is Mr. Sweeting, the pastry vendor, setting out the fresh butter and lump sugar and morning mugs of coffee for his breakfast display. And there is the grocer, Mr. Buckle, drawing down the shutters of his shop, just as a yawning, winking porter takes up his station over the way. Past them all glides the predatory form of the miser, seen, but all unseeing.

Arrived in Cobb's Court, Mr. Tusk pauses before an ancient pile of red brick with crow-stepped gables and a span roof crowned by nests of fantastic chimney-stacks. Up the steps and past the lumbering guard (whom he ignores) and through the doorway and into the moldering entrance-hall he goes. Ascending a flight of stairs in almost total darkness he emerges upon a narrow landing, and from there ventures into a dim passage lighted by sconces set at irregular intervals in the walls. About midway along the passage he stops before a filthy door, its surface garnished with the following inscription —

BADGER AND WINCH
SOLICITORS

The miser passes through the door and into a vast, poorly lighted chamber that at first glance appeared to be uninhabited. The walls of the room were lined from floor to ceiling with row upon row of dusty bookcases. Masses of legal paraphernalia of every description — jackets, folders, papers, ledgers, folios, octavos, writs, warrants, notices, correspondence, and other assorted memoranda — sprouted like malignant growths from every article of furniture. Ledger upon ledger, writ upon writ, folio upon folio, the most tremendous of these legal eruptions climbed towards the ceiling of the chamber; the ceiling itself being very high and blackened by tallow smoke, the tops of these monumental piles seemed to vanish into the upper darkness like volcanoes rising into the night sky.

Windows there were none, doors but two — the one by which Josiah had entered and another on the opposite side of the chamber. The sole means of illumination was an array of wax-lights distributed about the room — on an edge here or a corner there — some of which appeared in danger of toppling and igniting a litigious conflagration.

Mr. Tusk strained his eyes to peer about the stacks of legal writ, what with the seedy light and the tallow smoke adrift in the air. Turning round he beheld an extraordinarily tall and narrow writing-table, with spidery legs that carried it nearly halfway to the ceiling. Behind the table on an equally tall and narrow stool sat a legal clerk in a dark waistcoat, white false collar, and a blue shirt emblazoned with pink anchors. Drab knee-breeches and gaiters covered his legs, boots his feet. His abundant brown hair flared out from his head with many radiating points, like a sunburst; in it was nested an odd assortment of quill-pens.

"You," growled the miser, deigning to lift his eyes to meet those of the clerk, whose boots were resting on a rung of the stool a little above Josiah's hat-brim. "You there, Scribbler! Your master — he is in chambers?"

The clerk looked down on the black silk hat and white head of the visitor. His face wore an appearance of feigned disinterest, as though he were annoyed at the stoppage yet secretly welcomed any respite from his labors. Recognizing who it was, Mr. Scribbler mulled over his reply with a few preparatory lifts of his eyebrows. Growing very serious, he screwed up his eyes and jerked the feather of his pen towards the inner door of the office, cocking his head at the same instant, before adjusting his candle and resuming his lofty studies.

Mr. Tusk, recognizing this as an answer in the affirmative, proceeded in the indicated direction. At that moment the inner door blew open, as if by a stiff wind, and discharged a very fat man wearing a plum-colored suit and a fine linen shirt, with a heavy gold watch-chain at his generous waist. In one hand he carried a sheaf of legal papers, which he was scanning with the aid of an eyeglass suspended from his collar by a black ribbon. Unconscious of the miser's presence, he coughed loudly and addressed his vassal on the high seat.

"Ahem! Scribbler, I say — ahem — have you completed the quarter-sheets of the Puddleby accounts? We simply must have them today, you know — ahem — at once, I say. Ahem. There's word that Puddleby senior will be arriving by the late coach from Newmarsh — ahem — and you know, it would reflect very poorly on the firm if he were to discover that — "

"Winch, I am here," intoned the miser, with commanding directness.

The eyes of the attorney wrenched themselves from the clerk to Josiah. They were small eyes, dark and long-cut, and held a sleepy glitter. Another loud cough escaped the throat of Mr. Winch. His eyeglass fell from his eye and clicked against his waistcoat-buttons. He wiped his lips and passed a handkerchief lightly across his bald head. An ingratiating smile took charge of his features.

"Ahem," reiterated Mr. Winch, without elaboration.

"In there," said the miser, indicating the inner sanctum of which Mr. Jasper Winch was now sole possessor, the senior partner in the firm, Mr. Badger, having long since departed to that abode where all good gentlemen of the law reap their final reward. "An execution is imminent — you know the one. There are papers to be drafted, signed and sealed. All must be in perfect order for the sheriff and the execution men. There will be no mistakes. You know that as a man of business I don't stand for mistakes and I don't stand for dillydallying. You will have the papers drawn up and be lively about it, or you'll bear the consequences."

"Yes — yes, at once, Mr. Tusk," acquiesced the attorney. His eyelids quivered with nervous energy. "Ahem — our clerk Scribbler there will assist in — "

The miser shook his great white head. "We won't need him yet. You and I will ourselves prepare the preliminary drafts of the documents in your chambers. I tell you, Winch, every word must be chosen with care; nothing must be overlooked. You know the case. Afterwards that fellow" — one bony hand tossed in the direction of Mr. Scribbler, whom he viewed as an inconsequential but regretfully necessary article of humanity — "will prepare the final copies. As I am a conscientious man, I will see justice done. This action will provide a valuable lesson for our Mr. Bouncing and Coaches, up there on the fells. We will show that fellow what happens when he overreaches, and takes another man's hard-earned money with no intention of repaying it. *We shall teach him.* Be assured, Winch — it is going to be a very pleasant piece of work." And he laughed a grim little laugh, disclosing an abundance of hard white teeth.

Lawyer Winch laughed too, with his head cocked oddly to one side. His neck had a twist in it which caused his head to be screwed into a perpetual half-turn, as though he had been partly hanged. This oddity, combined with a certain reluctance to look his man in the face, but instead to fix his pupils on a spot somewhere about the chest region, lent him an air of slyness, as though — heaven only knows why — he was not to be trusted.

"Yes, yes, of course. Ahem. Won't you step in, sir?" he said, smiling greasily, and with one hand extended toward the door of his private office. "This way, Mr. Tusk. Ahem. Scribbler!" he cried, aiming a premonitory forefinger at the clerk. "Puddleby. Quarter-sheets. *Now!* And be prepared — ahem — to be of use to Mr. Josiah Tusk shortly."

The miser glided past, the fat attorney following with deferential alacrity, and so the two were closeted together.

Silence rolled like a wave through the outer chamber, flowing round and about the dusty islands of legal writ, splashing at the feet of the surgent volcanoes and washing back against the door of Lawyer Winch's private chamber. A sturdy door it was, too, of good solid oak, so thick and knotted that no sound could pierce it in either direction; those on the inside could hear nothing without, while those on the outside remained insensible of the plots and conspiracies being hatched within.

So silence spread her soothing waters among the volcanoes and past the fluttering wax-lights, which sparkled here and there like so many miniature

41

lighthouses amid the gloom. Not many minutes passed, however, before the door of the outer office opened again to admit a small figure, followed by a second, slightly larger one. Peering about, the visitors quickly ascertained the location of Mr. Scribbler, and stood observing for some few minutes as the youthful scribe busied himself with his work.

It was evident that Mr. Scribbler's interest in the quarter-sheets for the onrushing Puddleby was on the wane. Two flies, which had begun executing aerodynamic maneuvers about his candle, seemed ready-made to provide the clerk with a needed diversion from his studies. Eagerly he deposited pen in hair, placed his blotting-paper and wafer-box aside, steadied himself, and proceeded to make several vigorous but completely ineffective lunges at the insects with a ruler.

The two visitors crept stealthily forward, trying as best they could to avoid the radiance of the wax-lights. The smaller figure appeared to be that of a young woman; the other belonged to a wiry gentleman of middle years. Once or twice the pair dropped behind a desk or table so as not to be spotted by the clerk, who was by now engaged in fierce combat with the insects overhead.

At length the visitors reached the foot of Mr. Scribbler's writing-table. The female figure resolved itself into a very dimpled and a very pretty young charwoman in a dark smock and an apron of calico. Her golden hair was tied round her head with a kerchief, while her eyes of afternoon blue were tied to Mr. Scribbler. There was however a certain weariness in her otherwise bright features, a droop in her shoulders, a hardness in her hands, that tallied well with the bucket dangling from her fingers.

The gentleman with her was a short, dapper, wiry fellow in a black coat and trousers with narrow running pinstripes. His waistcoat was black, his shirt was black, his high-buttoned boots were black, his soft felt hat was black. He was in fact dressed all in black, and he had smoked lenses in his eyeglasses and so they were black too. Behind the lenses nothing of his eyes was visible; one wondered how he could see anything at all in those gloomy quarters. His face was clean-shaven and of a hardy, brick-red disposition. His nose was very sharp and narrow, as was his mouth, which was stretched into a grin as he watched the antics of the clerk.

High above, Mr. Scribbler was preparing to launch one final decisive campaign. The flies made their noisy approach, moving in separate circles round his head. Grasping the ruler firmly in both hands, the clerk wound himself up, reached back over his shoulder, and was on the verge of swinging away when a cheery voice softly cried —

"La, Mis-ter Scrib-bler!"

The arms of the clerk stood in place, his mighty lunge for the moment forestalled. His eyes swept the upper reaches of the room with a furious attention. Discerning nothing of interest at that altitude, the look of scrutiny was replaced by a vacuous stare. He scratched his head in some consternation, disturbing a few of the resident writing implements, knitted his brows, shrugged, and so squared himself again for the assault.

"La, Mis-ter Rich-ard!" came a second melodious call.

A look of fierce surprise from Mr. Scribbler. Again his eyes hunted about the corners of the room, and again they found nothing of significance. He inspected the ruler, the candle, the pen-knife, the blotting-paper, the inkstand and wafer-box, and ruffled through a few leaves of the enormous volume. He retrieved several quills from his hair and examined them closely. Convinced that none of these items was capable of addressing him by name, Mr. Scribbler scratched his head again and looked out across the vast smoky chamber with a forlorn countenance.

"La, Mis-ter Rich-ard!"

The light broke at last upon the puzzled clerk, as glancing down he beheld the two visitors. He stared at them very hard, looked round himself again, then stared at the two small visitors even harder, just to be sure, before a puckish grin overspread his face. He tossed a little embarrassed wave in their direction, which the young woman returned with a flutter of her fingers. This result caused him to grin all the more, which in turn precipitated a fit of laughter from the pretty charwoman.

"La, Mr. Scribbler!" she exclaimed. "You didn't notice poor Bridget down here, did you? Bridget, she surprised you, didn't she?"

The dapper man in pinstripes waved his hat in salutation. "Friend Scribbler — good morning to ye! And a wery fine morning it is in here, too. And if ye believe that, ye'll believe Samson Icks to be the richest cove in the city. Ha ha! What is it ye're up to, up there? Powdering away at yer studies again, are ye?"

Mr. Scribbler threw himself across his writing-table, resting his chin in the palm of one hand, and gazed at the visitors with an air of careless nonchalance. With the feathers of the quill-pens sticking out of his hair he resembled nothing so much as a species of weird bird lolling on its perch.

"Ah, friend Scribbler," continued Mr. Icks, with his hands in the pockets of his pinstripes. "Powdering away again, bright and early, I see. Well, don't ye make a habit of it. Ye know ye'll not get any consideration from that fat rascal for it, that ye can be sure on."

"La, Mr. Richard," smiled Bridget. "La! says I. You'll come down from there and give poor Bridget a kiss, now, won't you? She can't stay long — Bridget's got her charring to do, you know. She's only a few minutes now before she must get to her work. And hard work it is, too."

She regarded Mr. Scribbler with a mixture of sweetness, good humor, and undisguised affection. Her affection for the odd clerk in fact knew no bounds; but I don't suppose it was returned in like measure. Indeed, the clerk seemed not even to hear her entreaty, blithely shifting his chin to his other hand and ruffling his wild hair.

"Friend Richard," said Mr. Icks, in a more confidential tone, and with two or three furtive glances about the volcanoes and lighthouses. "I seen the tall nasty rascal on his way here. I seen him go up the stairs, and I followed him tight. I know he's in there" — a nod toward the inner sanctum of Mr. Winch, and a visible hardening of the sharp lines of his mouth — "with the fat rascal, no doubt."

Mr. Scribbler, intrigued more by this line of conversation than by the charwoman's, bent down from his chair to listen closely. Mr. Icks for his part clambered onto the nearest available table and there stood on tiptoe, steadying himself against a stack of dusty law-books. In this way they succeeded in closing the gap between them to a few feet.

"Aye, the tall rascal — Mr. Josiah Tusk. Winch's client. Ye know all about him, friend Richard, that's sure. Now there — there *is* the richest cove in the city, and a wery nasty one to boot. They's close, them two, but there ain't no doubt which one's master — it's the one with the money! Never a kind word from that tall rascal for Samson Icks, not one. Got all the coin any fellow could ever want on this earth, but it's not enough to soften him. No. The more of it he gets, the nastier he gets — mark that, Mr. Richard! Ungodly rich he is and owns half o' Salthead, and that half ready at the signal to cut out his heart for the way he treats 'em. And as for Icks — never a word for old Icks but it's a nasty one."

Here the red face of Mr. Icks grew redder, and his eyebrows darted up behind the smoked lenses.

"Now, I know why that tall rascal's come today. It's bad, bad, ye can believe that. A sorry case. Do ye know why that tall rascal's here, Mr. Richard?"

Mr. Scribbler conveyed his ignorance by a solemn shake of his head.

"It's an *ex-e-cu-tion*," said Mr. Icks, gravely, to which the clerk responded by enlarging his eyes and rounding his mouth into the shape of an "O."

Mr. Icks nodded briskly. "Aye, aye. Been watching it for weeks now. A simple matter of a loan that won't be repaid. And for that the tall nasty rascal is going to kick a man's livelihood out from under him and set him a-swingin', like the hangman. Just as I've seen him do to so many other kind folk. And that fat rascal's his instrument. And as for old Icks — why, he's the instrument of the fat rascal. And so I'll give ye one guess who it is they gets to carry out that execution, Mr. Richard. Who it is they gets to set the poor squit a-swingin'. Them rascals, so proud and mighty — they loves to discharge the orders, and I'll offer ye one guess, friend Scribbler, who it is they gets to do their nasty work. Aye, aye," he sighed, "it's a sad day, friend Richard, for the world belongs to the rascals."

Mr. Scribbler commiserated, after a fashion, and tried to look very sympathetic. The pretty charwoman commiserated too and wrung her hands, but her emotions for the most part were reserved for the clerk.

"Into the stone jug with 'em!" exclaimed Mr. Icks, with an angry toss of his fist. He stopped for a moment to reconsider; then a new light filled his eyes and he broke into a dry chuckle. "No. No. Not the stone jug. That's too soft for the likes o' them. There's a harder way. Aye! Why not give them rascals the same medicine as is doled out by the hangman? Why not treat 'em to a dose o' their own physic? Aye! Aye! There's justice in that. Why not treat 'em as them murderers is treated — them that swings from the gibbet?"

The gentleman in black drew himself up, still on tiptoe, and dropped his voice into a lower register. "Do ye know what's done with the bodies, friend Scribbler?" he asked, with a very significant inclination of the head. "The bodies of the murderers — after they hauls 'em down off the gibbet. What do ye suppose happens to them bodies, eh?"

Upon hearing such words as "murderers," "bodies," and "gibbet," Mr. Scribbler began to look very frightened. With his eyes riveted on the smoked lenses, he rolled his head slowly from side to side to express his ignorance as to the fate of those bodies.

"Them bodies, friend Richard," replied Mr. Icks — in a voice reduced now to a grim whisper — "them bodies is given up for *dissection*."

This dreaded word caused the eyes of Mr. Scribbler to grow very large indeed. He covered his gaping mouth with a hand and directed a horrified stare at Samson Icks.

"Dissected, aye. *A-na-to-mized*. Not coffined in the ground like good honest folk, but given up for dissection, Mr. Richard, for the young medical men to practice on."

The lips of Mr. Scribbler trembled violently and his eyes began to water. He shifted his frightened glance from Mr. Icks to Bridget, seeking confirmation of the horror that had been described to him. The pretty charwoman could only nod in assent.

"And that's how old Icks would make a go o' this execution — if things was up to old Icks, that is," said the dapper man in pinstripes, relishing with an artist's sensibility the portrait of justice he had painted for Mr. Scribbler. He rubbed his hands in delight before depositing them again in his pockets. "My acquaintance Bob, now — he'd find agreement with Icks on that. Bob ain't a social fellow, he'd tell ye so himself — he ain't a socialite. But he'd like to see that tall nasty rascal swing just as much as old Icks would. Do ye know that Bob, Mr. Richard? He's a character, that one. Lives along the waterside. Black circles round his eyes like a raccoon, and an ugly squint."

Mr. Scribbler indicated by a roll of his head that he was not acquainted with that unsociable character.

"Aye, but there's yet a third rascal, friend Richard — a deep one — what would give them two in there a good name by comparison. A gentleman he is, by the looks of him — but looks can be a wery bad indicator. For it's my studied opinion that this certain young gentleman is worse than them two in there and my acquaintance Bob put together." Mr. Icks stole another cautious glance into the dark corners of the office before asking, in a voice barely above a whisper —

"Do ye know what the fat rascal in there has had me a-doin'?"

As usual Mr. Scribbler did not know.

"He's had me a-spyin' on this certain young gentleman. Aye! For secret intelligence, o' course. And do ye know what else, friend Scribbler? This certain gentleman as I have mentioned — this same gentleman is the fat rascal's client. Aye, aye!" — (this last in response to the astonishment in Mr. Scribbler's face) — "He has me a-spyin' on one of his wery own clients! And this certain gentleman being one of his clients, it's quite plain that ye yerself, Mr. Richard, have seen this gentleman here in this wery office, and not so long ago, neither. He's new to town, and Winch has had me on him night and day, a-keepin' track of him, and a-sniffin' out things about him. But that certain gentleman, Mr. Richard — aye, what old Icks could tell ye about him, sir! For I think it'd make that fat rascal shiver in his breeches if he had the faintest notion what a deep one he was a-dealin' with there. And that's the pretty part of it!"

"La, I thought I were the pretty part of it," spoke up Bridget, with a laugh and a toss of her eyes for Mr. Scribbler's benefit.

"Ye are, Bridget, ye are, dear, but pray don't interrupt," said Mr. Icks, reprovingly. "As I was saying, Mr. Richard — the pretty part of it is this: that fat rascal has had me a-spyin' on one of his own clients, a young gentleman what you have seen in this wery office. The fat rascal, knowing the gentleman's a stranger to Salthead, sets old Icks a-sniffin' after anything dark, anything hidden, anything compromising, anything less than honorable, anything *not quite right* concerning that young gentleman, what might put that gentleman in the fat rascal's power. But the pretty part is that the joke, friend Scribbler, is on the fat rascal — for it's that certain young gentleman what is going to have power over everybody else."

Here Mr. Icks took to a heavy swaying of his head, what with the gravity of the knowledge held within it. "What I've seen in that certain gentleman's house, friend Scribbler! Aye, old Icks has been there — how or why ain't up for discussion, but I've been there, and I've seen something awful there that would make all yer hairs stand on end" — and despite his apprehension concerning the certain young gentleman, Samson Icks couldn't resist here a dry little chuckle at Mr. Scribbler's expense — "as if they wasn't already!"

Even if Mr. Scribbler could have comprehended this remark he would have had little time to do so, for the door to the inner chamber swung open and one of the closeted rascals — the fat one — appeared on the threshold. Seeing immediately how the land lay, he aimed a finger of warning at the clerk.

"Scribbler — Puddleby — *now!*" barked the attorney, his gold watch-chain a-jingle at his waist. He licked his lips and angled his crooked head in the direction of Mr. Icks, who was in the process of climbing down from the table-top. "Icks — you're here. Ahem. Stop distracting that young idiot — he has important matters to hand. Did you hear that, Scribbler? As you're here, Icks, be apprised that Mr. Josiah Tusk — ahem — is in my chambers at this very moment. He and I have been preparing the documents of execution — ahem — and they are nearly complete. Stay for me — there will be instructions directly regarding the disposition of the stock. Ahem. And stop pestering that young fool." He narrowed his eyes at Richard Scribbler, waiting until the clerk was again at his work before retreating to the inner sanctum.

Mr. Scribbler did everything he could to avoid the eyes of the two visitors. With great ceremony he spent some minutes busily ordering and settling the writing materials before him. He thumbed through the enormous volume, checking entries here and there and removing several loose papers he found

47

inside. He set the candle here, he set the candle there. Satisfied, he retrieved a quill from his hair and dipped the nib into the ink, ready at last to deal with Puddleby. No sooner had he begun scratching at the parchment, however, than a familiar voice came to him from below.

"La, Mr. Scribbler — why do you do everything that man says?" asked Bridget, with a sniff. "What's he, your mother?"

To his credit Mr. Scribbler made a great effort not to hear this, directing his concentration instead upon the important matter at hand.

"He ain't his mother, that ye can be sure on," said Samson Icks, scrambling back onto the table-top. "That fat rascal ain't got nothing of the milk o' human kindness in him. He's larded over with self-importance, that one is."

This effusion having little apparent effect on the clerk, Mr. Icks, in mountaineer spirit, launched himself onto the law-books and ledgers piled up beside him. Using his fingers and the points of his boots he picked his way carefully up the side of the volcano, until he had reached a spot nearly even with the edge of Mr. Scribbler's writing-table. There he clung like a lizard, staring very hard at the clerk through his smoked lenses.

"Powdering away again, are ye?" he chuckled. "Ain't that dainty!"

"He's a sensitive young man," said Bridget. "La, Mr. Scribbler, are you listening to Mr. Samson Icks when he asks you questions? He's your greatest friend except one, you know, and she's not going to wait for you forever."

"He's listening, he is," nodded Mr. Icks, with some justification, for he had observed that the concentration of Mr. Scribbler already was wavering — as denoted by a few intermittent stoppages of his pen, a drift of his pupils toward the corners of his eyes, a yawn, a ruffling of his hair.

"It's time for Bridget to be about her charring," said the pretty charwoman. "But she really shouldn't go without that kiss. La, Mr. Scribbler, won't you come down and powder away with Bridget a little before she leaves?"

"Scratch the kiss — Icks is talking coin," said Samson Icks, in a low voice, straining to draw the clerk's attention from his labors. "What it is, is a proposition, friend Scribbler — a proposition to undertake a small service. A wery small service — with, o' course, expectation of emolument."

At the mention of money Mr. Scribbler's quill stiffened. His eyes slid from side to side a few times, very slyly, under narrowed lids. His brow lifted and stretched. He laid his pen aside, straightened his waistcoat and bent down from his chair, folding his hands on his knees and gazing into the smoked lenses with an expression of renewed interest.

"Aye," exhaled Mr. Icks — half to himself, and half out of breath from clinging to the book-stacks — "I thought that would gain yer attention. Friend Richard — ye'll pardon my impertinence for asking — but what does that fat rascal give ye now? Can it be more than — eighteen bob a-week, eh?"

Mr. Scribbler's face sank and he shook his head, quite *triste*.

"Fifteen?"

Another gloomy turn of head and hair.

"Twelve?"

No, not twelve either.

"Ten, then?"

The clerk confirmed the figure with a dismal nod.

"A sad case. A wery sad case. Just ten bob a-week." A whistle escaped the lips of Samson Icks, but at a slightly higher pitch than he'd intended owing to the exertion of clinging to the stacks. "Tell me — do ye know the Cutting Duck, the old public house on Highgate Hill, Mr. Richard? The one as overlooks the harbor. Old Icks is often there, most days. Stop and see him later in the week — at yer convenience, o' course. There is something to yer financial benefit I have to propose to ye."

Their conversation was terminated by the opening again of the door to Lawyer Winch's chambers. Instead of the fat attorney, however, it was the long shadow of the miser that filled the doorway. As he glided into the outer room his eyes lighted on a pretty scene.

"Winch," said the miser, in his coldest manner, "what is that man doing up there?"

The attorney, who had followed Josiah into the room at a respectful distance, halted in his tracks. His eyeglass popped from his eye and his face wrinkled with displeasure, at sight of his agent hanging from the stacks. He wiped his bald head and waved a sheaf of papers in exasperation at the dapper man in black.

"Icks! Stop bothering that young scatterbrain and get down from there. Scribbler — ahem — Puddleby quarter-sheets — done?"

Mr. Scribbler promptly held aloft several sheets of parchment for Mr. Winch to gaze on at long distance.

"Excellent. Ahem. Puddleby senior will be most appreciative."

The attorney might have been less than gratified, however, had he known that the sheets championed by the beaming clerk were in fact covered with no more than the few stray lines he had managed to scratch out during the visit of Samson Icks and Bridget.

"Scribbler — ahem — your attention, please," said Mr. Winch, with cross-glances at a very stern-faced Josiah. "It is as you know — ahem — a tremendous honor for the firm to be visited by so noteworthy a client, so venerable a philanthropist, so eminent — ahem — a representative of the majestic world of commerce, as Mr. Josiah Tusk. Ahem. Mr. Tusk and I, in mutual consultation — ahem — and with due consideration, have now completed — ahem — the preliminary drafts of the documents of execution. I have them here."

With excessive formality he indicated the sheaf of papers in hand.

"Scribbler — ahem — you will prepare the required number of copies as rapidly as possible. Ahem. Once the documents have been signed and sealed, the execution order — ahem — from the sheriff will be carried out by Icks and his associates."

The attorney stepped round to Mr. Scribbler's chair and handed up the papers. Meanwhile the wiry Mr. Icks had completed his descent from the volcano. Brushing the law-dust from his coat, he adjusted his smoked lenses and hat in hand came to attention before his employer. Over them both hovered the tall form of the miser, a gaunt and sinuous spirit that seemed to darken all it surveyed.

Lawyer Winch cleared his voice. "It would seem, Mr. Tusk — ahem — that the necessary business of the morning has now been transacted. Ahem. Our house is in order, and the documents are being made ready even as I speak." (One uneasy sidelong glance at his clerk, who for now at least seemed to be busily at work). "Should there be any related service the firm can offer at present — "

"A word with your man Wicks, if you please," said Josiah, more in the form of a command than a request.

The attorney yielded at once, bowing his crooked head and extending a hand as though to say — "There's the fellow, have a go at him, do with him as you will."

The miser's boots creaked as he took a long step forward. "Now then, Mr. Sticks — "

"Ah — begging yer pardon, sir — but the name is Icks, sir. As is spelled I-C-K-S. Not Wicks. Not Sticks. *Icks*. As in *Samson Icks*. Always has been, always will be," said the dapper little man in black, with uncharacteristic sharpness. No expression could be read through the smoked lenses, though the cheeks of Mr. Icks had acquired a flush that pointed up the brickness of his brick-red complexion.

The attorney for his part turned a ghastly shade of white and stared at his agent in open-mouthed amazement. Mr. Scribbler, powdering away, ceased powdering and leaned across his writing-table to see what was the matter. Behind Mr. Icks the silent figure of Bridget visibly cringed.

Slowly, searchingly, the great white head of the miser swiveled on its turret, swinging round until the sharp falcon-eyes had fastened on Samson Icks.

"I know your name, sir," rumbled the head. "Do you think I don't? Do you think I'd address you if I didn't know you? What do you take me for? Well, you'll listen to me, Mr. Hicks, for I know you very well, sir."

"And I know ye," replied Mr. Icks, firmly, but adding quickly, "sir."

Lawyer Winch staggered back, wonder-struck, and wiped his head. His eyes darted rapidly from one figure to the other.

The miser responded with a malevolent frown that would have pierced the heart of the stoutest oak. For several moments he stood thus, immobile, as though considering in his mind whether to flay the miscreant now or let him squirm a little first. Then the frown dissolved into a look of predatory curiosity, by which he appeared to be sizing up the gentleman in black and taking the measure of his impertinence.

"I see. I see. Very well, Mr. Bicks," he said, with the grim little smile playing at the corners of his mouth. "You have made your pretty statement — it has been a long time coming, no doubt — and so I shall make mine."

Mr. Icks awaited this pronouncement in the full light of the miser's baleful glare.

"You know very well, Mr. Flicks, that I'm not a man for chatter. Chatter is not for me. But your case will prove an exception. To put the matter plainly: I don't like you — never have, never will." (At this cunning mockery of Mr. Icks, the grim smile fleetingly became a smirk). "You're an idler and a bungler and a dodge. Your conduct in affairs of business with which I have been concerned has been, more often than not, exceedingly unprofessional, while your sense of duty and responsibility to your employer — the firm that provides you with your daily bread and butter — has been, from my perspective, grossly deficient. You're a joker and a flash. Simply put, *you are everything I am not*. Because I am a man of business, Mr. Wicks, and am widely known as a conscientious man, I cannot in good conscience overlook such behavior."

"And ye," returned Mr. Icks, standing his ground, but with something noticeably a-tremble in his legs, "are a bully. Sir."

Lawyer Winch licked his lips and for a wild instant fancied that this must be a scene from a play, and these chambers a playhouse, and he a spectator in that playhouse, and that somehow, someone had neglected to tell him. He clamped a hand to the top of his head to keep his brain from boiling over.

"You object to an occasional liberty taken with your name. So be it; that is your prerogative," said the miser. "Object all you wish, it does not concern me. Let it instead stand as a lasting symbol of my disregard for you. Were it not for the years of fruitful service provided me by this firm, first in the form of Mr. Ephraim Badger, and more recently his successor, Mr. Winch" — here the plum-colored bulk of the attorney sighed in relief — "I would have quitted these chambers long ago. You say I am a bully. You are entitled to your opinion, as I am to mine. So be it. I am not your employer. But our opinions of each other cannot be allowed to color our actions in areas of mutual concern. We are hard men of business, sir. We have not the luxury of opinions. Do we understand one another?"

Every muscle in the body of Mr. Icks was straining for composure. A river of perspiration stung his face and eyes, his heart seemed ready to leap from his ribs, there was a prickly tingle in his ears, his breath came in short, hurried gusts. Despite his best efforts the struggle was wearing him down.

"Aye," he said at last, with a peculiar huskiness in his voice. This was followed by a little gasp of thanksgiving from Bridget, and a fit of head-wiping on the part of Mr. Winch. Mr. Scribbler rested his chin in his hand and watched in fascination.

"Now then, Mr. Ticks," began Josiah, in his jauntiest manner, as if nothing in the least remarkable had just occurred, "you will attend closely to your employer's every instruction regarding the matter that has called me here today. I needn't remind you that it is of the greatest professional interest to me. Your services as agent to the firm are required — see that you do not disappoint. Your associates are prepared to act?"

"Aye, sir."

"Then tell me, Mr. Kicks," said Josiah, folding his long bony arms upon his chest, "do you know how to drive a herd of thunder-beasts?"

Despite the incipient *rapprochement*, Mr. Icks bristled at the continuing ill-treatment accorded him and his name. It was not a new taunt for Josiah, but one that he had practiced and perfected over time. His resolve quickening, Mr. Icks comforted himself in the knowledge that, should his designs prosper, a far greater power than old Icks would soon confront Mr. Josiah Tusk.

"I know something of the creatures, sir — the big shovel-tuskers and the like — and I'm familiar with the Hoakum matter, o' course. Might I ask where we'll be driving 'em to?"

"South — the precise destination to be announced later. And so our friend Mr. Bouncing and Coaches soon will be taking leave of his precious beasts. We must show him, Mr. Jicks, what it means to honor one's financial obligations, what the consequences are of taking money that is not one's own. We will put a period to the existence of his little enterprise. That, no doubt, will teach him."

The miser abruptly whirled on his attorney — "Winch, I trust I shall hear from you!" — before launching himself with that bold superior stride towards the outer door of the chamber. He hurtled past Samson Icks and Bridget with the force of a whirlwind, a swirling vortex that seemed to sweep up all the darkness in the room and carry it along. "Many happy returns of the day to you," he smiled, without looking at anyone. The darkness followed him through the door; so that despite the smoky air and the lack of daylight, the chambers of Badger and Winch became noticeably cheerier for his absence.

The cheeriness, however, did not extend to the fat attorney in the plum-colored suit.

"Icks — in here — now," he growled, inclining his crooked head in the direction of the inner sanctum. The sour expression on his face was duly noted by Samson Icks. Not only did the attorney look as though he had just been hanged, he appeared to be anticipating a certain dapper gentleman's joining him in that exercise. Prepared for a raking-down Mr. Icks straightened his pinstripes, clamped his fists into his trouser-pockets, and followed the provider of his daily bread into the secret chamber.

"La, have you ever seen or heard anything like that, in all your life?" exclaimed Bridget, once the heavy door had shut. "I thought he was about to be perforated through the heart — such looks in that tall rascal's eyes! I can't believe what's gotten into poor Icks. `Never a kind word from that tall nasty rascal' — la! there's not many kind words been spoken in this place today, that's certain. And now poor Icks is getting his, I'm sure. Imagine him speaking that way to a client — and that the richest cove in Salthead! La, Mr. Scribbler — "

Her wandering monologue failed to catch the attention of Mr. Scribbler, who had returned to his labors and so was scratching away again at his parchments. Unable to lure the clerk from his high seat, the pretty charwoman abandoned the effort and took up her bucket. A thing like a sigh escaped her lips, and her eyes lost some of their blue.

"I wish you were kinder," she murmured, quietly. She looked at her feet and shook her head in disbelief of herself, before turning and going out.

Mr. Scribbler, meanwhile, had early set aside the drafts of the documents of execution, which were of such import to Mr. Tusk, to resume his work on behalf of the onrushing Puddleby. Such conscientiousness on the part of Richard, in so ordering his priorities in favor of the client expected by the late coach from Newmarsh, would no doubt have been applauded by Josiah, had he known anything of it. After all, Mr. Josiah Tusk was a man of business, and Mr. Richard Scribbler was a clerk of business; and was not Josiah widely known as a conscientious man?

Presently, a chastened Samson Icks emerged from the audience chamber of the attorney. A cloud lay settled on his features. His mouth was fixed in a straight line, with the upper lip tightly curled. It was evident that all his powers of self-restraint had been mobilized; though at present he seemed to be receiving from his employer nothing more censorious than a few instructions regarding the matter of the mastodons.

After a few minutes the plum-colored bulk of the attorney whirled round and secreted itself once more in its private vault. Mr. Icks slammed hat to head and moved thoughtfully toward the outer door, with his hands in his pockets. On the verge of departing he called out to the clerk —

"I trust ye'll remember Highgate Hill and the Cutting Duck, friend Richard."

Mr. Scribbler paused, quill in hand. By way of reply his eyebrows rose and a sly smile filled his lips. The sharp line of Samson's mouth lifted at the edges as something of his old manner returned.

No sooner had Mr. Icks opened the outer door, however, than he immediately whisked it shut and propped his back against it, with his arms outspread at his sides. A rush of wild imaginings stirred behind the smoked lenses, like a covey of startled birds taking wing. Slapping a hand to his hat he dodged beneath a lump of furniture in the nearest corner — one with a particularly large volcano perched on it — where he could safely observe without being observed himself.

The door swung open and the object of Samson's anxiety made its appearance. Mr. Scribbler peered down at the object — a fashionable young gentleman with a broad mustache, a finely-hewn chin, and large dark eyes that smoldered beneath a haughty pair of arched brows.

"Winch is expecting me," stated that gentleman.

The clerk, after appraising the visitor with a quick up-and-down, knitted his brows very severely and jerked his quill in the direction of the inner sanctum. The fashionable young gentleman in the bottle-green coat strode past and without announcement breezed into the private office of the attorney.

Mr. Icks, seeing the visitor safely deposited, crept from his hiding-place and with a wave of his arm caught the attention of Richard Scribbler. In great excitement he pointed to the door of the inner sanctum, hammering the air repeatedly with his forefinger. The clerk's eyes reflected only puzzlement at first; then his brows sprang up and his lips rounded themselves into an "O." He aimed his quill at the door with a questioning look. Mr. Icks nodded emphatically, mouthing the words — "*certain young gentleman.*"

Mr. Scribbler looked at the door with a changed attitude. Samson Icks, after directing his smoked lenses at that same door a few times more, passed out of the chamber with a scowl on his face, and the images of Mr. Josiah Tusk, Lawyer Winch and the fashionable gentleman haunting his cranium.

CHAPTER VI

In Friday Street

THE buckskin mare stepped lightly, and at an easy gait, nimbly picking her way among the cobbled stones of the road. As she jogged on, effortlessly, with her legs bounding beneath her, her graceful head poised and alert, her ears pricked forward, her dark mane whiffling in the wind, she glowed with that innate energy and confidence that is so marvelous to behold in a beautiful horse. Like any animal — or person — exercising a natural talent, the mare seemed absorbed in some private world of her own design, the essence of her elemental self; and so caught the attention of onlookers simply by her beauty and her motion and her power.

"This is my calling. This is what I do. There is no sense in being modest, for I am good at what I do. Nor have I any hesitation in showing you how well I do it. I am the best." So might those observing the mare's progress along the road have gathered, despite the improbability of their ever being privy to her inmost thoughts. Well, I suppose there may perhaps have been something more — at least some little bit more — on her mind, in the late afternoon of such a cold, cold day; something very much like — "I am hungry, and eager to be home."

Behind her the mare drew an old gig — still shiny in spots, grown rusty in others — which rattled along at a comfortable pace. The driver, with his rug and muffler wrapped about him, was maneuvering the reins and whip with less than optimal efficiency, owing to his having to raise one or the other gloved hand to his head, every few moments, to keep his hat from flying off.

The way led through an avenue of disheveled little houses — sadly tattered as to doors and windows, and rumpled as to chimneys and gable-ends — then into a crooked lane and along a narrow byroad. The ring of gig-wheels and the clink of shoes rebounded from the walls of the buildings. High overhead, the feeble attempts of the sun to burst forth in glory had long since come to naught. The afternoon was languishing under a drizzly gray shroud, which threatened every now and again to release a full-fledged torrent.

Beyond a far corner the road opened onto a broader prospect. The cobbled stones gave way to a muddied track, while still farther along, after a second turn, the buildings dropped back to reveal the lofty crags and wild soaring pinnacles that marked the eastern limits of the city. The road began to angle upward in a direction generally parallel to the mountains. The houses thereabouts were less numerous but noticeably finer structures, which stood in their own grounds and were abundantly supplied with greenery.

Before one particular villa the driver of the gig, attracted by something he had glimpsed from the corner of an eye, hastily drew rein.

"Well, indeed," likely ran the thoughts of the buckskin mare at this interruption in the journey. "I believe this would be an excellent time for a rest, excellent — on any day but this. This will only delay home and my feed-bucket. Oh, let me chase the wind again! What can he find so interesting about this dreary place?"

Dreary was just the word. Little resembling the other well-tended houses along the road, apart from its composition — blue-gray stone with facing elements of brick — it was an enormous, dismal, gloomy place, set well back from the road behind impressive area railings. Glacial arches, twisted chimneys and menacing gables sprouted from its time-stained frontage. From the roof, high above the entrance-door, a group of sullen stone angels glared at visitors. The rich mantle of ivy so common to the walls of the neighboring houses was nowhere in evidence; instead, desolation dripped from the eaves.

A general air of decay pervaded the entire scene. Even the old oaks in the yard looked to be wilting, the hedges seemed sad; the very grass emitted a melancholy. Still, it was the house itself that commanded the greatest attention. If one gazed at it long enough and hard enough, an imaginary transformation might take place in the mind's eye, in which the house seemed to come alive and be glowering like the face of a monstrous troll, rising out of the earth; with two oriel windows for eyes and a roof and chimneys for a hat, and a crumbling expanse of stairs beneath the front entrance like a mouthful of broken teeth.

What caused the driver of the gig to stop, however, was not the house or its joyless surroundings — for he passed them often on his way — but the lone figure of a servant who was dodging wildly about the grounds like a rubber ball. He had first been spotted charging from a side entrance, from where he vanished round a corner of the building. Re-appearing on the other side of the house he ran to the stable-yard, then to the back-garden. Then in at the side-entrance and out at the front door, now dashing to and fro between the pilasters and along the crumbling stone steps, wringing his hands — all the while calling out what appeared to be the same few indistinguishable syllables in a voice of growing agitation.

At some point he became aware of the driver observing from the road. He covered the intervening distance in a flash and threw himself against the gate in the area railing, clutching at the bars with white fingers.

"Have you seen him?" he demanded, in terrible earnest and nearly out of breath.

"Seen whom?" asked the driver.

"A large ferocious dog, of course!" returned the servant, who from his dress and demeanor was evidently a footman.

"Where?"

"Anywhere! A large ferocious dog — Turk — canine variety — the old man's mastiff. He's gone and disappeared — the dog, that is. You haven't seen him?"

"Oh, that one. Sorry — afraid not," said the driver, rubbing his gray bristle-brush head.

"This is dreadful. When the old man returns to find his dog has up and gone, it will be my turn to up and go. Thrown upon my beam-ends at my time of life! Oh, I just know it. I can see it all now, the whole dreadful panorama. It's all too dreadfully, painfully clear."

"I'm sure he'll turn up. More than likely he's just sniffing about somewhere," said Professor Tiggs — for it was he driving the gig — with one or two brief visual scans of the vicinity. "Someone is bound to recognize him. That's not an easy animal to forget."

"I know, I know," returned the footman, with wild staring eyes. "The dog listens to no one anymore, not even the old man. He's been a bad lot for years — the dog, that is — but of late he's gone positively unmanageable. Won't heel, won't obey — does absolutely whatever he pleases. You've seen him — would *you* care to discipline him? No one has any idea what's gotten into the brute. The veterinary left just yesterday, shaking his head. Wait until he discovers the old man has no intention of paying him, for want of a diagnosis — then he'll be shaking his fist!"

"How long has the dog been missing?"

"I don't know. He was here a few hours ago, sprawled like a drunken sot in the back-garden. I didn't take any particular notice of him. Perhaps I should have. Then he just seemed to be gone. Now I'll be paying for it, dreadfully. I just know it."

"But why should the dog be your responsibility? Surely, at least the groom — "

"What groom?" asked the footman, with a scornful laugh.

"If not a groom, then perhaps a stable-hand — "

"Stable-hand?"

"Or a kennel-boy — "

"Ha!" scoffed the footman.

The professor halted, gazing past the footman toward the dreary premises. The unkempt condition of the house and grounds, the known parsimonious habits of the master, the plight of the footman — all converged and connected and made perfect sense, as he saw just how things stood in the miser's household.

"You must have someone at least to prepare the meals, to wash up the plates and glasses, to — "

"Not a living leg. Look at these hands," lamented the footman, extending the indicated items through the bars for the professor's inspection. "Worse than a scullery-maid's!"

"I see. Sorry — didn't realize the extent of your predicament," said the professor. He resumed his seat and took up the reins. "As for that dog — he'll turn up soon, I should think. Should I spy him along the way I'll send word. Good luck. Perhaps it's a blessing."

"Obliged!" returned the footman, and hurried back to the house.

"Walk on, Maggie," said the professor to the mare, with a light touch of the whip. The last view he had, as the house glided by, was of the footman vaulting up the steps and calling loudly for the dog, his speech interspersed, I should imagine, with not a few unprintables.

The muddy track soon leveled off, and as the gig was negotiating yet another turn something large and dark passed overhead. Glancing up the professor saw that it was a huge black bird, something along the lines of a vulture. It wasn't just the size of the creature, but the brilliant crimson hue of the head and neck, that sent a disturbing chill through him.

It was unusual for teratorns to venture so close to the city. Ordinarily they avoided the coast, their range being restricted to the fells and the cold mountain meadows beyond; it was rare to find one seaward of the crags. They were odious creatures, vicious predators with a fearsome reputation. Unlike vultures they often forsook carrion in favor of living prey — and not simply small game. There were those far up in the mountains who claimed to have seen teratorns, in groups of two or three, set upon a full-grown saber-cat and drag it to ground. Whether or not such a thing could possibly be, however, remained for most people a matter for conjecture.

Superstition held that the appearance of a teratorn so near the city was a portent of evil to come. The professor watched the bird glide across the sky, like a black shadow on the clouds. The eyes in the crimson head searched the landscape below, meticulously, impersonally, as the creature circled round in the direction of the Tuskan villa. For a moment the professor found himself concerned for the safety of the missing dog; recalling however that animal's notable deficiencies of character, he very quickly found himself less concerned. When he looked again the bird was gone.

The road straightened out and the scenery grew increasingly wooded. A light rain had begun to fall as the professor directed the gig into Friday Street, then along a graveled drive beside a very pleasant house and so into the sheltered yard behind. There a narrow, wheezy old fellow in stable-clothes took the mare in hand, patting her affectionately on the shoulder, and greeted the professor with a tip of his black bowler.

"An unpleasant afternoon, I think, Tom," said the professor. He discarded his rug and jumped to the ground, plucking his thick valise from the floor of the gig.

"You saw the bird, sir?" asked Tom, a genial soul with a face like old boxwood. He had great puffy lips and flaring side-whiskers and was partial to clay pipes in addition to black bowlers.

"Yes, I did."

"It don't mean nowt that's good," asserted the groom. He released the buckskin from her harness and led her toward the stable.

"Ah, Tom — one thing. The miser's dog is on the prowl. You know the one — the big brindled mastiff. Keep a look-out for him, will you? The servant's frantic."

"Another bad sign," murmured Tom Spike, with a long shake of his head. "On a good day, that's a bad dog. Come along, Maggie dear," he said to the mare, "we'll have you all dry and comfortable, and then we'll see what dainties old Tom has prepared for you."

The professor hurried across the stable-yard to the house. It was a cheery, pleasant, smiling old house of modest proportions, and so in sharpest possible contrast to the miser's abode. It was a marvelously cozy half-timbered structure of three floors, with a tiled roof of many gables surmounted by picturesque chimney-stacks. It had lath-and-plaster walls, scrubbed very white, with black timber framing, and tiny lattice windows that glowed with a welcoming blush of firelight.

"Why, hallo there, young man," exclaimed the professor, coming upon an orange tabby cat perched on the back-stairs of the house. "And how did you pass your day?"

The cat responded with some excited murmurings in the feline tongue, and applied himself with great assiduity to the professor's trouser-legs. The professor scratched the tabby's head and ears and was rewarded with an explosion of vehement purring. He opened the door and the cat scurried through it into the house, noisily announcing his return.

"Hallo, Mrs. Minidew," the professor called out, depositing his hat and great-coat on a stand in the back-passage. He drew off his gloves and rubbed his hands together vigorously. "I see that Mr. Pumpkin Pie has not been a stranger to his food today," he said, observing the condition of the crockery bowl reserved for the orange tabby.

"It's your Mr. Rime, sir," said a good-natured woman with twinkling eyes, who turned to greet him from the kitchen fire where she was stirring a large pot of soup. She had bright strawberry hair and a bright strawberry complexion, a disarming smile, and a surfeit of dimples. She had passed through her middle years and acquired now a certain ampleness of form that often attends the journey. "He's at his rounds again and I'm afraid has been particularly generous to Pie. He seems to feel that he is more than ever in your debt, sir, considering the recent excitement."

The professor nodded without replying. Thoughts of the cat's-meat man, of the Misses Jacks and the dancing sailor who was dead, together with the appearance of the teratorn, filled his mind and added their weight to a subtle disquiet that had been gathering there. He caught up his valise and directed his steps toward the staircase, then abruptly pivoted on his heel and whisked back to the kitchen.

"Ah, Mrs. Minidew — I very nearly forgot. Young Mr. Kibble will be with us again for dinner. Will you set an extra place for him?"

His housekeeper cast him a knowing look. "I do suppose it's Laura, isn't it? I know when a young man takes a fancy to a young lady, and sir — your Mr. Kibble is one hopelessly smitten young man. Do you realize, Miss Dale has been with us barely these two months and this is already his fifth call?"

"Now, Mrs. Minidew, please don't read anything into his visit that is not there. Mr. Kibble has been applying himself to his work very diligently these past several weeks. Absolutely indefatigable he is, and a very polite and scholarly young fellow as well. He's remained behind to complete some memoranda I've asked him to bring along. You must agree, Mrs. Minidew, it would be very ungracious of me to have him ride clear out here, at this hour, and not invite him to dinner. As for your hypothesis regarding a supposed attachment to Miss Dale, I imagine you're exaggerating."

He spoke these last words with a glint in his eye and a rub or two of his bristle-brush head, which signaled to the widow Minidew that he understood very well what she meant.

At the staircase the professor was ambushed by a tiny figure, which leaped giggling from the shadows and attached itself to the sleeve of his mulberry coat. Setting down his valise he knelt and folded the child in his arms, kissing her cheeks and smoothing her lustrous hair.

"How are you, Fiona dear? Why, you certainly frightened your old uncle! What are you playing at now, eh?"

"I'm a bear, Uncle Tiggs. Didn't you recognize me? I've jumped out of my cave and surprised you."

"An exceedingly small bear, it seems to me. But I'm certainly glad you aren't a real one."

"I think it would be ever so much fun to have a bear. May we have one, please?" asked the child, with bright glowing eyes.

"Bears are very large and unruly creatures, I'm afraid, dear. They don't like people, you know, and they certainly wouldn't tolerate having a little girl about! What's more, our house is far too small — there isn't nearly enough space for a bear here."

"Not enough space?"

"Oh, no. Bears can't live in houses. They require lots and lots of room. That is why they live in those enormous caves far up in the mountains. You see, bears need all the meadows and valleys and forests and streams to ramble in."

"Oh," said Fiona, sorely disappointed.

"And so where is Miss Dale?"

"She has been helping Mrs. Minidew with the cooking, but now she is upstairs in her room with her books. She reads ever so much. She's very studious, you know."

The professor looked into the pretty face of his niece — his ward and sole living relation — with unqualified delight. "And so should you be," he whispered, nuzzling a tiny nose with his own far more substantial one, and so eliciting a flood of giggles. "Miss Dale is your governess, after all. She's your tutor. She's expected to be studious."

"She's very studious, but still ever so much fun — not like old Sledge," said the child.

"`Old Sledge,' as you choose to call her," returned the professor, with facetious gravity, "was a trifle too studious, I must admit, even by our standards." Then, in a changed tone — "But truly you mustn't speak of her so, Fiona. Mrs. Sledge was taken with brain-fever very suddenly, you recall, and it's Dr. Dampe's opinion there is permanant damage. It was only by the greatest of good fortune that we were able to engage Miss Dale in her stead. You do like Laura, don't you?"

"Oh, yes, very much!" exclaimed Fiona, without hesitation.

"Very good. Now, then, please run up and tell her that Mr. Kibble will be joining us for dinner tonight."

A seemingly innocuous request, it produced only a wince and a tired little groan from Fiona.

"What's the matter, dear?"

"Not your Mr. Kibble again! Oh, Uncle Tiggs, he's so — so — so very boring."

"Now, then, young lady — "

"And ever so unfashionable — those horrid green glasses, and all!"

"Fiona, dear — listen to me," said the professor, taking his niece's tiny hands in his. "Mr. Kibble is a very earnest young man, and a fine scholar, and very honest, and an exceedingly hard worker. I couldn't ask for a better assistant. And what is more, I've reason to believe he's grown fond of Miss Dale during the short time she has been with us."

"But he's so boring, and I'm certain Miss Dale must think so too — "

"Fiona," said the professor, firmly.

A pause, with the child twisting some few strands of her hair into a knot, while casting long repeated looks of entreaty at her uncle. The professor, however, stood his ground like a champion.

"Very well," sighed Fiona. With downcast eyes and slow-footed tread, she dragged her martyred self up the staircase to deliver the fatal message.

"Thank you, dear," the professor called after her. He fished up his valise and ambled down the adjoining stairs to a small library, very comfortably panelled in cedarwood, that served as his private study. He put off his coat, raked the low fire in the grate, and sat down to his desk to light a pipe. After several minutes' serene and thoughtful meditation, he took up pen and ink and set to work on some items of correspondence that had been awaiting his attention.

And so passed half an hour, perhaps a little more. The sky went black; the rain beat fitfully against the windows. A wind blew up from the sea and at irregular intervals could be heard whistling past a corner of the house. Lightning flickered, thunder boomed. For a moment something like a howl rose above the general clamor. It was sufficiently distinctive for the professor to raise his head from his writing, his normally frank and genial expression effaced by a contraction of his brow. He listened. He smoked his pipe and listened some more. He peered through the window beside him, drumming a devil's tattoo on the desk-top. He glanced at the fire, at the paneled wainscot, at the book-shelves, at the comfortable sofa. Yes, that could have been the cry of a mastiff. Or perhaps a dire wolf — they weren't unknown on the edge of the city. Dog or wolf, or what was more likely simply the wind. Whatever it was, it wasn't heard again.

After sealing the letters and placing them in the dispatch-box, he put on his coat and returned to the main floor. There he found his secretary in the throes of arrival, dripping with rain but with the professor's memoranda safe and dry in a leather satchel. Gratefully Mr. Kibble surrendered his hat, his coat, and his mackintosh to Mrs. Minidew, who laid them to dry beside the fire in the kitchen. He wiped his unfashionable green spectacles and pounded his hair into submission with a comb.

As he and the professor stepped into the drawing-room, through the arch that opened from the hall, a young woman in a blue dress appeared at the foot of the stairs. The eyes of Mr. Kibble were immediately drawn to her as though by some irresistible influence.

"Hallo, Miss Dale. It's very g-good to see you again," said that most earnest young man.

The governess responded with a polite smile and her hand. "Good evening, Mr. Kibble. I'm happy to find you've made it safely through the storm. It's certainly turning into a frightful one."

Young Mr. Kibble mumbled some few incomprehensible syllables, all of which were lost in his contemplation of the young woman's face — her soft gray eyes from which the light of a keen intelligence emanated, her pretty brow, her nose, her smile, her firm round chin, her golden-brown hair curling about her neck and shoulders —

The eyebrows lifted over the soft gray eyes with an inquiring expression. "Yes? What is it, Mr. Kibble?"

Completely absorbed in his thoughts, Mr. Kibble awoke with a jolt to the realization that he was gawking — scrutinizing the object of his unspoken adoration blatantly, openly, unabashedly, with his mouth limply a-droop; that he was clutching her proffered hand tightly in his with an adhesive squeeze, and would not let it escape; that all the while the professor was standing off to one side, trying not to notice by artfully shifting his attention from one corner of the room to another.

"Yes — yes. Yes, indeed, it's — frightful weather," sighed Mr. Kibble, relinquishing the hand of Miss Laura Dale to her own safekeeping. He cleared his voice with a nervous cough that came perilously close to a retch. "Why, I do believe the cats and dogs have been tumbling left and right tonight. And such thunderclaps and lightning bolts — it's a wonder my nag Nestor didn't shy, or stumble, or buck me straight off, by G-God!"

Poor Mr. Kibble! Having crowned his embarrassment by hurling an unfortunate oath — it had simply slipped out — into the young woman's face, I believe he wanted then nothing more than to crawl off — miserable, wretched, and alone — into one of those corners the professor had been scouting. To conceal his distress (as if that were possible) he pressed a hand to his cheek and rotated toward the professor. "Ah — Tom's put Nestor in the stable, sir — in the stall beside Maggie's," he managed to stammer out. "He'll offer him his feed later, once he's had a chance to cool down — "

A skipping tread was heard in the hall as Fiona came bouncing down the stairs. She ran smilingly to Laura who put an arm around her and kissed her. At the same time Mrs. Minidew stepped round from the kitchen with a most welcome announcement.

"Dinner, ladies and gentlemen, if you please."

They gathered round the cloth-covered table in the small but very comfortable dining-room. The professor assumed his place at the top of the table, with Fiona on his left and Mr. Kibble at the bottom. Mr. Pumpkin Pie as well made an appearance, leaping onto a nearby chair, from which position he could observe the diners and so be alert to any and all signs of generosity on their part.

"Hanna, I'm afraid, is away in attendance on a sick relative," said Mrs. Minidew from the kitchen-door, "and so Laura will be assisting with the meal this evening."

There followed much to-ing and fro-ing from the kitchen, much clinking of glasses and clattering of china, as the food was laid upon the cloth. First came the soup, then some caraway-seed biscuits, some fried soles and some shrimps, a butter-boat of shrimp sauce and a large dish swimming with potatoes. These were followed by a baked shoulder of mutton, with walnut ketchup, some roasted apples, a fruit salad, parsley sprigs, sundry dishes of vegetables and a platter of saveloys. The dinner was rounded out by glasses of porter and some hot elder wine, well qualified with brandy and spice. And specially for Fiona, a little seltzer water with mint and cherry.

The laying-on of the meal completed for the moment, the governess took her place at the table opposite Fiona, with the professor to her left and Mr. Kibble to her right.

"This is positively delightful," enthused the secretary, warming quickly to his shrimps and porter. He was continually amazed at the quality and quantity of the board laid on at the professor's house. "I can't remember when I've tasted such a glorious shrimp sauce. And such potatoes — such apples — "

"Thank you, Mr. Kibble, I'm very pleased you like them," answered Mrs. Minidew, beaming. "It's always a pleasure to have you with us." Through the open door behind her old Tom Spike could be seen lounging at the little table in the kitchen, where he and the housekeeper would enjoy their private share of the comestibles.

"Miss Dale," said the professor, after a little time spent in silent enjoyment of the food, "I should like to take this opportunity to acknowledge the marvelous progress you have made in the education of my niece. In the short time you have been with us, you have exceeded all my hopes and expectations on that head. And it is quite plain to everyone how completely Fiona has taken to you. I want you to know how very much your care and consideration of her are appreciated."

"Thank you, sir," replied the young lady, blushing deeply. "May I say for my part that tutoring Fiona has proved to be an enormous pleasure. Your niece is a very bright little child, and very clever, and takes instruction readily. Really, sir, she makes my task quite effortless."

"Uncle Tiggs," said Fiona, cutting through her saveloy with a thoughtful expression. "I should like very much to study French."

The adults at the table traded glances.

"Well," said the professor, lightly patting his lips with a napkin. "That's very laudable of you, my dear. Perhaps we can have Miss Dale include some bits of French in your lessons."

"I've heard Mrs. Minidew speak French. It's a very beautiful language, it seems to me."

"It's a dead language," remarked Mr. Kibble.

"What is a dead language?" asked Fiona, with a look of innocent inquiry.

Mr. Kibble glanced at the professor and Laura, both of whom seemed interested to hear his response. He laid aside his knife and fork and adjusted his spectacles.

"It's called a dead language because no one has needed to use it for a very long time — above a hundred years at least," he said. "Certainly no one in Salthead has any need for it."

"Why is that?" asked Fiona. "Why doesn't anyone speak it any more? Mrs. Minidew's French words sounded ever so pretty. Mayn't I learn to speak French, too?"

"Of course you may, my dear, of course, if you'd like," smiled her uncle. "At one time, you know, the French language was one of the most important in the world. In those days every educated person spoke French. It was the language of the law and the language of royalty. But that was a very long time ago — hundreds of years in fact, and long before the sundering."

"What is the sundering?"

A crackle of thunder erupted almost directly overhead. The professor looked from his secretary to Miss Dale, as though gathering an unspoken consensus whether or not to embark upon the topic in question.

"The sundering is — is a part of history, dear," he answered slowly. "A `sundering' is a separation or a breaking-apart of something. That is what happened to the world, you see. Many centuries ago, when people first arrived here from England, tall sailing ships were voyaging to all sorts of new and fascinating places all over the world. They went absolutely everywhere, bringing people from the home countries out to the new lands and transporting exotic goods back home. Then, about a hundred and fifty years ago, it all came to an end — after a great tragedy occurred."

"What is a tragedy?"

"A tragedy," volunteered Miss Dale, after a pause, "is when something terrible happens to good people. In this case, it was darkness and cold — a ferocious winter which lasted for many years, and which was very hard on many, many good people."

"Did they die?" asked Fiona, regarding her governess with solemn attention, her face softly radiant in the candle-light.

"Yes, I'm afraid they did. Many of them. Most, in fact."

"But why should they have died if they were good people?"

"I don't know, dear. No one does."

"Nor does anyone truly know what happened at the sundering," spoke up Mr. Kibble. "According to some it was a fireball — a meteor or a comet, perhaps — that dropped from the sky, while others contend that it was a huge volcanic eruption. Perhaps it was both; no one can say for sure. Whatever the cause, the sky was filled with clouds of smoke and grew very dark, and remained that way for months and months. Then the great ice sheets came down from the north and froze up the world."

"I've seen England in my geography atlas," said Fiona. "It's an island, is it not, and very far away?"

"Yes, extremely far away. Across a great continent and a great ocean."

"And I've seen Europe as well. That is where France is?"

"Yes, that's where France is. Or was."

"Did the smoke and darkness come to Salthead? Did people die here, too?"

"Very few," replied the secretary. "We were amazingly fortunate — the disaster did not much affect us here, and so the people were able to go on with their lives. But by then the tall ships had stopped coming, and so there was no one to bring news of the greater world. All contact with England was lost. Since then, no one who has set out for England has ever returned. Indeed, no one knows if England still exists, or any other country for that matter. No one knows what has gone on there or what remains, if anything. No one goes there any more, and no one has come from there ever since."

"Perhaps they've forgotten about us," suggested Fiona.

Mr. Kibble shook his head gravely. "Unfortunately, I don't believe there is anyone there to do any forgetting. All we know for certain is that here in Salthead, and north to Saxbridge and a little beyond, and east as far as Richford, and south to the islands in the channel, we were spared."

"I see," said Fiona, quietly considering all she had heard, while toying with the remains of her saveloy. "It's very sad."

There followed a decided lull in the conversation. Laura, resolved to disperse the atmosphere of gloom that had fallen on the company, looked to her pupil.

"Fiona, dear — would you care to help me with the wonderful dessert Mrs. Minidew has prepared in the kitchen?"

The child brightened at once. "Oh, yes, very much, Miss Dale!"

"Then come along."

IN FRIDAY STREET

They soon returned with Fiona bearing an enormous platter of sugar-plums, followed by Laura with a tray of hardbake and Mrs. Minidew with a pot of chamomile tea.

"I believe this to be," said the professor, on sampling these latest culinary treasures, "the finest meal we ever have had in this house. Mrs. Minidew, Miss Dale — you have outdone yourselves today. You're — you're — absolutely indefatigable!"

"It's all positively delicious," seconded Mr. Kibble, with an enthusiastic nod.

At which juncture a few plaintive cries were lofted by Mr. Pumpkin Pie, who had abandoned the nearby chair for a better spot at the professor's feet, and was peering up with expectant eyes.

"Begging, I see. Young man," said the professor, addressing the cat, "where on earth are your manners?"

The dessert was indeed delectable. As a result the conversation became more animated, and so the time glided away unperceived. At length the plates were cleared and the cloth removed from the table. The gentlemen retired to the drawing-room, where the professor took to smoking his pipe and gazing into the fire, while Mr. Kibble sipped the remains of his chamomile tea.

A short while later a very sad-faced Fiona drooped in to tender her good-nights. The professor embraced her and kissed her forehead. Mr. Kibble shook her little morsel of a hand with the self-conscious formality of a man unused to children. She turned then and left with Miss Dale, who had been watching from under the arch in the hall.

As Mrs. Minidew had concluded the last of her labors in the kitchen, the professor saw fit to propose a little game of whist, which was agreed to with alacrity by both the housekeeper and Mr. Kibble. As soon as Laura returned and had lent her consent to the proposal, they chose sides and sat down to play. Mrs. Minidew, who was regarded as a very cagey whist-player, naturally selected Miss Dale for her partner, leaving Mr. Kibble and the professor to fend for themselves.

The cards had been flitting about the table for perhaps half an hour, when the pleasant crackling of the wood-fire in the grate was interrupted by a wild shout, the roaring of horses, and other sounds of disturbance emanating from the direction of the stable.

The professor and Mr. Kibble immediately jumped to their feet and ran for the back-passage.

"What in heaven's name is the matter?" exclaimed Mrs. Minidew.

The professor grabbed his hat and leaped out into the night, followed closely by the secretary. As they clambered down the back-stairs and splashed their way across the yard, a flash of lightning illuminated the figure of Tom Spike as he emerged from the barn, a sputtering torch in one hand and a ghastly look of horror on his face.

CHAPTER VII

Night Walk

THE leathery sound of wind in the trees — the incessant clatter of the rain — a crash of thunder in the cold black air — the smoking torch in the hand of Tom Spike, illuminating the darkness where he stood just under the eaves of the stable — such were the elements of the scene that greeted the professor and Mr. Kibble on their dash across the yard.

And from inside the stable, the awful cries of terrified horses.

"What is it, Tom?" shouted the professor, breathlessly, the rain pelting his coat and hat.

"You'll not want to go in *there*," warned Tom, with a toss of his head toward the barn. His eyes had grown to the size of hens' eggs, and the hand holding the torch visibly trembled.

"What is wrong with the horses? What is wrong with Maggie?"

"And Nestor?" asked Mr. Kibble.

More frightened cries from the stable.

"What is it, Tom? The horses — they sound as if they've gone mad!"

"It's not *them* that's mad. Not likely!" said the groom, his voice faltering.

"We must calm them. It's the storm, of course. You know how Maggie detests thunder and lightning. They drive her to distraction."

"I wish it were just that!" cried Tom Spike; but he volunteered no more. His lips were quivering. He shuddered, his clay pipe dropped from his mouth, his eyes stared fixedly at nothing. His face was pale; he looked as though he had seen a ghost.

The professor and Mr. Kibble traded a pair of hard glances. For an instant a sheet of lightning blew away the darkness. Thunder exploded in the clouds.

"What is it, Tom? What did you see in the barn?"

The groom made no reply, but seemed about to faint.

"Let me have that," said the professor, plucking the torch from his hand. "You must steady yourself — you must not overexert your energies. You have had a terrible fright. Go in the house, Tom. Go! Mr. Kibble and I will resolve the situation."

"If you can, sir!" whispered old Tom. He broke away and staggered toward the back-stairs, his eyes darting crazily here and there as though terrible things were going on in the darkness around him.

The professor crept through the door of the stable, with Mr. Kibble at his heel. The rays of the torch penetrated the nearer nooks and corners, chasing away the shadows and casting an irregular glow upon the stalls where the horses were.

The buckskin mare flattened her ears and voiced a challenge, which was echoed immediately by Nestor, the secretary's black gelding in the adjoining stall. A terrible sheen was evident on the flanks, neck, and shoulders of both animals.

"They're sweating like the very devil!" gasped Mr. Kibble.

The professor nodded. He approached the mare with the intent of calming her, but this served only to heighten her anxiety. She rolled her eyes and snorted, then spun about with her heels in the air.

"Maggie, Maggie, what has gotten into you!" exclaimed the professor.

"Could she be mad?" asked Mr. Kibble.

The mare halted and faced them over the door of the stall, dripping lather, with her nostrils blown wide and her forelegs shivering. Mr. Kibble attempted to approach his own horse but was rebuffed in like fashion. The gelding furiously stamped his legs and rattled his head. He pawed the ground, whipping up the straw and slapping his tail against his rump.

Mr. Kibble turned to the professor and was about to speak, but no words came. Instead he found himself gazing earnestly at his employer, whose eyes had grown very shrewd and become fixed on a point in the middle distance beyond the secretary's shoulder.

"Do not move, Mr. Kibble," said the professor, sternly. "Do not move, and do not turn around."

"What is it, sir?" whispered the secretary, inwardly aching to disregard his employer's injunction. "What do you see there?"

There was little need of a reply, for Mr. Kibble's suspense was to be short-lived. He heard a coarse, malevolent growl behind him. The professor lifted the torch and advanced with a measured tread in the secretary's direction.

"Mr. Kibble," he said quietly, "after I pass you, you may turn round and look. But stay behind me, please. And listen very closely. There is a hayfork leaning against the wall, just inside the door. Beside the barrow. Do you see it? Good. Make your way there — slowly — very slowly, mind you — and grab it up."

With cautious but steady progress the professor moved toward and then past the anxious Mr. Kibble. The secretary revolved gingerly on his heel, his eyes searching for the thing that had so frightened the horses and old Tom.

It was not hard to find, nor far away. No more than five paces and there it was — an enormous brindled mastiff poised on its haunches in the straw. The hairs were raised all over its back and neck, the flesh underneath rippling like a sea of ship's cables. Heavy, rapid respiration through the dog's mouth had left a froth of saliva on the lips. The creature growled again, and the saliva bubbled. The eyes — evil, watchful eyes — glistened like black porcelain in the torch-light.

"It's Turk," said the professor. "The miser's dog."

"Surely it's the dog that is mad, and not the horses," said Mr. Kibble, backing away in the direction of the hayfork.

"I don't know." The professor paused and leveled the torch at the dog. For some reason the animal crouching there seemed even larger and fiercer — if such were possible — than its more insubstantial counterpart lodged in his memory. "Perhaps it *is* mad. There is, after all, that slobber from the lips — the shudder in the throat — the wicked look in the eyes — "

"But certainly, Tom Spike has had dealings with mad dogs before," said Mr. Kibble, as he took the hayfork into his hands.

The mastiff swung its hindquarters to and fro as though preparing to spring. The corners of its mouth were pulled back, displaying the evil points of the teeth.

At that moment something indescribably cold passed through the stable.

"Do you feel that?" said the professor, with a hushed intake of breath.

Mr. Kibble nodded, adjusting his spectacles and peering about the darkened recesses of the barn. "It's grown very cold in here. So much colder than it was."

"Yes." It recalled to the professor's mind a certain foggy night, not a week past, when he had stood at the open window in his chambers at the university and felt a similar icy vapor pass between the moon and the earth.

"What could it be?" asked the secretary.

The professor made no response, for already a new horror had gained his attention. Raising the torch he whispered —

"Look *there*, Mr. Kibble!"

Mr. Kibble looked, and promptly gasped at what he saw. It was the mastiff, reared up in a single powerful movement onto its hindquarters. Violent cracking and popping noises were heard as the the shoulders pulled back and squared themselves. The muscles of the legs and chest swelled with newfound strength. The massive head with its black muzzle rose up and snapped into position.

So there stood the creature before them, wholly upright, in what the professor could only describe as an awful caricature of the human form. Even more remarkable, he noted, was the brooding intelligence in the eyes of dark porcelain — as though the dog's brain had been infused with a new and cunning intellect quite alien to what had inhabited it before.

I know you. I comprehend you. I know who you are, but you don't know me.

That intelligence communicated itself now in the way the flesh of the head curled itself into the semblance of a malignant leer.

"I don't believe it," said Mr. Kibble, nearly dropping the hayfork on his foot. "I've never seen such a thing before. I don't believe it!"

"Believe it," said the professor, grimly.

"Is it a dog or a man?"

"I suspect something of both, yet neither."

"I've the feeling it knows what we're saying — that it can understand our words."

"Yes."

"But how can that possibly be?"

"I don't know."

"And what does it want?"

For answer the dog growled and lunged toward them on its hind limbs.

"I conclude, Mr. Kibble," said the professor, hastily, "that it's time we took our leave!"

The secretary agreed at once, and together they scrambled for the door. The mastiff threw back its head and emitted a mournful howl. As it lurched past the stalls, not yet certain of its footing, the horses cried out and pawed the ground in a frenzy. Maggie snorted and smashed her hooves against the panels of her stall, while Nestor whirled round and round with the salt-sweat dripping from his flanks.

The professor stepped backwards through the stable-door, waving the torch before the dog's eyes, until he found himself at that point under the eaves where he and Mr. Kibble had come upon Tom Spike.

"The rain!" exclaimed the secretary. "It will quench the fire, surely!"

"Yes, I know. Mr. Kibble, I want you to escape into the house now."

"Sir, I refuse to leave you in such a position — "

"Please do as I say, Mr. Kibble. You will hand me the hayfork, and then you will run as quickly as possible into the house."

Another howl from the mastiff.

"But, sir, it's my duty to — "

"To do exactly as I have requested, Mr. Kibble. Please — there isn't time for argument!"

Mr. Kibble saw the dog plunge through the stable-door, saw the slavering jaws, saw the cunning eyes of dark porcelain fastened upon him. Without further objection he surrendered the hayfork and bounded across the yard, up the stairs and into the house. Thereafter his face could be seen at the window, framed like an old portrait in the back-passage. Beside him were the faces of Laura and the housekeeper, both pale, puzzled, and apprehensive.

The mastiff snarled and rushed in upon the professor. One of its great grasping forelegs touched his elbow, and with alarm he felt the nailed digits close around it like the fingers of a human hand.

It was then he thrust the torch into the dog's face.

With a howl of pain and rage the mastiff leaped back against the stable. The forelegs thrashed about wildly with eerie, man-like movements, as they strove to damp the flames racing over its head and neck. An odor of burning flesh permeated the night.

As he backed away the professor drifted out into the rain, beyond the projecting eaves of the stable. Almost immediately the torch began to sputter. Casting it aside he stepped in again, this time jabbing with the hayfork. Another howl, another flailing of limbs. The dog lunged forward, beating and clawing furiously at the striking prongs. Blood in prodigious amounts could be seen flowing from the head and chest. The dog fought, growled, spit; but the wounds had taken their toll. After another few attempts at reprisal the monster turned and with a snarl loped off into the darkness.

The professor remained where he was, despite the rain thundering down around him, and watched the dog vanish into the storm. Vanish it did — but not before stopping long enough to cast a final, parting glance at him over its shoulder. For an instant the creature stood frozen in a burst of lightning, the look in its eyes of dark porcelain — anger, arrogance, evil, commingled with a deep and secret knowledge — fully as electrifying as the natural discharge that illuminated them.

Waiting no longer the professor rammed the stable-door shut and slid home the bolt, set the lock, and charged up the stairs into the house. In the back-passage he rejoined Mr. Kibble, Laura, and Mrs. Minidew, and at the table in the kitchen found old Tom Spike, an empty glass in the groom's one hand and a shaking fear in the other.

"We must see that every window and door in the house is securely latched. We must in fact be doubly certain. Mr. Kibble, Miss Dale — would you assist me, please?"

They set off on their mission. When he came to the upper corridor, the professor paused for a moment outside the room where Fiona lay asleep. Entering, he quietly checked — twice, thrice, even a fourth time — the security of the windows in her little chamber. Satisfied that all was well he knelt beside the bed, and leaning across it kissed the child gently on the cheek. He brushed a few stray wisps of hair from her forehead and found himself marveling, as he often did, at the miracle of her slumbering face.

For it was in that face that he saw again the face of his sister, Fiona's mother, as she had been in her childhood. His beloved and only sister, whose own features the living world never would see again, save by reflection in the face of her little living memorial.

Remember me. So had his sister whispered to him with her last breath. As he looked now upon her dear child, upon that placid, restful countenance, he saw that Fiona was smiling in her sleep. What a wonder was there! Oblivious to the late excitement, she was off on her own adventures in the wild land of dreams.

When he and the others returned to the kitchen, they found the widow Minidew brewing an especially rousing pot of tea, with which she hoped to improve the state of Mr. Thomas Spike's mind.

"Did you see it, sir?" cried the old groom, anxiously, as soon as the professor entered.

"Yes."

"Did you see what it done?"

"We saw, Tom."

"Then I weren't dreaming? I weren't crazy?"

"No — most definitely not."

Tom Spike bobbed his head, slowly at first, then more vigorously, mostly for his own self-assurance, as if to say — "Yes, yes, it's true, then, it must be true if they saw it, too."

"Are you feeling better, Tom?"

"My mind is all in a muddle," complained the groom. He turned round in his chair and threw a wild eye on all the party. "What sort of mad dog was that, eh? Call it a dog? *Not likely!*"

"What happened?" asked Laura of the professor. "We could see very little from the window. Mr. Kibble said it was a huge dog."

"It was a dog," affirmed the secretary. "A devilish one, but not mad. No mad dog living ever stood up and walked about like a man."

"Like a man," said the professor. "As though actuated by some force that had taken control of it."

"`Actuated' — that is the same word used by Miss Jacks to describe the movements of the dancing sailor."

"Yes, it is."

"And what of the horses?" exclaimed old Tom, banging his fist on the table-top. "I've heard nowt about them. What of Maggie and black Nestor?"

"The horses will be safe tonight, Tom," the professor assured him. "The stable-door is locked. Nothing can get at them now."

"Poor Maggie," wheezed the groom. He looked sadly at his tea-cup, his face of old boxwood wrinkling up like a prune. "Poor dear girl — frightened out of her wits she was. And who could blame her? It's my fault, it is — I should have stayed with her. I must go to her!"

"There's no cause for self-recrimination, Tom. Mind, you'll remain in the house tonight," said the professor, quite naturally vetoing the groom's removal to the stable. "And Mr. Kibble — you'll stay as well. It's very late and I'll warrant the storm isn't through with us yet. We'll certainly not have you venturing abroad, considering what has occurred this evening. Mrs. Minidew — can you see that the guest-room at the front of the house is readied for Mr. Kibble?"

"Yes, of course, sir," replied that good woman of the twinkling eyes and strawberry complexion, and bustled up the stairs to carry out the professor's instructions.

"Are you yourself again, Tom?" the professor asked, placing a reassuring hand on the groom's shoulder. Tom Spike finished the last of his tea, gained resolution thereby and nodded.

After a bit of drying out by the kitchen fire the professor and Mr. Kibble returned to the drawing-room, where they soon were joined by Laura and Mrs. Minidew. The professor stood for a while at the window, smoking his pipe and meditating on the unruly night. Although the lightning and thunder had receded the rain was still chattering away on the glass. Looking out, a picture of the mastiff seemed to rise from the darkness — a vision of the creature as it had stood in the yard, its head turned back over one shoulder and its dark eyes regarding him with a malignant intelligence.

"Has anyone seen Pie?" the professor asked, abruptly. "The young man seems to have disappeared."

"I believe he bolted when all the trouble began," said Miss Dale.

"Let us pray he did not escape from the house!" exclaimed Mrs. Minidew.

A hurried search quickly disclosed an orange ball of fur curled up beneath the sofa in the professor's cedar-lined study. No amount of prodding, however, by Professor Tiggs or Laura Dale or anyone else, could coax that frightened young man from his hideaway. So there he remained, his eyes shining their vivid green lights at his rescuers.

A short while later the fires were taken down and the members of the household retired, as best they could, to their uneasy beds. And so the weary night, lately grown so full of incident, limped tediously away.

CHAPTER VIII

A Wager and an Offer

"LET me tell ye," said Mr. Samson Icks; and so he proceeded to tell them, at his own leisure and after all due preparation.

They were a company of four, and had been ensconced for some time at a sturdy table in the common-room of the Cutting Duck public house. Their view, overlooking the wide front window of the house, gave onto the muddy carriage-road that ran past the establishment. The house being situated on Highgate Hill, the view beyond the road broadened into a grand sweeping panorama of Salthead harbor — *sans* fog, for when the fog was in, the panorama was out — that filled the lattice window with light and provided many a pleasing perspective for town-weary eyes.

The Cutting Duck was a venerable structure of hardy red brick — as hardy and red as the face of Mr. Icks, though not nearly so clean-shaven — streaked and crossed with old oak timber-work, full of antique-fashioned casements, yawning gables, and tall chimney-stacks, all wreathed in ivy. Well do I remember the features of that rambling house, though it is gone these many years — destroyed, existing now only in dreams, like the fleeting summers of my youth. Old friend, how changed are you now! Gutted by fire, your woodwork and furnishings reduced to cinders, the remnants of your hardy brick walls long since dismantled and carted away. It was rumored at the time that the blaze in the kitchen had been deliberately set, in retaliation against the implacable tyranny of the landlord. But more of this later.

"Let me tell ye," said Mr. Icks again — not yet having told them — and adjusted his smoked lenses, before reaching deeply into a pocket of his pinstripes for a sack of tobacco.

It was a bleak, cold afternoon with an unseasonably sharp wind. A turf-fire stood in the hearth, while at the sturdy table the company of four ruminated on the muddy comings and goings of the passersby, on the lumbering carts and wagons of the Salthead tradesmen, the grand carriages and lowly dog-carts, and the great flashing horse-buses that sailed past in the road beyond the window.

Still Mr. Icks had not told them, for he was busily engaged now in charging his pipe. A steaming pot of gin-and-water and several mugs of grog littered the table. Mr. Icks and his companions seemed at first glance to pay one another little heed, their attention drawn instead to the window and the passing sights of the road. Comfortably smoking their pipes and downing their grog, when they spoke it was as if they were communing by means of the window itself, their words reflected backwards off the glass and so showering the entire party with conversation.

"Let me tell ye," said Mr. Icks for a third time, having now lit his pipe and screwed himself up in his seat in anticipation.

"Go on and tell it, then. What're you waiting for?" said a hard-featured gentleman with a grizzled chin, who was seated on his left. "You've been sayin' you've got something to tell us. So tell it."

"Yea," said the diminutive fellow across the table, putting to his lips a tankard fully as large as his head.

"Gentlemen," said Mr. Icks, with a dry chuckle that barely disturbed the hardy red bricks of his complexion. "I will tell ye. Samson Icks is known in the trade as a wery observant individual. Aye! Now, mind ye, that ain't a boast; it ain't a fragment o' my own invention; it's simply a plain statement of fact, ye see, what I happen to have heard."

"Fact," repeated the first gentleman.

"He says he heard it," nodded the third gentleman. He was long and lean, with thinning hair and white side-whiskers.

"As I have heard, Lew Pilcher," said Mr. Icks, "from folks what I happen to respect. In the line o' work that engages old Icks, ye know, observation is a wery important trick o' the trade. Observation, gentlemen, in both word and deed. Why, it was just t'other day, it seems, when a young friend of mine happens to inform me that he's lost his fine black hat. `Where did ye lose it?' I asks him. `If I knew that,' says he, `I wouldn't be standin' here wasting my time with ye.' `Are ye sure ye haven't misplaced it, then?' I asks him. Now, in my studied opinion, gentlemen — "

"Hoo! `Studied opinion,' says he," broke in the gentleman with the grizzled chin.

"Sich formality," lamented Mr. Pilcher, the long and lean gentleman, smoking his clay pipe. "Must be one of them `tricks o' the trade,' as he's picked up from that fat attorney."

"Yea," said the fellow with the tankard.

"In my studied opinion, gentlemen," continued Mr. Icks, with heavy ironic emphasis upon the last word, "that certain young friend had not lost his hat.

Not lost it, gentlemen — simply misplaced it. There's a difference, ye see, atwixt the two, as an observant gentleman like old Icks might winkle out."

"I don't see no difference," said the grizzled gentleman, frowning suspiciously. "Show it."

"To lose a thing," said Mr. Icks, "is to be deprived of it by what is beyond a cove's control. A man what has lost his hat, for example, is deprived of it by someone else what don't give it back; otherwise, it'd be found in due course and returned to him. A man what has misplaced his hat, however, ain't deprived of it — he's only temporarily without it, owing to a minor slip o' the mind. It'll come back to him eventually. The first case is the result of an outside agent, the second the result of his own self. So ye see, gentlemen, by dint o' keen observation ye can distinguish atwixt the two. As ye'll note — they's not the same." He cracked a dry smile full of self-satisfaction, and his eyebrows darted up behind the smoked lenses.

"That's damned lawyer-talk!" roared the gentleman with the grizzled chin, jumping to his feet. "Billy knows damned lawyer-talk when he hears it!" And he knew it well, I warrant, for Cast-iron Billy, as he was called, had suffered much in his life from the depredations of the law-courts, from the craft and the costs of the revered minions of the law.

"Angels dancin' on pin's heads," drawled Mr. Pilcher, without apparent regard for his friend's outburst, and whose easy-going nature stood in defined contrast to that of the fiery Billy. "Splittin' o' hairs it is. A precious waste o' time — useless tommy-rot. But amusin' in a small way."

A much more philosophical view, this outlook of Mr. Pilcher's — a man who had lived long enough to see his own bloodsucking attorney, not two months since, coffined up and dropped into the churchyard, on account of a disagreement at supper with an unusually quarrelsome chicken-bone.

"Yea," nodded the diminutive gentleman — who for one knew nothing of law-courts, or lawyers, or their costs — and quaffed his tankard. His smirking face was all red cheeks and genial blue eyes. A wide cap of a nautical flavor sat far back on his head, effectively concealing the few threads of hair that still sprouted there. Born into this world one Nicholas Crabshawe, he was universally known as "Busket," for reasons so obscure that even Mr. Crabshawe could not tell you what they were. And as for what a "busket" might be, exactly, no one had the slightest idea. What was certain, however, was that Busket he was, and that the name fitted him perfectly.

"The point, gentlemen," pursued Mr. Icks, undaunted, as Cast-iron Billy grumblingly resumed his seat, "is as follows. Observation is a keen facility what must be developed. As I have said, old Icks is known in the trade as an observant individual, and it comes in wery handy — that ye can be sure on. And so, with such in mind, I have made an observation which, in my studied opinion, is worthy of a small wager."

"Hoo! A wager," exclaimed Billy. "`In my studied opinion,' I knew there was bound to be money in it, somewheres!"

"Money for old Icks, most like," observed Mr. Pilcher, narrowing his eyes and nodding at the window with comfortable assurance.

"Gentlemen — "

Before Mr. Icks could elaborate, however, a commanding voice, very loud and piercing, erupted from the depths of the kitchen.

"WHAT DO YOU THINK YOU'RE DOING WITH THAT BLOODY SKILLET, EH? COOKING, IS THAT WHAT YOU CALL IT? I DON'T THINK SO. AND YOU! DO EITHER OF YOU TWO ROGUES BY CHANCE KNOW THE FIRST BLOODY THING ABOUT COOKING? WHAT HAVE I ENGAGED YOU FOR THESE TWO LONG YEARS, EH? COOKS, YOU CALL YOURSELVES! BY GOD — YOU'LL BE THE BREAKIN' OF ME!"

The person responsible for this ear-splitting noise charged into the room. He was a tall giant of a man somewhere above forty years of age, with a broad chest and long muscular arms covered with fur. He wore a white cotton shirt, very wrinkled, a black waistcoat with metal buttons, a white apron over drab trousers, and leather high-buttoned boots. His face was full and long and smooth as marble, with enormous black staring eyes and a massive chin, very steely and very blue. He had a wide slash of a mouth, from the upper lip of which dangled a pair of huge mustaches resembling an inverted horseshoe. His hair was black and oily and parted in the middle. Tied round his forehead was a flaring red handkerchief.

This imposing apparition was accompanied by a youthful sprite in the form of an apprentice pot-boy, who kept well in the shadow of the tall landlord so as not to be noticed.

"SO! WHAT'S IT NOW, EH?" demanded the giant, peering about the common-room at the few customers taking their ease there. Receiving no answer he marched up to the table by the window, and hovered over the company of four with his black eyes starting from their sockets and his red handkerchief beaming from his forehead.

"COME ON, THEN — OUT WITH IT! LET'S GET IT OVER WITH. COMPLAINTS, NOW. EVERYBODY'S GOT COMPLAINTS — I'M

BLOODY UP TO HERE WITH 'EM! WELL, I'M READY FOR YOU, BY GOD! COME ON — COME ON — OUT WITH 'EM! SOMETHING'S ALWAYS THE MATTER. WHAT'S THE BLOODY MATTER HERE, EH?"

"Ain't nothing the bloody matter here but you, you great big fool," said Lew Pilcher, calmly swishing his pipe.

Cast-iron Billy threw a fierce glance at the landlord and hitched up his mouth in a sly smile. "Gervaise Balliol, you're as mad as a hatter and you always have been, and you damned well know it."

"Yea," agreed Busket, hiding his smirk behind his tankard.

"SO!" hissed the landlord of the Cutting Duck. "THAT'S HOW IT STANDS EH? ALL THESE YEARS O' HARD WORK, AND SHEDDIN' THE SWEAT OF ME BLOODY BROW, AND THIS IS WHAT IT ALL COMES TO! DO YOU KNOW THAT THEM PRECIOUS BLOODY ROGUES IN THERE — THEM AS CALLS THEMSELVES COOKS — BY GOD! — IS A-GOIN' AT IT WITH ALL THEIR MIGHT TO BLOODY POISON ME PAYIN' CUSTOMERS? AND WHAT DO I GET FOR REINING 'EM IN, EH? WHAT DO I GET FOR STANDIN' UP FOR THEM AS CALLS THEMSELVES ME CUSTOMERS, EH? BETRAYAL — BLACK TREASON — IS WHAT BALLIOL GETS! WHY, THEM BLOODY CUSTOMERS — MEANIN' THEM SUCH AS *YOU* — IS NOW A-GOIN' AT IT WITH ALL THEIR MIGHT TO INSULT BALLIOL AND THE HONOR OF HIS ESTABLISHMENT, WITH THEIR TALK O' HATTERS AND SUCH. SO THAT'S HOW IT BLOODY WELL STANDS NOW, EH?"

"That's how it bloody stands," nodded Billy, emphatically.

"Friend landlord," spoke up Mr. Icks. He was smiling pleasantly at the giant, with his eyebrows raised in an expression of good will.

Mr. Balliol bent lower and intruded his marble-smooth face into the brick-red one of Mr. Icks.

"WHAT DO YOU WANT, THEN, EH?" he demanded loudly, so that all present at the table received — as the landlord himself might say — a bloody earful.

"A wager, friend Balliol," said Mr. Icks, unperturbed by this noise. "A slight wager — a wery slight wager — is what old Icks happens to be proposing to these kind gentlemen here. Might ye be interested in hearing its contents, worthy landlord, and perhaps even venturing a little wager yerself?"

The landlord's eyes nearly leaped from his head. His blue chin got even bluer as the vessels in his neck surged and swelled.

"A WAGER — IS THAT WHAT I HEAR? IS IT A WAGER YOU'RE PROPOSING, EH? A WAGER — HERE, IN ME OWN RESPECTABLE HOUSE? I DON'T THINK SO!"

"Aye, but it is."

Mr. Balliol appeared stunned by this admission. His eyes froze into a sort of meaningless stare, and his mustaches drooped. He uttered a loud groan.

"From my long observation of town life," continued Mr. Icks, good-naturedly, "I've noticed a certain peculiarity concerning which I propose to make a little wager. The wager is this." He laid his hands flat on the table. "I'll wager, gentlemen, twenty to ten, that of the next thirty rascals as passes by this window here — twenty of 'em will have at least one hand in their breeches or coat-pockets. And what's more, I'll wager that of them thirty rascals, fifteen of 'em will have both hands in their breeches or coat-pockets. Aye! What do you think of that wager, gentlemen?"

"You're on," said Cast-iron Billy at once.

"You're daft," jeered Mr. Pilcher, narrowing his eyes again at the window.

"Yea," put in Busket, though it was quite impossible to decide with which of the two views he was agreeing.

"WHAT SORT OF WAGER IS THAT?" cried Mr. Balliol, with passionate intensity. "BREECHES AND COAT-POCKETS — ONE HAND OR TWO HANDS — WHAT BLOODY SORT OF WAGER IS THAT, EH? WHAT SORT — ?"

The landlord was prevented from commenting further by an abrupt crash and the sound of shattering crockery, from the general direction of the kitchen.

"PIGEON!" he roared at the tiny apprentice lurking in his shadow. "PIGEON! LOOK SHARP! YOU COOKS IN THERE! WHAT'S THE BLOODY ROW ABOUT NOW, EH? BY GOD — YOU COOKS — YOU'LL BE THE BREAKIN' OF ME!" Hot on the heels of the pot-boy he raced into the kitchen, where his voice could again be heard disparaging them as called themselves cooks.

"A finer man never put foot in stirrup-iron," smiled Mr. Pilcher.

"A finer loon, more like," said Cast-iron Billy, running a hand over his short grizzled beard. He had eyes like steel and a jaw like stone, and was laughing quietly to himself in that way I well remember. Across the table little Busket finished off another draught.

"That's the greatest goose I ever heard talk," said Mr. Pilcher, with a lazy inclination of the head.

"That rascal's a perfectionist, that's his problem," said Mr. Icks. "Everything gets his steam up."

"That's not our look-out," returned Billy. "After all, we ain't his keeper — his *zookeeper*, that is!" And he laughed very heartily.

"Aye. The day he regains his wits there'll be seven new moons."

"Fine weather, this," remarked Mr. Pilcher, ironically, looking out onto the dismal street.

"Hoo! Very fine," agreed Billy.

"Here he comes, gentlemen," announced Mr. Icks, rapping his knuckles on the table to gain their attention. "Here's rascal number one."

A severe gentleman in black, tall and well-kept, strode briskly past the window, being followed in that slight journey by the four pairs of eyes at the sturdy table.

"One pocket," said Mr. Icks, with a dry chuckle.

"Fine weather," said Mr. Pilcher, "for a fellow to leave his hands out in the cold, a-freezin' in the west wind."

"He's picked a fine day for his wager," grumbled Cast-iron Billy, with realization growing upon him.

"Gloves, gentlemen," said Mr. Icks, holding up his hands with the fingers outspread — "they's always gloves, ye know. No need for pockets if they's gloves available."

A second gentleman, a country-sort-of-fellow in breeches and top boots and a snuff-colored coat, plodded by the window.

"Two pockets," said Mr. Icks.

A third gentleman (two pockets) and a fourth (one pocket) passed by. (Interposed between them was a young woman in a cloak and bonnet, who had one hand on her reticule and the other on her umbrella, but who was disqualified by Mr. Icks on account of her failing resemblance to a "rascal"). It appeared that the wiry fellow in pinstripes was on his way to a rout.

"It's a humbug," growled Cast-iron Billy. He turned to Samson Icks with his steely eyes screwed into an awful configuration. "I know what it is — it's another o' them damned lawyer jobs! Why, he's got hundreds of 'em — thousands, most like. Comes from associating with them damned lawyers — them parasites — muckworms — them — them — them Badgers and Winches!"

"Tell me, Icks," said Mr. Pilcher, lazily tapping out his pipe, "why is it `Badger and Winch,' when there ain't no more Badger?"

"Don't ye recollect, gentlemen?" replied Mr. Icks, as though it were all perfectly clear to any thinking individual. "It's on account o' the fat rascal, Winch. Aye! Surely ye remember when old Badger pegged out, years ago, and the fat rascal was afeared of losin' the richest client in Salthead — that's Tusk, o' course — he said to the miser he'd swallow his pride and keep the `Badger' on. The miser didn't trust the fat rascal, ye see, what with Winch being junior partner and never in charge of the firm. So as it were beyond the fat rascal's power to resurrect old Badger, he kept old Badger's name in his stead. The tall nasty rascal don't abide change, ye see, and Winch knows it. Why, there ain't no more Badger in Badger and Winch than there's horses in horseradish!"

"SO! WHAT'S IT NOW, EH?" roared the landlord, returning from his latest skirmish in the kitchen. His black eyes sped round the common-room. Almost immediately they lighted on a promising candidate. "WELL? WHAT ARE YOU BLOODY STARING AT? WHAT DO YOU WANT, THEN, EH? MORE OF YOUR BLOODY BITTER?"

"If you please, sir," simpered the victim, a timid old fellow who had been perusing his newspaper, quite innocently, and who now sat cowering in his chair with the landlord bent over him and the bright red handkerchief shining in his face.

"NOW YOU'LL WANT YOUR BLOODY BISCUITS AND CHEESE, I SUPPOSE!" said Mr. Balliol. "PIGEON — MORE BITTER FOR THIS ROGUE!"

"Bitter, yes, sir!" exclaimed the tiny apprentice, swooping in and then just as quickly swooping out to fetch the requested item.

The landlord marched again to the table by the window, with his hands on his hips and a little disdainful swagger in his walk. "SO! STILL AT THE WAGER, EH? STILL TURNIN' ME RESPECTABLE HOUSE INTO A BLOODY GAMING PARLOR, EH? WHY, IT'S BLOODY ROGUES LIKE YOU — AND YOU — AND YOU — AND YOU — AS'LL BE THE BREAKIN' OF ME!"

"And is it you talkin' o' rogues?" retorted Mr. Pilcher, with a lazy laugh. "Ain't that the big ugly pot a-callin' the kettle black!"

General hilarity ensued.

"ARE YOU CALLIN' ME A BLOODY BLACK ROGUE, LEW PILCHER?"

"Black rogue?" returned Mr. Pilcher. "Ha! Black rogue is too grand for the likes o' you, Gervaise Balliol — you great bloody fool, you."

Thus assailed, the giant came dangerously close to launching himself into an apoplexy. Words failed him; the blood rose in his neck and his hairy arms fluttered with rage.

"Speakin' o' rogues, gentlemen," remarked Mr. Icks, nodding toward a stranger in ragged sailor's garments who, upon crossing the window, had come to a halt and was now peering in with a ghoulish leer — a visual feast accentuated by a tangled mustache and a gleam of gold in his mouth.

"No pockets!" exclaimed Cast-iron Billy, pounding the table.

As if in response the stranger retired a few paces behind and proceeded to execute a sailor's hornpipe, apparently for his own amusement — leaping about with wild abandon and an awkward flailing of his limbs, in what looked to be a horrid mockery of that well-known dance.

"Lord love him!" cried Billy. "That rascal's as daft as you are, landlord!"

At which point Mr. Balliol appeared to regain his composure, and striding up to the glass focused his wrath upon the dancing sailor.

"YOU THERE — CLEAR OFF!" he shouted, with a threatening wave of his hand. Wheeling round, he tossed up his chin and cast an ill-tempered glance at Mr. Icks and his party. "WHAT ARE YOU FOUR A-STARIN' AT, EH?" After which he marched back into the kitchen, where he could again be heard pillorying the cooks and the apprentice pot-boy.

"I have observed, gentlemen, that ye can't tell all the rascals by their looks," said Mr. Icks, rolling his head so as to emphasize this overflow of wisdom. "Looks, I can assure ye, can be a wery bad indicator — that ye can be sure on. The nastiest rascal is sometimes the properest cove, on the outside, what you'd ever care to meet — I can tell ye that from keen observation."

"Observation again, he says," drawled Mr. Pilcher.

"As for example," continued Mr. Icks, "there's one fashionable rascal I'd tell ye of, a certain young gentleman what I have watched for several weeks. This young gentleman — no names now, gentleman, no names — is one what asked me, not long ago, and strictly on the confidental side, to oversee a little job for him. Not to be too particular, it involved a fellow as I knows well, to do this job. However, this poor fellow — very feeble in the mind, true, but trustworthy that way, on account of it — couldn't quite manage to bring it off. Twice he tried, in point o' fact; both times, no result. So it then was up to old Icks to inform the certain young gentleman of the failures. Well, I can tell ye, that young gentleman he became wery agitated and upset when he heard it was no go. And when that happened — why, there's an awful yellow light what suddenly flashes on in his big dark eyes. A light from hell, is what I calls it!

He's a deep one, is that young gentleman — no names now, gentlemen, no names. Fashionable and prosperous he is on the outside — but that yellow light is not something ye'd care to gander at twice."

"A yellow light," grunted Cast-iron Billy, skeptically.

"From hell, he said," nodded Mr. Pilcher.

"Yea," said Busket.

"Aye, but that weren't the worst part of it," resumed Mr. Icks, noting the subsequent passage of several ladies by the window — beings who, again, did not appear to qualify for inclusion in his wagering universe. "What were even worse, gentlemen, were what I seen in that young gentleman's house, when that young gentleman had no idea old Icks was near. Ye see, gentlemen, one night as I just happened to be standin' aside his window — no need to say why, but it were full in the line o' duty — and it were bright that night, the moon was out — and as I slips forward to the door of that young gentlemen's study — his house as it were being situated in a distant part o' town — "

"No pockets!" exulted Cast-iron Billy, slapping at his thigh.

"As I were standing on the long gallery outside his window — which window looks in at his study — I happened to observe, on that particular evening, that the tall curtain of said window was just slightly parted. Not that old Icks had any such intention o' spying, now — "

"Course not!" said Mr. Pilcher, with a wag of his head.

"But it were as I said, Lew Pilcher, in the line o' duty. Ye see, the pretty part of it is that Winch — the fat rascal as gives me so much trouble — has had me a-watchin' this young gentleman, what happens to be his wery own client. Aye! So that night, as it were impossible to pass the window on the gallery without a-lookin' in, old Icks proceeded to linger there for a while and take his ease. And what, gentlemen, do ye suppose he seen there in the window?"

"Two pockets," said Mr. Pilcher.

"Not two pockets. Gentlemen, what I seen there — it were enough to shatter the marrow-bones of the strongest individual. It were a sight, gentlemen, as is once observed, is never to be forgot — a sight as is forever implanted in the mind." And he tapped the side of his head with a blunt forefinger.

"No pockets!" cried Billy, pointing.

"Yes, it were no pockets, gentlemen," said Mr. Icks. "That certain young gentleman — no pockets had he. For ye see, he were considerable changed since the last time I'd seen him, the time when the yellow light was in his eyes. For now it weren't his bottle-green coat, as he's right fond of, but a long purple robe what he wore, that run all the way from his neck to his feet, and splattered all over with gold stars and a strange, mysterious writing. It were a sight as ye'd never seen before in all yer life."

"A robe," drawled Mr. Pilcher, winking broadly. "And so the gentleman might just a-tooken his bath, eh?"

Which wise remark elicited no end of mirth from Billy and Busket.

"Gentlemen, gentlemen," said Mr. Icks, mildly irritated. "Ye'll not be listening. A robe it were — not one o' yer common dressing-gowns, but a robe as a great monarch might wear. A robe of state, a kingly mantle, as ye'd see in yer history books. A beautiful purple thing it were, with its gold stars and its strange characters. But, gentlemen — that robe weren't the worst part of it."

"No?" said Mr. Pilcher.

"Not by a long chalk. For ye see, gentlemen, it weren't the robe what claimed the most of my attention. Aye, the robe, it were grand enough — but it weren't terrible to behold. The terrible thing to behold, gentlemen, was his face."

"His face?" asked Cast-iron Billy, with sudden interest. "What about his face?"

"Painted, gentlemen," replied Mr. Icks, gravely nodding. "All of it smeared with the brightest red paint, a color like ye've hardly seen in all yer life. Like living, breathing blood it were! His brow, his nose, his cheeks, his lips, his chin, his ears, his neck — all of 'em dripping a blood-red! Old Icks had caught him at his secret arts. There he stood, with his arms held out afore him and his head back, and his eyes closed, and his lips a-mouthin' wild words in a language what I could not understand. And from that night, gentlemen, old Icks has done everything he can — everything — to avoid that fashionable gentleman. No names, gentlemen, no names! So as I have said — looks can be a wery bad indicator."

His companions glanced at one another, a little uncomfortable now.

"Mayhap he's got the scarlatina — the scarlet fever," suggested Lew Pilcher.

"Are you sure it weren't the mad Balliol, with his red handkerchief at his head?" asked Billy.

"It were not," replied Mr. Icks, firmly.

"And what about the little job this young gentleman tapped you for?" inquired Mr. Pilcher.

"The poor fellow as I employed gave it his best try, as I said, but it weren't enough. He needed the coin, for he's wery poor, but his mind — it's feeble, ye see, and he made a go at it but he weren't up to it. And I told the fashionable young gentleman so, in point of fact, and wery strongly put. But that was when the yellow light came on, and after what I seen that last time — what with the kingly mantle and the secret words and that bloody devil of a face — I ain't been back, and haven't the least notion what's a-goin' on. Likely he fingered some other cove what could do the job."

"And what was this job, by the by?" asked Cast-iron Billy, curiously.

Mr. Icks glanced downward at the table, smiling faintly and slyly. "I can only tell ye, gentlemen, that it were in a delicate and a wery confidential line — if ye gather my meaning."

Billy and Mr. Pilcher returned sage nods of understanding, while Busket finished another draught and threw his blue eyes on the company. Those eyes happening to drift toward the lattice window, he started. The others, noting this, turned to the window and found themselves similarly affected by an odd figure that had materialized there.

It was arrayed in an old brown coat with brass buttons, a white false collar, and a dark waistcoat. Abundant brown hair flared out from its head with many radiating points, like a sunburst. It was looking in at the window with a breezy nonchalance that alternated with an inquisitive stare — which changes were marked by a periodic screwing-up of the eyes and knitting of the brows, together with some nervous chewing on a forefinger.

"Now there's a pleasant rogue for you," cried Billy — "and *no pockets!*"

"Must be an idiot," drawled Mr. Pilcher. "Not much brain there, nohap."

"Yea," was the contribution from Busket.

"Why, gentlemen — " said the wiry Icks, leaping from his seat. "That pleasant rogue is, for yer information, my wery great and good acquaintance, Mr. Richard Scribbler."

"Scribbler?" returned Cast-iron Billy, with a suspicious frown. "From Badgers and Winches?"

"The same." Mr. Icks gestured to the clerk, urging him in pantomime to run round through the courtyard and so join them in the common-room. Mr. Scribbler finding these instructions uninformative, Mr. Icks was obliged to venture out and bring his great and good acquaintance in, where he was presented to the rest of the company. Mr. Scribbler nodded and bowed, knitting his brows very seriously and scratching his hair, and nodding and bowing again, until Mr. Icks took him by the arm and led him away.

"Mr. Scribbler and I, we've an important matter to discuss," said Mr. Icks to his companions, by way of explanation. "Keep yer pipes loaded and yer mugs at attention."

He steered the gawking scribe into one of the small private chambers that adjoined the common-room. As they passed the door of the kitchen Mr. Gervaise Balliol came hurtling through it.

"Friend landlord," said Mr. Icks, with his cheeriest smile.

"WHAT DO YOU BLOODY ROGUES WANT NOW?" cried the giant. "I SUPPOSE IT'LL BE SUPPER, EH? IT'S ALWAYS SOMETHING. WHAT! TIRED OF YER GAMIN' AND YER WAGERIN' AND YER ONE-POCKETS, TWO-POCKETS, EH? NOT BLOODY SATISFIED WITH YOUR GIN AN' GROG?"

"In point of fact," returned Samson Icks, "supper it is. But not for old Icks — supper for my good acquaintance, Mr. Scribbler, what has just this minute arrived at yer worthy establishment."

Mr. Balliol, conscious now of the newcomer, sniffed; then examined him closely, up and down, and with his hands at his back made a little swaggering turn or two around him, garnishing this inspection with some private murmurs of amusement.

"WELL, LA, LA! WHAT'S THIS HERE, EH?" he demanded. "WHAT'S THIS YOU'VE DRAGGED IN? LOOKS TO ME LIKE A BLOODY HEDGEHOG!"

Mr. Scribbler quailed; his heart took a dreadful dive.

"Landlord, ye see here Mr. Richard Scribbler, a great and good acquaintance o' mine, as is also clerk in the eminent firm o' Badger and Winch's. Friend Richard, ye see here Mr. Gervaise Balliol, as is landlord and Mine Host of this house," said Mr. Icks, in a very pleasant manner.

Mr. Scribbler peeped cautiously into the face of the landlord.

"WELL, LA, LA! BLOODY FORMAL, AIN'T WE, SIR? WHAT'S THE MATTER WITH HIM, THEN — CAN'T HE PARLEY FOR HIMSELF? PIGEON! PIGEON!" roared the landlord. "BLOODY TABLE FOR THE HEDGEHOG!"

He glared at Icks and Mr. Scribbler in grim and mirthful triumph; then the apprentice pot-boy flew past and showed the two guests into the private room, where they were attended by a solemn-faced waiter with a cold in his head. After receiving Mr. Scribbler's request — which was arrived at by the clerk's pointing out some of several delicacies crudely chalked on a board hanging against the wall — the waiter hastened to the kitchen in search of the meal.

"Friend Richard," said Samson Icks, with a little flourish of his hands on the table-top. "Old Icks thanks ye for taking him up on his offer to join him at this wonderful establishment of the Cutting Duck. And how is things at the home office? Not having had the pleasure for several days, on account o' some hot words between the fat rascal and yer worshipful servant, the place has been a stranger to me lately."

Mr. Scribbler, having regained his negligent air — so long as the horrid landlord was out of view — tossed his shoulders, indicating presumably that nothing of interest had transpired since he of the pinstripes had last set foot in those lawyerly quarters.

"Wery good. And ye, friend Richard — how are ye, now? Still powdering away at yer studies, I predict, at the bidding of the fat rascal. Well, I suppose it keeps ye out o' mischief. And mischief is a wery bad thing to be into — that ye can be sure on."

After a few more suchlike pleasantries the waiter arrived with Mr. Scribbler's supper, which consisted of a bowl of turtle soup, some slices of venison, a corner of cheese, a pair of deviled biscuits, and a glass of porter. Having deposited these treasures before the eyes of the hungry clerk, the waiter returned to the kitchen. Mr. Scribbler plunged into the meal with a hearty satisfaction and in a very short time finished it off, leaving only a solitary biscuit.

"Now, friend Scribbler, as to the purpose of this invitation," said Mr. Icks, with a dry smile and a tug at his smoked lenses. "As I mentioned to ye before, that day in chambers, there's something of financial benefit I have to propose to ye. What it is, is a small service what needs to be rendered, and I'm offering ye the opportunity to render it — with admirable remuneration, o' course."

Mr. Scribbler nodded gaily and flung himself back in his chair, crossing his arms and awaiting Mr. Icks' proposal with his usual flow of breezy nonchalance.

"This service," continued Mr. Icks, reaching into a pocket of his coat, "has to do with a certain letter, as I have here, what is to be delivered — in person — to a certain party." From the pocket he withdrew a flat object sealed with a large wafer stamp. "What I offer, friend Richard, is the opportunity for ye to deliver it."

The clerk looked questioningly at Mr. Icks, at the same time directing a thumb toward the dapper fellow in pinstripes.

"Aye — o' course, friend Richard, I understand ye," chuckled Mr. Icks. "Ye wery naturally wish to know why old Icks don't hand over the message himself. Why he's willing to sacrifice good coin — and it be good coin, ye're assured o' that, Mr. Richard — to have another deliver it for him and collect the brass. A fair question. An honest question. What I'll say to it, friend Scribbler, is this: were old Icks to deliver this letter himself, it might be considered — how's the word — *prejudicial* to the writer. Aye! Prejudicial — and so might place unnecessary suspicions in the mind of the person receiving the message, as to the motives of the writer. Do ye understand, friend Richard?"

Mr. Scribbler understood.

"What's more, there's a big, big job a-comin' on tight — ye know the one, involving the execution as ye knows about — what is going to take up a mighty parcel o' my time. And what's even more, Mr. Richard, knowing what the coin would mean to someone of yer limited finances — it's only fair that ye should have the opportunity to deliver the letter yerself. Ye see, I trust ye, friend Richard. I've known ye these two years and ye're a fine, honest cove. So, what the writer has given old Icks, Icks gives to ye — the letter, as well as the coin."

Mr. Scribbler — his doubts resolved to his apparent satisfaction — straightened himself in his chair, looking very bright and expectant.

"Now then, friend Richard, what the writer of the letter is willing to offer for its delivery — is this!"

Mr. Icks unfurled a closed fist to reveal a glittering pile of coins, at sight of which the clerk's eyes went wide and his lips rounded themselves into an "O."

"Ain't that dainty," smiled Mr. Icks, looking very pleased. "I can see, friend Richard, that ye have accepted the commission."

Mr. Scribbler nodded eagerly, whereupon Mr. Icks transferred to him ownership of the coins and the letter.

"Ye should know, Mr. Richard, that the writer of the letter is in no particular hurry for its delivery, so ye may feel free to take yer ease in relaying it. That writer don't care the crack of a cart-whip whether ye deliver it tomorrow, or the next day, or the next. If, however, ye can see that it arrives at the address what is written there, no later than this day week — why, that would be wery satisfactory to that person."

Mr. Scribbler smiled broadly, slipping the letter into his coat and the glittering coins into his purse.

"But, mind ye, friend Richard," warned the wiry gentleman in pinstripes, "not a word about old Icks now. Not a word about this present conversation, nor about the Cutting Duck, nor how that letter came into yer possession today. Ye understand that, don't ye? Not a word — not a breath! Such is wery important. All ye know is that ye came upon the letter at the home office — that ye'd seen it a-lyin' there for a fortnight or longer, undelivered — and that ye undertook it yerself to hand it over to the proper individual. Have ye got that, Mr. Richard? And remember, not a word about old Icks — not a syllable — otherwise there'll be wigs on the green, sure!"

Mr. Scribbler shook his head with energetic firmness, indicating of course not, never in a thousand centuries.

At this point the solemn-faced waiter reappeared, and having ascertained that the keen edge of Mr. Scribbler's appetite had been removed, turned to Mr. Icks.

"Is there anything I can get for you, sir?"

Looking very pleased with himself, Mr. Icks eased back in his chair and peered at the serving-man through his smoked lenses.

"Not a thing, thank ye," he answered, with a dry chuckle. "Not a thing. I believe old Icks has got everything he could possibly want at present."

CHAPTER IX

What Sally Saw

FROM the old public house on Highgate Hill I return now to the secluded environs of a certain leafy inn, beside an embayment of the river Salt. A greater contrast between two havens of hospitality could not be imagined — the Blue Pelican, which still stands, and the Cutting Duck, which does not. The Duck, with her hardy red brick and her ivy and her antique-fashioned casements, and the Pelican, with her pale plastered sides framed and crosshatched by beams of oak timber. Where the Duck was cold and windy, up there on her hill, the Pelican was warm and welcoming under her shade trees by the river. Where the landlord of the Duck was roundly disdained, the mistress of the Pelican was universally admired — and most certainly would never have been seen with a flaring red handkerchief tied round her head. And of course, where the Duck had her Pigeon, the Pelican had her Gosling.

But there was one thing the Blue Pelican had that the Duck never did, and that one thing was Sally Sprinkle.

"Who is Sally Sprinkle?" the pretty new chambermaid inquired of her companion.

"There's Sally," replied Mary Clinch, pointing toward the small figure seated in a wing-chair by the fire. "Come along, then, and I'll introduce you."

They glided to the hearth, where the small figure resolved itself into a frail old woman with head bowed, and hair like powdered snow.

"Sally?" said Mary, very gently so as not to startle her. "How are you today, Sally? Feeling better?"

The snowy head, whose cheek had been resting in one withered hand, lifted itself up and out of its reverie. What the new chambermaid saw beneath the powdery hair was an ancient but otherwise cheery face, with a great interlocking web of wrinkles and a pair of green eyes marvelously magnified through spectacle lenses. For a long minute the eyes searched Mary's with an uncomprehending stare, as if the young woman had just arrived from the farthest reaches of space.

"Sally? It's Mary Clinch, Miss. Surely you know me! It's Mary," said the head chambermaid of the Pelican, touching the fragile eminence of the woman's shoulder.

"Mary?" repeated a little voice, with an uncomfortable movement of the lips that indicated trouble with her teeth. The old woman's eyes fluttered away like troubled starlings, hovered briefly in the middle distance, then flew back to Mary. Her brow darkened; she gripped the arms of her chair and whispered earnestly —

"Who are you, child?"

Mary glanced significantly at her new companion.

"It's Mary Clinch, Miss, as is chambermaid here at the Pelican. You know me, Sally, don't you?"

Again the uncomprehending stare. The old woman's lips parted and her tongue absently roved about her poorly fitting teeth. Her gaze swept Mary's features — the pinched little eyes, the broad red cheeks, the full mouth, the upturned button of a nose — as if hunting for something, anything, that it found familiar. Then, at last, a faint light of recognition —

"Are you my mother?"

"No, Miss, I'm not your mother. I'm Mary — you know that. Mary. Mary Clinch, as makes up your bed each day and serves up your hot tea and cakes. Don't you know me?"

"I don't know anyone any more," replied Sally. She touched a withered hand to her brow and shut her eyes, as though the world had grown too confused for her and she were trying to dream it away.

Mary took the arm of her new companion, drawing her to the old woman.

"Sally — here's someone to meet you. Do you see? This is Bridget — our newest in service. You'll be seeing much of her from now on."

The uncomprehending look returned to Sally's eyes as they sought out the golden-haired Bridget. They found nothing familiar there, of course; and so her gaze drifted to a far window where the pink and melancholy light of autumn was standing.

As I sit here now, myself gazing across the vast gulf of years, I recall the Sally Sprinkle of my childhood. I recall her kind and generous nature, her thoughtfulness of others. I recall how fond she was of handing out sweets to those of us little children who happened by. Always a smile for everyone, always a laugh, always happiness. But her later years were hard ones; they wore her down and reduced that kind and generous nature to a vacant shell. For though she smiled at everyone with what seemed to be affectionate interest,

96

it was all trickery — a mean falsehood, aided and compounded by the appearance of those great magnified eyes, for the Sally of my story inhabits a world only thinly connected with our own. When approached she brightens, as by a reflex, without comprehending; when left to herself she falls back into a reverie, with bowed head, her spirit once more adrift among the scenes and forms of the past. She had watched her spring, her summer, and her autumn come and go; it was winter with her now.

Mary Clinch drew her companion to the great oak bar — that same hardy structure behind which the mistress of the Pelican could be found each evening, dispensing draughts of bitter for her admiring public. At the same time George Gosling, that most industrious of pot-boys, came charging by in the crispness of his white uniform, on one of his multifarious errands for his employer. Outside, the gruff tones of the ostler could be heard in the yard, while in one of the back rooms the authoritative voice of Miss Moll Honeywood herself was audible, providing instruction of one kind or another to one of her minions.

"Is she daft?" inquired the compassionate Bridget — referring not to Miss Moll, of course, but to Sally — as she watched the snowy head begin to droop.

"Not yet," replied Mary. "But she's right forgetful. She can remember, as clear as crystal, things as happened to her when she was a wee babe — but can't recollect who it was brought her breakfast this morning. She's nearly ninety, I'm told."

"And she visits every day?"

"Lord, no! Sally don't visit. Sally lives here."

"Lives here? La! At the Pelican?"

"That's what I'm saying. In a wee room in the back as was once used for storage. Likely you ain't seen it yet. It's at the corner of the house, and has a bonny view of the trees, with a wee bit o' the river thrown in. The Miss had it freshened up and painted just for Sally."

"And she pays no board?"

"Of course not!"

"That is unbelievably kind of Miss Honeywood."

"The Miss is a right kind person," said Mary, proudly.

"But why? Is Sally Sprinkle a relation?"

"Not as I know of. The story's a long and windy one, but I'll shorten it for you. You see, for years and years Sally lived just over the way, in the house of a weaver and his wife. Such a loving couple! She did a few wee odds and ends for them — a bit o' cleaning and washing and such — and so they kept a place in their house for her. Years past she'd supported herself making embroidered bonnets of silk and braid, but her eyesight failed her. Then the weaver and his wife fell on hard times. When they hadn't the rent on the quarter-day they were cast out of the house. Think of it! Such faithful tenants for so many years. Then one bit o' bad luck and it's out into the street with 'em, and the house scraped clean as a bone after a hungry dog."

"La, it's the way of the world," sighed Bridget.

"So the weaver and his wife left Salthead and went to live with her relations in the country, as I've heard. But Sally had no such place to go. The Miss, having known her for a right long time, took pity on her and found her a short way out of the thicket. But, oh! — it was an awful thing. Such bad work. Such bad, bad work."

"What was?"

"The eviction, o' course. It was enough to make a sane person weep. It was that wicked Bob — he's the one as done it, under orders of his master. Do you know Bob?"

Bridget shook her head. "Which Bob?"

"The horrid ugly one — Nightingale — the one with the black circles round his eyes. Now there's a varnished rogue — always hot and sulky, just like his master. It's his master, o' course, as held the lease on the weaver's house, and caused 'em all three to be thrown out. Tossed 'em out, he did, into the night, and Sally with nothing but her wee bag o' belongings, and sitting there in the muck, and sobbing, and likely to freeze to death, if it hadn't been for the Miss, who took her in and offered her a toasty room. And that's how it was Sally Sprinkle came to live at the Pelican."

"Does she sit there all day?"

"In the afternoon, mostly, when the common-room is quiet. She rattles in with her cane about noon and plants herself in the wing-chair. Then she has her dinner in the kitchen with Cook, and so it's off to bed early for her — before the Pelican begins filling for the evening."

"I'm sure I've heard of this Bob Nightingale," said Bridget, thoughtfully, "but I can't recall the details. A bad man, though, is what I've gathered."

"Right bad, particularly when he's in liquor. And for what he did to Sally Sprinkle the Miss won't allow him inside the Pelican. She's made it quite plain and public that he ain't wanted. Well, she caught him in here one night, only last week, and made him take water. And the rogue took it, too, for there's no resisting the Miss when she's got her steam up. There's no one like her! And as for his master — the one as evicted the weaver and his wife and Sally — not only don't she let him into the Pelican — as if he'd likely be seen here — she don't allow so much as the speaking of his name in this house."

"Whose name is it?" asked Bridget.

Mary glanced timidly this way and that, on the look-out for Miss Moll, who was known to have an ear like a hare.

"Tusk," she answered, in hushed tones. "Josiah Tusk. You know the one?"

"The miser!" exclaimed Bridget, with a snap of her fingers. "La! I know enough about that rascal. Mr. Josiah Tusk! Why, everyone in Salthead knows of that great ugly maggot — "

"Was that the forbidden name of a certain person I just heard spoken in this good house?" said a starchy voice behind them.

The two startled damsels leaped into the air. In the doorway behind the great oak bar stood the very tall and very angular proprietor of the Pelican — her brow contracted, her pale eyes narrowed behind her spectacle lenses, and her arms folded across her breast, with the long white fingers of one hand drumming on the elbow of the opposite arm.

Mary Clinch uttered a little cry and slapped fingers to mouth; while Bridget held herself rigidly at attention, uncertain what to make of this sudden confrontation with her new employer — a woman whom, as Mary had said, there was no one like.

"Oh! Begging your pardon, Miss — I'm sorry, Miss, for I spoke the name as you said not to speak — but not as I thought you'd be there to hear it," cried Mary. "Oh, no — what I meant to say, Miss, is — I was explaining to Miss Bridget, Miss, the history of poor Sally there, and how you saved her from a frozen death, Miss, when the miser — whose name is not to be spoken here, I know — and that wicked Bob Nightingale, they chucked her out into the night. Oh, forgive me, Miss!"

"I see," said Miss Moll, in her starchiest manner, unfolding her arms to adjust her smock. "Very well. Bridget Leek," she said, addressing her newest minion, "you will understand that the two persons whose names you have just heard are not wanted here. You will understand as well that the name of the one person in particular is never to be spoken in this house. Please see that you adhere to this instruction. You will learn that everything is either black or white at the Pelican; there's no gray here. And as for you, Mary Clinch — "

"Yes, Miss?" cried Mary, trembling.

"Fingers out of mouth, girl — don't slobber."

"Yes, Miss!" sighed Mary, with a gasp of relief, and dropped her hands from her lips.

"Now, then, Bridget," said Miss Honeywood, "we formally welcome you to the Pelican. We are a happy household here. You come to us highly recommended, and there's no doubt in my mind you'll find employment at the Pelican a far more rewarding experience. After all, a common charwoman of slender means has not a pretty situation."

"No, Miss," replied Bridget.

"Seeing that this is your first day in service, we shall overlook your transgression with regard to the name of the person that is not to be spoken in this house. As for you, Mary Clinch — "

"Yes, Miss?" cried Mary, trembling again.

Miss Moll paused long and hard, for maximal effect, before replying —

"You may resume your duties."

"Yes, Miss!" sighed Mary, quickly relieved again.

The mistress of the house consulted her watch. "I see it is nearly five o'clock. Mary, you and Bridget will help Sally to the kitchen at her usual time."

"Of course, Miss."

Whereupon Miss Honeywood gave them a parting nod and disappeared behind the bar.

Enormously relieved, Mary and her companion returned their attention to Sally Sprinkle, who seemed to be floating in and out of her reverie.

"Sally, is there something we can do for you?" Mary asked.

Another mystified look, followed by a stare of forced concentration, as though the old woman were trying mightily to understand the question. The look passed as it frequently did, the smile faded, and the great magnified eyes settled once more on the window through which the autumn was glowing.

"How brisk it seems outside — is it the fog?" she inquired, and promptly wandered off into an imaginary fog of her own design. "The trees are shedding their leaves — so sad — oh, where has my dear old pear-tree gone? — it was there but a second ago, beside the coach-house — and there's the moon — grand old moon! — oh, perhaps it's not the moon — I can't see anymore — did you hear that sound? — I believe there's someone there — someone at the garden wicket, asking to be let in — "

"Oh, Sally, there's no one there," said Mary, frowning. "There ain't no garden wicket. Not at the Pelican."

"Did you know that I was born and bred in Richford? Yes, yes. Dear old Richford! A Richford girl, straight and true. Did you know I'll be seventeen years old, come Saturday week?" She fixed a searching eye on Bridget, whom she appeared to be seeing clearly for the first time. "Who are you, child? Are you my mother?"

"No, Miss," replied Bridget, blushing. "My name is Bridget, and I'm new in service here."

"I see," said the old woman, gazing abstractedly at her frail folded hands. "I am sure Jamie will be quite happy to meet you. He'll be here directly, you know. He's coming to see me."

"Who is Jamie?"

To this there was no reply. Bridget looked round for Mary Clinch, but she had slipped away to the hearth-rug where the nut-brown tabby was busily washing his paws. Lifting the cat Mary gently transferred him to Sally's lap, where the tabby, after a few preparative curls and swishes and some comfort-seeking mews, settled down to resume his ablutions.

"Here you are, Sally — here's little Nutmeg, come to see you," said Mary.

A smile stretched the web of wrinkles on the old woman's face. She placed one of her hands on the cat's head and stroked it, slowly and methodically, with a heavy motion. Little Nutmeg, shutting his eyes, commenced purring at once.

"You see?" whispered Mary. "Even the Miss can't make that animal purr. Sally adores the poor wee thing. She's the only one he takes to."

"La, it's a pretty cat," said Bridget, admiringly.

They watched Sally as she rubbed the cat's head — rubbed it, smoothed it, burnished it, as though it were a rough little knob in need of polishing, all the while murmuring such soft and unintelligible morsels of talk as only the cat appeared capable of understanding. Looking altogether pleased, Nutmeg surrendered himself to the old woman's attentions with a regal and a sphinx-like serenity.

Turning to Mary Clinch, Bridget asked again —

"Who is Jamie?"

Still no answer to the question, as George Gosling now came bursting from the kitchen with a towel thrown across his shoulder. As he sped past, Sally Sprinkle looked up and into the pot-boy's face. At first there was no response; then, recognizing him, she stuck out her tongue. Still in the midst of his duties, the industrious George nonetheless found a spare second or two to return the favor.

"La!" cried Bridget. "Did you ever see the likes o' that?"

"Every day," laughed Mary Clinch. "Sally and George — those two don't get along. She claims he's always making faces at her, so she makes 'em back. Really, he don't mean to — he's just right busy, running about like that and all. It's her imagination. She ain't daft — she just don't like him. I think it's jealousy, I do, on account o' he's young and can skip about like a sparrow, while she's nearly ninety and can't barely walk no more. And she don't like his name, neither."

"Gosling? It is unusual."

"No, not Gosling — George."

"Why doesn't she like the name George?"

"I can't say, but the Miss thinks it must remind Sally of someone else she don't like, but Sally don't remember exactly who. She's nearly ninety, after all."

"And who is Jamie?"

For answer Mary Clinch nodded toward Sally herself. Having completed her polishing of the cat's head, the old woman drew a tiny object from her clothes. It was a shagreen locket, oval in outline and very much worn, with a gold clasp. The trinket popped open; of its interior Bridget was able to discern two painted portraits in miniature, one of a young woman and another of a young gentleman.

"It's a pathetic enough tale," said Mary, and so launched into it. "This Jamie was Sally's young buck when she was a lass in Richford, the great city in the east. He asked her to marry him. But before the marriage could take place he disappeared — vanished, utterly — and never was seen again. Sally's whole world was thrown upside-down. There weren't no letters, not so much as a note, to tell her where he'd gone. She heard nothing from him again. See! See her peeking at the pictures? She don't allow anyone close to that locket, but the Miss — there's no one like her! — has pretty much worked it out. She believes the young buck there is Jamie, while the young lass is Sally herself."

"La!" exclaimed Bridget, with an expressive sigh. "Did she never marry?"

"Never. She left Richford for Salthead, you see, to join her sister and begin a new life. But her sister died, and then her parents died, and so she was left alone. She's waited now these many years for her Jamie to return; she's convinced he will. Most every day she makes some comment or other about how he's to be here directly. She don't realize how much time has passed — she's nearly ninety — and that her young buck, wherever he may be, is dead and dust by now."

Bridget wiped her eyes with a handkerchief. "That is so tragic," she sobbed. "Look — look — she's speaking to it!"

It was true. They could see Sally's lips moving, as though she were communing with the faded image of the young gentleman. Then she raised the locket to those same lips and kissed the portrait.

"She don't let anyone near the locket," Mary went on. "It's her secret treasure. She keeps it close by at all times. Keeps it by her bed at night, and always carries it with her. Which does remind me now — as the Miss asked me to tell you — there's a particular cove you'll need to keep a watch for. His name is Jack Hilltop. He's here often in the evenings. You'll not miss him — he's got spots all over his face like the pox. The Miss has her doubts about him. About a fortnight ago there was a right bloody row when he tried to pinch Sally's locket. He'd come by early and spent some time jawing with the ostler. Then he crept in here, when he saw that Sally was all alone. He thought she was asleep, and sailed right up behind her and tried to lift the locket. She weren't napping, though, and when she realized what was a-goin' on — why, what a screaming and a howling there was then! I'll give her credit — she hung onto that locket like she hangs onto that cat there. And then George and the Miss came a-running in, and it was all up for Mr. Jack Hilltop."

"And still he's welcome at the Pelican?"

"He explained to the Miss as he only wanted a look at the tiny pictures in the locket, as he thought he recognized the young buck. Told her he didn't intend to pinch it. The locket's got no value, as you can see; why he'd want to lift it is anybody's guess. The Miss, she believes his story — for now — but she's got her suspicions. I say he was telling lies enough to break a bridge. So if you see a lyin' cove with a spotted face in here, keep a tight watch on him — especially if he pops in early."

By this time Sally had put away the locket and started in again to doze. Mary and Bridget still were engaged in quiet conversation when the door of the Pelican swung open and a lazy figure breezed in — an older gentleman of middle height, with a soft brown beard, brown hair, and hazel eyes. Beneath his sporty gray paletot lurked a dark velvet coat and a cherry-colored waistcoat. One gloved hand carried a small medical bag; the other held a pipe that the gentleman was smoking with a rakish air.

"Hallo, hallo there," greeted the visitor, making his leisurely way across the floor. "Very sharp afternoon in the city today, very sharp. Not snowing yet — but not far from it, actually. That mournful light in the sky tells me winter is coming on."

"Good afternoon, Dr. Dampe," said Mary Clinch, and proceeded to introduce him to Bridget, whom he acknowledged with a very professional bow of his head.

"And how are we today, Miss Sprinkle?" he inquired, turning his attention to Sally.

The old woman raised her eyes. "Good evening, Dr. Jenkins. Oh, I'm not well today. I'm not well at all, Dr. Jenkins."

"Come, come, let's not exaggerate. You're the picture of health!"

"Dr. Jenkins?" whispered Bridget, to Mary Clinch. "Why does she call him Dr. Jenkins?"

"Because," volunteered Dr. Dampe, as an aside, "she believes me to be an eminent surgeon who served her family when she was a child in Richford. Pity! Richford, you know — that once proud and opulent city in the east, now heavily decayed."

The doctor fell to an examination of his patient, removing her glasses to look into her eyes, inspecting her withered hands, feeling her pulse, to all of which Sally complied without resistance. Little Nutmeg remained in Sally's lap during the entire procedure, sniffing the air and gazing critically at the learned physician.

"Have you seen my Jamie?" asked Sally. "He lives in Richford, you know. He's very dapper and handsome, and has a lot of money."

"I have seen him," replied the doctor, blithely, "and I have said to him — `Jamie, young sir, you are a very lucky fellow.'"

The old woman laughed. "He'll be here directly, you know. He knows that I am waiting for him. I'm sure he had his reasons for going away. But he will be here, I know he will."

"And we'll all have a merry celebration when he arrives," said Dr. Dampe, winking covertly at Mary and Bridget. "Now then, Miss Sprinkle, I have ascertained that your pulse is as vibrant as a Thoroughbred's. Moreover, there's no evidence of jaundice and your eyes are clear. Really, you'll outlive us all."

The light retreated from Sally's face, as her eyes fell upon the hand the doctor had held when noting her pulse. She proceeded to examine the hand with an intense fascination, noting the wrinkled, transparent skin, the crooked fingers, the swollen joints. She then performed the identical operation on its companion.

"Oh, Dr. Jenkins, Dr. Jenkins — these can't be my hands. They simply can't be. These hands don't belong to me. Whose are they?"

"Those are your hands, Miss Sprinkle, I can assure you. Whose do you think they are?"

"Oh, I don't know. I don't know. Dr. Jenkins — are they my mother's?"

The doctor, knowing the course of this little conversation only too well, fished up his medical bag. "Look here," he said, with a very professional clearing of his voice, "I'm prepared to attest that you are in perfect health, Miss Sprinkle, and what is more, quite ready for your dinner. I'm sure these two young ladies will be happy to see you to the kitchen. As for your physician — well, he is prepared for a fresh pint of bitter."

"Come along, Sally," said Mary Clinch. Gently she eased the old woman from her chair, which action caused Nutmeg to spring from Sally's lap with a disgruntled mew. "Here. Here's your cane. Come along then, as the doctor says, for I'm sure Cook has your dinner laid on by now."

"Beg Jamie to come directly, when next you see him, Doctor," called Sally, in a faint over-the-shoulder kind of voice, as Mary and Bridget escorted her to the kitchen. There they found Cook — a great bear of a woman with an enormous frizzled wig and an inflamed countenance, but the gentlest of dispositions — who was indeed ready with Sally's meal. There too they found the mistress of the Pelican, busily supervising arrangements for the evening's ministrations, as well as the industrious George Gosling, who managed to avoid receiving another ugly face from Sally by rushing out through the opposite door as soon as she entered.

As the pale twilight faded the first of the evening's Honeywood regulars came grouping in, and were received at the great oak bar. With their pipes drawn and their glasses filled to brimming, they soon were prepared, one and all, to beguile the watches of this night with the usual free-and-easy conversation, joviality, and good-fellowship for which the Pelican was renowned. If you had been there you might have noted among the revelers Mr. John Stinger, the chemist, and bluff Donald Thompson, the plasterer — both of whom later provided me with vivid accounts of the disturbance that occurred that night. You might also have spotted Henry Duff, the carter, and George Starkie, the millwright, and Mrs. Starkie, and of course the Rev. Mr. Samuel Nash, the rector of St. Barnacle's.

The early part of the evening slipped uneventfully into the past. The esteemed Miss Honeywood spent her time at the bar, conversing with her faithful and coaxing long draughts of dark nectar from the beer-engine. She was in the midst of preparing one such draught for the rector, when she turned to find a worried Mary Clinch at her side.

"Excuse, please, Miss — but — it's Sally, Miss. She's taken a bit of a tumble from her bed. I — I believe she may have hurt herself. Could you please come quickly, Miss? And if Dr. Dampe might yet be here — "

The mistress of the house nodded curtly. She ran her eyes about the room until she located the figure of the doctor, where he sat in lazy conversation with a small group of regulars. She wheeled round from behind the bar — having recruited one of her accessory minions to take her place — and made her tall and angular way to his side. Apologizing for the interruption, she hastily outlined the situation. The physician immediately abandoned his pipe and glass and accompanied her, with the rector following in their wake.

They traversed a narrow passage toward the rear of the house, where the door to a corner room stood ajar. There they found Sally on the floor, with her back against the bedstead and her dazed eyes looking at the wall. Kneeling beside her and trying her best to comfort her was Bridget Leek.

"She must have fainted," said Bridget.

"Or she wanted to get out of her bed, Miss, and slipped on the floor," suggested Mary Clinch.

After a swift examination the doctor determined that no serious injury had been sustained, although a few scratches were evident on Sally's head and arm. For her part Sally volunteered nothing. Her eyes were staring fixedly ahead as though she were peering down a long tunnel.

"More than likely she fell asleep, and when she woke she thought it was the morning," said Mary. "She went to get out of her bed and took a tumble."

"Nonsense, Mary Clinch," replied Miss Honeywood, starchily. "Sally never has difficulty sleeping. She always goes straight through the night."

Bridget, looking about, spied the shagreen locket on the floor where it apparently had fallen. She was about to retrieve it when Sally emerged from her spell. One withered hand reached out and closed over the trinket.

"My poor Jamie," whispered Sally, and tremblingly gathered the locket to her breast.

The doctor stood back with a thoughtful expression. "Look here," he said, smoothing his beard. "She seems well for the most part, except for those few scratches. And there's that odd look in her face. It seems likely to me she must have fallen out of bed — took a bad turn, or had some sort of nasty dream perhaps. Happens to me now and then, actually — the dream part, not the falling-out-of-bed part. Well, come along, then — let's get her up and up."

Gently they lifted Sally from the floor and returned her to her bed, drawing the blankets over her. She paid them no notice, and lay there with her head on the pillow and her eyes on the ceiling.

The ruddy countenance and broad flappable ears of George Gosling appeared at the door, with the curious faces of John Stinger and Donald Thompson crowding the jamb behind him.

"What's a-goin' on?" he asked. "Has the old lady took a fit?"

"No fits, George Gosling," returned Miss Honeywood, sternly. "The doctor believes Sally must have fallen out of her bed. There's nothing damaged — she'll recover."

"I heard her gabbing," said George. "Who was it was in here with her?"

"What do you mean by that?" asked the doctor.

"Yes, what do you mean, George?" demanded Miss Moll.

"Well, Miss," replied George — a trifle uncomfortable, and fearing for his earlobes — "once or twice, just a short time ago, while I was a-running back and forth, outside in the passage — as I does so often around here — I heard the old lady speaking. The door was nigh shut, so I couldn't see what was a-goin' on inside, but I'm sure there was a body in here with her."

"Talking in her sleep, most likely," opined the doctor.

"Pardon for making so free, Dr. Dampe — but I don't think that was it," said George. "It seemed she was having a chat, she was, with somebody what was in the room with her."

"And did you hear this somebody's voice?"

"No, I did not. The old lady was asking questions. Now, why would she be asking questions, is my question, if there weren't somebody in here to ask 'em to?"

"Well? Was anyone in here?" asked Miss Moll, looking round at the others. Before anyone could respond, however, a desolate moan was heard from Sally.

"Oh — oh — don't tell my mother," she pleaded, with tears rising in her eyes. "Don't tell my mother — please — "

"There, there," said Miss Honeywood, her starchiness temporarily yielding to Sally's distress. "Not to worry. No one at the Pelican is going to tell your mother a thing, Sally, you can be assured of that."

"Oh — I'm old," cried Sally. "Where am I? Is this my room? Where are my teeth? I don't know what I'm about. I can't think anymore. I'm — I'm not myself anymore. I don't know who I am."

"You're Sally," said the kindly rector, coming forward to press her hand. "Miss Sally Sprinkle, of the Blue Pelican!"

"Pelican? Sprinkle? I don't know — oh!" exclaimed Sally, in rather a changed tone, and raised herself onto her elbows. "Where is my young scamp?"

"Who's that?" asked Mary Clinch, with a puzzled frown. "Who's that, Sally?"

"My young scamp — where is he off to now? Oh, he's such grand company!"

"What's she talking about, Miss? What young scamp?"

"Sally," said Miss Honeywood, "has there been someone here to see you? Who's your young scamp?"

"Why, that poor little boy, of course," smiled Sally. "The poor little scamp who visits me. The one who comes in the night."

Clouds of confusion drifted across the faces in the room — all the faces, that is, except Sally's, whose own now radiated sunshine.

"I knew I'd caught her gabbing!" exclaimed George Gosling.

"Oh, my young scamp is a darling little chap," Sally meandered on. "But he seems always so unhappy. Something is bothering him, I know it. What he needs is someone to cheer him! That's what I was trying to do, you know. Oh!" Here she became mildly agitated, as though an uncomfortable thought had infected her. "Now it comes back to me. He was standing just there, by the door" — one crooked finger extended in George Gosling's direction — "and I was wishing to get out of the bed to go to him. The poor little fellow — so sad! Then, while I was watching, his little fingers curled up into balls, and his eyes sharpened terribly, and he showed me his teeth. Then his little face turned green and his head melted off. Oh — it was a horrible thing to see — horrible — I was so frightened — I must have fallen from my bed — and now my poor little scamp is gone! Oh, I'm sorry, I'm sorry — please don't tell my mother — "

The effect this speech had on the listeners I leave to your imagination.

"A nightmare — oh, it's quite plain," concluded the rector, looking round. "What else could it be?"

"The old lady's gone crackers," whispered George, confidentially, to Mr. Stinger and Mr. Thompson.

"See here," said Dr. Dampe, "what did this young fellow look like? Can you describe him?"

"Oh, he's just a little boy — he's my little scamp — although he's come to me only three or four times," replied Sally. "He has such beautiful red hair and such wonderful eyes — such sorrowful eyes. Of course, that was before his face turned green and his head melted off. It's very sad — he's lame, you see."

Miss Honeywood interposed sharply —

"Lame, did you say, Sally? In what way is he lame?"

She threw a starchy look at Mary Clinch, who had grown visibly uneasy at Sally's words. Mistress and minion exchanged glances as if anticipating, through some shared secret knowledge, what the old woman was about to reveal.

"It's his little leg," said Sally. "His left leg. It's shriveled, you see, from the paralysis, and so he isn't able to use it. I suppose that's why he's so unhappy. Poor little fellow! Oh — I'm very tired now — I don't feel well at all — "

The mistress of the Pelican had no immediate response. She stood wrapped in thought, uncharacteristically absorbed in some remote inner vista. Mary Clinch, more characteristically, looked as though she were about to swallow her fingers. Blue-eyed Bridget watched them both, still quite at a loss, while Dr. Dampe, in an effort to resolve the situation, remarked to no one in particular — "My goodness, there's no little fellow in this house," then turned to Miss Honeywood and asked — "Is there?"

Miss Moll shook her head. "Not for many, many years."

"The old lady's off her nut," declared George Gosling. "What's all this talk about a kid, then? There ain't no kids at the Pelican." Here the youthful George squared his brow and assumed an air of excessive maturity, so as not to be mistaken for one of the aforementioned young people.

"I believe," said Miss Honeywood — growing starchy and angular, and so more like her usual self — "I believe it is time that you, George Gosling, returned to your duties. Kindly see to our good friends in the common-room."

"Yes, Miss," sighed George, unwilling to depart the scene, but resigned to it under threat of having his earlobes pinched.

"Look here," said Dr. Dampe, impatiently, "there's something odd going on and I'm going to understand it. Is there or is there not a young boy in this house?"

"There is no young boy," replied Miss Honeywood. "Not now, at any rate."

Unsatisfied the doctor turned his attention to Mary Clinch, who was biting her fingers and looking as anxious as it was possible for a head chambermaid to look. His eyes shifted to Bridget, then to Sally, who had now lapsed into a doze, and then to the rector, whose restless expression suggested he might be a vein worth mining.

"Rector? You're always remarkably well-informed about things. Is there some secret here?"

Mr. Nash shot a quick glance at Miss Honeywood, before tendering his careful reply.

"It sounds to me very much like the Lawson child," he said.

"And who might that be?"

"A lame little boy with red hair who once lived in this house. His family owned the Pelican, you see — in the early days, when it was a private residence. The father was a brewer, and consequently quite well connected in Salthead."

"Private residence?" returned Dr. Dampe, lifting his eyebrows. "This house has been the Blue Pelican for as long as I can remember — and my goodness, that's at the very least forty years!"

"Yes, so it is."

The doctor remained curious at his apparent reticence. "And the young boy? This Lawson child?"

"Lived in this very room," said Miss Honeywood. Her pale glance drifted about the snug, spare little chamber in quiet reflection. "It must be eighty years ago now."

"And?"

"He died in it as well, of a malignant fever. It utterly demolished the parents. He was their only child, you see, with no possibility of another. For years after they left the room just as it was, completely undisturbed, as though the boy still were living in it. They became quite insistent, in fact, that he hadn't died at all. Everyone in the parish was convinced they'd gone mad. After the house was sold the room was converted to storage, and has been used for that ever since — until Sally's arrival, of course."

The doctor responded with another cock of his eyebrows. "But surely Sally knows of this, and so dreamed of something with which she was familiar."

"Most unlikely," replied Miss Moll. "Few people today would know of it. The rector — who, as you know, is something of an antiquary — and Mary Clinch, to whom I once mentioned it in an unguarded moment — and myself, of course — were quite possibly the only ones until this evening. To my knowledge Sally has never heard of the Lawson child. She was not living in Salthead at the time the child died, and she certainly has never mentioned him."

Came a lengthy pause. Here, indeed, thought the doctor, was fresh matter for his colleague Titus Tiggs. Until now, spirits at the Pelican had seen fit to confine themselves to the vicinity of the great oak bar in the common-room. The doctor looked from Miss Moll, standing with her angular arms folded and her pale eyes steady, to the rector, then to the anxious Mary, then last to Sally Sprinkle who lay snoring in her bed. After a few moments' contemplation of the floor he cleared his voice, in that lofty manner so common to physicans.

"Extraordinary development," he said. "Wouldn't have believed it, actually, but for certain collateral circumstances. You'll recall young Mr. Rime — that wild tale of his and his reaction to the musk melon. I am afraid, Miss Honeywood, that an analysis of the situation will require considerable thought and reflection — which exercise can, of course, be aided by a glass of your best bitter. Rector — will you join me? If only I can remember where it was I laid my pipe — "

"I believe I'll require two glasses," said the rector.

CHAPTER X

Southward the Beasts

A big, big job — so the saying goes — calls for a big, big man.

Absent any evidence of the latter, a small wiry one in pinstripes would have to do. The small wiry man now urging his horse steadily forward, traversing the broad incline between two heath-covered hillocks, would have had no such thought, however. Such a thought, indeed, would never have breached his cranium, for Mr. Samson Icks, despite his height (or lack of it) considered himself to be, by very definition, a big man. Viewed as it were through the smoked lenses of his intellect, that definition encompassed, for Mr. Icks, a man of importance as well as a man of ability — a man of considerable personal experience — a man with knowledge of the world — an acknowledged leader of men — a man who could be trusted to get things done — in short, a line-by-line, point-by-point description of Mr. Samson Icks himself, the ideal man for a big, big job.

Presupposing, of course, that a man who could get things done had also the time to do those things right. And therein lay the key element — *time*. Ever since the latest rumblings of discontent between Mr. Icks and his bald-pated overlord, time had been in very generous supply for the dapper gentleman in pinstripes. Which was a good thing, in retrospect, for the big, big job that he had now embarked upon was likely to consume, as Samson himself had expressed it, a mighty parcel of his time.

Not that he would be venturing forth on such a mission alone. He and his horse, a bony, shock-headed hunter with one white stocking, comprised merely the vanguard of the party. Behind them jogged a second horse, a chestnut, bearing a hard-featured man with eyes like steel and a jaw like stone, who kept a watchful look-out, a cutlass and small-sword being much in evidence at his waist. The cold, searching eyes of Cast-iron Billy swept the road, across and across, grimly alert for anything at all the least suspicious — whether the perceived threat lay in human form, or in something else altogether, could not be determined.

A transport van of goodly dimensons followed. It was drawn by a sturdy pair of nags, with the driving-reins and whip in the capable hands of Mr. Lew Pilcher, his white side-whiskers streaming from beneath his hat brim. Behind the van, guarding the rear, was a young gentleman on a coal-black mare — a slight youth, trimly built, with faint pencil mustaches and tight, eager little eyes. A wicked rapier hung at his side, keeping company with a brace of daggers lodged at his belt.

Beyond the hillocks the frost-hardened road lurched and groaned to one side, and dropped into a narrow ravine. Walls of granite fleshed with pines and cedars rose up on either side. It was early morning — the sun had yet to appear — and the air was sharp. No sound penetrated the confines of the ravine, wild and somber that it was, apart from the clatter of horseshoes and the jingle of bridle-bits, and the rumbling growl of the van-wheels. The men themselves rode in purposeful silence, as men intent upon a mission often do, particularly at such an hour and with such a freshening breeze in their faces.

At the far end of the ravine the walls fell away, revealing a country of broad, sweeping uplands dotted with clumps of gorse and detached groups of trees — in brief, the country of the fells. A half-hour's travel brought the men to a long valley, richly verdured, and strewn with boulders of immense proportion. At the horses' feet ran a brawling stream, its ice-cold waters ringing fresh and clear in the mountain air. The valley stretched to the left and right in a general north-south direction, its opposing edge delineated by a range of jagged hills rising in bold relief out of the east. The sky behind the hills blushed as the sun rose, flooding the surface of the valley with morning tints.

As they rode along the men observed that a number of the huge boulders scattered about the distant landscape were in motion. Gradually, as their outlines grew more distinct and the details clearer, these stony giants acquired a set of unusual characteristics, *viz.*, a dense coat of red-brown hair, four massive legs like pillars, an arching pair of ivory tusks, flattened ears, and a grasping, pendulous trunk. Like galleons the boulders seemed to be sailing — slowly, silently, majestically — across the valley floor.

Such was the scene that greeted Mr. Icks and his grim party of execution men as they rode into the mastodon camp. The camp itself was little more than a loose assemblage of tents and sheds, barns, paddocks, tumble-down outhouses and a few other oddments, all of very rude design. The one substantial structure, a cabin, was a homely blend of weatherboard and log construction, with some cobbled stonework thrown in. It had tiny windows with lead lattice glazing, a slant roof, and a chimney with a curl of smoke rising into the air.

The travelers drew up before the cabin and dismounted. Mr. Pilcher rose in his seat and stretched his limbs, glancing about the camp with lazy eyes and a self-satisfied air, as if to say — "So this be it!" — before clambering down from the van.

"Hoo!" exclaimed Cast-iron Billy. "Uneventful trip. Just the way I like 'em!" He wiped his greasy hair and coughed once or twice, before attacking a muscle in his back made sore by riding.

"Sich splendor!" remarked Mr. Pilcher, winking broadly to his companions as he pointed out several of the more luxurious features of the camp.

The last rider, the slight youth with the pencil mustaches, looked disdainfully about the premises with his tight little eyes, but said nothing.

Having picketed their horses in a nearby field, the lesser members of the party now gathered round the acknowledged leader of men.

"Gentlemen," said Mr. Icks, reaching into his coat to retrieve some blue sheets of law scrivenry garnished with red ink lines and silver seals. "I have here, as ye can see, the instrument of execution, what has been duly and officially drawn up and notarized. In my studied opinion we'll have little trouble with the rascals here. We'll carry out the transfer as neat and tight as possible, and then be about the main business. There's nearly a dozen o' the stock as'll require tending and readying. Then there's a pile o' goods and chattels, as'll need to be inventoried and carted into the van. Last and longest, there's the big trek. So ye can see, there'll be wery little time for pleasant talk on this job."

"I hate pleasant talk," said the youth with the tight little eyes. "I hate it, I do."

"Now, then, Joseph," returned Mr. Icks, gingerly, "we'll have no outbursts from ye today, will we?"

"Hoo! An outburst from Joe Rooke? Ain't that a rarity," laughed Billy.

The youth threw him a ferocious glance loaded with menace.

"Joseph," said Mr. Icks, hardening his voice, like a father on the verge of disciplining a child.

Further discussion was prevented by the opening of the cabin-door and the appearance of a sturdy little man in greenish drab trousers and a checked waistcoat. Mr. Icks stepped forward to greet him, while the remaining members of the party stood aside to watch, Mr. Pilcher lighting his clay pipe and leaning with his shoulder propped against one big wheel of the van.

The two gentlemen who came together at the front of the cabin — the one all in black running pinstripes, the other in the shabby trousers and checked waistcoat — were nearly equal in height (they both were equally tall, or equally short), and so faced one another eye to eye, Mr. Icks looking into Mr. Hoakum's honest blue ones, Mr. Hoakum into the impenetrable smoked lenses.

Without ceremony Samson Icks extended a hand, displaying the calamitous sheets of law-scrivenry.

"It's an execution," he said, very simply, "as has come down from the sheriff. We claim possession upon a judgment for costs and money advanced by the aggrieved creditor, whose name ye see listed there, and there, and there too. Ye'll observe the official seals of the court — here, and here. Are ye prepared to give over, Mr. Hatch Hoakum, according to the terms as has been agreed on?"

Mr. Hoakum was about to reply when the door of the cabin swung open and another figure was deposited on the step. This one was, by contrast, strikingly tall, taking the form of a gaunt, goofish young fellow with strange watery eyes, a long slender nose, and a gaping mouth that would have looked at home on a bull-calf. He was clad in overalls of an underdone-pie-crust color, with the legs tucked into top-boots. A blue cotton neckcloth and a wide-awake hat with an enormous floppy brim completed the picture.

Mr. Hoakum, who had glanced back upon hearing the door, returned his attention to the wiry man in pinstripes, and to the dreadful instrument hanging from that gentleman's fingers. This document — representing for Mr. Hoakum the collapse of his dreams, the obliteration of his hopes, and the disappearance of his livelihood — he regarded now with a curiously resigned detachment.

"Mr. Benjamin Blizzard, as is nephew to Mr. Hoakum?" inquired Mr. Icks, of the gaunt, goofish figure.

"Blaster," replied that young man, sullenly.

"I see there's a mistake. Mr. Benjamin Blaster, then."

"Not Mr. Benjamin Blaster Then. Blaster."

"Blaster. Just — Blaster?"

"Blaster."

Such words left Mr. Icks a trifle disconcerted, and also a trifle annoyed at the interruption in the smooth flow of his official duties.

"Ain't that dainty," he muttered under his breath.

115

"I b'lieve, sir," spoke up Mr. Hoakum, not wishing to delay the inevitable any longer than necessary, "as it'll be a sizable undertaking, and busy gents like yourselves need to get to work, arter all."

Samson Icks answered with a dry smile, and returned the law-papers to his coat.

"That's wery thoughtful of ye," he said, expansively. "These gentlemen as ye see here are, like myself, wery experienced in such matters. They'll be as quick and professional about it as possible."

The gentleman in the checked waistcoat nodded to each member of the party. He acted like a man who had been drowning at sea for ages and was anxious now for a final release. Retiring a pace behind, he said to the goofish young fellow —

"Blaster, lad — call the beasts." He nearly added "for the last time," but found himself unable to form those particular words.

Blaster, examining the newcomers from beneath his greasy wide-awake, appeared not to have heard his uncle's request.

"Where might you be headed?" he demanded loudly.

Mr. Hoakum, who had been rolling and crushing his cap in his hands, stopped to look at his nephew for a moment, then shifted his attention to Samson Icks. "Ah — I had gathered, sir — from a previous conversation — that it might be south," he ventured. "Might that be — ah — still the case?"

Mr. Icks could see no harm in disclosing such a detail. "South to Crow's-end is what the orders say. Do ye know the place called Strangeways?"

The evenness of Mr. Hoakum's response to his predicament suffered a setback. For a moment the sturdy little man knew not what to say; the answer received from Mr. Icks was not one he'd been prepared for. Appalled, Blaster marched forward and stood just behind his uncle, hovering there like some guardian angel tending to his earthly ward. (Like no guardian angel with which I am familiar, however, with that gaping mouth and that great floppy wide-awake).

"That's a zoo!" cried Blaster, displaying the same horrified aspect as if the word had been *slaughterhouse*.

Mr. Icks nodded very attentively, rubbing his hands and smiling in what he hoped was a reassuring way; for he sensed that the relative docility with which he and his associates had been received was now threatened.

"Aye," he agreed. "It's a zoo. And rather a tidy one, too, and wery well known. They's agreed to take in the stock, ye see, for a decent pile o' coin."

"You can't put the beasts in the zoo!" protested Blaster, with a defiant wobble of his wide-awake.

Mr. Icks smiled again and tossed up his hands, indicating there was little more to discuss.

At this point the slight youth with the pencil mustaches stepped behind Samson Icks, and so the four gentlemen so placed formed a little tableau — the short sturdy man in the checked waistcoat overshadowed by his tall nephew, on the one side; on the other, the wiry man in pinstripes and smoked lenses, backed up by the sour-faced youth with the rapier. From several feet away Cast-iron Billy watched in fascination, massaging his beard, while Mr. Pilcher continued his leisurely smoke.

Mr. Hoakum seemed on the verge of making some reply, but evidently thought the better of it and said instead to his nephew, in a tone of dignified resignation —

"Call the beasts, lad."

"That I will not!" vowed Blaster, with another defiant toss of his wide-awake.

"It was a fair and honest bargain," said Mr. Hoakum. "Fair and honorable. Two honest men made an honest bargain, both in good faith. It was a gamble and now it's lost. My father, whose business it once was, would have done no different; for he was an honest man. The miser trusted us with his money, lad. It's his right to be paid. So call the beasts."

"That's right — call 'em!" said Mr. Rooke, glowering fiercely from a point just above Samson's shoulder.

The cheeks of Mr. Icks flushed deeply as this challenge reverberated in his ear. "Steady, Joseph," said he, turning his head aside in warning to the volatile youth. The smoked lenses darted from Mr. Hoakum to Blaster and back again.

"Call 'em!" pursued Mr. Rooke, undaunted. "I hate 'em. I hate 'em all! Brutes. Enormous, stinking, disgusting monsters. They're a dying breed, and it's good riddance to 'em, I say!"

"There may be some dyin' soon enough, but it ain't the beasts as'll be doin' it," returned Blaster, with a passionate wobble of his hat.

Young Mr. Rooke's hand dropped to his rapier. "Call 'em, you great bean-pole!" he hissed.

"Joseph!" barked Samson, loudly and sternly. "Ye'll kindly look after yer manners, sir, and ye'll keep yer hot words to yerself!"

He returned to Mr. Hoakum, trying his best to maintain an air of imperturbable professionalism. "Mr. Rooke, here, he's the eager sort, ye see — wery devoted to his craft. A noble competitor! But ye must admit, friend Hoakum, that there's just the slightest bit o' truth in what he has to say. Aye! Not that old Icks is agreeing with him *in toto*, mind ye, but what with the clearing of the roads and the coming of the coaches — why, surely ye must know there's wery little need for such creatures now. Their day is gone. But ye should not regard it as a personal affront. Ye should regard it as — as something of a favor. Aye! As a new opportunity for ye, in having the brutes taken off yer hands."

There followed a chilly silence during which Mr. Hoakum and his nephew attempted to digest these remarks. Resigned to his fate with an equanimity bordering on the marvelous, Mr. Hoakum had cause now perhaps to reconsider that position; while Blaster, his initial blast spent, braved the glances of Mr. Icks and Mr. Rooke with his watery eyes but with apparently little more to say. Wild plans and imaginative strategies flitted through the mind of Mr. Hoakum — all to no avail. Giving a few smart tugs and pulls at his checked waistcoat, he raised his chin and looked Mr. Icks straight in his smoked lenses.

"Call the beasts, lad," he said to his nephew, though his eyes were on Samson. "Call 'em."

Blaster did not obey at first, but maintained his watch on the enemy — particularly on Mr. Rooke, whose fingers were still on his rapier, though a restraining hand had now been placed on that young man's shoulder by a very grim-eyed Billy.

Another jerk of his wide-awake and Blaster plunged away, muttering, toward the cabin. He returned bearing an enormous elongated pipe or flute, nearly five feet in length, and of very primitive construction. He set off with it across the field, eyes averted from the execution men, and reaching a particular spot some distance away halted and raised the instrument to his lips. To the ears of the visitors the plaintive melody that emerged was as eerie and dreaming a sound as any they had ever heard. Its mournful cadence floated on the mountain air, up the valley and down the valley and into the hills. Wherever they happened to be, the huge boulders — shaggy red mastodons each — lifted their heads as the call reached them. Within moments, the earth could be felt to tremble with the tread of thunder-beasts approaching from every corner of the landscape.

Mr. Icks and his associates now entered upon a brief discussion with Mr. Hoakum, wherein it was determined how the job of transferring the movables into the van might be accomplished. It was decided as well that Cast-iron Billy, who had some experience of shovel-tuskers — the red mastodons' southern cousins — would assist Blaster in collecting the animals. While he strode off on that errand, Mr. Hoakum led Mr. Pilcher and a sour-faced Joe Rooke into the cabin.

Not long after, one of the small tents planted near the cabin was seen to rustle. The flap opened and a ragged gray figure appeared, stretching and yawning, and scratching at its woolly, mouse-colored hair. It had small nut-like eyes, a dingy beard, and a highly industrious mouth that mumbled and chattered of itself. The figure seemed taken with a nervous ailment that caused its limbs to twitch and squirm with exaggerated movements.

Mr. Icks, who was standing nearby writing in a pocket notebook, raised his eyebrows as he caught sight of the figure. He hesitated for a brief space as the line of his mouth firmed. A shrewd look arose behind the smoked lenses, and he put away the notebook. His glance strayed momentarily to where Blaster and Billy stood among the thunder-beasts. He saw the face of the goofish youth fill with a special joy as the animals crowded in around him, waving their trunks and lifting their ears inquisitively. He saw too that his colleague Billy, he of the eyes of steel and the grizzled jaw of stone, was himself visibly enamored of the giants. At first suspicious of him they seemed less distrustful now, owing to the acceptance of his presence by Blaster. So the two of them, goofish youth and grizzled veteran, together proceeded to lead the creatures toward the spacious paddock lying just beyond the cabin.

Rubbing his head to clear it of this vision, Mr. Icks turned to confront the other vision, that of the ragged gray figure, which had by now trotted up beside him.

"Good day to ye, friend Earhart," said Samson, with a brittle smile that was less than welcoming. "It was not that I was expecting to see ye here today, however."

The vision pointed with a wavering finger. "Look there! Blaster's called the beasts. Blaster woke Charley when he called them," said the gray figure — otherwise Mr. Charles Earhart, otherwise the Sheephead. He gave up another yawn, stretched his jerky limbs and adjusted his rags. "Mr. Samson, why are you here at the camp? Are you come to see the beasts?"

"Not in particular."

"Then why?"

"Business, friend Charles, business. It ain't important."

"What sort of business?"

Mr. Icks seemed uncomfortable with such persistence. He grinned dryly and buried his hands in his coat-pockets.

Charley, now fully awake, grew sly on a sudden and drew from his clothes a gleaming silver watch suspended from a ribbon — the very same bauble with which he had regaled Mr. Hoakum at the Blue Pelican not many nights before.

"Is it — is it — Mr. Hunter's business?" he asked.

"No names, sir, no names! What is it ye've got there?" demanded Mr. Icks, eyeing the timepiece suspiciously. "Where would *ye* get a thing like that?"

"Mr. Hunter's business," whispered Charley.

"Aye, I understand ye now," returned Mr. Icks, the light now shining upon him.

"Mr. Hunter! Mr. Hunter!" Charley exclaimed, swinging the watch from side to side and marveling at how its shiny carapace sparkled in the morning sun.

"No names, friend Earhart, no names! Trust me, friend Charles — trust me — ye'll not want to mention that young gentleman's name," said Mr. Icks, clutching the excited Mr. Earhart by the shoulders. "He's a devil! Do ye hear me? And ye'll not know when or how, but he may be a-watchin' ye. Ye'll not want to make such a rascal as that angry, eh? Ye remember what old Icks told ye, don't ye, concerning the rage of that young gentleman, when he learned as ye'd been unsuccessful — twice unsuccessful — at retrieving the certain object of his desire?"

Sheephead Charley, who had been only half-conscious of this sermon — his mental faculties, such as they were, being expended on the watch — looked into the face of Mr. Icks with a show of concern and a few feeble extrusions of his lips and tongue.

"And what's more," continued Samson, "it's my studied opinion that said young gentleman as likely blames old Icks for the loss as blames ye. As having entrusted the success of the job, and so my faith as well, in ye, friend Charles — well, if ye'd seen that yellow light from hell come into his eyes, it were a sight as ye'd never forget in all yer life. Ye'd not like to see old Icks come to a bad patch, now, would ye?"

"No, Mr. Samson, no bad patches."

"Good. For ye see, Mr. Earhart, it's only with the barest of luck that old Icks was able to escape that devil. Even now he ain't necessarily safe from the yellow light. Aye! And who would help Icks, I ask ye, friend Charles, if said young gentleman should choose to come after him? And he might, ye know, at any moment. If old Icks ended up a-roastin', who'd walk across the yard and take him off the spit?"

"Charley'd take you off the spit, Mr. Samson," murmured the Sheephead, a trifle absently, for already he had grown restless and was again admiring the silvery bauble. He held it to his ear and uttered a wild laugh. "You see? You see? Charley has time of day!"

"I wonder if you do," said Mr. Icks, with a doubtful frown. He found his own attention diverted by the glittering watch, by its brilliant sheen and intricate design, but most of all by its obvious value.

"Can old Icks have a peek at that lovely object, friend Charles?" he smiled. "Just for a moment, o' course. A friendly inspection."

Slyly, confidentially, the watch was presented — dangled, I should say, for a few seconds under the nose of Mr. Icks, before being quickly withdrawn. Not a long time for a look, certainly, but long enough for Mr. Icks to note the letters "H.J.B." engraved in flowery script on the case.

"I see how it is," declared Mr. Icks. "Ye lifted that watch from a certain party, didn't ye, Mr. Earhart? Ye took something as didn't belong to ye — isn't that what ye did?"

The Sheephead broke into another laugh, with his head thrown back and his limbs a-quiver. "Eaton Wafers! Eaton Wafers!" he exclaimed, stamping the ground repeatedly. "Mr. Hunter's business!"

"Ye will be quiet, sir!" cried Mr. Icks, grasping the jerky figure again by the shoulders. "Not a word, Mr. Earhart — not one word, sir! Ye'll not want anyone to hear that name. Believe me — ye'll not want that! Ye'll not want to stand and face the yellow light. Do ye want the very devil to call on ye — or perhaps yer friends there?"

The Sheephead quailed in sudden alarm. "Oh, no, Mr. Samson. Not Charley's friends — not Blaster! Not Mr. Hatch! Charley disremembered. Don't tell Blaster. Charley don't want Blaster to know what he's done."

"Ye pinched that watch, didn't ye, friend?"

Charley nodded, dropping his eyes and looking quite repentant. A little sniffle or two even escaped his nose.

"And ye're ashamed, aren't ye?"

"Ashamed. Busy Charley. Busy, busy Charley." He emitted a hollow, self-pitying sigh, swinging his head to and fro in rhythmic condolence with his predicament.

Mr. Icks replaced his hands in his coat-pockets. "Ye removed that watch from the premises, sir," he declared, as though propounding a point of law, "and yet twice — in two separate attempts, mind ye — ye could not come away with the object as ye'd been sent to recover. The property of the young gentleman, as ye were sent to reclaim, ye could not retrieve — and so ye took something what didn't belong to ye, merely for yer own selfish gain."

The Sheephead confirmed it all with a few mournful extrusions of the lips and tongue. "It weren't an easy job, Mr. Samson — it weren't like the others. Charley couldn't do it."

"The young squire as is master of that house — ye're sure he didn't see ye, is that right?"

"Charley's sure."

"And the object — to the best of yer knowledge — remains there?"

A sad swing of the head, which was abruptly transformed into a quick little nod.

"Which is it, sir — no or yes?"

A vigorous nod, then a shrug.

Mr. Icks paused thoughtfully. "I tell ye, friend Earhart, it's a good thing, for both ye and old Icks, that ye weren't detected. But it's a wery bad thing that ye couldn't recover the desired object. That devil of a young gentleman — anything he wants, somehow I know he'll get it. Ye say the object's there yet in the house, and ye may be right about that or ye may not. He may have clamped onto it already for all old Icks can tell. I ain't seen him since that last night, when he said as he'd resolve the matter another way. But it ain't healthy thinking o' such things. Ye'll not go off now, friend Charles, a-jabbering that name to everyone ye meet, eh?"

The Sheephead cast a furtive look round as he pocketed the watch.

"Charley's come to see the beasts," he said. "Did you know, Mr. Samson — someone's come to take the beasts away?"

Mr. Icks made no reply, but instead retrieved his pocket notebook and looked very hard into it.

"Who is it? Who's taking the beasts from Mr. Hatch?" asked Charley, watching the mastodons as they were led into the paddock. "Is it that one? That one there with Blaster, the one with the beard? Is that the one taking them?"

"One of 'em," grunted Samson.

"And the others — the ones in Mr. Hatch's cabin. Are those the ones, too?"

"Aye."

"Those are bad men. Charley should tell them what he thinks of them. Why don't you tell them what you think, Mr. Samson? What kind of men would take the beasts away? What kind of men would do that to Mr. Hatch?"

"Men o' business," returned Mr. Icks, uncomfortably.

"Business? Whose business?"

Out of the cabin came Mr. Hoakum, followed by long Lew Pilcher and Mr. Rooke. On seeing Mr. Icks they strode forward to join him for some moments of quiet deliberation. Mr. Pilcher nodded lazily a few times, then tapped the youthful Rooke on the shoulder and together they re-entered the cabin. After a brief space they returned with armsful of goods and supplies which they carried to the van.

Sheephead Charley observed all of this with rising agitation. He stumbled about, confused, one outstretched hand directed first at Mr. Icks, then at the van, then at Mr. Pilcher, then at everything at once.

"Your business?" he exclaimed, taking aim at Samson. "Charley thinks it's — Charley can't believe — is it your business, Mr. Samson? Mr. Hatch — Mr. Hatch — whose business — ?"

"It's all fine, Charles, it's fine," spoke up Mr. Hoakum, reassuringly. "Everything is perfectly tol'rable. Mr. Icks and these men are here to help with the move."

Samson Icks kept his eyes askance of the Sheephead, focusing his attention instead on the efforts of Mr. Rooke and Mr. Pilcher.

"Mr. Samson?" whispered Charley. His features were riven by dismay as the great and awful truth came home to him. "It's Mr. Samson's business? Mr. Hatch — tell Charley — please — is Mr. Samson taking the beasts? Is it Mr. Samson's business?"

"It's Mr. Tusk's business," said Mr. Hoakum, by way of correction. "It was a fair and honest agreement, Charles. But we lost our gamble, Blaster and I. And so we must live up to our side of the bargain — like honorable men, arter all. What's a man's life, sir, without honor? I b'lieve you're an honorable fellow yourself, Charles — surely you understand. Mr. Icks is here to help us."

The dapper gentleman in pinstripes — hearing these last words out of the corner of his ear, as it were — winced, unaccountably.

But Sheephead Charley was not to be dissuaded. Stumbling forward with his bumping, lurching gait, he took Samson Icks by the shoulder and swung him around — and so stood facing him, quivering in his rags and barely able to express himself.

"Your — your b-business?" he stammered out, between violent extrusions of his lips and tongue. Flecks of spittle stained his whiskers. "Your b-business, Mr. Samson?"

Mr. Icks did not answer. The hardy red bricks of his complexion grew very cold, the line of his mouth very sharp. An aura of estrangement oozed from behind the smoked lenses. He wrested himself from the vagabond's grip, straightening his pinstripes in a symbolic attempt, perhaps, to recover his dignity. He turned his back and walked stiffly away.

With a dismal groan the Sheephead watched as the belongings of his two great friends were hauled from the cabin and flung into the van. Hauled, loaded, carted, conveyed, carried, transported, taken away — however stated it did not matter — and all by strangers, led by a supposed friend who had betrayed him. At the same time the last of the thunder-beasts was seen entering the paddock. The swing-gate was fastened by Billy; and so the little world of the camp drew down into its final circle.

"You'll understand afore all this is done, Charles," said Mr. Hoakum. He wrung his cap in his hands, rolling it and mashing it, and at length returned it to his round gray head, where it lay crouched like some odd species of rodent. "You'll understand that a bargain's a bargain, and that the only thing a man can call his own in this world is his honor. Nobody's going to guard your honor but yourself."

"Don't speak to Charley — Charley don't want to hear no more," protested the Sheephead. He had grown full sick and sad, as though his last light had gone out. Nausea convulsed his stomach, dizziness his brain. He staggered into his tent and collapsed in a heap among his rags.

"Now, then, Mr. Hoakum," announced Samson Icks, clearing his voice. "As is plainly stated in the documents as ye've reviewed, dated the 24th instant, ye are to retain possession of two of the stock — one male, one female — as was yer own personal property, and as was by direction not stipulated in the loan agreement what has ended with such unfortunate consequences."

Mr. Hoakum nodded briskly, his blue eyes glowing. "Betty and the Kingmaker, that's true — they're Blaster's and mine arter all. Ye can't have *them*, and that's flat."

"All the rest is to go, as is reverting to the ownership of the said creditor, Mr. Josiah Tusk, of Shadwinkle Old House, Salthead. Are ye in agreement with this?"

Mr. Hoakum looked down at his little rodent of a cap, which he had taken from his head and was again mangling with his hands. "There ain't much. There's just the lad and me, arter all — and Mr. Charles, when he's with us, which hasn't been much these days. There's the equipages for the beasts — the harness and blankets and such, the saddles and surcingles, cruppers, bridles, and tug-lines, and the like — and o' course the passenger cabs and freight platforms, the cord-ladders and flutter-sticks. There ain't much left arter that, and so there ain't much more to sort out."

"Wery good. Nevertheless, the gentlemen will require a bit o' time to scrape out the premises. Once the movables are in the van, we'll take final possession of the stock, while ye retain possession of the two said creatures. At that time ye and Mr. Blizzard will be free to depart the camp. The remainder of the stock is to be driven south by the gentlemen and myself to Crow's-end. So, that's fair and plain. Have ye any questions?"

Mr. Hoakum had no queries and so the execution proceeded. It required several hours to dismantle the equipages and other relics of Mr. Hoakum's business concern — that once-burgeoning enterprise that had so precipitously slipped from his fingers into the jaws of a city shark. Said Mr. Hoakum and his nephew were not witness to this savagery, having chosen to spend the time instead at the paddock taking leave of their charges.

Taking leave of all but two, that is — the lofty red bull known as the Kingmaker, and gentle Betty. Though they and the other mastodons could not understand the words of apology and farewell offered by Mr. Hoakum and Blaster, nonetheless there was a realization of sorts among them that a change of substantial moment was at hand. Something was to take place that would alter the current of their lives forever. In their great soft eyes I believe they knew that.

Never more would they be as they were now. Never more would Blaster be there to call them together each day, at first light. At the close of *this* day, life would never again be the same at the camp on the fells, because the camp itself would be no more.

"Well, nephew," said Mr. Hoakum, "if there's a thing I've learned, it's you've got to look a thing straight in the face. Stare it down, lad! It's the only way that makes it tol'rable. We'll come out all right in time. Look, look — look about you! We've still our Betty and our Kingmaker, each as fine a companion as any man could ask for in this life. Never a hard word or a skew look, and true as steel. What more in life do you need, lad? And besides which, we'll turn up something."

"That we will," declared Blaster, with a purposeful jerk of his wide-awake. "That we will!"

"Things are never as black as you b'lieve 'em to be, nephew. Take that horizon there, by way of example. When you look at that horizon, you can see only so far — everything t'other side of it is hidden from view. You can't see the colors and outlines of the beautiful vista lying just beyond it."

Blaster acknowledged the truth of his uncle's words, as the trunk of gentle Betty wound itself lightly about his waist, the soft brown eye of the cow gazing on him from above.

"There's a deal of work went into the building of this business," continued Mr. Hoakum, resting his hands upon the fence rail. "First my father's work, and now ours. But it's just that, lad — a business. It ain't *life*. We've gone to the wall and lost — so what's to be done? Give it a `heigh-ho' and move along. It doesn't signify. There ain't no help for spilled milk, arter all. It was a fair and honest bargain and we held up our side of it. We're honorable men for that, and at the end of the day that's the important thing. Remember that, nephew."

The young man agreed, like a student receiving instruction from a great master — which in his eyes his uncle was, arter all — and with his arms wrapped feelingly about Betty's trunk. Mr. Hoakum peered up at the Kingmaker, in his view the finest and noblest member of the herd, whose dark eyes were looking out across the valley as though reading the future there.

"What I'm sorry for is the beasts," said Mr. Hoakum, with a careworn smile. "It ain't their fault, and they can't understand it any more than the man in the moon. They'll be all of 'em in a muddle. But the thought of 'em at Strangeways — in that lock-up — in that — that — " He stopped, unable to go on, as image upon image of the fate lying in store for the herd assaulted him. The preposterous injustice of it!

Blaster, concerned, placed a hand on his uncle's shoulder and bobbed his head again.

"What's besides," said Mr. Hoakum, regaining courage after a pause and a few smart tugs and pulls at his checked waistcoat, "on another topic, as is more agreeable, is this: I've been thinking. And what I've been thinking is this: that there's more to the business than the passengers. Ain't that so, lad?

Arter all, ain't there still decided advantages to the beasts, even without passengers?"

His nephew was a little puzzled how to receive this question, and screwed up his watery eyes to show it.

"What I mean to say is — do we need the passengers? Everything don't have to bounce over to the coaches, ain't that right? Ain't there still plenty to transport besides the passengers?"

Blaster stood fixed as an old pump in thought. "That is right!" he exclaimed, throwing open his big gaping calf's-mouth.

"Arter all, ain't we got all the means and the might for hauling?"

"We do!"

"And ain't we hauled before?"

"We have!"

"Which is why I've been thinking, nephew, and cogitating these past few days — cogitating very hard, night and day — and a definite strategy has formed itself in my mind. It's a strategy as'll work, too, and that's flat. Can you guess now what it might be?"

"That I can!"

Mr. Hoakum, noting how the eyes of the Kingmaker remained fastened on the distant landscape, turned to see what it was that had so captured the attention of the noblest of his herd. Blaster, observing this, disengaged himself from Betty's grasp and searched the valley as well. It was not long before he spotted it.

"What is it?"

"Coach and pair," replied his uncle. "Private drag, by the look of her. More visitors from the city, I b'lieve, on their way to the camp."

So it appeared. A light coach was speeding along the Salthead road, the very same road that earlier had been traversed by Mr. Icks and his party of execution men. As the conveyance drew near they could make out the driver sitting on the box, but no sign of outside passengers and no luggage heap.

"Who can it be?" wondered Blaster.

"Don't know their names, lad. Haven't a clue."

The coach rumbled to a halt beside the transport van. Mr. Icks, attracted by the sound of wheels and the snorting of horses, appeared at the door of the cabin and promptly stopped dead in his tracks. Odious vision! For what should he see but the bald head of his employer poking out of the coach-window.

"Icks! Icks! Where is the man? Ahem! Ah, Icks! — there you are at last. No need to interrupt. Ahem! Simply inquiring into the progress of the action. Ah — for our client, of course. Necessary, quite necessary — ahem — an execution as you know, Icks, can be a tricky business — ahem — and it would reflect very poorly on the firm should anything go amiss. Ahem. All is proceeding as expected, I trust?" said the eminent limb of the law, coughing loudly.

"Aye," said Samson Icks, half to himself.

Cast-iron Billy burst into a fit of muttering. "It's one o' them — them damned lawyers — one o' them damned Badgers and Winches, I think!"

"Keep yer wits about ye, now, William," cautioned Mr. Icks. "Think, as ye say. Temper yerself."

"Driver — let me out of this — at once, I say. Driver! Ahem — where *is* the fellow? Let me out of this coach, I say!" demanded Mr. Winch, pounding on the coach-door.

The driver — who was one of that species of coachman, much more prevalent formerly than today, who seems disposed never to do anything in a hurry — threw the apron off and eased himself down from the box, amid a flood of grumblings concerning his back and bones. Firmly settled on the ground he spit into the palm of each hand, rubbed the hands together and threw open the coach-door with a clang.

"All right, all right. Ahem. Now, then, Icks — " said the gabbling attorney, preparing to exit the vehicle while the driver was yet engaged in putting down the stairs. The outcome was dreary and predictable. Slipping on air where the step should have been, the attorney's plum-colored bulk went flying, executing an awkward little flip that landed him on his breeches in a puddle.

An explosion of mirth went off in the direction of Mr. Pilcher and Billy. Lawyer Winch clumsily gained his feet, pawing at his coat and trousers where the earth had befouled them.

Samson Icks observed these antics — not without a degree of enjoyment, I should think — from the periphery, but did not see fit to render assistance. So, ponderous overlord, ye've come to spy on me, was his thought. Come to check on me. Come to keep a close watch, aye, and see to it that old Icks is properly engaged about the business. So ye've been taken in by the charges of that tall nasty rascal, that old Icks is an idler and a dodge, and a joker and a flash, and a this and a that — and so ye had to come out here and see for yerself, that he was a-carrying out the matter of the execution just as it were arranged.

Whether such charges were true or false, of course, mattered little in Mr. Icks' view of the cosmos. What did matter to the dapper man in pinstripes was *trust*. If one were trusted by one's employer, it followed that one would be granted considerable leeway in the exercise of one's duties, such as choosing when and how to commence such duties, at such and such an hour, at such and such a place, in such and such a condition — or indeed, whether one need commence them at any particular time at all. Such flexibility being an indispensable condition of employment for Mr. Icks, the restriction now levied upon him by the presence of the fat rascal — and hence the dismissal of that trust he once enjoyed — must have troubled him deeply. But his dark mood soon lifted and he found the gristle of his situation easier to chew, when he considered how the wheels of his secret plot already were fast whirling away.

"Driver! Ahem. Driver! Lazy do-nothing — wool-gatherer — what do you mean by this? Look at this coat, sir — look at this — ahem!" sputtered the attorney, struggling to contain himself. "Ahem — Icks — Icks!" he shouted, clapping hands to gain that vassal's attention, like a farmer frightening crows. He screwed up his neck very severely, transferring his attention from the unrepentant driver to Samson, thence to the cabin and the surrounding tents and outbuildings, saying, with a rapid flow of breath —

"So this is the property!"

"Aye."

"Capital spot — ahem!"

"Aye."

"And the stock? Ahem. Where might they be?"

Mr. Icks indicated the paddock beyond the cabin, where Mr. Hoakum and his nephew stood at the rail.

"Ah!" exclaimed Mr. Winch, with a slender gasp. "Magnificent specimens! Ahem. Magnificent! That monstrous red bull there — ah! Quite takes the breath away," he added, wiping his head with his handkerchief.

Mr. Icks had himself a passing thought or two concerning an absence of breath, but wisely refrained from expressing it. He settled instead for flicking away, with his thumb and forefinger, a lump of sod still adhered to his employer's coat-sleeve. The attorney, blithely insensible of this action, screwed up his neck again and demanded —

"And the delinquent party? Ahem — the Hoakum person — the defaulter. Where is he?"

Mr. Icks pointed out the sturdy little man in the checked waistcoat. "There — a gentleman of honor, what has kept his side o' the bargain."

"So that's the one."

"Aye."

Mr. Winch regarded the little figure critically. "Overreaching," he murmured. "Always overreaching. Ahem! Will his kind never learn?" He whirled about, hands to hips, and looked the country round at long ranges, mentally inhaling the valley, the cabin, the tents, the outbuildings, the beasts, like a new landlord taking possession — which in a manner of speaking he was, in his position as attorney for the master of Shadwinkle Old House.

"So this is the camp!"

"Aye."

"Excellent acreage — ahem — fine view — remarkable, in fact — superb site — ahem — buildings must go, however — no doubt about it — absolute rubbish — worthless — total waste. All in all, though, quite a bargain. Ahem!"

That moment the Sheephead chose to come staggering from his tent, with Mr. Joseph Rooke and his rapier in hot pursuit.

"Clear off!" shouted that aggressive young man of the pencil mustaches. "Clear off! Stir your stumps!"

The Sheephead set his stumps obediently in motion. His ragged gray form careened past an astonished Mr. Winch on its way to the paddock and friends.

"What," demanded the attorney, "is that?"

"Undetermined," said Mr. Pilcher, with a meditative chew on his pipe-stem. "Sich ridiculosity!"

"An acquaintance o' the delinquent party," explained Mr. Icks. "No need to bother about that rascal. He'll be off soon enough with the others."

"I see," said Mr. Winch. "Ahem. Well, well — carry on, Icks. Not to worry about me; I'm not here. Ahem! Remember that — I am not here. I'll stay out of your way. Ahem. Have you any refreshment?"

"In the cabin," said Mr. Pilcher, motioning the attorney thereward.

"Capital. Ahem. Lengthy, exhausting ride from the city — thoroughly incompetent driver — thoroughly — no sense whatsoever."

"You've borne it like a brick, sir," smiled Mr. Pilcher, by way of commiseration.

"Yes — ahem — yes, that's very true. Very observant of you, fellow. So, Icks — you'll carry on, eh? Remember, I am not here. Ahem!"

The lawyer turned his muddied back to them and propelled himself into the cabin. The said incompetent driver, who had been leaning against the side of the coach, scowled and threw him a black look.

Mr. Icks glanced round moodily at his companions. "It were all a-goin' so smooth," he said. "Everyone powdering away so tight."

Cast-iron Billy nodded agreement, while Mr. Pilcher smoked his pipe out in the sun. The volatile Mr. Rooke and his rapier said nothing. The coachman, however, appeared to have something on his mind.

"Whar be the damned cats?" he growled, slapping his hat in anger against his leg. "Whar be the damned cats — when ye need 'em!"

CHAPTER XI

The Black Ship

THE same early hour that found Samson Icks and his band of execution-men negotiating the lonely ravine on their journey to the fells, ancient Salthead stirred.

Up comes the sun, and the old university town wriggles from its slumber — yawns — blinks — looks out at the morning — likes what it sees (for once) — and so elects to rise. Not a trace of fog to dampen this morning's spectacle, to fill the steep, narrow streets with a chilly vapor — and this, the city has decided, is good.

It is a crisp, translucent dawn that peers over the house-tops and into the courtyards and back-gardens, into the dim quadrangles and the countless crooked back-alleys. A hard white frost, the parting memento of the night, clings to the lofty gables and twisted chimneys, the ancient timbered walls, the cold gray stone. It glistens in the light, tickling the sleepy faces of the cottages and lodging-houses, the stables and coach-offices, and the slopsellers' shops. Equally clear looks the dawn over the counting-houses, over the long dark carcass of the debtors' prison; equally clear over the venerable churchyard yews, which through the night have kept their solemn vigil over those who, unlike the sun, will not rise today.

On the sweeping highlands at the back of town, another sort of vigil is kept over ancient Salthead itself; for there rise the seven lofty crags — wild soaring pinnacles, each with its dusting of new snow, standing up against the sky like granitized warriors, silent, eternal, keeping watch over the estuary on whose rugged slopes the old city clings to life.

There, at the foot of the nearest crag, lies the rocky channel through which the Salt River flows to the sea. And there is the graceful chain bridge, which crosses the river and so unites the city. And there — there is the magnificent bridge-house, and below it the docks and their water-washed piers curving round the harbor. There a sheltered swarm of vessels lies at anchor; there beside them, along the wharf, lie the outfitting warehouses, the blockmakers' and boat-builders' establishments, the slipways and rigging-loft, the boat-yards and sailors' inns, and the crazy waterside shambles.

A salt-breeze is blowing stiffly; the noise of the sea, a dull, monotonous surge, fills the air. Ah — the sea, the sea! There is so much of it, a vast, imperishable expanse of water lying in the light. As the day comes on the myriad melodious forms of sea-bird settle into their activities — gulls veering and looping, cormorants guarding their nests in the high rocks, sandpipers a-scurry at the water's edge, pelicans skimming and plummeting, coastal jackdaws grubbing for dainties.

On this particular day — at the very same time, in fact, that Samson Icks and his men are breaking apart the mastodon camp — something glides into view just beyond the breakwater. It drifts toward the mouth of the harbor, vaguely birdlike and mysterious. As it grows in size it assumes the form of a capacious, three-masted sailing vessel, carvel-built. So not a bird on the water but a brig, a merchant trader — but with her mainmast tottering and her rigging reduced to a tangled confusion of spars, ropes, and fallen gear.

The ship is drenched in foam; ropy threads of sea-moss lie dripping from every rail and bulwark. A shattered stump is all that remains of her foremast. The ship's coat of black paint is sadly blistered, her gilding tarnished as though by lengthy immersion in water. The bowsprit has been blasted away; the jib boom dangles without a trace of the spritsails. A naked spar rises in the stern where her ensign once waved.

The ship rises to the swell, leaning into the wind. White foam-spray bursts across her bows. No evidence of the crew can be descried amid the havoc littering her decks. As she lunges forward on the waves, straining and groaning, something quite remarkable is disclosed in her larboard bow, just at the water-line. There! Do you see it? A breach in the hull — a great yawning cavity, with a fringe of cracked and splintered timbers through which a profile of her inner compartments is visible. The sea, oddly enough, is repulsed from this defect; rather than rushing in and sending the hulk to the bottom, the water rushes *out*. No ballast, no rigging, no crew, a gaping hole in her side — and still she sails!

On she comes past the breakwater. Though she rolls with the swell there is purpose and direction in her movement, in the heel and lift of her prow, in the sluggish determination with which she holds to her course. Then, at a point about the middle of the harbor, in clear view of the entire city, she lies to and comes to a full stop as though riding at anchor. But no hook has been cast to steady her thus, for of her anchors there is no sign. She seems content to remain there for now, with the waters plunging against her in a smother of foam, rolling into the breach and rolling out again.

At length a flotilla of diverse small craft — lighters, wherries, and such — begins arriving, one by one, from the shelter of the wharves. Curiously, cautiously, they drift in irregular circles about her, a few of them drawing alongside, their crews regarding her with suspicion. Heighing and hallooing through their speaking trumpets, they receive no response. Shortly thereafter a medium-sized vessel flying the insignia of the harbor-master approaches. A couple of boats are lowered into the water and make for the black ship. Ropes and Jacob's-ladders are thrown across the bulwarks and secured, and men begin scrambling aloft.

Having gained the deck the boarding party commences its examination, roving about the ship like industrious insects inspecting an abandoned hive, their activities overseen by a commanding presence in a blue coat with rows of bright yellow buttons. As one eye they scrutinize the broken masts and sagging canvas, the rusted capstans, fragments of yards, the twisted tangle of ropes and cordage. Below, one of the diverse small craft noses about the breach in the hull, the callow youth in the stern sheets viewing this enigma with a mix of curiosity and astonishment.

Presently another vessel arrives and releases a skiff, which comes alongside the black ship. Two figures can be seen climbing gingerly aboard, the one a collegiate gentleman with a gray bristle-brush head, the other an earnest young man with orange hair and green spectacles. Once on deck they begin their own examination, the earnest young man drawing forth a small memorandum book in which he begins making detailed notations. Following an exchange of conversation with members of the boarding party, the newcomers are shown about the various compartments of the ship, fore and aft, by the commanding presence in the blue coat and yellow buttons.

Amid the maze of devastation belowdecks they come across the mysterious hole in the bow. The collegiate gentleman and his associate examine this defect with great interest, noting the shattered planks and the outward rush of water, and so looking out make contact with the eyes of the callow youth in the stern sheets, looking in — these very same eyes that look now on all of you; though they were brighter and clearer eyes then, and not yet hardened to the experience of life.

A few sturdy tars endeavor to take command of the ship's wheel, but the wheel, in its stubbornness, resists all such efforts. This, together with the breach in her hull and the absence of visible moorings, is profoundly unsettling to all the men, giving rise to much uneasy conversation, much massaging of chins and scratching of heads. All step aside as the commanding presence places his own hands upon the wheel, and huffs and strains, and huffs and strains; but even a blue coat and yellow buttons are insufficient for the task this day.

Unable to devise an explanation for the mysteries surrounding them, the boarding party decides, collectively and for the moment, to abandon the vessel. The collegiate gentleman and his associate, having concluded their own investigation, take their leave and descend to the skiff. The curious small craft begin to disperse, although some few of them are seen to remain in the vicinity of the black ship — perhaps out of idle curiosity, perhaps out of respect for her vanished crew, whose ultimate fate no one of the men could hold in doubt.

Did I mention that the ship resembled a bird on the water? In one sense I was quite correct in this — for look there! There at her prow, beneath the remains of her bowsprit — do you see it? *There* — the ship's figurehead, partially obscured by a coating of sea-moss.

Look closely at that effigy riding just above the water, that figure with one wing outstretched, its long, sinewy neck curling gracefully with the bill pressing on the breast —

Look closely at it! Inelegantly carved, but manifestly clear —

The figure of a gliding *swan*.

CHAPTER XII

Visitors at the Tuskan Villa

"*DITES-MOI,*" said the pretty governess, with a sweeping gesture of her hand toward the heavens. "Tell me, Fiona — what do you call that?" ·

The child thought for a moment. "*Le ciel,*" she answered. "The sky."

"*Bien.* And that?"

"*L'arbre.*"

"*Bien.* And that — across the road?"

"*La maison.*"

"*Bien.* And that?" said Miss Laura Dale, pointing into the sky again but with a more particular object in mind.

"*Le nuage* — the cloud."

"*Très bien!* And look there — do you know what he is called, Fiona?"

"*Oui, Mademoiselle.*"

"*Dites-le-moi.*"

"*L'oiseau,*" said Fiona. The bird sitting *en l'arbre* shook his feathers and discharged a very pleasant little song.

"*L'oiseau. Bien.* And what sort of bird? Think, now, of the new words you learned this morning."

A pause while Fiona considered this question. She wrinkled her brow and looked down at her feet, as though the answer might be written on the points of her shoes.

"*L'oiseau noir,*" she said, brightening.

"*Très bien!*"

"*Merci, Mademoiselle* Dale."

And so the black bird, in regard perhaps to the progress the child had made in her studies, respectfully dipped his wing and flew off into a neighboring tree.

"Come, give me your hand — let us walk. It is growing late."

They continued on, through a broad tract of woodland not far from the carriage-road leading to Friday Street. They had spent the better part of the day visiting in the city and were now making their way home.

"*Mademoiselle?*"

"*Oui?*"

"How long will it be before the French people come to Salthead?"

"French people?"

"The French people from France, who disappeared in the sundering."

The governess frowned, unsure how to respond. How to communicate it to the child so that she finally understood — that such people from the outside were unlikely ever to be seen again, having gone forever from the world?

"After all," Fiona prattled on merrily, "it will be ever so fine once I've learned my French — which I truly wish to do — but will there be anyone to understand me, apart from you and Mrs. Minidew?"

"Of course there will, dear," laughed Laura, folding her arm about the child as they walked along. "You musn't listen too much to what Mr. Kibble has to say about such things. He means well but he is sometimes given to exaggeration, you know. There are many people in Salthead who know the French language and with whom you may converse, including your uncle."

"My Uncle Tiggs?"

"I believe he has studied it. He is after all a professor, a very learned man."

"I think it a very beautiful language."

"*Oui, Mademoiselle*. And is that not, in and of itself, sufficient reason to study it?"

The child smiled happily. "You are always right, *Mademoiselle* Dale. You always know what to say! It's no wonder Mr. Kibble is so fond of you. It's a pity he's so boring, though. And he will persist in those horrid green spectacles — oh, I cannot endure them!"

The eyes of Laura strayed downward to the grass through which her feet were softly treading. She said nothing at first, and I imagine a shadow of some kind must have crossed her pretty face.

"And how is it, Fiona, that you should know the state of Mr. Kibble's affections?"

"My Uncle Tiggs told me. `He's very earnest, and a fine scholar, and very honest' — he told me that as well."

"Well, it's true that Mr. Kibble is all those things, and that the professor thinks most highly of him. But I'm afraid your uncle has been privy to only one side in the matter — Mr. Kibble's side."

"That is just what I thought," replied Fiona, with a very grown-up tilt of her head. "Indeed, that is what I have often told him — that he's so boring and unfashionable, and that you thought so as well."

"Told whom?"

"My Uncle Tiggs, of course."

"For a moment I thought you might have told Mr. Kibble."

The child winced and uttered a tired little groan. "Oh, good gosh, not Mr. Kibble! I'd never tell him that. I should think I shouldn't have to — I should think it was ever so obvious."

They proceeded in silence for a time, the child gazing about at the solemn grandeur of the woods, and Miss Dale wondering what other discoveries her bright little pupil might have made. She glanced away and noticed that the clouds were starting to gather, and that a sharp breeze was rippling through the tree-tops.

"Are there bears in these woods?" asked Fiona, suddenly.

"Bears? In Salthead? I should hope not, dear!"

"I wish there were bears. I wish I could see one, just once! I asked my Uncle Tiggs for a bear — so that we might have one in the house to keep us company — but he told me no. He said that bears must live in caves and can't live in houses with people. But I'd still love to have one, ever so much."

"A bear is not a pet, Fiona," said Miss Dale. "Bears are wild creatures and not very nice, I'm afraid. Actual bears, you see, are not at all like the ones pictured in your story-books. They can be cruel and vicious, and are never to be trusted."

"That is what my Uncle Tiggs said."

"And so you should listen to him."

"Look there!" exclaimed the child, pointing with one tiny finger.

For a terrible instant Laura thought it must be a bear; but on looking in the direction indicated, through the trees and toward the carriage-road, her fears were allayed. Some fellow was marching briskly along the shoulder of the road, parallel to their course, and so near that the tuneful air he was whistling was audible to their ears.

"I wonder who it can be?" murmured Laura.

Fiona uttered a joyful shout. "*C'est monsieur* Scribbler!" she exclaimed, waving excitedly.

The whistling stopped. The whistler stopped, too, and peered through the foliage with one hand cupped to his forehead — bent his knees and dropped into a crouch — screwed up his eyes and stared directly at Laura and Fiona, with his brows knit — stood again — repeated this little exercise — removed his hat — scratched at his wild head of hair — replaced the hat — then put two fingers to his lips and whistled.

"*C'est lui*," said Miss Dale — half to herself, and with a curiously ambiguous expression — as Fiona went skipping through the trees toward the carriage-road.

It was indeed Mr. Scribbler, he of the old brown coat, drab small-clothes and gaiters. He embraced Fiona as she ran to him, and lifting her into his arms spun her about several times like a top. Returning her to the ground he performed a little jig, very artfully, which Fiona imitated, not very artfully, after which they bowed and shook hands in a formal manner.

By the time Laura came upon them they were scrambling about the trunk of an old oak, Fiona peeping and laughing, and Mr. Scribbler with one hand covering his eyes and the free arm extended, in what looked to be a spirited interpretation of hoodman-blind. Every time he reached out for her Fiona would slip beneath his arm and tap him on the coat, giggling at the conclusion of each successful foray.

The governess watched in silence for some minutes. Peering again at the sky, however, and noting the lateness of the hour, she was compelled at length to intervene.

"Come, Fiona — that's enough play for now. We must be along home."

At the sound of her voice, and amid Fiona's protestations, Mr. Scribbler ended the game. His hand dropped from his face as his eyes fell upon Laura. She returned his look — briefly, and with that oddly ambiguous expression — before averting her gaze and gesturing to the child.

"Come along, dear — it's late. Your uncle and Mrs. Minidew will soon wonder where we are."

Unwilling to relinquish the company of the clerk, Fiona raised a mighty howl. But in the end authority won the day.

Mr. Scribbler, who had not moved since the governess had first spoken, whirled in a half-circle and set himself to roaming about the premises. He vanished behind a screen of foliage; on his return he crept playfully toward Fiona, with both hands hidden at his back. He shook himself like a cart-horse, and one of his hands magically appeared; in it was a pretty bunch of flowers, the last of the season, which he presented to the child. She accepted the gift eagerly, lifting the flowers to her nose to inhale their fragrance.

"What do you say, dear?" asked Miss Dale.

"*Merci, Monsieur*," said Fiona, with a curtsy to the gawking scribe.

Mr. Scribbler tipped his hat and bowed. His other hand appeared; in it was a second cache of flowers, wholly as splendid as the first, which he presented — a little timidly — to Miss Dale herself. She paused over the bouquet, so deftly retrieved from nature's waning garden, before looking into Mr. Scribbler's face — a face in which, at that moment, something like his whole heart must have been concentrated.

"Thank you, sir," she said, quietly. "They are indeed lovely. I wonder you could find them so late in the year."

Mr. Scribbler touched his hat-brim and made another bow, by which he meant to say that the task had been both effortless and pleasureful.

"Are you continuing in our direction?"

The clerk shook his head sadly, and pointed instead toward a darksome manor sitting in dismal grounds over the way.

"That awful place?" said Fiona, with a little scowl. "Why on earth would you want to go there?"

Mr. Scribbler shrugged to indicate he had but little choice in the matter. He gave a look of farewell to Laura and her small charge, lifted his hat again, and so turned and plunged across the road toward the gray stone mansion.

The two young ladies continued on their journey home — something changed, I suspect, with the thoughts of each in her own way revolving about the breezy clerk from Badger and Winch.

"And so — what do you call a great house such as that?" asked Laura, meaning the destination of Mr. Scribbler.

Fiona looked across her shoulder at the house but couldn't remember the word. She searched among the trees for a parting glimpse of the marvelous Mr. Scribbler, who was without doubt — aside from Laura and Mrs. Minidew, and of course her Uncle Tiggs — her dearest and most admired friend in the world.

"*Le château*," said Miss Dale, in answer to her own question. But Fiona paid little heed, what with the sudden tears glimmering beneath her lashes.

As he approached the damp and somber domain, Mr. Scribbler, for purposes of his own reassurance, resumed his whistling. By chance he threw an eye to the heavens, and there saw the very same cloud that earlier Laura had pointed out to Fiona. As he watched, the cloud underwent a subtle change — growing rounder, harder, and darker, acquiring a sort of celestial chiaroscuro until it came to resemble a human face, which frowned at him with a malignant intensity.

Mr. Scribbler's eyes went wide and he began to look very frightened. A brisk wind thrust itself along the carriage-road, causing him to shiver. When he found the courage to peep again at the cloud the face was gone.

He stopped before the area railing and gazed upon the mansion, with its discolored walls of blue-gray stone, menacing gables and twisted chimneys, and sullen stone angels glaring from the roof. Everywhere, disintegration and decay; and especially the house, so like the head of a monstrous troll poking out of the ground, with the roof for a hat and oriel windows for eyes, and the crumbling expanse of stairs like broken teeth.

Anxious to be about his errand, Mr. Scribbler rang the yard-bell at the gate and waited attentively. After a few minutes he rang it again; still no one appeared. He rang it a third time, and in frustration draped himself against the bars like a convict. Eventually a door in the side of the house opened and a footman in livery appeared, looking towards the gate to see who it was had disturbed him. Unable to identify the miscreant he charged down the steps and covered the intervening ground in a huff.

"Well? Well?" he demanded, crossly.

Mr. Scribbler dove into a pocket of his coat and withdrew a rumpled scrap of note-paper, which he handed to the servant. The man unfolded the shabby specimen — read the message through — looked with disdain into Mr. Scribbler's face, as if doubting such a fellow could have written it — could have written anything, for that matter — and read it through again. Mr. Scribbler did his best to maintain his customary nonchalance, but I suspect he avoided glancing at the cloud.

"You're a clerk — from Badger and Winch?" sniffed the footman.

Mr. Scribbler removed his hat and ruffled his hair, thereby acknowledging that illustrious connection.

"You're in luck — the old man's just arrived," said the servant, nodding toward the house. "Just back from the city and in a foul temper, I can tell you! On second thought perhaps you're not so lucky. He's a fearful old screw. What's this here about a letter?"

Mr. Scribbler rapped his chest twice in rapid succession, denoting the location of the pocket where that missive was safely lodged.

The footman scanned the note again and appeared to accept its legitimacy. Retrieving a large brass key from his clothes he unfastened the gate.

"This way," he said, opening the gate and standing aside for Mr. Scribbler to pass.

The clerk nodded and bowed, and tipped his hat, and nodded and bowed, and so swept triumphant through the portal and onto the withered grounds of the Tuskan villa.

"This way," said the footman, curtly, leading the clerk to the troll-house, up the rotting steps of teeth and into a darkened foyer. "Wait here — and don't touch anything, or it will be dreadful for you." Saying which he disappeared with the rumpled scrap of note-paper.

Mr. Scribbler scratched his head and tapped his chest, to reassure himself that the letter given him by Samson Icks was indeed in place. The next few minutes he devoted to an examination of the foyer. With brows knit and hands clasped behind him he roved about the dismal chamber, noting the ornate but dilapidated cornices, the cracks in the mirror, the gloomy busts frowning from their pedestals, the two formal piers with their dusty urns on top. He wondered, in his fancy, what might be in those urns — or who — and what they did all day, and how they passed the time. Did they ever laugh? Did they ever weep? Did they know someone was there in the room? Did they know anything at all? Such thoughts soon made him uncomfortable, however, and he began to fidget, deciding that eternity in an urn was far better than anatomical dissection.

Presently the footman returned and led him to the drawing-room. It was ungarnished save for a modicum of furniture, and its walls were badly water-stained. A single window looked directly onto a tall hedge, effectively shutting out most of the light.

A door at the far end of the room turned slowly on its hinges, admitting the long shadow of the miser, which darkened the room still more.

"Scribbler," said that conscientious man of business. Fresh from his daily round of high jinks in the city, he was attired in the magnificent black coat with resplendent buttons, very superior red velvet waistcoat, and richly lacquered strap-boots, which struck so much fear into the hearts of the common folk. The heavy boots creaked as he walked, and as he fixed his sharp falcon-eyes on the clerk one bony hand rose up, clutching the scrap of note-paper relayed to him by his servant.

"This says you have a letter for me. Show it."

The clerk dutifully obeyed. The letter being directed to Mr. Josiah Tusk, Shadwinkle Old House, Salthead, the miser broke the seal and unfolded the paper. Inside he discovered a second folded missive, this a blue one, addressed to him as well but directed instead to the care of Badger and Winch, Cobb's Court.

The miser's stern gaze descended on Richard Scribbler, who was affecting his usual attitude of careless indifference.

"What do you mean by this?" growled Josiah, a little fiercely. "What sort of trick are you playing here? I have no time for tricks. I am a hard man of business, sir, and tricks are not for me."

Mr. Scribbler — ignorant of the contents of the letter, and merely adhering to the instructions of Samson Icks — shook his head with energetic firmness to assure Josiah that no, no, it was no trick, and threw up his hands to validate that assertion.

Josiah inspected the blue letter, turned it over and was prepared to break the seal, when he came across these words scrawled in block capitals on the reverse —

SIR, —

THIS LETTER, HAVING BEEN RECEIVED IN THESE CHAMBERS ON THE 4TH INSTANT, AND HAVING RESIDED IN THESE CHAMBERS FOR THE INTERVAL WITHOUT HAVING MADE THE ACQUAINTANCE OF THE ADDRESSEE, IT IS THE CONSIDERED DUTY OF THE UNDERSIGNED THAT IT BE DELIVERED YE.

REGARDS,
R. SCRIBBLER

The great white head of the miser rotated in its collar like a socket.

"Is this your handwriting, Scribbler?"

Completely at a loss, and with no idea what labyrinthine plots and suspicions might be fermenting in the miserly brain, Mr. Scribbler threw caution to the wind and nodded agreement.

Josiah was about to break the seal of the blue letter, when he discovered it had already been broken.

"What is this?" he demanded, coldly. "You have opened this letter — my private correspondence — and examined its contents?"

Mr. Scribbler shook his head vigorously and clapped hands to face, to deny such an unwarranted accusation.

"You are prepared to swear an oath you did not break this seal?"

The clerk was more than prepared.

Mr. Tusk paused, studying the messenger and wondering just how far to trust his responses. He thought he might be lying; but Josiah always thought everyone might be lying. He looked thoughtfully at the broken seal, grinding

143

his teeth and so causing the swollen jut of his chin to protrude even more. What to think? What to think? From irritation he growled —

"Why is it you never speak? What is the matter with you? Are you an idiot?"

Mr. Scribbler managed only a pale ghost of a smile and a toss of his shoulders.

"I see. What value your employer finds in you is quite beyond my comprehension. I suppose there must be some function you perform adequately. You are a law-clerk, you are obviously able to write. And so you tell me these are your words here. Yes? No? Stop bouncing your head like that, sir! You're like some lunatic jack-in-the-box. What is wrong with you?"

Mr. Scribbler, blithely unaware that anything at all was wrong — or perhaps, unwilling to admit it — nor perceiving his likeness to a child's toy, nonetheless obliged.

The miser unfolded the blue letter and held it out before him. The contents, composed in a tall, businesslike hand, were fairly brief and dated some three weeks prior —

MR. JOSIAH TUSK,
Sir, —

It has come to my attention that a certain Mr. John Hunter, of Malt House, Raven Lane, being newly settled in this town, may be a person of some interest to ye.

He is, by all appearance, a young gentleman of excellent breeding; his holdings are substantial, but their source is difficult to trace; he spends freely and travels much of the year, no one knows exactly where; he keeps but a single servant, and that a rude, sullen rascal not given to discourse; he is a fellow client of the fat lawyer, Winch; and — which is wery interesting — he has been, in point of fact, under continual observation by this same attorney.

Knowing that such a matter, having attracted yer notice, may prove useful to ye — but wishing to remain out of the lights, as it were, owing to personal circumstance — I remain,

"A FRIEND"

The effect these lines produced on the mind of Josiah was not hard to discern. He conned the letter over twice, three times, in gloomy rumination,

144

and cast his eyes about the room in a long, thoughtful sweep. His flow of breath increased — his chin swelled — his mouth grew very sharp — his free hand began clenching and releasing at his side like a breathing thing.

"I put it to you again — you did not open this letter, and you know nothing of its contents? I warn you — I'm a man of business and I won't be gammoned, sir!"

Mr. Scribbler answered with another energetic shake of his head.

"I see. Very well, Scribbler," said the miser, blowing off his wrath with a testy laugh. "I shall believe you — for the moment. You seem ill-equipped for deception. I thank you for bringing this correspondence to my attention. Its dalliance may prompt a reconsideration of my long-standing relationship with a particular firm. And there are new things here, new things, which must be looked into."

So saying, Josiah folded the letter and thrust it into his pocket. "As a conscientious man of business, I am obliged to acknowledge such an exercise of effort and professional responsibility, in whatever low quarter it may arise. It is heartening, heartening. Here, sir — perhaps this will be of assistance to you."

Mr. Scribbler looked at the palm of his hand, into which the miser had placed a single brass farthing, and so waited, as if expecting the remainder. But nothing more appeared.

"Many happy returns of the day to you," said Josiah, pivoting on his heel. With the grim little smile playing on his lips, the miser and his mighty boots strode from the room. Mr. Scribbler, conscious of the footman posted behind him, closed his fingers over his prize — he could not help but contrast it with the largesse of Samson Icks — and so departed those dreary premises.

The long shadows of night drew on and enveloped the house. Soon, everywhere about, minute frigid pellets of moisture began falling from the sky. Not overly substantive in and of themselves, for they left little trace wherever they hit, yet they were cold enough and palpable enough to serve as reminders of the long, unwelcome season to come.

It had gone eleven when Josiah, lately translated into his dressing-gown and having consumed his solitary meal of cold chops and porter, settled into the cumbrous, high-backed chair in his bedchamber, beside the tiny spark glinting in the grate which he called a fire. The night was cold, the house was cold, the room was cold, the fire was cold, everything about the miser was just as cold, and as he sat down in the chair he seemed to give off a frost.

With his eyes upon the fire-irons and his slippers on the fender, he lapsed into a brown study. From one bony hand dangled the mysterious epistle brought to him by Richard Scribbler. He rocked it gently to and fro with a meditative motion, his black brows contracted in thought. His chin swelled, as he stared with a terrible fascination at the single glowing coal in the grate.

What meant this letter? Its contents he had revolved over and over in his brain, and now examined again in the glow of his candle, noting carefully the form and flow of the characters; but for all his effort he could discover nothing suspicious. The message itself was written in an odd but businesslike script; the handwriting on the reverse, in block capitals; the hasty note from the clerk, appropriately, in a scribbled hand. He compared the characters, one with another, and thought there might be some superficial resemblance between the block capitals and the businesslike script — then again, perhaps not. For a brief space he weighed the possibility that all three messages were the product of a single hand, but after inspecting them again he dismissed it. What, after all, would be the purpose? Still, there was something indefinably familiar in the reading of the message — in the general selection of the words, in their tones and accents; something that he couldn't quite put his long bony finger on.

And what of this person, this John Hunter? He knew not the man — had not heard of him, even. A young gentleman of independent means — a stranger to Salthead — making do with but a lone servant (an economy of which Josiah heartily approved) — and sufficiently promising to be a source of interest to Mr. Jasper Winch. The miser exhaled an icy breath as he fingered the broken seal. This very letter, directed to him, had been intercepted and its contents brazenly scrutinized by another — by all indications his own attorney! How many other items of personal correspondence, he wondered, had been violated in like fashion by that man? The thought of it caused the tide of his breath to rise, his eyes to sharpen, and his fingers to crush the offending document.

Up got Josiah, stiffly. His back was to the chimney-piece, his brooding gaze on the carpet at his feet and on the flowery blossoms inhabiting its surface. He began pacing beside the fender, the creak of his boots replaced by the quiet shuffle of his bedroom slippers. Back and forth he plodded, the huge shadow thrown by the candle miming his every movement like a sinister anthropoid.

He heard the clock at the stairhead sound the hour. Absorbed in thought his eyes drifted from the flowery carpet pattern to the fire-irons, and so to the ragged window-curtain, to the bed-posts, to the large old-painted press, to the dusty backs of the books ranged against the wall, to the grim sly portrait above the mantel-shelf. As he paced, the flower-heads in the carpet seemed to change into so many faces, staring at him from the floor. He snorted; and almost immediately his eyes glided to the chimney-piece, where he thought that the grim sly face in the portrait had drawn a breath and was observing him from the darkness.

He stopped to rub his brow, thinking he was perhaps more fatigued than he otherwise suspected and that his mind was taking liberties. When he looked again the flowers were flowers once more, and the portrait cold and lifeless.

He sent the footman for a glass of sherry. When it arrived he sat down again in his chair, feeling more composed. He smoothed the crumpled letter and placed it on the table beside him, resolved to think the thing over while he slept. It was certain, however, that the matter of Mr. Hunter should be looked into. Who knew what possibilities there might be for a conscientious man of business in a youthful swell, freshly arrived in town with an excess of capital at his disposal? What possibilities indeed! And if such a conscientious man devoted himself to his studies, and dug, and dug, might he not eventually dig out something of interest in the history of that young gentleman — something compromising, perhaps, that that young gallant would just as well prefer remained confidential?

Why should a young gentleman have come here to Salthead, unheralded and unknown, maintaining such a modest existence that not one word of it had reached the ears of Josiah? Was he in flight perhaps from some indiscretion, some mischance of fortune, the knowledge of which could be turned to a conscientious man's advantage? No doubt, similar possibilities had teased the brain of Lawyer Winch — at thought of whose deception the eyes of Josiah grew sharper than ever, and his mouth screwed itself into that grim little smile as he sat and contemplated his options.

He was resolved upon it; he would investigate — he would find out what there was to be found out about Mr. John Hunter — he would exact his revenge against the duplicitous attorney — and he had the perfect fellow in mind to do it. So it was settled, and so Mr. Josiah Tusk prepared himself for bed.

Having performed his ablutions and placed his nightcap on his head, he was bent on extinguishing the light when he became aware of a sudden cold that had invaded his bedchamber. Granted, the room already seemed frozen; but this new sensation was so thoroughly chilling, so overwhelmingly frigid, so much colder than cold, that even Josiah noticed it. He stood shivering in his night-clothes and felt it pass over him like a wave.

Wondering if the sash might be up he drew the curtain, but the window was tightly shut. He looked out into the darkness, and as he did so a flicker of lightning illuminated the face of man, peering in.

Mr. Tusk did not spring back in surprise — did not utter a strangled cry — did not rush from the room — did none of these things, for he was not a man to be shocked or frightened. He was a conscientious man of business; shock and fright were not for him. What he did do was grunt and calmly replace the window-curtain, just as it had been, and stand aside for a moment's thought. At the conclusion of that moment he parted the curtain again and waited.

The night greeted him and nothing more, apart from the idle tap of a hailstone upon the window. He looked to the left, he looked to the right; all was well. Certain now that he had been mistaken — he ascribed it all to an overworked brain, the price paid for being conscientious — he was about to close the curtain when the sky flashed, and he was confronted by the image of an old gentleman smiling through the glass.

He was appareled in clothing of an antique mode, very dusty and seedy. His face was like a drift of snow — pale, careworn — with milky eyes that looked not so much at Josiah as through him, as though absorbed in some hazy, far-off perspective. He was like a man wrapped in a spell, but one charged with a peculiar sadness and that something of regret that belongs to the past; as though he were dreaming on the scenes of his youth and reflecting on the loss.

Josiah grunted again, shut the curtain and turned his back on the face. He paced his bedchamber a few times more, stealing a look at the flowers in the carpet, which were still flowers but which in his mind's eye now seemed to be copies of the face in the window. And so it struck him that the face in the window was indeed the very same face he had earlier imagined in the carpet pattern.

He parted the curtain awaited the next flicker of light. When it came it revealed nothing more than a few drifting bits of hail blown about by the wind.

The miser harrumphed, and tossed his great white head with the nightcap on it. *Never mind*, seemed to be his conclusion.

Never mind that the window in which the face had appeared was on the third floor of the Tuskan villa, high above the carriage-way, with no adjoining gallery or other platform on which to stand.

Never mind whose face it was, even, though Mr. Tusk knew whose face it was very well indeed. In that initial flicker of light a suspicion had formed, and in the second flash that suspicion had been confirmed.

148

Never mind that the face of the old gentleman belonged to Mr. Ephraim Badger, founding senior partner and legal light of the firm of Badger and Winch, Cobb's Court.

Never mind that Mr. Ephraim Badger was no longer attached to that eminent firm; never mind, indeed, that Mr. Ephraim Badger was no longer *attached* in any sense whatsoever.

Never mind that Mr. Ephraim Badger had been quietly attending to his affairs eleven years this Michaelmas, beneath a headstone in a dark churchyard in a secluded corner of the city.

Never mind how absurd it was for Mr. Ephraim Badger, solicitor, to be floating, unsupported, outside a window of Shadwinkle Old House, three flights up, in Salthead, in the night.

Just never mind.

END OF BOOK THE FIRST

THE CALL OF TUCHULCHA

«☉»

CHAPTER I

News of Eaton Wafers

IT was Friday in Friday Street.

It was morning — gray, wet, and cold — and the fog hung in drowsy profusion about the windows of the house. Professor Titus Vespasianus Tiggs, fresh from breakfast and looking his usual sprightly self, was seated in the drawing-room with his newspaper in front of him and a cup of tea at his side. Settled in the very comfortable chair opposite was Dr. Dampe, in his cherry-colored waistcoat, his features hidden behind his own palisade of newsprint. The professor's physician colleague had arrived during breakfast — a convenient happenstance — to look in on Mrs. Minidew, who had the previous day complained of a mild headache, and having seen his patient and then beheld the breakfast spread upon the board, had elected to extend his professional visit. Then it was he spotted the newspapers strewn about the drawing-room, and so the visit was extended further. Faced now with a choice between the cheery fire and the newspapers and the comfortable chair on the one hand, and the uncomfortable weather lurking beyond the windows on the other, the doctor had found it expedient to light his pipe and so extend his visit further still, while he pondered the concept of departure.

The professor turned over several sheets of the *Gazette*, and in so doing discovered an orange cat-face peering up at him from the floor.

"Why, what is it, young man?" asked he — the professor, not the cat — "What do you want, sir?"

Here Mrs. Minidew happened to step in from the passage, just as the orange tabby flopped onto his side and spread his limbs and yawned in one grand enormous lazy stretch. Then sitting up again he directed his eyes first at the professor, then at the widow — not knowing from which easy mark the expected treat might come — but ignored the doctor, who was by and large not very fond of cats.

"Milk," concluded the professor, with scholarly certitude. "I believe that is his milk posture, Mrs. Minidew."

"But he's had his milk, sir," said that lady. "Twice already, to be sure."

"Ah," said the professor, brought up a little short by this disclosure. He meditated for a moment. "Perhaps, then, it is his `I must be off now, if you please' posture," he suggested.

"He's been in and out all morning. Been to the stable and bothered Tom and Maggie there, then back into the kitchen to play with Hanna, then upstairs with Fiona, then back out into the yard, then back in again, and out, and in, and so now here he is in the drawing-room with you and the doctor."

"Ah. Well, yes, so he is, indeed. Perhaps it's his play posture, then? No? Not play? Nor milk either, you mentioned. If not milk, then, perhaps something a bit more substantial?"

"Really, there's been no end of eating and playing, and playing and eating, ever since Hanna let him in at first light."

"I see," murmured the professor. A frown creased the space between his eyebrows as he rubbed his gray bristle-brush head. "Well, he's a very independent gentleman, you know."

"You are very learned in feline ways, sir."

"I have had years of study, Mrs. Minidew."

"Yes, sir," said the widow, dimpling. "Come along, Pie — oh, there now! Do you hear that? There is Mr. Rime at the back-stairs. I'm sure he's brought something very nice and tasty for you this morning. Shall we have a look?"

Mr. Pumpkin Pie, hearing these words and observing eagerly the path of the widow's shoes, bolted for the back-passage.

"That cat of yours," said the voice of Dr. Dampe, from behind his newspaper, "has a better life than I do."

"What do you mean?"

"Here he has one — two — no, three, four — five even — remarkably gullible persons in this house attending to his every fancy, to his every imaginable desire, while he does virtually nothing for it in return. Simply present the obligatory rodent now and then, freshly slaughtered, for the general admiration of the household, and you've absolutely got it made. Look here — it's not as if it requires real work, you know. They can do it in their sleep. It's instinctive."

"What you say isn't completely true. He has many fine points."

"And the run of the house as well. The housekeeper gives him whatever he wants, whenever he wants it, and the young niece of the household aids and abets her in the most scandalous fashion, while the master of the house — well, I could go on, actually."

"I'm sure you could."

151

The head of Dr. Dampe, with the soft brown beard and hazel eyes in it, appeared from behind a flap of newsprint.

"You're quite hopeless, Titus. Utterly gone."

"Yes, Daniel, I accept your diagnosis completely. Far be it from me to dispute it."

The doctor shook his head, releasing a cloud of smoke from his pipe, and resumed his lazy perusal of the columns. The professor took up his *Gazette* and together the two gentlemen pursued their researches for another half-hour, the quiet of the morning broken only by the rattle of crockery in the kitchen, and the soft tones of Mrs. Minidew murmuring to the cat, and the throaty chuckle of Mr. John Rime — thoroughly recovered now from his late escapade, and looking fresh and chipper in his coffee-colored great-coat.

The professor had just swallowed the last of his tea when a clatter of horseshoes sounded in the yard, with the insistent tread of a rider coming at a good lick. In due course the figure of the housekeeper reappeared in the doorway.

"Here's a letter just arrived for you, sir," said she, relaying that item into the professor's hand. "By special messenger. The gentleman says he's to await your written response."

"Indeed? Then it certainly is a matter of some urgency." The eyes of the professor lighted with surprise on a familiar name. "Why, this letter is from Harry!"

"Harry who?" said the voice of the doctor.

"Banister. A former student of mine at Swinford. You remember him — tall, good-natured fellow, given much to horses and hounds and all manner of field sports. Superb batsman — the absolute star of his club. A trifle negligent in certain of his studies, perhaps, but an engaging and very agreeable chap overall. Sensible head on his shoulders."

"Is he not the one who succeeded to an inheritance and consequently retired into the country?"

"The same. An aged relative passed on — an aunt, I believe — and left him her entire fortune, including an estate known as Eaton Wafers. A splendid place, as it has been described to me."

"Splendid isolation, I should call it. It is situated on the high moorland beyond the mountains, near a remote village called Pease Pottage," the physician informed him.

"You have been there?"

"I have seen it, from a distance. A number of years ago."

152

"It must be two days' journey at least, by traveling-coach."

"The mastodons are a good deal safer, though not so swift," the doctor said. "But of course, they're nearly gone now, what with the clearing of the roads."

Professor Tiggs, curious as to the motive behind Mr. Harry Banister's unexpected communication, broke the wax and silently scanned the letter, before reading it aloud for the doctor's benefit. It was dated the day previous, and its purport was as follows —

MY DEAR PROFESSOR, —

You will forgive perhaps, Sir, the imposition of a poor scholar on his old college tutor, but you are, I am sure, aware of my past and present admiration for you and your accomplishments. As you may recall I have come into some money, and so am now enjoying a comfortable existence in an as out-of-the-way spot as one can imagine. A far cry from the bustle of Salthead town! It is, however, a superlative living, the sport is excellent, and I find myself constantly engaged; so much so, in fact, that it is all I can do to maintain the few finer social obligations one incurs in such a quiet place. Quiet, that is, until the past several weeks.

I write, Sir, to request your assistance, with regard to a series of disturbances at Eaton Wafers that I absolutely cannot account for, and which have filled us all with concern and apprehension. At first unsure of either their validity or significance, I am now persuaded these incidents bear in some way on the recent apparitions in Salthead. I refer, of course, to the dead sailor who has been seen about the streets, and the damaged hulk standing in Salthead harbor, of which I have been made aware through the florid renderings of certain acquaintances in the city.

After due consideration I find myself convinced of a relationship between these extraordinary occurrences and the odd phenomena we have encountered here at home. Perhaps what I have to relate can throw new light on the matters in Salthead, and vice versa. Regardless, I find myself humbly requesting your aid, your guidance, your insight, respecting the events that have shaken us here, and left us with uneasy minds; and so, perhaps, may we, in some small way, be of assistance to you in return.

I will be forever in your debt if you would come to us at Eaton Wafers at your earliest opportunity. Have no concern, Sir, about either the travel or accommodation. Simply mention my name at Timson's coach-office, at the top of Bridge Street, and Mr. Timson will see to it himself that you receive a first-class booking on the eastern coach. As for our accomodations here at Eaton Wafers, they are — if I may be so modest — of the very finest. You may be assured of a most pleasant stay.

At the risk of repeating myself, I urge you, in closing — please come as soon as possible. We have no other recourse.

I am, respected Sir, yours truly,

H.J. BANISTER

Eaton Wafers, Pease Pottage
Broadshire

The doctor whistled through his beard and discarded his paper, bestowing on the professor the full measure of his attention — an indication in and of itself of the importance he attached to this latest development.

"So — are you going?" he asked, knocking the ashes from his pipe and dropping it into his pocket.

"Absolutely. This is most intriguing. It's possible, as Harry writes, that these 'disturbances' of his may in turn help us decipher the mysteries here in the city, and lead us to their source."

"I agree with you. You have first, as he mentions, the dancing sailor, which was viewed by your cat's-meat man and the sisters Jacks, and has since been spotted by at least a dozen others. And you have this same fellow's ship, the *Swan*, floating there in the water with a hole in her side — most extraordinary effect! Then you have your stalking mastiff — that's one I wish I'd seen. Then there's your little lame ghost-child (which story I brought you, you'll recall). And now these new incidents deep in the country. Pity he wasn't more specific about the nature of the phenomena. I'm positively ablaze with curiosity."

"Whatever has happened must be profoundly unsettling, for a chap of Harry Banister's free-and-easy nature to write a letter such as this. Now, indeed, I must draft a response for the post-boy," said the professor, gliding from his seat.

His task accomplished he conveyed the reply into the hands of the rider, who placed it in his satchel beside a brace of sandwiches and some cold refreshment (thoughtfully supplied by Mrs. Minidew), and leaped onto his horse — the "boy" being in reality a sturdy fellow something above thirty winters, of a rough-hewn but nonetheless obliging disposition.

154

"You are well-prepared for travel," said the professor, noting the frightful assemblage of cutlasses and small-swords that hung about the post-boy's saddle.

"One can't be too careful in the mountains, sir," returned the rider. He lifted his hat with a cheerful "Thank'ee," and turning his horse galloped rapidly away.

"Now I must arrange for the coach. But first I must see young Mr. Kibble and provide him with a brief summary, and inquire as to his interest in accompanying me. I've no doubt what his answer will be, but I'll not insist. Such an undertaking is quite beyond the normal duties and obligations of his position, and the journey to Eaton Wafers is not without hazard."

"Of course he'll accompany you, as will I," said the doctor, taking up his hat and sliding into his jaunty paletot.

"You? But, Daniel — what of your practice? Your patients? How will they manage in your absence?"

"Look here, Titus — we physicians, we're always grossly undervalued by these patients of ours. They complain bitterly when we're there, they complain bitterly when we're not there. They're never satisfied with a diagnosis, or a treatment, or a recommendation. It's as though they're always probing us, testing us, to see how closely our opinions match their own preconceived notions. No matter what the circumstance, they always know better. In my view, patients haven't the least idea when it is they're well off. It does them good now and again to receive a dose of physic from another dispensary. I believe I'll have Sweetman look in on them for me. One dose of that fellow and they'll appreciate their own physician that much more. See here, I can stop and brief Kibble for you; he's on my way. And I'll also arrange for the bookings at Timson's — it's on my way as well."

"But what of Harry? He'll be expecting only a single visitor. No doubt I can satisfactorily explain the presence of Mr. Kibble, as he is my personal secretary and assistant, but beyond that — "

"You say you have never before been to Eaton Wafers," said the doctor, pausing at the door with one hand on his hip and his hat cocked at a rakish angle.

"That is true."

"Well, I have — or at least I've seen it. It's an enormous place — quite spectacular, actually. You could easily stuff this tidy little house of yours into one corner of it. It is apparent to me, Titus, that you've spent precious little time among the privileged classes. Have no fear — I'm certain Master Harry and his staff can accomodate all of three visitors at one swoop. Well, I'm off now."

So saying the doctor marched out the door and into the fog. A few moments later came a growling of wheels, as the doctor's dog-cart rattled out of the stable-yard. The professor found himself glancing thoughtfully once more at the words of the "poor scholar" of Eaton Wafers, as the noise of the wheels faded into the distance.

After looking in on Mr. Kibble at his quarters and gaining his earnest consent to join the expedition, the doctor trotted off for the coach-office. The fog was starting to lift now, and as a consequence the drab gray streets of the city were becoming more animated. Passing through a little cobbled lane that led into Key Street, the doctor abruptly reined in his dun pony, in recognition of a tiny figure in the footpath beside the lane.

"Hallo — it's Miss Jacks, is it not?" he called.

The young woman so addressed raised her eyes but made no other acknowledgment, looking perplexed and a trifle hesitant.

"May I offer you a ride?" asked the doctor, politely doffing his hat. "It seems we are going the same way."

"Oh — it is you, Dr. Dampe," said the diminutive Miss Mona Jacks. "I didn't recognize you at first, with your hat on."

"But I recognized you immediately," returned the physician. "As a matter of fact, it would be most uncharacteristic of me to forget either a name, or a face, or a date, or a place, or just about anything, actually. Rather a study of mine — an old habit formed at university, very helpful for sitting examinations. And so — may I see you to your destination? Have you far to go?"

"That's very kind of you, sir, but I am simply out for my morning's walk," returned Miss Jacks, in that chirrupy voice the doctor found so engaging. "Indeed, I've just this moment stepped from the door. That's our house you see behind you there, beyond the area railing. My sister Nina remains quite despondent, I'm afraid — owing of course to the incident with which you are familiar — and has been unable to walk with me these several days, as is her usual custom. Normally we stroll down into Key Street, and on to the park that lies at its farther end."

"So this is the very spot where you and your sister witnessed the vision?"

"Yes. That is my sister's window, just up there."

"Extraordinary! Well, a morning walk is a fine thing, you know," said the doctor, folding his arms and nodding very sagely, as though he were delivering an opinion on a difficult case. "Everyone should have one — a morning constitutional! And the sharper the weather, the better. It charges up the blood, aerates the senses, and invigorates the spirit. It's excellent for degenerative conditions of the heart and the circulation. And I'm convinced the liver and intestines must profit from it as well, though I can't prove it yet. We'll have none of these sedentary layabouts — one must be active, active! You must urge your sister to reconsider. A little ramble in the morning can easily add years to one's life. It's common knowledge, really."

"I have little doubt you are correct. Have you by any chance seen Professor Tiggs of late?" asked Miss Jacks, attempting to redirect the conversation to a topic of more immediate concern, and at the same time arrest the flow of medical advice gushing from the physician. "Nina and I have not heard from him and are anxious to know if he has made progress in the matter. All of Salthead is talking about it now, as they are about the *Swan*."

"Ah, yes, our *'ghost ship,'* as I like to call it," replied the doctor, in his jauntiest manner; but observing the troubled look on the young woman's face, he abandoned his chatty good humor for a more sober tone. "I beg your pardon, Miss Jacks — an unfortunate choice of words on my part. We physicians, we're inured to this sort of thing, really. I fear it's the rough-and-tumble of our lives, the stress of the job. Occasionally we forget that such jocularity can be upsetting to the lay mind. Please accept my sincerest apology. Actually, there have been a number of developments, the latest occurring just this morning."

"And what might that be?" asked Miss Jacks, with a hopeful lift of her brows over her large moon-shaped eyes.

"An urgent communication, received by my professorial colleague not more than an hour since, regarding a series of disturbances of an as yet ill-defined character at a place called Eaton Wafers, on the high moorlands. I'm for Timson's just now to secure bookings for the eastern coach. Look here — why don't you come along to the coach-office? We can speak of these matters on the way. There are as I have said a variety of developments, all of which I'm certain will interest you."

The young woman paused for a moment to reflect. The tip of her pink tongue swept across her pretty lips. Coming at length to a decision she extended her hand to the doctor, who very gallantly assisted in raising her tiny form into the seat beside him.

"Thank you very much," said Miss Jacks, settling onto the cushion. "This is a very smart and comfortable carriage."

"Possibly the smartest and most comfortable dog-cart in all of Salthead, actually. You see, Miss Jacks, a dog-cart is a very practical and even necessary item for a physician. There's quite a good-sized louvered boot under there — normally it's for dogs, of course, but since I can't lay claim to a single pup, I use it instead to carry my medical paraphernalia when I'm on my rounds. A very practical vehicle, actually, and a very well-crafted model at that. The seats here, for example, can be slid forward or backward, for adjusting the balance. Suspension made of simple, semi-elliptical springs. And the shafts are hickory, for durability — less of a tendency to shatter. A broken shaft is unfortunately an all-too-common occurrence with your more cheaply-made conveyances."

"I see," nodded Miss Jacks, responding as best she could to this unexpected rush of information concerning vehicular transport. "I had no idea."

"Oh, yes, Miss Jacks — quite a necessary item for us physicians. Just a lowly dog-cart, however, to the uninitiated. Walk on!"

With this brief instruction to the dun pony and a leisurely flick of the whip, the doctor and his youthful passenger rattled off toward the coach-office.

As the dog-cart was negotiating the turn into Key Street, a dark smudge, which had until now remained motionless under the loom of a portico over the way, detached itself from the soft yellow stone. The smudge — seen now to be a man — ventured out into the misty lane, where his eyes stood fixed on the retreating carriage. With a smile of what looked to be triumph, or perhaps conviction, on his spotted face, the man drew his jerry hat down upon his brow and hurried into Key Street, following the same route as that taken by the dog-cart.

While the doctor was about his errands, the professor took time to explain to his housekeeper the details of the imminent and hastily arranged excursion to Eaton Wafers.

"There will in all probability be the three of us — Dr. Dampe and myself certainly, and most likely Mr. Kibble as well. The doctor himself will return later; he's gone off to the coach-office to arrange for the bookings. I am hoping he can secure three places for the morning coach on Monday. I estimate two full days of travel to reach the village of Pease Pottage, with a stop overnight at a posting-inn" — the professor consulted his atlas — "yes, here, most likely, at Mapleton Magna. There's very little else around for miles and miles."

"And you believe whatever it is Mr. Banister has to relate may aid you in your researches?" asked the widow. She seemed genuinely interested in what it was Mr. Banister might have to say, but there was no mistaking the concern that had infiltrated her bright strawberry complexion.

"I've no doubt there's some relevance. It's too great a coincidence for there not to be — though exactly how events at such a distant spot might bear on the current matters is beyond my understanding at present."

At this juncture a young woman in a blue holland dress appeared in the doorway.

"Pardon me, sir — I couldn't help but overhear," said Miss Laura Dale, looking in. "It seems you will be leaving us for a time?"

"Yes, I'm afraid so, Miss Dale. A brief journey of a week's duration at the outside. Here — " he fished up the letter from Harry Banister and passed it to the governess for her inspection — "here is a note received just this morning, from a young gentleman whom I once tutored at university. A very bright fellow and thoroughly engaging, but not given overmuch to scholarly endeavor, as he would be the first to concede. He came into an inheritance and is now master of a great house called Eaton Wafers, away on the high moorland."

"I know of it," said Laura, with her gaze dropped upon the letter, as though she were speaking to the paper rather than to the professor. "A very solemn and stately old place, given to endless runs of casement windows and chimney-stacks. Very beautiful, and very secluded. Lonely, even, I should call it. The loneliest house in the county — " She glanced up suddenly, as though just awakened to her breach of etiquette. "Forgive me, sir. It was rude of me to be speaking to you while my attention was directed elsewhere."

"Nonsense, Miss Dale," returned the professor, unconscious of any affront. This was not the first time the young woman's propensity to self-criticism had surfaced. "In my brief experience of you, you have shown nothing but kindness and graciousness to everyone in this house. No need to find fault where there is none."

"Yes, sir."

"So you have visited Eaton Wafers? Dr. Dampe has seen it, so he says, but only from a distance."

"Yes, I have been there," said Miss Dale, recovered from her brief discomfort. "My grandmother was for many years in service to Miss Nokes, whose house it once was."

"Miss Nokes. That would be Mr. Banister's aunt — the lady who died. And so perhaps you know Mr. Banister as well?"

"I believe we have met, on occasion." She folded the letter and returned it to the professor's hand.

The rumble of the dog-cart in the stable-yard signaled the return of Dr. Dampe. In he came, striding leisurely through the back-passage, with old Tom Spike behind him, and a very bright-eyed Pumpkin Pie riding on Tom's shoulder.

"Hallo, hallo, we're booked," announced the doctor, with a little snap of his fingers, expressive perhaps of the speed with which the transaction had been accomplished. "East country coach, Monday morning, six o'clock sharp. One word to Timson there respecting your Mr. Banister, and the fellow jumped to attention as though he'd been nipped by a flea."

"An inheritance must be a marvelous thing," said the professor, not a little envious.

"I went round to Kibble's as well and he's very keen on the idea. Excellent fellow! You couldn't hold him off with a stick if you tried."

"I thought as much."

"By the way," the doctor went on, almost as an aside, "there are one or two little addenda to our plans that may be of more than passing interest to you. Quite extraordinary, really, the way things have turned out today. It appears the size of our little party has grown."

The professor's brow rose. "Again?"

"Yes. But see here, it's quite a logical development, really. I happened to be jogging down into Key Street, on the way to Timson's, when whom should I spy but our Miss Jacks — she of the charming voice, you recall — out for a walk in the lane, next to her house, and my dog-cart there rattling over the very cobblestones upon which the dancing sailor had performed his merry hornpipe! Naturally the young lady was much intrigued by the course of the investigation, and wished to know more. One thing leading to another, I presented her with an invitation — and so she has agreed to come with us."

"Miss Jacks?" exclaimed the professor. "To Eaton Wafers? Surely, Daniel, you don't propose that that young lady — "

"Yes, yes, very sporting of her, very game, actually — though *Miss* Jacks isn't entirely accurate. No, no, I'm afraid you haven't the complete picture yet."

"Am I prepared for the `complete picture,' as you call it?"

"Of course. To be wholly accurate, it is the *Misses* Jacks who will be joining the party. That is, Miss Mona Jacks — our young friend — together with her older sister, Miss Nina Jacks."

The professor stood gazing in open-mouthed astonishment at his physician colleague.

"Really, Titus, you needn't look so stunned," ran on the doctor, blithely. "Miss Jacks — Miss Mona Jacks — felt it would do her sister a world of good. Apparently she has been moping about her room for days on end, suffering intense paroxysms of self-pity brought on in all likelihood by guilt at the sight of Mr. Pickering. Oh, yes, absolutely classic response. I've seen it more than a few times, actually. Then of course there's the maid — "

"Maid?" inquired the professor. "What maid?"

"The handmaiden Susanna, the sisters' companion and confidant. Well, you know, Titus, these young women today won't go anywhere without them! Oh, impossible, really. No, no, it's simply got to be."

"Ah," said the professor — making a little show of staring very conspicuously at the face of his watch — "and what might the grand total of the little party be, as of this hour? I've lost track of the count for some reason."

The doctor waved his hand dismissively, as though brushing away all earthly care and consideration. "Not to worry, Titus — it's not a problem. If you must know there are six, by my accounting."

"Six," echoed his colleague, with the gravity becoming such a pronouncement. "And Harry Banister expecting only one."

"As I explained to you before, it simply doesn't signify. Harry Banister is the master of a great house, a member of the landed gentry. These are fashionable people, Titus — they have visitors coming and going in shoals, all year round, what with the card-parties and the social get-togethers, the sumptuous dinners, the hunt balls! I've no doubt Eaton Wafers can accomodate such an insignificant number of guests as comprises our little party of sojourners. And don't overlook the salient point — he has *invited* you. He is requesting professional assistance, a private consultation with the recognized authority in the field. He needs your help. Look here — what are six visitors to the master of a great house, a fellow of Harry's stamp? What indeed are sixteen, for that matter?"

"Nonetheless I remain uncomfortable with this, Daniel. And now — now you'll have us shouldering responsibility for the safety of three young women on a hazardous journey through the mountains!"

"Two," corrected the doctor. "Two young women — the maid, I am given to understand, being quite beyond a marriageable age."

"And where is the father in all of this? He of the `old school'?"

"Gone to Fishmouth, for a fortnight at the very least, on a constituency matter. The session is on, as you'll recall from your *Gazette*. So the ladies will be safely returned to the bosom of their household long before he returns.

161

Really, Titus, the sisters Jacks are quite competent to make such a decision for themselves."

"All in all, I don't know that this is something I can condone. And I'm not certain Harry would condone it, either."

"If it will appease your busy conscience," sighed the doctor, waving his hand again, "I'll explain it all to your Mr. Banister for you once we've arrived. We physicians, we're experts at explaining things, you know. Absolutely top-notch. We're trained for it, actually — all part of the job. It's not a problem."

"Very good, then it's settled," said the professor, with a quick little nod. "Thank you, Daniel, for volunteering. I accept."

The doctor stopped abruptly with his hand in the air. He had not expected his offer to be taken up quite so readily. In truth, he had not expected it to be taken up at all. What he had expected on the part of the professor was, in order of appearance, modest surprise, grateful thanks, and a polite refusal. He got the thanks but little else, for here now was his collegiate friend sailing from the room with a sly chuckle, and the doctor at a loss for words for the first time that day.

In the doorway old Tom Spike stood grinning from ear to ear, while Mr. Pumpkin Pie, perched on Tom's shoulder, looked to be grinning too.

"Don't know nowt about it," wheezed the groom, the humor of the situation lighting up his face of old boxwood, "but it's not the professor as has been outflanked here. Not likely!"

162

CHAPTER II

Night and Nightingale

MR. Robert Nightingale was a man who stood in wholesome dread of his wife — as well he should.

For as redoubtable a figure as Mr. Robert Nightingale might be in the way of reputation, demeanor, and personal appearance, Mrs. Robert Nightingale was, I believe, his acknowledged superior on every point. Ever since their marriage — so long ago, it seemed now to Bob, that hardy men in suits of armor surely must have jousted at the wedding feast — she had exerted a power and a fascination over her lord and master that held him in thrall. In the early years of their bliss it was, of course, her beauty that possessed him; now, with that beauty run to seed, it was fear.

Many an honest citizen of Salthead had remarked on the perennial ill-humor of Mr. Bob Nightingale and chalked it up to a naturally villainous disposition. Many an honest citizen had remarked as well on his ugly squint and coarse, menacing voice, deeming them the consequences of a life devoted to questionable pursuits. Many noted his slovenly attire and carelessness as to personal hygiene, and pronounced them reprehensible. Others alluded to his oft-heard boast that over a long and celebrated career — interesting words to describe it — he had been brought up, at least once, before every sitting magistrate in Salthead and never received a conviction. Up and down the waterside Mr. Robert Nightingale was known as a slippery character. Yet I maintain in all these things it was Mrs. Nightingale who served as the model; for however bad her Bob might be, on whatever point under consideration — Mrs. Bob was worse.

Fortunately, Mrs. Robert Nightingale did not venture abroad nearly so often now as before, a clutch of little Nightingales, the result of her blessed union with Mr. Nightingale, keeping her enagaged most of the time. This brood comprised a total of five hatchlings, varying in age from two to ten years. They were on the whole a troublesome lot, given much to bickering, and pouting, and spitting, and biting, and sniveling, and kicking; to the tearing of hair and hurling of weighted objects; to the loud defiance of authority, and to melodramatic outbursts that not infrequently came to blows. In short, they were all that Mrs. Nightingale could have hoped for, or could handle. To vent her frustration and wrath in respect of these horrid children, Mrs. Bob turned quite understandably to her lord and master, whenever that gentleman was unfortunate enough to be found at home. It was for this reason, therefore, that Mr. Bob Nightingale was only rarely on the premises; it giving him a measure of personal satisfaction, and to some degree assuaging certain vengeful impulses, to know that as his wife terrorized him, so their offspring terrorized her.

In Mr. Nightingale's crooked eyes, then, there was some justice in his domestic arrangement. In the muddy dark circles that surrounded those eyes, some observers read evidence of the combativeness and pluck of Mrs. Nightingale. But in this they were wrong. Rather, the dark circles owed something, I think, to Mr. Nightingale's nocturnal habits, and his general aversion to the soothing balm of sleep; even more, perhaps, in consideration of his greasy hair, unkempt mustache, and declining forehead, to the fact that Mr. Robert Nightingale was just plain ugly.

One night, the wind being up and Mrs. Nightingale and the hatchlings in a particularly foul temper, Mr. Nightingale bethought himself of a little job that had lately come his way, concluding that a bit of energy expended in the exercise of his vocation — which was in the delicate and confidential line — might this evening spare him the rod of domestic bliss. So decided, he gathered about him the necessary accoutrements — a few small but ingenious instruments of iron, a coil of rope, a candle and flint, an empty canvas sack — and like a busy workman set forth on his errand, with his slouch hat upon his head and the sack thrown across one shoulder.

Sensing that rain was imminent, Mr. Nightingale made his way quickly to a distant part of town, there to do the bidding of his own lord and master — whose name I need not mention here, but who had a white head that swiveled on a turret, and a swollen jut of a chin, and two sharp falcon-eyes, and a grim little smile at the corners of his mouth.

He propelled his burly form along many a lonely terrace and darkened thoroughfare, and soon arrived at his journey's end — a melancholy, stoop-shouldered morass of a house, built largely of stone and half hid in ivy, at the top of a drafty lane marked by the sign of a raven. It was by now the hour of night when all decent citizens were comfortably lodged in their beds, with their shutters closed and their doors bolted. Mr. Nightingale, reflecting upon this, squinted ferociously and set to work.

He scouted the perimeter of the house and found three windows alight, all at the farther end of the building. Noting the long gallery that projected from a pair of French windows on the floor above, he initiated his assault by drawing out the coil of rope, one end of which he tossed over the balustrade; and having secured its tether to an old iron arabesque in the area railing, thereby hauled himself up.

With the implements of his profession in hand, it was but a short time before the windows of the darkened chamber stood open before him. Having detected no sound whatever from within — and thus sure he had not by chance ventured into some person's bedchamber — Mr. Nightingale fortified himself with a savage leer and prepared his candle, so that he might see just what sort of place it was he was in.

It was a most unusual place indeed. It was, to begin with, a very tall and a very spacious apartment, wainscoted in carved oak, with a marvelous stone chimney-piece mounting up and up to the ceiling. The walls were hung with a collection of primitive weaponry, among which Mr. Nightingale could identify javelins and lances, and swords and bucklers, all of bronze. Items with which he was unfamiliar included a mysterious double-headed ax, and a huge circular shield with the molded face of a cat, perhaps a panther, glaring from its center. The furniture in the room was adorned with an assortment of terra-cotta figurines, glossy black pottery, ceremonial urns, libation-vessels and silver plate. Ranged against the farther wall was a row of painted screens, with colorful depictions of warriors in battle, chariot-races, athletic contests, divers and wrestlers, pipers and acrobats; scenes of dancing, hunting, fishing, feasting, the artistry lithe and graceful, and unquestionably ancient — a vibrant panorama of life in the morning of the world.

In a corner of the room, near a half-opened door leading to an inner passage of the house, stood a life-size statue of a young man in terra cotta — a figure of quite striking appearance, with dark hair falling in rope-like braids about his shoulders, hypnotic black eyes, and a mystical smile. He was clothed in a short white tunic or toga with rippling purple borders, and in his hand was a walking-stick. The figure was inclined at a sharp angle toward the viewer, as though in vigorous forward motion — an effect which added to Mr. Nightingale's surprise on first seeing it. Beside the figure were a bronze tripod, an incense-burner, and a mobile brazier on wheels, each decorated with a multitude of fantastic animal designs.

The effect these artifacts must have produced upon Mr. Nightingale — intensified no doubt by the utter silence of the place, and the chilly shadows cast upon the old oak wainscot — can well be imagined. It was as if he had been transported to the bottom of the sea and were viewing the scattered remnants of an ancient shipwreck, forever frozen in time. The entire apartment lay cloaked in a solemn aura of antiquity.

A jug of wine and a libation-cup were resting on an ornate altar of volcanic tufa, which occupied a cleared space in the middle of the room. Propped against the altar was a staff in the form of a shepherd's crook. The altar had a wooden door in it which resisted Mr. Nightingale's most assiduous efforts. Frustrated, he turned his attention instead to the heavy, old-fashioned writing-desk that stood beside the chimney. He ran through the papers lying atop it and searched the drawers, on the look-out for anything that might be of interest to his lord and master. There seemed to be little there, however, apart from some worn parchments, some letters, and a few odd coins, the likes of which Mr. Nightingale had not before seen; unevenly rounded and very worn, they bore faint markings that defied interpretation.

Odd might be the word as well for the parchments, which were covered with a script so fanciful and queer that Mr. Nightingale spent the better part of five minutes turning the sheets this way and that, upside-down and sideways, in his attempts to decode it. He soon gave up in disgust and deposited the items in the canvas sack, along with the letters, reasoning that his master with the great white head might perhaps understand what they were and so somehow make use of them.

There was in addition to these things a map, which he spent some time studying. Spread out before him was a vast landscape he did not recognize, with a long narrow coast on either side of it, and mountains in the middle, and what appeared to be twelve cities marked out at various locations, their names inscribed in that same fanciful script. Unable to make anything of it, he threw the map in with the parchments and the letters — seeing to it, however, that some of the coins found their way into his own pocket. He had thought at first that this place might be some kind of museum; given his natural proclivities, however, this idea was soon discarded in favor of a new and far more likely explanation — that the objects in the room were the spoils of plunder, and that the plunderer was none other than the master of the house. So if booty already, what harm in thieving from the thief?

A twinge struck the burly neck of Bob. He pricked up his ears, listening intently. There was a quiet patter of rain now on the gallery, but nothing more — or was there? Squinting horribly, he thought he heard footsteps in the passage outside the half-opened door. Fearing that the light of his candle had been spotted, he blew it out and dove behind the writing-desk, squeezing his bulk into a crevice formed by the desk and the wall, where on knees and elbows he waited.

He heard the door of the apartment swing open, and saw the light from another candle fill the room. His ears detected a laborious sort of breathing, as is often found in pensioners who have smoked far too much for far too long. Peeping round the corner of the desk, he had his first glimpse of the candle-bearer — a hoary figure in dusty black tails (an ancient retainer, thought Bob), who had approached the French windows (which now stood open to the night, thanks to the industry of Mr. Nightingale) and was examining them with a slow and deliberate curiosity.

A flash of lightning electrified the sky, bathing the gallery, the museum room, the servant, and Mr. Bob Nightingale in a vivid radiance. The resourceful Bob fell back into the safety of his hideaway, just as the thunder boomed overhead. Not knowing when the next flash might come and perhaps reveal his presence to the servant, he decided to forego his peeping until such time as the ancient retainer saw fit to leave the room.

That time, as it turned out, would not be soon. There were more sounds of examination and inspection, a ragged cough, a wheeze, a shuffling of feet. Bob could tell by the way the candle-light was directed along the walls and ceiling, approximately where the old servant was and in which direction he was moving. It was with some concern then that he realized the bearer of the light, he of the laborious breath, was approaching the writing-desk.

Nearer came the light, nearer the breathing. The candle floated above the desk, casting a succession of ghostly rays upon the floor, as the servant examined the desk-top for signs of disturbance. Mr. Nightingale tensed his muscles, prepared at any moment to spring from his refuge. Then he saw his own shadow on the wall beside him, and it alarmed him, for he was sure the bearer of the candle would see it too. So the burly Bob held his own breath and gathered his legs under him, readying himself for the moment of discovery.

But the light went away, and might have gone away altogether had it not been for the arrival of a second person in the room. The tread of this individual was quick and lively, with a deliberate stride. As Bob heard him enter from the passage he could not resist a peep round the corner of the writing-desk, to size him up and determine exactly who he might be. What he saw was a youthful figure in a bottle-green coat and black velvet collar, white shirt and buff kerseymere waistcoat, and black trousers. The face of the man was unusually handsome, with a finely hewn chin, a broad mustache, and large dark eyes that smoldered in their sockets beneath a haughty pair of arched brows. After due consideration Mr. Nightingale decided that this fashionable young gentlemen must be Mr. John Hunter, master of the house and plunderer of ancient artifacts.

The young gentleman spoke to his servant in low tones. Taking the measure of the man from beneath his slouch hat, Mr. Nightingale drew a picture of a youthful swell who was something of a dandy, fresh from the country, and so no match for city sharks of the mettle of Mr. Nightingale and his lord and master. No, they should have no trouble with *this* monkey!

Another vivid flash of light forced Bob back into his shell. What he saw when he looked again greatly surprised him — for there was the monkey, Mr. John Hunter, standing just outside the French windows with his coat off and the shepherd's crook in his right hand, pointed at the sky.

Another flash. Instantly the shepherd's crook was directed towards it, tracing the descent of the lightning and noting the place where it struck. Thunder boomed. Another burst of light, another tracing, another boom. This same cycle was repeated a third time, a fourth time, a fifth, and so on. With each flash the direction and character of the thunderbolt were called out by Mr. Hunter, as though he were divining from them some secret intelligence. Bob, observing from the safety of his hideaway, was duly impressed, and now certain that not only was the master of this house a thief and a dandy, but a lunatic as well.

How long this exhibition went on Mr. Nightingale could not say. Eventually, however, the discharges grew less and less frequent, the thunder moved off, and so Mr. Hunter put away his staff. He slipped into his coat and exchanged a few words with the ancient retainer, who, after preparing some lights, obediently withdrew from the room.

Mr. Nightingale pricked up his ears, for now it was Mr. Hunter who approached the old-fashioned writing-desk. The shoes of the young gentleman were only inches away from the canvas sack, with the slippery Bob himself pressed into his little crevice between the desk and the wall, scarcely daring to inhale for fear of alerting the lunatic. There was a shuffling of papers above him and a noise like a sigh, and the ticking of a clock somewhere in the room, which Mr. Nightingale thought must be his heart beating.

After a time Mr. Hunter stepped to the altar of tufa. Removing a key from his waistcoat-pocket he unlocked the stubborn door, and took from inside the altar an elegant cedarwood chest decorated with lions' heads. This he opened, and lifted from it another object which he placed with great reverence upon the altar. Bob could not see clearly what the object was, as the body of Mr. Hunter was obstructing his view. After attending to another few matters, however, the young gentleman obligingly quitted the apartment, leaving Mr. Nightingale to his proclivities.

Bob decided that the time had come to abandon his hideaway. He gathered up his sack and crept forth, his momentary glimpse of the object from the cedarwood chest having fired his curiosity. Arriving at the altar he stopped, and so stood looking down on what it was that rested there.

What it was was a pair of tablets, linked by a series of clasps along their common border like the leaves of a book, and held open on a stand. The tablets themselves were no thicker than blotting-paper, and composed of some lustrous, unidentifiable material resembling gold. Engraved on the pages of this slim metallic volume was a treasure-trove of those same fanciful characters seen on the parchments and the map. As he moved closer Mr. Nightingale's eyes went wide and his squint became more pronounced — for here surely was some sort of devilment! He saw that the opalescent sheen of the metal was not due to the reflection of candle-light, but was instead a property of the substance itself; that the metal was glowing with an eerie, inner light entirely of its own creation, independent of any external source.

Marvelous strange! Mr. Nightingale swallowed hard and wiped his mouth. What trickery was this? What magic? Here, he knew, was something his master with the great white head would be most interested in! Perhaps his master could sell it — for it was quite plainly an object of incomparable value — or demand a reward from Mr. John Hunter for its return. Either way there was money to be made, and Bob could smell it.

He leaped into action. He took up the glowing tablets — they did not burn him or poison him or electrify him, as he thought they might — and placed them in the canvas sack. He made his way quickly about the apartment like a housewife on market-day, grabbing up other documents that might be of use to his master, as well as a quantity of finer items such as a bronze hand-mirror, some votive figurines, a libation-vessel, and a black cup carved in the face of a demon — an ugly, bearded, grinning thing, with the beak of a vulture and ears of an ass, and snake-infested hair. Some of these items he would give up to his master, some he would not, the latter serving as consideration for services rendered.

He tied up the sack — which had grown quite bulky and rattled now of its contents — and threw it across his shoulder, stepping toward the French windows and the long gallery and freedom. It was then that a noise in the passage caught his attention. Another moment and he would have been clean away! With a grunt and a growl he bounded, as noiselessly as possible, into a corner where the light did not penetrate, shrinking against an old press and holding what remained of his breath.

A man entered the apartment, very slowly, with his head bowed and his features hidden. He was attired in royal raiment — a wondrous purple cloak littered with gold stars and more of those fanciful characters Mr. Nightingale found so perplexing. On his feet were curious soft shoes of maroon cloth that curled into points at their tips. Advancing at a stately, ceremonial pace, he paused to bow before the smiling figure with the hypnotic eyes. Three times the supplicant inclined his body, on each occasion murmuring a single low word that sounded like "Aplu" to Bob, though he couldn't swear to it.

The stranger turned round and in full view raised his head and hands. Mr. Nightingale froze on the spot, and felt his own toes curl inside his boots — for he saw that the face and throat and arms and hands of the man were painted a ghastly, lurid red, the very color of blood, like the image of a warrior-king drenched in gore.

The ghastly apparition moved to the altar and was about to place his blood-red hands upon it, when he discovered that the tablets were gone. He looked round quickly, several times, as if perhaps they had walked off of their own accord; but he found them not. A torrent of indecipherable words escaped his lips. He sped from the room, through the door and into the passage, perhaps in quest of the dusty servant. Only now, hearing the sound of that raised voice, did Mr. Nightingale equate the ghastly apparition with the lunatic who had counted the lightning-bolts. Only now did he see it was John Hunter.

Rallying himself, Mr. Nightingale lifted his burden and fled toward the gallery. The storm, which had eased up for a time, struck with renewed fury. A blinding light flashed upon the gallery, revealing the bulky form of Bob crouched there like a guilty thing — which, of course, he was. As the thunder crashed, the greasy hairs on the back of his neck rose in one accord, and throwing an ugly eye over his shoulder he beheld Mr. Hunter standing at the French windows.

The ghastly apparition stepped forward onto the gallery.

"Give it to me," he said, in level tones.

"Give you what, then, young gentleman?" returned the resourceful Bob, figuring in his brain the distance between his current position and the point where his rope lay wound about the balustrade.

"You know very well. What you have in that sack, and which does not belong to you."

"This sack? I ain't got nothin'," laughed Bob, with a vicious squint.

"Don't lie to me, sirrah. Who sent you?" demanded Mr. Hunter. "Was it *he?* He knows I am here."

"And who might that be, young gentleman?" asked Bob, throwing out the words to gain time while he edged toward the balustrade:

"Don't lie to me, I say. You fool, you've no idea what you're playing with here. I ask you again — who sent you? Ah!" The eyebrows of Mr. Hunter flew high above his eyes in a blood-red spasm of recognition. "It is you! The same one — the low fellow at the inn, that night the stricken man was carried in. That is where I have seen you. And he was there that night as well. So do not lie to me, sirrah. I know who sent you — only he, who was once my friend — *Avle Matunas!*"

"I don't know what the devil it is you're gabblin' about, young bloody gentleman," said Bob, "but I'm hanged if you ain't mad as a hatter — if by chance you ain't somethin' worse. Nobody sent me — I come o' my own accord, when I will, and I works alone, I do. I ain't a socialite!"

"Nothing occurs by chance," smiled Mr. Hunter, with a strange, sardonic gladness. "Every event under heaven — even this — is ordained by the shrouded gods. Everything that has ever happened, or is yet to happen, has been decreed."

The ancient retainer appearing at this moment behind Mr. Hunter, the latter's attention was briefly diverted — long enough for Mr. Nightingale to grasp his sought-for opportunity.

"Then you and your shredded gods ain't gonna mind," growled Bob, with a backward glance, "if I turns and cuts my lucky!"

He darted — as best his burly form could be said to dart — toward the edge of the gallery, one hand clutching the sack, the other reaching for the rope.

The ghastly apparition lunged after him. Poised for one last second on the balustrade, Bob glanced up and so found himself staring straight into Mr. Hunter's onrushing eyes. An eerie yellow light flared; the painted face of the young gentleman turned black, like a mask, with the yellow light glowing through the eyes as though live coals were burning inside his head. He barked out something that sounded like an oath — again it was uninterpretable — just as Bob, surprisingly nimble, dropped from sight over the balustrade.

As Mr. Hunter reached that spot and seized the rope he felt the tension upon it slacken, and heard the noise of Mr. Nightingale's boots striking the ground below. The burly ruffian fled into the night, attended by the rattling of his trophies in the canvas sack; and the darkness received him.

CHAPTER III

Then and Now

I⊤ was in the afternoon, on the day following the arrival of Mr. Harry Banister's letter, that Miss Laura Dale excused herself for some little while from the professor's household, begging attendance on a matter, as she framed it, of considerable personal concern — Mrs. Minidew engaging the attention of Fiona in the interim with the baking of cookies in the kitchen — and was shortly on her way into the heart of old Salthead. At the top of Friday Street she boarded a horse-bus, which carried her through the winding avenues and chilly gray boulevards — how well I remember them! — of the old city, past Great Wood Street and the Angel Inn and Fishmonger Lane, along the High Street and down among the well-worn courtyards of Snowfields and the Exchange, then across the chain bridge and bounding up and away from the docks, and so on to the coach-road that runs along the curving shoulders of the city — where, at a particularly dismal corner not often frequented by the lights of society, she found herself deposited.

All about her, buildings of brick in a crazed and faded state thrust upward toward the clouds, straining as if to tear themselves from their sorry foundations and so collectively fly away; between them, every now and then as she walked, a view could be glimpsed of the salty harbor below. As she made her way up the street, which was tilted at an alarming angle, she was accosted by a beggar demanding money. With the pittance received from her clutched in his fist, he staggered into a low ale-house over the way. It seemed to Laura, shivering and a little unnerved by this incident, that the air hereabouts was growing very sharp and thin, the higher she climbed — up and up, and still further up she went — but she soon dismissed this as nothing more than fancy, attributing it to her growing weariness with the effort and depression brought on by exposure to these melancholy precincts.

At length she arrived at a clump of ancient apartments, a stony shambles of a place dotted with innumerable tiny windows, and with the imposing title "FURNIVAL BUILDINGS" stamped on a circular brass plate affixed to one of the walls, like an eyeglass stuck onto a dreary brick face — a shambles, by the by, which was there at the time of my story but isn't there now, so don't bother

173

looking. Pausing at the gate-house to gain instruction from the surly porter, the governess entered the hall and found there just what the porter had described — a yawning flight of stairs.

Another climb! She set to it as best she could. Coming to a landing, she ascended the next flight of stairs, at the top of which was another landing, and then another flight of stairs — a total of five flights in all, to the very tip-top of the soaring old structure, at which point she emerged onto a dim passage lighted by sconces. Guided by the numerals on the dingy doors she came to one particular door, the dingiest of all, where the number "9" ought to have been. The door was unmarked, however, save for two tiny drill-holes, one above the other, where presumably the number in question had once been attached.

She hesitated only long enough to re-examine the numbering of the rooms, to assure herself that this was indeed the apartment she sought. She knocked at the door — a light, brisk rap, delivered with the urgency of one embarked upon an unpleasant task that, with a little luck, would be concluded as quickly as possible. As no answer was received she knocked again, more loudly this time, and a trifle more insistently. A scraping noise was heard on the other side of the panel, as of a chair being pushed back; footsteps sounded; the door swung inward and the breezy face and startled hair of Mr. Richard Scribbler appeared in the opening.

For the briefest instant Laura thought she must turn and go, so awkward seemed her mission now; but almost immediately her resolve came surging to the fore. Mr. Scribbler for his part radiated surprise and delight. He threw wide the door to admit her; she dipped her head in acknowledgment and passed silently into the room, which was in truth nothing more than a garret.

Breezy and careless was Mr. Richard Scribbler, law-clerk, and breezy and careless were his chambers. Careless, in that every item looked as though it had been cast into the air with wild abandon, coming to rest in a place and manner of its own devising rather than by any rational design; breezy, in that the cold wind from the harbor was seeping through the cracks and seams in the windows — the sashes drawn down tight, no doubt, to guard against this invasion. High windows they were, too, at the top of a high building perched on a hill high above Salthead town. For know you that this ancient pile of stone and brick called Furnival Buildings, now long demolished, stood upon the very summit of Whistle Hill, a place where the unbridled gusts from the sea rage and howl with a fury that can take your head off. There lived Mr.

Richard Scribbler those many years ago, at the top of the world — or perhaps he was above it.

Those gusts were starting to blow now — Laura had felt them in her face several times on her journey up the tilted street, but undoubtedly they blew with greater force up here in the clouds — such that a little piping squeak was heard now and again as the air found its way through the sash-boards.

Despite the disorder that characterized the garret apartment of Mr. Scribbler, there was, in fact, little of real substance in it: a deal table, upon which rested a pair of wax-lights, a bowl of fruit, and a book; a few chairs, very down at heels; some desultory items of china languishing on the mantel-shelf; a sagging chest of drawers; a wash-hand stand and ewer, both cracked; and a low settee that evidently doubled as a bed. A shabby floor-cloth beneath the table did little to amend either the warmth or the domesticity of these desolate surroundings.

Mr. Scribbler, somewhat formally, waved the governess to a chair at the deal table. She sat down, putting off her cloak and bonnet while the clerk raked up the fire. The chairs and table were so placed as to avoid the rush of air that periodically leaked into the room; and being as well near the fire it was possible, here at least, to avoid the cold without fear of catching one at the same time.

Mr. Scribbler made a motion toward the bowl of fruit, but the governess chose to decline his hospitality. She avoided his eyes, keeping her own fine gray ones lowered upon the floor, where they wandered from one dreary section of the cloth to another, then to the legs of the table, then to the hands fidgeting in her lap. This entire undertaking was hugely distasteful to her and she made no attempt to hide the fact. She appeared to be gathering within herself the strength to get on with it, whatever it might entail. An overwhelming desire to have it over with drove her forward, such that she continued to reject the clerk's offers — which by now entailed some bread and cheese, a pasty, a neat's tongue, and a glass of porter, all of which he retrieved from the chest of drawers standing against the wall.

"Mr. Scribbler," said Laura, determined to arrest these overtures. "I thank you for your kindness, but I really must speak with you now."

The clerk's features registered disappointment. He replaced the half-loaf of bread on its platter and dropped lifelessly onto his seat, shoving a hand into his wild head of hair. He seemed to know what was coming — indeed, it seemed he had known all along, the offers of food and drink to Miss Dale representing in part an effort to forestall the inevitable.

175

Without a word — which of course was the normal state of affairs for Mr. Scribbler — he laid his elbows on the table and rubbed his palms together, flicking his eyes this way and that; while Laura gazed absently at the floor-cloth, wanting, and yet still not wanting, to get on with it. It was so difficult to find the words! Mr. Scribbler — after a little passage of time and no progress made in the unpleasant direction he had anticipated — began to brighten, hoping for a change of heart in his visitor. Encouraged for the moment he seemed to recover something of his old spirits, folding his arms and smiling at the young woman with the kindliest of aspects.

"It seems we have come to yet another of those unfortunate crossroads on life's highway," said Laura, at last. "I wish — truly I wish — that I could have altered the course of things, for there is, as you know, nothing now to be done. You know as well, sir, my feelings in the matter, and so I won't repeat them here. I merely state that nothing whatsoever has changed with respect to our relations. But I fear this is a conversation we have had more than once before."

The light in Mr. Scribbler's eyes faded at these words. They were not such words as he had hoped to hear from her. They were not soft words, but they were not totally unexpected words. His shoulders drooped and he sank in his chair.

"It is," resumed Miss Dale — noting these changes in Mr. Scribbler, but plunging on nonetheless — "it was very difficult for me to come here today. Whenever we have met, it is as though time has gone all topsy-turvy and we are again back where we once were. But the past as we both know is the past, and we must live with its consequences. Although I harbor no ill feelings toward you — you do not believe me, I know, but regardless it is the truth — our relationship cannot be anything other than what it has become. The past prevents it. The terrible events that changed our lives so completely are as real to me now, today, at this instant, as they were seven years ago. The memory of that day is implanted deep in my consciousness; I never can forget it. But once again, these are things we have discussed before."

The clerk looked down at his fingers, which were playing with the pages of the book. Laura could not see his face, only the top of his wild sunburst of hair, in which, she noticed, a quill-pen was lodged.

"You think me unreasonable in this," she said, straightening, "but I assure you that is not the case. The past marks us, Richard, and there is nothing either of us can do about it. This is the way I am; I can no more change myself and my nature than I can change these candles into something they are not.

Can't you see that? I know I am somewhat rigid and fixed in my ways, but I've never meant at any time to hurt you. That is what I want so much for you to understand! If it were possible for me to change the things that have occurred, I would change them. If there were any way I could change, I would do it. But such miracles are quite beyond our power."

Mr. Scribbler raised his eyes and gazed at her with the most dismal of expressions. His cheeks were turned the color of custard; his brow was sorely ruffled; his normally free and breezy disposition was nowhere in evidence.

There followed an awkward pause, which was brought to an end by a blast of air through the sash-boards. Mr. Scribbler reached into his hair for his pen, with which he began scraping at a crumpled sheet of note-paper. He passed the paper to Laura, who read the message through quietly.

"Of course I remain your friend," she replied. "I will be your friend always, but friend is all. There will be no return to the ways of the past — there can be no question of that. It is pointless to discuss it. However, this subject does bear directly on the matter that has brought me here today."

Mr. Scribbler drooped even lower on his seat. He felt like a puppet in a verbal puppet-show, every volley from the governess punching him in the nose, or boxing him about the ears, or rapping him on the head; every unwelcome word from her lips beating him down, lower and lower, squashing him on his chair.

"When I first discovered the extent of your acquaintance with Professor Tiggs and his niece, I was not a little surprised. After all, what were the chances for such a coincidence? As I have come to understand it, you and Fiona have been friends for some time — a friendship originating, I believe, in some kindness bestowed upon you by the professor. He is a very kind man, and a generous employer. It was quite clear, the first time I observed you and Fiona together, how much your companionship means to her. She is a dear child and looks forward so much to your visits. I believe she has never met anyone quite like you."

Seeing Mr. Scribbler squashed on his chair, with his wild hair flaring out from his head and the quill-pen once more stuck in it, the validity of Laura's claim could scarcely be doubted.

"You are aware, of course, that I have been in my present situation in Friday Street for but a short time," she continued, a trifle hesitantly. "Here now is where I find myself stumbling, for as a relative outsider I am placed in the awkward position of — forced into a position that is — distasteful to me, and thoroughly unjust to — "

She halted in mid-sentence, one hand pressed to her face, as she searched for the words that eluded her.

Another stroke of Mr. Scribbler's pen, another scrap of note-paper passed to Laura. She smiled when she read it, but the smile was a transient one and not very encouraging to his prospects.

"Yes, the flowers were lovely. Fiona has put hers in a little vase by her window, and cares for them every day. It was very kind of you."

The light momentarily returned to Mr. Scribbler's eyes. A fond remembrance danced before them like motes in the sunshine.

"But here, you see, is the very thing I must discuss with you," said Laura, with sudden energy. "That afternoon by the carriage-road — our chance meeting there, you and Fiona and I — has made the matter quite clear to me. And lately your expeditions to the professor's house — oh, Richard, how shall I put this to you? I find myself in the position — the awful, horrible, unjust position, I know — of begging to impose upon a friendship over which I have no prerogative. You see, I should like to remain on terms with you — in spirit at least — but I should prefer to avoid those occasions on which we might happen to meet. Oh, how can I express myself? I must simply say it, although I know you will misunderstand. *I ask that you not come to Friday Street any longer.*"

There it was, then — the cruelest volley of all. His heart took a fearful leap; again her words pounded him into his chair.

"You see, Richard," Laura went on, undeterred, "I have acquired at last a measure of calmness and equanimity in my life, and that is of great importance to me. Had I known beforehand of the friendship existing between you and Fiona, I would under no circumstance have accepted the offer of Professor Tiggs; indeed, I would have declined it outright without either hesitation or regret. Perhaps my entering the professor's household will prove a mistake. Nevertheless, his niece's upbringing and education are now in my hands, and so I ask you, Richard — beg of you, if you will — not to disturb my new-found tranquillity with your periodic appearances."

The look in Mr. Scribbler's face was indescribable — although the term *macerated* comes to mind — as the full force of what Laura was asking of him struck home. Not come to Friday Street! Not see Fiona! He hardly could believe it. He hardly could hear it, either, what with the throbbing deep in his ears. Her voice sounded as if it were traveling down a long tube from very far away.

"I realize I have no right to ask such a thing of you. It is despicable of me, I know, yet I ask it anyway — in memory of how things once stood between us, and of the affection we shared. Please, Richard, do not be angry with me. There are times when I think it is all my doing. I am selfish, I know, and far too rigid. It is my nature; I cannot alter it. I am so fixed in my ways and unable to bend — or unwilling — and in this I am accursed. Please grant me this single request, and have my assurance it will be the very last request I ever make of you on this earth."

The cheeks of Mr. Scribbler were as white as turnips. His lips quivered. His staring eyes filled with tears, so full that it seemed his very soul might at any moment come pouring out of them. All manner of thoughts and desires, sad and gloomy, came welling up through the stormy channels of his heart.

Laura, moved by this demonstration of feeling, and to some extent alarmed by her own apparent deficit in that regard, covered her mouth with her hands — in awe, perhaps, of her own callousness — and returned his stare. It required little more for the false edifice of her self-control to collapse; she moaned and flung herself back in her chair, weeping silently.

Much affected first by her speech and then by her evident regret of it, Mr. Scribbler offered her a handkerchief. She accepted it with thanks and wiped her eyes. The clerk was perched on the edge of his seat, watching, hoping against hope that the abrupt flow of tears might produce a change of fortune. It did not.

"I am frightfully ashamed," sniffled Laura, her voice falling an octave as a result of her cry. "I am so thoughtless — so wicked — so cold and unnatural — so — so — "

Her words ran slowly down like the spring of an old chimney-clock. She swallowed a couple of times, and brushed aside a lock of hair that had strayed upon her forehead. Mr. Scribbler reached across the table and touched her hand, shaking his head gently and knitting his brows, thereby signing to her that her concerns were needless.

Laura made answer by shaking her own head in a most dejected fashion.

"Why are we made this way?" she asked, of no one in particular. "Why can't it be otherwise? Why? Who has done this to us? Why can we never change our hearts and minds?"

Here Mr. Scribbler took up a sheet of note-paper and dashed off another dispatch.

Not to worry, he wrote. *I understand — Friday Street.*

Laura lifted her head, hardly daring to believe. "Thank you, Richard," she said, in a rapturous whisper. "Oh, thank you! God bless you."

Mr. Scribbler managed to get up a little smile but it was a perfunctory effort at best, tainted with the melancholy of resignation. He folded his arms and deposited his gaze upon the table-top, where he kept it trained for some few minutes. He appeared to be reconciling within himself a whole host of conflicting emotions, sorting them and categorizing them, retaining some and discarding others, yet holding them all at a distance, like a philosopher contemplating the folly of humankind. The past is the past, Laura had said, and that was certainly true; it was the future now he must learn to accept. Underneath it all he was happy for her, no doubt, but such happiness did not come without a price.

And what of little Fiona and her own feelings? Had she no say in the matter? What would be *her* response? Ah, but I suppose that grown-ups always know better; such are not the concerns of childhood. Leave to the children their toffey, toys and penny-books — isn't that what the pedlar sings?

"I must go now," said Laura, gaining her feet — unsteadily at first — and taking up her gloves and bonnet. *How unkind of you*, whispered a chiding voice in her ear. *How very, very unkind of you.*

As she lowered her head and swept her curls aside, to put on her bonnet, a scar was by accident exposed, running from behind her ear and down her neck and so vanishing beneath the collar of her garment. A restless, ugly thing it was, this scar, like a meandering river with many tributaries, standing apart from the smooth white plains of her flesh. Mr. Scribbler shrank from it — though it was not the first time he had seen it — and uttered a scarcely audible gasp, his lips rounding themselves into an awful "O." He had not forgotten the existence of that terrible stain, only its violence; the shock of seeing it again touched him deeply.

Laura turned up her hand to draw on her glove, and so another scar was revealed curling about her wrist and up her arm. It had the same features as the other though they were not as much in evidence, as this second blemish was mostly hidden by the sleeve of her jacket.

Conscious of Mr. Scribbler's reaction, Laura tied the ribbons of her bonnet and lifted her eyes to his.

"You see how the past marks us," she said.

Mr. Scribbler, in the grip of an overwhelming sorrow, desired to do he knew not what. Unable to think, unable to speak, unable to fathom how to make amends to the poor creature who stood before him, unable even to move, he saw everything now as though in a dream: saw Laura put on her cloak, saw the door open, saw her pass through without a word, saw she was gone.

The pain of remorse is a bitter pain, and in the moments that followed Mr. Scribbler endured the torture of its sting. He gazed stupidly at the door through which Laura had disappeared. A minute went by, then two. Gone? Had she really gone? He couldn't remember. Had she ever been there, or was it indeed all a dream? He found he couldn't answer any of his own questions.

It was a squeal from the sash-boards that brought him round. He stepped to the drafty window and there looked out upon the world, examining it with folded arms and knitted brows from the safety of his chambers high above Whistle Hill. So in much the same manner did he survey, on a daily basis, the wide legal world of Badger and Winch from his high seat. Above it all, aloft and aloof — whether as a consequence or by design, I cannot say; but in either case looking down upon the world from a remote perspective, at once apart from it and so safe from it as well.

Safety. Why should he have known safety in his life, and not she? What had he done to deserve safety? Safety gained for him had meant safety forfeited for her, with a terrible consequence. And what of the others, those two dear lost souls? What right had he to such safety from the world when he'd had so little care for theirs?

Grabbing up as many stray sheets of note-paper as he could find, he rushed to the table and threw himself into his chair. He began to write on the papers, on the front and on the back of them, repeating over and over the single word that, to him, seemed to define now the essence of his character, the sum total of his existence, the very nature of his being. Again and again, without pause, the same letters dropped from his pen upon the note-paper, filling the available space with the one word that seemed to describe, for all time, what it meant to be Richard Scribbler.

COWARD was that word.

When he had tired of this little exercise he ripped the sheets of note-paper into a hundred fragments and tossed them aside. Slumped on his chair he stared at the table-top in gloomy rumination, absently fondling and pinching his lip between a thumb and forefinger.

What to do now? How to mend a hopeless situation? Never was a fellow driven harder to the wall! There was, simply put, nothing to be done. The days of his life would wheel on as they had before, but now and forever more they would be empty days. Was there nothing else to be done, however futile it might seem?

Abruptly he shook himself from his reverie. Taking up one of the few remaining sheets of note-paper left intact, he stuck his pen into his hair and bolted from the room.

In the meantime Laura had descended the five long flights of stairs to the entrance-hall, and having endured the rude stare of the porter while passing through the gate-house, emerged at last upon the tilted street. There to greet her were a charcoal sky and a blustery wind, keen offspring of the elements that earlier had kept her company on her way to Furnival Buildings. She turned into the road, and had very nearly reached the bottom of Whistle Hill, where the bus-stand was, when she heard rapid footsteps gaining on her from behind.

Mr. Scribbler came clattering to a stop, not more than a foot away. Heedless of the weather he had forgotten to don his coat; he was nearly out of breath and smoking at the mouth with cold. Before Laura could respond he motioned her to silence, and clutching the sheet of note-paper bent low and scraped out another message — this a very short one — using the ink that still lingered on the nib of his pen, and his thigh for a writing-stand.

He handed the message to her and awaited her reply with a beating heart. Scratched upon the paper, in dim and crooked letters, were three words —

Forgive some day?

Laura glanced up with that same odd, ambiguous expression that had crossed her face the day she and Fiona met him in the road. Gaining courage, he very gently touched her arm — the one with the scar — and lifted her hand to his lips. Laura said nothing. She placed the message inside her cloak, and without any measurable reply walked off in the direction of the bus-stand. Mr. Scribbler remained where he was, watching her small dark form until it vanished round a bend in the street. After a final scratch or two at his hair he retraced his steps toward Furnival Buildings, with his eyes on the ground and his thumbs hooked in his waistcoat-pockets.

As luck would have it, a young man mounted on a black gelding — just one of several riders amid the traffic in the street — happened onto this little scene. Recognizing one of the participants he drew bridle and stood observing from the front of a pork-butcher's over the way, with his muffler pulled up to hide his face and his hat pulled down to hide his orange hair. Such feeble attempts at camouflage proved unnecessary, however, as his presence went all unnoticed by the participants. The young man's gaze fell softly on Miss Laura Dale, and held there until the moment she disappeared round the corner. It was a frown, however, that attended the progress of Mr. Richard Scribbler as the sad-faced clerk pivoted on his heel and trudged up the tilted street.

Welladay! Despair clouded the eyes behind the unfashionable green spectacles. Mr. Austin Kibble, unfortunate enough to have witnessed certain events, urged black Nestor on through the traffic; and so made his troubled way home, away from the sights and sounds and anything at all that might remind him of a place called Whistle Hill.

CHAPTER IV

The Fall of the Leaf

"BUT why must you go?"

"I'm very sorry, dear — we didn't mean to wake you. Not to worry, then! I'll be away for only a short time. No more than a week, in fact."

"Yes, but why?"

"Really, Fiona, I thought you understood. Don't you recall our little conversation last night, after dinner?"

"It's ever so cruel for you to be going away into the country, all by yourself, and not take me with you!"

"Dear, I thought I explained that all to you quite clearly. In the first place I'll not be alone, for Dr. Dampe will be with me, as will young Mr. Kibble."

"Boring Mr. Kibble! Why take him? Why can't you take me instead?"

"Now, then, dear, no more remarks about Mr. Kibble. In the second place, while it's true we're going into the country, this will be quite a lengthy excursion — across the mountains, you know. It's not as simple as one of our little afternoon rambles down to Grigsby or Butter Cross. Oh, no. We're going to the high moorlands. They're very far away, as you'll recollect, I'm sure, from our look at the atlas last evening. Two days by traveling-coach is not an easy journey for a young child."

"But I'm not a young child."

"But you are," insisted the professor, kissing his niece on the forehead. "Even if you don't realize it. And so we'll have no more arguments — agreed? It's far too early in the morning for that sort of thing. I'm sorry, dear, for waking you at such an hour; it wasn't intentional. Pray go back to sleep now, and be assured, Hanna is here — " he nodded toward the ruddy young farm lass, Mrs. Minidew's helper in the kitchen, who was watching from across the bed with a sympathetic expression — "and she, and Miss Dale, and Mrs. Minidew will look after you most admirably while I am from home. So we'll have no more talk of your coming along. Such nonsense!"

"Nonsense!" agreed Hanna, bobbing her head.

Fiona lay back on her pillow with a little groan of capitulation. "If you won't take me with you," she said, calculatingly, "will you bring something back for me?"

"What would you like?" the professor asked.

"Will you bring me a bear?"

"A stuffed bear?"

"No, a real bear. From the mountain meadows."

Professor Tiggs, well knowing the futility of dissuasion when it came to this particular topic, laughed softly and bid his young ward farewell on the cheek.

"Good-bye, dear," he whispered, with a good-natured sigh. "I'll see what I can do about it."

"Thank you, thank you!" exulted Fiona, entwining her little arms about his neck and squeezing with all her might. "*Bon voyage, Oncle* Tiggs. *Je vous aime!*"

At this moment Mrs. Minidew looked in at the door, saying in a low voice —

"Tom's ready for you, sir."

"Ah — thank you, Mrs. Minidew," smiled the professor. With a last farewell to his niece, who already was sinking back into the dreamy clutches of sleep, he left her to the care of Hanna and descended to the back-passage. There he donned his muffler and great-coat, and his hat and gloves, and gathered up his valise and umbrella. Tom Spike came in from the stable-yard to fetch the professor's portmanteau, which he carried out to the waiting gig. Waiting there too was Maggie, the buckskin mare, looking resplendent in harness. She snorted and shook her flanks, jingling a little and emitting a white steam from her nostrils.

The professor took leave of the remaining members of the household and descended the back-stairs, at the bottom of which a plaintive voice betrayed the presence of one Mr. Pumpkin Pie.

"Good-bye, young man," said the professor, rubbing that spoiled dependent about the ears. "See that you don't get into any mischief while I'm away."

"Ha!" laughed old Tom, from his seat in the gig. "That one? Not likely!"

The professor settled himself on the cushion beside Tom, who took charge of the reins, and so away they went. On the landing beside Mrs. Minidew, watching them go, stood Miss Laura Dale, her lips tightly drawn and a look of steady concentration in her gray eyes. What thoughts could have been running through that young woman's mind to fix her face so, as though it were cut in stone? What scenes, far removed in time yet fresh in memory, could have been passing before those eyes as they stared off into an immeasurable perspective?

I can venture a guess, but only a guess; and at this point in my story, a guess it needs must remain.

It was a brief and wordless journey through chilled and darkened streets. Neither the professor nor Tom seemed much inclined to conversation at such an hour. The clatter of the gig-wheels echoed through the silent boulevards; the ring of Maggie's shoes sounded clear and sharp on the frosty air. Already the darkness was beginning to recede, revealing the first faint traces of daylight in the silver-gray contours of the hills and houses.

Eagerly the buckskin mare carried them along the empty avenues, in the general direction of the chain bridge, until at length they were arrived in Bridge Street and so came to a halt before the coach-office. This turned out to be a fair-sized establishment of half-timbered plasterwork, the area immediately in front being lighted by oil lamps over the window. Inscribed upon the glass was the image of a coach drawn by four spirited horses, high-flying it through some imaginary wilderness panorama. Above this delightful image was the single word "TIMSON'S" in an elaborate script. Maggie, if she could have been queried on the subject, would I'm sure have argued that the four horses were not all that spirited; and that any one of them, on a good day, could have been beaten by any nag with half her mettle.

A brisk wind was blowing in the street and scattering the withered leaves. The professor drew his coat closer about him and stepped from the gig. Old Tom collected the portmanteau from the boot and followed him into the booking-office — a damp, dreary chamber, whose walls were posted with enormous bills advertising the routes and fares of the Timson coaches. A long wooden counter dominated the center of the room; to the left of it a welcome fire was burning in the chimney. The groom laid the heavy portmanteau on the counter, while the clerk — little more than a youth, he seemed to Tom — noted the professor's name and checked his booking, and wrote out his ticket, and stamped his portmanteau, all at the same time and with equal dispatch.

"Lug it out!" shouted the clerk, in a voice considerably out of proportion to his slender frame. In response a porter — a great hulking Hercules of a man, with muscles like watermelons — appeared in a door at the back of the room. He gathered up the heavy portmanteau with ease and whirling round launched himself out at the same door, which led presumably to the coach-yard. The professor inquiring upon just this particular point, and also as to the general safety of the transport, the clerk informed him that the coach was even that moment up the yard, and that the horses were being watered, and that Timson coaches were as safe as any coaches could reasonably be expected to be, and that the equipage would be brought round now in something under twenty minutes. Thus assured the professor bid farewell to old Tom, who tipped his bowler and breezed out of the moldy office just as Dr. Dampe was breezing in.

Despite the extremity of the hour and its not inconsiderable chill, the doctor was looking his usual splendid self, with his jaunty paletot over his dark velvet coat and his hat cocked lazily above one eye.

"Hallo, hallo," he sang out in greeting, with a little flourish of his walking-stick. "Lovely morning, isn't it? The air hereabouts is sharp, very sharp. Excellent for the heart and circulation. Did you know there's a ginger-cake seller's over the way? I didn't. Pity they're shuttered-up yet. Some coffee would be nice."

"Rather crisp this morning," agreed the professor, warming his hands at the fire. "And rather early as well."

"I've been up for hours, actually," said the doctor, and tossed his carpet-bag upon the counter. "Dampe," he announced to the clerk.

"It certainly is," returned that young person, with a yawn. "Sorry — no help for it."

"No, no, no — *Dampe* — Dr. Daniel Dampe — physician. I have a booking."

"You are one of the passengers going out by the early coach?"

"Exactly. Booking — on Friday last — here," said the doctor, tapping his finger upon the booking-list.

"You're right. I see it now," said the youth, glancing over the names. "`Close personal friend of Mr. Harry Banister' is what it says here. Hmmm. That's impressive."

The doctor threw a look of inexpressible significance at Professor Tiggs.

"Lug it out!" roared the booking-clerk; then turning back to the physician inquired, apparently in all innocence —

"Who's Harry Banister, then?"

"Never 'eard of 'im," boomed a voice from the back door. It was Hercules, who, having appeared again, scooped up the doctor's carpet-bag and removed it to the coach-yard, so that it might keep company with the professor's portmanteau.

"Look here," said Dr. Dampe — in that same condescending tone he adopted whenever explaining a difficult medical point to a patient — "Mr. Harry Banister happens to be one of the most eligible and fashionable members of the landed gentry. He is a graduate of that famed institution, the University of Salthead, as well as being a very wealthy gentleman and master of a great estate on the high moorland called Eaton Wafers. No doubt you've heard of it. My friend and colleague, Professor Tiggs there — himself a distinguished professor of metaphysics and fellow of Swinford College, Salthead — and I are off to see him on the coach this morning."

"I don't see Mr. Banister's name here," said the clerk, frowning. "If you're going to see him on the coach, his name had better be on the list!"

"I don't mean to say that Mr. Banister will be *on* the coach," explained the doctor. "What I mean is that we're taking the coach to see him."

"Go on, then!" jeered the clerk, with a little whisk of his hand. "That coach out there can't see nobody."

"Look here," said the doctor, irritated at having to confront such impenetrability of mind so early in the day, "would you by any chance happen to know whether that other fellow might be about somewhere? That *older*, much more *experienced* fellow, who was taking the bookings on Friday morning last?"

"Oh, him," said the youth, shaking his head mournfully, with a few sympathetic clucks of his tongue. "Sad. Sad. Very sad."

"What do you mean?"

"Crushed."

"What! Thrown beneath a carriage? When? How did it happen?"

"Worse," said the clerk, clucking again. "Crushed — to learn he weren't a close personal friend of Mr. Harry Banister's."

"I see how it is," said the doctor, very slowly and emphatically, and by now persuaded that clotted cream — or was it vinegar — must constitute a sizable proportion of this clod's cerebral hemispheres. "I see how it is. Might I have your name, my good fellow — if it isn't too much trouble?"

"Brittlebank, sir. But you must return it, once you've finished with it. That's the law."

"If I may be so bold as to inquire, Mr. Brittlebank," said the physician, coloring, "whether Mr. Abel Timson might be about the premises this morning?"

"Mr. Abel Timson? Who's that, then?" asked the youth, with a puzzled stare.

Here it was that the professor — who had been eavesdropping on this little tête-à-tête with a fascination approaching wonder — became the recipient of a knowing wink, discharged from the clerk's eye; and so they both at the same instant burst into laughter. The doctor, realizing he'd been gammoned by a practitioner of the first water — youthful though he might be — threw back his head and laughed very heartily.

So it happened that sounds of merriment accosted the ears of Mr. Austin Kibble, as that uncharacteristically somber young man entered the coach-office. After surrendering custody of his luggage to Messrs Brittlebank and Hercules, he stood for a time at the fire, saying little to either Professor Tiggs or the doctor, apart from a polite greeting and one or two terse comments regarding the dreariness of coach-offices. The professor, noting his secretary's altered demeanor, questioned him briefly on the subject; Mr. Kibble's reply consisting of a few mumbled words to the effect that he was "Sorry, sir — kept up all night — indigestion — excitement of the journey — neighborhood cats — etc., etc."

Consulting his watch in the interim, Dr. Dampe wondered if the other members of the party might have encountered some unforeseen delay. It was ten minutes before six, and he knew that Timson's had a reputation as a punctual service. Six o'clock departure meant departure at six o'clock. He began to pace the room, glancing now and then at the details of the timetables posted on the walls. The professor found himself pacing too, with his hands at his back and his head lowered, watching his shoes measure out length upon length of the sawdust-littered floor. When a newspaper vendor blew in voicing the cheerful cry — "*Gazette*, gen'lm'n! *Gazette*, gen'lm'n!" — the fellow was rewarded with the gift of a coin from the professor's pocket, in return for a copy of the sunrise edition.

The doctor, standing at the window beside the spirited horses and the high-flying coach, suddenly brightened and moved to open the door, thereby admitting the diminutive form of Miss Mona Jacks. He lifted his hat in salutation, saluting as well the young woman behind her, who was introduced as Miss Nina Jacks — a taller, paler version of her younger sister. They were accompanied by a maidservant in a patterned shawl and the severest of bonnets, who was given much to sniffing and the casting of fussy looks.

The professor and Mr. Kibble were introduced, and so the little traveling party of six was now assembled for the first time. The belongings of the Jackses were brought in by a servant and laid upon the counter, where the youthful clerk proceeded to scratch the names from his list; all the while paying rather closer attention to the two pretty sisters than was otherwise warranted — arching his brows and indulging in a few offhand witty remarks, smiling excessively, and inclining his head at rakish angles — while completely ignoring the fussy maidservant, who sniffed several times in his direction.

For her part the maidservant Susanna busied herself mostly with Miss Nina, now and again taking her hand, or arranging this garment of hers or that, or whispering some little word of encouragement in her ear; while Miss Nina kept very much to herself, saying nothing to anybody and gazing about the coach-office with an anxious expression. Thus it fell to Miss Mona Jacks to serve as ambassador of sorts to the gentlemen members of the party.

A peal of bells rang out from the steeple of St. Skiffin's Church, announcing the magic hour of six. The coach was in the yard, and the four horses harnessed and pawing the ground in anticipation. Where all had been quiet, all was now noise and bustle, as Hercules and the helpers made their final dashes back and forth from the office, bearing items of transport for the boot and box.

"Six o'clock!" cried the guard — as if the holy bells of St. Skiffin were not inducement enough — "Make haste, there! Make haste! Six o'clock!"

The lone outside passenger — shrouded from head to foot in his great-coat and boots, and his hat and muffler, like a modern mummy — climbed to the top of the box and took his place beside the luggage heap. The inside passengers were loaded in, the sisters and the fussy maidservant on the one side, the gentlemen on the other. There followed a clank of steps and a clang of doors; and so the insides were secured for the first leg of the journey.

The coachman mounted to the front of the box. Behind him, on the little seat at the back, rested the guard, with his feet upon the boot, and the grim necessary armaments — cutlasses, small-swords, rapier, and a wicked poniard — in easy reach at his elbow. Between the two men sat the outside passenger, huddled on his cushion like a second luggage heap, with his face buried in his muffler as though he were already asleep.

The coachman undid the buckle that held the driving-reins and seized the whip. The guard shouted from behind —

"All right, Jemmy — give 'em their heads!"

The coachman nodded to the helpers, who pulled the horse-cloths off and backed away. The guard blew his little curly key-bugle — the driver gave a flick of the whip to the off-leader — there was a clang and a jerk — the body of the vehicle shuddered — the walls of the coach-office began to glide away — and so amid shouts of farewell from the helpers and Hercules, the eastern coach gained speed and rumbled out of the yard.

With consummate skill the coachman drove the horses due east along the river, then north along the main coach-road and so up and onto the high ground at the back of the city. The dark and narrow streets were yielding to the light of dawn. Soon the shops and houses flying by were replaced by broader vistas of field and hedgerow, glade and hollow, richly clothed in timber; and so, in very little time at all, the familiar environs of the city were left far behind.

Past the lofty crags and wild soaring pinnacles thundered the coach-and-four. They were now well on course to the nearer highlands, threading their way through avenues of majestic oaks and the misty woods that led to the fells. Inside not a word had been spoken since leaving the yard. Professor Tiggs, quiet as always at this hour of the morning, had coiled himself snugly into his corner of the coach and was looking out upon the passing scenery. The corner to his left was occupied by an uncommonly drowsy Mr. Kibble. Between them sat the doctor, gazing with rapt attention at every passing tree or shrub, whatever its nature, and in whichever window it happened to appear.

On the side opposite, Miss Mona Jacks was dividing her thoughts between the woodland vistas and the face of the subdued Mr. Kibble. The maidservant Susanna, with a sister on either hand, had thrown herself back against the cushion and was toying with sleep. Her mouth hung open like a feed-sack; every now and again her eyelids fluttered as she strove against the charms of Morpheus. Miss Nina Jacks meanwhile had succumbed completely to the rhythm of the wheels, lying against the maid's shoulder with her eyes closed and curls of her chestnut hair spilling from her bonnet.

Such, in my experience, is the usual case with early coaches. There is the initial excitement of waking at just the right hour — neither too early (for then you remain exhausted and unrefreshed) nor too late (then you might as well sleep some more, for the coach has gone without you). It is the balance between the alternatives that provides the tension. Once awake and into your clothes and cab and at last at the coach-office, it is the bustle and excitement of departure that dominate. Then into your vehicle and onto the road, and almost at once some of the passengers become rather dismal and sleepy, as the vibrations of the coach work their magical effects — which, I might add, are more potent than any stock remedy of chaomile or valerian known to humankind. And so the temptation to doze is a hard one to resist, particularly when the light is so dim, the air is so cold, and the year is so late.

Thoughts something akin to this, I venture, may have been passing through the mind of Mr. Kibble — still on the mend from a certain late experience on a certain windy hill — as he pondered the diorama of hills and woods rushing past his window. Occasionally the outline of a gable or chimney on some distant farmstead could be glimpsed through the trees. Everywhere squirrels were scampering among the red and yellow leaves, gathering their provisions for the coming season. The bleak and somber days of winter, the end of another year, the conclusion of yet another cycle — what changes of life, wondered Mr. Kibble, might the new year's cycle bring?

Onward flew the eastern coach, climbing slowly into a range of hilly upland. Far away, purple mountains of fir and pine rose against the horizon. The rumble of the wheels threatened to extend its influence now to Professor Tiggs; by dint of active resistance, however, he conquered it, by focusing his attention on the columns of his *Gazette*.

"Extraordinary thing," said a voice from nowhere, which, coming as it did after a period of quiet, sounded a good deal louder than it actually was. The voice belonged to Dr. Dampe, who seemed determined that, with the rising now of the sun, he and his conversational powers should rise like a second sun within the carriage.

"What is?" inquired the professor.

"This transportation system of ours. Just think of it, Titus. It wasn't very long ago that a place like Eaton Wafers was virtually inaccessible from Salthead, except to the hardiest of travelers. Now here we are, flying along the highway on a brilliant morning, hopping from one stage to another, with a fine night's stay at a cozy country inn in the offing, and so by late tomorrow we arrive at our far-away destination! Most extraordinary thing, I say."

The others nodded in agreement, save for Miss Nina, whose sleepy head still rested on the maidservant's shoulder.

"When I was a young fellow in medical training," said the doctor, rambling comfortably along now like the coach itself, "I once arranged a little holiday for a week or so at Fishmouth. Now, I needn't tell you that the road from Salthead to Fishmouth is today about as well-traveled a path as can be imagined. Virtually no trouble at all. But in those days — well, such a trip was quite another thing, actually. No long-distance coaches then — oh, no. Those were the days of the thunder-beasts! I still can recall, with vivid intensity, the exhilaration of that adventure among the mastodon men."

"It was a different world, and a world of difference," nodded the professor, guilty perhaps of a bit of reminiscing himself. "Things we take today for granted were scarcely thought of then."

"There was a mastodon in Salthead last month, and my sister and I went to see it," spoke up Miss Mona. "It was the most enormous creature — very shaggy and red, with a long trunk and sweeping tusks. Yet for something so vast and powerful, it was possessed of the most soulful eyes one ever could imagine. They shone like two mirrors, and it seemed to me I could see its inmost thoughts reflected there. I have no doubt the creature felt deeply the indignity of its situation — the fall from grace — for you see, it belonged to one of those horrid traveling shows. The proprietors had chained it to an oak, where it was compelled to perform silly, inconsequential tricks for the delight of an audience. It was almost cruel."

"It is virtually all they have left now," said the doctor, reflectively. "With the clearing of the roads and their accessibility to coaches, demand for the mastodon trains has all but vanished. It's a pity, actually. There are a few teams yet in existence, here and there — but they are rapidly disappearing."

"There are zoological gardens, I believe, at Crow's-end, where a number of the animals are displayed," said the professor. "But as you have so aptly pointed out, Miss Jacks — it is a sorry spectacle, and a sad end for a noble race of creatures."

Mr. Kibble, who had been listening rather indifferently to the conversation, rose abruptly in his seat, his attention arrested by some distant object. He straightened his spectacles — as if that simple action might somehow put to rout the disbelief in his eyes — and ran his fingers through his orange hair. He pointed to the window, exclaiming in amazement —

"Thunder-beasts — look there!"

Everyone looked in the direction indicated — everyone, even a startled Miss Nina Jacks, whose pretty head bounced up from the maidservant's shoulder at the sound of Mr. Kibble's voice. A momentary hush enveloped the little party.

"Extraordinary thing!" cried the doctor.

"Absolutely splendid!" cried the professor.

"Magnificent!" cried the secretary.

The coach had by now ascended to level ground, from which elevation a clear view was obtained of the distant fellside. At the base of the hills, before a dense wood studded with evergreens, a fleet of red mastodons was sailing. There appeared to be about a dozen of the creatures. They were led by three men on horseback, two of whom held aloft long poles from which bright red pennants were fluttering. It was by means of these banners, explained Dr. Dampe, that the animals were guided, for they had been trained from earliest infancy to follow them. In the rear came a transport van of moderate dimensions, driven by a gentleman urging on a pair of horses.

"It looks to be an entire team," observed the doctor.

Even the fussy Susanna was transfixed by the sight, rising up on her cushion with her eyeglasses tightly pinching her nose and her bonnet tightly pinching her head, and uttering a little "Ooh! my stars" under her breath.

"What are they doing?" asked Miss Nina, speaking now for the first time, and revealing a voice at once mellifluous and affected.

"Where are they going?" asked her sister.

"They're moving south along the old fell trail," said Mr. Kibble, regaining some of his earnestness as his mind was deflected from other things. "But they've no passengers, and the only freight seems to be in that van. Devilish thought! Can it be they're for Crow's-end?"

"Oh, I hope you are wrong!" exclaimed Miss Mona. "See how majestic they are, how graceful, like swans on the water — yet each and every step is laden with power. If we were standing on the ground I have no doubt the earth would be trembling under our feet."

It was the carriage that trembled now, however, as the road veered to one side, the coach following suit, and so their view of the thunder-beasts was obliterated by a lengthy ridge of pine woods.

The travelers settled back in their seats. The spectacle of the mastodon train had lifted their spirits; so that now, with the emergence of the sun and a full flood of daylight about them, the drowsy swaying of the coach had less of an effect. They began to chat among themselves on a host of topics — small talk mostly, concerning this or that, with much to-ing and fro-ing of eyes as the conversation passed from one person to another — and so they came to know each other a little better.

It soon became apparent that Miss Nina Jacks was a wholly different type of Jacks from her younger sister. Whereas Miss Mona was forthright and affable, Miss Nina was distant, speaking relatively little and nearly always when spoken to; whether from shyness, or discomfort, or innate reserve — or a form of coquettishness even, so far as the gentlemen were concerned — was not readily apparent. Miss Mona was in the main cheerful and attentive to all, while Miss Nina seemed less interested in her companions than in herself. How much of this could be attributed to her natural disposition, how much to the strain of the journey and the presence of strangers, how much to the trauma of her encounter with Mr. Pickering, could only be conjectured. Miss Mona was ingenuous and unassuming, and given to little flights of humor — often at her own expense — but her sister most definitely was not. She laughed at nothing anyone said, and accordingly took her own views rather seriously, not hesitating to point out her good qualities to others; and so appeared to be a young lady who cherished a most agreeable opinion of herself.

Physically the two sisters differed as well. Miss Mona was much the smaller, and wore her dark hair short and curled, which left it for the most part hidden under her bonnet. Her sister's hair was of a lighter tint and a good deal longer, with a portion of it lying rather fashionably about her shoulders. This overflow she spent much time fondling and inspecting, and winding stray curls of it round her fingers. The doctor thought she must be one of those young women he had observed, who were excessively fond of their tresses. In this as in everything she was aided and abetted by Susanna. It was clear from her reliance on Susanna's constant attention that Miss Nina was, to paraphrase her sister's words, ever their maidservant's favorite. The fussy Susanna in fact paid little or no heed to Miss Mona at all, devoting her ministrations almost exclusively to the elder sister.

Despite the general brightening of the atmosphere inside the coach, Mr. Kibble after a while seemed to lapse again into whatever it was he had lapsed into before. He pressed his head back against the cushion and cast long vacant stares upon the passing scenery.

"Are you quite all right, Mr. Kibble?" inquired Miss Mona. "You seem indisposed today. I hope it is nothing serious?"

"It is nothing at all, I assure you, Miss Jacks," replied the secretary, rousing himself with an effort from his languor. "Indigestion, I believe — nothing more serious than that."

"Dyspepsia," diagnosed the doctor, nodding sagely.

"Yes. Exactly. A disagreeable piece of beef at dinner last evening, that's all. A bit too much whistle for one's liking."

"Whistle?" repeated Miss Mona.

"I — I meant to say *gristle*, of course — too much gristle for one's liking. I believe it's made me hill — I meant *ill* — "

Poor Mr. Kibble! What indeed could he be thinking of? Should prizes ever be awarded for dissembling, I'll wager he needn't fear winning one.

"I must say, sir, I am happy to hear it was the beef, and not one of those `green culinary vegetables' you and the doctor had your little row about. Oh, no need to worry, Mr. Kibble — I've quite recovered from that discussion. And from my late talk with you as well, Dr. Dampe."

"Ah, the young lady has recovered!" exclaimed the doctor, rapping his stick upon the floor by way of approbation. "Bravo, Miss Jacks! I had complete faith in you."

"And for which I must apologize to all three of you, for being so faint-hearted upon such topics," she continued. Her sister was watching her uncomfortably from the corners of her eyes, as she ventured now into delicate territory. "After all, I came seeking your aid in regard to the affliction that has been visited upon Nina. And so we cannot shrink from the consequences, no matter how disagreeable. Indeed, that is why we are here now. As I have made clear to my sister, we have no choice — we must face the matter directly if we are ever to understand it."

The professor, once more impressed with the strength of character exhibited by this tiny young woman, fairly beamed.

"Dr. Dampe has informed me," she went on, "of other exceptional events that have transpired in Salthead, of which my sister and I were unaware. When he told me next of your intended journey to Eaton Wafers, I confess I could not restrain my curiosity. He was then kind enough to invite us to accompany you, and I haven't until this moment had the courage to ask your pardon for burdening you with our presence."

"Why, it is no burden," said the professor, in a prolonged tone of surprise — though the expression on the face of Dr. Dampe seemed to recall another conversation, not so long ago, the tenor of which was quite the opposite. "We were fortunate to have been able to secure a coach so promptly, through the auspices of Mr. Banister."

"There is an answer to all that has happened, and we will find it out. We simply cannot allow Mr. Ham Pickering — I'm sorry, Nina, but I must speak my mind — we simply cannot allow Mr. Pickering, whether alive or dead, to dictate the course of our existence. Perhaps, as the doctor has suggested, your friend Mr. Banister can aid us in solving the problem. It is urgent that it be resolved, if for no other reason than to restore the well-being of my sister."

Looks of commiseration were bestowed upon Miss Nina by the gentlemen. That young lady accepted them as the tribute due one of her youth and beauty, who had suffered so; and dropping her eyes, twisted another few curls of chestnut hair about her fingers.

"I shall survive, Mona," she said, in a faintly reproving tone; then added, with a skillful drawing-up of her brows and that affectation so alien to her sister — "It is simply too much, when I think of that horrid experience — the fog — the sight of him — poor Mr. Pickering — the sound of his shoes — "

"That's quite all right, Miss Jacks," said Dr. Dampe, with the confident matter-of-factness of the physician. "Be assured, yours is a very natural response to a shock of such magnitude. Quite understandable, actually. Look

196

here," he laughed, "it isn't every day one encounters a dead sailor with a gold tooth in his mouth careening about the streets!"

At which point Miss Nina abruptly burst into tears and threw her head on Susanna's shoulder. The maidservant folded an arm about her while the doctor hastily apologized — apologized again, but to a different Jacks sister this time — blaming it all, of course, on the stress of the job, and subsequently relieving the tension with a few comic anecdotes drawn from his practice. This proved sufficient to quell the waterworks, at least for now; and so the travelers continued on their way, a little more subdued than before, and with the physician resolved to choose his words with finer care.

Just past noon they arrived at the first stage of the journey, a quiet roadside inn. The travelers alighted from the coach to partake of a brief but welcome refreshment while the ostler supervised the change of horses. All participated in the meal but the outside passenger, who remained stubbornly on the box and declined all invitations to join them.

"Horses on!" came the cry from the yard. "Horses on!"

Out came the travelers — up sprang the coachman and the guard — in got the insides — "Farewell!" sang the landlord and his assistants — "Off we go!" sang the guard, by means of his key-bugle — and off they went.

The road thereafter climbed steadily upward as they penetrated farther and farther into the mountains. It was a tough, long pull, and the freshness of the horses was a clear key to gaining the summit; it was obvious why the stage had been positioned at such a spot. The spaciousness of the landscape gave way to soaring curtains of rock. The air grew colder and sharper, and very still. The sky, when they could see it, was filled with that liquid blue light so characteristic of the mountains. The proximity of the looming crags on either side of the road became stifling at times, and together with the melancholy overhang of the trees contributed no doubt to a certain claustrophobia in some of the travelers.

As the rocky crags now and again retreated, a dense screen of fir and pine could be seen blanketing the higher elevations, with glimpses of snow on the loftier peaks. The terrain grew very wild and strange, and the air frostier still, as they began to approach the summit.

"Have you been to Eaton Wafers, sir?" Miss Mona inquired of the professor.

"No, I'm afraid not. I haven't seen Mr. Banister in a few years — since he left the university, in fact — although we have had occasion to correspond. It was an elderly aunt who passed on and left him her legacy. As I understand it he's quite enchanted with the place, and exceedingly popular with the local families. Given the distance, the ties to Salthead have grown fewer; though I should think the opening of the coach-road will improve the situation."

"These little communities of the high moorland can be rather insular," said the doctor, speaking with great authority. "You won't find many Salthead folk in the area. No, no. Most of the visitors will be drawn from towns to the north and east — Saxbridge and Winstermere, Uxton-on-Dawling, Blore, and the like. Their social get-togethers and hunt parties can be quite splendid things — oh, it's a way of life for these fashionable country people in Broadshire and Chestershire."

"I was surprised to learn, just on Friday," remarked the professor, "that our governess, Miss Dale — she has charge of my young niece — has been more than once a visitor to Eaton Wafers. A relation of hers, a grandmother, was in the employ of Mr. Banister's late aunt."

At mention of the name of Laura Dale, the face of Mr. Kibble underwent a transformation. Just as he had been coming out of his brown study, he went straight back into it; seemed to lose interest in conversation; and lay staring through the window of the coach as if the end of time had arrived and he didn't in the least care.

The doctor responded to the professor's words, not with dejection but with surprise and a lift of his eyebrows.

"Your charming Miss Dale? I had no idea," he said, smoothing his beard. "When was she there?"

"Several years past, from what I was able to gather. It's my impression she has not returned since the transfer of the property; however, I don't know that for certain. She was not at all keen to discuss the matter. She is a most competent and gracious young woman, and I have complete faith in her with regard to the education she is providing for Fiona. Nevertheless there are, every now and then, these little episodes when she seems to withdraw into herself, without explanation, becoming strangely austere and remote."

"I see. I'll wager there's more there than we comprehend at present."

"Moreover she is apparently on terms with Harry Banister. At the very least, she intimated they had met on occasion over the years."

"It's a little odd," mused the doctor. "Harry Banister is not the sort of fellow one easily puts from one's mind. Has she never mentioned this before?"

"Never."

"Not the slightest hint?"

"No. But she has been a member of our household for only a few months. The topic has never arisen until now."

The doctor was about to comment further when a cry rang out from the coachman, followed almost at once by an excited snorting of the horses. The coach rattled and shook; the trees and boulders passing by slowed to a crawl; the wheels ground to a halt. Questioning looks formed on the faces of the passengers. They had traveled not nearly far enough to reach the next stage. What could be the stoppage?

They could hear the sounds of the coachman and the guard dropping from the box, the sounds of the horses anxiously stamping and pawing the earth. The professor let down the glass and put his head out, to see what was going on. He saw, and his eyes grew very round indeed.

"They'll need to clear the road," he reported to the others.

"Why?" asked Mr. Kibble.

"Carcass," announced the learned physician, whose turn it was for a look through the coach-window.

"Of what?"

Neither Dr. Dampe nor his collegiate friend made any immediate reply. Instead the doctor drew in his head, threw open the door and put down the stairs. He and the professor jumped to the ground, followed by Mr. Kibble, who with this distraction was once more in danger of rallying. Miss Mona nerved herself and peered through the door of the coach, one tiny foot planted on the step, and there gained a view of the obstruction.

What she saw was a tangled mass of brownish-gray hair, very thick and wiry, sprawled across the road a short distance forward of the horses. It was the body of some huge animal, lying on its side with its back to the coach; as a result she couldn't make out just what kind of animal it was. She could see, however, that there were large syrupy patches of blood on it, and on the frost-hardened earth surrounding it. This, then, was what had frightened the horses — the sight and smell of death.

The men formed a little circle about the corpse while they talked over the situation. The guard then retrieved a tow-line from the fore-boot of the coach and attached it to the limbs of the creature. By the combined efforts of all five gentlemen the body was slowly pushed, tugged, shoved, and at last dragged to the verge of the road.

As it was drawn into the underwood the body became turned partially around, revealing a long, heavy face with massive jowls, squared-off nostrils, and tiny ears planted far back on the head. The eyes were gone, plucked out by marauding birds. The throat and abdomen had been slashed open and the underlying tissues exposed. The oddest thing about the creature was its limbs, which were large, paddle-like affairs, very queerly angled, with an unusual inward curvature.

"What's wrong, Miss?" asked a frightened Susanna. "What do you see there?"

"I must confess — I don't know," replied Miss Mona, venturing another few inches onto the step. "I've seen nothing like it before. It is enormous, whatever it is."

"You're sure it's dead, Miss?"

"Quite sure, Susanna."

She watched the doctor as he knelt in the brush and performed some small operation on one of the stiffened forelegs. After a moment he rose, folding an object into his handkerchief; then he and the others returned to the safety of the coach. The vehicle shook, the trees and rocks began flowing past the windows again, and they continued on their way.

"What was that animal?" she asked.

"Megathere," answered the doctor. "Not a full-grown specimen, though. No, not by a long chalk. A juvenile — most probably orphaned, actually. It looked to be a fairly recent kill."

At mention of this last word Miss Nina shuddered.

"Megathere?" asked Miss Mona. "I'm afraid I don't know the term."

"A ground sloth," the professor explained.

"Exactly," nodded the doctor, briskly. "Most unusual creatures. You'll only rarely find them near the coast; they much prefer the colder, drier climate here in the mountains. They're reclusive by nature and very slow-footed, existing on roots and leaves. Harmless, for the most part, and not particularly intelligent."

"What could have — killed it?" asked Miss Nina, in a small voice.

"Hard to say, actually. It may have been any one of several predators. Not to worry, though — whatever attacked it is most likely far off by now. It's a good thing for us it was a young specimen. If it had been an adult, well — we'd have had a jolly time dragging *that* out of the way, I can tell you! A full-grown megathere is easily the size of a yearling mastodon. Oh, by the way —" He dove into a pocket and retrieved his handkerchief, which he gave to the professor.

"Here you are, Titus — a little something for Fiona."

Mystified, the professor undid the cloth. There upon its white surface lay a single large claw, no less than two fingers across at its widest diameter, and wonderfully smooth and sharp at the tip. The ladies gasped; the professor looked surprised; the doctor seemed pleased.

"Ooh! my stars," breathed Susanna, releasing a little of her pent-up anxiety.

"It's true it's not a bear's claw, but it's a reasonably good facsimile," said the doctor, triumphantly. "After all — isn't that what she's always going on about? Bears?"

"But this isn't from a bear," said the professor, stating the obvious.

"Pish! Who'll know?"

"Why, I will."

"Really, Titus — you must learn to be more imaginative," smiled the doctor. "We physicians, we're the most imaginative of people. One of our greatest gifts, actually. Oh, it's common knowledge. We use our imaginations every waking day in practice. We've absolutely got to — patients come to expect it."

"Why don't I simply tell Fiona it's from a megathere — a ground sloth — and not a bear?"

"Pish again! Oh, all right, all right — go ahead and spoil it, if you must."

"Thank you, Daniel," said the professor, depositing the souvenir in his coat. "I suppose I'll have plenty of time to think about it."

"You know," remarked the doctor after a little while, to remedy an ensuing lull in the conversation — "it seems to me that the horses should have quite settled down by now. If you listen closely you can hear them snorting into the air, and from their tread it's clear they're jostling one another. The coachman's being unusually vociferous as well. And there's a tug of the vehicle to one side, every so often, as though the off-leader is shying a bit or kicking at the traces. If you ask me they're as edgy as all get-out. I wonder why that is?"

"I've noticed it too," said Mr. Kibble.

The professor made it three at least who had noted this phenomenon, but he said nothing about it, as he had no serviceable explanation on offer.

Edgy horses notwithstanding, the coach rumbled on toward the next stage. An hour whirled past. The curtains of rock, held back for a time by the more spacious woodland through which the coach had been traveling, were again crowding up along the road. There was, in the professor's mind at least, something ominous in the way the thick fir woods and towering rock faces conspired to close in around them.

"Is it much farther to the posting-inn?" asked Miss Mona, having perhaps the same troubling thoughts as the professor.

"Not far now, surely, my dear," he said. A frown of concern creased the space between his eyebrows. "By my estimation the inn should be, I believe, just beyond the next — "

A roving dark form drifted across the landscape.

"Did you see that?" said the doctor, gliding to the door. From this position he managed to catch a glimpse of some black feathered wings and a flash of crimson, which were gone in a trice.

"Teratorn!" he exclaimed.

The professor was at once reminded of the bird he himself had seen in the skies over Salthead.

"And I believe I spotted a red fox, scuttling away into the underwood," said Miss Nina, with one dainty finger pressed against the glass.

"As most likely did the teratorn. Rather meager fare, however, for one of those creatures. Extraordinary!" The doctor looked again for the bird but was unable to locate it, and so returned to his seat.

"Thank goodness for that, Dr. Dampe," said Miss Mona. "Such terrible birds! They're said to be harbingers of bad luck."

"Harbingers of superstition, I say," returned the doctor, with a tap of his walking-stick. "Magnificent fliers, though. That's why I wanted a good look at the fellow, but he seems to have wandered off somewhere. Probably after that fox."

"What is that?" cried Miss Nina, pointing.

"What did you see?" asked the professor.

"I thought for a moment there was a silhouette — something huge and dark and very tall, with horribly long arms — on a ledge far up the side of that hill. It was just standing there, watching us."

"There's your bear," said the doctor confidently to his collegiate friend. "Some final scrounging before winter closes in. Incredibly powerful animals, these short-faced bears, and very wicked — far more dangerous than any megathere. My goodness, we're certainly getting into some wild country now! All sorts of creatures running about in these hills and meadows. Bears and foxes popping up like jack-in-the-boxes. Hallo — there's a rhyme! `Foxes' and `boxes.' Do you know, there are people who live their entire lives up here? Mine Host of the posting-inn we'll be stopping at tonight ought to have some interesting tales for us. It requires a special kind of pluck to survive in such environs. No false gingerbread glitter here, I can tell you!"

"It's colder now," said Miss Mona, shivering.

"Altitude. The horses have had quite a stiff pull for the last mile or so. But we should be coming to the summit here very shortly. After that, it's down the mountain all the way. We should be in the Vale of Broadshire by morning, and from there it's due east, gain a bit of ground again, and so onto the high moorland by afternoon. We ought to be arriving at Eaton Wafers just in time for dinner, I should think."

"You have been this way before, Doctor?"

"Not on this particular road, it wasn't much more than a bridle-path in those days. I spent a few years of practice in and around Saxbridge — now there's a chilly spot for you! — and so was often engaged in traveling to the various towns scattered about the moorlands. It's quite a fascinating place, actually. The woods can be a bit isolated and lonely at times — though you can't let them get to you."

"That is just how Miss Dale described Eaton Wafers," said the professor. "It would appear to be a common — "

There was an abrupt wrenching of the carriage to one side, followed by a shout of frustration from the box. Once more they felt the coach slowing, slowing, slowing down, until it came grumbling to a stop on a barren patch of earth at the bottom of a dismal ravine.

"Not another carcass, I trust," said the professor. He let down the glass and called out to the guard, who tossed him a brief, mumbled explanation from the box.

"What's the problem?" asked the doctor.

"The off-leader's thrown a shoe. It shouldn't be more than a few minutes and we'll be off again."

The coachman leaped down to retrieve his implements and a cold shoe from the fore-boot. The guard, ever vigilant, stood in his seat and maintained a roving watch, his eyes prowling about the hidden recesses of hill and wood on either side of the road. His fingers tapped nervously on the hilt of his cutlass. The horses, skittish after their encounter with the megathere, had settled down after warming into their run. But they were skittish again now.

A roar sounded from the darkening hills, resonating with an unpleasant fervor through the ravine. In its wake came an eerie stillness. The horses started to tremble, including the off-leader, whose leg was held by the coachman as he worked at the shoe. They sniffed the air, and finding something not at all to their liking pawed the ground and laid their ears flat against their heads. All around them, nature seemed to be listening and waiting — for what?

The near-wheeler, more affected than the rest, uttered a strange, unearthly cry, and fell down with every appearance of terror. As a result the guard was forced to abandon his look-out and render assistance. The horse subsequently regained its footing but insisted on moving about, stamping and snorting, despite the presence of the guard at the bridle.

"Make it quick, Jemmy!" urged the guard of his coachman friend. His eyes darted wildly about the ravine, as a presentiment of doom came washing over him. "They's somethin' not right here. I know it — I can feel it!"

By way of confirmation a falling leaf brushed his cheek. He started back in surprise, further alarming the near-wheeler.

"Gi'e me time — I'm rappin' away as fast as I can," grunted the coachman, with the heavy foot of the off-leader between his knees. Another few minutes passed, the cold breath streaming from his mouth and nostrils as he worked. A few more sharp blows of the hammer and the final nail was driven home. The points were quickly wrung off, and the clenches drawn up and smoothed with a rasp. The coachman dropped the foot to the ground with a thump.

"Done, Jem?" asked the guard, champing at the bit.

"Done, Sam. All's right as a trivet."

"Not if we stay here it ain't. Let's for the box and give these damned cattle their heads!"

In haste they vaulted to their positions. The coachman took up the driving-reins and the carriage rolled forward, with the nervous horses more eager even than the guard to be away from these unhealthful precincts.

A few minutes later one of the ladies inside the box — Miss Nina, to be exact — peering through the window saw, or thought she saw, in uncertain glimpses, something in motion among the trees beside the road; a huge, four-legged something striding through the gloom, keeping pace with the movement of the coach.

"There is — there is some creature — *there!*" she gasped.

The horses cried out and broke into a gallop. The travelers were flung from their seats as the vehicle lurched forward. The coachman, straining at the ribands, fought valiantly for control. It was a futile effort, though, and he well knew it, for there is no fighting horses that are running for their lives.

As the coach bounced over the road a deep-throated howl erupted somewhere close at hand, and a shadow sprang from the underwood. The coach was shaken by a tremendous jolt that rocked it from side to side, as the shadow — insubstantial it most certainly was not — plunged upon it. A great quantity of yellow fur could be seen pressed against the glass on the off side, where the professor and Miss Nina had been sitting.

Frantic shouts and imprecations broke out on the box. The maidservant Susanna uttered a piercing scream and fell down in a heap. Unable to make any sound herself Miss Mona clapped hands to mouth, while her sister cringed in fear beside her. Looks of atonishment abolished all other expression on the faces of the gentlemen.

Professor Tiggs, who was nearest the window, watched in fascination as the monster reared back, swinging its head and eyes upward as though contemplating a leap onto the box. As he saw what it was that was clinging to the side of the vehicle, a cold breath of horror raced from his scalp to his heel. Three dread syllables escaped his lips —

"*Saber-cat!*"

CHAPTER V

A Road Less Traveled

Dr. Daniel Dampe, physician, who had been known to do some surprising things in his day, now did another surprising thing. It was a reflex, actually, as he himself would later explain, involving brain, and hand, and eye; he didn't stop to think about it ahead of time. Indeed, given the present dire circumstance, there was no time ahead of time. Recollecting his collegiate friend's late encounter with the mastiff, the doctor let down the glass — lowered the very window against which the body of the saber-cat was pressed — and laying his walking-stick perpendicularly on the sash, drove the sharp point of it into the mass of yellow fur.

The cat flinched and cried out, looking round for the source of the irritation. For a moment it lost its grip on the coach, sliding down so that its head came level with the open window. Green glowing eyes of evil fastened themselves on the doctor. The mouth opened to reveal the full horror of its paired saber-teeth, which the doctor could see had serrated edges like carving-knives. The hot breath of the cat struck him squarely in the face, which greeting he managed to return with a petrified stare. One swipe of a paw dispatched the bothersome walking-stick, casting it aside with a force of motion that left the doctor gaping. The cat found itself slightly off-balance as a result; forced to release its hold on the coach, it leaped away.

The doctor pivoted round to discover eight goggle eyes regarding him with something akin to awe. Only Susanna, who was recovering from her swoon in the arms of Miss Nina, had failed to witness the doctor's extraordinary performance.

"*Never — liked — cats*," he stammered out, between hurried rushes of breath. Swallowing hard, he pulled up the glass and wiped his brow with an unsteady hand. Though determined to present a bold front, the doctor clearly was affected by his confrontation with undiluted nature. "Never liked 'em," he mumbled, in as level a voice as he could muster. "No, never did, actually. Never did."

There followed a crash and an anguished cry. The coachman shouted to the guard, the guard shouted to the coachman. The vehicle bounced and swayed before lurching to a standstill in the middle of the road. At the window Miss Mona opened her mouth to exclaim —

206

"The cat has pounced on the near-wheeler!"

"Don't look, dear, don't look!" implored the professor, taking hold of her arm.

Miss Mona could not help but look, however, as the cat's jaws tore into the horse with vicious, scissor-like movements, while with its feet and claws it sought to wrestle the animal down. The fierce assault by the carving-knives laid open the throat, releasing a bright red stream from the severed vessels. The horse stiffened as though seized with a fit — threw back its head — shuddered — voiced one final, plaintive wail — swayed eerily on its hooves — and dropped to the ground. Miss Mona tore her eyes from the window, sick at heart and shaking uncontrollably.

The other horses had flown into a panic and were struggling to free themselves from the confines of the harness. The daring coachman had dropped from the box and was working desperately now to release them.

"Look there!" cried Mr. Kibble. "There is another cat — there — over the way!"

It was true. Saber-cats were widely known to hunt in pairs; so it was not unexpected that another cat should come bounding upon the scene. The guard and the outside passenger, both armed with cutlasses, scrambled off the box. The coachman, having run out of time in his effort to free the horses, had no choice but to join the two men in making a stand. With their weapons drawn they waited, grim-faced, for the next cast of the die.

The second cat tucked in its belly and proceeded to stalk them. It growled, its tail swished to and fro, its fur bristled. It favored the men with a menacing show of teeth — it was indeed an impressive display — as it crept stealthily toward them. The first cat, having consumed a bit of horseflesh, was evidently in an expansive mood; it looked up, intrigued by what it saw, and abandoned its prey so as to join its partner in the revels.

The horses could endure it no longer. With a sudden surge they raced forward, drawing the coach and the body of their fallen companion along in a jumbled mass of confusion. In the process the pole splintered and the swingletree broke apart as the last of the restraints gave way. One wheel of the coach plunged into a rut at the roadside, burst from the axle and went spinning away as the vehicle tumbled over. The three horses sped off into the underwood, with remnants of the traces and driving-reins fluttering in their wake.

"Anybody damaged?" cried the doctor, looking round at the dazed faces of his companions. All replied in the negative. The pale Susanna uttered a familiar "Ooh! my stars" with evident alertness, as though the bouncing and jostling of the crash had revived her. This hypothesis was tempered, however, by her spectacles having flown off somewhere, as a consequence of which she could see no farther than her own nose.

The coach lay fallen on its side. What had formerly been the floor and the roof of the vehicle were now walls. One of the coach-doors was serving as the floor, while the other looked down on them from above. It was like being imprisoned in a dungeon, an oubliette, with a trap-door at the top, through the window of which the only available light was streaming. As if this were not inconvenient enough, one of the saber-cats had leaped upon the trap-door and was blotting out most of that light. Nostrils and whiskers quivered at the window. The cat stamped and danced upon the coach, rocking it to and fro and growling contemptuously at the prisoners.

The body of the vehicle appeared capable of withstanding such ill-usage. The door, moreover, was securely fastened; it didn't seem possible the cat could open it. The window, however, was quite another matter. A minute passed; the travelers cringed and prayed. The cat sniffed, beat its paw against the door, placed its feet on the glass. For a terrifying moment the window seemed about to give way. Then the cat stepped aside; unable to make headway it lost interest and dropped to the ground.

"What of the men on the box?" cried Miss Mona. "They are all alone with those creatures!"

"We've got to help them!" declared Mr. Kibble, valorously.

"We first must see what has happened," said the professor, not nearly so enthusiastic as his secretary, but perhaps wiser.

Cautiously he drew the glass aside. Standing on an assembled pile of cushions, he and Dr. Dampe raised their heads through the open window. The three men, they saw, had not ventured from their previous positions. One of the saber-cats was pacing restlessly before them, while the other lay extended on its belly, contemplating the scene with an evil countenance. Evidently the monsters preferred slow-moving humanfolk to speedy horses when it came to agreeable playthings.

Without explanation the outside passenger snatched the cutlass from the guard's hand. So astonishing was this act that the startled guard did not resist. The passenger then directed both the guard and the coachman to withdraw a few paces behind him, all the while murmuring under his breath, quite calmly —

"Not to worry. Get behind now, get behind — and stay where you are. If you turn to run you'll not get far, don't you see."

He put off his hat and muffler. With a cutlass in either hand he strode toward the cats, swinging the weapons round and round and over his head, displaying very considerable skill and agility in the process.

"*Is that fellow completely mad?*"

It was Dr. Dampe. Still affected by his own encounter with the saber-cat — I'm afraid the snarling face at the window would haunt his dreams for some nights to come — what this stranger was doing seemed to him incomprehensible. The man was either incredibly brave or incredibly foolish, which fact the doctor communicated to his collegiate friend.

"Mad," he concluded, thereby solidifying his diagnosis. "He must indeed be mad."

"I admit, I can find no other word for it," agreed the professor. "I am sorry for him, for his actions are inviting certain death."

"That's the most senseless fellow who ever stood in shoes. I suspected there was something peculiar about him, actually, at the inn, when he refused to come off the box."

The cats circled warily round the outside passenger and his weapons, with which he was holding their attention by means of various threatening gestures and poses. At the same time that daring gentleman was seen to be inching his way farther and farther up the road, gradually distancing himself from the coachman and the guard. A new thought — and perhaps a new diagnosis — struck the learned physician. Could it be that the outside passenger was trying to draw the cats off, so that the two men might gain the safety of the coach?

The cats by turns raised and lowered their heads, fascinated by this newest plaything. They orbited round him like a pair of twin moons, treating him to many little snarls of affection and displays of their own frightful cutlery.

When he had gotten far enough away the outside passenger, never removing his eyes from the monsters, called to the coachman and the guard to direct their steps slowly, slowly, towards the coach. To his dismay, neither of them seemed inclined to take instruction; either from fear (which was highly unlikely), or from sheer wonder at the bravery of this anonymous, foolish man. In short they mutinied, refusing to retreat.

The cats, still pacing round the anonymous fool in broad circles, began now to close those circles tighter. Emboldened, one of the animals stretched an inquisitive paw toward the shiny weapons, before making a sudden lunge at the bearer of the weapons himself. The outside passenger darted instantly away, but not instantly enough. A stream of blood went shooting from his hand as it was grazed by a flying claw. Strangely oblivious to his injury, he responded at once by turning the tables on the cat. The poise and quickness with which he accomplished this were beyond marvel, as he reached in and with a single deft motion slashed the muscles of the cat's foreleg.

The monster cried out in pain and leaped back, glaring stupidly at the wound. Without slackening his pace the outside passenger raised both his weapons and — wonder of wonders! — rushed in upon the cat, with a ferocity and strength of purpose as though an entire battalion had been condensed into a single individual.

Before the outcome of this rash act could be decided the ground underfoot began to shake. A series of thunderous vibrations, one after another, rattled the legs of all who happened to be standing. The guard and the coachman traded uneasy glances, thinking it to be an earth tremor; such events were, after all, not uncommon in the mountains. Even the saber-cats paused to lift their noses in the air — the very air that next was shattered by a pair of trumpetous roars from somewhere just beyond the road. Several tall trees at the verge were seen to split and crack asunder, as though struck by invisible lightning; from behind them, two immense forms came bursting through the underwood.

"What is it?" cried Mr. Kibble. "What is that noise? What is happening?"

"Extraordinary!" was the doctor's reply from above.

"I want to see!" begged Miss Mona, eagerly. "Help me, Mr. Kibble, if you would, please."

Mr. Kibble, ever courteous even when in the brownest of studies, came to her assistance by assembling an extra few cushions — in consideration of the young lady's diminutive stature — on which she might stand. By this means she was able to insinuate herself between the professor and Dr. Dampe, and so raise her head above the level of the window. Almost immediately her large moon-shaped eyes went wide at what she saw there.

Two shaggy red mastodons in full harness and with cabs at their backs were standing at the roadside. In the cab atop the smaller of the two was a sturdy little man with a rumpled gray cap and a checked waistcoat. In the other cab — on a gigantic bull nearly twice the size of the cow — was a goofish youth with strange watery eyes and a gaping mouth, who was urging the animal on in strident tones. Next to him was a bearded figure with small nut-like eyes and a profusion of fleecy, mouse-colored hair.

210

"Yow!" was the shout from Mr. Benjamin Blizzard, otherwise Blaster. "Yow! Yow!"

"Cats! Look there!" exclaimed the gentleman in the checked waistcoat. "Pitch into 'em, nephew — the Kingmaker knows what to do!"

"That he does!" cried Blaster, with a ferocious wobble of his wide-awake. "Kingmaker — *strike!*"

The lofty red bull, spotting the two cats — whose size paled now beside his own imposing bulk — knew indeed what to do. He first raised his trunk and sent another trumpet-blast flying from his lungs. The men on the ground quickly scattered as the thunder-beast came charging in upon the cats.

"*Strike, Kingmaker!*" commanded Blaster.

"Charley says to strike!" chimed in the Sheephead, with a wild laugh and a wave of his clenched fist.

One forefoot of the Kingmaker rose and struck the earth with such force that it stunned the landscape all around. Everyone could feel it; the overturned coach even tilted a little on its side. Sadly for one of the cats, its wicked skull had been occupying the space between that forefoot and the ground, and as a result lay crushed out of all recognition.

Hesitating not a moment, Blaster turned the bull short and gave him the reins, making straight for the dead cat's companion.

"Kingmaker — *strike!*"

The remaining cat, seeing its comrade so rudely dispatched — flattened, as it were, by fortune — and presented now with the specter of a bull mastodon bearing down under full steam, recoiled, snarling and bristling, and flashed its gleaming sabers as though to say — "Ye may have whipped me this time, ye pluckless rogues, but I'll live to whip ye next!" — before turning round and with a flick of its tail slinking off into the trees.

A shout of victory went up from Blaster. He waved his hat in the air, which triumphant salute was returned by his uncle in the other cab. The dingy figure of the Sheephead exploded in exultation; he clapped his hands, threw back his head and laughed in a wild fashion, while hurling all manner of dismissive epithets at the retreating saber-cat.

By their combined efforts the professor and his colleagues managed to extricate the ladies from the coach. While they were engaged in this activity, Mr. Hoakum and his fellows descended from the cabs, to be greeted by the coachman and the guard and the outside passenger.

Expressions of gratitude flowed from the travelers to the mastodon men. The unassuming Mr. Hoakum removed his cap and began mashing it with his hands, saying in all honesty how he didn't see as they'd done anything special, and that if anybody at all ought to be thanked it should be the Kingmaker and gentle Betty. "Arter all," he said, with a nod toward his beloved mastodons, "nothing stops the beasts, sir."

Professor Tiggs and the doctor both recognized Mr. Hoakum from his occasional visits to the Blue Pelican, though they had never been formally introduced; likewise they were familiar with the antic Mr. Earhart, alias Sheephead Charley. The doctor had, in fact, once diagnosed Mr. Earhart's unusual condition, out of professonal interest, by an observation of his actions and by reports of his behavior from others whose opinion he valued; which of course would have come as a great surprise to the Sheephead, had he known of it, as in his eyes he had no recognizable condition to speak of.

Inevitably they came to the outside passenger, who had by now reclaimed his muffler and his jerry hat, and was standing a little off to one side with his eyes averted, listening to what was said but trying not to attract attention.

"You are a very brave man, sir," said the professor, stepping forward. "I have not heard of many who would challenge a saber-cat to single combat — but two of the brutes!"

"I b'lieve there ain't much sense in that, howe'er," remarked Mr. Hoakum with a shake of his head, before replacing his little squashed cap upon it — "but it were a grand way to go out, all the same. Considering the cats, arter all!"

"I quite agree, that was an extraordinary display of courage," said the doctor, thereby contributing his twopence to the conversation. "Might I shake your hand, Mr. — ?"

"My hand don't need a blessed shakin', but you're welcome to it," was the interesting reply. The outside passenger turned and extending the requested item, added — "Jack Hilltop is my name. Your servant, sir."

So the professor and the doctor were confronted with another face — this a spotted one — known to them from the Pelican but unknown by name until now.

Once the introductions had gone round, the doctor, intrigued, returned immediately to Spotted Face.

"You are very familiar to me, Mr. Hilltop. I believe I have seen you at the Blue Pelican of late," he remarked, with a narrowed gaze — "though I never much saw you there *before*."

"Because I was never much there before. Salthead is new to me, don't you see."

"You are a stranger to the city?"

"Say it how you will. I am — something of a traveler, sir."

"As are we."

Mr. Hilltop conceded this point with a wry smile.

"Another thing, Mr. Hilltop," said the doctor, his hazel eyes wandering to the hand he had just shaken. "Your wrist there — is that not the one injured by one of the cats? I'm quite sure I saw you bleed."

"True, I saw it, too," nodded Mr. Hoakum.

"Belike you've imagined it, gentlemen — for there is no wound, don't you see," said the outside passenger, removing the glove from the hand in question. "Examine it for yourself. As I have said, you're plainly mistaken in your assumption."

The doctor stood back thoughtfully, looking quite puzzled. There was congealed blood on the man's wrist, to be sure; but there was also, as Mr. Hilltop had stated, not the faintest trace of an injury.

"What you have said appears to be true. There is no wound — there is no way to hide *that*. But there is most definitely blood, both on you and on the grip of that cutlass," he observed. "See here, how some of it was transferred to my own hand when we shook."

"It's from the cat, sir, what I cut with my blade."

"And there is as well a rent in that glove, where the cat's paw — "

Here the doctor stopped, knowing in his heart that his senses could not be deceiving him. The foible of the blade — that part from the middle to the point — was indeed bloodied, from the wound it had inflicted on the saber-cat. There was as well blood on the handle. But the forte — the portion of the blade between the two — was clean. How then came the blood on the grip and on the man's hand? And what of the torn glove? There was something very odd here, and though the doctor didn't know what it was he vowed to himself he would find it out.

"Yes. Yes, of course. From the saber-cat. What else could I have been thinking?"

"Are you for Pease Pottage, Mr. Hilltop?" asked the professor, having noted the very same inconsistency as the doctor. "Have you business there?"

"No, sir, no business whatsoever," replied the outside passenger. "I have a holiday there, a little excursion for my health. The fogs in Salthead — they're very unwholesome this time of year, as I have lately discovered. I have been advised to seek out a drier climate, don't you see, to recover some of my old dash and vigor."

213

Dash and vigor, mused the professor, glancing at Dr. Dampe, whose expression made it clear he was thinking along the same lines. If the spectacle of Mr. Hilltop facing down the cats was not indicative of dash and vigor, he didn't know what was. But with nowhere else to take it, the matter was left where it lay.

It was agreed all around that the services of Mr. Hoakum should be engaged for transport to the posting-inn, which that small sturdy man assured them was not far ahead. The goods and luggage, however, had first to be transferred from the coach to the mastodons. To accomplish this, the two animals were instructed by Blaster to drop to their knees and rest their bellies on the ground, so as to facilitate access to the cabs. The bulkier items were drawn up by means of rope and pulley to the Sheephead, who, despite whatever shortcomings he might have, proved himself an excellent porter, ordering the luggage into neat rows in the boot of each cab.

The passenger cabs were mounted on blanket cushions between the shoulders of each mastodon, just behind the head. The boot was a lengthy rearward extension of the cab, in essence a freight platform comprised of several individual compartments stretching along the back and flanks of the animal. These compartments were surprisingly spacious, and it was evident that a considerable store of goods could be transported in them — more, in fact, than could be pressed and squeezed into the upset coach.

"This is a highly efficient operation you have here, Mr. Hoakum," said the professor, admiring very much the way his heavy portmanteau was hoisted in a trice onto the back of the Kingmaker.

"Yes, very!" enthused Mr. Kibble. The doctor was energized as well, what with the excitement of a new adventure among the mastodon men to look forward to.

In the morning the passengers would be able to hire a post-chaise at the inn, and so continue their journey to Eaton Wafers. (At mention of the name of Mr. Banister's estate, it was noted that the Sheephead removed from his rags a large silver watch, which he held to his ear). The coachman and the guard would return with Mr. Hoakum and his fellows to the site of the upset, making such repairs as they could, and with the mastodons' assistance return the coach to Bridge Street.

It came time at last for the travelers to board the cabs. This operation involved the use of long cord-ladders that were unfurled from the cab-doors. Everyone found this exercise exhilarating, even Miss Nina; everyone, that is, except the fussy Susanna, who uttered no fewer than ten "Ooh! my stars" as she swung and plucked and bobbed and twisted her way up. Once all were safely aboard the ladders were drawn up and the doors secured. The thunder-beasts rose to their feet. Little gasps of wonder passed the lips of the travelers as the earth fell away below, revealing a vast twilight vista spread out before them.

"I once booked passage with a mastodon train between Salthead and Fishmouth," remarked the doctor, who was riding in Betty's cab with Mr. Hoakum and the ladies. "In former days, before the long-distance coaches. I was a young medical student at the time, and very much absorbed in my studies, as you might expect — always sitting up late, reading wild books and drinking strong coffee to all hours of the morning. The leader of the train was an enterprising old fellow, about your size, actually, Mr. Hoakum, and with a great fund of knowledge concerning all manner of fascinating subjects. He was, as might be expected of one in his occupation, widely traveled through the counties. You seem to me now very like that man."

"That was undoubtedly my father, sir," replied Mr. Hoakum, his tiny blue eyes gleaming. "It's been a family business, arter all, sir. You'll note that's very common among the mastodon men — what's left of 'em."

"My goodness — then most likely you were along on that journey as well! I seem to recall now there was a son of the old fellow, who assisted with the management of the animals. Yes, indeed, I believe we may have met before, Mr. Hoakum, on the road to Fishmouth those many years ago."

"I b'lieve that's not unlikely, sir."

"Although we were both a good deal younger then."

Mr. Hoakum looked shyly askance, and gave a few smart tugs and pulls at his checked waistcoat. "Some of us still is, sir," he smiled.

At which remark the physician laughed very heartily, and his admiration for the sturdy little man grew that much more.

"And how do you like our new enterprise, sir? Though I b'lieve it's ironic, arter all, as here we are temp'rarily out of the passenger business — as the passengers and such have temp'rarily bounced over to the coaches — so we sets up ourselves in the freight business, and what is it we see here? Two full cabs loaded up with passengers! It's a very strange situation, I say, and that's flat."

"I am surprised, but very pleasantly. I had thought you men were nearly gone from the land now — apart from some of the old northern and eastern routes, of course."

"Most of us are, sir, and that's a sad fact. But there's a few as'll survive, here and there. The lad and I — the young man's my nephew — we'll make another go at it and see where it lands us. If it don't work out — well, sad as it might be, for busy gents it ain't the end of the world, arter all."

"We passed a train of red mastodons today, Mr. Hoakum, on their way south," said Miss Mona, quite innocently volunteering this information without the least conception of the effect it might have. "I don't suppose you might know where they were going? There were no passengers that we could see. The creatures were being shepherded by four men, two of whom were leading with bright red flutter-sticks."

Something of the luster departed from Mr. Hoakum's eyes, though he of course did not permit any of the others to see it. Considering the situation he made no reply at first, but gave another few tugs and pulls at his waistcoat — somewhat perfunctory tugs and pulls, I should think, rather than smart ones — and followed up with another round of cap-mashing.

"Prob'ly," he answered, "prob'ly one of the old teams, removing to another camp. Prob'ly it's been taken up by new masters. It's — it's common now."

"They were all splendid specimens. Mr. Kibble thought they might be bound for Crow's-end — the zoological gardens. But that couldn't be true! Could it?"

"I wouldn't know about that," said Mr. Hoakum, a little peremptorily, and so a little out of character as well. He made a show of adjusting the driving-reins and keeping his eyes on the way ahead. After a few minutes of reflection, however, he turned to the young lady and with a kindly smile added —

"It ain't none o' my business, arter all, Miss."

The travelers noted that the coach-road had been left far behind, and that the mastodons were following an ancient trail that they appeared to know very well. Mr. Hoakum explained that this route was actually more direct than the winding coach-road, but harder on horses — though much easier for thunder-beasts, who were bred for mountain travel.

The ride itself was much smoother than expected. From their swaying vantage-point above the earth the passengers were treated to exemplary views of the surrounding countryside, where long shadows of night now were creeping. Presently they emerged onto some high ground overlooking a darksome valley, with lighted windows here and there and curls of smoke from cottage chimneys. On the horizon their first faint glimpse of the high moorland was visible, with the melancholy hues of twilight fast receding from it. Stars were blinking and staring in the dark sky, into which a cold white fragment of moon had risen.

"Ah, the lovely Diana!" rhapsodized the doctor, with his eyes on that heavenly wonder. "The queen of the night greets us upon our arrival. That's a favorable sign, actually. Most propitious! And there — there is the Vale of Broadshire, just over there."

"And there's the inn, just over there," said Mr. Hoakum. Within minutes they were arrived at their destination — overdue, but luckily not much the worse for wear considering the nature of the afternoon's adventure. The landlord and his wife welcomed them with some relief, as they had grown concerned when the Salthead coach failed to appear. The hostelry, the travelers noted, was appropriately named — it was the Cat and Fiddle — and was a most well-fortified mountain inn, with a great oak door, high narrow gables, and iron bars guarding the small lattice windows. A colorful sign depicting a saber-cat — uncomfortably well-rendered by the artist — smoking a pipe while scraping away at a violin, hung over the entrance.

Well-fortified themselves later that evening with a hearty meal and plenty to drink, the travelers and Mine Host gathered round the fire to talk over the events of the day. And just as the doctor had predicted, the landlord of the Cat and Fiddle concluded the entertainment by regaling them with tale upon harrowing tale of everyday life in the mountains, tales which at least one of those present — the landlord himself, of course — found immensely enjoyable, but which sent a few of the listeners quivering to their beds.

Thankfully the night passed without incident. The morning — the radiant sunrise having dissipated the lingering effects of the landlord's nightmarish recollections — saw the departure of Mr. Hoakum and his party, with assurances from the coachman and the guard that a reliable Timson's coach would be in Pease Pottage at the appointed hour, several days hence, to bring the travelers home.

As anticipated a chaise-and-four was available for hire from the Cat and Fiddle, to allow the professor and the others to post on to Eaton Wafers. The ostler and stablehands were in the midst of loading the boot, and making other such preparations for departure, when Mr. Jack Hilltop — who was going on to Pease Pottage as well — walked out into the cold sunshine. A flutter of birds, startled perhaps by his sudden appearance, hurled themselves into the air from an adjacent hedge. Mr. Hilltop immediately arrested his step. He touched a hand to his brow and extended the opposite arm before him, fixing his eyes on the birds with a piercing concentration. He remained in this posture for some few moments, as though reading something written on the sky by the fleeing sparrows.

"Is anything the matter, Mr. Hilltop?" inquired Miss Mona, as she and the doctor emerged from the inn.

"Ah — Miss Jacks — Dr. Dampe — nothing whatsoever at all," said the man with the spotted face, abruptly abandoning his odd endeavor. "I was observing the changing signs of the season, don't you see. I suppose it will rain today, very late."

"And how do you know that?" asked the doctor. "There isn't a cloud to be seen and quite unlikely to be any. These climes are, for the most part, very dry and hardy this time of year. As you yourself have affirmed, the unhealthful fogs of the coast do not penetrate. Apart from the crispness of the air, the weather today is exceptionally fine — and has been for the past few days, according to the landlord."

Mr. Hilltop shrugged, and dropped his eyes. "Take it or leave it," seemed to be his response, which he didn't bother to fashion into words.

"Look here," pursued the doctor — resplendent this morning in his jaunty paletot and cherry-colored waistcoat, with his favorite pipe commuting very sagaciously between hand and mouth — "I've heard tell of soothsayers with a gift for divining the future — or the will of the gods, as it were — by the observation of certain natural phenomena, such as the flight of birds, or flashes of lightning, or the color and configuration of a sheep's liver. Augury, haruspicy, the fulgural science — they're arcane interests of mine, actually, since my days as an undergraduate in the tutelage of Professor Greenshields of Antrobus College, Salthead. Do you know of him? He's a distinguished professor of classics, retired now, though still highly regarded, and quite knowledgeable in the civilizations of the ancients."

"Such folk as you mention there — they disappeared long ago, don't you see," replied Mr. Hilltop, smiling with half-closed eyes upon the gravel at his feet. "They're all dead and done now. And about a distinguished professor of classics — well, I'm not familiar with that, don't you see."

"Yes, it's true — most of them are gone, and have taken their knowledge with them. Ah, dear old Antrobus! I was bred up in that college. My salad days, Mr. Hilltop! There was nothing that could not be discovered, nothing that could not be deciphered, so long as one devoted one's mind wholly and solely to the effort. How well I remember those many pleasant evenings at table, spent in high chat with witty young fellows from all over the land.

218

Where are you from, Mr. Hilltop, by the by, if you don't mind my asking? You never have said, actually."

"Elsewhere," was the tendered reply.

"That's plain, though not very specific. It's also plain you're not too keen to tell us."

"Here and there," elaborated Mr. Hilltop, thereby narrowing the field considerably.

"As distinct from `elsewhere'?"

"Exactly. Let's say I've been many places, but that I'm lodged in the city of Salthead for a time, and that now I'm on holiday. What's the good o' life without holidays?"

"On holiday? Alone?"

"True," said Jack Hilltop, throwing back his head a little, and stroking his mustache with a thumb and forefinger. "Too true, in point of fact. I'm a solitary kind of fellow, sir, though not by choice. Fortune has knocked me about some, don't you see."

"I believe I can understand that, Mr. Hilltop."

The physician directed one final meditative glance upon the outside passenger, which scrutiny was answered by a look of disinterest that told him nothing. Neither seemed to know exactly what to say next or how to proceed, but it was just as well; for the call came now from the yard, whereupon the two gentlemen and Miss Mona joined the others in the chaise, and so in a short time they all were off.

Late in the day the chaise rolled into the picturesque hamlet of Pease Pottage, along a quaint cobbled street of stone-built shops fronting a wide village green, and pulled up before the genial hostelry known as the Pied Horse. The professor and his companions were about to take their leave of Mr. Hilltop when a gentleman on a gray hunter came riding up, and touching his hat called out in greeting —

"Hallo — Professor Tiggs! There you are at last. Welcome, sir!"

"Why, it's Harry!" exclaimed the professor.

The rider hurriedly dismounted at the foot of the inn and ran to take the hand of his former tutor. The grip of the young gentleman was warm and firm, and charged with a youthful energy. It did not take long for the two university men to renew their acquaintance.

"How do you do, sir, how do you do? It's good to see you again!"

"You're looking very well, Harry. It is clear indeed that the country life suits you admirably."

"And you, my dear sir — you have not altered an iota since last we met, in your chambers there at Swinford."

Young Mr. Banister was a striking figure in his trim dark riding-coat, single-breasted with silver buttons, striped canary waistcoat, sky-blue cravat, and leather breeches above mahogany-colored top-boots. He was tall and lean, with an athletic frame and an engaging spring in his step; a wide intelligent brow; large eyes, very bright and lively; a handsome chin, with a cleft in it; and hair worn short about the ears and nape in the country manner. By temperament he was generous, frank, and cordial; free and easy; cheery and unaffected — all of these, and more.

He was attended, the travelers now observed, by another man, a servant in the costume of a verdurer or groundskeeper — an older and very kindly-looking man with enormous side-whiskers that met under the chin, deep solid eyes, and the quiet, self-assured manner of one who spends much time in the company of nature.

"Dr. Dampe!" said Harry, not a little surprised, as he exchanged greetings with the learned physician. "It has been some time indeed since last we saw one another. What! Have you taken leave from your practice to join my mentor on the expedition? Excellent! You are welcome, most welcome, sir!"

The doctor turned to his collegiate friend with a smile on his lips, as if to say — "What did I tell you, Titus? It's not a problem."

"And here," said the professor, endeavoring to ignore this — "here is my young secretary, Mr. Austin Kibble, who assists me now in my researches. I took the liberty of asking him to accompany us."

"Welcome as well, Mr. Kibble!" exclaimed the enthusiastic Harry, wringing Mr. Kibble's hand with such animation that the secretary's spectacles shook like an infant's rattle. "You're keeping a close eye on that old tutor of mine, eh?"

"And the doctor, I believe, has some related intelligence he wishes to convey," said the professor, deftly passing the reins of the conversation to his physician colleague. So it was that Dr. Dampe, recalling his vow in Friday Street to "explain it all to your Mr. Banister," found himself at stage center.

"Yes, well, it's — it's all rather simple, actually. Allow me to introduce our traveling companions," he began. "Miss Mona Jacks — and of course her sister, Miss Nina Jacks — "

The bright and lively eyes of Mr. Banister grew ever brighter and livelier, as surprise after surprise was laid before him.

"What! Dr. Dampe — Professor Tiggs — have you brought half of Salthead with you?" he cried, peering with mock astonishment into the chaise, as though expecting to find a vast crowd of townsfolk secreted there.

"The sisters Jacks, I hasten to add, are intimately involved in the mysteries afflicting Salthead," explained the doctor. "They have, in point of fact, been witness to one of the singular apparitions referred to in your letter. I confess it was I who took the very considerable liberty of asking them to join us, owing of course to their great personal interest in the resolution of the phenomena. As matters stand, I felt this experience of theirs might be of help in our inquiry into the disturbances that prompted your letter to Titus here."

"I see," said Harry, massaging his chin with respectful amusement; though his face darkened for a moment at mention of the clouds gathered at Eaton Wafers. "Well! What reply can a gracious host make to this but welcome? Welcome, all! I am simply delighted to see you — all of you. You are most welcome to our little part of the world. But you must tell me, Professor — whatever has become of Timson's coach?"

Whereupon the previous day's adventure on the road was sketched out for their host, in quick detail, by Professor Tiggs, and the doctor, and Miss Mona, and Mr. Kibble. Mr. Banister, hearing this news, grew by gradual degrees very sober — very concerned — then alarmed — dismayed — distressed. By the end of it he looked as though he were ready to fight someone.

"I should have fetched you myself!" was his impassioned response. "The coach-road can be hazardous on occasion, it's true, although of late we have had few problems. This is most disturbing to me. Please, my friends — accept my humblest apologies. I am so thankful for your safe arrival. Your presence at Eaton Wafers will be doubly — triply — quadruply appreciated!"

Having learned in the course of discussion of the uncommon bravery of Mr. Jack Hilltop, Mr. Banister issued an invitation to that gentleman to accompany the rest to Eaton Wafers, if he so desired. Mr. Hilltop at first protested mightily, saying he had no business there, that he was on holiday for his health, don't you see, and that he would not dream of imposing. Mr. Banister pressed, Mr. Hilltop resisted, Mr. Banister pressed again; Mr. Hilltop, glancing round at the others as if seeking their guidance, relented.

"Excellent! Well, there it is, then," said Harry, clapping hands together with evident relish. "I assure you, Professor — we have been awaiting your arrival with great anticipation. I cannot tell you how much it relieved my mind to hear that you had agreed to come to us."

"I hope we may be of some assistance," smiled the professor.

"Ah! Of that I have no doubt. Again — please accept my apologies for the trial you and your companions have been made to endure. Oh! My word, I've failed to introduce my man here," said Mr. Banister, pausing to indicate his servant. "This is my chief groundskeeper, Ned Vickery. Ned has been with the family, believe it or not, for longer than I can remember, having served my late aunt, Miss Caroline Nokes, in that same capacity for many years. His eyewitness testimony respecting the disturbances should be of considerable interest to you. But more of that later! Let's get you home. Professor, Ned and I will guide you. Bid the postilion follow us. The road is a trifle unsure in places."

So they set off on the final leg of the journey, the travelers in the chaise, the postilion on the near horse, and Mr. Banister and Ned Vickery leading on their mounts. Just beyond the village they entered a tall wood thick with spruce and pine. The air grew very sharp and quiet; no sound but the rolling of the chaise-wheels and the ring of horses' hooves disturbed those tranquil and sylvan solitudes. A cool amber sun, fast receding, cast bare switch-like shadows on the road, which effect contributed to the brooding and melancholy atmosphere of the forest.

After negotiating a few more twists and turns in the carriage-road, they drove through a gate framed by two time-honored piers of stone, and so down a lengthy avenue of trees at the end of which they found Eaton Wafers. Its proportions were so enormous that it was not much visible from this angle, apart from a long row of battlements, a profusion of lighted casement windows, and the outline of a soaring roof infested with chimneys. It was a very large house indeed.

They came to a stop in the drive, where they were met by a flurry of servants who began removing the luggage from the boot. The travelers debouched; gathering before the vaulted entrance, the size and grandeur of the great house became even more apparent.

"This is a magnificent edifice," enthused Mr. Kibble, looking round in several directions at once, with one lens of his spectacles held between a finger and thumb like an opera-glass. "Absolutely wonderful."

"Indeed, Mr. Kibble, you are quite accurate in your assessment. A baronial estate," smiled his employer, not without a little pride at thought of the good fortune that had befallen one of his young men.

In the entrance-hall they were greeted by an equally imposing work of art. It was a full-length portrait, much larger than life, of a gentleman of ancient

222

appearance, with a full-bottomed wig and narrow mustaches, and the light of a cultivated intelligence shining in his eyes. He was attired in the extreme of the prevailing fashion of the day, with one hand on his hip and the other on a globe of the earth. Surrounding him were books and busts, and scrolls and parchments, and a collection of dusty stone monuments, the remains perhaps of some faded civilization.

"It's a stunner, is it not? There you have Mr. Thomas Vane Scarlett — plain `Tom' to his familiars, meaning the household. Without question the most illustrious master of Eaton Wafers, and one of the first. It was his uncle, Mr. Vane Eaton — that's his rather more modest portrait over there — who built the original manor house, which has been considerably enlarged since his day. Tom Scarlett himself flourished something above three hundred years ago. But we'll more of him tomorrow," expounded Mr. Banister, a little mysteriously.

A plump, elderly servant with a white beard, a bald head, and large inquisitive eyes, approached with a rustling step.

"Ah! Mitton," smiled Mr. Banister. "We seem to have acquired some additional guests. Here is Professor Tiggs, from Salthead — and these are his colleagues, Dr. Dampe and Mr. Kibble — and here are Miss Mona Jacks and Miss Nina Jacks, and their maidservant — and Mr. Hilltop, also of Salthead. We'll need a few rooms more — perhaps the row of apartments along the side gallery, above the gravel walk. There's a superb view from that part of the house, and it's most convenient as well."

The servant nodded and went off about his mission to instruct the chambermaids.

"We'll let you refresh yourselves for a time before dinner is laid on. After the late excitement of the journey a bit of relaxation is most definitely in order. No business this evening, to be sure! We'll let you get in a good night's sleep, then on the morrow, after breakfast, I'll summon your collective expertise, if I might, to assist us with our little problem here."

This plan was most agreeable to everyone concerned. Soon after they were shown by Mitton to their respective chambers. In the spacious room prepared for the sisters Jacks — a room replete with sofas and ottomans, and dim soft lamps, and rich tapestry curtains, and old portraits, and a profusion of carved oak wainscoting — Miss Nina removed her bonnet and went immediately to the dressing-table to inspect her appearance, attended by Susanna. The ordeal of the expedition had apparently loosed her tongue; during the day, in the chaise, she had become positively voluble, and so much more her usual self — her pre-Pickering self, as it were. Sitting now before the mirror she prattled on about this and that, about how very impressed she was with Mr. Harry Banister, and with his splendid house, and with his splendid servants, and with these splendid accommodations. Miss Mona, observing from the cushioned sofa behind, reacted somewhat critically to all of this — thinking, as Nina proceeded with her toilet, how perhaps *too* much like her old self her sister was.

Ah! Why so critical, Miss Mona? Did you not press your sister into service to rid her of her dismal mood? Now that this had to all appearances been accomplished, why such surprise — or disappointment — at having your old sister returned to you? Did you actually believe change was possible?

"He's very handsome, don't you admit?"

"He is handsome, I suppose," Miss Mona replied, with some ambivalence — "in a certain dashing sort of way."

"Well, what other sort of way is there?" asked her sister, turning round from the glass with a look that allowed only one answer to such a question.

"One can be handsome, in different ways," returned Mona, quietly.

"He also is immensely rich," said Miss Nina. Applying some artifice to her eyelids, she became distracted by the attentions of Susanna, who was attempting to brush her mistress's curls. "Really, Susanna, I haven't the faintest notion what it is you're doing there. I don't know why I put up with you. As usual it's all your fault, Mona. But about Mr. Banister — do you suppose he is married? Does he seem married to you?"

"I have no idea. I suppose he is not married, for he has not mentioned a wife and we have not been introduced to one. Perhaps we shall meet her this evening."

"He does not seem married to me," opined Susanna, pausing in the midst of her duties.

"Minx, he would never be married to you!" cried Miss Nina, with a playful rap of the maidservant's wrist, to which Susanna reacted with considerable hilarity. "It would, however, be too bad if he were married." Here Miss Nina stopped to view her reflection in the glass, a little dispirited.

"You have only now been introduced to the gentleman," her sister pointed out. "What! Are you forming another attachment so quickly?"

"Mona, Mona," said Miss Nina, shaking her head. "Little sister, you really are too much to bear at times! A lady must be sociable, don't you see, and to be sociable a lady needs to know her ground — must know exactly where she stands and what her chances are. It's protocol; it's expected. It's nothing whatsoever to do with an `attachment,' as you call it."

"Perhaps, chick-a-biddy, the wife is a madwoman, and he's hidden her away, a prisoner, somewhere in the bowels of this house!" exclaimed Susanna, with a lively cackle.

"Minx, you are wicked, wicked!" laughed Nina, rapping the maidservant's hand a second time. "You are in high feather this evening, I see."

"And have been reading your romantic novels again," added Miss Mona.

"Simply because Mr. Banister is handsome and rich, and lives in a splendid house, and is plainly a sort of prince in this region — really, Mona, you know so little of life! You are the one, it seems to me, who is guilty of far too much reading in our house. It's very well known, after all, that too many books can paralyze the mind — can focus one's attention upon such dreary, inconsequential things as nouns, and verbs, and infinitives, and past participles, and indefinite articles — upon people who have never existed, and events that never have happened, or ever could happen — all this at the expense of daily social interaction — can load the brain with foreign precepts and propaganda, and render one completely incapable of independent thought."

"I prefer to think of books as old friends, who never die or change. They're always the same and they won't run off. They treat you as an equal, and always show you the same honest face. And you, it seems to me," said Miss Mona, as a new resource struck her, "have been guilty of far too much moping."

"Do not remind me of that, I caution you, Mona."

"You say Mr. Harry Banister is handsome and rich. As handsome as Mr. Pickering, perhaps? Surely not as rich!"

"Mr. Pickering was hardly handsome, and as for — "

Miss Nina brought herself up short, aware of having given herself away.

"It's so very plain, is it not?" said Miss Mona, with a knowing smile. "Father was right. Mr. Pickering was not for you — aside from the fact you didn't care a pin for him. He flattered you in every possible way, was very well traveled, and showered you with gift upon gift. He also was unfortunate enough to believe you when you told him you loved him — which instantly set him apart from your usual sort of beau."

"Really, Mona, I have no idea what it is you mean," returned her sister, after a little pause, with her eyes cast slyly downward upon the dressing-table. When she resumed prettying herself it was with a renewed purpose, and as well with renewed distraction from Susanna, who had not yet finished with her hair.

"I doubted you would," said Miss Mona. She slid forward to the edge of the sofa. "And when Mr. Pickering signed onto the *Swan* — because of the hurt you'd inflicted on him — you protested, not because he was going away but because all the attention, and the gifts, and the other compliments to your person would stop if he left you."

"Have a care, Mona. You have no notion or experience of such things, and so should not speak of them."

"And when next you saw him — from your window that evening, in the fog — when you knew very well he couldn't possibly be there — your guilty heart overwhelmed you at last."

"I wonder you can speak that way, sister. What do you know of such matters?"

There followed another pause, which Miss Mona spent looking at the floor and contemplating the ironies of her life.

"Why did you not marry George Curle?" she asked, curiously.

Which question elicited a laugh from her sister, who tossed up her pretty chin. "Marry `Grandfather' Curle? That dry old cake? You can't be serious. Oh, I'm sure he must've been quite charming, about a hundred years ago. Really, Mona, I've never for one moment in my life cared for Mr. Curle. Wherever did you get that idea?"

"Neither did you care for Mr. Pickering."

"Very well, I never cared for Mr. Pickering," said Miss Nina, a little exhausted now by such persistence. "There! I've said it. Does that satisfy you? I never cared for Mr. Pickering. Never, never. But I did like him quite a lot." She rose from her chair with sudden energy. "Really, little sister, what have you been doing with your time? You must hurry and refresh yourself. Musn't appear late for dinner, after all. It most definitely would not do."

She glided from the room, leaving Miss Mona alone with Susanna, who looked at her and sniffed a few times, but otherwise exhibited little inclination to assist her in her preparations.

"Yes, of course," said Mona to herself, as she took her sister's place at the dressing-table. She peered into the mirror, at her clear oval face and moon-shaped eyes, and wondered if perhaps there wasn't something in what her sister had said. *We have time enough to be wise* ran the old proverb. A host of unrelated thoughts drifted through her head in a winding melisma of introspection.

She was plucked from her reverie by the sound of water, dripping. Unable to identify the cause at first, she glanced in the direction of the window. The prophecy of Mr. Hilltop came at once to mind, for lo! as if from nowhere, a chilly rain had begun to fall.

CHAPTER VI

Harry Banister's Story

BY morning the rain had given way to a subtle mist, which enveloped the great manor house and all its environs. The azure skies of yesterday were reduced to a memory; a vast blanket of gray — that peculiarly leaden shade of Salthead gray — had fallen upon the battlements of Eaton Wafers. Still, there were birds twittering in the coppice and fires roasting in the chimneys — which, together with the general warmth and good cheer of the company gathered at the great house, did much to dispel the morning's gloom.

The dinner yestereve in the banqueting-hall had been a delight, what with the convivial glow from an army of wax-lights, the sumptuous furnishings, and the wealth of food and drink upon the board, the travelers had been greatly heartened and refreshed. Even Mr. Hilltop, reluctant guest though he might be, had appeared to enjoy himself. But whenever word of the "mysteries" of Salthead or the "disturbances" at Eaton Wafers was lofted on the air, a keen observer might have noticed the ears of Mr. Hilltop prick up, and a look of shrewd attentiveness slip into his eyes.

And so breakfast was laid on — the guests having scarcely recovered from the effects of dinner — with all manner of good and breakfasty things, with ham and eggs and old-fashioned potatoes, and a goose-pie, and warm brown bread, a plum cake and sillabubs, and plenty of hot tea and coffee. Once the travelers' hunger — what remained of it — had been assuaged, the plates and glasses were retired to the scullery, and the company retired to the drawing-room. There they settled themselves in a host of cushioned chairs at the fire, with a shield of screens for background, and beside them a great oriel window overlooking the misty wood — which chilly view made the warmth inside all that more precious. There it was, amid these congenial surroundings, that Harry Banister told them his story.

"As you undoubtedly recall, Professor — and which I relate again now, for the benefit of your companions — I came into my inheritance when the mistress of Eaton Wafers, my aunt, Miss Caroline Nokes, passed away a few winters ago. It was rather a shock, I can tell you — a real stunner! — when the news of her death reached me at Salthead, for I dearly loved my aunt, who had always been very kind to me. It did prepare me in some fashion, however, for the shock that followed: after having led such a cavalier existence for most of my young life, to be presented with such a monument as this" — he made a little gesture to indicate the noble house wherein they were gathered — "for safekeeping! Nonetheless I have grown to love and respect this wondrous place. Having visited my aunt many times in my youth, I was of course familiar with the house and grounds, so that when I arrived to claim the estate it was really more a matter of reacquainting myself with an old friend.

"As you might expect, a manor such as this has passed through a number of families over the years — three of them, in point of fact. The Eatons and Scarletts were the first — you'll recollect certain of their portraits in the entrance hall — followed by the Gyffords, and most recently the Nokes and Banister line, which, I might add, is now sadly reduced. The years have inflicted their depredations; I fear I must have been poor Aunt Caroline's final choice respecting the matter of an heir, simply by default! Regardless it's an excellent living and the servants all top-notch, as I'm sure you've discovered for yourselves in just the few hours you have been here.

"Of those families I mentioned it is the Eatons and the Scarletts who are of greatest relevance to our discussion — there being, I propose, a causal relationship between this ancient lineage and the disturbances that have afflicted us. It is in fact Mr. Thomas Scarlett himself who, I believe, started it all. Let me expain what I mean by that.

"About five months back my chief verdurer, Ned Vickery, whom you met yesterday, was inspecting the park for signs of damage. There'd been a frightful storm, with gusts of rain and a vicious, howling wind that had thrown down trees all round the county. I thought it wise to make a complete survey of the property. When Ned came to the stream that runs through the park — you can see a portion of it from this window here, when there's no mist — he found that one of our oldest oaks, hard by the stream — it had been in an ailing condition for some years — had become uprooted and fallen completely over.

"Tradition holds that this particular tree had been planted by Mr. Thomas Scarlett himself, about three hundred years ago; for this reason it has been known as the `Scarlett oak.' It was sad to see this companion of my childhood in ruins. The ground wherein the roots were buried evidently had softened over the years, perhaps through flooding and erosion from the adjacent stream; the storm had merely applied the *coup de grâce*. As a result, a goodly quantity of soil had been thrown up along with the roots as the tree collapsed. It was in that rich brown earth that something attracted Ned's eye. He explored it with his cutlass and felt the blade tap against solid stone, at which juncture he came to fetch me here in the house.

"Generally speaking it is not uncommon to find buried stone about the estate — foundation works, mostly, of vanished barns and outbuildings. But it was unusual to find buried stone beneath a large tree and so near the stream. I should add here that the stream did not naturally flow in that place; many years ago, my aunt's great-grandfather had had it redirected from the nearby wood. At the time the tree was planted by Tom Scarlett, there was no stream in the vicinity.

"Well, Ned and I got about it straightaway, but we soon found the stone to be more than we could manage ourselves. It looked to be a kind of sarcophagus — so we thought at first — and though the upended roots had done quite a decent job of unearthing it, the job wasn't finished and more work was needed. We secured a length of rope and some implements and a few more sturdy hands, and after some chipping about and a heave-ho managed at last to dislodge the object from the ground.

"It was a block of stone in the shape of a cube — not a sarcophagus, certainly, but very old nonetheless. It had been hewn from some of our local yellow limestone — you'll note that half the house is fashioned of the same material — so whoever had made it, made it here. Once we had it out of the earth we could see an inscription on the top — the initials `T.V.S.' and a date some two hundred ninety-six years previous. The plainest explanation was that the block had been commissioned by Mr. Thomas Vane Scarlett. There were other inscriptions as well on the four sides of the block, each consisting of the single word `*NUNQUAM*' — which of course is the Latin for *never*.

"Mr. Scarlett buried the block near the tree, I presume, to make it simple to locate again, and simple as well to keep watch over, as any disturbance of the site would be instantly apparent. What is more, I believe the tree was put there expressly to mark the location of the block. Of course, he hadn't anticipated the later diversion of the stream and the effect it might have on the soil and roots. We had no idea why he'd buried the object, or what its function was, or whether he'd left instructions for its disposition; if he did, they have not come to light."

"Perhaps, considering the nature of the Latin inscription, he did not want the object found," suggested Dr. Dampe.

"That is a most reasonable possibility," agreed the professor.

"Yes. And I believe, after all that has occurred since, it may be the correct one," said Harry Banister, grimly. "As it turns out the object was not a solid block of stone after all. It had no obvious lid, you see; it was in fact quite a clever piece of work, designed to frustrate a potential plunderer. In the end it was Ned who uncovered the secret of its mechanism. There was a lever hidden very cunningly in the base of it — evident once we'd got it turned on its side — so that the means of access was from underneath. Even then it was hard work getting it open, let me tell you, although at last we managed it. Inside we found a beautiful cedarwood chest, about a foot across, wrapped up in linen and decorated with carved lions' heads. Even to my untutored eye I could see it was a valuable piece of work. Naturally we opened it and had ourselves a look inside.

"Resting there, on a worn velvet facing, was a pair of wafer-thin metallic sheets or tablets. They were joined along one edge by a series of clasps, like the pages of a book, and were covered with an odd sort of script with which I was not familiar. Certain of the characters bore a resemblance to signs from the Greek and Latin alphabets, but it was quite plain the language was neither Greek nor Latin. That, however, was not the oddest thing about the tablets — not by a long chalk."

"Why do you say that?" inquired the doctor, ablaze with curiosity.

"What was the oddest thing?" asked the professor. Beside him the earnest Mr. Kibble glanced up from his note-taking.

"It was the very metal itself. It was of a rich golden hue, though it wasn't gold, and shone with a pale luminosity that it seemed to derive from its own substance. Yes, yes, it's the very truth; there's no mistake. We did indeed think at first it was reflected light, but that was quickly disproved once the tablets were brought into the house and put in a darkened corner, where they proceeded to glow with a soft, even radiance. It was a real stunner! I was nearly afraid to touch them, I can tell you."

"Extraordinary!" exclaimed the doctor.

"Yes, indeed," said the professor, his voice rising with excitement. "We should very much like to examine these tablets."

"I wish I could show them to you," said Harry Banister, with a rueful expression, "but they are no longer here."

"How do you mean?" asked the doctor.

"They were stolen from this house."

"Stolen! How?"

231

"Pray let me continue, Doctor, and you shall hear all. It was apparent, upon viewing this object, that we were in possession of something quite remarkable. But how to explain it? Not understanding the language of the tablets, it was impossible to read what was written there. There was nothing in the stone repository to provide a clue — no documents or letters of any sort, nothing but the tablets themselves, and the linen wrapping, and the chest of cedarwood.

"I should like to emphasize here that irrespective of their origin or purpose the tablets were extraordinarily beautiful. The innate luminescence of the metal was wondrous to behold. Having not the slightest inkling of what was to follow, I assumed that what we'd uncovered was a lost work of art; that Tom Scarlett — who was a noted collector of antiquities and fashionable art objects — had hidden this particular treasure away for himself, but had died without informing his assigns of its existence. Naturally the question passed through my head — why conceal such an object in the first place? At the time, however, I gave scant attention to this aspect of the matter.

"I placed the tablets in my private study, which normally is locked whenever I am from home, and where I judged they should be quite safe. The tablets were a most attractive item, as I have said, and there were many evenings, sitting there at my work, when my thoughts would drift and my eyes wander to the tablets — how lustrous, how curious, how very strange they were! The metal had an opalescent quality to it, shining with different colors of the rainbow depending on the angle from which it was viewed — which was quite a remarkable thing in itself. Add to that the mystery of not knowing what the tablets signified!

"On certain occasions, however, they caused me a degree of apprehension as well. Now and again, at night, with the crackle of the turf-fire beside me, I would look up as my ears registered a sound that appeared to emanate from the tablets. Yes, yes! A soft, low-pitched hum, of a peculiar resonance such as I'd never heard before. It would last for a few moments and then subside, after which I would be left with doubts. Perhaps it was nothing more than my unruly imagination, influenced by the leaping shadows on the wall. It is, after all, very quiet here in the country, and sometimes the mind plays tricks.

"I now relate how it was the tablets came to be lost. It was very much my own fault, and I'll tell you why. About a month after their discovery, a hunt was organized by Captain Fogg and myself. He's a retired naval officer living just beyond the village, and an excellent sportsman as well as a fine

MFH — that's Master of Foxhounds. As you're probably aware a hunt's quite the thing here in the country, and not simply for the excitement of the ride or the thrill of seeing the hounds work. It's a social occasion as well — an opportunity for the county families to come together, for the gentlemen, young and old, to display their mettle and their hunting-pink, and for the ladies, young and old, to display themselves! Needless to say, most everyone has a smashing good time. The meet itself is almost secondary, in a way, though most of the farmers round here are very keen on it. But I digress from the point at issue. I fear it was this particular hunt that set in motion the disturbing events that followed.

"As you might imagine, I found it impossible to resist temptation — I simply had to show some of the fellows what it was we'd found under the Scarlett oak. Most everyone who saw the tablets expressed complete astonishment. As I'd expected, no one knew quite what to make of them, or how it was the metal glowed as it did. Old Pycroft hinted that the inscription must be a prayer of some type, the tablets having come perhaps from a ruined church; but we pointed out to him that the language wasn't Latin. Mr. Revesleigh, who fancies himself something of a comic poet, thought it a eulogy for glow-worms. Tom Hudson put even money on it, it was a three-hundred-year-old practical joke; while Captain Fogg said it looked suspiciously like his wife's handwriting.

"Everyone had either a suggestion or a witty remark to contribute, except for one fellow whom I realized I'd never laid eyes on before. He'd arrived with someone else, an attorney from Salthead named Winch — an oily character if ever there was one — whose firm had long handled my aunt's affairs in the city. He's not exactly our sort of chap, but he's the sole remaining partner in the firm, and I'm afraid I've maintained the connection simply from idleness. This fellow manages to find some pretense, every now and again, to attend one of our hunts — they're subscription, you see, and his account's been in arrears for ages — although it's my impression he's attracted more by the hunt dinners and the opportunities to curry favor, than by the joy of following the hounds.

"The senior partner in the firm, Mr. Badger, now deceased, had served my aunt very admirably for many years — now he was an interesting old rascal! His successor Winch is, I fear, just a rascal. Winch's companion that day was introduced to me as a Mr. Hunter, a well-to-do young gentleman newly arrived in Salthead, who had engaged the firm on some matters of property. Evidently Winch brought him along on what amounted to a whim, to provide him with an introduction to some of the landed gentry."

"Hunter, is it?" said Professor Tiggs.

"Yes, sir. Mr. John Hunter."

The professor frowned and shook his gray bristle-brush head. The doctor and the ladies as well denied knowledge of the man.

"This Mr. Hunter said nothing while viewing the tablets. I could see he was thoroughly fascinated by them, however; he stood there, completely absorbed, long after the other fellows had wandered off. At the time, though, as with certain other things, I gave it no more than a passing thought.

"A fortnight later the first attempt was made to steal the tablets. It was a very clumsy affair and as a result nothing was taken. As I have said, my study ordinarily is locked when I'm not on the premises. On that particular day I'd ridden over to Fridley on a social call. Whoever it was had struggled mightily with the latch, but was unable to get in; marks from the implement he'd used were visible on the door. None of the staff had seen anything unusual, and I must admit we were a bit shaken by it.

"The very next day, while my huntsman and I were out riding, a second attempt was made, this one very bold. The door to my study had been left ajar, thanks to my hurried preparations of the morning. Fortunately, Mitton happened along just in the nick of time and caught the fellow. Well — caught at him, but couldn't restrain him. It was quite plain what the fellow was after, for he had the very tablets in his hands! When Mitton surprised him he dropped them and scampered off like a new barrow with the wheel greased. Nonetheless he managed to snatch one of my silver pocket-watches as he fled. Judging by his appearance he seemed to be a vagrant, but not one of our locals. He was a complete stranger to Mitton and Mitton knows everyone round here. What I believe is that he was dispatched from Salthead expressly to rob me of the tablets."

"The jackanape!" said the doctor, heatedly. "He deserves a good thrashing."

"Another fortnight passed without incident, and another meet was on the docket. Most of the usual crowd were in attendance. To my surprise I discovered Mr. Hunter among them. He explained that his friend Winch was indisposed in chambers at Salthead, and so he, Hunter, had come in his stead. Well, it was a raging cock-and-bull story and I should have known it. After dinner that evening he complained to me of an indifferent state of health, and

234

asked if he might be excepted from the hunting-field next day. Of course I obliged him, being wholly insensible of his true motives.

"Sadly, my good bay horse Thunderbolt — one of our very finest stallions — broke down next morning after clearing a hedge. I led him gently to the stable, where the groom and I had a good hard look at him, but in our hearts we knew already it was very bad. Blinkins, the veterinary surgeon from the village, happened to be in the field that day, and came running once he'd heard the news. He concurred — there was nothing more to be done. We put Thunderbolt down immediately, for he was suffering badly. I tell you — to have seen him there in his final moments of life, so courageous, with his leg horribly bruised and swollen at the break — and he so patient, regarding me with so noble an eye — so trustful, so valiant, so much the champion — and whinnying softly to me despite his dreadful injury — ah, poor Thunderbolt! That was a rare horse, my friends, the likes of which comes round but seldom in a fellow's life. It was the darkest of suns that shone upon our house that day.

"Feeling dismal and low I retreated to my study, and what do you suppose I found there? It was Mr. John Hunter — none the worse for his ill-health, which was of course a monstrous humbug — creeping like the thief that he was from my study with the tablets and the cedarwood chest in his arms. His portmanteau lay just beyond the door, and what do you think? It was empty. Yes! He'd brought little or no in the way of clothing, you see, because he never intended to stay. His plan was to use the portmanteau to conceal the tablets, and so make off with them while everyone was in the field.

"Well, it nearly knocked me to smash — first Thunderbolt and now this! I was feeling terribly dispirited on account of the horse, and perhaps this slowed my reflexes, for we tussled, Hunter and I, and he bested me with a ringing blow to the chin that knocked me flat. The next I knew I lay extended on the floor with Mitton and some of the other servants hovering about me, and Mr. Hunter and the tablets nowhere in sight. Ned and I set off in pursuit, taking the carriage-road into the village, but by that time it was too late. Mr. Hunter and his private chaise had last been seen by the landlord of the Pied Horse, streaking along the High Street in the direction of the Salthead road."

"Have you made inquiries in the city?" asked the professor. "Is there anyone acquainted with this Mr. Hunter? And what of his attorney?"

"The fellow Winch was contacted by one of my friends in town, but he claimed utter ignorance as to the activities of his client. An agent of the magistrate, as a favor to my friend, went to see Mr. Hunter at his residence, but was rebuffed by a rude serving-man who informed him that the master was away indefinitely on important business. There's little else that can be done there, I'm afraid. The crime was perpetrated here in Broadshire, and, well — there's no jurisdiction in Salthead, of course. The magistrates are in the main uncooperative when it comes to matters outside their own sphere of influence. And so — there it is, then."

"But you know where this Hunter lives," Dr. Dampe pointed out. "In all likelihood that is where the tablets are, irrespective of what a lying servant may have to say."

"Yes, I see your point, Doctor. But let me tell you now why I am not particularly anxious to have them back — in fact, I'm quite relieved they're gone! For you see, I believe they lie at the root of the disturbances, which began soon after the theft. Within the week, in fact."

"And what," asked the doctor — still burning with curiosity — "is the nature of these disturbances?"

"They began in the crypt of the chapel. You cannot see it from this vantage point, but beyond that corner of the house there is an ancient stone chapel that was built by Mr. Vane Eaton. It still receives occasional use, whenever a member of the clergy happens to be visiting. It has a number of attractive architectural features — voussoirs decorated with hounds and horsemen, above the north door — quite appropriate for this part of the country — as well as some decorative brickwork, some terra-cotta portrait plaques and the like, and burnt bricks set in a zigzag or diamond-pattern, in the Jacobean style. The crypt of the chapel is, however, not the repository of the ashes of Mr. Tom Scarlett or any of the members of his family; their remains lie in the village church. I must admit, I'd always thought that a curious circumstance.

"In the crypt was a most enigmatic piece of sculpture. It was rather a large thing, fully twice a man's size in all dimensions, and carved from a kind of porous rock that's been identified for me as tufa. I'm told it is of volcanic origin. There are no such deposits in the area of Pease Pottage, or anywhere in Broadshire that anyone knows of for that matter. An unusual thing about this statue was its color — a dark, steely blue, with a few long narrow streaks of gray or black. On first sight you'd think it was simply painted rock; on closer examination, however, it was apparent that the very rock itself was blue.

"This piece was just one example of Tom Scarlett's impressive store of antiquities. As I've mentioned, he was quite an avid collector of such things. Much of his collection — vases, votive figurines and other statuary, bronze mirrors, rhytons, coins, papyri and the like, gathered from all over the world — centuries before the sundering, of course — much of it can be found in the museum rooms in the north wing of the house. We can view them later today, if you'd like.

"It has been a singular stipulation of the freehold of Eaton Wafers, first instituted by Thomas Scarlett himself, and devolving upon each successive family as the estate has changed hands, that this particular item of sculpture was to remain in the crypt and never be removed from it. Indeed, I have here the very words of Mr. Scarlett, to the effect that — here, I've copied the words exactly —

"'Y^e blew Figure w^h lyeth in ye Chappel shall remayne in y^t holy House, in Perpetuitye, *viz.*, for ever & ever, never to forsake ye sanctifying Presence of ye holy Reliques.'"

"Holy relics?" echoed the doctor.

"Of an obscure saint, one Malfius, together with a purported fragment of the True Cross, which are kept in the chancel. As you know, the presence of such objects in a house of God is believed by the faithful to offer protection against evil."

"Something like an amulet was to pagans, actually."

"Yes. But that was not all. Mr. Scarlett evidently did not trust all to Providence or the benign influence of a little-known martyr. The statue — being as I have said very large — was placed in a corner of the crypt in a horizontal position, and chained to the stone flagging by a series of sturdy iron links. The crypt itself was then sealed. It is, in point of fact, only in the past generation or two that this chamber has been reopened, and that anyone has set eyes again upon the statue itself."

A momentary hush went round the room.

"Chained to the floor!" exclaimed Mr. Kibble, looking up for a moment from his notebook.

"What does this item of sculpture depict, exactly?" asked Dr. Dampe.

"That is a very good question, Doctor, to which no one has a very good answer. The best I can muster is that it appeared to be some kind of bird. It was pretty much all wing — two gigantic wings to be precise, folded over the length of the body like a shroud, with the head drawn down under them and so rendered invisible. At the base of the statue, below the level of the wings, was a pair of large, wicked-looking talons."

"From all you have said, with reference to this statue," said the professor, "are we to assume it is no longer in the crypt?"

Harry Banister did not reply immediately, but got up from his chair and went to a nearby cupboard. He returned with a small tin porringer filled with a quantity of fine blue powder, and set it before the visitors.

"This," he said, "is a small portion of what remains of the statue. About a week following the theft of the tablets, a loud crash was heard in the night. At the time we took it for thunder, for there had been a storm earlier that evening. In the morning Ned found that the door to the crypt had been forced open. Ned — why don't you recount for the professor and his friends exactly what you saw there."

The groundskeeper, who had entered quietly during this last discussion, cleared his voice and took up the tale, plainly and succinctly —

"Well, now, I can say it war like this. I thought at the first it war vandals, for there's trouble as that every now and then in an isolated spot such as this. Once I gone into the crypt, though, I soon seent it warn't no vandals as done it. There warn't nowt left o' that statue but great heaps o' blue powder scattered round the floor o' the crypt, and the great iron shackles as once held the statue all broke apart. There warn't one solid piece o' that statue nowhere, no, sir. It were nowt but powder — like in that pot there — like it war exploded from inside, and blowed itself to atoms!"

"You can well imagine how puzzled we were by this incident," said Mr. Banister. "Later that day a perishing cold descended upon the house and grounds, such a cold as is unusual even for Broadshire. A cloying, unhealthy business it was, penetrating into every corner — even the fires in the chimneys failed to dispel it. Naturally we assumed it was an aberration of the weather; but upon venturing into Pease Pottage we discovered there was no such cold there, beyond what would be considered normal for the season."

"This is most interesting," said the professor, "for we have experienced something very like this in Salthead, on at least two occasions."

"You see how it is — here and in town — the very same phenomenon, just as I have supposed!" cried the master of Eaton Wafers.

"What was next?" asked the doctor, eagerly.

"Over the next two months we were visited by a succession of disturbances, one upon the other. The perishing cold was wont to come and go, quite at will; often its arrival meant something out of the ordinary was about to occur — unexplained noises in the night — a tapping at the window — the movement of furniture when no one was in the room — the unexpected snuffing of a candle — a subtle motion of the eyes in a painted portrait. One of the maidservants saw an evil face in her glass and heard mocking laughter. On another occasion the groom was walking in the park, at dusk, and came upon something kneeling at the edge of the stream. He thought at first it must be an animal, but it couldn't have been, for it laughed at him and scuttled away at his approach. By then we were fixing to proclaim ourselves a madhouse and advertise for patients, so certain were we of our imminent insanity."

"Incidents such as these can be characteristic of hauntings," said the professor. "Jealous spirits making mockery of the living, as a way to ease their torment. You have never before encountered such things here?"

"Never in my recollecton, nor in Ned's. And I certainly do not recall hearing any such stories from my aunt."

"And these disturbances continued?"

"Yes, and worsened as well. I myself witnessed several of them. One evening, while lying in my bed, I heard the mocking laugh. Taking my candle I stepped into the passage, where I thought the sound had originated. There was nothing there but the cold. Suddenly something brushed against my leg — I must have leaped ten feet into the air, I can tell you! I found it was one of the cats, scurrying past in the dark. As it ran down the passage it stopped to look back at me, and for just an instant I saw it had a human face."

"Exactly which cat was this?" inquired the doctor, glancing uncomfortably round the drawing-room.

"Not to worry, Doctor — he's safely out and about this morning. But now it is I come to the most fantastic part of my story. On another evening, not more than a month ago, I was seated in the downstairs parlor attending to my correspondence, when the vast cold came over me. A short time later I heard the sound of a horse grinding its teeth. Looking up I beheld the face of Thunderbolt peering in at the window. It froze me to my chair. I tell you, everyone — it is a shocking thing to see the risen dead."

"You're sure it was this same horse?" asked the professor.

"Perfectly. The mark upon the face which gave him his name, the general form and carriage of the head — it was Thunderbolt. Not wishing to alarm him, I rose slowly from my chair and went to the side door, which I cautiously drew open. From that position I was able to obtain a full view of him. I identified all the familiar details of conformation: the graceful, arching neck, the well-shaped chest, the powerful hindquarters, the white stockings upon three legs — included among them his shattered leg, which he now stood upon quite boldly, as though the flesh itself were benumbed. And so I was convinced more than ever it was my horse.

"There was a particular whistle I had always reserved for him, to call him from the meadow, and which he knew intimately. I reasoned that if I voiced that whistle now and he responded, I'd have conclusive proof. On the first attempt I failed, my mouth being so dry from fear and apprehension that I could utter not a single note. My very hands were trembling. Nonetheless I placed my unsteady fingers to my lips and managed to sound it out.

"There was indeed a response, but not the one I had anticipated. The horse immediately swung round on his heels and faced me, with his head lowered and his ears flat and the most fearsome look in his eyes. I hardly can describe it — a look of such venom and malignity, such foulness, such proud disdain. I thought he meant to run me down. It was indeed my Thunderbolt, but Thunderbolt all horribly changed!

"I shut that door pretty quick, I can tell you, and ran for my sword. I called up the manservants and gave them weapons as well, for I knew what had to be done. By the time we took the field, however, the horse had vanished. In the morning we searched the area thoroughly but could find no trace of him. Not a single blade of grass had been disturbed. It was as if the horse had never been there."

"A phantasm," concluded the professor. "It has all the appearance of reality, but its substance is not real."

"We examined the place where we had buried Thunderbolt and found it to be undisturbed. You must accept my word upon it — Thunderbolt did stand there at the window that night, and I did see him, just as plainly as I see all of you now. It was not a dream."

"Of course we accept your word, Harry. Your story is most intriguing. I have the impression, however, that there is at least one more surprise," said the professor, quite obviously fascinated by what he had heard thus far.

"The next disturbance was — if you don't mind my phrasing it thus — the most disturbing," said Mr. Banister, rubbing his chin. "Again it occurred after dark, but this time under a full flood of moonlight. I was in my study, poring over the monthly accounts, when the perishing cold overcame me. I looked round but saw and heard nothing. I drew the curtain across the window, however, so I would not be disturbed that way, and turned the mirror to the wall. All of this was of course precautionary. A fire was blazing away in the grate yet the cold persisted, as was its habit. My study, you should be aware, is situated in a far corner of the south wing, at the very top of the house, from which there is a quite spectacular view. As I returned to my accounts, trying to lose myself in the work, there came a sound from above, as though something had landed on the roof directly over my head.

"Below stairs I happened upon Ned, and together we went outside to see what there was to see, both of us taking up our weapons on the way — another precaution. As we stepped from the door we parted, agreeing that each should examine half the building. As I have said the moon was quite brilliant, and as a result the main features of the house were awash in light. If there were something up there we stood a doubly good chance of spotting it, as the roof rises very steeply above the battlements. I had found nothing thus far on my half of the route, which encompassed the south wing, but as I came round to the opposite side there was a distant shout from Ned."

Here Mr. Banister signed to Ned Vickery.

"What I saw there — I vow it war the truth," said the groundskeeper, in sober tones. "It war at the very edge o' the roof, it war, atwixt the battlements, with the moonlight streamin' full upon it. It warn't my imagination, no, sir — I seent it clear. It war the figure of a man — or what I took at the first for a man — with great arms o' muscle, and a beard, and an ugly countenance. But there came an end to the resemblance, for it had a beak like a vulture's where its nose should be, and ears like an ass, and the hair on its head — why, it was up and wrigglin' like a sea o' vipers! On its back it wore a huge pair o' wings, and on its two feet war claws like a bird's. There war summat curled round one of its arms — I took it at the first for a length o' rope, but then I seent it squirm and slither, and I realized it war some kind o' serpent it had there. Then I thought for sure it war the Foul Fiend himself, as was perched on the battlements of Eaton Wafers."

"What an extraordinary image!" cried the doctor.

The professor was wholly transfixed, his gaze riveted on Ned. Mr. Kibble's pen lay stilled; he was too astonished to write. Miss Mona and her sister were holding each other's hands. Behind them all sat Mr. Hilltop, with his arms folded and a look of dark significance on his spotted face.

241

"I thought I war gone mad," said Ned Vickery, swallowing, "but I war hot, too, so I shouts at the thing — 'Hi! Ye there! What business have ye here, ye devil, on good Christian ground?' Then I bethought myself that warn't quite right to say, for the thing it warn't stood on no ground at all. But I war so worked up, so hot at the trespass, that I warn't thinkin' clear. Well, sir, that thing turned its ugly face in my direction, and I thought at the first it war aimin' to come at me. Then it throws back its head and laughs, long and hard, and flings itself from the battlements. But instead o' breakin' its neck on the gravel walk it turns in the air, light as can be, and flits round to the other side o' the house. Then it war that Mr. Harry reached me — but he had no chance to see the crayture, or the devil, or whatever it be, as it war far off by then."

"Hallo — a flying man!" exclaimed the doctor. "How remarkable!"

"It was a real stunner," said Mr. Banister, quite obviously affected, as was everyone else, by this electrifying recital. "It was during the period of these latter disturbances, I believe, that mysterious events began to be reported in Salthead. As soon as I received word of them from my friends in the city, I sat down to my desk and wrote off to you, Professor. I could not put any of this in my missive; I thought it too fantastic. I needed you to come to Eaton Wafers, to hear the story for yourself, and to show you what there is left to see. I must take you to the chapel and the crypt, and have you speak with a few of the servants, to hear the reports from their very own lips."

"Look here — it's a pity the tablets aren't available for an examination of the writing," said the doctor, taking the opportunity to recharge his pipe. "They could have provided a great deal of useful information, actually."

"Ah! Doctor, that's where I've got you," said Harry, with barely suppressed enthusiasm. He sprang to his feet and went to an escritoire in the oriel window, from which he withdrew a scroll of white parchment. "For you see — before the tablets were stolen, I of course took the precaution of transcribing a detailed copy of the inscription for myself."

"Magnificent!" exulted Mr. Kibble, looking round then a little sheepishly, as though embarrassed by his own exuberance. He could see, however, that both Dr. Dampe and the professor were just as delighted at Mr. Banister's words.

"May we examine the copy?" asked the professor.

"It's not a particularly artful interpretation, but it should suffice," said Mr. Banister.

242

He unfolded the parchment and laid it out before them. All eyes looked upon the exotic script with a curious stare — some marveling, some registering confusion, some consternation, some faint recognition — while a pair of eyes in a certain spotted face registered triumph, colored with self-congratulation.

"Yes, yes," the professor was heard to mutter as he perused the inscription, the first few lines of which are reproduced here —

ᴲᴎV : TV : ᴎᴲ⟩ : Ĵ⟨⟩

AↆↄↄↆVᴛ : ᴲᴎVↄAᵮ⟩

"I'd hoped you might recognize the writing and be able to translate it," said Harry. "I'm sure if we could simply read the thing, we should gain a considerable understanding of the situation."

"It is unquestionably Italic," said the professor. "Of that much at least we can be certain. Having said that, nonetheless there is a marked Greek influence — for the Greeks, as you know, colonized much of southern Italy in pre-classical times. And if I am not too far wrong, the text is meant to be read from right to left. But unfortunately, linguistics is not my specialty."

"Professor Greenshields!" exclaimed the doctor, with a snap of his fingers. "My old tutor, from Antrobus College. He's a renowned expert in the classics and philology — retired now, actually. There's no doubt he could translate it for us."

Professor Tiggs nodded his assent immediately. "Christopher Greenshields. A noted polymath, he remains the leading authority in Salthead on classical civilization and letters. Yes, surely he will know what to make of this."

"Then we must show it to him," declared Mr. Banister. "Given a reading of this inscription, together with an account of the disturbances, an explanation should be forthcoming."

"I am in complete agreement with you. And what is more, I am myself persuaded now — even as you have been since the outset — of a connection to the apparitions in Salthead. The events you relate began soon after the theft of the tablets, with the destruction of the statue in the crypt. What I

243

believe is that the tablets were used to liberate something from that statue, and it is that which has unleashed this torrent."

"And so it follows, then, that Mr. Tom Scarlett knew indeed what he was about when he buried the tablets."

"Yes, for he interred them in a spot just where he might keep an eye on them. Likewise he confined the statue to the guardianship of the holy relics — not to protect it, but to protect himself and others from it. He must have happened on these artifacts in the course of his travels, and recognizing what it was he had acquired, hid them away where they could do no harm."

"It must be true, for I tell you, Professor, if you had seen the remains of that statue as we saw them that morning in the crypt — "

"I can imagine the effect of it, Harry. The statue blew apart because something inside it had been released. With it came the perishing cold, the phantasms of the dead, and the flying man. How interesting that both the statue and the flying man had wings and talons."

"Exactly so!"

"These disturbances — as they have unfolded here and in town — are almost mischievous, actually," mused the doctor, with a leisurely draw on his pipe. "Every event is so very random. It's as if someone were making at play — having a little fun, perhaps, or trying his hand at things."

"Or reviving his powers after a very long absence," said Miss Mona.

These remarks occasioned a period of silent reflection, which was broken finally by the master of Eaton Wafers.

"Well, there it is, then! I believe we have a strategy," he said, with a brisk clap of his hands. "I must show you now the various places where these events occurred, and have you speak to the servants who witnessed them. Then tomorrow we must leave for Salthead and a conference with Professor Greenshields."

Professor Tiggs and the doctor both attested to the excellence of this proposal.

"Kit Greenshields is the man for the job," nodded the doctor.

There followed another pause, which time the professor spent looking closely again at the scroll. A ray of light shone across his face. "Do you know, I believe I have indeed seen this particular script before. Yes, I'm sure of it. This character here, and this one, and this one here — yes, yes, I do know what this is! It's quite clear now."

"What is it?" asked Mr. Kibble, earnestly.

"Perhaps I should say first what it is not. As we've already observed it's neither Greek nor Latin, though it has elements of both. See for example this sign here, which resembles the Greek *theta*, and this downward-directed arrow which I'm sure is related to *chi*, and these more familiar letters here. Neither is it Oscan — one of the chief languages of ancient Italy, covering the territory of the Samnite tribes — nor Umbrian, I don't believe."

"What is it, then?" asked Harry.

"It is Etruscan," said the professor.

CHAPTER VII

High Jinks in the City

MR. Josiah Tusk, that close-fisted and conscientious man of business, feeling now the keen edge of appetite after the fatigues of a day in the city, bursts forth from the shadows of the Exchange like a specter of doom — which every citizen of Salthead knew he was, of course. Striding that bold superior stride through the well-worn courtyards, his tall gaunt form cleaves the night air, left and right, as cleanly as a broad-ax through blood pudding. From the Exchange he directs his booted steps down into Snowfields, to a nearby chop-house he occasionally frequented when detained by affairs in town. There, finding his way to a table beside a goodly fire, the miser hangs up his hat and draws a city newspaper from his coat, and so sitting down begins to pore over the chronicles of life.

The waiter — a mere youth, a stripling, and clearly new to the profession — approaches. His eyes grow very large as he sees who it is who is seated there, gracing the establishment with his icy presence. Clearing his voice the youth recites the bill of fare for the miser's benefit, and is about to depart when Josiah, having made his choice, intones —

"Waiter."

"Yes, sir?"

"The fire. It is much too hot."

The youth, uncertain at first what to do with this remark, or where to stow it, says nothing; which ensuing silence Josiah interprets as either stubbornness or insolence, and more than likely both.

"Waiter! I say to you again — the fire is too hot."

Having never received such a complaint before — it being usually the other case, in the experience of his brief career, that the fire was *not hot enough* — the waiter glances round at the patrons of the establishment; looks then for one or another of his fellow attendants, but none happens by; as a last resort stares dismally at the water-decanter on the miser's table.

"Waiter," says a very stern-faced Josiah. "What is the matter with you? Are you deaf? Didn't you hear what I said? The fire is too hot."

"Yes, sir, I heard, sir," replies the youth, and with a tremulous hand proceeds to offer Josiah another table some distance from the offending chimney.

In response the great white head of the miser swivels on its turret; the jet-black brows contract; the falcon-eyes sharpen themselves on the object of their displeasure.

"Waiter," says Josiah, leaning forward on his chair with a stupendous frown. "Tread softly. Do you know who I am?"

"Yes, sir," answers the youth, quivering up to the very tips of his fingers. As an afterthought he blurts out, in an owl-like stammer — "Who — who — who is it who don't, sir?"

"If you know who I am, then do as I say," instructs the miser, with an imperious nod toward the fireplace.

"But if I take down the fire, sir, it will freeze most everyone in the house," protests the waiter, quite sensibly. "It's very cold these nights, sir, and we must keep the fire up for comfort."

"Comfort? Cold? What cold might that be? There is certainly no cold here. Show it to me; I feel it not."

"Please, if you would, sir, it's not for me to — "

"And suppose it were cold, what should be done then, eh? A simple case — let 'em freeze! Cold won't hurt you. No, it is fire that is the scourge of business. Fire, the destroyer of property. Do you own property, sir? I thought not. Let me ask you a question. What do you suppose is the end-effect on this house, sir, of a freezing night in winter?"

The youth, dumfounded, has no response.

"Nothing," answers the miser, with a bony forefinger raised for emphasis. "Nothing, whatsoever. Now I put it to you — what would be the effect of fire on this same piece of property? For how long do you suppose this house would survive, sir, should those flames there light upon some combustible material — that ancient settle, for instance, or those curtains, or the hearth-rug — and so escape the confines of their stony prison? I'll give you the answer — not long. And as for the result? The loss of business, the loss of custom — the loss of your situation. We are both men of business, sir, in our different stations. Fire, not cold, is our greatest enemy. Always remember that."

"Yes, sir."

"Let me put it another way, one that is perhaps simpler for you to comprehend. Would you rather die, sir, sweetly and quietly, on a calm, cold winter's night, or wake to find your house burning down around you — your lungs smothered in wood-smoke — the hot flames eating at your body — the flesh hissing and crackling as it drips from your bones — and the bones themselves blasted to cinders?"

"Please, sir," gasps the horrified youth, blanching, "I'd rather not die at all, sir, if it could possibly be avoided!" His heart leaps into his throat. What next, he wonders, oh, what next from the miser's fund of cheerful ideas?

"An admirable attitude. Keep it in your mind, sir — cold is your ally. Never shrink from it. But enough! I'm not a man for chatter and I won't be gainsaid, do you hear? I am a man of business and am accustomed to service. So you'll take down that fire, sirrah, or I'll take my business elsewhere. I ask you — is that what your master, Mine Host of the chop-house, would wish to hear? Shall we summon him and put the question to him directly?"

The waiter appeals with pleading eyes to the other customers, some of whom are looking on with incomprehension, some with compassion, some with disbelief; some unconsciously urging him to do as he was told, some not to do so; with one or two here and there plainly resentful of the situation, their emotions held in check, however, by their common dread of the miser.

"No, sir!" answers the youth, making up his mind at last. He goes immediately to the chimney and takes down the fire, leaving nothing but a few dusky coals to shiver there behind the grate; and so returns to Josiah's table.

"Is — is that how you wanted it, sir?"

"Indeed," says Josiah, grimly triumphant, and not unconscious of the discomfort that would soon be visited upon those around him. "That is a great improvement. The fire was much too hot. The season itself has been uncomfortably warm of late; I'm told it will be a fine winter."

"Yes, sir!" says the waiter, scurrying away and mumbling under his breath — "Fine winter, aye, sir!"

With his dinner being assembled in the kitchen, the miserly keeper of the frost returns to his paper. There he sits, frozen to the seat of his chair, as his eyes dart about the columns, eagerly searching for news of evil events that might have befallen anyone he knew. With the grim little smile playing at the corners of his mouth, he comes to the "obits" — a particular favorite — and at intervals can be heard chuckling with glee over the fate of some late unfortunate, leavening his humor with such refrains as —

"That fellow certainly deserved it!"

"Faugh! That settles *his* hash."

"Too bad — that one ought to have swung!"

"Insolent minx! I should have known she'd leave it all to him."

"What a jolly ass *he* was!"

"There's justice — that hound cut me once."

"I see he had the good sense to restrict the cost of his funeral to ten pounds." (Frugal Josiah! He was not a man to spend a shilling where a penny would do).

"Ha, ha! `Put a period to his existence, by precipitating himself from the window of his attic.' Good, good — it saves the rest of us the trouble."

Chancing on one particular name the miser's brow abruptly darkens. The grim little smile dissolves into a livid scowl, as in a low voice he mutters —

"That fellow owed me money!"

While the miser is engaged in this pleasant ritual, a gentleman in a plum-colored suit crosses the threshold, and locating Josiah's table approaches it with reverential steps. He is a round, fat man, with a bald head cocked queerly to one side and small dark eyes, long-cut. He comes to a respectful halt a few paces from the table and removes his hat, waiting for Josiah to acknowledge him; the miser, however, takes no notice. The visitor utters a polite cough behind his hand, to attract the miser's attention, but sees this stratagem fail as well.

"There's one," mutters Josiah — who is, by the by, fully aware of the presence of his solicitor, Mr. Jasper Winch, and who consequently takes a fierce and ill-natured pleasure in ignoring him — "There's one. That buffoon has lost everything!" (He had by now completed his survey of the obits and moved on to items of more general interest). "Serves him well. Extravagant living! He's ruined, completely ruined, and I for one am glad of it. He called it down upon himself. It's a simple case — if he can't take care of his money, he shouldn't have it."

Hearing these tender concerns Mr. Winch coughs again — a little more insistently this time, but still with the same deferential restraint. Even this is insufficient to coax the eyes of Mr. Tusk from the columns. The attorney thinks busily for a moment, licking his lips and screwing his neck into a knot. He leans a little to the left, then a little to the right, then to the left and to the right again, hoping this motion might attract the miser's gaze; it succeeds, however, in attracting only a little sea-sickness. Upon his recovery the lawyer coughs, loosens his collar and engages in a fit of head-wiping — all to no avail.

At this moment the youthful waiter comes flying in with Josiah's dinner. The miser is obliged to put down his paper. Glancing up he catches sight of Mr. Winch at last, and so finds it necessary to acknowledge the presence of that eminent limb of the law.

"Ah, Winch — you're here," he grunts, peering at his watch. "And late, as usual. I should have expected it."

"Late!" retorts Lawyer Winch. He massages his head again, and it seems that each stroke of his palm is loaded with a deep and secret resentment. "Late! I was just on time, you ugly scarecrow, if only you'd noticed me." He doesn't actually say any of this, of course; instead, it comes out curiously translated as —

"Ahem! At your service, Mr. Tusk. May I sit down, sir?"

With a sly look the miser motions the attorney to a chair, while he himself applies knife and fork to his meal. He says nothing more for some minutes, being engaged in the consumption of his dinner. The food is excellent, and consists of some gravy soup, roast beef with greens and mustard, a deviled biscuit, some potatoes, onions, and some bread, capped off by a glass of fine sherry. Mr. Winch watches with an unhealthy fascination, struck now by the resemblance of the gaunt Josiah to a teratorn picking over its prey, an effect enhanced by the miser's black coat and red velvet waistcoat.

Having little else to occupy him, the attorney glances round the chamber and so observes the struggling fire in the grate.

"It's deuced cold in here," he says, rubbing his hands together. "Lazy do-nothings — ahem! — thoroughly incompetent — can't believe they haven't a decent fire in this house. I'll see to it for you, sir."

Here the waiter stops to ask Mr. Winch if he requires anything from the kitchen. Mr. Winch says no, he's already dined, but does request an improvement in the condition of the fire. The waiter pales at this, and looks to Josiah for instruction; turning again to Winch he assures him he'll see what could be done about it.

"Ahem! Well, sir," smiles the attorney, obsequious as always but anxious now to get to the point. "I received your kind offer — ahem — in my chambers at the firm, to meet you here tonight. Ahem. You have perhaps a specific proposal in mind? Is there some service — ahem — the firm can perform for you, sir?"

Mr. Tusk nods, champing mightily on a wad of beef. "Indeed. I have good news for you, Winch!" he exclaims, and so proceeds to load his mouth with more food.

"Good news?" echoes Mr. Winch, with an impatient shuffle of his fingers on the table-cloth.

The miser nods again, smiling and chewing.

"It had better be good news," is the response of Mr. Winch. "It had better be capital good news, old man, for I'm certainly not tickled to be wasting my evening here with *you!*" (Of course he does not say any of these things either,

250

but in their place coughs a few times, and makes a complete study of the oak timbers in the ceiling).

Josiah, having exhausted this little bit of fun with his solicitor, takes a sip of sherry, and devotes himself now to the matter at hand.

"It has lately come to my notice, Winch," he begins, "that there is a young gentleman, new to town, a person quite well-connected and possessed of independent property, who finds himself in an unfortunate circumstance. He is from a distant city and has few friends here. When he arrived he engaged an attorney to attend to his affairs, but in the interim has become dissatisfied with his counselor. The young gentleman tells me this attorney has set a spy on him. Monstrous! What do you say to spying, Winch?" Here the miser leaves off chewing for a moment, the better to observe the other's reaction.

Despite the growing sharpness of the air in the room, a few beads of perspiration can be seen sprouting from the forehead of Mr. Winch, like rain leaking from a water-butt.

"Spying? Ahem! On a client?" he returns, his eyes squirming beneath their heavy lids in furtive calculation. "Never heard of such a thing."

"The young gentleman's name, by the by, happens to be Hunter. John Hunter. Do you know him?" (Another pause, and a flash of the grim little smile.)

The lawyer stiffens as though he had just been clearstarched. He thinks swiftly and so does again what lawyers do best — he lies, claiming total unfamiliarity with the name. Even as he speaks he can feel himself being pressed back into his chair by the miser's sharp falcon-eyes.

Did the ugly scarecrow — a touching appellation! — know already that John Hunter was his client, and so know as well that he, Winch, was a liar? Surely Hunter must have divulged his name. And if it were so, how by God had Hunter discovered the truth? A hundred million thoughts flash through the attorney's head, all in the matter of a second, as he tries to reconcile the conflicting lines of evidence. The obvious suspect was of course the spy himself, Samson Icks. But that possibility is soon dismissed, as the attorney recalls that his agent — he of the smoked lenses and narrow running pinstripes — had for some time been engaged in the disposition of the Hoakum case, and so was most likely out of the picture. Who else, then, and how? How?

"I didn't think you knew him," resumes Josiah, sliding the blade of his knife through a fat potato. "Otherwise I would have been aware of it, wouldn't I? A young gentleman of Hunter's considerable wealth, new to the city and wishing to establish himself, and desirous of favorable local connections. You would have seen to it I'd been informed — wouldn't you, Winch?"

"Yes, of course, Mr. Tusk. Ahem!"

"Having received assurances that I am a conscientious man of business, and one familiar with the law-courts, Hunter came to me in hopes of obtaining a recommendation for fresh counsel. A noted solicitor of stature in the community — someone reliable, someone honest — someone who wouldn't betray him — someone trustworthy — these were the particular qualities he described for the individual he sought."

"When did this conversation take place?" inquires Mr. Winch, still baffled how it was his secret had been discovered. "When did you speak with him — ahem — with this Mr. Hunter?"

"Last evening, at Shadwinkle Old House."

"And who," continues Mr. Winch — determined to get it all out in the open — "who is the lawyer representing him? The one with whom he is — ahem — dissatisfied?" He pulls out a handkerchief and wipes his head and neck. Did the miser know? *Did he know?* The attorney shudders to think of the waiter's returning at any moment to bolster the fire, as it has suddenly grown far too hot in the chop-house.

Another lengthy pause while Josiah ruminates over his meal, which strains the nerves of Mr. Winch still further. At last the reply —

"He would not give me the name. He considers himself an honorable gentleman, and so looks upon it as a matter of some confidence — which is more than can be said for his double-dealing attorney. Nonetheless the young gentleman was quite distressed — oh, yes. Imagine it, Winch — setting a spy on one's own client! It must be assumed this pettifogger was seeking knowledge of Hunter's private affairs, to extort money from him, perhaps, on account of some prior indiscretion. To be played false by one's own counsel reflects very poorly upon the profession, wouldn't you agree? The sort of man who would stoop to that is the sort of man who would stoop to anything. It would not surprise me in the least, if such a man might not stoop even to the intercepting of a client's private correspondence! What do you say to *that*, Winch?"

This barb the miser hurls directly into the face of his attorney, awaiting its effect with piquant anticipation. The face, however, registers only confusion. His disappointment at not scoring a hit does not seem to bother Josiah; instead, it fuels his wrath and provides even more assurance that the fat attorney was deceiving him.

"This young gentleman, this Hunter," continues Josiah — tearing apart his deviled biscuit with inordinate ferocity, as though the biscuit were the body of Mr. Jasper Winch and the miser had just dismembered it — "has a remarkably good head on his shoulders. He is very sharp — all business. He is possessed of excellent references and seems to me a most conscientious young man. I admire that, Winch, as you well know. What is more, in the midst of our conversation we discovered certain avenues of mutual interest, richly deserving of exploration, and which should prove of considerable benefit to both our houses. To speak truth it was a surprise, but a very pleasant and professional one.

"And so here is your good news, Winch. Documents — contracts and agreements — memoranda of understanding — must be drawn up to initiate this cooperative endeavor between Mr. Hunter and myself. I have indicated to the young gentleman that my own trusted solicitor of many years' standing would attend to this matter personally. You'll do that for me, won't you, Winch? I shall moreover propose to Hunter that he consider retaining you as his own counsel. So! That is good news, is it not, Winch?"

Lawyer Winch coughs loudly, and clamps his hand to the top of his head. "Contracts — ahem — and agreements? Personally?" he gasps, too staggered for the moment to offer more than this.

"I shall see you at your chambers on Monday next. We will draft the papers establishing a joint enterprise between Hunter and myself, and which you will deliver yourself to Mr. Hunter for his approval. He is residing presently at Malt House, Raven Lane — you're familiar with the district, of course? I needn't underscore the fact that this is a very important matter to me, Winch. I trust you will not disappoint."

"Personally!" cries Mr. Winch, his brain a-swirl with images of the confrontation with Mr. John Hunter — nostril to nostril, eyeball to eyeball, and, very likely now, fist to fist.

"Of course. I've said as much already. What is wrong with you, Winch? Aren't you listening? As my solicitor you're expected to carry out such duties — that is what I pay you for. So I shall expect you to meet with Mr. Hunter at Malt House exactly as I have described. I am providing you with an opportunity to gain an important young client — what more could you want? I'm sure Mr. Hunter will be pleased to receive your services. At the very least you'll not be spying on him like that other villain!"

"Spying? No, no — ahem! — of course not."

"Very good. Many happy returns of the day to you, Winch!" smiles Josiah, by way of dismissal. He is finished with the attorney for now, and so proceeds to cast him aside like a discarded card in piquet; then takes up his newspaper and returns to his dinner.

"Yes — sir," mumbles Lawyer Winch, rising from his chair with the ghastly look of a man going to execution. "Many happy returns — ahem — to you, sir."

He stumbles out into the darkness of Snowfields, whence he manages to find his way, somehow, to a cab-stand, and so is driven home in his stunned condition, barely able to raise hand to purse to pay the cabman his fare. He totters into his house and asks his servant for a gin-and-water, very hot; whereupon he falls backwards upon the sofa, to contemplate with a vacant stare his impending rendezvous with Fate.

Mr. Tusk, seeing the attorney's plum-colored bulk vanish into the night, throws down his paper and uncorks an explosion of laughter — like a brisk ritornello to his little song of deceit — in admiration of the device he had set afoot.

"That will teach you, old short-and-fat," growls the hypocrite Josiah, with a wag of his mustard-spoon toward the door. "Yes, yes, yes. That will teach *you*, sir!"

CHAPTER VIII

Gods Float in the Azure Air

HAVING lately encountered the name of Samson Icks whirling its way through the mind of Lawyer Winch as that legal light sat perspiring in the chop-house, it is time we renewed our acquaintance with the dapper gentleman in pinstripes — the elusive agent of Messrs Badger and Winch, Cobb's Court — the big, big man for the big, big job — namely, with Mr. Samson Icks himself, whole, hardy, and in the flesh. Accordingly I shift the scene now far to the south, along the old fell trail, and so begin drawing the disparate threads of my story together. The time I know is short and my story long, and I fear some of you may hasten off ere I finish it; but I urge you — stay a while! Fortify yourselves with the cordials upon the board, and listen a few hours more to my tale of old Salthead, remembering always that every word of it is true.

The day was gliding swiftly by. The heavens were clear and blue, and the distant surrounding country in all its manifestations — its folded hills, its undulating meadows, its trickling streams, its breathtaking vistas — served to captivate the eye. In short the weather was fine, albeit cool; all nature seemed to be enjoying one final brief "*Huzza!*" before the irrevocable decay into winter. But though the countryside certainly provided some spectacular views, no such view could compare, in *my* view, to the spectacle of the mastodon train as it surged and thundered down the road.

At the head rode Samson Icks in his black traveling-clothes, his black hat upon his head and his smoked lenses upon his eyes, jogging his horse forward, with Cast-iron Billy, very grim-eyed and watchful, riding at his side. Each of them held aloft a tall wooden pole, or flutter-stick. These devices, with their bright red pennants flying high above, were anchored to the horses' saddles by a series of leather rings, from which they could be released quickly in an emergency. Marching behind came the thunder-beasts — their bodies swaying, their shaggy heads nodding, their massive limbs pound, pound, pounding the earth like a solemn drum-beat upon the land. Despite the monotony of the trip, the soft brown eyes of the animals remained marvelously alert; for the mastodon is a wary creature, and relies as much on its wits as on its great size for its survival.

The grizzled Billy, with his eyes like steel and his jaw like stone, glanced over his shoulder to assure himself for the moment that all was right. Farther back, beside the lead bull, rode a youthful figure on a coal-black mare. He was a trimly built young gentleman, with faint pencil mustaches and tight, eager little eyes. Billy cast his eyes with peevish sullenness upon this youngster — Mr. Joseph Rooke, with whom he had already had sharp words, on more than one occasion, since the start of the journey — and broke into mutterings.

Billy didn't approve of Mr. Rooke. Billy didn't approve of anybody who was young, for he considered all young things to be empty vessels devoid of knowledge, sense, and judgment. Such infants he treated with a mix of humor and derision. In his mind the young hothead riding beside the bull was a know-it-all and a smarty-pants, and that was that; nothing more to be said. Mr. Rooke, having felt the sting of Billy's animosity before, no doubt returned these feelings in kind. So Mr. Rooke remained a little back of the two leaders, moody and self-absorbed, intent only upon performing his duties — it was Icks, after all, to whom he owed allegiance, not the prejudiced Billy — and collecting his coin, before heading off on his own business until the next call for his services went out.

Behind the train rolled the transport van, driven by long Lew Pilcher, with his white side-whiskers streaming from beneath his hat-brim. Mr. Pilcher had an air of self-satisfaction about him always, which was particularly evident now that they were on the road. In the van were their provisions for the journey, together with various items of equipage scavenged from the mastodon camp for delivery at Crow's-end. The remainder of the movables left behind by Mr. Hoakum — such as the passenger cabs, cord-ladders, freight platforms and the like — would be sold as scrap, for hardly anyone had use for such things any more.

"I say it again, it's not our lookout," grumbled Billy, moving his horse closer to that of Samson Icks, the better to facilitate communcation between the two gentlemen without being overheard by Mr. Rooke. "I say it's his last job with us. He leaves us at Crow's-end, at Strangeways, when the beasts are delivered. Jettison him there, I say, and it's good business. He's a damned trouble-maker and don't fit with the rest of us."

The smoked lenses of Mr. Icks kept to the road ahead, but the ear of Mr. Icks inclined itself toward Billy, out of respect for that grizzled gentleman's valued opinion.

"Now, then, William," returned Mr. Icks, in tones of conciliation, "ye'd not like to see the young rascal there come to a bad patch, would ye? He's a restless young cove, that's true, but wery devoted to his craft. He's a perfectionist, that's what he is, and he don't like his devotion questioned — that ye can be sure on. In my studied opinion his resistance to the imposition of authority is wery high. I seen it before. So ye'll need to get along with him for just a while longer, at least till we're in tight at Strangeways."

"There ain't no joking with a young pup like that one. He's got no common sense and no feelings. He's a zero, apart from his reflexes, which ain't connected as yet to no brain. He'll threaten you some time, Samson, mark me. He thinks he knows it all and that he ought to be running this show. And him barely twenty-one — the damned insolent young rogue of a pup!" He spat sideways into the air with scornful pride. "Remember what I'm telling you."

"Aye. I understand ye, William, I understand. It ain't escaped my notice as he's been more than a little sulky on this job."

"Sulky? Hoo! He's more than sulky. He's an ingrate, he is. After all the jobs as you've given him, when nobody else would touch him on account of his reputation. He's got a reputation, you know, and it's not one as I'd be proud of. And him barely twenty-one!"

"Aye, he's a brash young cove, it's true, but he'll learn in time. He's got something in him, ye see. He's got the makings."

"But he's got no heart in him — that's what I'm telling you! There's nothin' in him but a foul temper. He's got no heart, I say, and he's the sort as ain't likely to get none — with his history he's not bound to live long enough!"

"Ye needn't judge him so harsh. He's a useful individual, as has proved himself on several occasions. Ye'll recollect wery well the nasty incident with them two rascals, Tinsley and Graff, at King's Bottom. Ye need the young blood every now and then, William — it's handy to have him in the party. He ain't much more trouble than most other rascals his age and occupation."

Cast-iron Billy shook his head, and with a growl of disgust tossed his eyes into the middle distance, as if he were forever through trying to convince Samson Icks of anything in this world.

They rode on in silence for a time. Silence it was only with respect to conversation, for there were plenty of sounds to attract the ear — the rattle of harness and the clink of horses' shoes — the jingling of bridle-bits, light and airy — the feathery rustle of the banners high overhead — and from behind the rhythmic boom and crash of the plodding behemoths, firing salvos of expired air from their mouths like jets of steam. Mr. Icks made several comments about the fine weather, which Billy heard but saw no reason to return, for he had pitched himself headlong into one of his moods.

Mr. Samson Icks was a man who was altogether rather pleased with himself at the moment. He had, by his own admission, taken on the big, big job, which had thus far consumed a mighty parcel of his time, and pulled it off. There had been few problems of any consequence. Now they were well on their way to Strangeways — the zoological gardens in the great metropolis of Crow's-end, atop a mighty headland overhanging the coast — there to deliver the beasts to their new keepers. The city was called Crow's-end, Samson believed, because it was so full of crows it was thought all such birds ended up there; though this was probably incorrect. Once, in my youth, I saw at Strangeways a mighty imperial mammoth, more than twenty-five feet at the shoulder, with soaring tusks and a massive, furry head. It perished long ago, and I believe there has not been another since. There are those who claim that tribes of imperial mammoths still roam the vast frozen wastes of the north, far beyond the cities and beyond the reach of man. If there be any truth to this, however, I have not seen it.

All in all, then, Mr. Icks was quite taken with himself at this point in time, and with the progress of his latest assignment; so he looked forward to ample remuneration from the rascals as employed him. At thought of them his eyes narrowed behind his smoked lenses, and he smiled a dry, brittle smile of satisfaction. Without doubt the wheels of his little plot were well in motion by now. Who knew what he might find once the big, big job was over, and he had ridden back into Salthead? It gave him no end of pleasure, the thinking on it. It was in fact the memory of the yellow light in the eyes of a certain young gentleman, that now provided Mr. Icks with a measure of comfort, rather than terror, for he knew the fury in those eyes would soon be directed at a wery different target!

"Why not Busket?" asked Billy, emerging from his black mood and growing conversational once more.

"Busket?" echoed Samson, not sure of his intent in mentioning their diminutive companion from the Cutting Duck — the gentleman with the perpetual smirk and the tankard as large as his head, who was known to say little more than "Yea," by way of agreeing with everything said by most everyone around him.

Billy nodded and thrust out a grizzled chin. "Busket!" he said again, for emphasis.

"Ye mean — Busket for Rooke?"

Another nod, and a sly roll of the eyes like steel.

Mr. Icks looked the countryside round about, as though half-expecting some passing tree or shrub to comment upon this absurd proposal.

"Ye're not serious!"

Billy threw him a wicked grin, followed by a confidential wink. The result of this was an outbreak of chuckling, which gathered momentum by degrees, and which both gentlemen enjoyed immensely; but which Billy concluded with the unfortunate words —

"Hoo! Might as well draft that damned sheep-headed fool!"

This remark appeared to cause Samson a degree of discomfort, for he abruptly broke off his humor. He had an odd feeling, that kind of odd feeling that someone somewhere once had told him was called a conscience. "Ain't that dainty," he murmured, and crushed the feeling at once. It was not in the scheme of Mr. Icks to think of the sheep-headed rascal just now — most certainly not now, in the expansion of his triumph. Everything was going so well, he wanted no clouds to obscure the bright sun of his success.

Poor Samson! It was not to be. At that precise moment something like a physical cloud passed over the mastodon train. Mr. Icks and Billy looked into the sky as the shadow touched them. There they saw the broad, black wings and crimson hood of a teratorn gliding overhead.

"I don't like the look o' that," said Billy, frowning grimly. "It's an evil thing, seeing one o' them creatures. It means there's no damned good to come!"

"What it means is nothin', except to a superstitious mind," returned Samson — who nevertheless watched the teratorn closely as it went drifting off, not a little apprehensive himself, though he chose to cloak his anxiety in dismissive terms. "It ain't got no basis in fact, ye see. They stays away from the city 'cause there ain't nothing there for 'em, o' course. Out here it's wery different. This is their place, so it's wery natural to spy one of 'em on the road."

His companion remained unconvinced. "I say again it's an evil token. Everybody says it!"

Mr. Icks shrugged, and turned his attention elsewhere. The sky was a darker shade of blue now; the party would need to think soon about a place for the night. A wind came up and brushed Samson on the face. The temperature of the air plummeted, growing icy-cold all in a moment, as though a great frigid ocean had washed over him. He searched the heavens with a mystified countenance, expecting to find a wall of rain-clouds or a thunderhead; but all was perfectly clear. He glanced next at Billy, who nodded slowly several times in affirmation that something bad was on the way.

"I haven't any idea what's a-goin' on," said Mr. Icks, "but I knows as it can't be — "

His companion held up a gloved hand as a signal for all to stop. Mr. Icks, unprepared for this, reined in his horse very short and dropped his flutter-stick in sign to Mr. Rooke. That sour-faced young man obediently slowed his horse beside the lead mastodon, tapping the beast's foreleg with his quirt. Gradually the entire train came to a halt, one animal after another pausing in its tracks and so propagating the stoppage down the line, until it reached Mr. Pilcher in the transport van.

"What is it?" asked Mr. Icks, riding in close.

The grizzled veteran appeared to be listening intently. His eyes swept the countryside like a lighthouse beacon.

"What is it?" asked Samson, again. "What do ye hear?"

"What do *you* hear?" countered Billy, hoarsely.

"Nothing."

"Are you sure?"

"Aye."

"Then listen!"

At first there was nothing but the rustle of Billy's flutter-stick in the air overhead. With one hand steadying the pole and the other on his cutlass, Billy and his eyes of steel scanned the distant landscape, searching, searching.

Mr. Icks himself peered through his smoked lenses at the far-off purple hills. Undulating purple hills, very drowsy and pleasant under the afternoon sky, but a little melancholy and perhaps menacing now as well.

"There!" cried Billy, straightening in his saddle. "Do you hear it?"

Samson heard it — the distant sound of laughter, deep and hollow, mocking and arrogant, rising from the hills and spreading everywhere like a contagion, yet coming from no one place in particular.

"Aye," said Mr. Icks, in a hard whisper. His face solidified into one single red brick. "I hear it plain. Where is the rascal?"

"Don't know. He's all over the damned place!"

"Who is he? I don't see no one. There ain't no one there."

"It's the very devil," declared Billy, under his breath.

"It's wery unusual," said Mr. Icks. "It's some rascal what is having a bit o' fun. That's it."

"That's not it. That's not anywheres close to it!"

They listened again, but this time there was nothing; the purple hills spoke to them no more. Samson Icks glanced at the lead mastodon, who before this had been content with his plodding lot, but who was now quite clearly anxious and on edge. The bull repeatedly stamped his feet and bobbed his head up and down, making abortive roaring noises in his throat. Similar signs were being exhibited by other members of the train — signs that, to Mr. Icks, appeared to support Billy's hypothesis more than his own.

"Hoo! Lord love 'em, they're spooked. They can sense it!" exclaimed Billy.

"Nothing ruffles the stock," said Mr. Icks, noting a restiveness now as well in his own horse. "What can it be, as worries 'em such?"

But neither he nor his grizzled companion had any solution to the problem, unless —

"You know the thing in Salthead?" asked Billy, his eyes still hunting about the landscape.

"What thing in Salthead?"

"The sailor. The one as we spotted dancing like a madman in the street, as Balliol shook his fist at."

"Aye."

"When that fellow what they took in at the Blue Pelican — the cat's-meat man — recovered his wits, he told 'em he heard `proud laughter' in the dead o' night, just after he run into that sailor. He told 'em the laughter rose up out o' the fog like a voice from hell. Like the very devil! And there were others astir at that hour as heard it too."

"I recollect some talk about that," said Mr. Icks, uncomfortable with the general idea of anything rising out of the infernal regions. "Talk, it was. Wild talk."

"And there were teratorns seen in town. Teratorns in Salthead! It's them that's behind it. It's the call of evil, that's what it is."

"It ain't nobody a-callin'," said Samson, persisting in a vain attempt to deny his true feelings, which were remarkably similar to Billy's. He was, after all, the leader of this enterprise. He was the big, big man on the big, big job. He couldn't be seen as anything less than masterful and in full command of the situation. "What it is," he decided at length, by way of compromise, "is the weather. Aye! The weather. A wery unusual phenomenon."

With this quaint diagnosis — which of course flew in the face of his own belief — Mr. Icks appeared outwardly content, and so raised his flutter-stick and motioned the train forward. Talk of devils did little for his inner composure, however; so little that the yellow light in the eyes of Mr. John Hunter — so lately subdued, at least in theory — began to torment him once more.

They continued on their way, though at not nearly the same efficient pace as before. The trepidation of the lead bull was infectious. Many of the animals now were rearing and jibbing like unruly horses. Trumpet-roars were sounded — loud, plaintive wails, saying please, please, don't make us go on. Others shied this way and that, seemingly intent on disrupting the flow of the cavalcade. Whether it was the cold, or the ill-omened bird, or the mysterious laughter, or something else that only they could detect, it was becoming more and more difficult to maintain order.

Young Mr. Rooke, racing his horse madly here and there in his efforts to maintain order, grew frustrated with the stubbornness of his charges. His temper, always near the point of boiling, was threatening to bubble over. Having pinpointed the lead bull as the chief instigator of the rebellion, he galloped squarely toward that animal, quirt in hand.

"Hey! Walk on, you!" he cried out, angrily. "Walk on! Walk on, I say!"

Instead of complying the mastodon redoubled his resistance, in direct proportion to the vehemence of the commands from Mr. Rooke. Like Cast-iron Billy the animal seemed to have little use for the foolish youngster with the pencil mustaches.

"Walk on, I say!" snarled Mr. Rooke, lashing out heatedly with his quirt. He struck the bull upon the face and shoulder. The mastodon uttered a loud roar and veered to the edge of the road, where it came to a dead stop, halting the forward progress of the train.

Cast-iron Billy, observing this latest activity on the part of Mr. Rooke, turned to the big, big man.

"There's your Joseph!" he harrumphed, with a jerk of his head toward the aforementioned insolent young rogue of a pup.

"Pardon old Icks for makin' so free, but he ain't my Joseph, as ye choose to word it," replied Samson.

Both riders reined in their horses. Mr. Icks had a premonition that something distasteful was about to occur that he was powerless to avert.

"He ain't?" cried Billy. "You took him on, didn't you? You and them damned lawyers — them Badgers and Winches!"

"Aye," murmured Mr. Icks, conceding this rather inarguable point. "I did, that's sure."

Mr. Rooke became ever more impatient as the lead bull refused to submit. He dealt it another blow with his quirt, this time on the flat of the ear, and then another, leaving the mastodon shuddering at the sting.

"Walk on, you brute!" cried Mr. Rooke, with a peremptory wave of his hand. He was about to deliver another gentle reproof when the bull spun round and lunged for him.

It was only by the hairs of his pencil mustaches that Mr. Rooke evaded the animal's tusks — so long, so broad, so sharp — as those mighty weapons came flying past his head. Somehow he was able to dodge them, whipping his horse aside and avoiding what in all likelihood would have been an outcome incompatible with life.

The rush of air from the mighty weapons was still hurtling by when the flood from his beating heart reached his brain. Enraged, the young hoodlum stood up in the stirrups and struck the mastodon upon the face repeatedly with his quirt. The creature recoiled in pain, crying out as blood spurted from the delicate tissues of the eye and ear.

"Walk on, you stinking, disgusting creature! Walk on, I say! All of you! Stir your stumps!"

Cast-iron Billy, who in a short time had grown very fond of the beasts, and who as we know was not fond at all of Mr. Rooke, had seen and heard enough. Without pausing to consult Samson Icks, he wheeled his horse around and rushed to the scene, dropping his flutter-stick on the way. He leaped from the saddle and strode with cold decision toward the black mare and her rider.

"Climb down off that mount," he said, slowly and emphatically, his grizzled face flushed with emotion. He jabbed the air once or twice with a angry forefinger to indicate the ground at the mare's feet. "I'm telling you now. Get down here!"

The tight little eyes of Mr. Rooke glowered fiercely from on high. Calmly he kneaded his quirt, as though having half a mind to use it on something else he now found stinking and disgusting.

"You don't talk that way to me — *old fool*," said he, in a voice charged with menace. "You ain't Icks."

"Ye'll climb down off yer horse now, just as he says," obliged Samson, riding up, with a look of shrewd inflexibility behind his smoked lenses. "Ye'll do that for old Icks — won't ye, Joseph?"

"Why should I?" demanded that impudent young man.

"Because I can't knock the daylights out of you while you're a-sittin' up *there!*" roared Billy, with an impatient flourish of his balled fists. He then proceeded to give Mr. Rooke more than a lick or two with the rough side of his tongue, in words which I simply cannot repeat here.

Mr. Rooke, uncertain how to receive this tirade given the participation of Mr. Icks in the attempted dethroning, laughed coolly under his breath.

"You've got it in for me," he said. "You've always had it in for me. Joe Rooke is the one as works the hardest on this job, and takes the punches, and gives it his all, and for that you've got it in for him. For that you give him the go-by. So that's how it stands!"

"That's how it bloody stands!" returned Billy, scarcely able to restrain himself. "Now climb down off that damned mare or I'll peel you off!"

Having determined that a serious defense of his honor was called for, Mr. Rooke swaggeringly dismounted. He turned to face his challenger, one hand on the hilt of his rapier and the other grasping his quirt.

"You'll not treat the creature so," said Billy. "You're more the coward for it. It's not the fault of the animal. Can't you see he's spooked? You'll not treat a damned cur that way, let alone a great thunder-beast."

"I treat 'em any way I like — which is the same way I treat you, old idiot," replied the vengeful Mr. Rooke, who suddenly drew his rapier and stormed in upon Billy. His tight little eyes, so intent upon their target and running it through with the point of his sword, failed to observe the point of the old idiot's boot. As he drove the rapier straight at the body of Billy, that body turned swiftly aside like a lever. The legs of Mr. Rooke dropped out from under him; hat, rapier and quirt all went flying. Billy, chuckling quietly to himself in that way I well remember, snatched up the fallen hero's arsenal as a brittle smile overspread the face of Mr. Icks.

"Joseph," said Samson, viewing his young assistant sprawled so inelegantly upon the ground. "Stand up, Joseph, will ye. Mind, ye'll not be damaging the movables, please. The stock is to be delivered up at Strangeways in prime condition; it's a stipulation o' the contract, ye see. Aye, I'll not have 'em damaged, and so ye'll not be a-rappin' on 'em that way again, sir — not while you're employed by old Icks and this enterprise. Now, we'll have no more outbursts from ye today, will we?"

"Maybe I ain't employed by this enterprise no longer!" growled Mr. Rooke, as he stood and brushed the dirt from his cheeks and clothing. "What's more, I know I ain't. This enterprise is a damned joke. Everybody in Salthead knows it. Everybody in Salthead knows as it's run by a bungler and a dodge. I'm telling you — Joe Rooke won't take water from the likes o' such, he won't. He quits this job, and good riddance to it!"

"That's wery thoughtful of ye. If ye take yer leave," warned an abruptly indignant Samson — his minion having turned on him now, just as Billy had predicted — "it's the last time I'll have anything to do with ye. And old Icks is nearly the only cove in Salthead what will, ye know."

Mr. Rooke retrieved his hat and slammed it down upon his youthful head, like a lid on a simmering hot-plate.

"You've always been against me," he sneered. "You've always been against me, you have, the both of you. I never asked for nothing and I never did nothing to you. I never complained. I just did my job, better than any other cove ever could. You resent it now just 'cause Joe Rooke is the best there is. Well, if that ain't good enough for you, then you ain't good enough for Joe Rooke."

Having delivered this humble testimonial to himself, Mr. Rooke marched up to his horse. A very grim-eyed Billy handed him his rapier and quirt — a very courageous Billy, I might point out, considering the state of Mr. Rooke's mind and body at that moment. But Billy knew his man, or boy; and so the rapier was sheathed and the quirt taken up, as the youthful warrior sprang upon the mare.

"Joe Rooke'll trouble you no more," said he, by way of farewell. "He hates you. He hates the lot of you, he does."

This was apparently intended as a sort of general indictment, implying hatred of Samson Icks, and Billy, and probably Lew Pilcher (if he'd been there, rather than in the transport van), and the stinking, disgusting beasts, and the very ground under their feet, and the distant purple hills, and the sky overhead. He was a very equitable young gentleman, one who hated everything and everyone in equal measure.

So Mr. Rooke went riding off, disdainful of all he surveyed, with his tight little eyes turned toward the north and Salthead town.

"Hoo! Modest Joe Rooke. Ain't that a rarity," remarked Billy, hitching up his mouth in a sarcastic leer. "He's not our look-out. It'll be damned easier without him."

Mr. Icks, now that the gravity of the situation had struck home, bethought himself what the shortage of one man would mean now to the handling of the stock, and thus the success of the entire enterprise. The hardy red bricks of his complexion paled momentarily, as the vision of yet another botched job rose up before his smoked lenses. How would they manage it now? The beasts were nervous and he didn't know why, and so he didn't know what to do about it. Despite Billy's assurances it would be no easy task driving the train with two men rather than three. He expressed this concern to his hard-featured companion, who scoffingly waved it aside with a flick of his hand.

"I'll ride guard," said Billy, leaping onto his horse. He raised his flutter-stick and fell back to take up Mr. Rooke's position beside the lead bull, who acknowledged his presence by nodding and pawing the ground a time or two with a huge forefoot. "You see? The beasts know me — they'll not linger now. Why, I'll venture it was Joe Rooke they was skittish of all along."

Mr. Icks, fervently wishing that this might be so, wasn't so sure — neither was Billy — but said nothing about it. He urged his horse forward, and to his surprise and delight discovered that the lead mastodon, with Billy at his side, walked on without hesitation. A ray of comfort darted across his face; perhaps, thought Samson, things were not so wery bad after all. The vision of the botched job had been just slightly premature.

With this auspicious beginning they took up the journey where they had left it off. Despite the valiant efforts of Billy, however, the animals in the train remained skittish. The grizzled veteran tried calming their anxiety by speaking to them in soothing tones, patting them, reassuring them, resorting at one point even to song; but as this latter exercise seemed to frighten more than it reassured, he quickly abandoned it.

They came to a turning past which the road widened, and emerged at length into a broad, roughly circular basin, well-watered, with clumps of gorse and loose rough shrubbery, a scattering of red and golden grasses, and numerous fragrant patches of wild onion. It was framed on the left by an irregular wall of limestone that stood glowing in the amber light. On the right was a steeply sloping hill, beyond which the sun lay crouched on a distant ridge. It was in the main a thinly-wooded country, overhung by a loneliness that seemed to pervade every nook and prospect.

Mr. Icks signed for the train to stop, believing in this secluded valley to have found the ideal camp for the night, ideal both for safety and for guarding the stock. Ideal, that is, apart from the cold, which it seemed was greatly intensified here. He was on the point of dismounting when he heard a peal of laughter, very faint at first, but rising quickly in volume as it rebounded from the wall of limestone. The lead bull raised his head and uttered surely as strange and haunted a sound as has ever escaped a mastodon's throat.

Mr. Lew Pilcher, having rightly interpreted the occasion for the stoppage, had driven the transport van to the head of the train and was climbing down from his perch, as Samson Icks and Billy dropped from their horses.

"Sich ludiocrity!" exclaimed Mr. Pilcher — in that single concise phrase combining his delayed response to the departure of Mr. Rooke and his reaction to the unearthly phenomenon that surrounded them.

"Where's it a-comin' from?" demanded Mr. Icks, shivering, with his hands thrust deep into his pockets and his smoked lenses searching the distance.

"There!" cried Billy, pointing.

Mr. Icks peered in the direction indicated — toward the top of the sloping hill, where he saw something black standing out against the sunset. It looked to be a monument of some kind, planted by persons unknown in this solitary spot — a spot where it was very unlikely to be disturbed, as the old fell trail was but little used now. A monument, aye, thought Samson, but to what? And for what purpose?

"Why, it's a statue," declared Mr. Pilcher, with a lazy nod. "That's what it is. It's a statue — all the ways out here, where there ain't nobody to see it. Who'd set a thing like that up? Not much brain there, nohap. Sich ridiculosity!"

"There's some bloody daft rascal up there, hiding out behind it," asserted Billy, clenching his fist. "It's him what's been laughin' such!"

"And so what would he be doing up there? Explain that. Must be an idiot."

"And why would he be a-laughin' at us?" said Mr. Icks, thoroughly at a loss. He could not believe what his ears heard, or what his eyes saw through the smoked lenses. "It ain't sensible. It ain't logical. Who is the rascal? What's his name?"

Mr. Pilcher scratched his white whiskers and shook his head.

"Let's have a look!" said Billy, drawing his cutlass. "Lew — stay where you be and keep a watch on the beasts."

"Aye," said Mr. Icks. "And see that ye keep yer wits about ye."

Mr. Pilcher smiled amiably at this, standing with arms folded and eyes crinkling as his two companions began their ascent.

The sun was sinking below the distant ridge. As he and Billy picked their way up the hillside, Mr. Icks found himself reflecting upon the peculiarity of their situation. Something was telling him that things were not quite right here. It wasn't sensible, after all. He had the uncomfortable feeling that what he and Billy were engaged upon was not a good idea, yet for some reason he chose not to stop. Everything had been going so well; everybody had been a-powdering away so tight. Then came the fierce cold and the proud laughter, the trouble with the stock, the rebellion of Mr. Rooke. And now this! What sort of rascal, he wondered, would put up a monument in this somber place? And why hide behind it?

The cold was even more powerful at the top of the hill. If he hadn't thought it ridiculous Mr. Icks might have concluded that the cold was emanating from the monument itself. The thing had all the appearances of a statue, despite its unusual blue color. As they moved closer they could see it was made neither of stone nor metal, nor of anything else they could identify, although a certain resemblance to leather came to mind. Neither could they understand what it was intended to depict. It looked to be a sort of headless bird, the entire figure swathed in a pair of huge wings folded over. Of feet there were two — ugly vulture's feet, their wicked sharp talons resting directly on the ground in lieu of a plinth or pedestal.

"What in damnation is it?" asked Cast-iron Billy, staring the thing up and down with his jaw thrust out.

Mr. Icks had no answer, and communicated this fact with a roll of his head. He decided then and there that the direct approach might be best.

"Hallo!" he cried out, to whomever lay concealed behind the monument. "Hallo! What do ye mean, friend, by affrighting the stock?"

"And what is it you find so damned laughable, you great goose?" chimed in Billy, flourishing his cutlass.

There was no response to these pleasant overtures. The wiry Samson was examining again the form and outline of the statue, or whatever it was, with a thoughtful expression, when from below came a shout of inquiry from Mr. Pilcher.

"Is it animal, vegetable, or mineral?" called that gentleman, with a lazy grin splitting his face.

"It's none o' that lot!" returned Billy.

Mr. Icks, determined to bring the business to a conclusion, crept boldly forward and behind the statue, and there pounced upon — thin cold air. He made a complete circuit of the monument, which was more than twice the size of any normal human person, and reappeared on the opposite side, where he stood gazing at Billy, perplexed and grim-faced.

"No rascals here," said Samson, thrusting his hands into his pockets. He looked behind him, he looked at the ground, he looked round behind the statue, but still he could find no rascals. "Ain't that dainty."

Here it was that Billy — in a less combative mood now that the threat of conflict had evaporated — sheathed his cutlass and pulled out his flint, in preparation for lighting his pipe. After inspecting the dottle he struck a light and applied the glowing flame to the bowl.

This innocent action, otherwise unremarkable, the monument appeared to find of some interest. The leathery wings parted slowly and a blue head lifted above them. This head had two human eyes in it, which opened now and looked down upon the gentlemen with a dark and frightful aspect. The monument had also a human brow, and a human chin with a human beard, and a mighty human chest, over which a sleeveless tunic was draped, and great muscled arms and hands; but there all humanness ended. In place of a human nose there was a vulture's beak, sharp and curving. In place of human ears it had the ears of an ass; in place of human hair the top of its head wriggled and squirmed with a confusion of vipers. Round one muscular arm was a coiled serpent, which glared for a second at the two very surprised gentlemen before opening its jaws and hissing in their direction.

Mr. Icks and Billy fell to their knees in speechless wonder. The blue monster threw back its head and discharged a sample of the mocking laughter they had heard rising from the purple hills.

Not waiting to hear the laughter again — or to discover what shocking words might follow — the two gentlemen beat a hasty retreat to the foot of the hill, and together with an equally astonished Mr. Pilcher made a dash for the horses. Glancing across his shoulder as he ran, Mr. Icks saw the blue being vault into the air, then heard the leathery swish of wings as it came sailing overhead.

Like some nightmarish bird of prey it swooped down upon the mastodon train, cackling and gesticulating. A mad scramble of horses and thunder-beasts ensued, with the monster describing circles in the air while taunting the animals with its arrogant laughter. The mastodons, in a frenzy of panic, scattered in all directions. Even the lifeless transport van managed to escape, as the horses harnessed to it galloped for the old fell trail. Mr. Icks and his companions saw it all but could do nothing except run for their lives.

The serpent coiled round the monster's arm lifted its head. From the gaping jaws came a bolt of yellow flame, which struck the ground at the feet of the stampeding mastodons. Two, three, four times liquid fire poured from the serpent's mouth; each time great cratered pockets opened up in the earth where the bolts came down. At each hit the winged apparition roared out a stream of triumphal words in a language neither Mr. Icks nor his companions could understand.

It required but another few moments for the animals to disappear, vanishing one by one among the cracks and fissures of the landscape. Soon neither mastodon nor horse remained for man to claim.

The monster made one final circle about Mr. Icks and his party — all of whom were cowering now behind a rather substantial boulder — before it flew off into the sky. As it went, so too went the great piercing cold that enveloped it.

At least ten minutes of the clock ticked by — ten silent and uneventful minutes — before Mr. Icks, and Mr. Pilcher, and Cast-iron Billy, after consulting one another by means of various grim looks and nods, thought it safe to venture forth from their refuge. This they did, and so took stock of their situation. Nearly dusk, in the midst of a wilderness, with virtually nothing — no horses, no thunder-beasts, not even the transport van, which had carried all their provisions. Nothing left but the very clothes they wore, and the two flutter-sticks, both of which had been trodden on by the beasts as they fled.

It was no less than complete defeat for Mr. Samson Icks. Disaster. A total botch, a fiasco. An utter rout. He stood and revolved these concepts in his mind, looking at them from all sides, trying to extract what brighter shades of black he could from them, while gazing upon the empty landscape through his smoked lenses and wondering what there was to be done now. It had all been going so well, he heard himself repeating, all going so well. It was all too good to last. He knew it, he knew it. Something had to happen to deprive him of his victory, and it did, and he knew it.

Cast-iron Billy, having miraculously retained possession of his pipe, now clamped that object firmly between his teeth and glared a single full look upon his two companions. He was conscious of some small measure of complicity in all of this — he and his pipe — and so quite naturally reacted to it by assigning the blame elsewhere.

"Bad!" he growled, with a stab of his finger toward Samson Icks. "I warned you — that teratorn was a *damned bad token!*"

Taking his lead from Billy, Mr. Pilcher lighted his own pipe and so took up his usual stance, clucking his tongue in comment upon the ludiocrity of the situation.

What to do now? Plainly the first order of business was to retrieve the horses. And if they managed to accomplish this, what then of the beasts? How to recapture the mastodons and reassemble the train? It was true, the herd instinct of the beasts might bring them together on their own. But Billy, knowing the minds of such creatures from his experience among the shovel-tuskers, could not discount the possibility that the entire herd might set course for home.

And so how might the gentlemen themselves reach that distant and now longed-for seat of paradise — *home?* And what to do, asked Mr. Icks of himself — what to do, once arrived there? How to present the situation to his ponderous overlord, Mr. Jasper Winch? And what of the response of the tall nasty rascal? Perhaps the seat of paradise might not be the most hospitable abode for Mr. Samson Icks at the moment. Might it not be better to fade from view for a time — to vanish amid the wilderness, like the beasts? Simply drop off the edge of the earth (or the trail) so that none might know what had transpired? The delivery at Crow's-end simply would not be made — there would be no trace of men or beasts — some catastrophe would be assumed — the transaction would be nullified. How then could the rascals in Salthead exert their wrath, if the object of that wrath were unavailable to be exerted upon?

And what of the flying man, and the serpent, and the bolts of yellow flame? What hell had *these* things come out of? How to explain them, and set them clear in one's mind? They clouded the brick-red complexion of Mr. Icks like nothing else could, for they came from a world completely outside his own — a world which, like this one, probably belonged to rascals too.

All in all it might be necessary for Mr. Icks to keep well-earthed for a time, at least until the state of affairs could be more objectively appraised. But first he and his companions would need to locate the horses, which was something they couldn't do in the dark, so the thing to do now was to find shelter for the night. This they soon discovered in the form of a narrow opening — a small cave — some few dozen feet off the ground, in the wall of limestone on the farther side of the valley.

The sun went down in a halo of purple light. They built a fire for warmth, using the remains of the flutter-sticks, and conversed in low tones while they smoked out their pipes. Then Billy and Mr. Pilcher lay down upon their stony cots, and were instantly asleep — for they had few worries to speak of, such men as they, such lucky men. The mill of anxious thought ground no corn in that quarter.

But Mr. Icks remained awake for many hours, standing at the entrance to the cave with his back to the fire and his hands in his pockets, and the scent of wild onions in his nostrils, while he pondered the moonlit landscape, and the vicissitudes of circumstance, and the parlous state of his own fortunes, with a new devil — and this a very real one — haunting his cranium.

CHAPTER IX

Chance Encounters

"AND there she lies," said Mary Clinch, head chambermaid of the Blue Pelican, "riding in the harbor without a soul aboard, and a right shocking hole in her timbers!"

"It's a mystery," admitted her companion, with a solemn nod. Miss Bridget Leek was that companion — she of the golden hair and eyes of afternoon blue — hurrying there beside Mary at the edge of the busy street.

"It's wicked. It's the work of the Foul Fiend — that's what the rector says. It's plain to see, too. What honest explanation can there be for it, I ask?"

Her friend shook her pretty head, and shifted the bundle in her arms — three dressed pullets from the butcher's, destined for the Pelican's kitchen.

"La, there's no honest explanation in the wide world."

"Which does remind me," said Mary, rearranging her own unwieldy burden — two more pullets, and a few other necessaries gathered along the way — "as the rector told us Sunday last, if there was any good behind the thing, any good at all, it would've shown itself by now. Instead, there she floats on the water like a dead bird — like this pullet here! A blasted hulk, giving no sign to Christian souls as to her purpose or intention. It's right plain it's wicked work."

"It's a very hard thing to understand," said Bridget. "I do wish it weren't all so difficult."

These two young maidens of the Pelican, trotting side by side down a busy thoroughfare near the river, did not trot alone, but were hastening to keep pace with the very tall and very angular woman — a woman with narrow beams of spectacles framing her pale eyes, and a quantity of starched white hair drawn together in a knot at the back of her head, like a hornet's nest — who was sailing majestically before them.

"The Miss," said Mary, confidentially — by which she meant Miss Honeywood, whose wake they were navigating — "she ain't said a word about it, nor about the dancing sailor, nor the poor crippled child. Think of it — a ghost at the Pelican! She ain't said nothing at all. I think she knows more than she's telling, but she's a-keepin' it to herself."

"What was that, Mary Clinch?" said the commanding voice of Miss Honeywood. The mistress of the Pelican wheeled to face her minions, arresting their progress along the street. "What are you babbling about, girl?"

"Begging your pardon — nothing as is of any importance, Miss!" replied Mary, clutching her pullets tremblingly to her breast. "I was saying only to Bridget — telling her, as regards the dead ship in the harbor, how the rector said it's right bad work — evil work — and how the Foul Fiend is a-keepin' watch on it — I know it — "

"Now then, Mary," returned Miss Honeywood, sharply. "You'll not be filling Bridget's head with such ideas. The Foul Fiend may have his mischiefs, but lifting a ship from the bottom of the ocean is not one of them. There is an explanation for what has occurred. There is always an explanation. Not to worry — the answer will be found out in time. There's no doubt in my mind whatsoever."

"Yes, Miss!"

"Bridget — you will pay no heed, none whatsoever, to what Mary Clinch has told you of this matter. She knows nothing of it. Do you hear that, Bridget?"

"Yes, Miss," acquiesced that maiden.

"You will keep your own counsel. And you will both see to it that you do not run about spreading unsubstantiated gossip. I tell you, tongues will keep going like bells on a sheep-walk. Do you hear?"

"Yes, Miss!" was the combined reply.

"Good. End of conversation."

So they continued on their way, the two servant-girls with their burdens of poultry, trailing behind the majestic figure of Miss Moll. All about them was noise and bustle — the noise and bustle of one of the liveliest thoroughfares in the neighborhood of the docks, over which a cold haze that was not quite a fog had drifted in from the river. On they went, past the shop-fronts of the fishmongers, of the nautical instrument-makers, the marine-store dealers, the wholesale chemists and druggists. Past the taverns and oyster saloons, the tea rooms and gin-sellers' establishments, the pawnshops, the shabby boarding-houses and sailors' inns, the outfitting warehouses. All about them thronged the denizens of the waterside — pilots and skippers, common merchant sailors, half-pay officers; shipwrights and sailmakers, bargees and watermen; fish porters with their fantastic headgear; rag-merchants, carriers, and cheap jacks; a muffin man, ringing his bell — all jostling one another on either side of the muddy street, while the street itself rang with the cracking of whips and the jingle of harness, the rattle and slosh of cabs and coaches, the growl of wagons and transport vans, and the occasional thunder of a passing omnibus.

"Begging your pardon again, Miss," said Mary Clinch, taking up the subject after a lapse of a few minutes — for Mary was always uncomfortable with long stretches of silence, even in a noisy thoroughfare — "but what I was telling Bridget was that there's right little reason for it all. The dead sailor, you know, and — and the poor young child in Sally's room. And the others as have since appeared, like the head of the convict as was impaled on the iron spike atop Dinger's gate. Ain't there just a wee bit more you can tell us about such things, Miss?"

"End of conversation, Mary Clinch. I know no more than what I see in the *Gazette*. And you'll not be infecting Bridget with any of your notions. Bridget Leek!" said Miss Honeywood over her shoulder, without any slackening of pace.

"Yes, Miss?"

"You are an exceptional young woman with a nice brain for thinking, and I am most gratified by your performance thus far. See that you keep it up. I repeat, pay no attention to what Mary Clinch there has to say about these matters. She knows nothing of them and neither do I. We must allow the magistrates and the harbor-master and the other authorities to manage the situation — it's their job. Please see that you adhere to this instruction."

"Yes, Miss," replied Bridget, with a sidelong glance at Mary. "I shall, Miss."

"Good. End of conversation."

So on they went apace.

"To be sure, Miss," ventured Bridget after a time, taking up Mary's line of argument, "these are very mysterious matters. How can a dead person rise up from the grave, but at the Resurrection? That's not to come until the end of the world. Is it the end of the world now, Miss?"

"And how can a dead ship be raised from the ocean, Miss?" chimed in Mary, unable to restrain herself. "Who else could do such a wicked thing but the Foul Fiend?"

"They say it's the dancing sailor's ship — the *Swan* — the ship he was serving on, as went down in the terrible storm."

"And the poor little lame boy. A ghost at the Pelican! It's got me all a-tremble, Miss. Ain't you afeared of it? I'm right shy now to go anywhere near Sally's room. It's accursed. How can she sleep there?"

"Yes, Miss, how? I know I couldn't."

"And what of Dinger's gate, Miss?"

Despite the incessant chattering of her minions, mention again of these phenomena left Miss Honeywood oddly silent. For once she offered no reprimand. They pressed on in silence, weaving their way among the passing throng and endeavoring to avoid a tumble into the busy street.

A tall giant of a man with a long face and a mammoth pair of mustaches, and with a flaring red handkerchief tied round his brow, backed himself out of a doorway, still in the midst of a spirited discussion with some unseen person within. As Miss Moll and her minions hurried by, he turned and glared at them with black burning eyes that threatened at any moment to leap from his head.

"COOKS!" he exclaimed, in a very loud key, as though the object of this outburst were self-explanatory. "BLOODY DAMNED COOKS!"

Mary turned at once to Bridget, who promptly turned to Mary; both threw looks of protest at the staring man, to deny that either of them had ever gone by the name or occupation of cook.

"Gervaise Balliol," said Miss Honeywood, placing hands on angular hips. "You'll be complaining about your cooks for as long as you live. Every honest soul knows it's all in your head. It's a habit with you."

The landlord of the Cutting Duck burst into an hysteric laugh. "AYE, THEY'LL BE THE BREAKIN' OF ME!" he roared. The vessels in his neck bulged; his black eyes searched the street with distrust and suspicion. "BETRAYAL. BLACK TREASON. THE BLOODY ROGUES WOULD HAVE ME SCRAGGED IF THEY COULD. ME, GERVAISE BALLIOL, HIM AS EMPLOYS 'EM AND GIVES 'EM THEIR SUSTENANCE. BLOODY INGRATES!"

"Stow the gammon, Gervaise. Out of the way there, double-quick!" returned Miss Moll, all starch and frost. "Most likely your cooks have missed you by now. You'd best be returning to that drafty house of yours on the hill."

"AYE, IT'S BLOODY LIKELY," allowed Mr. Balliol. "THERE'S LITTLE ANY OF 'EM WILL DO UNLESS GERVAISE BALLIOL IS THERE, ALWAYS PUSHING, PUSHING, PUSHING AT THEIR BACKS TO DO IT. WAITERS — DRAWERS — POT-BOYS — AND DAMNED BLOODY COOKS! ALL IT'S COST ME IS THE SWEAT OF ME BLOODY BROW, AND SOON ME LIFE. WELL, IT'S ENOUGH TO MAKE A PERSON MAD!"

"He's already mad — touched in the upper story," whispered Mary Clinch, tapping the side of her head with a forefinger.

"It's tragic," returned Bridget, sympathetically. "He was so normal, once upon a time."

"You're daft, Gervaise, and I don't care twopence about it. Step aside!" With this peremptory command Miss Moll shouldered her way past Mr. Balliol and his mustaches, leaving the landlord of the Cutting Duck bitterly reproving himself for ever having hired cooks in the first place.

"That's the queerest cove," remarked Mary Clinch. "There's folks as say his eyes are a-goin' to jump right out of his head one day, if he's hotted up enough. Likely they'll find the pair of 'em rolling around in the street, gaping and gawking at nothing!"

"He is a very disturbed individual," said Bridget.

"And one you'll want to keep a tight watch on."

"Just as Jack Hilltop?"

"What's that I hear about Mr. Hilltop?" rang out the voice of Miss Moll, clear and sharp as a bell.

"I only was asking about him, Miss," replied Bridget. "Mary told me once I must keep a watch on him if he shows his face at the Pelican. That's the rascal as tried to nick poor Sally's locket. But I've no idea what his face looks like, apart from the spots."

"I'll watch for Mr. Hilltop," Miss Honeywood assured her.

"It ain't likely you'll need to now, Miss," offered Mary, "for Mr. Hilltop was seen leaving Salthead on one of Timson's coaches, Monday morning last."

"How do you know that, girl?"

"Begging your pardon, Miss," said Mary, her cheeks coloring, "but it was Mr. Brittlebank. You'll recollect young Mr. Brittlebank, Miss — him as has been spoony on me these past months — Mr. Frederick Brittlebank, as is booking-clerk at Timson's. It was Fred told me that Mr. Hilltop was on that coach. The same coach as took away the professor and Dr. Dampe."

"And where were they off to?" inquired Bridget, who knew nothing of this.

"To the high moorlands. If we've any luck he's gone forever — Mr. Hilltop, I mean. He's another strange one. It's still a mystery why it is he tried to pinch Sally's locket."

"Now then, Mary Clinch," said Miss Honeywood, "you will understand that Mr. Hilltop has explained his actions — "

"Look there!" exclaimed Bridget, who very nearly lost her pullets in her haste to point out something over the way.

There, on the other side of the street, a tall gaunt figure was striding its bold superior stride through the multitude. Looks of fear and wonder attended this apparition on its progress. The black felt hat and flowing white hair, magnificent black coat with resplendent buttons, very superior red velvet waistcoat, and richly laquered strap-boots were all too familiar to the people of Salthead. As it strode that bold superior stride the multitude about it parted and gave way, miraculously, as though the figure were the incarnation of some unspeakable plague that no one wanted to come near. *Unspeakable* plague in one sense it was, for the name of it was never to be uttered at the Blue Pelican or in the presence of Miss Honeywood, save by Miss Moll herself, pursuant to her own directive.

"Oh, Miss — it's — it's — !" whispered Mary, remembering not to put too fine a point on it.

"It's the tall nasty rascal!" said Bridget, closer to the truth but still within the bounds of propriety. "He's after someone. Look at his eyes, Miss! I do believe he's already got a body singled out. It's a little sport of his — the great ugly maggot!"

By now the two servant-girls and Miss Moll had reversed course, and were following to see who it was had become the latest target in the miser's little game of feints, that congenial pastime which he found so pleasing to inflict at intervals upon the citizenry.

"Why, it's only a babe!" cried Mary, with a hushed intake of breath.

"The nasty rascal is aiming for a child — a little girl!" said Bridget.

"Oh, the poor wee thing!"

Too true! But was it not children that the master of Tusk & Co. found abhorrent above all things in life, and for which he reserved the greatest number of points in his scoring system? Did not the sultan of superiority rejoice in a positively festive manner, whenever some unsuspecting urchin fell victim to his canny leg? Was he not amused to be seen hurtling at full velocity toward some such innocent among the crowd?

Mary Clinch shuddered and with a cry dropped her bundle, for she recognized the tiny figure who was on a course for collision with the towering white-headed potentate.

"It's Miss Littlefield, the professor's niece," she gasped, her heart leaping into her mouth. "Oh, Miss, what's to be done? If that horrid man tumbles her into the street — what with the rush of the traffic — the carriages — the horses — oh, Miss — "

They watched in helpless fascination as the canny Tuskan legs bore down upon the child. Behind Fiona walked her governess; but the eyes of Miss Dale were upon the more mundane hazards of the thoroughfare — the wheels of the

278

passing carts and coaches, the feet of the trotting horses, the press of human flesh immediately around them, anything that might prove a danger to her young charge — and had not yet caught sight of the oncoming Josiah.

"What's there to do?" cried Mary. "He's so quick. There's no stopping him!"

A three-horse omnibus lumbered by just at the moment the striding Josiah closed on his victim, obstructing the view of Miss Moll and her companions. Certain that the child would be driven into the road, Mary Clinch emitted a screech of horror and filled her mouth with fingers. Likewise Bridget clapped hands to face and awaited the outcome, sure as well that it would be very bad.

The horse-bus rumbled past. The outcome came; it was not as they had expected. Far from being run into the street the child was standing her ground, and peering up, up, up at the miser with a most militant expression. Behind her stood Laura, her hands resting protectively on Fiona's shoulders. The townsfolk around them continued moving along — sneaking along, creeping along, slinking along, slouching along, alonging however you will — maintaining their distance from Josiah and wholly indifferent to the fate of the child, afraid only that the sharp falcon-eyes of the miser might at any moment light on *them*.

It was too much for Miss Honeywood.

"Stop! Stop! Stop, I say!" she ordered — in tones of such authority that even Mr. Balliol would have obeyed — and extending her arms in a warning gesture toward the conveyances and the riders on horseback, stepped boldly into the road. "You there! Stop! Out of the way! Let me pass! Stop!"

Amazingly they did stop. An irregular passage opened up in the traffic, and through it marched the proprietor of the Pelican, making her very tall and angular way to the other side of the road. Extreme displeasure was written on her face; already her hands were reaching unconsciously for her spectacles. Seizing the opportunity before the traffic began to move again, Mary and Bridget quickly followed with their pullets.

"Oh, what did I tell you, Bridget!" exclaimed Mary, excitedly. "It's the Miss — there's no one like her!"

Laura's reaction was one of surprise when she saw them. The miser, whose back was to Miss Honeywood and her minions, remained wholly unaware of their approach, caught up as he was in verbal combat with his very tiny but very determined opponent.

"You're a bully," Fiona was heard to say, as the vanguard from the Blue Pelican arrived within earshot. "You're a mean, nasty old man, and ever so ugly."

"I am not old," said the miser.

"Yes, you are. You're *ancient!*"

"And you," said Josiah — bending down from his great height to look the child squarely in the face, with his black brows knotted together in a most threatening fashion — "are a disrespectful little creature who deserves to be punished."

"I'm not frightened of you," replied Fiona, deflecting his menace with her bright eyes. "I know all about you from my friend, Mr. Scribbler. He knows what you are. You're an awful man, a scoundrel. I know what he and everyone else in Salthead thinks of you, and I'm not frightened."

"And you," said the miser, with the grim little smile playing on his lips, "are an insolent little brat who should be silent before her betters. I am a hard man of business, and insolent little brats are not for me. It is plain you need to be taught your place, Missy. And as regards your colleague, Mr. Richard Scribbler — as useless and insignificant an excuse for a law-clerk as ever I have seen, and a dunce to boot — be assured, he will live to pay for his misdeeds."

"You will kindly allow us to pass now, sir," said Laura, breaking in upon this little exercise in tit-for-tat. Though inwardly resolute, there was no mistaking the quaver in her voice. "You have no authority to detain us here. What do you mean, sir, by attempting to harm this child?"

It was then that Laura felt the stern gaze of Josiah upon her — a cold, cloying, malignant sensation, as though a flood of venomous syrup had been poured over her body. The miser reared back upon his heels and raised himself to his full height. The flow of his breath increased; his eyes sharpened; his hands with their long bony fingers began breathing at his sides.

"Who is attempting to harm this child?" he retorted, with feigned innocence. "Not I, certainly, Little Miss Governess, if that's what you are. It's plain you've much to teach your brat here in the way of manners. I have no quarrel with you. It is you, indeed, who are standing in my way, hindering my progress. Stand aside and let me by!"

"*Shame upon you,*" said Miss Honeywood.

The miser abruptly spun around, anxious to see who it was had dared to interrupt him. His sharp falcon-gaze fastened upon the mistress of the Pelican, standing there with her angular arms folded and her pale eyes narrowed behind her eyeglass frames. Recognition spread slyly across his features.

"Shame upon you," repeated Miss Honeywood. "How dare you speak to these good people so? They have done nothing to you. And what are your intentions regarding this blameless child? You can't fool me — it's you who are the villain here. Everything is either black or white with me, sir; there's no gray in it, particularly where you are concerned. Yours is the blackest of black hearts in my book."

"Ah! It is the renowned Miss Blunderwood — a common barmaid," was the miser's riposte, delivered with a magnificent sneer. "Not to worry. I recognize you, Mine Hostess of the Blue Buzzard. You are well known to me. You make a proud show, but inside that dry husk of yours you are as weak and malleable as all the rest. I could crush you like so much chaff."

"You know nothing of me, sir," returned Miss Honeywood, looking at him steadily and fiercely. "You couldn't begin to know anything of me. You may believe you have power over me, but you have none, sir."

"I see. I see. You are very sure of yourself, Miss Tapstress. Take care your overconfidence is not your downfall."

"You are an ill-bred, insupportable person, and I'll not take sauce from the likes of you," said Miss Moll, touching her fingers to the sides of her eyeglass frames and emphatically leveling lenses. "Do not fool with me, sir, I warn you. You will regret it."

"Words of intimidation from a common barkeeper! I am warning you not to provoke me, for your own sake, Miss Muddlehead. Beware — you stand at danger's threshold."

"And your words are wind, sir."

The miser ruffled up his magnificent black coat, like feathers. The current of his temper was running so high it was all he could do to keep down his choler. But there was something inexplicably persuasive in this tall, narrow, angular woman with the starched white hair and ominous spectacles that seemed to restrain him, if only for the moment. Before he could formulate a counterstroke, however, they both were interrupted by a small voice from below.

"*L'oiseau noir!*" exclaimed Fiona.

"Eh? What's that?" demanded Josiah, suspiciously, for the miser's *français* was not what it used to be. In fact it never was anything, if the truth be told.

"The child calls you a black bird," explained Miss Moll. With the utmost gentleness she nudged Fiona into the arms of Miss Dale, so as to interpose her own angular frame between them and the miser. "You have said something in reference to a buzzard, sir. What I believe the child meant was a vulture. Or perhaps a teratorn would be more appropriate."

"I see how it is. Well, I shall teach you. If you continue to get up my nose — " sputtered Josiah, looking as though he were about to burst an appendix.

The miser stopped, glancing sharply from one hostile female face to another. Five hostile female faces they were, ranged there against him — from the insolent child to the insipid governess, to the two ignorant servant-girls with their bundles, to the rather more formidable mistress of the Blue Buzzard. They stood frozen together as a block in their opposition to him; or perhaps they simply were benumbed by his chilly presence. He was about to say something in response, but decided instead to say nothing; decided not to expend the effort on such petty and inconsequential beings as women. It galled him, though, to think that his little game of feints had been scuppered by one uncooperative brat and a low tavern-keeper, leaving him without a single mark to etch upon his mental scorecard.

"I am a conscientious man of business," he declared. "I'm not a man for such chatter. Chatter is not for me — "

"Stow the gammon, Josiah, and clear off! We've had enough of your merrymaking. End of conversation." So said Miss Honeywood, folding and refolding her arms in a combative manner, prepared to do anything necessary to defend herself and her friends.

"Bah!" scoffed the miser, with a sideways sweep of his hand. "Good day to you. I haven't the time to waste on such — such — !"

Whatever he meant to say he was unable to find the proper word for it; so he clamped his hat tighter upon his great white head, and with a lofty air of contempt plunged away in the direction he had been traveling.

Before more than a few seconds had elapsed, a little whimper was heard from Mary Clinch.

"Oh, the Miss! She made him take water. Him — the miser! What did I tell you, Bridget — there's no one like her!" she cried. One huge shiny tear, a composite mixture of joy and disbelief, was standing in each eye — a testament to the indescribable awe in which she held her employer.

"Thank you, thank you, Miss Honeywood!" cried Laura, relievedly brushing Fiona's hair and cheeks with her trembling hands. It looked as though the child had survived her encounter with the unspeakable in a better condition than her guardian.

"He's a bad man," said Fiona.

"A nasty rascal, true, but it's a wicked world," said Bridget, taking an even greater interest now in the child after hearing her speak the name of Richard Scribbler.

Miss Honeywood supervising these proceedings in her usual starchy way, appeared now to lose some of her starch as she said to Fiona —

"Would you like some hot punch and scones, dear, to warm you up on this cold afternoon? A little something from the Blue Pelican?"

"Oh, yes, very much!" rejoiced Fiona.

"Then come along," said Miss Moll, taking up Fiona's hand in hers. "We've been to the butcher's — see there, those fresh pullets Mary and Bridget are carrying — and are on our way to the Pelican. But we must of course first obtain permission from your guardian. Please do come and join us in some punch, Miss Dale. Or perhaps tea? And scones as well."

Laura accepted gratefully on behalf of herself and Fiona, mindful though that they must soon return to Friday Street or Mrs. Minidew would worry. She took up Fiona's other hand, and so the child found herself safely ensconced between her two protectors, as they all set off for the Pelican.

"How is it you know Mr. Scribbler?" inquired Bridget, shyly.

"Oh, Mr. Scribbler is my best friend in the world," replied Fiona. "He's ever so much fun. We play lots and lots of games, and he brings me presents. When will Mr. Scribbler come to us again, Miss Dale?"

"I don't know, dear," replied Laura, after a brief pause. "I'm afraid I am not privy to his plans."

"I do hope he will come soon. I miss him ever so much."

They turned from the busy thoroughfare into a quieter street filled with tall half-timbered houses, gabled and venerable. They were approaching a bend in the lane, which inclined at a slight elevation toward the more secluded environs of the Pelican, when a fashionable young gentleman in a bottle-green coat, with his head down and his face hidden by his hat, came rushing round a blind corner. He was moving at so rapid a pace, he didn't notice the ladies until he was already upon them; at the last moment, to avoid crashing into Miss Dale, he leaped aside and into the road, where his coat, boots, and trousers were immediately spattered with mud by a passing trap.

"Oh, I am sorry!" cried Laura, reaching out to help the gentleman to safety. "Forgive me — I'm very clumsy. I wasn't looking. Are you injured, sir? Your clothes are ruined! Oh, I am sorry, sir."

"No, no, I assure you, I am not hurt in the least. It was entirely my fault. Please don't bother," replied the young gentleman.

Miss Honeywood presented the stranger with one of her searching looks, and adjusted her eyeglasses — not in a threatening way, but simply to clarify her vision. "Do I know you, sir?" she asked.

The young gentleman raised his head. He was uncommonly handsome, with a broad mustache, a long narrow nose, a finely-hewn chin, and dark eyes that smoldered in their sockets beneath a haughty pair of arched brows.

"I don't believe so," he answered.

"You are the gentleman," said Miss Moll, as recognition dawned upon her, "the gentleman who discovered Mr. Rime in the dock-road. It was you and Henry Duff who brought him to the Pelican. He very nearly popped off, but in the end was saved, I believe, by the ministrations of Dr. Dampe and my young girl here, Mary Clinch. We looked for you so as to thank you for your efforts, but you had disappeared. Am I not correct in this?"

"Yes, that's true. If you'll excuse me, now, I must retrieve my mare from the stables — "

"The name is Honeywood. I am the sole proprietor of that good house of the Blue Pelican. And your name is — ?"

The young gentleman hesitated, but quickly realized there was no antidote powerful enough to counteract the scrutiny of so many female eyes.

"Hunter," he said, relinquishing. "John Hunter."

"Mr. Hunter, we are in your debt. You'll be pleased to hear that Mr. Rime has made a complete recovery. We are grateful for the part you played in it. The poor young man might have gone off the hooks that very night, had you not come upon him when you did."

"I assure you it was accidental. I saw him there in the dock-road as I was riding past. I thought at first he was a pedlar or a vagrant, or more likely a drunkard. Mr. Duff then happened along with his cart. He mentioned your house, which he said was nearby, and that is how we brought the fellow to you. You say you are Miss Honeywood, the owner of that establishment?"

"Yes, indeed," said Miss Moll, always quick to acknowledge the fact. "Do you know, Mr. Hunter, now that I've seen you clearly I've the distinct impression I've seen you before — on some occasion other than the night in question. Could that possibly be?"

"No, I don't believe so."

"I can't dispel the sense of familiarity. There's no doubt in my mind it's real; there's no gray in it. Tell me," she continued, after introducing her companions, "are you new to Salthead?"

"Yes. I have only recently taken up residence in the city."

"Ah, like our Mr. Hilltop."

On hearing this name Mr. Hunter's demeanor abruptly altered. His face darkened.

"What do you know of *him?*" he demanded, coldly.

"Very little. You needn't be cross, Mr. Hunter. I merely remark upon the coincidence — two gentlemen recently arrived in Salthead, both strangers, and both of whom we've had occasion to observe at the Pelican. In the case of Mr. Jack Hilltop, he at least has been obligingly conversational. A bit too much so, at times."

"You must be wary of that man," blurted out Mr. Hunter. Almost immediately he checked himself, as though regretting the disclosure.

"Why is that, Mr. Hunter? Is he very dangerous?"

"That is all I am free to tell you. Do not listen to him. Give no countenance to his lying words. Above all, do not trust him."

"The cove as tried to nick poor Sally's locket," said Mary Clinch. "I knew he weren't to be trusted, Miss!"

"It would seem you know much more of Mr. Hilltop than we do," said Miss Honeywood. "He is an acquaintance of yours?"

Mr. Hunter dropped his eyes for a peep at his watch. "As I have told you, there is little more I can say. I am sorry, Miss Honeywood. I merely offer a bit of advice, based on my own unfortunate experience."

"What's plain is plain, Mr. Hunter. We're grateful, nonetheless, for your help in the matter of Mr. Rime. Perhaps we may return the favor some day. Here, we're very nearly at the Pelican. Come along and have some hot punch. It's unseasonably cold this afternoon — I'm afraid the winter will be upon us sooner than ever. And we'll see about your garments."

"Thank you," said the fashionable young gentleman, regaining something of his former composure. "To speak truth, there is a small matter in which you might be of some assistance to me."

"Indeed?" said Miss Moll, a little surprised at this. "And what might that be, Mr. Hunter?"

"There is a man I must find — a low fellow who was present at your house that same night. His appearance is quite distinctive. An unkempt, burly ruffian, with a mustache and greasy hair, a sloping forehead, and crooked eyes with great dark circles around them. Perhaps you know this man — who he is, and where he might be found?"

The question elicited a half-suppressed inhalation of breath from Mary Clinch. She aimed a quick glance at Miss Moll.

"Is this man known to you?" asked Mr. Hunter, looking round at the ladies in general. "What is he called?"

"Indeed," replied Miss Honeywood. She had by now surrendered care of Fiona to Miss Dale and was once more striding majestically forward of the little group, her pale eyes fastened on the way ahead. "We are only too well acquainted with that man. He is one who has been banished forever from the vicinity of the Pelican on account of his black deeds. The night you saw him there he was discovered and routed."

"I was in hopes you might tell me who he is and where I might find him. There is a matter of some concern I must discuss with him."

"Whatever business you might have with that man is of no possible interest to me. What is of interest to me, is why you should have business with such a man as that at all?"

Mr. Hunter allowed a few moments to pass before answering, so that he might sculpt his words into their most presentable shape.

"This man has something that belongs to me, and which he removed from my house one night without my consent."

"Ah! That does not surprise me in the least, Mr. Hunter. The man is a nefarious thief and burglar — a criminal of the first order. There's no doubt in my mind he belongs in the lock-up. Unfortunately, he is far too slippery for the magistrates to convict. I believe his master may exert some influence there on his behalf."

"As I have in general surmised, from my encounter with this fellow the night he broke into my house. I came upon him in the midst of his activities, you see, and so got a clean look at his face, which I recollected from the Blue Pelican. So might I ask you again, Miss Honeywood, for his name and a place where I might seek him out, and so recover what he has taken from me?"

"His name," said Miss Moll, "is Robert Nightingale. He has lodgings in Dogpole Lane, with a wife and several children, but you'll not find him there. He prefers to take his ease in certain low houses of refection near the docks — in Water Street, or Turbot Gardens, or at the Ship public house. Ask for him there."

"And who might this master be you spoke of?" asked Mr. Hunter, pressing a little. "I have the impression that it was someone else who dispatched him to my house. For whom does he work?"

Here it was Miss Honeywood's turn to hesitate before replying.

"Yes, he has a master. Mr. Josiah Tusk is that man."

At mention of the unmentionable Mary dropped her bundle, and her fingers flew into her mouth.

"He is a well-known financier in this city — a very conscientious man of business. We have, unfortunately, just now encountered him in the street. You may call upon him at Shadwinkle Old House. It is he, and only he, who has power over Bob Nightingale," said Miss Moll — growing starchy and angular as she turned to Mary Clinch, enjoining her to pick up her pullets and not to slobber.

"Oh — I am a butter-fingers, Miss!" cried that obedient damsel.

Mr. Hunter appeared either confused or puzzled, as though the answer provided by Miss Honeywood were not the one he had been anticipating.

"You are certain of this?" he demanded, sternly. "You are certain as to the employer of Mr. Nightingale?"

"Of course," said Miss Moll.

"There is no mistake?"

"There is no mistake, Mr. Hunter. None."

The gentleman shook his head. "I know nothing of this conscientious financier. How does he know me? How does he know I am here? Perhaps he in turn was directed by another?"

"I should consider that a most unlikely possibility. The miser of Salthead receives orders from no one but himself. I'm afraid this is a mystery you must resolve on your own. As for the nature of the rivalry between you and Mr. Hilltop — for that is what I interpret it to be — it is no concern of mine. I'm not one of your common prying persons, who looks upon the private affairs of others as her own. Come along, then! Our hot punch awaits."

"And scones?" piped up Fiona, to be sure this important item was not overlooked.

"And scones, dear! Then we'll settle by the fire, and perhaps Mr. Hunter will tell us how he proposes to recover his property. You never have said, Mr. Hunter, just what it is that was taken from you."

They were traversing now the humble precincts of St. Barnacle's Church. As they came round to the parsonage a door opened and a clergyman appeared on the step.

"Hallo there, rector," called out Miss Moll.

"A lovely day, Miss Honeywood!" returned the kindly Mr. Nash, with not a little irony, as he tipped his hat to the filmy gray mist that was serving today for a sky. "Just by chance I was on my way to your fine establishment to see Miss Sprinkle. Might I join you?"

287

"Of course. Let me introduce Mr. John Hunter, whom you may not know. Mr. Hunter, this is our rector, Mr. Nash. Mr. Hunter is new to Salthead, rector."

"I don't believe we've met," said Mr. Nash, extending his hand. "Welcome, welcome, Mr. Hunter. And where are you from?"

"From Lye — most recently," replied Mr. Hunter.

"Mr. Hunter is on his way to the Pelican as well," said Miss Honeywood, by way of firming up that young gentleman's itinerary. Mr. Hunter, looking very much as though he would rather be somewhere else, nonetheless surrendered to Miss Moll, while she explained to the rector the circumstances behind the state of his clothing.

"What a delightful coincidence," smiled Mr. Nash. "To think that you and your companions would be passing by the church, just as I was walking out the door. Such a marvelous, chance occurrence, Miss Honeywood."

"Nothing occurs by chance, my dear rector," said Mr. Hunter, in a strangely offhand but dogmatic sort of way, as though this were the plainest fact in all the world.

"Is that so? Oh. Why, I had concluded, from my limited range of observation, that chance plays quite a substantial role in our everyday affairs."

"Everything that occurs has been pre-ordained. Every event is foreseen and unalterable."

"So you are an adherent of the doctrine of predestination, Mr. Hunter?" said the rector, with kindly curiosity. "It is I admit a rather fascinating subject, but at its heart, it seems to me, an illogical one."

"You must remember that logic is a construction of men, not of gods."

"Gods? By this you refer to the mystery of the Holy Trinity, I assume — the union of three Persons in one Godhead."

Mr. Hunter did not answer, appearing uncomfortable with the tenor of the conversation.

"Predestination," the rector went on, pleasantly enough, "is, I'm afraid, one of those annoying little thorns in the side of the Faith. Oh, yes. If you carry the argument to its logical extreme, you must conclude that the Lord is rather a cold-hearted Old Fish, having determined from all eternity whom He will save and whom He will not, regardless of merit. Of course I suppose the answer all comes down to grace. But I'm not well-versed in such difficult arguments, I'm afraid. Oh, no. I love the simple life of our little parish, and prefer to leave the finer points of the Faith to men more qualified than I. You have perhaps special knowledge of this doctrine, Mr. Hunter? Do you find predestination compelling?"

"I do, but not as you Christian folk envision it."

At this, most everyone in the party looked very hard at Mr. Hunter — everyone save Fiona, who was busy whistling little airs to herself and observing the movement of her shoes. An odd expression crossed the face of Miss Honeywood.

"Oh," said the rector, a trifle uncertain how to proceed. "Well, in its broadest sense I suppose predestination can be traced back to the pagan mythologies. In ancient Greece, for example, you have Klotho, Lachesis, and Atropos — the three Fates, or goddesses of Destiny. A most mysterious trio of ladies, the weavers and spinners who determined the course of events in human lives. Their workings were absolutely unalterable, as you say. Well, I look forward to chatting with you further on this subject, Mr. Hunter. It is one I confess has always intrigued me."

Mr. Hunter seemed to be regretting his impulsive words and what they might have revealed. "I have nothing further to offer on the topic," he said, brusquely. "I'm very late. I must retrieve my horse — "

"Really, you musn't," urged Miss Honeywood, touching his arm. They were standing now before the door of the Pelican, beneath the great oak sign with its colorfully droopy seabird. "For you see, we've arrived. Mind the board on your way in!"

CHAPTER X

In a Mist

THE gloomy cold mist comes swirling in from the river, from the harbor, and from the long sweep of ocean beyond, extending its reach into the dock-yards and sailors' haunts before creeping, eel-like, into the very heart of town. It steals in through the chain bridge to invade the narrow crooked streets and back-alleys, growing thicker as the daylight fades. Unseeing it feels its way among a confusion of winding lanes and byways — slides smoky gray fingers along the building walls, along the stone-built cottages and their brick dressings, over half-timbered houses with tiled roofs and jutting eaves — drifts past mullioned windows with their lead lattice glazing and diamond panes — wreathes itself round graceful gables and barge-boards pierced with tracery.

When night comes on the mist condenses into a salt-laden fog, which clings to every structure and every tree and every animal and every human person it comes across. There is a particular chill in this fog — a keen, sharp thrust — that heralds the onset of winter; a characteristic tingle in the nostrils happening to inhale such fog, which banishes all warm and pleasant memories in favor of the harsh cold reality coming on.

As darkness settles in over the landscape the rush and bustle settle with it, and soon, apart from a few scattered outposts here and there, the city draws up its collective blanket, puts its collective night-cap on its collective head, and settles in for the night's collective sleep. An uneasy sleep it will be, however, for the events of recent weeks — the sinister phenomena that had made their presence known, one by one, by means of evil deeds in the night, and glimpses of the forms and faces of dead folk about the streets — leave it an open question, as Bridget Leek had posed, whether or not this were Resurrection time and the end of the world were at hand.

From all about the city reports had been received, by rector and alderman and magistrate, watchman and landlord alike, of sights and sounds both horrid and reprehensible. Vivid accounts of things seen in churchyards, of unearthly voices laughing in the night; noises of invisible animals drinking at troughs or sniffing at windows; mysterious rappings and tappings where no one was, with morning evidence of a whole catalogue of nightly mischiefs; the ominous shadow of a teratorn; tales of a fearsome mastiff that walked upright like a man. And now, most recently and most ghastly, the claim of six frightened individuals, honorable citizens all, to have seen perched one night upon the spire of St. Skiffin's Church the figure of a man-like creature with great leathery wings, who laughed derisively at them and flew off into the darkness — creating a most credible impression, as Ned Vickery might attest, of the Foul Fiend himself.

Such are the uneasy thoughts that occupy the minds and quicken the hearts of the good people of Salthead as they huddle in their beds this night, while the thick fog rises from river and sea like a leviathan and swallows up their city.

Such uneasy thoughts do not occupy one mind, however — that of the gentleman now stumbling along a certain tilted street in a certain dismal part of town. It is night, and correspondingly dark — as I have said — but this gentleman doesn't care. It is foggy and cold, but this gentleman doesn't care. It is dark and so the ghouls are out, but still he doesn't care. He doesn't care in part because he knows nothing of ghouls, or churchyards, or flying men; mostly, though, he doesn't care because there is nothing left to care *about*.

As he directs his unsteady steps on and up the tilted street, toward the top of Whistle Hill, the gentleman says nothing — does not speak or mumble to himself, does not sing, does not whistle, even — despite having consumed a frightful quantity of grog at a nearby ale-house, the place where he has lately spent his hours and most of the coins in his purse. He staggers forward at a limpish pace, believing this to be the way home but in truth caring nothing whether it is or not. He is attired in an old brown coat and dark waistcoat, a blue shirt with pink anchors, and drab knee-breeches and gaiters. He is not dressed for the cold but neither is he feeling it, in his present interesting condition. He stops to pull off his hat and scratch his head, revealing a crown of abundant brown hair that flares out in all directions like a sunburst.

The glow from an oil-lamp illuminates the fog at an eerie street-corner, and as Mr. Richard Scribbler (for so it is he) lurches past this landmark he is arrested by a voice that demands harshly in his ear —

"*Are you pleased with your station in life, man?*"

From out of the gloom slides a tall figure, a merchant seaman to judge by his garments, all of which had seen better times. Mr. Scribbler screws up his eyes at sight of this inquisitive stranger, squinting through a fog of fog and malted ale.

"Well? Say something, man! What's wrong with you?" growls the interrogator, vehemently. "Have you no thoughts? Have you no feelings? Have you no desires? Have you no regrets, man? Is there nothing stirring inside that puffed headpiece of yours?"

The clerk responds with only the faintest alteration of expression. Puffed headpiece! He doesn't much like the sound of that. It could very well be an affront; then again, in his present state it might not. He scratches his hair, knitting his brows very severely, and with a mighty effort retrieves himself from the brink of unconsciousness. Memory of the evening's wassail is cast aside; the present is very suddenly the present, and Mr. Scribbler becomes convinced that at some time, in some place, in some capacity, he was acquainted with this nautical fellow. If only he could recollect the finer details...

"Are you satisfied with your life, man? Is it all you'd hoped it would be? Are you happy tonight? Are you unhappy? Damn it — you've got to be either one or the other, or you're not living!"

Mr. Scribbler is acutely aware of the fact that he is not happy, so who is this interloper to put him in mind of it? Had he not trickled away the very last of his coin at a low ale-house, this very night, in an effort to blot it all out? What business had this rude fellow to bring it up now?

"Have you no regrets? Are there no words left unsaid, no deeds undone? Is there nothing you'd like to change in your life? Is there nothing you'd like to do over again, if given the chance? Speak up, man! Is there no one you've left behind?"

Mr. Scribbler grows sad-faced at this speech, as voices and pictures of the past come storming into his head. The bitter beer had for a time purged him of such nightmares; now here they were again, rushing at him with unprecedented ferocity. All at once the eyes of the law-clerk are feeling very hot and briny, so he draws out his pocket-handkerchief and buries his face in it.

"Ah — there it is!" exclaims the stranger, with a glare of triumph. The glare dissolves into a fiendish leer, the gleam of a gold tooth shining in his mouth. "That's all fine and good. That's fine and good for the little grammar-school boy, for the little scholar. We'll be bawling soon now if I'm any judge. Where's your backbone, man? Where's your self-respect? This ain't the school-room now, lad. This is the world, man, this is the world!"

These words from the sailor produce now a definite effect. The heat and salt abruptly drain from Mr. Scribbler's eyeballs. The handkerchief drops from his face; he sniffs once or twice, wipes his nose, scratches his head, knits his brows, and looks upon the stranger in a new light. *Schoolboy*, he ponders. *School*. Yes! *Grammar school*. Yes, yes, oh yes! He raises a timid hand toward his interrogator, and if he could have spoken, then and there, I believe he would have.

"Do you know how to caper, man? Young scholar like you ought to know how to caper. Caper, caper! Very useful for catching the pretty girls, after all. Capered much myself in my school days. Caper, you see? Like so!"

The stranger is on the point of executing his ghastly hornpipe, but at the last moment something in the face of the law-clerk deters him. For a time he says nothing at all, his eyes darting nervously this way and that, but lighting very often upon Mr. Scribbler, as though the sailor, too, has seen a thing he is just beginning to comprehend.

The clerk offers his hand in a gesture of friendship; then taps his chest with the flat of his palm several times, in quick succession, as if to say —

"*Don't you know me?*"

The sailor swings his arms to and fro — long, gangly arms hanging far too stiffly from their joints — and instead of launching into his hornpipe performs a spin round on his heel.

"So, man," says he, "what do they call you? Is it anything even remotely remarkable? For you see, you've got to do something remarkable with your life, man, while you can. Do something — anything — that makes a difference to someone. Don't go tumbling into your grave without that! Listen to me, listen to me, I know what I'm talking about. Why — "

At which point the sailor leaps into the air toward Mr. Scribbler, one hand thrust out and its extended forefinger aimed squarely at the gawking clerk.

"It's — it's Dick Scribbler, ain't it?" he says, in tones bordering on accusation.

Mr. Scribbler nods energetically, with an eager smile on his lips.

"It's Dick Scribbler — little Dick Scribbler, the stationer's boy — as sat beside me those many, many days in the old grammar school, at Monks Minster. My old school-fellow! Do you remember me, Dick? Do you know who it is? It's Ham Pickering, man!"

Mr. Scribbler continues to nod and smile, happy that he too has been recognized, that recognition now is mutual between them. How long has it been, he wonders, since he'd last seen this old friend, who had gone far away to sea and so drifted out of his life?

"So how are you, Dick? Flourishing, I see. Come to Salthead to seek your fortune, no doubt! Well — have you found it? And what of that pretty young sister of yours? She ought to be a monstrous fine girl by now. How many years, Dick, how many years since those golden days on the green? Too many. Golden days in Fridley — long dark winters filled with Latin, logic and learning, and bright summers chock-full of escapades. And all the old fellows, too — Will Poplar and Bob Simpkins — Tony Sparke — Hugh Clopton — such game lads! And you, Dick! You and your joking, and those wild pranks we'd play on the poor squits in the almshouse. Such mischievous lads we were, such mischievous lads — the most mischievous lads in all of Broadshire!" The corners of the sailor's mouth rise up beneath his mustache in a ghoulish grin. "Well, look at us now, Dick," he adds, with something like a sneer. "Look at us now!"

Mr. Scribbler remains enthusiastic, and oblivious of the irony.

"So what are you doing here, Dick? What's going forward? What are any of us devils doing here? Do you have an answer for that, man? Because if you have, you're a better lad than Ham!"

Mr. Scribbler tosses his head and shrugs. But it is a half-hearted effort, as if he isn't totally clear on the question.

"Ah, I didn't think so," says Mr. Pickering, his nervous eyes scampering from the oil-lamp to the depths of the gloomy street, to the timbered frontage of the shops across the way, and back to Mr. Scribbler. "You won't find it in your Latin grammar or your rhetoric. Nobody has the answer, that's it, Dick — because there ain't no answer. But at least you're able to rest, man. You can sleep and forget. You can put it all out of your head for those blessed few hours. Sleep! What Ham Pickering wouldn't give for one instant of sleep. One instant of peace. For you see, there ain't no rest for such as me, Dick. No, no, man. There ain't no rest for any such as me!"

The clerk offers him a look of compassion mixed with curiosity and not a little fear.

"What's happened to us, Dick? What's happened to *me?* Ah! There's a fine question. Do you see me standing here, Dick? Ah, so you do. Well, how can that be, man? Don't you know I'm dead?"

Mr. Scribbler did not know this. As a result his underlip takes to trembling, his eyes blow up and he begins to look very frightened.

"This is it, man!" exclaims Mr. Pickering, with a little flourish of his anatomy. "It's death that stands before you — death without peace. What's that! There's something in my ears now, Dick. Listen! It's the noise of a great thunderstorm at sea. Can you hear it? Can you see it? Can you feel its power, man? Wind and rain — entire sheets of rain! The swaying of the deck, the cracking of timbers. Then comes the salt-water all over you. Icy cold water, racing in. Salt in your nostrils, salt in your throat, salt in your lungs — salt-water, everywhere. The cries of drowning men. It's terror, man, real terror! Darkness — paralyzing cold — paralyzing fear — and so it's Ham's turn to drown — "

Mr. Scribbler is both startled and horrified, his heart beating wildly against his ribs.

"And so there's the last of it. Utter darkness. The next I know, here I am in Salthead town without so much as a word of explanation. Ha, ha! Can you tell me what it's all about, man? Can you let me in on the joke? Because damn me — I ain't got the least notion myself!"

The sailor bursts out in a great laugh, and whirls round again on his heel. As if by magic a letter, crumpled and water-stained, appears in his hand.

"Can you do me one kind favor, Dick?"

Mr. Scribbler agrees to this with some anxiety, fearing the result should he decline.

"Take this and deliver it for me, if you would. It's for a young lady as once I courted. Do you know her, man?"

The clerk glances at the name inscribed on the letter, and indicates that he is unfamiliar with that person.

"A wonderful girl, Dick, a wonderful girl! We would've been happy, but it's all mine to regret. That's a hard lesson to learn. It's too late for me, but not too late for you. Give her that letter, and she'll know at least I'm sorry for the causing of so much trouble. She's not to blame herself. For you see, she loved me, Dick, she loved me — with all her heart."

Poor Mr. Pickering! What do the dead know of love? What, for that matter, do the living?

"I had a mind she'd betrayed me, and so my pride kept me from her. She begged me to hear her out. Begged me, man! Instead I signed aboard that foul ship, and so that was the last of Ham Pickering. I know she's grieving for me, Dick. I've seen her! Give her that letter for me. It's all I've left to give her."

Mr. Scribbler makes it clear he will do as instructed, and deposits the letter in his coat.

"Thank you, Dick," says the sailor, turning round and round a few more times, like an ungainly skater disporting himself on the ice. "Thank you, Dick

Scribbler. For Dick the scribbler you be, no doubt. No lying there with a name like that. Just the common truth. Just a common fact. And facts, after all," says Mr. Pickering, in rather a changed tone, "are *FACTS.*"

This abrupt transition produces in Mr. Scribbler a growing sense of discomfort.

"This is the world, Dick. What do you know of the place? I've seen plenty of the world — what's left of it — in my travels. And what do you think? Everywhere, everyone is all the same. The whole lot of 'em!"

Mr. Scribbler allows how this might be true, although he hasn't witnessed it for himself.

"So do something remarkable with your life, man, while you've got the chance. Don't be just another of those everybodies everywhere else. Take a stand! Do something remarkable with your life, before it's too late. Believe me, Dick, I know what I'm talking about. Do as I'm telling you, and you'll be remembered long after the dust and silence."

Mr. Scribbler, with some trepidation, agrees to follow this precept.

"Well, then, man," continues the inquisitor, rubbing his hands together stealthily, and with a faint gleam of his unpleasant smile thrown upon the ground. "Well, Dick, I think it's all been fine and good, but now it's time to present you with something remarkable in your life. Here, Dick — take this, man, and blaze away!"

First it was a letter, and now it is a lighted match that materializes in the hand of Mr. Pickering. The clerk, fearful again of disobeying, nonetheless hesitates.

"What! Why so frightened, Dick? Ain't you never seen a flame before? Take it!"

Gaining courage, Mr. Scribbler accepts the offering. The head of the match is brightly aglow, a blue and yellow teardrop that flutters as it burns. As the clerk watches, Mr. Pickering proceeds to pass his arms and hands through the flame, by which means those portions of his anatomy, like the driest tinder, are immediately ignited.

"Look at me, Dick," says he, very calmly raising his arms for Mr. Scribbler's inspection. "Look at this! Isn't this remarkable, now? Ha, ha! Why so puzzled, man? There's no mystery here. No rest, no peace. The fire couldn't hurt old Ham even if he wanted it to. What can it hurt him — when he's already dead?"

The match falls from the clerk's hand. He stares, gapes, recoils in shock and horror at sight of the hot, eager flames.

"It's only the beginning, Dick. We've just started. Look at this now, man!"

Laughing the sailor touches his arms to his chest and legs. Within moments most of his body is alight, crackling and smoking, like a scarecrow burning in a crop-field.

"What's the matter, Dick? Always the timid one, eh! Always the runaway. Never one to face the world, were you? That's the way it's always been with you, man — you can't take the world, so you fly from it. You can't face your own shame. You haven't changed, man, you haven't changed! That's why you don't speak no more, ain't it? The world has struck you dumb. Well, look at me, Dick!"

Mr. Scribbler obeys, cringing as Mr. Pickering delivers a farewell salute in his most nautical manner.

"Look at me, Dick!"

The sailor touches hand to brow; immediately his head explodes in flames.

"Look at me!" cries the voice of Ham, from somewhere. "This is the world, man — this is the world!"

Unable to bear it any longer, Mr. Scribbler falls to his knees in the street. The body of the sailor is flooding the area with light like a celebratory bonfire. The noise and heat, the suffocating odor of smoke and burnt flesh, the fog, the disembodied cries of Mr. Pickering, all mix together like the elements of some grand apocalyptic vision.

This is the world, Dick!

In time the nightmare subsides, and the clerk wakes to find himself in another place.

It is a quieter place and a much softer place, not so cold yet far from warm. There is a deal table there, and a down-at-heel set of chairs, and a sagging chest of drawers. There is a chimney, too, with some small items of china clinging to the mantel-shelf, but thankfully no fire; no, no, that had burned itself out some time ago. There is a window there, which looks out onto a dismal gray perspective. There is a low settee in front of the dog-grate, and Mr. Scribbler finds himself reclining upon it. It is a very familiar and a reassuring place. It is his own garret apartment.

The clerk rises with a shiver and glazed eyes and senses only half-awake. There is something unhealthy squatting in the hollow of his stomach, at the very center of his being. He turns his mind back to yesternight, to the carouse in the ale-house and the encounter with Mr. Pickering, and marvels at his success in finding his way home. He rubs his cheeks and forehead and pours a little water from the ewer to splash over his face. Behind him a squeal erupts from the sash-boards in the window. He turns round and goes to that window. Looking with sad strange eyes into the mist, he finds there nothing more remarkable than the usual view from Whistle Hill.

He delves into his coat-pocket for his purse, knowing already that there is no money left. To his very great astonishment he finds that every coin is still in place. Not an empty purse, but an ample one; and so it flashes upon him that he never spent the money because he never was in the ale-house, and because he never was in the ale-house there was no carouse and so no Mr. Pickering and no bonfire. He sees now the opened book on the settee, and looks again at the condition of the grate, and so grasps the fact that *yesternight* is in actuality *tonight*; that he had fallen into a deep sleep while reading but a few hours ago, and that it is now late afternoon of the same day.

A terrible sickness comes over him. The words of Mr. Pickering return in full force, together with the horror of Mr. Pickering's incineration. The first surge of nausea is followed quickly by a second, a third. His face turns white as sea-foam. He swallows thickly several times, but there is no resisting the expulsive force rising in his stomach.

He makes a rush at the window. Up goes the sash; in blows the cold air, but Mr. Scribbler cares little for that now. He leans out, bending forward at the waist and preparing to relieve himself of his misery. He drapes his body over the window-ledge like a human antimacassar, his head and outspread arms hanging down with the palms of his hands flat against the side of the building.

His eyes have time to roam about the adjacent houses and the tilted street far below, and the mist swirling around them. Ordinarily he would be rather frightened now; but considering his state of mind one might forgive an allusion to Mr. Josiah Tusk — *fright was not for him*. It is the recollection of his dream that concerns Mr. Scribbler, for the surges of nausea are but reflections of his own self-contempt and the awful truth brought home to him by his former school-fellow.

This is the world, Dick. The world has more meaning than ever for Richard Scribbler as he dangles there above it, from the ledge of his garret window in Furnival Buildings. It would be so very easy now, he muses, to lift his feet from the floor and so precipitate himself into the world below — a world from which he has for so long held himself aloof, and looked down upon in a rather more figurative sense. *Go! Go!* Simply lift your feet and slide from the ledge, and all will be better for everyone concerned. Then will come at last a blessed end to guilt and self-reproach. *Slip!* — go on now, man, and slip — and so become part of the world once more.

Gravity is forcing the heavy blood farther and farther into his head. A rush of hot tears streams down his brow and into his hair. He shuts his eyes, and so too shuts his mind to all earthly things in preparation for what is to come. But at that moment — the very moment he is ready to carry out his design — a murmuring of voices intrudes itself upon his consciousness.

What of Laura and little Fiona? What, indeed, of them? For they would learn of his death and its manner, in time. It was true, letting himself drop now would bring a swift and longed-for conclusion. But what of them? What pain might not be inflicted upon them, after he'd gone, once they discovered what it was he'd done? What, indeed, of little Fiona? How to break the news to her that her best friend, Mr. Richard Scribbler, had done away with himself? What to say to her? How to explain such a ghastly event to a child?

And what of Laura, who, once she'd recovered from her distress, would certainly say to herself, oh, Richard, Richard, how true to form, you've gone and put a period to your existence. Killed yourself, and so taken the easy road. Richard Scribbler — ever and always a coward!

Do something remarkable with your life, before it's too late.

The eyes of the clerk pop open. Looking down now they see a very different world, and one very much farther away. Gone is the expulsive urge in his stomach, replaced by a frenzy of alarm that perhaps already he has slipped too far for saving. For one heart-stopping moment his shoes leave the floor. Madly he throws back his arms; just as he feels himself going over his fingers contact the window-ledge. It is only by the most desperate and awkward of efforts — aided of course by blind panic — that he succeeds in fighting his way back in.

He shuts the horrid window with a bang; the window in a fit of pique responds with a blast of air through its sash-boards. He shivers again and it strikes him how very cold it is in the room. Overcoming the horror of his dream, he prepares a small fire in the dog-grate. He drops onto the settee as the apartment begins to warm and tries to interest himself again in his book. The endeavor is not very successful. After a time he casts the book aside, finding himself strangely drawn to the flames — finds himself fire-gazing, blissfully, soothingly, meditatively, but without a single thought of Mr. Ham Pickering bothering his head.

Until, that is, he recalls something he'd felt earlier in the pocket of his coat, when he had examined his purse for its contents. Mystified, he reaches into that pocket and draws forth a crumpled letter, addressed in a hand he knows very well is not his. Peering at its water-stained surface he reads the direction there —

Miss Nina Jacks
Boring Lane, Key Street

CHAPTER XI

Professor Greenshields Renders an Opinion

CAME the rustle of a lady's garments, followed almost at once by the lady herself. Looking in at the door she stepped forward into the drawing-room, and so into the presence of an elderly gentleman of a faintly green and Jurassic appearance, who was seated in an invalid's chair. He was looking out through a tall window that gave on to a silent back-garden, and did not at first perceive her approach.

"Christopher?"

The elderly gentleman turned his head. He had clearly been a very imposing fellow in years gone by, but his body now was considerably reduced in scope — shrunken, I might even say — with no longer any trace of the elasticity and strength that had characterized it in his youth. Despite his age and enfeeblement he was decked out rather smartly in a black coat and day waistcoat, low collar and broad necktie, and checked trousers, with a wrap of tigerish tweed across his legs for warmth. His wrinkled hands lay folded together in his lap. Though the body may have withered the eyes in the once-handsome face had not, remaining restless and alert beneath a fringe of the gray hair that was still rather generously arrayed about his head.

"Yes? Yes? What is it, Amelia?" he inquired, in a voice once so full of suppleness and learned authority, but hoarsened now by the agents of time.

"Daniel Dampe and Titus Tiggs, and some of their friends, are come to see us," replied the lady — who, as you may have surmised, was the elderly gentleman's partner in life.

The eyes of the old collegian sharpened with evident interest. He nodded his head briskly a few times and rolled his chair forward, propelling its wooden wheel-rims with his hands. "Where is Hobbes? Have Hobbes bring them in immediately. Daniel and Titus — here! My, my, this is a most unexpected surprise. Yes, by all means, Amelia — have Hobbes bring them in!"

His lady smiled agreeably and departed the room. The room itself, like the window giving on to the back-garden, was very tall, but of a more shadowy constitution, apart from the area where the light from that window penetrated. The walls were taken up with bookcases, very dry and stuffy, on the top of which stood a procession of alabaster busts, their grave sightless eyes forever fixed on eternity. Despite these effects it was nonetheless a neat and comfortable apartment, very nice I should imagine on the coldest of cold winter nights, what with the splendid chimney of cobbled stonework, the quaint mahogany doors and generous floor-cloths, the shiny rosewood tables, and the cushioned chairs and ottomans that adorned it.

Dr. Dampe and Professor Tiggs soon appeared at the door, escorted by the aforementioned servant Hobbes — a very prim and efficient individual with a little squeezed-up raisin of a face, and oiled hair swept far back onto his head — and accompanied by the sisters Jacks, together with Mr. Kibble and Mr. Banister. Bringing up the rear, beside the lady of the house, was Mr. Jack Hilltop — the same Mr. Hilltop who had flown off to Broadshire professedly for his health, and who concluding that the present mystery was too curious a one to let pass, had abandoned all thought of his own dash and vigor to return with the others to Salthead.

"Yes, yes, this is a most pleasant surprise. Daniel! Titus! How are you both?"

"You're looking well, Kit!" exclaimed Professor Tiggs, warmly taking the old gentleman's hand in his. "It's not the same without you. How long has it been now since your retirement? Two years? Three?"

"Four, I'm afraid. Four, going on five — and not getting any less. And Daniel — so good to see you again! You haven't changed. Your practice is thriving, I trust?"

"It's extraordinary, actually," said the doctor, looking rather pleased as he always did when the topic of conversation was himself. "Thriving is not the word. You wouldn't believe it. I've absolutely no time left for philosophical pursuits these days. Patients *will* be calling! There's simply no stopping them, I'm afraid. But, pray — let us introduce you and the lovely Amelia to our companions here."

Once the acquaintances had been made and the raisin-faced but highly efficient Hobbes had supplied the members of the company with refreshment, they settled down in a semi-circle round Professor Greenshields and his wife, near the tall window, where the gray light of afternoon was peeking in.

"We have just now come from Broadshire," began the doctor, with an air of immense importance. "We arrived in Salthead not more than an hour ago, actually, and at once hired a private chaise to trundle us out here. We've come straightaway from Timson's coach-office — for you see, there's a matter of the utmost urgency that we must discuss with you."

"Ah-*hah!*" exclaimed Professor Greenshields, not a little fascinated to be the object of such attention, and not a little excited too that so many people had traveled so far, on a mission of gravity, to confer with him. As a professor of classics, retired, it had been some time since he had been an object of importance to anyone other than the fair Amelia.

"We are in need of your assistance, Kit — your wealth of knowledge concerning the ancients and their world," said Professor Tiggs, his usual sprightly radiance eclipsed now by a dogged seriousness. "We've come for your expert opinion, as Daniel has said, on a matter of great significance to everyone living in Salthead."

"Ah-*hah!*" exclaimed Professor Greenshields again, glancing for a moment at his wife. It seemed he was even more fascinated than before. "But this is most unusual, Titus. My, my, I'm afraid I don't see how I can be of any help to you at all. My studies are of the dim and distant past, of lost worlds of bronze and iron that disappeared long ago. It's rather a puzzle how they could be of importance to anyone."

In short order a general outline of events — from the discovery of the relics at Eaton Wafers, to the visitation of the sinister phenomena upon that house and upon the people of Salthead — was sketched out by several members of the party, each of whom contributed his or her own salient points to the discussion. With each new revelation the restless eyes of Professor Greenshields grew sharper, and he became fired with enthusiasm as he was drawn deeper and deeper into the story. He was particularly intrigued by the finding of the square stone block at Eaton Wafers — ("Was it a cippus?" he inquired of Mr. Banister, who replied by saying he had no idea what a "cippus" might be, exactly, apart from the Latin for *post*) — and by the blue statue that had blown apart in the chapel. He asked numerous questions about Mr. Thomas Scarlett and his collection of antiquities, and on the whole appeared delighted with the entire business, from an academic point of view, but a trifle wonderstruck as well that all of this had been going on around him without his knowing the slightest thing of it.

"We're very isolated here, you know," explained Amelia, who was seated beside her husband and had been listening as intently as he. She was a most intelligent, cordial, good-natured woman, not unlearned in her own right, and who retained yet something of that winsome beauty that had captivated a certain university don so many years before. "We mix so little now with the world. Although the house sits not more than a mile from the Salthead road, it might as well be the back of beyond! Our relations are few and we see them only rarely, and given Christopher's condition it is very difficult for us to travel. What with friends being friends and having their own families to attend to, we simply don't receive many visitors."

"Certainly not so many as we have here!" exclaimed her husband, delighted at receiving such visitors as these on this or any other day. "It reminds me of our old tutorials at Antrobus — eh, Daniel? My, my, some of my lectures were attended by fewer scholars than this!"

The doctor laughed and discharged a volley of smoke from his pipe. Despite the urgency of the situation, he and Professor Greenshields took now a moment to indulge themselves in a few brief reminiscences of college life. At first pleased to be again in the presence of his old tutor, the doctor soon found himself growing a little uncomfortable. So accustomed was he to his way of life now, to his practice and his professional standing in the community, to having been completely his own man for such a long time, that it was unsettling to be returned — however briefly, however real or imagined — to the position of a subordinate, to be once more under the watch of one so senior, and who once had held such sway over him. Unlike Harry Banister, who appeared quite unaffected by the companionship of Professor Tiggs, the doctor was too old to be a student again. So it goes with many of us, I think, that past affinities and attitudes must remain forever past and can never be restored — nor should they.

"Yes, yes, I believe we have heard something of these events in Salthead," said Professor Greenshields, returning the current of conversation to its earlier flow. "The strange ship in the harbor — the *Swan*, I think it is — yes, we've heard of that, haven't we, Amelia? My, my — utterly mystifying! But these other matters you relate — they're most interesting as well."

"We believe," said Professor Tiggs, "that these events are all related in some way to the tablets and the blue statue that were discovered at Eaton Wafers. Everything derives from them. The disturbances began only after the tablets had been appropriated by this fellow Hunter, who it appears is a resident of Salthead, and who insinuated himself into Mr. Banister's household for the sole purpose of stealing them."

"I see. And you say you have brought me a copy of the inscription on the tablets?"

"Here it is, sir," said Harry, hastily proffering that document for Professor Greenshields's inspection. The professor clipped his gold pince-nez to his nose and fell to an examination of the writing. Almost at once his brow lifted and a little gasp of surprise escaped his lips. The look on his face was something akin to love — the love that only an academician who has chanced upon some rare, hidden jewel of scholarship can know.

"Can you read it, Kit?" asked Professor Tiggs, still impressed after so many years by the depth of learning evidenced by his former colleague.

"It appears to resemble both Greek and Latin," put in Mr. Banister. "Professor Tiggs has suggested it may be of Etruscan origin."

Professor Greenshields raised his head and looked into the eyes of his collegiate friend.

"You're right, you know," said he. "It is Etruscan, without question, indeed. My, my!" He nodded gleefully to himself and resumed his perusal of the document. "Ah — marvelous, marvelous! Look at this, Amelia. Approximately third century B.C., don't you think?"

"Some of these characters that so resemble our own," said Professor Tiggs — "they're derived from the Greek, are they not?"

"Indeed. They were adapted from an early alphabet, which the Etruscans learned from Greek traders who began colonizing the south of Italy in very remote times. The Etruscans in turn handed their new alphabet over to the Romans, from whom it has come down to us. So you see, were it not for influence of the Etruscans our own alphabet today might very well be Greek! The Etruscan language itself, however, is most peculiar, being unrelated to any other known language or language family of the world. It is not, for example, a member of the great Indo-European family, which includes Greek, Latin, French, German, and our own hearty English. The origin of the Etruscan language, as well as of the Etruscans themselves, remains a mystery with no prospects for solution. `A very ancient people resembling no other in language or customs, very proud and reserved toward outsiders' — that was their reputation in antiquity."

"But what is the inscription, actually?" asked Dr. Dampe, unable to rein in his curiosity any longer. "What does it say?"

"It is an invocation. More precisely, an invocation to the mighty god Apollo — or *Aplu*, as the god was known to the ancient people of Etruria — that's his name you see written here — to permit his servant — that is, Aplu's servant, presumably whoever is reading this — to call forth Tuchulcha from the underworld."

"Tuchulcha," repeated Professor Tiggs. "I have heard that name before in some connection."

"Tuchulcha," said Professor Greenshields, "was an Etruscan demon of death. The keeper of the gates, who greeted the souls of the Rasna upon their arrival in the underworld."

"Rasna?" asked Miss Mona, with a quizzical frown.

"The name the Etruscans reserved for themselves as a people, Miss Jacks. The Greeks knew them as *Tyrrhenoi*, while to their Roman conquerors they were *Tusci* or *Etrusci*. The term *Rasna* was a very general designation, more cultural and religious in connotation than political, for so far as we know a unified Etruscan `nation' never existed. Instead, the Etruscans formed themselves into an alliance of fiercely independent city-states, which occupied the whole of central Italy at a time when Rome was little more than a collection of thatch huts along the Tiber. For one hundred years, in fact, a dynasty of Etruscan kings ruled at Rome. Etruscan history is dominated by twelve of these city-states — their exact identities tended to vary over the years — which were known as the twelve sacred cities of the Rasna. Among them were Caere, called by the Etruscans *Cisra*; Veii, or *Veia*, Rome's great rival across the Tiber; and Volterra, or *Velathri*, one of the ancient world's wealthiest communities.

"The Etruscans were a seafaring people and at the height of their fame absolutely commanded the coast. They had command as well of the great iron and copper mines of Italy, and these factors combined were the source of their early power and wealth. Despite such promising beginnings, however, their aspirations faltered, for the independence of the individual city-states was jealously guarded, and in the end counted for more than did unity as an Etruscan people. The twelve sacred cities of the Rasna formed in no sense a unified state or empire — and this, I believe, is what led to their downfall, when the period of their spectacular rise was over and they were threatened with invasion. Every year at a great festival the leaders of the city-states chose from among themselves a titular head of the Etruscan people, a strictly ceremonial or religious office with little or no influence I believe over political matters. The Etruscans were either unwilling or unable to make common cause, you see, and so there was no way for them to unite and repel an invader; it was, in a very literal sense, every city-state for itself. Of course, such a tenuous alliance could not hold together in the face of relentless aggression."

"Over time the city-states succumbed one by one to the Romans, their rivals and former subjects to the south, and so eventually the Etruscan people became citizens of the Roman Republic," said Professor Tiggs.

"Yes. Now stop a bit. What of the tablets themselves, and this unusual material of which they were made? You say they were composed of a metallic substance that resembled gold. Could you describe it further?"

This task fell to Harry Banister, who proceeded to relate in greater detail the mysterious qualities of the tablets — their peculiar innate luminescence, the rainbow of colors of which the glow was composed, and the resonant, low-pitched hum that at times was emitted by the metal. As he spoke, he saw the restless eyes of the old college don slowly working themselves into a frenzy of excitement.

"What you say is very nearly incredible," Professor Greenshields exclaimed, as though the greatest wonder on earth had just been laid at his doorstep. "A priceless, priceless treasure, Mr. Banister, is what you had there. A treasure that until now was considered simply an invention of mythology. No one thought it could possibly be real. These tablets, linked together in the form of a hinged diptych, represent I believe a sample of the rarest of rare minerals on earth — nothing less than Tyrrhenian electrum!"

"What might that be, sir?" inquired Mr. Kibble, his hand racing to get it all down in his notebook. "And how exactly do you spell it?"

"Tyrrhenian electrum — quite unmistakable, Mr. Kibble. The legend of electrum is a legend no longer! The ancient authors who described it knew very well what they were writing about."

"But what of it? Does this material have any special significance or value, apart from its intrinsic beauty?" asked Dr. Dampe.

"Ah, indeed, Daniel — and `priceless' is hardly a sufficient word for it! According to legend, Tyrrhenian electrum was a personal gift from Apollo. The opalescent glow and low-pitched sounds were thought to be emanations from the other world, the tablets representing a means by which those living on earth and those beyond it might communicate. A very particular brand of electrum it was indeed — not an alloy of silver and gold, but an alloy of this world and the next! It is recorded that Tyrrhenian electrum was entrusted to the Rasna so that a chosen few among them — their great priest-kings, called *lucumones* — a *lauchum*, as the Rasna referred to their leaders, being transliterated in Latin as *lucumo* — so that these great kings, as I say, might petition for Apollo's aid in times of trial.

"The Etruscans, you see, were an inordinately religious people, believing that all manner of phenomena they observed in the natural world were in reality signs or omens dispatched to them by their gods. Livy wrote that they were `a people more than any other devoted to religious customs.' Life, the

307

Etruscans felt, was a fleeting dream that every day brought them into close contact with deities. It was the responsibility of the soothsayers — some of whom were lucumones — to interpret these signs or omens and so divine the will of the gods. The nature and direction of lightning flashes, malformations of the liver of sacrificial animals, the flight patterns of birds — all held special meaning for the Etruscan soothsayer."

Hearing this, Dr. Dampe and Miss Mona somehow managed to resist turning round and having a hard look at Mr. Jack Hilltop, who they knew was sitting somewhere behind — for they both could feel, or supposed they could feel, the pressure of his eyes upon them.

"A highly superstitious society," said Professor Tiggs, with a rub of his gray bristle-brush head. "So very much so that many ancient writers in addition to Livy commented on it. Even among the most zealous of religious cultures in those times, the Etruscans stood out from the rest. They were a people set apart."

"Exactly. Their religion was characterized by a fatalism unmatched in the ancient world. To an Etruscan, you see, it was useless to struggle against one's destiny; everything that had happened or was ever going to happen had been decreed by the *dii involuti* — what the Rasna referred to as the `veiled' or `shrouded' gods. Very mysterious forces indeed, which existed on yet another plane above what we would call the more `common' deities such as Apollo, as well as Jupiter, whom the Etruscans called *Tin* or *Tinia*, and Bacchus, known to them as *Fufluns*. To paraphrase Seneca, the Etruscans believed not that things had significance because they had occurred, but that they had occurred because they had significance. They saw divine intervention in every aspect of nature."

"So what we have in this glowing metal — this Tyrrhenian electrum — these tablets — is what might be called the personal stationery of the gods!" remarked Dr. Dampe.

"Every event or phenomenon of nature, rather than being given a logical explanation, was interpreted as the direct intervention of a deity. Following Seneca's example, an Etruscan soothsayer who observed a lightning-bolt would see in it some message that must be deciphered. In many cases it was believed that such natural phenomena could predict future events. It was after all an Etruscan soothsayer, one Spurinna, who warned Gaius Julius Caesar to beware the fifteenth of March — though little good it did Caesar, of course, as his fate had already been decreed."

"But if this Tyrrhenian electrum does exist, sir," said Mr. Kibble, homing in on a point, "then it implies that the god Apollo exists as well. And that in turn implies that the gods of the classical world were not imaginary beings, but real flesh and blood — or whatever it is they had — or have — or so to speak — "

"Ah-*hah!* Yes, that would be one possible conclusion, Mr. Kibble. But who is to say whose gods are real and whose are not? My, my — that is certainly one thing I have learned from a lifetime of study. The gift of electrum was intended as a means for the chosen leaders of the Rasna to communicate with Apollo, to learn his will or request his intercession. I cannot believe, however, that every lucumo of Etruria had simply to recite an invocation inscribed in electrum and be awarded this power. No, no, such authority could not be so common. This must have been a very special talent — if I may be so bold in my hypothesis — bestowed by Apollo upon a few, very special lucumones.

"It was of course not unusual for gods of the classical world to favor particular human beings over others. All one need do is consult Homer or Vergil to find evidence of this. Ah! I can visualize it now, in my mind's eye, the spectacle of one of these great priest-kings of Etruria, beloved of Apollo, in his sacred tunic of purple sprinkled over with stars of gold, his face and hands drenched in ceremonial crimson, standing before the tablets of electrum and calling upon the mighty god to hear his prayer, to grant him his wish — "

"Yes, but what does our inscription here say, precisely?" asked Dr. Dampe.

"Here — here — I shall translate as best I can," said Professor Greenshields, taking up the scroll of parchment again and pointing out various characteristics of the text with a wrinkled finger. "It must be read from right to left, of course. Here — here at the very top, these first few lines serve as a brief introduction. See this here — I shall copy out the text in the reverse orientation, to make it simpler to read — please hand me my pen and ink, Amelia, and a fresh sheet of writing-paper, and my letter-board, too — thank you, dear — and so as I say I shall re-write the text in the reverse configuration, and then provide a translation beneath the Etruscan characters. These double dots you see here and there serve merely to separate the words. So. And so. Ah-*hah*. And here we have it — "

He held out the sheet of paper for his visitors' collective inspection. What they saw there was this —

⟨IƷ : ⟨ϝN : VϮ : VNϝ

ϟϝɑLVNϝ : ϮVↆVLↆA

In another few minutes he had completed the translation, and so the long-forgotten words of a vanished people were laid before the eyes of the company. A solemn voice it was, remote and mysterious, speaking to them from across an unimaginable gulf of years, from a dim, unremembered time long before the sundering —

CIZ	:	CEN	:	UT	:	UNE	SVALUNE	:	TUCHULCHA
Three times		this		perform		and then	will live		Tuchulcha

"There! Do you see the meaning? `Perform this three times and then Tuchulcha will live.' There then follows a lengthy votive tract — a few of the words I cannot make out, unfortunately — they're very obscure — but it is without question a summons. I interpret it to mean that the lucumo was to pronounce the entire text of the invocation three times, after which the demon Tuchulcha would make his appearance."

"Tell us more about this Tuchulcha fellow," said Dr. Dampe, champing on his pipe. "Who was he, and what was his job?"

"He was the keeper of the gates of Achrum, a great city lined with towers which the Etruscans identified with the realm of the hereafter. The departed souls arriving there by chariot or on horseback were escorted by Charun with his mighty hammer and greeted by Tuchulcha, before passing through the gates. The details here get a bit muddied, however — so much must remain conjecture because so few Etruscan texts survive — but it would seem that the demon performed some sort of welcoming function, approving or disapproving admission of the soul to the underworld, or perhaps simply frightening it. The ancient Greek and Roman writers are not clear on this point. Perhaps they didn't understand it themselves.

"We would know a great deal more about the Rasna and their beliefs, you see, had it not been for the fire that consumed the celebrated library at Alexandria. No original Etruscan literature has come down to us, apart from the relatively small series of inscriptions on bronze tablets and hand-mirrors, on coins and ceramic ware, on votive figures, and on the Etruscans' peculiar stone sarcophagi and cinerary urns. It is from these that we have pieced together most of what we know of their language. The folded linen on which their literature was written disappeared long ago, and the works were no longer copied once the language ceased to be spoken. But in that library of Alexandria, among many other precious works now lost, was a great history of the Etruscan people in twenty books, composed by the Roman emperor Claudius. His first wife, one Plautia Urgulanilla — a rather troublesome woman of turbulent passions — was of Etruscan stock, as was the poet Vergil himself on his mother's side, by the by. In some circles in imperial Rome, it was considered quite fashionable to advertise one's descent from these ancient people."

"And what did this demon of the underworld look like — this Tuchulcha?" asked Mr. Banister, leaning forward in his chair. Miss Nina Jacks — who had at the outset managed to appropriate the chair beside Harry's for herself, and in the interim had been lofting sidelong glances, every now and then, toward the handsome master of Eaton Wafers — leaned forward as well.

"There are only one or two known representations of him, from the colorful wall-paintings in certain Etruscan tombs. The originals, of course, were all destroyed at the sundering, but fortunately we have the copies made by early visitors. Amelia — would you please bring me Mrs. Standish White's book? Ah, no, I'm sorry, dear — the sketch I'm thinking of — it's in the first volume of Mr. Ottley's excellent text, I believe — thank you — it's on that shelf just over there — "

"Here it is!" said his wife, returning with an ancient volume, very much worn about the spine and edges, which she handed delicately to her husband.

"Thank you, dear. Let me see here, let me see. Ah-*hah!* Here he is. The demon Tuchulcha, in the company of Theseus and Pirithous, as depicted on the wall of a tomb at Corneto. Look at that face! My, my. He is depicted you see as part man and part bird, with a monstrous bearded head, a sharp beak like a vulture's, the ears of an ass, and snake-infested hair. On his back are two huge leathery wings, and round his arm is a coiled serpent that exhales liquid fire."

The visitors peered into the book, where they were confronted with a rather fearsome sight —

"That is he!" exclaimed Harry Banister, with rising excitement. "That is the very creature seen by my chief groundskeeper. That is the flying man!"

In finer detail now he described for Professor Greenshields the events of that night — the noise on the roof — Ned Vickery's moonlight encounter with the creature perched on the battlements — how the creature had laughed derisively at Ned, and gathering its wings floated off into the sky.

Professor Greenshields grew visibly uneasy and took a few sips of his tea. The fair Amelia seemed troubled as well. She reached for a newspaper on a nearby table and passed it to her husband.

"Here is this morning's *Gazette*. I don't believe you've seen it, dear. There is something you and our guests must read — this article here."

The restless eyes of Professor Greenshields scanned the indicated paragraphs. A shadow came over his face, and the paper slipped from his fingers.

"My, my," were his only words.

Dr. Dampe, his curiosity burning at a fever pitch, took up the fallen paper and quickly conned it over, before handing it on to his collegiate colleague.

"What is it?" asked Miss Mona.

"The flying man," said Professor Tiggs, paraphrasing from the columns, "was last night observed by a group of citizens, who watched the creature

312

launch itself from the spire of St. Skiffin's Church, in Bridge Street — hard by Timson's coach-office."

"We were just ourselves at the coach-office," said Miss Nina.

"So the demon is here in Salthead!" said Mr. Banister.

"But this is still so much conjecture," protested Mr. Kibble. "There aren't any of these ancient gods, these — these deities. There is no such being as Apollo. There is no kingdom of Achrum, and there are none of these devilish lucumones. The Etruscans disappeared two thousand years ago!"

Professor Greenshields shook his head indulgently. "Their great city-states may have been conquered, the Etruscans may have ceased to exist as a separate people and been consumed politically by Rome, but they themselves — the Rasna — did not disappear from the earth. Far from it! Some were absorbed into the general population of Italy, it's true, but in many pockets of old Etruria, in the hill country, Etruscan families lived on, worshipping the ancient gods and perpetuating many of their customs and rituals. As late as the fifth century A.D. a pope of the Christian Church is said to have enlisted the aid of Etruscan soothsayers to scatter lightning upon the invading Visigoths. Rome may have conquered the Rasna but she did not destroy them. It is possible that some could have survived the sundering. Indeed, there may be people of Etruscan descent dwelling among us even now."

"But what of the invocation on the tablets? What purpose would be served by calling forth this demon?" asked Miss Mona.

"And how does it relate to the disturbances at Eaton Wafers, and the apparitions here in Salthead?" asked Mr. Banister. "The phantasms of the dead? The black ship in Salthead harbor?"

"You say there could be descendants of Etruscans living in Salthead," remarked Dr. Dampe. "But certainly there are none of these vaunted priest-kings! There are no more Etruscan city-states and so no more lucumones. Who is it then who has called Tuchulcha? Who, in your opinion, could have such power?"

"As I have said," answered Professor Greenshields, "the duties and abilities of the demon Tuchulcha must be inferred mostly from second- or third-hand sources. Without direct knowledge of Etruscan literature we are left with little else but these indirect accounts. And few even of these have survived. But to answer your questions, Daniel — I'm afraid I have no idea who may have called the demon. To the best of my knowledge, none but a mighty lucumo of Etruria could have this power."

"And so it is that the only one with the power is the one who can't possibly exist," observed Mr. Kibble, adjusting his unfashionable green spectacles.

"Nonetheless there remains one thing of which there can be no doubt — that the flying man, whether or not he is the demon Tuchulcha, has come to Salthead," said Professor Tiggs. "We must proceed on the assumption that his summons was not without a specific purpose. It seems far too much to believe, all in all, that he is not associated in some way with the disturbances here and in Broadshire. These things, as we have hypothesized, must be tied together. Don't you agree, Kit?"

"Completely," responded his former colleague.

"And how do we send the irksome fellow back?" asked Dr. Dampe, in his most practical and physicianly manner. "Perhaps an extinct lucumo will be required for that as well."

"A very gifted and powerful one," said Professor Greenshields. "But as to how he would go about it, I don't know. This is not child's play, as the ancients — and, I believe, your Mr. Scarlett — well knew. The keeper of the gates of Achrum is loose in our world, but what his intentions are I haven't the least notion."

"Clearly our search must focus on this Mr. Hunter," said Professor Tiggs. "We must find him at once. If he is not at his residence we shall speak to his attorney, this fellow Winch. Surely he can't be involved in any of this. Once it is fully explained to him what his client has been up to, I'm sure he can be persuaded to assist us. He can't be such a bad fellow. We must assume that Mr. Hunter is the driving force behind all that has occurred. Whatever he is scheming at, he is no doubt well on his way to achieving it. We know for a fact that he removed the tablets of electrum from Harry's study; soon after that the disturbances began in earnest. The evidence to me seems clear. Whoever or whatever this Mr. Hunter is, we must conclude that it was he who called the demon."

"But why?" asked Miss Mona, her eyes reflecting the perplexity on the faces of nearly everyone present. "What is it he wants here?"

Blank looks for replies, followed by a lengthy pause; until a voice from behind said —

"I can tell you what he wants."

CHAPTER XII

Somebody's Return

MR. George Gosling, that most industrious of pot-boys, was not enjoying one of his better days this day.

It all began with a crash, literally. In the midst of his busy preparations for the day's influx of Honeywood regulars, he had without assistance managed to shatter several large jugs of porter, one of the Blue Pelican's finest offerings and a staple of the luncheon board. Emboldened by this achievement, his next action was to inflame the countenance of Cook — albeit not a hard thing to do — by inadvertently toppling a fresh goose-pie from its perch and then treading on it, while racing through the kitchen on one of his multifarious errands. Soon after this he was reminded of his failure to engage Mr. Drinkstone, the brewer, to replenish the Pelican's supply of that gentleman's best bitter, the house reserves being now perilously low. To round it off, a cask of cranberries being brought up from the cellar had chosen that very moment in the history of mankind to spring a leak — surreptitiously — such that a lengthy blood-red trail, like the drippings from a new-slaughtered corpse, had been laid down through a fair portion of the establishment. So it was not the most even-tempered of pot-boys who now burst from the kitchen, a load of linen in hand, to be accosted by a terse whisper from the back-passage —

"Georgie! Georgie!"

"Who's that?" snapped George, peevishly.

The whisperer came forward, revealing herself to be Miss Lucy Ankers, one of two rather charming upstairs chambermaids who functioned under the general supervision of Mary Clinch. There was an oddly anxious cast to her pretty features, and when she spoke again it was in tones just barely above her prior whisper.

"Georgie!"

"What is it?" demanded George, his own voice immoderately loud — in requital perhaps for this latest interruption in the flow of his official duties. "What's a-goin' on?"

"Shhh!"

"What's wrong, then?"

"Oh, Georgie — I seen 'im! I seen 'im, I did!"

"Seen what?"

"Not what — who! You don't know 'alf the fright of it. I'm shiverin' in me shoes to go back in there!"

The dutiful Mr. Gosling, hearing such talk, laid his cargo aside and proceeded to roll up his white sleeves, very crisply and professionally. He folded his arms upon his chest, squared his brow, and frowned in a most condescending manner, thereby conveying the opinion that I'm dead against believing whatever it is you've got to tell me, but being the mature, contemplative soul that I am I'll stop for a minute and listen anyhow.

"What are you gabbing about?" he asked. "Who'd you see? And what's this you're saying about a fright?"

"I seen 'im — the poor crippled boy — the same one as visited Sally Sprinkle — you know, Georgie — 'er `little scamp' — the little chappie with the red hair an' the green face, whose head took an' melted off!"

Immediately George could feel his own hair begin to rise at the back of his neck. Nonetheless he maintained his attitude of cool skepticism, to bolster not only his own self-confidence but also his standing in the eyes of the pretty chambermaid.

"What do you mean, you seen him?" he asked, doubtfully. "And where was that?"

"I seen 'im, Georgie. It's 'im, an' 'e's in Sally's room this very minute! I come ramblin' round that corner — you know, the spot in the passage where it's so dark — an' the door to Sally's room bein' open, I seen 'im there — driftin' beside 'er bed with his little feet six inches above the carpet, like he were glidin' on a cloud — an' such a regretful look on 'is little green face!"

With this disclosure the strength of Mr. Gosling's constitution began to be tested.

"Is the old lady in there with him?" he inquired, tossing one or two wary looks across Lucy's shoulder, as though he expected the little crippled boy at any second to come floating through the passage.

"No. She's a-sittin' out there by the fire with Nutmeg in 'er lap. I suppose she's clean fell asleep by now."

The contemplative George paused while he considered what action to take. What could a ghost possibly want in Sally's empty bedchamber?

"Ain't the Miss back yet?" he asked.

Miss Lucy replied in the negative. She was an uncommonly handsome girl, even for an upstairs chambermaid. She had lovely large dark eyes and beautiful dark curls, and a little turned-up nose like a leprechaun's, and fine red lips — all of which qualities had not gone unnoticed by young George.

"And where's Mary Clinch?"

"Gone off with the Miss and Bridget. To the butcher's, George — to fetch pullets for the kitchen."

Ah, yes, George remembered now. He'd lost track of Mary, and of Bridget too, what with his absorption in his duties, with bustling here and there about the Pelican to attend to the numerous and annoying little cock-ups that had dogged him all the day. He looked at the clock and wondered why it was that the Miss and her minions had not yet returned. How very much more convenient for George if they had!

"What about Jane, then?"

"Gone to visit 'er mother at the lunatic hospital. It's 'er free day, you know. Jane's, that is. So, then — what you gonna do about the situation, Georgie?"

Unsure how to answer, the industrious pot-boy resorted to one of his more reliable stratagems.

"That old lady's crackers," he drawled, with a dismissive roll of his head. "She's all the time gabbing to herself. Ain't she always talking to that cat or jabbering into that locket o' hers? She'd have a chat with the bloody wall if you'd let her. She's all muddled in the head. She's daft, she is."

"But I seen 'im, Georgie!" protested Lucy, with such altogether appealing helplessness that George had not the heart to disbelieve her. Moreover, despite his lowly-sounding status as pot-boy, he was nonetheless a publican's assistant and at the moment *de facto* Man of the House; in the absence of his formidable employer, he, George Gosling, was in command of the Pelican and all that transpired within its precincts. It was his responsibility, then, to find out just what was a-goin' on. And he certainly did not want to create an unfavorable impression in the eyes of the delightful Miss Lucy Ankers — no, that simply wouldn't do.

"All right," mumbled George. He stole a glance into the common-room to confirm Lucy's observation, and saw there the frosty white head of Sally Sprinkle nodding by the fire.

And so he was determined to do *something*, though he didn't quite know what.

"All right," he said again, bunching up his sleeves still further, as though this action in and of itself might accomplish something toward a resolution of the crisis.

"What's the matter with you, George Gosling?" demanded Lucy, placing hands on hips in a manner not unlike that of the starchy proprietor of the house. "Ain't you gonna peep into Sally's room? It's your job. What's the matter, Georgie? What! You ain't *afeared* to go into that room, are you?"

"Afeared?" retorted George, scornfully.

"That's it."

"Why, what's there to be afeared of, girl? If there's anything there it ain't nothin' but a grotty little kid. And who's afeared o' that, I ask? Out of the way!"

Saying which the pot-boy marched himself past a staring and oddly smirking Miss Lucy. Before him lay the back-passage, reaching for him like the gaping jaws of a saber-cat. Directly ahead was the dark corner, beyond which there was another passage, and then another corner containing Sally's chamber, where — supposedly — lurked the immortal remnant of a little lame boy with bright red hair, who had lived and died in this place, and who it seemed was missing it so much he'd come back for a visit.

"Selfish little blighter," thought George, appalled by such inconsideration for others.

He stepped cautiously down the passage, praying that no eerie unseen hand would suddenly lay itself upon his face, that no glowing apparition would come leaping at him from the darkness. But nothing even remotely eerie occurred, so he reached the corner and had a look beyond it. There lay the second length of passage, and at the end of it Sally's room with the door ajar and the faint gray light of afternoon standing in it.

Soundlessly the young George crept along the passage, looking very crisp and professional in his white uniform, but with his pulse racing madly and his heart flailing away like a tom-tom. He could make out a small portion of the room's interior but saw in it nothing unusual. He drew closer, scarcely daring to breathe. If there was a spirit wandering about in Sally's chamber, he wanted to retain at least some element of surprise in confronting it.

He paused at the threshold to gather his courage. It seemed that ages upon ages had gone by since he'd last taken a swallow. He leaned in through the doorway, aiming for a look round toward the bed. He had no real notion what he expected to see there, apart perhaps from the decapitated body of a little ghost-child and a puddle of green slosh that had once been a head.

One silent step, two steps, three steps and he was in the room. The pounding of his heart had grown even louder, and there was a buzzing now in his ears as well. He held his breath. Careful — careful, now —

Where was the poor little crippled boy? Not there!

He caught the sound of furtive movement. Immediately something cold and pointy was thrust against his back, and the voice of Miss Lucy Ankers was heard to exclaim —

"*I see you, Georgie!*"

So startled was George by this that he shot fully three feet into the air, turning as he did and landing awkwardly on his heels, to confront the laughing, giggling figure of the upstairs chambermaid.

"I see you, Georgie!" she crowed.

What *he* saw was that there was absolutely nothing extraordinary about the room — nothing supernatural, nothing the least bit ghostly or sloshy — nothing there resembling a little ghost-child — nothing but Miss Lucy Ankers, the pretty prankster, who it seemed was finding the look on George's face the most extraordinary thing to appear at the Pelican in a very long time.

"I see you, Georgie!" she cried out again, between deep gulps of hilarity. She wagged a cold and pointy forefinger under his nose. "See there! See now, that'll serve you, George Gosling, for playin' your tricks on poor Lucy. If you'd not affrighted me with that mad dog walkin' like a man — if you'd not scared me half out o' me wits with your growlin' and your scratchin' at the door — well, it was all I could do not to pitch you into the water-butt, straightaway!"

"Agh!" fumed George, his face burning with excitement and indignation — and perhaps not a little embarrassment at the recollection of this prank, which he had levied against the charming Miss Ankers not two nights past, and which evidently had served as the catalyst for her retaliation.

"You ain't upset now, are you, love?" asked Lucy. She was trying to calm herself but it was difficult going. "Lord, if only you'd seen the gawk on your red face! What with those big monkey eyes o' yours an' them sticky-out ears — you've just not seen the like!"

George felt another blush at mention of his ears — those large, flappable appendages that the mistress of the house found so convenient for pulling whenever a dose of discipline was called for, which these days was rather often. Embarrassment notwithstanding he straightened both his shoulders and his very professional white uniform, gathered up as much of his shattered dignity as he could, and prepared to take his leave. Miss Lucy watched him quietly from the doorway, her head tilted against the doorpost and a few residual gleams of mischief in her eyes.

"That old lady's off her nut," said George to no one in particular, as though this were sufficient explanation for what had occurred.

He turned to go just as a thin but no less alarming cry arose somewhere in the house, resembling in both timbre and character the voice of that ancient lady so lately disparaged.

Mr. Gosling looked with dismay into the eyes of Miss Ankers; she returned his gaze in kind. Neither said a word to the other. For a fleeting instant George had an impulse to kiss the pretty chambermaid, thinking perhaps that a catastrophe had struck and that this might be his last and only chance to do so; thankfully for both of them the instant passed. Instead they raced back along the passage to the common-room, and there came upon a most interesting tableau.

Standing inside the door was first and foremost Miss Honeywood, just ahead of Mary Clinch and Bridget and their load of pullets. Behind these three stood Miss Laura Dale and Fiona. The rear guard was comprised of the rector and a haughty-eyed stranger in a bottle-green coat, whom George Gosling recognized at once as the young gentleman who had discovered Mr. Rime — or as George himself had so artfully framed it, "the gentleman what found the dead gentleman."

Miss Sally Sprinkle evidently had cried out upon seeing Miss Moll and her companions enter at the door, and then struggled to her feet, scattering little Nutmeg in the process. She stood leaning now upon her crutch-handled cane and scrutinizing the newcomers. Her great magnified eyes seemed ready to burst through her spectacle lenses.

She raised her free hand — a gnarled, claw-like thing — and extended it toward the others in a sort of greeting. All the while her lips were moving silently, as though she were murmuring to herself — or might the trauma of something she'd seen robbed her of her voice?

"There, now, Sally," said Miss Honeywood, stepping cautiously forward a pace or two. She didn't want to frighten her for fear the old woman might take a tumble. Carefree perambulation was not one of Sally's strong suits, and had not been for a very long time. "Not to worry. What's the matter, Sally?"

It was Sally's turn again to surprise Miss Moll and the company. Supported by her cane she began to walk, slowly and deliberately, toward the newcomers. Her great magnified eyes had fixed themselves on something or someone in the party, but it was not possible as yet to determine what or whom.

No one in the room spoke. Even the kindly rector, who had come to pay his usual call on Miss Sprinkle, was speechless with amazement. Ordinarily it required some effort to extract Sally from her bed, to get her walking to the kitchen or the common-room. Yet here was Sally not only walking at her own insistence but gaining energy at every step. With each thrust of the crutch-handled cane it seemed another few of the accumulated years were shed from her life. Her features radiated blissful sunshine. What, oh what could be the source of such happiness?

As Sally drew near the mistress of the Pelican stepped aside to let her pass, for it was clear that Miss Moll was not the object of Sally's attention. Mary and Bridget withdrew as well, their eyes riveted upon the shuffling figure. Laura Dale, who was unfamiliar with Sally and her ways, looked on with some apprehension, while tiny Fiona presented a study in frowns, not a little piqued that so much attention should be paid to someone so ancient and unintelligible. The rattle of Sally's cane against the floor accentuated the oddness of the scene and the silence that otherwise pervaded it.

When Sally came to the rector, he too was passed by — which left only the fashionable young gentleman whose clothing had been spattered with mud from his late encounter with the trap. And indeed, there it was that the rattling of the cane ceased. Pausing before Mr. Hunter, the old woman looked up and into the eyes of that young man with what could only be described as a rapture of affection.

She placed a claw-like hand upon his breast. Instinctively Mr. Hunter started back; nonetheless he allowed the hand to remain where it was, very near his collar. He stared at the old woman with an ill-humored fascination, at those great magnified eyes, at the interlocking web of wrinkles that was her face — it was as though a fisherman had drawn a net over her head — and at her powdery white hair, so sparse now but once so dark and luxurious, and at the smile that stretched her withered lips. How much of mind or sanity lay hid behind that ridiculous expression, Mr. Hunter could not tell.

The hand of Sally rose to touch his cheek. He recoiled again; but this had no effect upon the old woman, who clearly had been transported to a realm quite separate from our own. Completely absorbed, she was looking into the face of Mr. Hunter with something like a soul's contemplation of paradise.

A gnarled finger caressed his cheek, drew a little circle round it, then was joined by the remaining digits. Together they scrambled crab-like down the side of the cheek to the chin, which was explored in loving detail. The contrast between the ancient leathered surface of Sally's hand and the youthful flesh of Mr. Hunter, so vibrant and glowing with life, could not have been more profound.

"What is it, Sally?" asked Miss Honeywood. "Do you know who this gentleman is? This is Mr. John Hunter."

"No, it isn't," replied the voice of Sally — a teasing, playful voice it was now, with the childish accents of a maid of seventeen.

"Who is it, then?"

"She thinks he's her mother!" snickered George Gosling; which comment being overhead by Miss Honeywood, she cast the pot-boy a look that carried with it all the force of an ear-lobe tug.

"No, it isn't," insisted Sally. "It's my Jamie."

Mary Clinch uttered a little groan and dropped her pullets, as her fingers went flying toward her mouth. Tears of compassion rolled from her eyes, compassion for a lonely old woman on whom the snows of life had fallen too thickly.

"That's not your Jamie, Sally dear," said Miss Honeywood, touching Sally's shoulder. "That's Mr. Hunter."

"Oh, you may call him what you like," laughed Sally, "but I shall call him Jamie, because that is his name. Dear Jamie — how long you've been away! I knew you would return to me. They doubted me, you know — all of them — but I knew. I always knew. Let me see you now."

She lowered her hand from his face to his shoulder. The crablike fingers scuttled down the length of his arm, smoothing and patting the fabric of his coat. Just as her great magnified eyes had so carefully explored his face, so now they examined his garments with a like degree of tenderness and solicitude.

"I do believe she's mistaken Mr. Hunter for her beau," whispered Bridget to Miss Dale, who had inquired into the identity of the aforementioned Jamie. "Her fellow, her young buck, as run off and left her when she were a young girl in Richford. They were engaged to be married."

"That's very sad."

"And very odd, too."

"How do you mean?"

"He went missing, you see, and was never heard from again — never so much as a letter of explanation to ease her mind! Because of this Sally never married. La! You should hear her. Every day she's prattling on about how her Jamie is going to do this or is going to do that."

"How long ago did this happen?" asked Laura.

"I don't know, precisely. I suppose it does depend on how old Sally is. Mary Clinch tells me she's nearly ninety."

"And she believes Mr. Hunter is this Jamie, the one who abandoned her — seventy years ago?"

Bridget sighed. "It's so tragic, don't you think, Miss Dale? Love has such strange, strange ways. Whatever it is we want in life, that is what we cannot have. And whatever it is we do have, it's not what we want. It's a sickness! What is the point of it all, I ask? But I do suppose it's the way of the world."

"She looks ever so much in love!" exclaimed Fiona, having exchanged her frowns for guileless wonder.

The industrious George Gosling was unable to hide his disgust. "Agh!" he cried, turning away from what he considered a most grisly exhibition, with a grimace and a squeeze of his nose between thumb and forefinger.

Having tired of the novelty afforded by an eccentric old woman, Mr. Hunter began to protest. But Sally cheerfully ignored him, persisting in her minute examination of chin and hands and cheeks and clothing. Droplets of liquid joy stood quivering in her eyes.

"Jamie — always so dapper and handsome! I knew you'd come back to me. All of Richford town will know you're here — Dr. Jenkins and I will see to that. And so now we can be married! Dearest Jamie, you've returned from your travels, as I knew you would. Where have you been, Jamie dear? You must tell me all! Oh, Jamie, Jamie Gallivan, you scamp — you've come home at last! Why — is something the matter? Why don't you speak? Don't you remember me, Jamie, dear? What! Have you forgotten your little Sally Sprinkle so soon?"

At mention of these names Mr. Hunter's face underwent a series of amazing transformations. Initial surprise melted into puzzlement — darkened toward suspicion — moved on to a fierce and ill-natured curiosity — then dawning recognition — disbelief — horror — unqualified revulsion. Not one of these changes escaped the notice of Miss Honeywood, who though she said nothing was thinking very deeply about what she saw.

Sally turned, and observing the doubting faces that surrounded her, pounded the floor with her cane several times in succession. From a pocket of her clothing she removed the shagreen locket, undid the clasp, and in a singular display of openness — considering her former zealous guardianship of that object — held the locket up for everyone's inspection, with the portraits of the two people inside clearly visible.

"Here! Here is my Jamie," she said, her voice rising. "Don't you see him standing there now? Look at him! Why is it you don't believe me?"

"I'm afraid this woman is mistaken," said Mr. Hunter, coldly. He had recovered himself now and was glaring at the others through a most unpleasant pair of eyes. If one had looked closely, I suspect one might have glimpsed the momentary flare of a yellow light in those eyes.

"Of course we believe you, Sally," smiled Miss Honeywood, without an ounce of starch. It wasn't disingenous on that good woman's part; there was in her voice that which said she did believe, howsoever it were possible. Howsoever indeed!

"You don't believe me," whimpered Sally. Distress, confusion and something like a palsy swept her body. She faltered, released her crutch-handled cane, staggered backward and would have landed on the ground had not Mary Clinch flung hands from mouth in time to catch her as she fell. Together she and Miss Honeywood guided Sally back to her chair, where the old woman sat with her great magnified eyes locked in place, as though engrossed by some scene or object faint and far away in memory.

Mary bent to retrieve the shagreen locket, which had dropped from Sally's hand. It was still unclasped and so she could not help but observe the two miniatures inside — the painted portraits of a young woman and a young gentleman in the costume of an age long gone by. Very intently did Mary examine these images, and one in particular; the result of this effort was a troubled wrinkling of her brow.

"Begging your pardon, Miss, but could you have a wee peep at this picture?" she asked. "This one here, Miss — the picture of the young buck. Look at his face now! You'll think I'm right daft, Miss, I know — but ain't it just like Mr. Hunter's?"

Miss Honeywood took hold of the locket and peered very hard into it.

"Where is Mr. Hunter?" asked Bridget, suddenly looking round.

The hushed response provided her with her answer — there was no Mr. Hunter now. Just as he had the night Mr. Rime was brought in, the fashionable young gentleman had hastily decamped, the open door of the Pelican bearing silent witness to his departure.

The sense of familiarity Miss Honeywood had experienced on meeting him puzzled her no longer. She had seen the pictures in Sally's locket before, quite accidentally of course, on a few occasions; now it was clear why the face of the handsome gentleman in the bottle-green coat had bothered her so.

"Yes, Mary," said she, looking again at the portrait of Sally's young buck, he of the mustache and the smoldering eyes and the haughty pair of arched brows. "It is like Mr. Hunter. *Most like!*"

END OF BOOK THE SECOND

THE LAST OF THE LUCUMONES

《⊙》

CHAPTER I

What Lives On

HEADS turned, and eyes with them, in the drawing-room of Professor Greenshields and his wife. The eyes searched inquiringly for the owner of the voice that had spoken with such assuredness from behind.

"Yes? Yes? What was your name again, sir?" asked Professor Greenshields, from his invalid's chair. "And how is it you know what Mr. Hunter wants?"

The owner of the voice unfolded himself and rose to his feet, laying one outspread palm upon his chest.

"The name is Jack Hilltop — your servant, sir. As regards Mr. Hunter, I know what I know because I know the fellow far too well, don't you see. I've known him, in point of fact, for a blessed long time."

Dr. Dampe gazed with indignation and surprise at the gentleman with the spotted face. "Hallo! What's this, sir? Here we've been pondering among ourselves the motives and methods of Mr. John Hunter ever since our conversation with Mr. Banister at Eaton Wafers — and all the while you yourself have had the answers to our questions, but kept your own counsel? What sort of knavery is this? What do you mean by such deception?"

"What do you know of these matters, Mr. Hilltop?" asked Professor Tiggs, wrinkling his brow very severely.

"More than he has volunteered thus far, I'll warrant," said Harry Banister.

"Gentlemen, gentlemen — truly, it's not deception, if you'll but let me speak," returned Mr. Hilltop, with an odd sort of grin. "There's uncertainty and there's investigation, and that's what it is, to be sure. You see — I've been on the track of Mr. John Hunter for a very long time, as I've said, and so it's clear to me what it is he wants. But as to the attainment of his desire — well, that's been something of a waiting game, don't you see. Believe me, no deception of any consequence was intended; but there were certain points what needed clarification. And you'll pardon me, Mr. Banister, but one of these involved yourself, don't you see, and required a call at your handsome estate. I've been following Mr. John Hunter, you see, watching and waiting, watching and waiting — waiting for him to make his move, and hoping to find the means to stop him before he did. He's a mysterious gentleman and not given to confiding in his pursuers, don't you see."

"Stop him from doing what?" asked the doctor.

"That, as I have mentioned, sir, is one of the particular points what required clarification. And as respects the narrative provided by Mr. Harry Banister, that point was indeed clarified."

"Might I say that you yourself are a mysterious gentleman, Mr. Hilltop," remarked Professor Tiggs, coloring a little. It troubled him that this man who had been dwelling in their midst, the recipient of their blind trust, was in reality a sham, an actor playing a role for his own ends. What perhaps disturbed him more, however, was that this actor had so thoroughly gammoned him — had gammoned all of them. "It was rather ungenerous of you to have used us so. Perhaps you should explain yourself, sir."

Mr. Hilltop promptly assented.

"I'm heartily glad of the opportunity. You're correct, Professor Greenshields, sir, in your identification of the inscription as Etruscan. I myself can vouch for the authenticity of the tablets, don't you see. You're right as well in your belief that there are men of Etruria among us even now."

"You refer of course to Mr. Hunter," said the old college don.

"In the main, yes."

"Ah-*hah!* So it is true. He is descended from that noble race?"

The man with the spotted face hesitated, the odd smile flickering on his lips. "Yes, it's true, but not quite as you picture it, sir. When I say that Mr. Hunter is a man of Etruria, I don't refer to descent. I mean simply what I mean. He is an Etruscan."

"I'm not certain I understand your meaning."

Mr. Hilltop stopped again, at pains to choose his words so as to convey their import in the clearest possible way.

"His name," he said at length, "is not John Hunter. Oh, that's the name what he uses and by what he's been known for some little time now. But before that, you see, he was Mr. Oliver Blackwood, and before that Mr. James Gallivan, and still before that Mr. Frederick Chandos. And long before that — a blessed long, long time before that — he was known as Vel Saties. That is, in point of fact, the name what was given to him at his birth, don't you see."

"Vel Saties? What sort of name is that?" asked the doctor. "A kind of nickname?"

"Vel Saties!" exclaimed Professor Greenshields, his restless eyes afire with scholarly enthusiasm. He nodded his head briskly several times. "This is utterly marvelous. Yes, yes! `Saties' was the name of a prominent and very ancient aristocratic family in the Etruscan city of Vulci."

"Or *Velca*, as that city was known to him and to all others living in the shadow of her winding walls," said Jack Hilltop.

Mr. Kibble glanced up from his note-taking. "What is it you are implying, Mr. Hilltop?"

"What I'm implying, Mr. Kibble, is nothing. What I'm *tellin'* you, don't you see — and what your colleague Professor Greenshields there has rightly perceived — is that Mr. John Hunter is indeed a noble son of Etruria, and has been since his birth in the sacred city of Velca twenty-three centuries ago."

The response that greeted this revelation was thunderous. It enveloped the entire drawing-room and everyone in it in a maelstrom of confusion and disbelief. If one of the solemn busts of alabaster ranged along the tops of the bookcases had chosen that moment to speak, the company would not have been more surprised.

Mr. Hilltop for his part seemed rather pleased with the effect his words had produced. The residual indignation of Dr. Dampe drained slowly into his shoes, and for once the learned physician found himself *sans repartie*. In its own way, this announcement by Mr. Hilltop was to the good doctor nearly as staggering as his encounter with the saber-cat in the coach-window.

"It's a quelling thought," murmured the fair Amelia, once the shock of realization had passed.

"A real stunner!" admitted Harry Banister, massaging his chin.

"Vel Saties," resumed Mr. Hilltop, "was *lucumo* — as you know the term in its debased Latin transliteration — of the sacred city of Velca. The beloved of his people, he was a wise and noble man; remarkably wise, in point of fact, for his youthful years. He succeeded his father, Achle Saties — what was himself a noble man — at a very early age, you see. The father had served but a twelvemonth when he was cut down by a malignant fever. The people of Velca mourned; they clamored for the son, whose success was sure from the start. He secured many beneficial compacts with rival cities of the Rasna, and it was an unspoken assumption that in future he'd be chosen *zilath mechl rasnal* — lucumo among lucumones, the symbolic head of the Etruscan people. In those bright days before Rome, you see, the lucumones of the twelve sacred cites came together each year at the sacred grove, the sanctuary of the god Veltuna, near the city of Velsna. There, amid the great festival, they chose from among themselves their spiritual leader, whose first task it was to drive the ceremonial year-nail into the wall of the temple of Nortia, the goddess of destiny, in acceptance of the inevitability of divine fate.

"And so it happened that Vel Saties indeed was chosen. But following his acquisition of this signal honor, an even more exalted honor lay in store. The shining god Aplu — what you know as Apollo, the lord of the sun — favored him, and in his glory smiled on him. Through the medium of his messenger, the demon Tuchulcha, the mighty Aplu bestowed upon Vel Saties that rarest and most precious of gifts what in the whole history of the Etruscan people has been awarded but three times — the gift of life."

"By this you mean the gift of *endless* life," said Professor Tiggs, with a raise of one eyebrow. "Which is to say that Mr. Hunter cannot die?"

"That's it, you see. Like the rays of light from what Aplu's shining spirit is made, Vel Saties was granted immortality on this earth. Nothing can harm him — ever. He does not sicken and he does not age, retaining forever his outward appearance at the time the gift of life was received. Retains forever his old dash and vigor, don't you see! He's the chosen of Aplu. As I have said, this is a gift what was awarded to but three lucumones among all the sacred cities of the Rasna."

"And are we correct in assuming that one of those three fortunate men is among us at this very moment?"

Laying the palm of his hand flat upon his chest, Mr. Hilltop gracefully bowed his head in acknowledgment of this fact.

"Exactly!" exclaimed the doctor. "I watched the saber-cat snare you on that very hand there. I saw the blood rush from it in a little fountain; yet when you removed your glove no trace of any wound remained. It's medically impossible, I can assure all of you — we physicians, we're trained in such matters. Extraordinary! So the explanation is clear. Wouldn't have believed it, actually."

"That is why you leaped so readily to the defense of the coachman and the guard," said Professor Tiggs. "You placed yourself in `mortal' danger — if I may use the term — in an effort to drive away the cats, because you knew that you yourself could not be hurt."

"That's it," smiled Mr. Hilltop.

Another hush swept the room. Professor Greenshields, struggling mightily against the confines of his wheeled chair, found he could no longer restrain his excitement.

"My goodness, my goodness! What we can learn from you, Mr. Hilltop, what we can learn from you, and from your associate Mr. Hunter. The secrets of the ancients! Here you are today, in this very room — in our very own house, Amelia — a living, breathing man of Etruria. And a lucumo as well! What knowledge you must possess, Mr. Hilltop. What deeds you must have witnessed in your long life. What history! What mysteries you could unlock for us. What it has taken me a lifetime of study to learn — a lifetime spent scrutinizing dusty parchments and faded inscriptions — what it has taken me a lifetime to discover, you could have told me in a heartbeat. And so much more! So many mysteries. Your history, your literature, your traditions — all lost, until now! There are so many, many questions I have to ask you. It is almost too much for me to grasp at present."

"For a start, what might your true name be, Mr. Hilltop?" asked Dr. Dampe, folding his arms upon his cherry-colored waistcoat in a vaguely defiant manner. "I don't believe that `Hilltop' can be proper Etruscan, actually."

"I was born Avle Matunas, the son of Sethre Matunas and his second wife Velia Veliiunas, and was named lucumo of the sacred city of Cisra," was the reply. "I was more than forty years of age when I received the gift of life from Aplu."

"A lucumo, but with the powers of a soothsayer as well. Ah, I see you recollect the incident. Miss Mona Jacks and I chanced upon Mr. Hilltop in an act of divination. He was standing in the yard of our very hospitable mountain inn, observing a group of birds in flight. It was on the morning of our departure for Eaton Wafers, Titus. We spoke then of certain gifted people with an ability to divine the future, or the will of the gods, by the observation of natural phenomena. `They're all dead and done now,' I believe, was his sage remark at the time. Do you recall it, Miss Jacks? Well, it seems they're not nearly so dead and done after all."

"There were many lucumones with the power of divination, don't you see. It weren't unusual," said Mr. Hilltop.

"And what did the flight of those birds tell you?"

"That it would shortly rain."

"And so it did," exclaimed Miss Mona, with a look to the others for confirmation. "From a beautiful clear sky — very fine weather — it showered all that evening. You remember, certainly."

"Is Mr. Hunter — Vel Saties — a soothsayer as well?" asked Professor Greenshields.

330

"A powerful one," replied Mr. Hilltop. "A *fulguriator*, or interpreter of lightning and thunder. An adherent of the doctrine of the nymph Vegoia, who revealed the fulgural science to human folk. But more importantly, don't you see, Vel Saties was once my good friend."

"So he is no longer?" said Professor Tiggs.

Again that odd grin spread itself over Mr. Hilltop's spotted face. "He discovered that the powers entrusted to his keeping — first by his own people, and then by the shining god — were not without risk. Great responsibilities — they're always attended by great temptations, don't you see. And as with so many in the sad history of this world, it was the temptation what got the better of him. The corrosion leaked into his soul like salt-water into iron, rusting him out. He grew deceitful in his dealings with others, and found sport in playing his brother lucumones the one against the other. In so doing, he betrayed his sacred vows to Veltuna. He imagined conspiracies round him everywhere and strove to crush all opposition to his will, growing rich in the process. When a few of us sought to temper his violence, he threatened to harm those what were dear to us. In some cases, I'm told, he did far more than threaten.

"At this same time, the cities of Etruria were engaged in a war of survival against the arrogant upstart savages of Ruma — what you call Rome — what were intent upon seizing the wealth of the sacred lands. Against such a background, the activities of Vel Saties became intolerable. By uniform decree of his brother lucumones, he was removed as the symbolic head of the Etruscan people, and it was I, the lucumo of Cisra, what was chosen in his place. So our friendship came to a miserable end. Belike it was for the best; there's no contending with the dictates of the shrouded gods, don't you see. And in the light of history it's of blessed little consequence. The enemy what threatened the sacred cities was too powerful, our people too hopelessly disunited and quarrelsome to resist; one by one they fell, city after city, all surrendering territories and tribute to Rome — what had once herself been ruled by mighty lucumones of Etruria.

"My former friend and brother lucumo vanished among the multitude, and for a long time was lost to my sight. He fled first, I believe, to the northern cities where resistance to the arrogant upstarts remained strong. Across the centuries he traveled to many foreign lands, growing harder, colder, and more determined than before. He refused to accept the harsh judgment of his brothers and his gods, you see, and had resolved that in future he would restore to earth the glorious rule of the Rasna. That, gentlemen and ladies, is what Mr. John Hunter wants from Tuchulcha."

"And just how does he propose to accomplish this?" asked Dr. Dampe, skeptically.

"With the tablets of electrum, Doctor, and the access they provide to the world beyond. The tablets were bequeathed to the Rasna so that in times of great distress their immortal lucumones might seek the aid of Aplu. The Rasna, you see, were the adopted favorites of Aplu; he was and is the secret guardian of the Etruscan spirit. So it is that the shining luster of electrum is like a conduit to the shining god himself. The demon Tuchulcha, one of the gatekeepers of the nether world, was his chosen messenger. The nether world, you see — the many-towered kingdom of Achrum, ruled by the lord Mantus — is the place where all Etruscan souls, apart from those of the three immortals, now reside. The eclipse of the Rasna on earth was not countenanced by Aplu; but even such as he can't overrule the decrees of destiny and the shrouded gods, what determine the fate of humankind. So Aplu gave to the Rasna electrum, as a means to temper the judgment of the shrouded ones."

"And so what is Mr. Hunter's aim, precisely?" asked Professor Tiggs. "I'm afraid you haven't made it clear yet."

"His aim, sir, is nothing less than the establishment of Etruscan power over the surviving cities of the world."

The features of Mr. Hilltop offered proof that he was in complete earnest; thus he was not prepared for the burst of laughter that came from Dr. Dampe, who in the throes of his hilarity lost hold of his pipe and so managed to scatter ashes down the front of his cherry-colored waistcoat.

"You find this a comical proposition, Dr. Dampe?" asked Mr. Hilltop, in a lofty tone.

"No — no — a preposterous proposition, actually," replied the doctor. He laid his pipe aside and brushed away the ashes, before resuming his former posture of attentiveness.

"He's serious, you know," said Professor Greenshields to his former pupil, endeavoring by dint of various looks and nods to convince him of that fact. "It's a thought to conjure with, Daniel."

"What you're telling us, Mr. Hilltop," spoke up Mr. Kibble — who to all appearances was nearly as disbelieving as the doctor — "is that an immortal priest-king of Etruria is looking to revive a horde of dead Etruscans, so they can lord it over the lot of us?"

"In your own inelegant way, Mr. Kibble — that's it," smiled Jack Hilltop. "To restore to earth his allies and comrades-in-arms, and with them the shining glory of the Rasna. But you'll permit me to return to my narrative. The tablets of electrum, you see, were kept in the sacred sanctuary of Veltuna, and represented the most precious possession of the Rasna. But the sanctuary was laid siege and plundered by the Romans, what removed the tablets and many other objects to their own temples in the city on the Tiber. Once they recognized the full significance of the electrum, however, their priests had the tablets buried in an unidentified spot on the Capitoline Hill. They couldn't o' course destroy them — electrum's eternal, indestructible — so they had no choice but to hide 'em away. The tablets were harmless and of no danger to Rome, you see, so long as they were kept from the hands of an immortal lucumo. None but an immortal might command them; none but an immortal had power to speak the sacred words and summon the gatekeeper of Achrum. Might I point out, gentlemen and ladies, you've witnessed already the power of Tuchulcha. I need but remind you of the disturbances at Eaton Wafers and the apparitions in town, don't you see, and of the black ship standing in Salthead harbor."

"And so Mr. Hunter — Vel Saties — went in search of the tablets in order to accomplish his mission," said Professor Tiggs.

"Not at first," replied Mr. Hilltop — his face growing so very sober and retrospective in character, one might have been forgiven for taking the thoughts and feelings he was about to recount as his own. "For a blessed long time he brooded, I believe, and in his travels from place to place, fought mightily with his convictions and his conscience. He knew deep in his heart, you see, that to kick over the traces and struggle against destiny was a vain endeavor, if not an outright dangerous one. All things, you see, have their cycle; there is first gain, then loss; the world rolls ever on, without mercy, and all things — even the glory of the Rasna — must in time give way. The great law of change and succession is at work, continually and everywhere. To defy the will of the shrouded gods was to invite reprisal, but in the end the desires of his heart overwhelmed him.

"During his exile he witnessed first-hand the long, slow decline of his people and their way of life, the dispossession of their lands, the triumph of the fierce and ruthless civilization across the Tiber. He watched the accumulated wisdom of the Rasna trickle away and all memory of the Etruscan people fade from the world, till the very word `Etruscan' itself stood for nothing but mystery and puzzlement. All round him his comrades and allies, being mortal, turned to dust; yet he lived on. All of this he watched. And when it came time at last to end his brooding, he was resolved to challenge the destiny what had been meted out to his people by the lady Nortia and the shrouded ones.

"But to return to the tablets of electrum. Their value was o' course self-evident to anyone, so like any priceless treasure what's been lifted they were kept well-earthed and out o' sight, passing discreetly from hand to hand through the centuries. During the pillage of Rome they were captured by the victorious tribes and taken to the cities of the East. For years upon years they were lost to history; I've been unable to trace their whereabouts during this time. Vel Saties, having by now settled on his goal, took up the search but even he could not find them. Since those dark days he has sought out every clue, every hint, followed every possible line of evidence, using his wealth to track the tablets of electrum across the world."

"And all this while you have followed him?" asked Harry Banister.

"Not always. For a time we traveled together. We happened to meet, you see, through the perverseness of circumstance, and so resolved to forget our differences. He told me he was searching for the great terra-cotta statue of Aplu what had once adorned the god's temple at Velca. At the time I believed him. I didn't see what his true aim was, till we came upon a dealer in antiquities at Damascus. By mistake this old fellow's servant approached me, believing me to be Vel Saties, and told me his master had that day acquired the `shining tablets' what I had been searching for. So we nearly had 'em, then and there, don't you see — they were nearly in our hands — and I would've known nothing of it! When I confronted Vel Saties he flew into a passion. High words followed, and his entire scheme came tumbling from his lips. This encounter occasioned a delay during what time another gentleman — an attorney what was passing through the city, and acting as agent for an anonymous collector possessed of astonishing wealth — offered ready cash for the tablets. The dealer thus had the collector's brass in one hand, and simply a promise from me in the other — and so what do you suppose was the result of that, gentlemen and ladies?"

"It seems painfully clear," said the doctor.

"That's it. Now that the true motive of my supposed friend had become known to me, I had no choice but to dissolve the partnership. I succeeded in tracking the attorney for a short time, only to lose sight of him in the Low Countries and without learning the identity of the anonymous collector. Since then Vel Saties and I have kept a wary distance from one another, each seeking the tablets for his own purpose, don't you see. Along the way we've thwarted each other more than a few times, it's true, the upshot of it being just what you'd predict — the tablets of electrum have remained in the hands of others. Until recently, o' course. By the by, the collector represented by the attorney — the anonymous gentleman what actually purchased the tablets — I know now to have been a resident of the county of Broadshire. I believe we are ourselves acquainted with this gentleman — you a bit more intimately than the rest of us, Mr. Banister, sir."

"Of course," replied Harry Banister, clenching his fist. "Mr. Thomas Scarlett."

"Fascinating!" exclaimed Professor Greenshields. "Fascinating, is it not, Amelia? Please continue, Mr. Hilltop — ah, Mr. Matunas — by all means."

"Yes, pray continue," urged the fair Amelia. "Hobbes — will you fetch more tea?"

"For a blessed long time after that my efforts proved fruitless, and I very nearly gave up the chase. Then it was a great disaster struck, a tragedy of near-incomprehensible proportions. I happened to be lodged in Medlow town, near Chedder, you see, at the time of the sundering. A blazing, fiery death it was what came roaring out o' the night — a thunderbolt hurled by Cilens the thunderer — then a mighty crash — the hammer of Charun, by command of the shrouded gods, ringing down such a judgment upon the world as had never been seen before. The words to describe what I've witnessed are not readily come by. The seas boiled over; the land was laid waste, scorched and shattered by the comet. It had been seen in the sky for some time, in the lower latitudes, you see; and so it came not without warning. No need to question the extent of its effects, gentlemen and ladies; no need whatsoever. Put a period to the existence of nearly everything in your geography books. I myself have viewed the devastation and can attest to it."

"Is there nothing left?" asked Miss Mona. "Nothing whatever?"

"Nothing worth the having, Miss — apart from these long narrow lands at the far edge of the continent, o' course. It's fortunate we've the fells hard by, and beyond them the high moorlands and the farther mighty mountains. I do believe they may have saved us. Everything beyond Richford and the mighty mountains is a waste, don't you see."

The contemplation of so much destruction, the surety now of what had but moments before been unproven suspicion, the chilling nature of Mr. Hilltop's testimony — above all the image of so many innocent lives snuffed out in an instant — acted together to produce an atmosphere of introspection, which accorded well with the sad gray light from the back-garden. Surely something more must remain! Surely something more than these narrow outposts of land, from frozen Saxbridge in the north to the islands in the south to decaying Richford in the east. General reflections on the preciousness of life — and on the corresponding fickleness of the life-giver, no doubt — informed everyone's sensibilities at that moment. No one seemed to know quite what to say; whereupon Mr. Hilltop took the liberty of resuming his narrative.

"When I came at last to Salthead, not so very long ago, I made the acquaintance of any number of publicans and their fine establishments. Such persons and places can be treasure-houses of secret intelligence, don't you see, and much of what I've learned in my travels I've acquired from such sources. Say it how you will, moreover, a gentleman does feel the want of a drink now and then. In one establishment in particular I came across what looked to be a portrait of Vel Saties — a miniature it was, hidden in an old woman's locket. Learning what I could of the old lady's story, I found that in her springtime she had known this gentleman at Richford. That tallied well, for I knew that as James Gallivan he had lodged in that city, long ago; unfortunately it told me nothing more. Further inquiries about town, however, disclosed that a fashionable young gentleman answering to his general description had lately been observed in Salthead. Having been disappointed many times over in like regard, I held out little hope that it was indeed Vel Saties; nonetheless I decided to remain in Salthead for a time, on the likelihood that something might turn up.

"One night, in this very same establishment what is called the Blue Pelican — you yourself were there, Doctor, with your friend Professor Tiggs — it was the night the cat's-meat man was carried in, half-alive — what should I spy standing in the door but the fashionable figure of Vel Saties, in his bottle-green coat? Our eyes touched for just an instant; a shadow came over his face, and without a word he disappeared — leaped onto his horse, it seems, and rode off into the fog at a ringing trot. So I knew now for a fact he was here. Then the story told by the cat's-meat man was circulated, and soon, one by one, other tales came to light. Dark laughter was heard in the night sky, and a sunken wreck came floating into the harbor. It was apparent to me then that Vel Saties had found the tablets of electrum. He'd spoken the sacred words, don't you see, for it was plain that Tuchulcha was here.

"It was then I overheard your conversation there, Dr. Dampe, with Miss Mona Jacks, one cold morning. I happened to be passing through the lane fronting your house, Miss, when the doctor came driving by in his dog-cart.

I recognized him from the Blue Pelican, and from your conversation it occurred to me that the high moorlands might hold the treasure I sought. I decided to follow you — you'll pardon me both for the boldness, I'm sure, but you can see now what it was I was about — and took an outsides booking on the coach to Pease Pottage. That's why I traveled on to Eaton Wafers — what with the sudden disturbances reported by Mr. Banister, I thought perhaps the tablets might have been taken there. Then I heard his story and learned they'd indeed been in his possession, but that Vel Saties — John Hunter — had come himself and pinched 'em. Not to worry, though; at the very least I'd discovered the name Vel Saties had appropriated of late, and so could now search for the tablets where they were most likely to be found — at his residence in Salthead."

"So Mr. Scarlett understood very well what it was he had acquired through his agent in Damascus," said Professor Tiggs. "It is as we thought. He buried the tablets under the oak tree so that no one would ever make use of them. That surely is the explanation for the word `NUNQUAM' inscribed on the stone receptacle in which the tablets were hidden."

"But what of the blue statue in the chapel?" asked Mr. Kibble.

"Ah!˙ That's another story in itself, that is," said Mr. Hilltop. "The shining god Aplu, you see, and the lord Mantus, prince of the nether world, had themselves a bit of a row. The lord Mantus, so full of pride, took objection to the god's choice of Tuchulcha — what he considered to be within the sphere of his own dominion, you see — as a messenger. Tuchulcha, being the haughty sly devil what he is, angered the lord Mantus so with his gibes and his mockeries, that in requital the prince caused him to be imprisoned in a block of volcanic tufa. This monument once resided in the great sanctuary of Aplu at Veia, where it was captured by the arrogant Roman upstarts. Years passed and it found its way to Campania, where for a short time it was lodged at a villa in Herculaneum. Thereafter its history is obscure; much later it was reportedly seen in a churchyard in France. Belike that is where the enterprising Mr. Scarlett happened upon it. Most probably he had it removed to Eaton Wafers before he'd discovered its true nature. He must have feared the statue mightily, for he had it sealed in the crypt of the little chapel there, to be guarded by the relics of a Christian saint. And there it was the demon remained until awakened from his long sleep by the call of Vel Saties."

"But what of the disturbances there, and the apparitions in Salthead?" asked Professor Tiggs. "Surely these are not Etruscan spirits returned to life."

337

"No, that they are not. What they are, you see, are manifestations of Tuchulcha himself. Upon his liberation from the tufa there was the need, I believe, for the testing of his powers, the exercise of his abilities, the simple enjoyment of freedom after the long centuries of repose. So now as he's been released by the power of the electrum, it's for him to decide when he'll take action and when he will not, and what the course of that action might be. He's something of a rascal that way, don't you see; a prankster, too; and in this he's not unlike many of those from the world beyond. A human person, you see — even a lucumo — can never command a god, or a god's minion, either to perform some action or to refrain from such. A human person can humbly request, petition, pray, plead, offer appropriate sacrifice. A human person can wait and hope. It is the prerogative of the god or the god's minion as to when and how to render assistance. And the demon Tuchulcha, I'm heartily glad to say, has been less than obliging. He's a mischievous fellow by nature, as befits his role. Capricious he is, too, very capricious — it's a trait common to all gods and their minions, don't you see. He is, I imagine, ignoring Vel Saties at this moment, and that's a good thing for it's prevented my former friend from carrying on with his scheme. Tuchulcha is not unintelligent, and I believe he may resent the position what he's been placed in; but that o' course is only my opinion on the matter. A demon, you see, whether intelligent or not, is capable of many things. He can for instance infuse his personality and will into any object, into an animal, or into a human person."

"The miser's dog!" whispered Mr. Kibble, with a look to his employer.

"He can as well refashion a dead form, such as a body, or raise a sunken wreck from the ocean bottom. Such dead forms as he may choose to animate — a sailor, a child, a horse — well, they're not the actual bodies themselves, o' course, for they've long since fallen to dust. It's more precise I believe to call 'em impressions — images — reflections, as it were, given certain of the qualities they had in life by the life-force of Tuchulcha. Phantasms, as you say. They live, they have a kind of substance, but they're only castings, you see — an extension of Tuchulcha himself, molded by him into the general shape and character of the beings they resemble.

"And so the demon has been amusing himself with these little tricks, I believe, while gaining strength and rejoicing in his release from the tufa. There's no doubt, however, that soon he'll address himself to the serious business what he's been called to. And if it's to his liking, he'll make his way to the gates of Achrum and gather to him the souls of the Rasna, what then will be free to return with him to this world and acquire for themselves new bodies by dispossessing the souls residing there. Hungry for life the dead are, you see, and fiercely jealous of the living. They can be vicious, savage — oh, there's little question of the outcome. So you see there's bound to be a mighty struggle, gentlemen and ladies, and I fear you'll all be in some trouble. It's certain Vel Saties has by now made several attempts to petition Tuchulcha by means of the electrum. I've no doubt he will succeed, given the time."

"You say the gift of life was bestowed upon three fortunate lucumones, you and Mr. Hunter included in that number," said Dr. Dampe, looking very profound.

"There is that tradition, sir — that three were chosen."

"And so who was the third?"

Mr. Hilltop shook his head. "He is unknown to me."

"Could he be known to Mr. Hunter?"

"It's possible, I suppose."

"Could he be here now — in Salthead?"

"He could be anywhere, don't you see," returned Mr. Hilltop, with a throw of his hand.

"So why do you think the shining god did this, actually? What was the basis for his selection? Why should he choose Mr. Hunter? Why should he choose you?" asked the doctor, training his hazel eyes upon the lucumo of Cisra.

"Who's to say, Doctor? They're questions without any answer, don't you see. No human person can hope to comprehend the mind of Aplu, or of any god. What is decreed by the unfathomable powers will come to pass; nothing can alter it. If it is meant for a thing to happen, it will happen. The gift of life was a blessing bestowed by the god for his own purposes, you see, and I've no desire to inquire into it further."

"A blessing you may call it, sir, but I should call it a curse," said Miss Mona, her chirrupy voice sounding strangely hollow in the gray stillness of the drawing-room. "I'm not certain I'd want to live for twenty-three centuries. Think of the sorrow one must endure, watching one's family and friends die, one after the other, time after time, century after century. An endlessly repeating cycle of loss — oh, it must be horrid! No one can possibly remain secure for long in your presence, knowing the advantage you possess. How do you endure it?"

"But this is all so much mythology," protested Mr. Kibble, running a hand in frustration through his orange hair. He could not accept the possibility that such myths at their heart might conceal elements of fact. "How can these things you've described possibly be real? How do we know they exist? How do we know what you've told us is the truth?"

"Do you doubt the evidence of your own eyes and ears, Mr. Kibble?" returned Mr. Hilltop, with some asperity. "You've heard Mr. Banister's account of the events at Eaton Wafers. You've seen and heard the evidence for the apparitions in Salthead. You and Professor Tiggs have yourselves visited the dead ship in the harbor and personally confronted the mastiff. You've seen and heard evidence for the reality of Tuchulcha. Yet you see fit to question me, and ask what is real?"

"I'm afraid I don't know what reality is any more," complained the secretary. He threw off his unfashionable spectacles to rub his eyes. Poor, unswerving Mr. Kibble! His whole world was bending and twisting before those eyes; he prayed it would not break.

"There are, you see, gentlemen and ladies, a preordained number of ages what all mortal human persons, and what all civilizations pass through; this — and no more — they're allotted by destiny and the shrouded gods. Having come to the end of their appointed span all things, even the glory of the Rasna, must give way. The dead folk can't be allowed to return, don't you see. If Vel Saties succeeds, the world as you know it would be changed beyond your recognition of it. That I'll assure you!"

"And what do you gain by this, Mr. Hilltop?" inquired Dr. Dampe, very reasonably. "You are an Etruscan — a lucumo, and an immortal. You yourself are one of the Rasna! Look here, it seems to me you should positively welcome the change of regime. Don't you look forward to seeing all your old colleagues again? Or is it that your own fortunes may not be so bright once your rival Mr. Saties takes command?"

Mr. Hilltop shook his head slowly, smilingly, like an indulgent parent might when a child, ignorant of the world at large, offers some naïve opinion on it. Granting the doctor nothing more than this in reply, he turned his attention to Miss Mona.

"You're right, and blessed close to the truth there, Miss, when you speak of a curse — a curse of *life*. Like my friend Vel Saties, I can no longer accept my fate. No one, as you say, can be secure for long in the presence of an immortal, for it forces 'em to look their own mortality straight in the eye. The fear, the jealousy, the rage what come after — well, they're inevitable, don't you see, given the human condition. I've witnessed it more times than I care to recall. As a result you must tell no one who or what you are. You're forced to lie, you see. You lie about one thing and so you must lie about another thing; soon you're lying all the time. You conceal your true self and live your life under an illusion of normality. You live your life, that is, till those around you are seen to age.

"Do you know what it is, gentlemen and ladies, to watch as your own dear child grows old, withers, and dies in front of your very eyes, while you yourself are not changed at all, and powerless to help? Can you even in your dreams conceive of such a thing? So it is, if you're wise, you'll tell 'em nothing about yourself from the start, and when the time comes you'll quietly disappear, you'll move along, without so much as a fare-you-well to your loved ones. You'll vanish, cloak yourself in a new identity like a change o' garments — and so on it is to the next life, as it were. But now I am resolved that this way of living, like all other things, must give way.

"So you see, Doctor — there is something I intend to gain from this, apart from preventing a great catastrophe. I'd be less than honest to deny it. It is my aim to petition Tuchulcha and the shining god on my own behalf, you see, to revoke the gift of life what was dropped upon my head so many years ago. I want now nothing more than to live out my allotted span of time, like any other human person. It's only right and just, don't you see. I was allowed no choice; I couldn't put a period to it myself if I tried. A blade to the heart, in my case, is no more injurious than a scratch on the arm is in yours, and but a small matter in the repair. It's my intention to use the tablets to seek the lifting of this blessed affliction, don't you see."

Somewhere a clock was ticking. No one spoke; even the doctor seemed impressed by the power of Mr. Hilltop's confession. After a while he glanced round, and noting the downcast thoughtful looks on the faces of the listeners, determined that something must be done.

"I once knew a gentleman who was convinced he was immortal," he offered, to rally the conversation. "A patient of mine, actually. To prove it to his fellows, he downed three pints of grog and a noggin of whisky, and precipitated himself from his window into the street below. I regret to report he is immortal no longer. And no longer is he a patient!"

The humor of this physicianly anecdote fell flat, nearly as flat as the unfortunate patient upon the stone flagging; but given the atmosphere in the room it was perhaps the best that could be expected.

341

"An interesting piece of experience. So we are resolved then to seek out Mr. Hunter and the tablets?" said Professor Tiggs, gathering consensus from those around him. They were resolved. But presuming they were successful, how then to dispose of the demon Tuchulcha? How to send him back? Would he return now, permanently, of his own accord? Mr. Hilltop, scratching his chin, admitted that he frankly didn't know, don't you see; that even if he himself had the means, he doubted whether he had the power to do it; then he tossed up his shoulders and declared it was all in the hands of Aplu — which response gave little encouragement to the others.

It was determined that the sisters Jacks should be driven home in the private chaise hired at Timson's, while escorted by Harry Banister on his gray hunter; Mr. Banister himself would then secure lodgings at his old club in town. Professor Greenshields graciously offered the use of his dog-cart, which was brought round by one of the servants, to convey the remaining members of the party to their respective households — a circumstance which Dr. Dampe, a great proponent of dog-carts, found highly agreeable.

Meanwhile Mr. Hilltop — Avle Matunas, lucumo of Cisra — agreed to remain at the house of Professor Greenshields and his wife for a few hours more, to indulge the curiosity of his hosts.

"There is so much you can tell us," exulted the old collegian, smoothing his hands one over the other in anticipation. "So much about your life history — your civilization — your culture — your art. For instance, were your people always in Italy, or did they emigrate from another land? What was the procedure for choosing a lucumo's successor? Who were your great artists? What was your literature? Your music? Was there poetry, drama? So much to learn, Mr. Matunas, so much — and always so little time!"

"Hobbes, can you fetch more tea?" called out the fair Amelia, brightly.

Mr. Hilltop very generously acceded to the wishes of his hosts, and replied to all their inquiries as best he could. To Mrs. Greenshields he was unfailingly courteous and obliging, complimenting her now and again on this or that point, on her hospitality and her not inconsiderable charm, and comparing her many fine qualities most favorably to those of other ladies he had known in his long life. Which laudatory words prompted her husband to respond —

"You'll recollect, Amelia, how freely men and women mixed in Etruscan society, and the exalted position accorded the female sex. You'll recall the sketches in Mr. Ottley's book — the delightful wall paintings, dear, from the Etruscan tombs — with the elegant young women on their banquet couches,

342

reclining at table beside their husbands, surrounded by musicians and dancers and all manner of servants to supply them with food and drink. My, my! The freedom and social status enjoyed by the women of Etruria was really quite remarkable. A wife dine with her husband? Why, such doings positively scandalized the whole remainder of the ancient Mediterranean world. Am I not correct in this, Mr. Matunas?"

"That's it," replied Mr. Hilltop, smiling into his cup.

CHAPTER II

Catch That Catch Can

"SO we shall see you again, Mr. Banister?" said Miss Nina Jacks, perched upon the steps of the house in Boring Lane, with her sister beside her and a glow of expectation lighting her pretty features.

"You may depend upon it," returned Harry Banister. He drew his horse forward so as to accomodate the passage of the empty chaise. The servants having collected the belongings of the sisters from the vehicle, the driver now touched the horses with his whip and away went the chaise for Timson's, rumbling and clattering down the narrow lane into Key Street.

Looking resplendent (particularly so in Nina's eyes) in his trim dark riding-coat, leather breeches, and mahogany top-boots, the youthful squire paused for a moment to adjust his pack-saddle, before springing into it. There he gathered up the reins and directed a cheery grin toward the ladies on the stairs. "You'll find me at Longstaple — my club — while I'm in town, Miss Jacks — and Miss Jacks. Once Professor Tiggs and Mr. Hilltop have pursued their deliberations and formed a plan of action, we shall be calling on you. Not to worry, then, not one iota. Once those two gentlemen have gotten their heads together, I'll lay fifty guineas they'll have a smashing good strategy for getting at Mr. John Hunter — and my tablets!"

"Your tablets, Mr. Banister? Isn't that a trifle proprietary of you? Perhaps you meant Mr. Scarlett's tablets. Moreover, I seem to recollect your telling us you were quite relieved they'd been stolen."

"My word, I'm afraid you have me there, Miss Jacks. I did indeed say something to that effect, didn't I? Perhaps it was the emotion of the moment. Believe me, once you've seen Tyrrhenian electrum for yourselves you're not likely to forget it — it's a stunner! And as for Mr. Thomas Scarlett, I suppose the tablets really are not his either, although he laid out a pretty sum for them. In truth I suppose they belong to the people of Etruria. Or perhaps they're the property of Apollo? I must confess, it's all a bit confusing for me. Well, there it is, then. I'll be off now," said Harry, dancing his horse a little, as though he were uncertain whether to go or stay. Settling finally on *go*, he raised his hat and turned the gray hunter into the road.

"Very good, sir," Miss Nina called after him. "We shall look forward to hearing from you. Very much so!"

They saw Mr. Banister's arm raised like an ensign in acknowledgment, as he trotted round the corner into Key Street. They were about to enter the house when they caught sight of an elderly gentleman, who was attempting to alight from a carriage that had pulled up before the next house but one. He was assisted in this inelegant maneuver by a spindle-shanked old servant, who seemed nearly as ancient as the gentleman himself and little better able to aid him. The elderly gentleman was none other than Miss Nina's chronic suitor, the attentive Mr. George Curle — who, once he'd gained the security of the ground, directed a tremulous shuffle of his fingers toward her, by way of greeting, followed by a monstrous wink of his one good eye.

Miss Nina returned his salutation with a smile and a graceful wave.

"Very fine weather we're having, Miss Jacks," enthused Mr. Curle, his voice squeaking like a hinge crying out for grease. "Very bright and lively!"

Miss Nina, noting the persistent crabbiness of the gray sky, nevertheless responded as though she were in complete accord with his estimation.

"A splendid day, Mr. Curle," said she, engagingly.

"*Hypocrite!*" whispered her sister into her ear, before plunging into the house.

"Now then, Mona — " remonstrated Miss Nina; but as by then her sister had disappeared from view, her fragmentary protest went unheeded.

All was stir and bustle within as the household welcomed the sisters home from their journey. Conspicuously absent was the master of the house, he of the old school, who remained at Fishmouth on a parliamentary matter; his return, however, was expected within the week. Without her father to greet her, then, Miss Nina ascended the staircase at once and made her way to her bedchamber. She was followed by Mona, who was by turns amused and curious to hear what her sister might volunteer next regarding the subject of Mr. Banister. Entering the apartment they found that the maidservant Susanna had already taken charge, and was busily at work returning her mistress's traveling-clothes to their proper quarters.

Miss Nina sat down to her dressing-table and began to repair her image in the glass. Then it was she confided very earnestly to both her companions that she had received the most encouraging signs from Mr. Banister, with regard to his interest; that she was certain he had detected her attachment to him; and, what was more — she now was certain as well that an attachment on his part was a most credible possibility, if not an outright assurance.

"So now you have set your cap at him," said Miss Mona, folding her arms, "I pray for your sake you are not disappointed."

"You must keep it ever in your mind, Mona — all is permissible in love. It's catch that catch can, little sister! It is all such a game, and a lady must play it if she ever is to succeed in this world. In the matter of Mr. Banister, I've no doubt there are girls enough on the catch for him. So it is, you see, if I don't snare him someone else most certainly will. And I cannot allow that to happen. One must think of the future, Mona. The mistress of Eaton Wafers! You saw what an absolutely splendid estate he has there in Broadshire. He is immensely rich, so there'll be no hindrance from Father. If one is to make one's way in this life — did you see, for instance, how Mr. Banister looked at me with those handsome eyes of his, before riding off?"

"I saw it, chick-a-biddy," exclaimed Susanna, nodding and smiling. A little cackle escaped her throat. "Ooh! my stars — it was most encouraging!"

"Thank you, minx. There now, Mona. Do you see?"

"You speak of love as a game, as though it were a competition like backgammon or piquet," returned her sister. "Is this how you would have it? Is this your ideal? Mr. Banister's conduct toward you, I believe, was simply in harmony with his natural graciousness and good manners, the same as he so lately bestowed upon Mrs. Greenshields — or upon Professor Greenshields, for that matter," she added, dryly.

"That may be your interpretation of Mr. Banister's conduct, but it is not mine. You'll note, for instance, how he chose to remain seated beside me the entire time, this afternoon in the drawing-room of Professor Greenshields."

"That is because you took possession of the chair beside his — the very chair in which I was about to sit down."

"Now there you are imagining again. It is an unfortunate trait of yours, Mona. An imagination, you know, can be a terrible impediment. It's well known that imagination derives from an excessive reading of books. Need I go on? It is a habit you have exhibited ever since you were a small child."

"And there are times I believe you still are one."

Here Miss Nina seemed to take some offense, Susanna even more; the maidservant uttered a faint "My stars!" and aimed a glare of disapproval in the direction of the littler sister. Miss Nina, twisting and coiling her chestnut hair about her fingers, for a moment seemed mindful of her sister's words; but the moment passed quickly, being hurried off with a whisk of her hand.

"I wonder you can speak that way, Mona; it's most distressing. But sufficient for the day are the censures thereof. For the present I am very, very tired. It has been a most exhausting interlude, this to-ing and fro-ing from

346

town to country, over the mountains. I simply must retire and refresh my eyes."

Finding herself in accord with this proposal, Miss Mona made ready to quit the room. As she was passing through the door an addition to the little group made its appearance in the shape of a dour servant, with hard white cheeks, a prim mouth, and lazy lids beneath a pair of ill-fitting eyebrows, lushly overgrown.

"What is it, Epsom?" inquired Miss Nina, gazing upon the reflected image of this minion in her glass. "Is something the matter?"

"Yes, what is it?" asked Mona, unaccountably on the alert. Something about this interruption alarmed her, she knew not what, nor could she say how she came to know it. She peered into the servant's face, attempting to discern in its hard lines something, anything, the slightest morsel of which might ease her fears.

The servant relayed the information that there was an *individual* below, Madam, a man, who was highly desirous of seeing Miss Nina. This man indicated he had a message for Miss Nina, Madam, one that must be delivered to her personally. Because the man would not entrust the message to me, Madam, I've left him soothing his heels in the foyer.

"What is this man like, Epsom — his characteristics? Is he well dressed? Is he handsome? Is he someone I'd wish to be seen with? Did he give you his card?"

He was — not quite handsome, Madam. And he was certainly *not* well-dressed, not in the least; so much in the least that his attire might best be characterized, Madam, as *disheveled*. For indeed he was something akin to a mendicant, or a bumpkin, nearly, or a vagabond perhaps, though not quite. He *seemed* to be intelligent, or marginally so, though he spoke not a word and from his outward appearance could be mistaken for a lunatic. And he had no card, Madam, but did have in his possession a brief note, written in his own hand, in which was related the purpose for his call. Will Madam see this man herself, or shall I send him away?

"Madam will not!" exclaimed Mona, with sudden fervor. She appealed to her sister. "There is something odd here, Nina. I can sense it. Do not see this man, I pray you."

"I shall be there beside you, Madam," said the heroic Epsom, with a flutter of his eyebrows — "in the event the gentleman proves fractious."

Miss Nina paused to consider her options, to inspect herself in the glass and make a little face; then she rose and walked to the door, ignoring her sister's protests.

"No, no, Mona, I shall see him. Perhaps he is an acquaintance of Mr. Banister's. People, you know, they're very rustic there in the country. Yes, yes, this could be one of Mr. Banister's Broadshire acquaintances, seeking him perhaps here in the town. This will be a splendid thing for me. I shall need to become accustomed to country people and country ways."

Mona found herself staring open-mouthed in disbelief; oblivious, her sister breezed by her into the passage. Sweeping confidently down the stairs Miss Nina arrived in the foyer. There, upon the black and white diamond-shaped tiles, with his hands to his back, gripping his hat, stood a smiling, gawking fellow in an old brown coat, dark waistcoat, knee-breeches, and gaiters. The most remarkable thing about the fellow was his hair, which was very thick and flared out stiffly in all directions from his head, like a sunburst. What looked to be a quill-pen was lodged behind his right ear. This fellow was, I need hardly state, Mr. Richard Scribbler — appearing just a trifle more devastated than usual, perhaps, as he was yet in the throes of recovery from a wild dream that had afflicted him earlier that afternoon.

Miss Nina started at the sight. It crossed her mind that Epsom might have been correct in regard to beggars and vagabonds. But she could not openly acknowledge the fact she might have been mistaken.

"Yes? Have you a message for someone in this house, sir?"

Mr. Scribbler directed his attention first to Miss Nina, then to her diminutive sister, unsure for which of the young ladies the message was intended. Miss Mona, with a nervous chirp, indicated it was the taller of the two. Mr. Scribbler thanked her with a smile and a polite nod, and so delivered into Miss Nina's hand the water-stained letter he had found in his coat-pocket. This motion he completed with a polite bow and a flourish of his hat.

Miss Nina accepted the missive and glanced at the direction. Her features froze; she uttered a nearly inaudible gasp; the color drained from her face.

"Where did you obtain this, sir?" she demanded, in a strained voice hardly above a whisper. "Is this your notion of a joke? Who are you? Who gave this to you?"

Mr. Scribbler appeared alternately startled, confused, frightened and offended. His eyes went wide; he knitted his brows and shook his head vigorously, denying all accusations. He pointed to the letter several times, which action Miss Nina did not at first comprehend. To make his meaning plainer he tapped with a finger at the handwriting and nodded. Then it was she understood. A terrible pall spread over her, enveloping her from head to foot.

"What is it?" asked Miss Mona, seeking a glimpse of the handwriting.

"It is nothing, Mona. It is nothing at all. I shall survive." Addressing Mr. Scribbler, in a voice as cold and featureless as an ice floe, she said — "Thank you, sir, for bringing this to me. You have discharged your obligation. Epsom, please give Mr. — Mr. — give this person something for his trouble." She spoke as one in a trance, as though feeling too much for speech.

"Yes, Madam."

Some shiny coins found their way into Mr. Scribbler's palm. He took little notice of them, however — in contrast to his previous commission as transporter of the mails — and was instead watching Miss Nina's face, which, having taken on the appearance of china, very white and fragile, seemed about to shatter. It was then his study came to an abrupt end, as he found himself propelled backward out of the house at the steady urging of Epsom.

Miss Nina ascended the staircase, looking vacantly before her and disregarding all her sister's inquiries. She went directly to her room and shut the door. A minute later Susanna came scooting from the apartment, like a fly chased off by the switch of a horse's tail. She glanced at Mona with an expression of alarm, sniffed a few times to regain her composure, and trotted off down the passage.

Once alone in her chamber Miss Nina cast the letter upon the floor, as though it were something loathsome and vile and not to be touched. She started in to pace with her arms crossed, eyeing the letter fearfully at each turn, as if it were a corpse she expected any moment might spring to life. Twenty times, thirty times, forty times she trod the carpet, her feet plowing their way through a mire of indecision. She wanted very much to know what was in that letter, she recognized, but at the same time she wanted very much not to know.

At length, concluding that such efforts would provide little in the way of comfort, she attacked the problem more directly — she plucked the vile object from the ground and with trembling fingers unfolded its contents. She read the letter through where she stood, at a point not far from her dressing-table. Her brow furled, her mouth opened wide, her eyelids quivered. Her breathing grew rapid, coming now in little gusts. She swallowed uncomfortably, blinked, swallowed again, raised a hand to her lips, then to her forehead, in astonishment at what she saw written on the paper.

She lifted her eyes and the letter slipped from her grasp. Everything about her seemed bathed in a wondrous new light. She looked straight into the glass with an intensity of vision unmatched in her former experience, as though she had bored a hole through into her very soul and were seeing it clearly for the first time. Her face recorded a kind of violent inner reaction; apparently she liked not what she saw there.

Hastily she retrieved the letter and hid it again in her clothes. Her flesh was pallid and drawn and she was starting to feel sick. Her legs could no longer support her weight, so she took to her bed. The delirium sweeping over her was worse even than that before, when the sound of a sailor's shoes on the cobbles beneath her window had worried her with fear and panic. Her head sank upon the pillow and the wondrous new light dissolved in a cloud of darkness.

A knock — a very tentative, very plaintive sort of knock — was heard at the room-door. There was no response; the knock came again. It was the maidservant, who by now had garnered sufficient courage to return to the scene of her dismissal, to inquire into the state of her mistress's well-being.

"Miss? It's Susanna, Miss. Chick-a-biddy — are you ill?"

Still receiving no reply, she entered boldly.

"Pardon, Miss — "

Susanna recognized at once the grievous condition into which her mistress had fallen. With a horrified gasp she scampered into the passage, calling loudly for Miss Mona. Where, oh where, she cried, was the master of the house when he was most needed?

Upon her arrival the face of Miss Mona turned instantly as white as her sister's. She hurried off a servant for Dr. Strathclyde, the family physician. Then, on impulse, she abruptly recalled the servant and sent him off instead for Dr. Daniel Dampe of Sawyer's Green, Crescent. The doctor had barely set foot in his lodgings, and was in the midst of a relaxing turn at his pipe, when the servant arrived. Fishing up his medical bag he came at once, and so commenced his examination of the patient.

Miss Mona stood anxiously by, observing this exercise with an expression of violent concern. At her ear she could hear Susanna whimpering into a handkerchief. For the moment their differences had been submerged, as together they kept watch over the poor limp form lying on the bed.

"What is your opinion, Doctor?" asked Mona, after a time. She could not bear the waiting. She had but one sister and would never have another. She knew her sister was shallow and childish at times, and selfish, but for all her faults she loved her *very* much; the thought of life without her was something she could not begin to contemplate.

"I'm not entirely certain," replied the doctor, standing away from the bed and smoothing his beard in thought. "A most puzzling phenomenon, Miss Jacks. There was a letter, you say? Well, I suspect whatever was in that letter has given her a stupendous shock. It's quite overpowered her, as you can see. Extraordinary thing, actually. It's neither syncope — that's a swoon — nor coma. Yet she can't be roused. It's as if she's made up her mind to sleep for a time and absolutely refuses to be disturbed. Most likely her constitution has been weakened by the rigors of the journey. Of course, since the visit of Mr. Pickering she's not taken part in the customary morning rambles you and she once shared. Lack of proper exercise, I can tell you, Miss Jacks, will sap you of your strength as surely as lack of nourishment. Oh, it's common knowledge. If the heart and lungs and the great vessels are not challenged by exertion, you see, they'll grow limp and weary, and this impedes their function, so that after a time you can go off — just like that!"

He concluded this oration with a little snap of his fingers, at which sound Miss Mona shut her eyes and covered her face with her hands. Susanna uttered a little groan and burst into sobs, from out of which the word "Chick-a-biddy" emerged at irregular intervals.

Dr. Dampe, seeing that he'd committed yet another physicianly *faux pas,* was again at a loss for words. The doctor was not one for affected delicacy or the politeness of restraint; it wasn't the physicianly way. In his rounds he daily made acquaintance with every conceivable form of human frailty and infirmity; was confronted with relentless suffering, pestilence, and death. As a result he often appeared unsympathetic — not so much by design, as by necessity — toward matters that the laity might deem sensitive. The doctor did not mince either his nouns or his verbs; too often he spoke out and said exactly what he meant, without regard for the listeners. Here, however, was a different situation altogether, and only now did he begin to see it. What he saw was the diminutive Miss Jacks dabbing at her tear-stained eyes, sniffling and trembling, while striving mightily to contain her emotions in the face of adverse circumstance. Beholding her in such a vulnerable condition, something akin to compassion struck at the doctor's heart.

"Please accept my sincerest apologies, Miss Jacks. I'm certain all will be well," he said, with absolutely no basis for such an assurance.

Miss Mona turned her face toward him with an imploring gaze.

"Oh, Dr. Dampe — *I cannot lose my sister!*"

In the quiet of his room that evening — it had been decided that he should stay the night, so as to be near the patient — the doctor smoked out his pipe and contemplated the fire. It was a bitter cold evening, one well-suited for rumination, and the doctor found no shortage of material to occupy his spacious mind. Over the course of the succeeding hour he reflected on all manner of events that had transpired during the past few busy weeks. After a time he lay down upon the coverlet, still in his shirt and waistcoat, and certain that he would be unable to rest. It was a very comfortable coverlet, however, with a very comfortable mattress beneath it, and so — as is often the case — he found himself instantly asleep.

His dreaming mind floated lazily for a time before coming into focus. There was a scene laid out before him. There was a dog-cart in the scene and he was in it, on the rear seat facing back, with his feet on the hinged tailboard. It was not the dog-cart of Professor Greenshields, which had conveyed him home to the Crescent, nor was it his own sturdy vehicle. It was someone else's dog-cart, and it was in motion along a narrow, rutted track that was unfamiliar to him. He saw that it was a well-crafted dog-cart, three-springed, with slatted panels for the dogs; the shafts however were of lancewood rather than hickory. There was a dog-cart driver, too, who was handling the horse smartly with his whip and reins. This driver was protected against the chill — for it was bitter cold in the dream as well — by a succession of heavy coats, one drawn over the other, and a monstrous sugar-loaf hat which totally concealed his head.

The doctor, impatient as always and not knowing where he was, turned round in his seat to address the reinsman.

"Driver! Where are we? Where are you taking me?"

Nothing.

"Hallo — driver! My name is Dampe. Dr. Daniel Dampe. I'm a physician. Would you kindly tell me where it is you're taking me?"

Still nothing.

"Look here," said the doctor, with a mind to tap the driver on the shoulder. As he reached forward his hand passed completely through the body of the man, as though through air. The doctor leaped back, startled. The driver turned round and doffed his enormous hat, offering the doctor a sly smile and a sidelong glance from the corners of his eyes. The head of the driver, the doctor saw, was the head of a young child with red hair and a green face. Without so much as a *by your leave*, the head melted down over the back of the seat like candle-wax, oozing and dripping.

Undeterred by such loss of face, the body of the driver applied whip to quadruped and away the dog-cart bounded at a high rate of speed. Faster and faster it flew, jolting in and out of the cart-ruts at a pace that threatened to break all existing records for the dog-carts of history. The doctor, terrified of an upset, could do nothing but grip the rail and utter a few solemn prayers for the preservation of life and limb.

Then came a thumping sound, which was repeated several times, and indicative the doctor thought of some instability about the vehicle. *Thump thump thump.* Perhaps it was the axle, or one of the wheels, or the lancewood shafts. There would shortly be a breakdown, he was certain of it now. Why couldn't they have used hickory? *Thump thump thump!*

With a start the doctor bounced into wakefulness, his ears filled with the noise of someone rapping at his door. It was the loyal Epsom, he of the lazy lids and festive eyebrows. The doctor called out, inquiring into the condition of the patient; the servant replied that Miss Nina, sir, appeared to be coming round. The doctor brushed the sticky sleep from his eyes and realized that it was morning. He slid from the bed to perform his ablutions, telling the servant to expect him at Miss Nina's side directly.

What Epsom had reported was true. After what had evidently been a very bad night, the patient was starting to rally. The doctor bent down and performed a rapid examination. His conclusion: she was improving — for the moment. The doctor had been present at too many false recoveries during his career to be more encouraging than this.

Miss Mona too had experienced a fitful sleep. Tired, impatient, a little exasperated, equal parts of each perhaps, she stood at the bed and asked —

"What is it, Nina? What has happened to you? What was in that letter?"

The sound of her chirrupy voice appeared to stimulate the patient. Nina's eyes flickered open, and drifted about the room a time or two before settling finally on Mona. A smile appeared — a most welcome sign, even to the doctor. Her hand fumbled weakly for something under the bedclothes.

"What is the matter, dear?" asked Mona. "What are you searching for?"

In response her sister withdrew something from inside her gown. It was the water-stained letter, which she offered now to Mona. Eager for an end to the suspense, to quell her doubts, to know at last what it was that had driven her sister into such a state, Miss Mona unfolded the papers. Immediately her brow contracted into a frown.

"What is it?" asked Dr. Dampe. "Is it bad news? See here, it isn't about your father — ?"

"I cannot say," replied Mona, with a mystified countenance. She handed the letter to the doctor. "There is nothing there."

"What!"

The doctor stared at the empty pages. He turned them round and round. He looked at the direction — or rather where the direction ought to have been — or had been — but it too was blank.

"Her name was there yesterday — the direction — we saw it," said Miss Mona. "And now today it is gone. It's faded away, and taken with it whatever else was inside."

"Extraordinary! Your sister was correct. It looks to be a kind of prank."

"A terrible one if true, Doctor."

Entrusting care of the patient for a time to Susanna, the doctor and Miss Mona descended to the breakfast-parlor. This parlor was a very bright place, a veritable temple of light — despite the grim and ghostly clouds haunting the sky — due to the large ornate windows that occupied its walls, according a very pleasant view of the kitchen-garden behind the house.

The breakfast was laid on. Few words were exchanged between the doctor and Miss Jacks during the course of it. The suddenness with which the crisis had overtaken them, its nature and severity, lingering doubts about the prospects for recovery, Miss Mona's lack of sleep, the doctor's recollection of his dream — all served to dampen any sustained effort at conversation. At one point the doctor made some few attempts at physicianly humor, but abandoned the effort almost at once. There was something intriguing about the tiny young woman sitting at table with him which he could neither define nor explain. It was positively strange, it was mysterious, inexplicable even, but lately he had found himself saying and doing all manner of foolish things in her presence. Or was it perhaps that he always said and did these things, and that it was only her presence that caused him to notice?

He sampled the generous helpings of food spread across the board, but found himself curiously dissatisfied with everything he touched. The new-laid eggs, the rashers of fried ham, the plates of hot buttered toast, the wheaten griddle-cakes, the lump sugar, the oranges and biscuits, tea and sundries, the black coffee standing in the kettle — nothing seemed to excite his appetite. He tried a little of this, he tried a little of that, but it did not please. Ordinarily, as in Friday Street, he would have launched into such a meal like a trencherman; today, here, he felt himself oddly at odds with it, oddly enough.

They were nearly done with their meal — as done as they were going to be this particular morning — done nearly with chewing in silence, having consumed very little of what lay before them, the doctor crunching a wedge of toast and sipping a little of his coffee — which was very good coffee, by the by — when Susanna came scurrying into the parlor.

"Ooh, Miss — Doctor — it's Miss Nina — I — I believe she's mended her spirits something remarkable. She's making to get out of her bed, and asking for her clothes — and — and asking for you, Miss!"

Mona and the doctor erupted from their chairs. But before they had a chance even to reach the door, there was Miss Nina standing in it. She was clearly weak but otherwise much improved, the color having returned to her features; the face as white as a plate was nowhere in evidence. Her eyes were lucid and shining, and full of life. The whole of her demeanor was unmistakably cheerful.

"I do believe we're home and dry," whispered the doctor, getting up a little smile of confidence, which sentiment was relievedly echoed by Mona.

It was then however that Miss Nina opened her mouth to speak, and what she had to say amazed all of them.

"I am resolute in my mind," said she, looking first to her sister, then to Susanna, then to the doctor, then to all three at once. "I am determined to waste no more of my life — not one day more. I wish to do good things. I will go today to the rector, and he will help me do these things."

"What good things, dear?" asked Miss Mona, gently.

"Useful things. Noble things. I wish to do things that will be of service to the common people, Mona. Helpful things, charitable things; so that in future I will be remembered for my kindness, and my good works." Her eyes roved about the table, noting the generous supply of food that remained there. "Have you finished with your breakfast?"

"Why, yes, actually," returned the doctor, clearing his voice in surprise. "Are you hungry? Of course, Miss Jacks, you must be very hungry. You must eat a little something, you know — "

"No, no, Doctor, it is not for me, but thank you just the same. This is splendid. This will be my very first good work. Epsom!"

"Madam!" responded that worthy retainer, appearing from out of the air.

"See that the food is gathered together. Place it in a nice wicker basket, together with some fresh-smelling flowers and some peppermint, some of Meg's hardbake, a case-bottle of milk-punch, and a few other oddments — Meg can help you in this — and send it round to the rector. He'll have in mind, I'm sure, some deserving family in the parish, in straitened circumstances, who could benefit from such a meal on this fine morning."

"At once, madam!"

Miss Nina turned and smiled on the others.

"You see? I am resolute. And it is a fine morning — a splendid morning!" This she said, in perfect defiance of the grim and ghostly sky sailing overhead.

"Nina," said her sister, "from whom was the letter you received yesterday?"

Miss Nina dropped her glance for the briefest instant, as though from embarrassment, but quickly recovered herself. "If you must know, Mona, it was from Mr. Pickering — yes, Mr. Pickering — and it has opened my eyes." She left the room without another word and mounted the staircase. Trailing in her wake was Susanna, who as she ascended the stairs glanced repeatedly over her shoulder toward Mona and the doctor, with an expression that exclaimed — "*My stars!*"

Miss Mona and Dr. Dampe were themselves far from resolute upon anything at that moment, being sorely perplexed; though the rector, they knew, would be very much pleased.

CHAPTER III

In Which Mr. Kibble Is Further Troubled

WHILE the breakfast just described was in progress in Boring Lane, another breakfast was being laid on — the one the doctor would have leaped into, if given the opportunity — at a certain cozy house in Friday Street. A house with a tiled roof of gables and chimneys, a house of white lath-and-plaster walls and black timber framing, the whole of it sprinkled over with tiny lattice windows, and very prettily situated among sheltering trees; in short, at the house of Professor Titus Vespasianus Tiggs.

It was to this shady lodge that Professor Tiggs had the previous day returned in triumph. There to greet him were his housekeeper, the widow Minidew, with her bright strawberry hair and her bright strawberry complexion and her surfeit of dimples. There too was his groom, Tom Spike, he of the face like old boxwood, on whose shoulder the regal Mr. Pumpkin Pie had lately established his royal seat. As they approached, Mr. Pie sniffed the air, a little suspiciously at first; then, recognizing who it was had stepped into the room, hurled himself from Tom's shoulder into the arms of his master. There too were Hanna, the ruddy young farm lass who often assisted Mrs. Minidew in the kitchen, and Miss Laura Dale, with her golden-brown hair, her soft gray eyes, and her pretty brow; and at Laura's side, her little charge and the professor's most valued possession.

"Welcome home, Uncle Tiggs!" exclaimed Fiona, and rushed into her uncle's embrace with an impetus that sent Mr. Pie scampering. "It has been ever so long since you left us."

"Hallo, dear, hallo," said the professor in his sprightly way, kissing his niece upon the cheeks two or three times over. "Have you conducted yourself like a proper young lady, while I have been in the country?"

"Very much so, Uncle Tiggs," replied Fiona; though the pleading glance she flashed in Laura's direction admitted perhaps to some flexibility in the interpretation of this response.

"She has been in all ways nowt but good, sir," said old Tom, who always rose to the defense of Fiona in such matters. He wagged his head and scratched his side-whiskers. "She's a model child, I do say. She's helped me

357

this week with polishing of the gig, and of Maggie's harness, too, her buckles and silver bits and such. Miss Fiona, she's a particular fondness for the snaffles, as I've noticed."

"And she has been of great help to me as well, sir," said Mrs. Minidew. "She has mastered now a great many useful skills, to be sure, as for example the preparation of the table, the arrangement of the tea-things, the squeezing of lemons, the making of macaroons, and most recently use of the nutmeg-grater. And just yesterday she has taken upon herself entire responsibility for the care and feeding of Pie."

"And she has been most assiduous in the matter of her lessons," Laura chimed in. "She absorbs everything so quickly. Each subject is taken up with equal ease and readiness. She really is quite remarkable. Her knowledge of the French language is increasing so, I believe we all must begin practicing our *français* to make her feel at home."

"This is most encouraging!" exclaimed the professor — who knew very well he was being gulled, just a little, and plied with exaggeration, and was enjoying it all immensely. He reached into his coat and withdrew a small package wrapped up in brown paper. "Here you are, dear, this is for you. Something to reward you for your diligence. It is from Dr. Dampe and myself."

"Thank you, Uncle Tiggs!" cried Fiona, receiving the gift into her tiny hands. "I was sure you would bring me something. But it seems to me much too small for a bear from the mountain meadows."

"No, it is not a bear," laughed the professor. "Although it is derived from something nearly as large and fine."

Hastily Fiona undid the wrapping, and so held in her palm the great shiny claw that had been removed from the ground sloth by Dr. Dampe.

"What is it?" she marveled, peering at the mysterious object from all angles.

"It is a claw from the forepaw of a megathere," her uncle announced, not without a little self-satisfaction.

"What is a megathere?"

"That," said the professor, smiling, "is for you to investigate and to discover. I am quite certain you will be able to locate the answer among your books. I offer it to you as an assignment! Miss Dale — might I ask you to supervise my young scholar in her researches?"

"Of course, sir," said Laura.

"A megathere," Fiona repeated, thoughtfully. A frown crinkled the little space between her eyebrows, forming an expression not unlike that which often engaged the brow of her uncle. "I have heard of it, I am sure, but I can't picture it. A megathere. Is it truly in my books, Miss Dale?"

"I believe it is. Not to worry, dear. I'm sure you will find it."

"Is a megathere as grand a thing as a bear?"

"A megathere," asserted Tom Spike, with a clearing of his voice and a long shake of his head — "is a mighty beast!"

"A mighty beast, yes, and a peculiar one, too. I myself have seen several of them," said Laura.

"How wonderful!" cried Fiona. "Where did you see them, Miss Dale?"

"Round Broadshire, where I was born."

"And have you seen bears as well?"

"Yes."

"And dire wolves?"

"Yes."

"And saber-cats, too?"

The face of Laura unaccountably darkened, as did the professor's — for he had not as yet contrived how to present to the household certain unpleasant particulars of the journey. But this, he knew, could not be the cause of Miss Dale's reaction, and so it intrigued him a little just what that cause might be. The governess for her part did not respond, preferring instead to alter the flow of conversation; and so the topic sank rapidly from view beneath the waters.

Professor Tiggs rose early the next morning, far in advance of daylight, to spend some few hours alone with his correspondence in his cedar-lined study. His busy mind, though intent upon the letters at hand, was unduly preoccupied with thoughts of Mr. Hilltop's story and the danger that threatened. He managed however to put his fears aside for a time, trusting that he and his colleagues would be able to devise a solution.

At length he quitted the study and returned to the drawing-room, where he found that Mr. Kibble had arrived, having been asked to breakfast along with Dr. Dampe and Mr. Banister. Shortly thereafter Mr. Banister himself appeared. Looking more than usually handsome in his trim dark riding coat, with an engaging sparkle in his eyes and a healthful spring in his step, he was introduced by the professor to Mrs. Minidew and Tom Spike. The housekeeper was most favorably impressed with the tall master of Eaton Wafers, and as a result suffered a fit of dimpling; while old Tom found much to like in the free-and-easy manner of the young squire, in his cheery and generous temperament and his affinity for horses and hounds.

It was then that Laura and Fiona entered the room. Almost at once, looks of recognition were exchanged between the governess and Harry Banister. This meeting of eyes was observed by Mr. Kibble, who had been stricken once more with that disconcerting consciousness of self brought on by the presence of the young woman he so admired. He recollected now the conversation in the coach on the road to Eaton Wafers, when the professor let fall that Miss Laura Dale and Mr. Harry Banister had been acquainted in days gone by.

"Hallo — upon my word, it's Miss Dale!" cried the astonished Harry, appealing to the professor for an explanation of her appearance in his house, which to the squire was no less surprising than if the tablets of electrum had been found there.

"Miss Dale is presently serving as governess to my young niece Fiona. She has been with us for some few months now."

"Well, sir, you could have knocked me down with this surprise! But what a delightful one it is, to be sure. It is good to see you again, Miss Dale. I trust you are well. It has been such a long time!"

Laura offered her hand, somewhat tentatively, but to Mr. Kibble's fevered imagination it seemed she was offering her entire self. It seemed too that she was as affected by the presence of Mr. Banister as Mr. Kibble was by hers. What could it signify? When she cast her eyes upon the squire it was, the secretary thought, with a subtle blend of delicacy, pleasure, and self-deprecation, mixed with something like gratitude and perhaps something like pride, all of it held in check by her rather extraordinary reserve. He had never before seen the like expression on her face, ever.

"Yes, I believe you two know one another," said the professor. "Miss Dale mentioned it in passing only last week."

"Yes, we do, indeed," returned Mr. Banister, looking altogether very happy. "What a stunner! I had absolutely no idea you were here in Friday Street, Miss Dale. None! You must believe me."

"Of course I believe you, sir. I am as always — most obliged to you," replied Laura. She was feeling her self-consciousness now — her face had crimsoned over — and begged leave for a short time, explaining that there were matters to which she and Fiona must attend before sitting down to breakfast.

"It's very good of you, sir, to look out for her," said Harry, once Laura and her charge had departed the room. A retrospective serenity filled his eyes, which were like two shiny pebble-stones on the shore, with thoughts of former times washing over them. "I had a notion she was in Salthead, though my last firm intelligence of her was from a few years ago. She is an excellent young woman, excellent, that I can tell you — extremely bright, extremely sensible, extremely prudent, and completely devoted to her work. Absolutely top-notch. You and your niece are very fortunate to have her, sir."

"That, my dear Harry, is scarcely half the story," said the professor, his face fairly glowing. "She is a most gracious and knowledgeable young lady, remarkably selfless, and as a consequence highly esteemed in this household. And as you mention, absolutely indefatigable in her exertions on behalf of my niece. We are all quite taken with her. Her grandmother, she has informed me, was in service to your late aunt?"

"Exactly so. Miss Dale and I have known each other since we were very small. Living close by in Fridley, she was regularly at Eaton Wafers to visit her grandmother — a very sweet old lady who did sewing for my aunt. As children we occasionally played together — Laura, her sister and brother, and I."

This last statement caused the professor some confusion. "I'd no idea she had either a brother or a sister. It seemed to us — well, drawing on what little she has told us — the way she has framed it — it seemed there was always an implication she was the only child in her family."

"Indeed? There's a puzzle," remarked Mr. Banister, giving the professor the strangest look. He was about to offer something more when Mrs. Minidew came in from the kitchen to announce that breakfast was served. The professor glanced at his watch. The hour was late and there was no sign of Dr. Dampe. There was, however, an impending engagement in the city; which fact led him to conclude it would be best to proceed with the meal.

It was during the course of the breakfast that the professor, with the aid of Mr. Kibble and Harry Banister, related certain of the events pertaining to the recent journey. By common agreement the incident of the saber-cats was omitted; in its place, the professor described how a dead megathere had been found on the road and its claw removed by Dr. Dampe — who, because he had still not made his appearance, was presumed to have had an early call on a patient.

On hearing of Mr. Hunter, Laura took occasion to relate all that had transpired the previous afternoon — the excursion to Salthead market; the encounter with Mr. Josiah Tusk, and the bravery of Fiona in facing him; the confrontation between the miser and the formidable Miss Honeywood; the meeting with Mr. Hunter and the subsequent walk to the Pelican, with Mr.

Hunter's odd inquiries and remarks along the way; and the even odder affair involving the aged Miss Sprinkle, Mr. Hunter, and the portraits in the locket. Joining this information to that gleaned from Mr. Banister and Professor Greenshields, a more complete understanding of things presented itself. It was apparent that Sally Sprinkle had had the great misfortune of becoming engaged to Mr. Hunter, in his earlier identity as James Gallivan, when they both had lived at Richford; so it was indeed his picture she carried in her locket beside her own youthful one. It was apparent as well why the marriage had not taken place, why it was Mr. John Hunter had abruptly abandoned Richford and his intended bride, without explanation, having no doubt received fresh intelligence regarding the tablets of electrum.

"I wonder at some of the particulars, however, as they concern Mr. Hunter," said Laura, calling to mind the figure of the handsome young gentleman in the bottle-green coat. "My knowledge of him is of course minute; I speak from but a first impression. His constitution appeared so very vigorous and strong, so forceful, so bursting with energy — is it possible he can be so unimaginably old? As regards his demeanor, it was without question moody and severe in certain respects, but more it seemed to me from self-command, and perhaps annoyance at being interrupted in his daily affairs. He was quite apologetic after nearly crashing into me; he fell into the road, after all, to avoid the collision. And on that foggy night was it not he who rescued poor Mr. Rime? Are these the actions of the creature described by your Mr. Hilltop?"

"My p-point exactly," said Mr. Kibble, bravely presenting his eyes to Miss Dale across the table. "How can we be certain that all Mr. Hilltop has told us is true?"

"Surely we cannot doubt the veracity of what Mr. Hilltop has told us about himself," returned the professor. "After all, Dr. Dampe — and Mr. Hatch Hoakum too, as I recollect — witnessed the injury to Mr. Hilltop's hand, as inflicted by — " Here he stopped.

"What injury?" asked Laura.

The professor, disgusted with himself for very nearly mentioning the saber-cats, could only grope helplessly for a reply. His distress was short-lived, however, as he was very conveniently delivered of it by a feline of another stripe — more specifically, by an orange cat-face that appeared beside the table. It was Mr. Pumpkin Pie, who, having tired of his usual fare, had wandered in to see what in the way of *haute cuisine* might be extorted from his master and the visitors.

"Why, what is it, young man?" inquired the professor, grateful for this timely intervention. "What do you want, sir? The clanking of the bowls will always bring him in, you see. Ah, Mrs. Minidew — has Mr. Pie received a proper breakfast this morning?"

"Twice, sir," said that good lady, looking in at the room-door.

"I see. And was it — ah, were they — of sufficient quantity as to satisfy him?"

"Most sufficient, sir. To be sure, he's hardly paused in his eating long enough to draw breath, since coming in from the stable-yard with Tom."

"So there can be little doubt he has not wanted for food today?"

"Not likely!" came the voice of Tom Spike from the kitchen. In a trice his genial countenance appeared beside that of Mrs. Minidew. "The young lad there has had more than his fill of dainties this morning."

"I see." The professor rubbed his gray bristle-brush head and frowned on the young lad, whose ears were raised in anticipation of some dainty from the breakfast-table. The professor, to his credit, would have none of it; he was determined that discipline should rule. "I'm very sorry to inform you, young man," he said firmly, "but you have had quite enough. There will be no begging today. I have nothing for you."

"Come here, Pie, and have some of this!" cried Fiona, letting drop a morsel of ham at the foot of her chair. The cat dashed over and inspected the object with quivering nostrils. Satisfied, he lowered himself onto his haunches — inclined his head — champed — crunched — swallowed — and the morsel was no more. He raised his eyes and glanced round, a little cunningly, while licking his mouth. After this he sat up and revolved his head this way and that, on the watch for more manna from above.

"Fiona, you should not have done that," whispered Miss Dale. "Did you not hear your uncle?"

"But Uncle Tiggs did not say that *I* should not feed Mr. Pie," protested Fiona.

"But it was of course implied, dear," said the professor.

"I fear your niece has a valid case, sir," chuckled Mr. Banister. "My man Glitters in the city could gain her a judgment at the quarter-sessions in his sleep. Absolutely cataleptic, on that score!"

"I'll believe it," wheezed old Tom. "There's nowt plainer than that for the lawyerfolk. What say, Mrs. Minidew?"

"I do suppose," returned the housekeeper, "that Mr. Banister, being a graduate of university and the master of a great estate, and a very learned gentleman in the ways of the world, knows what he's about."

"Is there none but Miss Dale prepared to second me?" exclaimed the professor, with feigned indignation. "First it is my niece, then my young friend here, then my groom, and now my own housekeeper! Mr. Kibble — surely *you* remain in my corner?"

"Of course, sir," replied the secretary.

"Very good. Thank you, Mr. Kibble."

"Boring Mr. Kibble," Fiona was heard to mumble; which remark prompted another reprimand from Laura and a warning look from her uncle, but very little reaction from the secretary himself, who I suspect was too far gone in admiration of Miss Dale to notice.

"You'll wish to have Maggie put to the gig now, sir?" inquired Tom.

"Yes, indeed," said the professor, comprehending the hour. "There is the engagement in town shortly."

"Yes, sir. She'll be ready for you. The poor dear girl has been all in a muddle since your excursion into the country. Come along, Pie!"

The cloth was removed from the table to allow the professor, Mr. Banister, and Mr. Kibble to outline a strategy prior to their meeting with Mr. Hilltop. It was agreed by all that the shortest route to Mr. Hunter and the tablets of electrum would be the most direct one — a frontal assault on Mr. Hunter's house in Raven Lane. What better and more off-putting approach, they reasoned, than simply to assemble *en masse* at the young gentleman's door?

"Suppose the same rude serving-man should answer?" asked Mr. Kibble, recalling Mr. Banister's account of the unproductive visit of the magistrate's agent. "Suppose he should lie about his master's presence in the house, and refuse us entrance?"

"I don't believe the fellow would resort to that, particularly if Mr. Hilltop is with us," replied the professor. "I have no doubt Mr. Hilltop will be our key to success in calling out Mr. Hunter. By sheer weight of numbers Mr. Hunter's hand will be forced — though our prospects could suffer if Dr. Dampe is not with us."

The hour being late they rose to leave, despite the absence of the doctor, who had planned to accompany them to the coffee-house and the meeting with Mr. Hilltop. An interesting sort of farewell passed between Mr. Banister and Miss Dale, which was spotted by the watchful Mr. Kibble. Harry seemed for the most part his cordial self, but there was an awkward formality to Laura's leave-taking, as though the two of them shared a secret bond which she acknowledged, but nonetheless wished should remain unperceived by the others. Jealousy squeezed at the heart of Mr. Kibble, who sensed now in Mr. Harry Banister another rival for the affections of Laura. Here was a powerful and a very persuasive rival indeed! The secretary might have stood a chance against that scruffy fellow from Whistle Hill; but what chance, he wondered, what chance against the wealthy and handsome squire of Eaton Wafers? How bleak were Mr. Kibble's prospects now! He wondered too, in a flood of despair, why someone in Mr. Banister's exalted position should take such an interest in a governess. And what did it reveal of Laura's character that she should return that interest?

Professor Tiggs climbed into his coat and then into his gig, which was waiting in the stable-yard with Maggie between the shafts. The buckskin mare was eager to be on the road, eager to be abroad in the world and show everyone what she 'and her bounding limbs could do. She seemed even more anxious than usual to be off, and demonstrated it by a little impatient stamp of her foot and a snort and a toss of her dark mane. So Mr. Banister leaped upon his gray hunter and Mr. Kibble upon black Nestor, and away they all went down the graveled drive that led to Friday Street.

From his perch on the back-stairs Mr. Pie watched them go. He blinked his green eyes once or twice, wishing perhaps that he could go too and so enlarge the sphere of his experience. After a yawn and a stretch, however, he decided it might be easier to go instead into the house, where it was warm and snug, and there contemplate the truly important things in life — namely the fire and his food bowl.

After a brisk and refreshing trot the professor and his companions arrived at the coffee-house, which was situated among the maze of courtyards down in Snowfields, and had been recommended by Mr. Hilltop as a convenient meeting-place. They managed to secure a comfortable table in the spacious commercial room, the professor settling into a high-backed chair, Mr. Banister and Mr. Kibble each into an easy ditto. The walls of the room were richly wainscoted in oak, and garnished with maps of the out-counties and pictures depicting scenes of the hunt, thereby providing an illusion of country life (very appealing of course to Harry) in the midst of city bustle.

The gentlemen informed the waiter they were anticipating the arrival of the fourth and fifth members of their party, one of whom happened to be a Mr. Jack Hilltop. Was he known here? No, sir, was the reply of the waiter, no one by that name. By the by, did he happen to know a Mr. John Hunter, of Raven Lane? Which inquiry produced a similarly negative response.

The gentlemen waited; the appointed hour came and went. Each new entrant through the door was closely examined as to face and figure. Not only was there no Mr. Hilltop, there was still no Dr. Dampe. The professor felt the stirrings of concern. A short time later the waiter approached, bearing a letter that had been delivered by anonymous messenger. The direction was to Professor Tiggs, who hastily unfolded the missive and ran over its contents.

The letter was from Mr. Hilltop, begging their forgiveness and their understanding in the name of charity, &c., &c., but regretting to say he would not be joining them. As it happened he had, upon further deliberation, become persuaded that the professor and his friends should not be associated with him in the enterprise, fearing as he did for their well-being were this alliance to become known to Mr. Hunter. If it were brought to the attention of Mr. Hunter that they were colleagues, don't you see, it might be very bad for the professor and those in his circle. Far better then, in Mr. Hilltop's reformed opinion, to work separately toward their common goal. In this Mr. Hilltop dropped hints as to the existence of certain methods, which he meant to employ to the fullest extent, and invited the professor and his associates to employ their own. Striving independently they could perhaps accomplish far more, with far less danger, don't you see, than striving together.

So wrote Mr. Jack Hilltop.

The professor was sorely disappointed, and Mr. Banister too. Mr. Kibble uttered some few words about the general unreliability of anything said by Mr. Hilltop, then abruptly stopped short. A lady who brought to mind something of Miss Laura Dale wafted past, drawing his eyes; which occurrence caused the secretary to reflect again on the state of his situation, more particularly on Mr. Harry Banister and that fellow from Whistle Hill. A chilly shadow descended, obliterating his hopes. So Mr. Kibble started in again to brood, to wonder how, how, how in this world he stood any chance in anything at all. The chilly shadow called attention to the ache in his heart for the young woman he so highly prized, and who to all appearances took no notice of him whatsoever. With a spasm of grief came the realization that his wounded heart would mend ne'er so readily as Mr. Jack Hilltop's wounded hand.

CHAPTER IV

A Cup of Kindness

THE scruffy fellow from Whistle Hill was not on Whistle Hill at present, but was instead occupying an equally lofty eminence — his high seat, among the dusty bookcases and the soaring volcanoes of legal writ, amid an array of wax-lights, here and there shining out like miniature lighthouses, in the vast dark sea that was the outer office of Badger and Winch, solicitors. There he sat scratching away at a parchment, a memorandum of understanding between a principal client of the firm — one Mr. Josiah Tusk, of whom I need not say more — and a certain young gentleman whose appearance in that office, on one occasion, had been pointed out to Mr. Scribbler so vividly by his friend Samson Icks. A memorandum of understanding between that venerable philanthropist and representative of the majestic world of commerce, Mr. Josiah Tusk, and the certain young gentleman with the yellow light in his eyes, called John Hunter.

Mr. Richard Scribbler was not alone while toiling at his labors. True, the surviving partner of the firm, the fat attorney with the bald head and the plum-colored suit, was not in the room, but he was not far away — hunkered down in his inner sanctum like an unfortunate gentleman in a prison-yard, knowing that the seal of his doom was at that very minute being set to parchment by the gawking scribe in the outer office. He sat rigidly at his desk, as if he had sprouted there, with his neck screwed up and his eyes staring off into what I imagine was a pretty uncomfortable future. This, combined with a general paleness of face and wretchedness of expression, gave him every resemblance to a corpse that had just been hauled from the gibbet. As if to dispel this fiction the corpse licked his lips and wiped his head, and began drumming on the desk-top with the fingers of one hand. Once the memorandum of understanding had been prepared, he knew, it would be his job, by direct command of Josiah Tusk, to have it ratified by securing the vital signatures of the two parties involved. The signature of the first party, that of the towering white-headed potentate himself, could be gotten without incident. But as for the signature of the second party — well, Lawyer Winch was most uneasy in that regard, for it entailed the dreaded personal encounter — face to face, nose to nose, and most likely fist to fist — with Mr. John Hunter.

How Mr. Hunter had come to learn that a spy had been set upon him by Mr. Winch — that is, by his own attorney — despite many long desperate hours of pondering and sweating and head-wiping, remained for that attorney an insoluble mystery. He had at first suspected that his man Samson Icks might have betrayed his trust, and divulged to Mr. Hunter the nature of those secretive rambles in the neighborhood of Malt House, Raven Lane, in return perhaps for some form of emolument. But upon greater reflection he dismissed this as improbable, for a whole host of reasons, most of which boiled down to the notion that his agent with the smoked lenses simply lacked the requisite courage. (This was personally reassuring to the attorney, for it implied that if their roles had been exchanged, he, Jasper Winch, certainly would not have lacked for the quality at issue.) Joined to this was the belief — a creation solely of the mind of Mr. Winch — that his agent Icks, despite occasional lapses, was nonetheless extraordinarily thankful for his present employment, which he found sufficiently rewarding as to render him immune to temptation. Lastly, of course, was the reminder that this same agent was even now upon the road to Crow's-end, overseeing the disposition of certain valuable goods and chattels, and as a consequence had been removed for some while from town.

So the mystery for him deepened.

As I have said Mr. Richard Scribbler was not alone while toiling at his labors, but I refer not to Lawyer Winch. For there was in the vast outer office that day, having arrived not above ten minutes before, another individual of sinister countenance, one who, despite his considerable bulk, was content for the moment to slither and glide among the volcanoes and lighthouses like an ugly frigate running under a press of canvas. This was an enterprise most congenial to him, for in his daily affairs he did much in the slithering and gliding line, and was known to be very good at it. (The city magistrates at least had found little fault with him). This individual had a salty air, from long association with the docks; or perhaps because his instincts as to personal hygiene were, like some vestigial organ, but little developed. He was of a burly, hardened, brutish cast, with an unkempt mustache, a declining forehead, and greasy dark hair matted down beneath a slouch hat. His eyes — very large and protrusive, and surrounded by black circles — were twisted into an ugly squint. His every feature exuded ill-humor, owing something perhaps to the terrible brood hen and the clutch of villainous hatchlings who shared his nest.

This ruffian — Mr. Robert Nightingale — in sailing through the door of Badger and Winch, had of necessity disturbed Mr. Scribbler in the midst of his studies. The clerk had seen fit to glare at him from on high for a full ten seconds, before resuming his copying. The burly Bob, as I have related, was more than satisifed to wait out the completion of that effort. Under sail, the ugly frigate could be observed now and again to slip a hand here or a nimble finger there, furtively, among the law-papers, his crooked eyes as always quietly searching, searching for anything that might be of interest to him or his master. One never knew where items of value were going to turn up — particularly in a lawyer's chambers — and as Mr. Nightingale was, by his own admission, not a socialite, such solitary employment suited him well.

At length Mr. Scribbler came to the finish of his assignment, and so the completed memorandum lay before him in all its glory. He scratched his head with his quill, and fell to an examination of the sheets with a breezy nonchalance. No sooner had he begun than his attention was drawn off by a tiny object that came flying at his head. Knitting his brows he set his wafer-box and blotting-paper aside, laid the cover on the ink-well, and taking up his ruler made a series of unproductive lunges at the fly wheeling about his candle.

"Listen here, listen here, I'll take that now," said the dark voice of Bob Nightingale, from below.

Mr. Scribbler paused to screw up his eyes and tap an inquiring finger upon the parchment, unclear whether it was the memorandum or the ruler that was being demanded.

"O' course it's the papers I mean, you monkey! I've got to get the old 'un's signature. He's got to sign 'em or they ain't legitimate. What, didn't ye know that? He's at the chop-house over the way, and sent me for 'em when they was ready. He'd like a gander at 'em afore he signs."

Mr. Scribbler digested this speech with a lift of his brow and an expression of feigned disinterest. Happening to glance at the vacant line awaiting the signature of Mr. Tusk — the very line he himself had scratched upon the parchment not many minutes before — the clerk was compelled to admit the logic of Mr. Nightingale's argument. Accordingly he slid the memorandum into its envelope, and bending down from his high seat dropped it into the greasy grasp of Bob.

"That'll do it," said Mr. Nightingale, with a grunt of satisfaction. "That's just fine. I'm headed out now, but I'm gonna be back directly. Don't you leave this hole."

Mr. Scribbler shook his head to assure Bob that the hole — whatever and wherever it might be — would not be abandoned, and watched as the fruit of his day's labor was carried off. There was a little something of weariness in his face, before the nonchalance reappeared; though it was by no means the old nonchalance he had been wont to exhibit in former days, for more than weariness had afflicted Mr. Richard Scribbler of late. A general confusion of mind and lowness of spirits, brought on by certain unsettling events, was threatening to overwhelm him — having evolved to such proportions that confusion and low spirits seemed now part and parcel of his existence. He could scarcely recall a time when things were different.

Once Mr. Nightingale had left the ancient pile of red brick, with its great mullioned windows and fantastic chimney-stacks, he went not to a chop-house but to a publican's establishment, where he regaled himself for above half an hour with the finest grog his coin could purchase. After this he took from his coat the memorandum of understanding, and smoothing out the freshly transcribed pages before him, made a brief examination of their contents before crushing the lot of them in his fist. From the same coat he retrieved another few sheets of parchment — these having been given him earlier in the day by his master — and deposited them in the envelope in place of the memorandum. The envelope he then sealed with wax. Throwing aside his glass he sallied forth from the public house, retraced his steps to Cobb's Court, and there returned the envelope to the waiting hands of Mr. Scribbler.

"You'll see to it Winch *gets it*," said Bob, squinting horribly at what he fancied was a very clever *double entendre* on his part. "He's to deliver it himself to the young bloody gentleman. It's by the old 'un's command, and Winch well knows it. It's two parties what's needed to make an agreement."

Mr. Scribbler nodded from his high seat, a little haughtily I should think, for this was a legal matter and he knew legal matters well, for was he not a law-clerk and what after all did this burly ruffian know of the quips and cranks of the law? So he frowned and waved a hand in the direction of the outer door, to hurry Mr. Nightingale on his way. Hurry Bob did, with a low chuckle, and obligingly vanished from sight.

If one had seen fit to pursue the greasy footsteps of Mr. Nightingale, subsequent to his departure, one would have discovered that they led, not surprisingly, to the docks at Salthead harbor. Down a dirty lane of outfitting warehouses and nautical establishments they went, past the swivel bridge, past the boat-yards and provision-shops to another public house, this one distinguished from its many fellows in the neighborhood by the sign of the Ship. There, in a private room, amid the odor of rum and sugar, Mr. Nightingale fell in with a number of his compatriots — men of equally slippery reputation and character, sly men, unsavory men, the raff and refuse of the waterside shambles, who welcomed him with drink and their own version of good-fellowship, which comprised a medley of ugly laughs and ribald jokes, churlish insults, sneers, and taunts, mock quarrels, and a host of wild oaths.

After a time the jolly tosspots were interrupted at their revels by the landlord, a pinguid gentleman with a scar decorating the side of his head, who begged to inform Mr. Robert Nightingale that he had a visitor.

"A visitor? Who's that, then?" demanded Bob, the ugly frigate by now running under a considerable press of liquor.

"It's a gentleman, by the look of 'im," returned the landlord, with a jerk of his head toward the door behind. "Didn't give 'is name."

"Ah, a gentleman!" cried a possum-faced fellow in a sou'wester hat, who occupied the table beside Bob's. "What's the story there, eh?"

"Bob ain't got no truck with no gentlemen," declared a second fellow at that table.

"Mayhap it's a member o' the quality," suggested a third.

"I always smells the quality, miles off," said Bob, patting the side of his nose with a knowing significance. He drew a hugely exaggerated breath, as though searching the molecules of inspired air for a trace of his visitor. "I've got a nose for it!"

"But have you the time for a gentleman of the quality?" asked the fellow in the sou'wester hat. "Is there a vacancy, perhaps, in your busy engagement-book?"

"My engagement-book is chock-full," said Bob, squinting, "but I'll see him anyhow, that's certain. I'm hanged if I'll disappoint the monkey, as he's taken the trouble to seek me out. Send him along!" He flung an unsteady arm toward the landlord and downed another swallow of grog.

The publican obligingly departed. In due course the figure of Mr. John Hunter appeared in the doorway.

As the eyes of Bob lighted upon the visitor his brain told him who it was, and the cup in his hand found itself stayed in mid-passage toward his lips. He uttered a little drunken laugh, half to himself.

"Well, now, if it ain't *him*," said Bob, in a hard whisper. He raised his cup toward the visitor. "A drink to the young bloody gentleman!"

Remarkably cool and brazen of Bob, I warrant, to salute in such a way the very person whose effects he had rifled not so very long before. Brazen though he was on the surface, there was yet something of restraint beneath — owing to the recollection, perhaps, of a certain bloodied face and an awful yellow light that glowed like living coals.

Mr. Hunter came forward. His haughty gaze swept the room and all its contents.

"Well, young gentleman," said Mr. Nightingale, after a few moments of this scrutiny. "What is it you want here in this fine establishment?"

"You are the one," said Mr. Hunter, as matter-of-factly as if he were at a country fair, selecting sheep. "The low fellow with the crooked eyes. You are a thief, sir."

"That he is," avowed Possum Face. He shook his head in mock commiseration, by way of admitting that no words could be closer to the truth.

"A thief, what is larger than life," said the second fellow, admiringly. "A ve-ri-ta-ble co-los-sus in the ways of thievery."

"Larger than life? Stow that gammon! Bob's just large," guffawed the third.

Mr. Nightingale slid his eyes all over the figure of Mr. Hunter, taking in his fashionable attire — from the bottle-green coat and black velvet collar to the white shirt, buff kerseymere waistcoat and fine black trousers, to the polished riding boots, to the doeskin gloves and turf hat the gentleman held in one hand — and performing a few mental calculations as regards the profit that might be realized in exchange for it all.

"Thievery," returned Bob, bridling up, "is an awful serious charge, young bloody gentleman."

"You will return all that you took from me," said Mr. Hunter, with the confident manner of a headmaster.

"And what might that be?" inquired Bob, squinting ferociously.

"You know very well. I need not enumerate the items for you. I offer you this opportunity to reform yourself."

"You're awful bold, young gentleman, awful bold. You runs in here with your sails filled, to call out Bob Nightingale like he was one of the crim'nal element. Well, young bloody gentleman, I ain't never been a member of the crim'nal element." Here the innocent Bob looked round to see his loyal compatriots, who had but moments before testified as to his villainy, abruptly putting about in their opinions.

"The young gentleman's sailing close to the wind now," avowed the sou'wester hat.

"Aye, he's close-hauled," said the third fellow.

The redoubtable Bob shrugged and turned his head gently from side to side, to profess his utter ignorance of the subject of Mr. Hunter's concern. "I ain't got nothin' what belongs to you."

In response the eyes of Mr. Hunter fastened themselves on a certain object Mr. Nightingale held in hand. It was the cup — an ugly black ceramic thing, formed in the likeness of a head. The face was charmingly grotesque, with the beak of a vulture and ears of an ass, a thick beard, wide staring eyes, and snake-infested hair. The lips were twisted into an unpleasant smirk, full of cunning, and offering to view a collection of sharply edged teeth.

Mr. Nightingale's own eyes traced the path of Mr. Hunter's. Not a drop of guilt leaked onto his brow despite such clear evidence of his perfidy. What a varnished rascal! For the cup he held in hand was the very cup which, among other things, he had removed from the house of Mr. Hunter that night, one of several such items he had chosen to retain for his personal use.

"I see what it is you're gawkin' at, young gentleman, and it don't signify," growled Bob, nonetheless nettled by this slip-up. There was no sign of any slip-up on Mr. John Hunter's part, however; he stood before the ruffians with his arms folded, superbly confident and unmindful of any danger, the very picture of power and self-assurance.

"Don't lie to me, sirrah," he warned. "If you do not return the tablets of electrum, which you yourself took from my house, it may affect you most adversely."

"Affect him *adversely?*" cried Possum Face, with a sharp tug at his sou'wester. "What's he mean by that, Bob? What's his tack?"

"Adversely," said the second fellow, "means whatever happens, it damn well ain't gonna be nice."

An outbreak of hilarity attended this remark, though Bob did not share in it with the same enthusiasm as his companions. As difficult as it was for him to admit, internally, there was something about this fashionable young gentleman, quite apart from the yellow light, that affected him. It was the sense of something so far above him, so potent, so remarkable, something so completely peculiar to its own person, as to be beyond all ordinary understanding. There were not many things in this world — apart perhaps from the inimical Mrs. Nightingale — that could affect Bob in such a way.

"And what if I ain't got these tablets o' whatever, as you're gabblin' about?" asked Bob. "How can I turn over what ain't mine to turn over?"

"I know who your master is. If necessary, I shall obtain what I seek through him."

Another outburst of laughter, as the revelers speculated on the chances of the fashionable young gentleman's wresting anything of value from the miser of Salthead.

"Well, I ain't got no tablets o' yours, that's certain," said Mr. Nightingale. "I don't know nothin' about 'em. I don't know what the devil it is you're gabblin' about. And as for this cup here — well, it's mine, and that's a fact."

"A fact," echoed the sou'wester.

"O' course it's Bob's," said the second fellow. "Can't you see it's got his face on it?"

"Aye," crowed the third. "It's 'is portrait!"

Mr. Nightingale did not appreciate the humor of these remarks, and so did not give in to the laughter that accompanied them. He had by now determined that several of his compatriots — two in particular — stood in need of serious correction, a matter he would attend to later in the day.

Mr. Hunter calmly unfolded his arms and laid his hat and gloves aside. The makings of a smile — albeit cold and transient — graced his lips. He placed his hands very casually at his waist, addressing Bob and the company of revelers with a look of strange, sardonic gladness.

"I see how it is. Very well, you have had your opportunity. All things in this life are foreseen and unalterable. I should have known better, I suppose, than to waste time upon such a low fellow."

"Ah, that he is, he's *low*," said the second fellow. "I'd disremembered, till now."

"Aye, it's the truth," nodded the third. "He's low, but he's wide, too, which means he ain't tall."

"The shortest o' the crew," said Possum Face.

"You have persuaded me, and I see now I have been laboring under a false assumption," said Mr. Hunter, growing magnanimous. "It is clear what you have said is true, that you do not have what I seek. Moreover, it is clear to me now who does. I thank you for confirming my suspicion. Shall we pledge, you fellows, and drink a toast to the very useful Mr. Nightingale?"

"A toast!" exclaimed Possum Face, waving his empty cup. "And who's to lay down coin for it?"

"Landlord!" Mr. Hunter called out. "A fresh round of grog for these men. I shall cover it."

"And so we're friends now, is that it, young bloody gentleman?" murmured the useful Bob, far too fly to relax his guard while Mr. John Hunter was on the scene. His eyes were locked in a wicked squint, with trying to pierce the motives and methods of the fashionable young gentleman. Something in Mr. Hunter's manner, suddenly so conciliatory, left him ill at ease. He cursed himself for inadvertently owning the truth, that the strange tablets he'd removed from Mr. Hunter's lodgings were no longer in his possession. But why should this knowledge lift the gentleman's spirits so? There was, after all, little hope of success in confronting Josiah Tusk. He wondered again whether Mr. John Hunter might not be as mad as a hatter. Hunter, hatter. Hatter, hunter. The thinking on it severely strained his cranial resources; but in the end he had to admit there was precious little evidence for lunacy on the part of Mr. Hunter. And certainly, lunacy didn't square with the yellow light.

A drawer arrived with the liquor. The glasses were charged and hoisted in the direction of Mr. Nightingale. Mr. Hunter himself led the toast.

"To the health, to the prolonged life, and to the generosity of Mr. Nightingale," was his pledge.

"Aye! Aye!" roared the companions of Bob.

"Let us drain the liquid from our cups, and thereby demonstrate that no ill feelings remain between us."

"That's it," exclaimed the sou'wester hat. "Drink up, Bob. It ain't your coin. He's offerin' the cup o' kindness, after all!"

"Well, I'll tell ye," said Bob, sniffing at his grog — the thought crossed his mind that Mr. Hunter might have had it poisoned — before venturing a swallow. His ugly features registered surprise. "It *is* the sort what I likes."

"Aye, he's got a nose for it!" laughed the third fellow.

"No ill feelings," said John Hunter, and finished off his portion. "As you have nothing for me, I shall instead reclaim my property at Shadwinkle Old House. That is the place, is it not? I thank you again for the intelligence."

So Mr. Hunter gathered up his hat and gloves, and with a parting glance took leave and went away.

There followed another explosion of mirth, as the revelers pictured in their minds Mr. Hunter facing the miser — that sultan of superiority, that towering white-headed potentate — and demanding the return of his property. All laughed save Bob, who drank his grog in sour rumination and kept his crooked eyes fixed, as best they could be fixed, on the door through which Mr. Hunter had vanished. Though the words had been spoken lightly, Mr. Nightingale understood that the young bloody gentleman was grimly in earnest.

He finished the remainder of his drink in silence. His companions observed his mood and chided him roughly for it. Gradually, however, their noses slipped farther and farther into their glasses, as the liquor slipped farther and farther into their brains. Still Bob sat quietly, patting the table-top with his empty cup. He heard someone laugh — a harsh, cynical, mocking laugh. For some reason he found his eyes drawn to the cup in his hand. Peering curiously at it, he thought he saw the carved face of it move.

He blinked and looked again. It was no illusion. The smirking face on the cup was smirking still, but the lips were farther apart now, revealing something more of the sharp-edged teeth than had been visible earlier. And as the smirk had expanded, the staring eyes had narrowed themselves into crafty slits.

"What sort o' monkey tricks is this?" growled Bob, scratching at his greasy head in consternation.

He lifted the cup for a closer inspection, bringing the ugly image to within inches of his own. Squinting horribly, he examined the other features of the carving for changes. It was then he heard again the mocking laugh, and with startled astonishment realized it came from the cup. Before he could react, however, he felt the cup move in his hand — felt the jaws close down on his nose, felt the sharply chiseled teeth bite into it.

The howls of pain awakened his companions, who despite their condition jumped to their feet at once in alarm. Glancing anxiously this way and that, they demanded to know what was the situation and who was in danger, for there was nothing to be seen but Mr. Nightingale with a cup to his face. Then they saw Bob release his hold on the cup, and saw the cup retain its position, adhering to his nose like a sort of ceramic excrescence. What was worse the cup appeared to be trembling, ever so slightly, as a result of the force it exerted on Mr. Nightingale's physiognomy.

In the meantime the shouting had drawn the landlord and the drawers, and several curious patrons of the establishment, into the private room.

"*Take it off me!*" cried Bob. He leaped up and performed a little dance about his chair, hopping from one foot to the other and shaking himself like a cart-horse. No result. He spun round and round in a transport of frenzy, flailing his arms, as if the discharge of energy might somehow ease the pain. It did not.

"Take it off my face!" he roared.

The landlord strode boldly forward. He took hold of Mr. Nightingale by the shoulders to steady him, then seized the handle of the cup and pulled on it with considerable violence. Despite his efforts he managed only to pull the cup toward himself, and a tortured Bob with it.

"No! No! No!" cried the enraged sufferer. Tears streamed from his eyes, and blood from his nose. "Back off! Back off! That ain't gonna work, you monkey!"

The startled publican retreated a pace or two. He had thought at first it was all a prank of Bob's, as had Bob's compatriots, and said as much.

"This ain't no prank!" exclaimed Mr. Nightingale, hopping about in his boots as though the floor were strewn with live embers. "Oh, God, God, God — somebody take mercy on me!" A greasy handkerchief came flying from his pocket to stanch the blood. "Oh, God, God, God!"

"What's 'e callin' out to God for?" demanded one onlooker, but one of many who still could neither believe nor understand what was happening. "It's right game of 'im, though. I've never known Bob Nightingale to 'ave any use for religiosity. If 'e's expectin' aid from that quarter, 'e's like to be disappointed, *I* think."

His companions could do nothing but stand apart and watch. Four or five times the terrified Bob grasped the cup, as if to wrench it from his face. Each time his fingers closed on it, however, the pain became blindingly worse. The cup was no more than an inch from his eyes, and as he looked at it, one of its narrowed eye-slits shut and opened in a mischievous wink.

"What sort o' tricks is this? Oh, God, God — young bloody gentleman — what sort o' tricks is this? *Is this the tricks o' your shredded gods?*" he cried out to the departed John Hunter.

No one helped him now, not only because no one *could* help him, but because no one cared to, even among his closest compatriots. The lone exception was the landlord, but even he was concerned far less for the welfare of Bob than for the welfare and reputation of his establishment. The problem with Bob, I venture, was that he had compatriots and acquaintances and business associates, but not being a socialite, little in the way of friends.

He tried to arrest the flow of blood by clamping his handkerchief round and under his nose. Thus the onlookers were presented with the spectacle of a howling Bob Nightingale, a drinking-cup attached to his face and a blood-soaked pocket-handkerchief stuffed beneath it, cavorting about the room in a frenzy of panic.

A physician, one Dr. Sweetman, who happened to be passing in the street outside, was called in by the landlord to give an opinion. Having examined the patient, he gave it.

"He's got a cup on his nose," he said.

The doctor then put a cigar between his teeth and departed the Ship public house, leaving with the patient instructions as to the disposition of his fee, which was payable by the 30th instant.

The landlord chased the doctor down in the street, protesting this result. The physician whirled on him with a look of fierce surprise.

"But, Doctor — 'ow's 'e supposed to git it off?" cried the landlord. "The cup, I mean?"

"Oh, he don't need me for that; I'm strictly a medical practitioner. What he needs is a cut-and-thrust man, a *surgeon*. Very well. Have him apply to Croker. That's Dr. Samuel Croker, of Darting Hill. He'll snip it off for him — the nose, I mean. Here's my card; tell Croker I've referred him. Croker's the finest surgeon on earth, and as a consequence his fees are considerably elevated. Good day to you, landlord."

So saying the doctor walked off with his cigar in his mouth and his hands at his back, exuding an air of self-congratulation.

"A murrain on it!" growled the landlord. He stared after the physician for some moments in disbelief, then dashed back into the Ship to offer whatever aid and assistance he could to the suffering soul within.

CHAPTER V

Something at the Window

MALT House, Raven Lane, afternoon. Mr. John Hunter is now at home, having played out his little scene at the Ship public house — by all accounts a success — and so confirmed what it was he needed to confirm. On returning he had gone directly to his study, that very wide and spacious apartment with its musty odor of the past — the very same apartment with which Mr. Robert Nightingale had become familiar not so long before — and giving his coat to his servant, had taken his seat at the massive, old-fashioned writing-desk, the same desk in which the same Mr. Nightingale had discovered some few odd coins, some letters and some parchments decorated in a fanciful script, and a map of twelve cities. Those items were of course no longer at hand, thanks to the curiosity of Mr. Nightingale and his canvas sack, which recollection caused Mr. Hunter to pause over matters for some time with an inner grimness of will. Soon, however, a mist rose before him — who can tell what far-off scenes were drifting past the retina of his memory — and his attention shifted to the French windows leading onto the long gallery without. On impulse he went to the windows and parted the curtain, to examine the day.

It was, all in all, a bleak and cheerless prospect. The weather had grown colder by degrees, literally, as Mr. Hunter had trotted home on his horse. The atmosphere in Raven Lane was alive now with an icy wind that was tossing the trees about. The low dark clouds had a ragged, unsettled look, as though searching for a place to drop their snow. These signs appeared to have little effect upon Mr. Hunter, however, apart perhaps from highlighting the insularity of his position, and the extent of his removal from nearly everything and everyone familiar to him.

He turned and sent his gaze roaming about the apartment — that remarkable study of his with its wondrous assemblage of objects, each bearing silent and mysterious witness to the past. To Mr. Nightingale the room had resembled a museum, a house of homage to the dead; but to Mr. Hunter it was a living, breathing world. There on the walls hung the arms and armor he had earned in his springtime, the javelins and lances, swords and bucklers, all of bronze; the double-headed ax, the huge circular shield stamped with the face of a cat.

There on the tables were a scattering of artifacts not plundered by the burly Bob — the remains of Mr. Hunter's collection of libation vessels and terra-cotta figurines, and the glossy black pottery so characteristic of the Rasna. In the center of the apartment stood the altar of tufa, which once had held the tablets of Tyrrhenian electrum and which held nothing now but stale air. His eyes traveled from these objects to the colorful screens beside the chimney-piece, with their painted depictions of chariot-races and athletic contests, banquets and celebrations. Divers diving, wrestlers wrestling, riders riding; scenes of dancing, hunting, fishing, feasting. Happy times — oh, happy, happy times! And above all the striding figure of a lithe and youthful piper, rendered by the artist with such grace and vigor that the room seemed to ring with the strains of music.

With sudden decision Mr. Hunter disappeared behind the screens, returning presently with two identical tubes of yellow wood — long, slender, tapering things, a pair of musical pipes, marvelously wrought. Moving to the desk he perched himself on the edge of it and raised the instruments to his lips.

For above a quarter of an hour he played, his fingers dancing nimbly about the finger-holes of the double-pipe, varying the pitch and texture of the notes with considerable refinement. Carried on the stillness of the air, the plangent song of the pipes found its way into all the hidden recesses of the apartment. From the quality of the sound it was evident that, in addition to being a soothsayer, Mr. Hunter was a musician of some achievement. Absorbed in his performance, with his eyes shut and his brows responding to the passion of the music, the face and form of Mr. John Hunter, fashionable gentleman, could very easily have melted away, leaving in their stead the face and form of Vel Saties, lucumo of Velca.

On the other side of the room stood the figure of the young man with the hypnotic eyes and mystical smile — a young man who, at any moment it seemed, might leap into a dance in response to the music, so real did he appear. But this young man was content, as he always was, to remain simply an image in terra cotta — the earthly representation of Aplu, shining god of the sun. On went Mr. Hunter with his song, some of it sweet, some of it joyous, some of it regretful to the point of despair; a celebration of sorts, a hymn to the memory of a magnificent, gifted people long vanished from the earth.

So Mr. Hunter passed the time for a little while more, until the appearance of his servant causes him to take the pipes from his lips, and so the music comes to an end.

"What is it, Salop?" demands Mr. Hunter. He lays aside the double-pipe, having satisfied for now some pressing inner need. "Is there something amiss?"

The ancient retainer in dusty black tails draws his breath hard, as though even that simple exertion were too much for his smoke-weary lungs.

"A visitor," says he, in a gravel voice.

"And who might this visitor be?"

"Winch," responds Salop, who never uttered more than a few syllables at any one time.

Mr. Hunter wonders what possibly could have drawn the comfort-loving attorney out to Raven Lane on such a day. The answer for the moment eludes him.

"Very well. I'll see him."

The servant nods, and with a shuffling tread removes himself from the apartment. After a time the body of the fat attorney and his plum-colored suit fill the doorway.

"Come in, Winch, come in. This is something of a surprise. I'm afraid you have me at a loss to understand the purpose of your visit. Pray enlighten me."

Lawyer Winch fawns his way into the room, keeping his eyes mostly averted from Mr. Hunter. He seems unduly anxious or tentative, or perhaps embarrassed, or a little sheepish, or all of these at once; licking his lips and smiling greasily, with lowered head, as though fearing the response of Mr. Hunter to his very presence. He comes near to cringing as he removes his hat and makes an awkward little bow, like a schoolboy prepared to accept a punishment. To the attorney's surprise Mr. Hunter seems unperturbed by his call. There is no evidence of displeasure in either voice or expression, something Lawyer Winch finds troubling. There is, he concludes, something not quite right here. Where was the wrathful indignation? Not there! His anger at being spied on by his own attorney? Not there! What mischief, wonders Mr. Winch, what mischief could his fashionable young client be up to?

"You're — ahem! — you're certain, ah — you're certain you're not — ah — distressed in any way, sir? Ahem!"

"Distressed? Concerning what? I'm not sure I understand your meaning. Well, Winch, don't stand quivering there. What business has brought you out? Or is this one of your occasional social calls?"

Mr. Winch, convinced now of mischief, cautiously hands Mr. Hunter an envelope, saying that it contains the initiating document — a memorandum of understanding — with regard to the cooperative endeavor into which Mr. Hunter was preparing to enter with Mr. Josiah Tusk of the firm of Tusk and Co., Salthead. Mr. Hunter, aware of the relationship between the miser and Mr. Bob Nightingale, and of the current position of Mr. Tusk as regards the tablets of electrum — but knowing nothing whatsoever about a memorandum of understanding — is now himself perplexed and suspicious of mischief.

"A cooperative endeavor? Tusk and Co.? What are you talking about, Winch? You're making no sense."

With swiveling eyes the attorney gives a jerk of his head toward the envelope, to indicate that the enclosed document would supply all answers. Accordingly Mr. Hunter extracts the item in question. His face assumes an expression of puzzlement, which is quickly followed by signs of a mounting choler, as he runs across these interesting words —

MY DEAR SIR, —

I know you. Yes, yes. I know your history, and whence you come. I know what you are. I know as well why you are in Salthead and what you are searching for. My agent, in point of fact, has for some weeks been observing you, Sir, at my direction, and has provided me with various items of information that I believe will be of interest to you, *viz.*, information a gentleman of honor would not wish disclosed to an unfeeling public.

Let us discuss this matter at some length, so as to reach an amiable settlement that will be of benefit to both parties. For a consideration I shall see to it myself that the offending items are quickly and quietly withdrawn, never to be resurrected. Your secret, Sir, shall be safe in my hands, you may depend upon it.

Discretion is ever my watchword.

I remain, Sir, as always, your humble Servant, &c., &c.,

J. WINCH

Mr. Hunter raises his head slowly. "This was prepared by you?" he asks in a low voice, remarkably controlled. For answer Mr. Winch's eyes glide swiftly away, exhibiting again that characteristic reluctance to look his man straight in the face.

"Ahem! Of course," says he, staring at the floor. "It's all in capital good order, is it not, sir? If there are imperfections, that clerk of mine will pay dearly for them. Ahem. Lazy do-nothing. Scatterbrain. Ahem!"

"Oh, it's in particularly good order," returns Mr. Hunter. He sits down to his desk, maintaining his scrutiny of the note while a careful forefinger strokes at his broad mustache. He must think, think now, and so work the matter out. How could Mr. Jasper Winch of Salthead possibly know who or what he was, and why should he deliver his ultimatum in such a way? Who was this agent — this spy — to whom he referred? How could anyone be aware of his motives? How could anyone know his history? Not one person in ten thousand thousand could possibly —

Hold on! Unless Avle Matunas —

"Tell me, Winch," says Mr. Hunter, "are you acquainted with a man who calls himself Jack Hilltop?"

"Who? Hilltop? Ahem!"

"I thought not. What of this Mr. Josiah Tusk, the financier? You are acquainted with him, I assume?"

"Ah, Mr. Tusk! Of course. Ahem! Very well acquainted indeed. I am his attorney, sir. Yes, indeed. Ahem. Mr. Josiah Tusk is one of the chiefest and most esteemed clients of the firm. A captain of industry. A marvel."

"I see. Then it is becoming vastly more intelligible to me," says Mr. Hunter, rising. "You are acting, I expect, with the full knowledge and consent of Mr. Tusk? You are of one mind in the matter?"

"Of course," replies Mr. Winch, with an ingratiating smile and an inclination of his bald head. He is feeling more at ease now, with talk of financiers and marvels. Perhaps he was wrong about Mr. Hunter. Perhaps what Mr. Josiah Tusk had told him was speculation, a lucky guess, or simply a lie. Perhaps the fashionable young gentleman knew nothing of Samson Icks's activities. Perhaps he was in the clear!

But Lawyer Winch's deliverance does not last long.

"Then I shall require very little time to consider this — this memorandum, as you call it," says Mr. Hunter, his manner turning suddenly cold. He flings the paper upon the desk with a wrathful motion. "I had not honestly thought it of you, Winch. When I came to Salthead I placed my affairs in your hands, as my trusted representative. Your service has in fact been of some value to me, for your introduction to the household of Eaton Wafers allowed me to reclaim an object that once belonged to my — that once was mine. Now I see the truth of it, however. You have betrayed me. Your supposed representation was an elaborate design to uncover what you could about me — a search for blemishes and vulnerabilities, for levers of opportunity that might be pressed to your advantage. It was your express desire from the outset to cheat me, a stranger to your city. You are indeed a pretty picture, Winch — an ornament of your profession! You are a falseheart and a recreant. You are a man completely without honor."

The reaction of the pretty picture is immediate and telling. The edges of his eyes start to quiver, uncontrollably; his tongue licks his lips, his hand wipes his head.

"H-How do you mean, sir?" he exclaims, casting long suspicious looks toward the discarded paper. "How do you mean? Ahem! What is in that document?"

"You know very well!" retorts Mr. Hunter, contemptuously.

Mr. Winch fixes his eyeglass in his eye and examines the supposed memorandum. He plunges through the unfamiliar text, line by line, word by word, syllable by syllable, with a stupified countenance. Here, here was a memorandum of understanding like none he had ever seen! He reads it through again, gaping at sight of his own name at the close. In the process his face turns a ghastly shade of white, with drops of perspiration scattered round it like the smallpox.

"Your agent, as you call him, whom you sent to spy on me," resumes Mr. Hunter, "is Tusk's man — a low fellow, this Nightingale, who broke into my house and stole my goods. I see how it fits together now. In addition to your other accomplishments you are a scoundrel, sir. I need hardly tell you that the services of your discreditable firm are no longer required by me."

The eyeglass of Mr. Winch pops from his eye like a cork. He quails beneath Mr. Hunter's searching glance, fearful of fist to fist. But — what had that slippery character Bob Nightingale to do with anything?

"This is not the document I had prepared," exclaims Mr. Winch. "Where is the memorandum? Not here! This is not mine. Ahem! Who has done this to me? Scribbler — wool-gatherer — ingrate — a black plot to destroy me —" He rummages madly through the envelope, searching for another paper that is not there, turns the one paper he does have this way and that, sideways, upside-down, curls it into a tube and peers through it like a telescope, looking for the slightest bit of anything that resembled a memorandum of understanding. Surely, surely, one must be here somewhere!

"Don't bother with denials, Winch. Your guilt is evident in every word you have written there — "

Abruptly Mr. Hunter checks himself. He frowns and turns his head aside, listening intently, as a gust of wind brushes against the French windows. An atmosphere of intense cold invades the room. Oblivious to it, he looks toward the attorney with the faint gleam of a smile on his lips.

"It would appear," says he — "it would appear we are not alone."

Fearing Mr. Hunter's wrath and perhaps another plot, Lawyer Winch glances nervously about the room, mentally inhaling its solemn and mysterious artifacts and wondering what to expect next. He finds himself shivering. "N-Not alone? Ahem! Who is with us?"

Mr. Hunter approaches the French windows and there pauses for a moment, looking out.

"It is as I thought," he says, and draws back the curtain. He opens the windows, allowing a blast of fresh air to enter the apartment, and with one hand upon the latch turns round to the pretty picture. "Look here, Winch. Here is someone come to see you."

The attorney — confused, embarrassed, frightened, dismayed — peers in the indicated direction. What he sees coming first through the windows is another rush of air, as manifested by a ruffling of the curtain; then following it in, an old gentleman with a face like a drift of snow, gray milky eyes and a careworn expression. He is dressed in clothes of the sort that had been *de rigueur* perhaps fifty years before. It is, however, not so much that the elderly gentleman *steps* into the apartment as *floats* into it, as though he were riding the gust of wind. A swirling fog envelops the lower half of his body, leaving to view only his upper torso, arms, and head. The body itself is very gently rising and sinking, rising and sinking — suspended in air as though the gods of gravity held no sway over it.

The torso glides stealthily toward Mr. Winch, bringing with it the perishing cold. As it approaches the benign expression on the face is transformed into a grimace of hideous malignity. The milky eyes grow huge and fierce, directing themselves at the attorney — who, if he were one to wear a wig, would most certainly have flipped it.

The torso utters no word but raises a hand — as if its direful presence alone were not sufficient to gain the attention of Lawyer Winch! Their eyes meet, holding for no more than the briefest second before the anguished Mr. Winch thrusts his away. The attorney manages a grimace or two of his own, reflective of inward torment, before at last crying out —

"What is this rubbish? Ahem! What is this rubbish? His k-kind can't be here!" He appeals dumbly to Mr. Hunter, who has been standing off to one side with an indifferent expression.

"You are surprised to see *my kind*, Winch?" exclaims the apparition. "Just what do you mean by that? Explain yourself."

"Very — ahem — very surprised, Ephraim!" gasps Mr. Winch. He loosens his collar, twisting his head from side to side. "Very surprised — to see you — " Again he turns in appeal to the impassive John Hunter. "That one — dead!" he says, with a fat finger aimed at the torso. "Stone dead — apoplexy — churchyard — Michaelmas — these eleven years. Ahem!"

"My kind?" reiterates Mr. Badger, smiling sourly — for Mr. Ephraim Badger it was indeed, or at least the shadow of him. "You have not satisfied me at all, Winch. What do you mean?"

The attorney screws his head around and attempts to shake it, to express his disbelief in the reality of the torso. But the head merely sits there, quivering in its socket.

"Do you mean because I am not alive? Because I am no longer like you, a covetous worldling? Is that what you say?"

Drawing back a little, Mr. Winch manages a strangled cough in reply.

"I thought as much. How it suits you! But your time will come, Winch, as did mine. Here you are one moment quite well, awake in the world, and then a sickness comes and turns you off like a spigot! So there you go, and nothing left behind but your good name. What have you done to *my* good name, Winch? What have you done to *me?* To all I lived for, to all I accomplished in my life? How dare you blacken the reputation of the firm — *my* firm, my life's endeavor — with your greedy machinations, your trickeries, your sly ways, your vanity, your selfishness. What! Do you think I haven't seen you, you blunder-headed clod? Well, I'll tell you now — *I have seen all*."

Mr. Winch manages to nod his blunder-head in agreement.

"You entered my employ as a young man with a most problematical future. I gave you opportunity, as my own benefactor had given me. I gave you my trust. In time I appointed you junior partner in the firm, and so made you guardian of my good name. See how you have repaid me, Winch. Spying on our own clients! Betraying *their* trust! Is it not, as this young gentleman here has described it, a pretty picture? You were nothing before I took you up. You are nothing still."

Lawyer Winch appears offended by these remarks, but can find no basis on which to deny them; nonetheless he makes a motion as though to object. But the chilly torso of Ephraim Badger, gliding closer, would have none of it.

"None of your chaff, Winch, and none of your lies — I don't care twopence for 'em! I am too old, too sensible, and too *dead* to be gammoned by a poor practitioner such as you. I have no desire now other than to recover the legacy of my reputation. Mark me, I *will* have it — so that people of Salthead will again pause in sign of respect at mention of Badger's name, and say *there* was an honest rogue! You, Winch, will recover that legacy for me. It will be your charge. You will restore to the firm of Badger and Winch the high regard it once commanded in every quarter of this city."

The air surrounding the fat attorney grows colder still, as the shadow of Ephraim Badger descends upon him like a winter frost. A most uncommon winter frost, however, one which looked and spoke like a decayed solicitor.

"You will restore it," declares the frost, not as a request but as a command.

"Yes, indeed, Ephraim," replies Mr. Winch, shivering.

"Have a care! You will restore my name, or you will see me again. That will be your reward, Winch, if you fail — *to see me again.* Not once, not twice; you will see me *everywhere.* Every way you turn, there I shall be. In every room, along every gallery, on every terrace, every staircase, at every window, in every doorway — you will see me. Day and night I shall be with you, forever in your company, never from your sight. Your every waking and sleeping moment will be plagued by my vengeful presence. In every face that passes on the street, you will see my face. Every voice you hear will be my voice. When you examine your face in the mirror — any mirror — it will be my face peering at you from the glass. Is that not a pretty picture? *Have a care!*"

This litany of terror freezes every part of Mr. Winch that the cold had not gripped already. The room begins to heave and roll — greenly — sickly — like a ship preparing to go under. The attorney slaps a fat hand to head, fearing at any moment his brains will explode. He wonders whether this might after all be nothing more than a sinister dream, a creation of his own fancy. He makes a little battling motion with his clenched fists, as though ready for a knuckle-to-knuckle with the shade of Ephraim Badger. But his resolve quickly fades — his eyelids flutter — he gives up a groan — a sigh — lapses into a swoon, and so goes crashing to the floor in a plum-colored heap.

When his servant arrives to trundle him home, there is of course no explanation on offer other than an untimely seizure or fit, brought on perhaps by exhaustion from overwork, by excessive devotion to duty — an hypothesis which the sullen Salop relays in the fewest words possible. With his minion's aid and a quantity of hartshorn, complimented by sal volatile, the attorney is partially revived, and with glazed eyes finds himself evacuated into his carriage, which vehicle promptly removes his shattered bulk from the vicinity of Raven Lane.

Not above half an hour later, despite the severity of the weather, a party of four gentlemen assembles at the door of Mr. Hunter's residence. They huddle closely together as a group, awaiting a response to their collective rap upon the door. The sullen servant answers and without emotion gives ear to their request. There follows a lengthy pause, after which the servant informs them, with consummate sparseness of verbiage, that the master was not at home, would not be home for a very long time, and how long that very long time would be, precisely, he (Salop) had no knowledge. The door is then abruptly shut in the faces of the four gentlemen, who spend the next few minutes gazing at one another in consternation — the professor and his secretary, Dr. Dampe, and Harry Banister. The doctor, personally indignant at the reception afforded them by a lackey, pounds several times on the door to register his displeasure.

But the melancholy stoop-shouldered morass of stone and brick known as Malt House, half-hid in ivy, frowned upon them in the late afternoon light, and welcomed them not.

CHAPTER VI

When the Miser's Away —

WINTER has come to Salthead.

A tremendous storm — offspring of the restless sky described in the previous chapter — rises up out of the east and buries the old city in white drifts. A bone-chilling wind howls all the day and night, spraying the snow about as it whistles past Whistle Hill and past every other eminence in town as high at least as a human head. The seven lofty crags, those granitized warriors standing watch over Salthead from the highlands at the back of town, wake to find themselves draped in sheets of powder, blind, inert, unable now to stand watch over anything. It is a grim and ghostly business. And as the days progress, the business only worsens.

Soon the mails are stopped, and the coach traffic comes to a shuddering halt. Bonfires are lit in the streets, not for celebration, but for the warmth and comfort of those poor souls without other recourse. Chimneys smoke like tobacconists, so desperate are they to generate the heat needed to satisfy their human companions, most of whom have taken to the wearing of layered shirts and bodices and woolen stockings, flannel waistcoats, heavy cloaks and wrappers, and all manner of well-insulated gloves and boots, shawls and mufflers, and oddly furred hats. Blankets and comforters come flying from wardrobes and presses as though by magnetic attraction, to find their way onto sofas and bedsteads and shivering shoulders. Kitchens, with their wide blazing fires, their kettles on the hob and their cozy ingle-nooks, once more become places of entertainment and social discourse, as drawing-rooms and dining-rooms lose their appeal. Horses are kept well stabled, except when needed for some inescapable errand, while dogs and cats all but vanish from the snow-lined streets. Ominously, reports of a teratorn seen in the leaden sky begin to circulate about town, leaving people to wonder whether this might not be the cruelest and most inhospitable winter to strike the ancient city in many a twelvemonth.

The council of aldermen, meeting in haste at the Guildhall, formulates its recommendation to the citizenry, which is then distributed by means of the parish watchmen, that none should venture out until the fury of the present storm had spent itself. Nonetheless, word is soon received of the inevitable strandings and other such tragedies, which are irrevocably linked to life in a frigid clime. A traveler whose horse had dropped from exhaustion is found sitting bolt upright in a ravine, frozen through and through, having evidently leaned for a moment against a snowbank to refresh himself, and so gone to sleep. A young child, escaping unnoticed from the arms of her large family, and unrecking of the dangers of the world, gets no farther than the nearest by-street before she collapses. And on his rounds a watchman, patrolling the margins of his parish, comes upon a fallen comrade who, with the exception of the point of one shoe, is completely immersed in snow, with his faithful spaniel lying under his right arm.

Such was the scene and such the sights, when there appeared on the high ground at the back of the city, along the main coach road, which was otherwise now unused, a caravan of two. Under most circumstances, two of anything would hardly qualify for a caravan; as for instance, a pair of cart-horses or a brace of carriages. But the sheer size and grandeur of the two creatures emerging now from the gloom, tirelessly striving, tirelessly plodding, their hot breath expelled in great rising pillars of steam, surely satisfied that description. There were, I say, two in the caravan, red mastodons both — their shaggy coats spattered with snow dust, their legs like tree-trunks plunging with rhythmic force through the drifts, creating muffled tremors in the earth at every step. A pair of red mastodons, the one a gigantic bull with two of the grandest tusks ever seen upon any creature in living memory; the other a cow, smaller in size, marching just behind.

Upon each of the mastodons were mounted cabs and freight platforms. In the cab behind the bull's head rode a gaunt, goofish young fellow with a gaping mouth, strange watery eyes and a greasy wide-awake. Beside him crouched a bearded figure with small, nut-like eyes and a profusion of mouse-colored hair like fleece. The other cab was occupied by a sturdy little man in a checked waistcoat — the waistcoat being submerged at the moment beneath a considerable depth of outer wear — with a rumpled cap perched atop his round gray head. All three travelers sported gloves and mufflers, and weary faces bleached white by the cold. So it was the coaches were stopped, the mails were stopped, civilization was stopped, nearly everything in the world was stopped but mighty red mastodons, which were in their element; for as Mr. Hatch Hoakum was fond of telling anyone within earshot, *there's nothing stops the beasts*.

On this particular occasion the beasts would stop, however, though it would be at the direction of their drivers. Having negotiated mountain snows and silent woods for the past two days, the drivers responded with cries of delight as they beheld the familiar outlines of the ancient city; and as their shaggy charges marched down into it, the equally familiar lines of the inn known as the Three Hats, which was situated in generous grounds at the brink of town, under the shadow of the lofty crags.

This inn of the Three Hats was well known to Mr. Hoakum for its spacious stable-yard and its proximity to the coach-road, both of which were of advantage under the present circumstances. As they drew rein and unfurled the cord-ladders, the mastodon men waved their greetings to the ostler and his helpers, who welcomed them heartily in return, and who extended their salutations as well to the Kingmaker and gentle Betty. Having concluded another successful transfer, and being arrived now in Salthead with freight compartments void of cargo, Mr. Hoakum and his companions were looking forward to a respite at the comfortable old inn, to the warmth of its generous hearth, to its good food and drink, and to the lively company of its inhabitants.

And a very apropos name it was, too, as the three gentlemen removed their own three hats and placed them on pegs in the gallery, before setting foot in the common-room. Two of the gentlemen doffed theirs quite willingly, whereas the third, Mr. Earhart by name, required the urging of Blaster to dislodge the ragged specimen from his head.

"The city, from one end t'other, she's shut up today," remarked the landlord, who had entered from the kitchen and at once joined Mr. Hoakum and his party. He was a little squab figure with a large discolored nose like a strawberry and fleshy ears like prunes. A calico smock-frock was fastened at his ample waist. "She's right dirty weather, justabout. Aye, that she is. Everything, why she's locked down tight. She's doone for now. She's all stopped. Nowt is a-goin' nowhere."

"Nowt that is but the beasts," Mr. Hoakum reminded him, with a few smart tugs and pulls at his checked waistcoat. His blue eyes fairly twinkled.

"Aye, ye've lodged 'em in the yard, have ye? They'll like it there, justabout. An' there's more snow to be fallin' afore this 'un is doone with us. So ye'll want a room?"

"I b'lieve so, sir, if it can be spared," replied Mr. Hoakum, noting the great number of travelers in the common-room. "If it don't work out, well, the lad and Charles and I, we'll put up in the loft."

"Now, I'll hear nowt o' that," said the landlord, with a solemn wag of his head. "Ye'll have yer room, justabout. But what ye'll be wantin' now is some hot grog. Eileen! Eileen! Three hot 'uns for Mr. Hatch Hoakum an' his mates."

The pretty plump girl at the bar, who just happened to be the daughter of the landlord, smiled briskly as she got about the task. Soon three steaming cups of hot elder wine, well qualified with brandy and spice, were set before Mr. Hoakum and his companions — an elixir against the chill, and a most efficacious one too, which never had tasted so good as it did that cold, cold day long, long ago.

"There's nowt runnin' upon the roads," resumed the landlord, idly tearing at a thumbnail while standing by in attendance on his patrons' needs. "She's all shut doone, justabout. Aye, she's locked up tighter than the good wooman's corset."

"Not much running, that's flat," agreed Mr. Hoakum. "As the passengers and such have temp'rarily bounced over to the coaches, well, it's a bad situation. But there ain't no help for spilled milk. We've come from Newmarsh and she's shut down too, as you call it. As cold as an ice locker."

"There's say there's ice already on the river. On the upper reaches. Likely they'll be a frost fair this year! Aye, with streets o' booths set up, an' oxen roasts, an' slidin' with the skates, an' sled races an' such. Aye, she's the coldest blast we've taken in some time, justabout."

"Well, it's winter, arter all," Mr. Hoakum pointed out. "It's the time o' the year for it."

"Aye, an' if this were midsoommer, an' the day like this — like that soommer not long ago, ye'll recall — well, the good wooman an' the daughter and I, we'd be packed up tight an' on our ways to Headcorn. Aye, past Headcorn, likely — all the ways to Nantle an' the southern islands. That's where we'd go, justabout, an' devil take this cold!"

"Can Charley go to Headcorn, too?" asked the Sheephead. "Charley would go to the islands. Where are the islands, Mr. Hatch?"

"Aye, I'll wager ye would!" laughed the landlord, merrily. "Ye do that, sir, an' send us yer best wishes, justabout!"

"The weather's fine there, Charles," explained Mr. Hoakum. "But the islands, they're very far away."

"Aye, ye're dead right about that, sir," said the landlord. "She's far, far away!"

"So we'll stay just where we are, Charles, temp'rarily at least — for today and tonight, and enjoy the hospitality of this good house. And so in the morning — well, we'll see to the morning when the morning comes. It's likely some busy gent will require our services. The coaches won't run, but that won't stop the beasts."

"That it won't!" declared Blaster, with a defiant nod. His wide-awake was missing from his head, and so it was strange to see him nod that head without the added emphasis of his wobbly hat-brim.

There was in progress in the common-room a lively game of *vingt-et-un* at twopence a dozen. Mr. Hoakum and his nephew, noting one or two acquaintances among the players, drifted over to the table to tender their regards. Invitations were quickly issued by the participants. Mr. Hoakum was not above a game of chance, now and then; besides which the stakes were low, and the game itself merely an excuse for conversation and the promotion of good fellowship within doors, while the storm raged without. So Mr. Hoakum and Blaster took up their cards and soon were immersed in luck, most of it good, in their quest for twenty-one pips; and as for the conversation, it was mostly good as well.

Sheephead Charley knew nothing of cards and games of chance, and even if he had, would have been unable to fathom the principles and regulations by which their play was directed. As well he lacked the necessary powers of concentration; so a round game was not for him. Instead he occupied himself with a favorite device — having *sprung* it, as it were, on Mr. Hoakum several times before — which was to parade before the unsuspecting that great silver watch he had removed from Mr. Harry Banister's study at Eaton Wafers. As was his custom he first would withdraw the watch, very slyly, and dangle it from its ribbon before the astonished onlooker; then quickly hide it again in his rags, and closing his eyes, throw back his head and laugh in a wild manner.

"You call that a valuable?" scoffed an excitable fellow, who had been observing Mr. Earhart's antics for some little while. The excitable fellow was spare and wiry, with dark, shiny eyes, a wrinkled face and a remnant or two of pale hair. Attired in a faded corduroy jacket with a button gone, a coarse-striped waistcoat and blue neckcloth, and fustian trousers, he gave every appearance of a servant on his day off. The excitable fellow had consumed a good deal of hot grog, though it was only mid-day; but being shut up at an inn and at the mercy of the weather, it was perhaps a not unreasonable state of being.

The Sheephead threw back his head and laughed. "Valuable. Charley has a valuable. Turnip, turnip. Time of day. Charley has time of day!"

"That isn't much of a valuable, I can tell you," returned the excitable fellow, scornfully. "It isn't worth the shake of a fist, in comparison to what I've got. No, sir."

"You have a valuable?" asked Charley, moving closer, with that odd bumping and jostling motion of his limbs. "What kind of valuable? Does it make a noise, like time of day?"

"It does make a noise, at times, but it's a secret. Do you hear? The old man's secret, not mine," replied the excitable fellow, after a brief silence. His shiny eyes darted warily from side to side, as though he feared the "old man" might be close at hand, listening. "That's what it is. It isn't mine, but I can get to it whenever I want — only *he* doesn't know that! He'd be in a foul temper if he did, I can tell you, and I'd be paying for it. But the fearful old screw is from home now."

"What is it?" asked the Sheephead, fascinated, though slightly confused by the other's vocabulary. "What valuable of the old man's? What are you paying for? What old screw?"

The servant paused to examine the ragged and fidgety figure more closely.

"You look to be a solid sort," he concluded, thereby testifying to the extent of his intoxication. He swallowed another quantity of grog, wiping the residue from his lips with the sleeve of his corduroy jacket. "What's your name?"

"Charley's name."

"Yes, but what is your name?"

"Charley's name," reiterated Charley, with a frown.

The servant put down his drink and looked the Sheephead straight in his nut-like eyes.

"Well? Well? Your name. That's what I'm asking!"

"His name's Earhart. Charley Earhart," spoke up the daughter of the landlord, from the bar, where she had overheard the latter stages of this interesting conversation. "But he's generally called Sheephead."

"That fits," nodded the servant.

"Pa says he was tossed from the workhouse years ago, on account o' his condition. He's got more than a few tiles loose, too, if you'll catch my meaning," said the girl, tapping a finger against her temple. She spoke quite openly, as though the Sheephead were some insensible object like a door or a post, incapable of understanding her words. But the servant in his present state did not understand them either, being so taken up with the particulars of his own situation — and his hot grog — that the import of her words passed him by.

394

"There are more than a few tiles loose, and bricks as well, at that dreadful dark old monastery of a prison-house where I'm obliged to labor, hour after hour, day after day," said he. "And for what? Look at these hands. Worse than a scullery maid's!" He held them out to view, at which point the Sheephead took one of them in his own hand and shook it, by way of greeting.

"Fallow," said the servant, returning Charley's grip.

"Fellow," replied the Sheephead. "Fellow. Charley's a fellow, too."

"Not fellow. *Fallow*," enunciated the servant. "James Fallow, footman to that fearful old screw, the miser of Salthead, otherwise Mr. Josiah Tusk." He made a little satiric salute with his cup, the remaining contents of which he dispatched in one swallow.

"Mr. Tusk? That's a bad man! Charley knows that. Mr. Hatch and Blaster have told Charley all about it. That's a bad, bad man."

"There's no way you could possibly know," returned Fallow, with a hopeless shake of his head. "No, no. It's more than one person should be allowed to suffer in this dreadful world. The old man's a complete terror. Nothing ever pleases him. Nothing ever is in proper order, or above criticism. Nothing satisfies him. There's no help for it — and no one else to blame! It's terror every day, terror every night. Complete oppression. It's too much to bear at my time of life. But there's no avoiding it, apart from a day like this when the old man is from home. Just look at this weather! Dreadful. When I saw him leave the prison-house this morning I knew I must get clear of the place, at least for a time. It's dreadfully hard to breathe there. So I locked the doors and leaped through the woods and the snowy field to the Three Hats, to escape the gloom and decay. For that's what it is, you know. Gloom and decay."

The footman sighed and propped his chin in his hand, looking philosophical. Or perhaps it was just the hot grog making him sleepy.

"But where is the valuable?" asked the Sheephead, persisting in a line of inquiry that the footman had abandoned. "Will you show Charley the valuable? Will it give you time of day?"

The footman appeared to make some sort of calculation in his head, then took to the tracing of abstract circles on the table with the heel of his cup. Should he? Shouldn't he? The fearful old screw, after all, had ridden out into the snow hours ago — on business, of course. Never let it be said that the harshest winter storm in recent memory should keep Mr. Josiah Tusk from the transaction of his daily affairs, for Mr. Josiah Tusk was, after all, a conscientious man. There was no danger of his returning — or very little danger — till nightfall. The footman had claimed access to something far more valuable than a silver watch; now he had been called on that claim. How could he reverse himself without losing face?

"All right," he said, dealing the table-top a thump as evidence of his determination. "You're a solid sort and no friend of the old man's, that much is plain. Come along, then, and have a look at the dreadful secret. What should I care? There's no harm in it. We'll hie to the old man's chamber and unlock the press, then cut our lucky and be back to the Hats before my glass knows I'm gone. This way!"

"This way!" echoed the Sheephead, waving a gaunt arm at no one in particular, apart perhaps from the pretty Eileen, as he and the footman set off on their mission — which activity went all unnoticed by Mr. Hoakum and Blaster, who were too busy counting pips to witness the departure of their friend from the premises.

The path led through a broad expanse of field overlain with a coverlet of new snow, as vast and empty as the universe. There followed then a lonely wood where all but the evergreens had long since shed their leaves. The bare black outlines of these trees, gaunt and grim, stood out against the white powder and the soaring mountains beyond. The air was very sharp, and the snow crisp and hard underfoot.

Presently the servant and his companion gained the carriage-road, and there came upon a gloomy park with a large gloomy house set in it — a house with broken stairs and ragged windows, with menacing gables and twisted chimneys, and sullen stone angels glaring from the roof-top. Sheephead Charley, whose teeth had been chattering all the way from the Three Hats, shuddered when he saw this house, where desolation like icicles dripped from the eaves.

Did he know this was the place called Shadwinkle Old House? I think not; and it would have made no difference if he had, for its appearance alone was enough to raise shivers. Then he recalled what the footman had told him, that his master was the conscientious Mr. Josiah Tusk, the miser of Salthead. So it broke upon the mind of Charley that the "old man" and Mr. Tusk were one and the same, and that this was his house; which caused him to shudder all the more.

They passed through a gate in the railing. The Sheephead gazed in wonder upon the desolate scene, which even the bright snow could not enliven. It was indeed, as the footman had said, as though gloom and decay lived here. Several times he struggled against an urge to flee; once he very nearly did, but found his curiosity had gotten the better of him. What was the valuable, the deep secret of Mr. Josiah Tusk, that the drunken footman intended to show him?

They climbed the rotting stairs of the Tuskan villa and entered its dark interior, where the footman prepared a taper. They wandered through the outer foyer, with its gloomy busts frowning from their pedestals, and the two formal piers with their dusty urns at top — the very same foyer in which Mr. Richard Scribbler had passed some time the day he brought a letter to the miser. And it was that letter, provided by Samson Icks, that had set off the chain of events which, unforeseen by Mr. Icks and not at all part of his plan, had led Charley to Shadwinkle Old House this day.

"This way, this way," said the footman, mounting the staircase. He signed to the Sheephead to follow. "Watch your step. The boards are loose hereabouts."

"Charley watches," mumbled the Sheephead. He had both hands upon the handrail, to maintain his balance on the stairs against the constant squirming of his legs. He couldn't help himself, the turmoil was quite beyond his control; nonetheless he worked at it very hard, edging slowly upward, a step at a time, until he found himself at the stairhead beside the footman and a pendulum-clock.

"This way," said Fallow, scowling. Clearly he was bothered by the delay. Moving rapidly down the corridor, he halted before a door at the end of it and placed a warning finger to his lips.

"Mr. Tusk — not here?" whispered the Sheephead, in some confusion.

"Of course not!" scoffed the footman.

"Then why — ?" The Sheephead put an unsteady finger to his own lips to question the need for silence, for he had seen or heard no one in the house, and the miser was supposedly from home.

The footman tossed concern aside with a wave of his hand, but his shiny eyes betrayed him. He was no longer so sure of his boast as he had been in the common-room of the Three Hats. To hide his fear he retorted —

"Of course he isn't here! It's just as I told you. But it would be dreadful if he were."

He drew from a pocket his ring of keys and unfastened the lock. The hinges complained as the door swung open. The footman's shiny eyes darted about at the sound, and his ears listened attentively. Satisfied, he led the way into the darkened room. There was a bedstead there, and a cumbrous, high-backed chair, and some dusty books, and a wash-hand stand, and a large, old-painted press, and a flowery carpet, and a grim sly portrait above the mantel-shelf, and windows curtained close — a place colder and gloomier even than the rest of the house, for it was the bedchamber of the miser.

Again the footman motioned for silence, and crept on tiptoe — as best a drunken man can creep — toward the old-painted press, which stood against a far wall.

"It's here," he whispered, over his shoulder. "This is where he keeps it. Why, if the old man knew you were in here, seeing this, it would be dreadful for you!"

A chill electrified the Sheephead, and he fought down another impulse to run. The footman seemed to take an ill-natured pleasure in alarming him, perhaps because it allayed his own fear of discovery.

"Not to worry, though. Fallow's here! If the old man happens on us unexpectedly, well — well — it will be dreadful for you, all the same." With these reassuring words he selected another key from his ring. Before applying it, though, he turned to Charley, who was keenly dreading whatever might come next from the servant's mouth.

"The old man has no notion I've a key to his press," said Fallow, with an uneasy chuckle. "If he knew of it, it would be the end of things for me. Thrown upon my beam-ends at my time of life." (A frown, followed by another chuckle). "But I'll teach him, sir. No, there's no mistake. This round will belong to James Fallow. With this key we shall break into his treasure trove, here and now, and he'll be none the wiser. Ha, ha! The *miser* none the *wiser*. The big pippin-squeezing old fool will be repaid for his treatment of me. For years and years of it! Did you know it was the dog that did it — the great mastiff? That was the final provocation. Did you know that dog? That Turk?" (A terrific denial from the Sheephead). "When the dog disappeared, the old man flew into a rage and blamed me for it. Why, what did I have to do with the business? He was a wicked, ferocious brute, not one you'd choose for a friend. Not one to call on in a pinch! There's a rumor" — he lowered his voice for a moment, close to a whisper — "there's a rumor as the dog's been seen in town, walking about on his hindlegs like he's been taken with the very devil. Yes! Well, devil or not it's good riddance, I can tell you. The dreadful brute, I'm glad he's gone. He can trot all the way to Nantle for what it's worth. What's it to me? The final provocation. Now I'm the one the old man treats like a dog."

The footman paused as the truth of this statement struck him. He bit his lip, and felt a strengthening resolve in his heart.

"I'll teach him, keeping me on the trot to all hours," he growled. He stabbed the key vengefully in the lock, and the doors of the cabinet magically opened. The Sheephead uttered a little gasp when he saw what lay within.

It was a kind of book, a slim volume of just two leaves. Each leaf was composed of a wondrous metallic substance that looked to be gold, but surely wasn't — for unlike any earthly gold it gave off light, creating an eerie, opalescent glow inside the darkened press. Engraved upon the leaves of the book was a host of fanciful characters, a cortege of mysterious scratch-marks that defied interpretation. The Sheephead stood quivering in his rags, hardly able to believe what he was seeing. Was this not the very object he had been dispatched to Eaton Wafers to obtain — the very object that on both occasions had eluded his grasp?

With a clumsy effort that owed something to the hot grog, the footman removed the tablets of electrum from the press and laid them on the miser's wash-hand stand, next to his shaving-glass.

"What do you think of it?" he asked, stepping back with folded arms. "It's a marvelous thing, isn't it? And extremely valuable, I can tell you."

"Very strange," murmured the Sheephead. "Very, very strange." Looking at them, he compared the tablets again to the description given him by Samson Icks. His conclusion was the same as it had been in the study at Eaton Wafers — that the description did no justice whatever to the reality.

"We'll drink to it!" said the footman, quitting the room, to return with a pair of wine-glasses and a bottle. He offered one of the glasses to his companion and charged it with a measure of Mr. Josiah Tusk's finest sherry. "Drink up," he urged. Suiting the action to the word, he downed the contents of his own glass at a stroke. The force of the wine hit him quickly — coming as it did on the heels of the hot grog — and sent him staggering toward the chimney-piece, gasping and coughing.

"Dreadful!" he exclaimed, by which of course he meant quite the opposite. A facetious grin split his wrinkled face from ear to ear, as he poured himself another glass. With eyes shining he pointed to the bottle of sherry and sniggered, in a conspiratorial tone —

"Drink up! We'll teach him. We'll drink all of the old man's sherry — ha, ha! — every drop of it — and in his own bedchamber to boot!"

The Sheephead peered at his own glass a little uncomfortably. It was loaded to the brim, and with his unsteady hands he couldn't help but spill a quantity of the liquid onto the miser's carpet. Terrified, he emitted a hollow, self-pitying sigh, poking his lips and tongue through his dingy beard.

"Drink up!" cried Fallow. "What's the matter with you? Do you want the old screw to walk in and see you with that? Drink up!"

The Sheephead most certainly did not wish to see Mr. Josiah Tusk walk in, now or at any other time, but neither did he wish to drink up. The footman's words began to haunt him, and shame overtake him; he looked again at the spot on the carpet, then toward the open door, half-expecting to see it blocked up by the figure of Mr. Tusk. The grim sly portrait glared from the chimney-piece. There was no sound in the house apart from the distant rhythm of the pendulum-clock on the stairhead. The footman had said the miser was from home. But how could he be sure the old man would not return sooner rather than later?

Having exhausted his reserves of energy for the time being, and also his third glass of sherry, the footman slumped into the miser's chair. He lay there with his eyes tumbling lazily in his head and one listless shoe on the fender, as the collective strength of the liquor overtook him.

"Dreadfully beautiful, isn't it?" he murmured, by which he meant the tablets. "What do you suppose makes it glow?"

Charley had no idea what made the tablets glow, though he had wondered himself much the same thing. He thought he heard a moan come out of them, and pressed his hands to his cheeks in amazement. Hearing the sound again, however, he realized it was more a snore than a moan, and that it came not from the tablets but from the high-backed chair. Turning, he saw that the footman's head had fallen aside, that his eyes were shut and his lips were drooping; saw that consciousness for the moment had left him.

Such stillness in the room, such stillness in the house! Could it be there was no one else here at all? Charley had seen or heard no one else since arriving. Where were the other servants? Perhaps the miser of Salthead was living up to his reputation. Thinking again of Mr. Josiah Tusk, he thought he heard a sound in the passage, some furtive movement perhaps, and looked guiltily toward the door — but again there was nothing.

He laid aside his glass, spilling more of the sherry along the way, and stumbled toward the wash-hand stand, toward the tablets and the curious, unfamiliar script that covered them. Of course, script of any kind would have been unfamiliar to one such as Charley. He had seen the tablets only once before, on his second attempt at entry into Mr. Banister's study, had even had them in his arms when Mitton surprised him. Now he touched them again with a nervous finger, and felt something of their power.

At which point the gaunt visage of Mr. Josiah Tusk rose up before him.

He staggered backward and nearly fell across the legs of the dreaming footman. He hid himself behind the chair; some few minutes going by, he heard nothing — no stern reprimand, no fearsome oath, no vile denunciation, which struck him as odd. Gaining the courage to look up he saw that the face was gone. No face, no figure, no miser. There were the tablets, there the wash-hand stand, just as before. He approached them again, cautiously — then jumped, as his gaunt reflection appeared in the miser's shaving-glass. He clasped his hands to his heart. It was this he had seen, then — his own face crossing the mirror! In his fear and shame he had mistaken it for the avenging image of Mr. Tusk, come to smite the invaders of his bedchamber.

So a tile fell into place, and a plan formed in the brain of Mr. Charles Earhart. Quickly, quickly, he must execute it quickly. There was nothing to prevent him now from implementing that earlier scheme that twice had failed, nothing but his own sense of honor, whatever that might be. Another tile fell; he shut the doors of the press and locked them with the footman's key — an operation which, for the unsteady Sheephead, required an aching length of time. Gathering up the tablets in a shawl he found lying on the bed, he fled the apartment.

No shame now, no guilt, none at all, for Samson Icks had turned against him and was no longer his friend. Was it not Samson Icks who had forced Mr. Hoakum and his nephew from the mastodon camp? Was it not Samson Icks and his business that had caused the downfall of his two friends? Was it not Samson Icks who had sacrificed a friendship? All of this was so. No guilt now for the Sheephead; nothing but a turning of the tables on Samson Icks and the cruel miser of Salthead. The treasure in the shawl was to be his gift to Mr. Hoakum and Blaster, in return for the loss and suffering they had endured, and for the kindness they had always shown Charley Earhart. The debt of gratitude he owed them would not go undischarged.

So the Sheephead flew from the mouth of the dreadful dark old monastery of a prison-house, jerking and squirming his way down its crumbling expanse of stairs, and set off through the trees for the Three Hats, across the white field as vast and empty as the universe.

CHAPTER VII

The Cupboard Is Bared

A rap on the door — a muted, hollow sound, like a bell rung at the bottom of the sea — foretold a visitor to the Tuskan villa. As no response was elicited the rap was repeated twice, thrice; still it was a time before the summons was answered. When it was, the gentleman on the steps offered his card and requested an audience with the master of the house. The tall, gaunt servant with the streaming white hair looked with contempt on both visitor and card, though he read the name that was written there.

"You greatly mistake me, friend," said the servant, haughtily, "for I am Josiah Tusk."

The gentleman on the steps was taken aback by this announcement. Nonetheless he recovered quickly, and sent his dark eyes roving about the face and form of the miser of Salthead, who had answered a knock at his own front door.

"No need to wonder long. My servant — a bungler, a reprobate, and a drunken coward — has chosen this time to run off," said Josiah. His chin was swollen and his falcon-eyes were sharp. "As well I have been disappointed in the city today. Thus I am in no mood for pleasantries. I am a hard man of business and pleasantries are not for me. Despite these impediments, however, I welcome you, for I have been anticipating your call. Come in, Mr. John Hunter."

The young gentleman eyed him warily, as the miser led the way through the foyer and into the drawing-room, with its sepulchral, water-stained walls, and its gloomy window overlooking a snow-covered hedge.

"It has been a matter of some speculation to me, when I might expect you here," said the miser, looking majestic in his black coat and very superior red velvet waistcoat, black trousers, and richly lacquered strap-boots. "So tell me, Mr. John Hunter — how goes it with you?"

"Goes it?"

"Yes. Your occupational activities. How go your occupational activities this day?"

"Let's not be disingenuous, sir. You care nothing how `it' goes with me. You are a financier — a roving city shark, so I understand — and not given to

402

pleasantries, as you yourself have stated. If you are a man of business, then let us get to the business. I suppose you forget you have here something of mine, something of very considerable value, which your creature Nightingale removed one night from my house," said Mr. Hunter, thereby getting to the business.

"I see. I see. So this is how it is. You are very sure of yourself, young Mr. John Hunter. Take care your confidence does not overwhelm you and leave you vulnerable. It is a prevalent condition, readily observed among the common chaff. But I believe you have misspoken, sir. Whatever I may hold in my possession is owned by me, for it is in fact *in* my possession and that makes it mine. Never forget that guiding principle. And so the true situation is this: that as master of the property, it is I who have something of mine, which may be of very considerable worth to you."

"Regardless how prettily you word it, sir, what you have rightly belongs to me. I demand its return."

"`Rightly' has no currency here; it is, I say, all a matter of possession. And you'll refrain from making any demands in my house, sir. If you're looking for justice and rights here, you're looking in the wrong place."

"As was the opinion in the city," said Mr. Hunter, cooling a little. "It appears you are a gentleman of quite formidable reputation, sir."

The miser bowed his head obligingly, and Mr. Hunter did the same, each perhaps from a certain grudging respect for the other's qualities. With strap-boots creaking Josiah stepped forward and offered his visitor a cigar, which Mr. Hunter accepted. They stood apart and smoked in silence for a time. The miser did not yet know what to make of his fashionable visitor, while the visitor seemed ready to wait the situation out, and allow it to evolve after its own fashion.

"Yes, I have had a sizable disappointment in the city today," said Josiah, with his black brows knotted together. "Most disturbing intelligence has been conveyed to me, now that the blizzard has passed, with regard to a consignment on the road to receivers at Crow's-end. The consignment failed to reach its destination; it seems the entire contents were diverted somewhere in transit, at the loss of a very considerable sum to me. Responsibility rests apparently with the agent overseeing the operation. It will be too bad for that fellow, I can tell you, should he choose to return to Salthead. There is, I believe, a magistrate's warrant issued now for his apprehension. Should he enter the city his prospects would be very dim indeed. The moment he is taken he will receive a visit from me, and very simply put — *he shall see stars!*"

Mr. Hunter listened with silent attention, looking calmly on the miser and smoking. His face revealed nothing, but he noted with some internal pleasure the irony of the miser's predicament.

"But enough of my business. I am, you see, a conscientious man, Mr. John Hunter. It's widely known I'm not a man for chatter. Chatter is not for me. Very good, then. Let us proceed to the subject at hand."

"The subject at hand, sir," returned Mr. Hunter, promptly, "is ignorance."

"Ignorance? I fail to see your point."

"And so with that single remark have you verified my assertion. The subject here is ignorance — ignorance on your part, sir. You may be a conscientious man of business and knowledgeable in the conduct of your own affairs, but in certain other matters you are utterly at sea. In brief, you have no idea what you're playing with here, none whatsoever. You could not possibly understand."

"You are a very cocksure young gentleman, Mr. John Hunter. On what do you base such presumption?"

"On long years of experience."

"I see." The miser smiled, noting the clear difference in age that existed between them. It amused him to hear this insolent young pup bark in so confident a manner, perhaps because it called to mind something of his own youthful self.

"I see," said Josiah again. "And so you are a most experienced young gentleman as well. Given the circumstances that is an extraordinary statement."

"Simply because one is unaware of a thing, sir, does not negate its being. There are in this universe entities and forces lying far beyond either your or my poor comprehension. Forces of such a nature cannot be controlled, because they themselves are all-controlling. They may however be made the objects of supplication, entreaty, or offered sacrifice, by such as we. They have no particular cause or desire to be of assistance to you, or to me, or to anybody, other than as it pleases them. However, if they are so disposed, they may at times accede to our requests."

"Your words are riddles, Mr. John Hunter," retorted the miser, looking cross. He disliked it when he didn't understand what a man was talking about; it annoyed him, made him angry, because it left him bereft of advantage. "I believe you are a little desperate, perhaps. That is not such a bad thing. It is good to see desperation. It is a mark of devotion to duty, which, as a conscientious man, I can well appreciate. You are zealous concerning your business, sir, as am I. Ah, but there is the question. Just what is your business, I wonder?"

"My business," said Mr. Hunter, "is my business, and mine alone. A mighty power has been released into this world, sir. Its presence here is my doing, my responsibility, and it must be governed by none but myself. This is vital. For the security of every living body the property you hold in possession, which your man Nightingale took from my house, must be returned to me at once. It cannot be allowed to fall into hands other than mine."

"You're jabbering like some accursed churchman," said Josiah, with a cynical grunt. "But I'll not be gammoned by a priest. Ha! Is that what you are, sir? A roaming papist, seeking to convert others to your idolatrous creed? Ostentation, always ostentation! Perhaps therein lies the secret of your purple cloak, your painted face, and your shepherd's crook. Oh, not to worry, Mr. John Hunter — I am kept well-informed of such details. But you will not proselytize in this house, sir; no, no, your derelict Church of Rome is not for me. I thought your kind had been stamped out at the sundering! No matter. What other details, you wonder, might not have found their way into my possession, eh? As for instance — what your true business is, and why you are here? From where do you come, sir?"

Mr. Hunter did not answer at first, but responded with what looked to be a reflection of Josiah's own grim little smile, while keeping his eyes firmly trained on the miser.

"From farther than you can possibly imagine," he said slowly.

Josiah grunted again. The smoke from his cigar encircled his great white head like a halo, through which he returned the other's scrutiny in equal measure.

"Are you acquainted with a gentleman who calls himself Jack Hilltop?" said Mr. Hunter, after a time.

"Is there some advantage in my knowing him?"

"I said nothing about advantage. I merely asked a question."

"Then I will merely answer it, if it will satisfy your curiosity. No, sir, I am acquainted with no man called Jack Hilltop. But if I were it would be no business of yours."

"Nor Avle Matunas?"

"Eh? What kind of name is that? A Romish name — one of your brethren, perhaps?"

"As I have in general surmised," said Mr. Hunter, shaking his head gently. "You are a bluffer. You know nothing of me or my history. Your `details' are composed of equal parts theory and conjecture, and in these you are, as in many other particulars, hopelessly at sea."

With this latest hit scored in their verbal thrust and parry, the two combatants withdrew, and stood again observing one another from their respective positions across the room. The miser ground his teeth. It was difficult for one such as he to contain himself in the face of an assault. Nonetheless he did it, for there was something odd in the eyes of the fashionable young gentleman that had caught his attention and gave him pause — something yellow, a smoldering glow that lacked perhaps only a proper spark for full ignition.

"You underestimate me again, Mr. John Hunter. It is an error I advise you not to repeat, for your sake. But I am a forgiving man. Let us move on. What is it, I wonder — what could this bit of property be that concerns you so?"

The miser went creaking in his strap-boots to a rosewood chiffonier standing by the empty fireplace, and drew forth a number of objects, which he placed on a low table for Mr. Hunter's inspection.

"I show you these items, sir," said Josiah, with a flourish of his long bony hand; after which he began to pace before the grate, his sharp falcon-eyes maintaining their surveillance of the visitor. "They are familiar to you?"

"You know they are."

"Coins, Mr. John Hunter. Old coins, and odd ones at that. Bronze and silver coins, but not of this realm. See there on that one, a bull with a dove flying above it, and a star — there a young male head — there a swimming hippocamp. See there the legends, inscribed in an alphabet of quite mysterious provenance. Is this all not the case?"

"You know it is."

The miser answered with the sourest of laughs. "Yes, yes. I see. You are not a man to be trifled with. You are not a man for sport. You are a man of duty, a man of business. I admire that, Mr. John Hunter."

"Whether you admire or don't admire is of no concern to me."

"Ah! And what is this here? Here we have a map, to all appearances a document of some antiquity. But a map of what, do you suppose? Here we have a lengthy peninsula, with mountains down the middle and waters on either side, and several large islands, and here twelve cities marked out upon the peninsula in a curious script — in an alphabet very much like that found on these coins. No doubt they are the same. What do you say to this, Mr. John Hunter?"

Mr. Hunter smoked in silence and said nothing.

"I see. It is quite apparent to me, judging by the contours of the peninsula and the several large islands, that this is a map of Italy. I put it to you — am I not correct in this? Moreover I put it to you that these coins, these ancient coins of bronze and silver, are of Italianate origin as well. What do you think of my hypothesis to this point, eh?"

"Any educated person would recognize the features of that peninsula. It can be found in any common volume of geography. I compliment you on your perception, sir."

"Then I needs must restate my hypothesis," said the miser, raising a bony finger. "It is a map of the land that once was Italy. For at the time of the sundering — as any educated person would know, Mr. John Hunter — this land of Italy and all its unfortunate inhabitants disappeared from the earth. Think of it — gone in an instant! Let us consider the state of affairs as they exist today, from your perspective. No Italy — no Rome — no pope!"

Mr. Hunter continued his watching and smoking, but for a brief second his eyes wavered — just the slightest attenuation of their steady piercing power, at mention of the sundering and the horrific fate of its victims.

"That is your conclusion, sir. You are free to express it."

"You think me wrong?"

The miser was observing Mr. Hunter just as hard, and smoking just as hard, while he paced to and fro before the grate. He raised again the long bony finger and shook it lightly.

"Not to worry, sir. I shall offer further evidence." He returned to the chiffonier and brought forth a magnificent vase of glossy black pottery — a beautiful, delicate, timeless work of art, with an incised design of porpoises leaping from the sea — and laid it on the table beside the coins and the map. "A respected specialist in antiquities at the Plaxtonian Museum, at Salthead University, has very generously taken of his time to examine this piece for me. *Bucchero*, he calls it, a characteristic ceramic of Italian antiquity. Of Etruscan origin, to be precise. Absolutely authentic — no question about it — and very, very rare. He was rather excited about it. How might you have happened upon Etruscan bucchero pottery, Mr. John Hunter?"

The eyes of the fashionable young gentleman wavered again as they lighted upon the vase. He seemed about to reply, but checked himself by clamping his cigar in his teeth.

"Yes, yes, it is all quite plain, Mr. John Hunter. It is just as I have hypothesized," exulted Josiah, with the grim little smile playing at the corners of his mouth, an effect magnified by the relentless clenching of his fists and the creak of his strap-boots. The miser clearly was savoring his rush to victory. "I know your secret. The motive is self-evident, though I admit to some small effort in the decipherment of it. Simply put — *I know what you are.*"

Mr. Hunter took his cigar from his mouth and looked at it in his hand, rolling it a little between his thumb and finger. He lifted his eyes and asked softly —

"What am I?"

"It is a simple case. Here we have these ancient coins, bronze and silver. Here we have a map. Here a vase. All archaeological treasures of an age long gone by. And we have as well a purple cloak, a bloodied face, a shepherd's crook — all of them emblems of the defunct Church of Rome. Here you are come to our town of Salthead, a youthful stranger of independent means, in possession of such items and a great many others you well know of. Where did you get them? A legacy from a maiden aunt, is that it?"

"Perhaps."

"I see. I see. As a conscientious man I am obliged to put the question, Mr. John Hunter, how a *very* young gentleman such as yourself, with no connections and no traceable lineage, should have acquired such things. I for one have never heard of you. None of my associates in the worlds of commerce and public affairs has ever heard of you. No one has ever heard of you. There are no records — none at all — despite a most thorough and competent search by confidential sources in town and country." The miser halted his pacing. "All of which leads me to a single unfortunate but inescapable conclusion."

"Yes?"

"That you, Mr. John Hunter, apart from being a recusant, are a fraud and a thief."

The fashionable young gentleman offered no defense, but kept to his watch through the clouds of cigar smoke. His eyes did not waver now, for a dull amber glow was stirring in them.

"It is as well the only reasonable conclusion. It is, I reiterate, a simple case. A dissembler, a heinous plunderer of art and artifacts — that is your black little secret! You journey from here to there, from city to city, altering your name and your background as you go, thereby leaving no traces. You acquire these objects by stealth from their lawful owners — those persons whom you and your kind consider heretics, and so feel justified in cheating — and offer them to others at a substantial profit to yourself. Very sharp, sir!

And so you practice your false religion, seeking converts from among the chaff, while financing yourself and your rather lavish existence by trade in these valuable pieces. Ostentation, always ostentation with your kind! That, sir, is what you are and that is what you do. What think you now of my hypothesis, Mr. Treasure Hunter?"

Crossing his arms the miser hurled at Mr. Hunter a single ferocious glare of triumph. The hypocrite Josiah was evidently pleased with himself and his tidy summing-up of the case. He stood there before the grate like a sort of chimera, a ghastly hybrid of attorney and teratorn, superior of course in every way — tall, gaunt, and spare, all in black apart from the flaring red waistcoat, with bony fingers locked at elbows, the swollen jut of a chin, the falcon-eyes under their jet-black brows, the streaming white hair like a barrister's peruke.

A simple case, or so he thought it to be, until Mr. Hunter stepped forward to duel with him again.

"I care neither for the coins nor the map, nor even the pottery — they are mortal constructs and like all such things will fall to dust in time. What you and your vassal Winch choose to believe is a matter of perfect indifference to me; I'll deny or affirm none of it. I have nothing to offer on the topic. There is but one topic of interest to me, one reason alone why I am here, and you know very well what it is."

"I see. I see. There is indeed one item more that may solicit your attention, Mr. John Hunter. An item of quite transcendent value, concerning which we may perhaps, after due discussion, come to an equitable arrangement," smiled Josiah.

The fashionable young gentleman shook his head. "There will be no arrangements."

"An item of such magnificence, such uniqueness, that its attainment would reward every exercise of effort, every grain of purposeful consideration. A worldly gentleman of independent income, Mr. John Hunter, surely would find such consideration well within the limits of his pocket-book?"

"Allow me to understand you, sir. You offer me an occasion to purchase my own property, that which belongs to me already, and which your blundering menial conveyed from my house?"

"You may call him blundering, but I remind you, sir, it is you who are come to me. I did not invite you; you are here of your own choosing. Very well. It is once again a simple case. I have that which is desired by you. As a man of business it is only right that I should profit from the situation. I am widely known as a conscientious man, Mr. John Hunter — or whatever your name may be — and greatly respected for it in this city and beyond."

"Business?" returned Mr. Hunter, coolly. "Larceny, more like — is that not what your magistrates call it? Burglary. Theft. Sheer villainy. It is you who are a fraud and a thief, sir. You and your creature Nightingale and that duplicitous attorney you have ensconced in your waistcoat-pocket."

"I have no quarrel with you, Mr. Hunter. We are both men of business in our own ways. Surely we may arrive at an equitable settlement. Let's have no talk of magistrates or false charges, and no talk of thieves, particularly from such a successful artist as yourself."

Mr. Hunter exhaled a sharp stream of smoke, and brushed a finger across his mustache. His brows were proudly arched, more proudly even than the miser's, and the glow in the eyes beneath them was gaining strength.

"How can I be certain you have it?" he asked. "You've shown me nothing as yet but these comparatively trivial objects — really, they are of little consequence all in all. How do I know there is something more? How do I know you haven't long since disposed of it?"

"There is more, sir, you may depend upon it," snapped Josiah, for once speaking the truth, or so he believed.

"Then allow me to see it, if such be the case."

The black brows of the miser contracted — his arrogant jaw swelled — his wristbands bristled — his breath came in rapid flows, proud and deep — his huge hands clenched and released at his sides like breathing things — in short, his every agitated movement brought to mind the ruffling-up of a teratorn's feathers.

"Very well, sir," he said, flicking the stub of his cigar into the empty grate. "I'll not have my word challenged by one such as you. I'm not a man for chatter. You will accompany me, Mr. John Hunter."

It was a very grim Mr. Hunter who followed the grimmest of misers up the grim staircase, past the grimly ticking pendulum-clock at the stairhead, then along the grim passage and so at last to the grim dark door at the farther end of it. A key drawn from the miser's pocket gave access to the grim chamber beyond. The visitor followed Josiah into the room, saw it was a bedchamber, saw the miser pause in his steps before a large, old-painted press standing against the far wall.

"I am a conscientious man, Mr. John Hunter," intoned Josiah. "You will see that I am not the man for fooling. Fooling is not for me. Very well, sir.

I will indeed show you what you have come to see. It is a quite astonishing prize, and worth, you will agree, a pretty sum."

Deftly he unlocked the press, and turned round to face Mr. Hunter, so to view that fashionable young gentleman's reaction as the doors of the press swung open.

"What do you think of it?" he crowed, expansively. "Is it not magnificent? Is it not worth a fortune?"

There followed a short pause, after which Mr. Hunter whispered —

"*It is worth nothing.*"

The great white head of the miser swiveled on its turret. His sharp eyes fell upon the press, and gave it a look that might have knocked it to pieces. There before him lay the interior of the cupboard, very dark and very nearly empty. No fortune, no astonishing prize. The astonishing prize was astonishingly gone.

For the first time in the history of his life, the conscientious man of business found himself completely at a loss. Feverishly he raced through every inch of air within the press, fumbling among its various nooks and recesses and hurling their slim contents to the floor, thinking perhaps he was mistaken, that he'd merely mislaid it, that the astonishing prize was lurking there, somewhere. But it was not to be. As a final desperate measure he lifted his key and examined it closely, as though he suspected it of having a secret life and of liberating the prize on its own initiative. When no answer to the mystery was forthcoming, he turned once more to Mr. Hunter, and so found himself confronted with yet another phenomenon for which he had no explanation.

For lo! the handsome face of the young gentleman had undergone a startling metamorphosis — had hardened and darkened into a black substance like charcoal, forming a mask of sorts where the face had been. Through the eyes in the mask an awful yellow light was shining, as though a furnace as bright and hot as the sun were burning inside his head.

The proud jaw of the miser fell; the sharp falcon-gaze was riven with surprise; the great bony fingers hung motionless at the ends of his arms. The towering white-headed potentate, the sultan of superiority who so humbly exulted in his supremacy over others — the thief who now had found himself thieved upon — was left speechless by evidence of a power so far superior to his own.

You have no idea what you're playing with here.

Abruptly the light in Mr. Hunter's eyes went out, and his face was restored to its normal appearance. Almost at once he broke into a low chuckle, which was drawn out rather slowly and quietly, rising and building by degrees until it blossomed into one great hearty peal of laughter — a strange, sardonic laughter, part of it no doubt at Josiah's expense, but an equal part clearly directed at Mr. Hunter himself.

"You're a keen one, sir," said Mr. Hunter, "but there are those who are keener. All this was foreseen. I confess — I was once more too absorbed in my search, too blinded to recognize the purpose there is in every event. In every leaf that falls, in every act of nature, in every beat of the human heart. Nothing in this world occurs by chance, sir, you may be sure of that. The shrouded gods have spoken and I hear them. All praise to the shrouded ones, the great and good givers of life. By the by — I'll send you a cheque."

So saying Mr. Hunter took leave and strode briskly down the passage, down the staircase, through the drawing-room and foyer, past the urns and the heads, and so down the crumbling steps of the Tuskan villa, where he mounted his horse and rode off into the gloom.

All of which left Mr. Josiah Tusk peering with grim determination at the empty press, at the wall, at his books, at the flowered pattern in the carpet. Confusion and puzzlement had taken hold of him and there was no help for it. He folded his arms and paced, and paced, plucked at his lip, broke into mutterings, brooded. He cursed his servant and he cursed his minion, the rebarbative Bob. He cursed his attorney, cursed his attorney's firm, cursed his lost dog, cursed his pork-butcher, cursed entire strangers to his person; in short, cursed nearly everyone in Salthead but himself. Here were mysteries, dark and unfathomable; but Mr. Tusk was a conscientious man and mysteries were not for him.

He threw himself into his chair and spent the remainder of the afternoon staring fixedly into the grate, restless and dissatisfied. How? How? Not surprisingly, the mystery of Mr. Hunter troubled him far less than the mystery of the empty press. How? How? *How?*

He heard the clock at the stairhead strike, hour after hour. All the time the grim sly portrait watched from the chimney-piece, and I'll wager it was smiling.

CHAPTER VIII

Who Was Changed and Who Was Not

THE snow ended, the clouds were carried off, and as the skies cleared the temperature sank precipitously. As a result the shallow reaches of the Salt River found themselves completely frozen over. Not long after, just as the landlord of the Three Hats had predicted, a frost fair was declared by the aldermen of the city. The ice on the river had grown so thick that avenues of booths were opened on it, containing within their precincts diverse shops and stalls for the vending of wares, the roasting of fowls and the imbibing of punch, the staging of puppet plays and comedic interludes, and suchlike entertainments. Upon the broader sheet of ice lying between the fair and the chain bridge, sledders could be seen disporting themselves, while parties of skaters whirled about describing circles and cutting fancy figures of eight. A more spirited diversion was provided by the horse and coach races in furious progress beside the riverbank. Such revels as these naturally attracted large numbers of people from town, all of whom, despite the chill, were overjoyed to be sprung from their homes after the suffocating snows.

There was among the citizenry another cause for rejoicing — and this a more uneasy one — for with the departure of the storm the apparitions plaguing the ancient city had to all effect departed as well. No new horror had been reported now for some few days; nothing more was seen or heard, no dead sailors danced about the streets, no flying men darted about the steeples of parish churches. Reverend gentlemen in pulpits delivered solemn pronouncements that the air had been cleansed of its affliction by the harsh cold breath of winter. The air was indeed cold; so cold, perhaps the ghouls were frozen too. All the ghouls but one, that is, for the black ship with the breach in her hull still clung to her invisible moorings in the waters of Salthead harbor.

It was amid such scenes as these that a horseman was one day observed crossing the chain bridge, late in the afternoon, as an orange ball of sun lay poised on the horizon of the sea. The rider jogged his mount at an easy pace while viewing with interest the festivities taking place on the ice below him. His horse was a bony, shock-headed hunter with one white stocking; the rider a compact gentleman in black traveling-clothes, with a soft black hat covering his head, and a monstrous black beard covering his face like an overgrown shrubbery. Little of his eyes could be glimpsed in the crevice between the brim of his hat and the curl of his beard, the available space being taken up by spectacles.

The horseman continued his steady jog through the streets — taking care to avoid the major thoroughfares by confining his route to the smaller, less populated byways — until he arrived at a certain public house situated on a high hill overlooking the harbor. The house was constructed of hardy red brick and old oak timber-work, with antique-fashioned casements and yawning gables, all of it wreathed in ivy. Dropping from his horse the rider was seen to be a wiry short gentleman, who in his instructions to the ostler was most discreet, offering few words and avoiding lengthy conversation while attending to the provision of his mount. He kept his traveling-clothes wrapped tightly about him and his hat drawn very low over his brow. His huge beard concealed nearly every aspect of his face apart from the spectacles, which were seen now to have smoked lenses.

Putting his hands into his pockets he cast a furtive look or two about the courtyard, before making his way through a side-door and into the Cutting Duck, which public house indeed it was. With no evidence of the daunting landlord in view, he took a seat at the sturdy table by the window, near the smoking turf-fire, in as calm and casual a manner as possible. There was however an impression about the gentleman in black, that if he could somehow have merged with the furnishings of the room, so as to make himself more inconspicuous, he would have done so.

Some little time passed before he was joined by a hard-featured gentleman of middling height, with dark greasy hair and a grizzled beard cut very short. He had eyes like steel and a jaw like stone. He said nothing to the gentleman in black, but settled himself nearby in a comfortable wing-chair. A bystander might have observed that his glance drifted occasionally toward the other gentleman, and that he offered now and again a subtle nod or some slight clearing of the voice, to indicate to the gentleman in black that his presence was duly noted.

The atmosphere in the house growing warm relative to his traveling-clothes, the gentleman in black proceeded to unbutton his heavy cloak and pull off his gloves. He also pulled off his hat, which he placed very neatly on the table before him. The enormous beard he could have pulled off as well, for in the light of the turf-fire it was apparent that the mass of curly hair was a sham — so flagrantly false that it left the wearer looking like a poor play-actor from an even poorer play. The clothing of black, the lenses of black, the nose very sharp and narrow, the traces of a red-brick complexion poking through the false shrubbery — all confirmed that the gentleman at the sturdy table was Samson Icks; though Mr. Icks himself appeared unconscious of this evidence, being confident that the beard concealed his features so well that none could possibly guess who he was.

Cast-iron Billy — the grizzled veteran in the wing-chair — coughed, and mumbled a few words concerning the weather and the daftness of the landlord, who had yet to make his presence known. Mr. Icks responded with a barely perceptible nod, thereby signing to his colleague that he had heard and understood.

Soon they were joined by a third gentleman entering the Duck. The newcomer was very long and lean, with lazy eyes and great white side-whiskers, and was puffing contentedly on a clay pipe. He acknowledged the two others with an easy movement of his hand and settled into another chair by the turf-fire. When questioned by Billy about the weather presently on display in the window, Mr. Lew Pilcher (for it was he) laughed softly and exclaimed —

"Sich frigidosity!"

A conversation in muted tones then ensued among the three gentlemen.

"How is things?" began Mr. Icks, pleasantly enough, but with an edge to his voice that bespoke more than usual interest in the response. "Have ye any news? Any sort whatsoever? Have ye heard what's a-goin' on — any news from the home office, or how the situation stands with a certain party?"

"Not too damned well," answered Billy.

"No, no, no," chimed in Mr. Pilcher, with a shake of his head and a few sympathetic clucks of his tongue. "It don't stand well, nohap."

As these words did not sound very encouraging, Mr. Icks requested some elaboration.

"There's a warrant out from the magistrates' court, Samson. If the sheriff's men find you're in town, it'll be days and nights in the lock-up for you. The stone jug! It's all the miser's doing, o' course — theft of the stock, or so he claims. The muckworm! You'd best keep your sharpest look-out. Them damned sheriff's men have got their eyes marked for you," said Billy, and narrowed one of his own steely dittos.

"A warrant! Ain't that a silliness? Sich ludiocrity!" exclaimed Mr. Pilcher, clucking again, as though he had never heard anything so absurd in his lifetime.

This information was received by Mr. Icks with something approaching equanimity. Outwardly he told himself he didn't care much, for he'd expected it and taken steps, and so was sure of his disguise; but behind the smoked lenses there rose a feeling of disquiet, a forewarning perhaps, which he could neither define nor deny. And despite his best efforts, his mind roiled at the very thought of the miser.

"What about ye?" he inquired.

Both his colleagues answered vigorously in the negative, to indicate that no warrants touching the theft had been issued for them, and probably never would be.

"Aye, it's the tall nasty rascal, that ye can be sure on," remarked Samson. "He's one what thinks the world and a half belongs to him. Aye! And he'd take the moon along with it, if he could only reach it. He and the fat rascal, what's his instrument — they's close, them two. Men o' business! So high and mighty, and never once a kind word for old Icks. Well, I say, and wery nicely put — into the stone jug with 'em!"

"The stone jug," drawled Mr. Pilcher, calmly swishing his pipe.

"Hoo! The stone jug is too good for 'em," objected a very grim-eyed Billy. "There ain't no sparing rogues such as that. Them Tusks, and them damned lawyers — parasites — them Badgers and Winches!"

"A scragging, mayhap, would be nice," said Mr. Pilcher. "Haven't had a look at a good tight scragging in many a fortnight. What do you think of a scragging, Icks — set 'em both a-swinging, eh?"

"Still it's too good for the likes o' them," growled Billy.

"Gentlemen, gentlemen," interposed Samson. "At one time, I'm forced to admit, old Icks thought as ye do — thought o' the hangman's noose and its consequences, and it made him smile. The gibbet — the noose — the prayer — the drop — the last dance — and the bodies given up for dissection. Aye! But I'm sure you'll recollect, gentlemen, as how they say that dead mice feels no cold. What's the good o' dissection, then, after a short swing? There ain't no feeling it. No — not scragging. The stone jug it is, and the stone jug it must be. In my studied opinion, gentlemen, it's the *claustrophobia*, ye see, as gets to 'em after a time. Aye! A medical term is what that is, as I see ye're a-scratchin' yer heads there. The jug, ye see — the lock-up — it's far better than the noose, on account o' how long it lasts. They's all the more time to think on it! So ye can see I've had a change in my opinion. Imagine it, gentlemen — the tall nasty rascal and the fat one, knotted up together in the cold dark jug, with nothing to occupy their minds but thoughts o' their condition, the both knowing there ain't no reprieve for 'em, ever. There ain't no end to it till it's all ended. The two rascals a-molderin' there in the jug, with nothing but each other for company, for years upon years. Imagine it, gentlemen, and tell me that ain't the pretty part of it!"

"It ain't the pretty part of it," Billy told him, with a turn of his head. "I say scrag 'em."

"Aye," agreed Mr. Pilcher. "The noose is nicer."

"Jettison the both of 'em!"

"Finer men never put necks in halter rope."

"There's not a truer statement on this earth, Lew Pilcher — though the blade of my cutlass would be even quicker."

"That's a fact, and as for the fat one, he's got the look o' being half-scragged already."

"For you see, the pretty part o' your scheme, Samson, is the part you haven't yet explained," Billy said, "which is how to coax the two rogues into the stone jug?"

Mr. Icks was on the point of replying when he felt a hand touch his shoulder — which action caused him very nearly to leap from his chair, his mind aswarm with images of magistrates and sheriff's officers. He whirled round, almost dislodging his beard in the process, to behold a diminutive gentleman full of red cheeks and genial blue eyes, with a smirk on his face, and a wide blue cap of a nautical flavor crowning his nearly bald head.

"Hoo! Busket — would you not be a-frightin' Samson in that way!" growled Billy, fiercely, but tempering his voice so as not to attract undue attention.

"Sich impetuosity!" snorted Mr. Pilcher.

A wounded look usurped the countenance of the inoffensive Mr. Crabshawe. For his part Mr. Icks was relieved to find it was only Busket, and not the sheriff's men come to subdue him; which relief greatly augmented his pleasure at seeing his friend. After a preparatory shaking of hands, he offered the diminutive gentleman a chair at the sturdy table. So the conversation of Samson and his colleagues was shortly resumed, with the smoke from the turf-fire tickling their nostrils.

In the midst of the discussion Busket found himself staring openly at the false beard of Mr. Icks. The entire shrubbery remained motionless whenever Samson spoke, for it was adhered to his face at only a few points about the ears, and so was always in imminent danger of falling off. More than once Busket was obliged to quell an outburst of hilarity, for to him the curly "disguise" was so transparent — as indeed it was to Billy and Mr. Pilcher — that he was nearly overcome by its *ridiculosity*. How could anyone fail to spot Samson Icks behind the black clothing and the beard and the smoked lenses? The other two gentlemen had until now withheld comment; in the end it was left to Billy, the most forceful of the group, to raise the matter.

"Samson," said he.

"Aye."

"What's your object, then, as to the wearing of that play-beard?"

"How is it ye mean?"

"Your purpose. Your motive."

"Motive? Ain't it plain?"

Billy glanced significantly at Lew Pilcher, who shook his head in commiseration with Samson's plight.

"It's plain, it is. Too plain!" exclaimed Mr. Pilcher.

"Yea," said Busket.

"You see, Samson, it — it ain't the handsomest of articles," continued Billy, absently massaging his own chin, the whiskers of which were rather more firmly attached. "If you understand me, that is."

The smoked lenses of Mr. Icks darted swiftly from one face to the next. Until this moment it hadn't occurred to him that his disguise might be less than perfect. The thought that it wasn't — that its falseness was plainly evident — sent a tremble through his body.

"What are ye jabbering about?" he demanded. He threw a host of anxious glances about the room, but no one there seemed to be paying the least notice. Leaning forward he whispered, confidentially —

"It ain't askew, now, is it?"

Despite the gravity of the situation, his companions found themselves unable to restrain their humor.

"Askew!" cried Billy.

"He wants to know if the curly-beard's gone a-crooked!" cackled Mr. Pilcher, slapping at his leg. "Sich ludiocrity!"

"Yea!" said Busket.

Their laughter just as quickly subsided, however, as a pair of sober-eyed gentleman in city suits passed by, on their way in from the courtyard. They didn't look like sheriff's men, but one could never tell. Nonetheless an imprint of their sobriety was retained upon the faces of Mr. Icks and his companions for some time after.

"Samson," said Billy, at length, "if you persist in the wearing o' that object, and not altering yourself in any other way, then you'll need to revise your scheme as regards the Duck. Mark me, Balliol won't stand for it. You and that nag with the white stocking had best vacate the city. Remember what I'm telling you."

Mr. Icks, aware now that his identity could at any moment be discovered by a passer-by, donned his hat and hunched forward in his chair, in the hope that these efforts might contribute something toward his obscuration.

"That's wery thoughtful of ye, William," said he, with a flutter of his fingers on his knees.

No one knew quite what to say next, for the hat was Samson's own soft black one, which was well-known to others and so did little more to shield him from identification.

"Fine weather it is we're having," grumbled Billy, resorting in his desperation to irony.

"Very fine," nodded Mr. Pilcher.

"Yea," said Busket.

"Finest day of the week, mayhap."

"That's a true statement if I ever heard one," said Billy.

"Never spoken truer."

"Fine weather — just the way I like it."

"Yea," said Busket.

"Two pockets!" exclaimed Mr. Pilcher, lifting a hand toward a figure that went hurrying past the window.

"What's that?" demanded Billy, startled.

"Two pockets," reiterated Mr. Pilcher, slowly and emphatically, in the event the hard-featured Billy could not grasp simple English.

"Hoo! Do you think I'm daft?" retorted that gentleman, setting his jaw at Mr. Pilcher with grim ferocity. "What sort of wager be that? In this cold, it's everybody's got two pockets!"

"Yea," said Busket.

"In this cold, it would be three pockets if such were humanly possible. Lord love you, Lew Pilcher — "

"Gentlemen, gentlemen, temper yerselves," said Mr. Icks. He was interrupted, however, by the appearance of a waiter at the table. The gentlemen delivered up their order of hot gin-and-water — it did little to allay the concern of Samson that the waiter addressed him by name — and awaited its arrival in silence. Once the steaming jorum and mugs had made their appearance, the four gentlemen spent some moments certifying the quality of the liquor, and once settling into it, began to converse again in level tones.

"There ain't no sign — no sign o' that flying devil?" asked Samson, lowering his voice to an important whisper. Mention of the miser or the fat attorney was nothing now as compared to the mention of this monster.

"No sign," said Billy.

"None o' that foul laughter?"

"None."

"Ye're sure o' that, William?"

"Damned sure!"

"Aye. Well, that's wery good. For let me tell ye, gentlemen — let me tell ye — I couldn't get the sound of it out o' my ears for days after. It ain't a wonder how it affrighted the stock. What was they to do but run? To see that blue rascal a-flittin' about, and the snake hurling fire — well, it ain't hardly a picture o' comfort to a Christian soul. And it ain't proper, neither — the present situation, that is. Not by a long chalk! Aye. The total loss of the stock — that ain't the fault o' no human alive!"

"No human as I know," said Billy.

"What could've been done about it, I ask ye?"

"Not a damned thing."

"Nothing, no way, nohap," agreed Mr. Pilcher, with a reflective scratch at his side-whiskers. "An inavoidable happenstance."

"A magistrate's warrant! But it don't surprise me," growled Samson. The invisible eyes behind the smoked lenses wandered off into the middle distance. "But it don't surprise me. Aye! It don't surprise old Icks in the slightest, what action the tall nasty rascal has took. Magistrates! Sheriff's men! Into the stone jug with 'em, I say — the lot of 'em!"

So saying he peered anxiously about, hoping that his intemperate words had not been overheard by some minion of the law.

"No sign o' the stock, neither," said Billy, not a little saddened at the memory, for he had grown quite fond of the huge shaggy creatures. "No report on a herd o' thunder-beasts marching into this city, at any rate."

"*There's* news," said Mr. Pilcher, eyes closed and head nodding as he smoked.

"Yea," said Busket.

"So what's the more general picture, then, gentlemen?" asked Mr. Icks. Cast-iron Billy and Mr. Pilcher had returned to Salthead soon after the disastrous events on the old fell trail, to begin smoothing his way. Having now crept in through the city gates and arrived at the appointed rendezvous, Samson was anxious to learn something more of the watchfulness of the people, of the strength of the warrant and the likelihood of spies; for his disguise, which it appeared was less than impervious, would offer him little now in the way of security.

"Hoo! It weren't good. The blizzard stopped everything cold, so to say," replied Billy. "Anybody what was coming or going, they were likely to be watched closely on account o' the aldermen's order to the parishes. But in the past week it's lightened up, particularly as the frost fair was opened on the ice. Such a thing diverts the mind, you know, and gives the people other things to think on."

"Other things," echoed Mr. Pilcher.

"Aye, that's wery good," murmured Samson, more to himself than anyone else. "Something what keeps the eyes and the minds occupied, so as they're not always watching and reporting. Aye! How stands it then with Balliol? He'll give me a place?"

"Ain't seen him," mumbled Billy, masking his words with a cough and a hand to his mouth.

This statement caused Mr. Icks to pull up short.

"He don't know I'm here?" he asked. Naturally he had assumed that his temporary concealment at the Duck, courtesy of the landlord, would have been arranged prior to the rendezvous; that if it had not, if the landlord had denied his appeal, then either Billy or Mr. Pilcher would have warned him off. Who knew now what the reaction of the mercurial Mr. Gervaise Balliol would be to the presence of a hunted man in his establishment?

"He don't know you're here," admitted Billy, after an embarrassed silence.

Mr. Icks was too shocked for the moment to respond. He looked toward Mr. Pilcher calmly smoking, and Busket grinning into his cup, and lastly toward his colleague William, who avoided his eyes, and realized for the first time that he was truly alone. His friends had failed him in his most needful moment. Here he was, agent in command and so solely responsible for the loss of the stock, for the failure of the mission to Crow's-end, and with a magistrate's warrant issued for his capture. Here he was the sole responsible party, and yet not responsible — for was it not that laughing devil, that flying man, who had engineered this calamity?

"Ain't that dainty," was the only reply he could muster.

"He'll be agreeable," Billy assured him. "He's daft, but there's a heart in him somewhere. He'll take it, once it's been explained to him."

"Aye," murmured Samson, not overly comforted. "But why weren't it all explained to friend Balliol afore this?"

At this point, events supervened to bar Mr. Icks from pursuing his inquiry further. He rose to attention and sniffed the air. "Do ye smell that?" he asked, with a mystified countenance. "Gentlemen, it's my observation as there's a mighty parcel o' smoke in here — "

"It's that fire there, in the dog-grate. Too much turf," said Billy.

"Yea," said Busket, wrinkling his nostrils.

The odor from the turf-fire had indeed grown very strong, such that the gentlemen found it necessary to consider a removal from the sturdy table. An ugly suspicion formed in the mind of Samson Icks; but before he could give it utterance a chorus of frightened shouts erupted that quickly confirmed it. Confusion and alarm filled the common-room of the Duck, with chairs being pushed back and booted feet striking the floor. Mr. Icks and his associates looked for the cause of the disturbance, and found it in the columns of smoke pouring from the kitchen. Voices from within cried out —

"Help! Help!"

"Help us!"

"Fire! Fire!"

Frantic figures charged from every direction — from the coffee-room, from private rooms, from the gallery, from below stairs, from above stairs — making a rush toward any and all available means of egress. From the more clear-headed members of the company came shouted commands to summon Mr. Mainwaring and the fire brigade at their offices round the hill.

A wall of flame erupted in the kitchen. Two gentlemen in linen came rushing out — cooks, by all appearances — and hot on their heels a great hulking giant of a man, the unmistakable Mr. Balliol, waving his hairy arms and turning the air blue with imprecations. As the pair in linen fled toward the courtyard, the landlord halted in the midst of the common-room and shook his balled fists after them. His black eyes bulged from his head; the veins in his neck swelled and throbbed. The perspiration on his face shone like melted butter in the fire-light.

"COME HERE, YOU COOKS, AND PUT OUT THIS FIRE!" he cried. "COWARDS! ARSONISTS! IT'S BLOODY MURDER, IT IS! BETRAYAL! TREASON! BY GOD, YOU COOKS — YOU'LL BE THE BREAKIN' OF ME!"

"You'd best cut your lucky, Gervaise," advised Billy, as he and his companions prepared to join the exodus. Cast-iron Billy knew a catastrophe when he saw one, and he saw one now.

"Ain't you got no water?" cried a frightened patron, running for the courtyard. "Ain't you got no buckets? What kind of a place is it ain't got no water and no buckets?"

"WATER, IS IT? BUCKETS, YOU SAY? NOW, JUST WHERE DO YOU THINK ALL THE BLOODY WATER IS, EH? WHERE DO YOU THINK IT IS? *IT'S DOWN THE BLOODY WELL!*" retorted Mr. Balliol, with a blinding stare at the miscreant.

"Why don't you get stuffed?" was the testy rejoinder.

"Nothing to be done here now," said Billy. He shook his head violently, coughing from the smoke. "Get out, Gervaise, you shatter-brain. This whole place is a-goin' down!"

"GO ON, LET IT! IT'LL SERVE THOSE BLOODY COWARDS RIGHT! YOU COOKS! YOU BLOODY INGRATES! COME BACK HERE AND PUT DOWN THIS FIRE! ARSON! ARSON! THEY'RE A-KILLIN' ME IN ME OWN ESTABLISHMENT, BY GOD! MURDERERS! PIGEON! PIGEON! STILL HERE, ARE YOU?"

"By your leave, sir!" replied the tiny apprentice pot-boy, flitting past just as an explosion rocked the kitchen. The entire building rattled and shook; the kitchen-door was flung from its hinges; smoke and fire came shooting into the common-room like breath from a basilisk. The strength of the explosion was so powerful that it threw even the mighty form of Gervaise Balliol to the ground.

This was quite enough for Mr. Icks and his colleagues. Together they helped the dazed giant to his feet and led him out into the night — for it was now dark — and so to safety across the carriage-road, where they joined the gathered throng to stand and watch.

At first the blaze was confined to the ground floor of the house. It was burning brightly in the wide front window, behind the sturdy table Mr. Icks and his friends had just vacated — the same table at which they had, over the years, spent so many idle hours in conversation while observing the traffic in the street. One pockets or two pockets, gentlemen? Never more! The fire was licking at the table now with a greedy hunger, and in a very little time it was gone. By then the flames had discovered the ivy cloaking the house, and soon the hardy red bricks and the old oak timbers and antique-fashioned casements were enveloped in a fiery lacework. A glow of wax-lights appeared in the upper windows — no, not candles but an extension of the fire, which was moving rapidly now through the fine wood interiors of the building.

Mr. Icks removed his hat to guard his face from the sight. Amid the darkness the blazing house shone out like a new star, its image reflected in the smoked lenses of Samson and in the eyes of the other onlookers. Billy and Mr. Pilcher stood reverently by, with the giant Balliol propped between them. The landlord for his part could barely comprehend what was going on around him. Struggling for composure, he could do little but gaze in speechless disbelief at the extinction of his life's endeavor.

For indeed his entire existence had been devoted to the Duck; always, always with him it had been the Duck. What would he do if the Duck was no more? He shut his eyes, and fixed his wide slash of a mouth in a straight line; then was overheard by Mr. Icks and Billy to utter a groan, followed by a single remark, resolutely, and without the slightest agitation or bulging of vessels —

"IT'S ENOUGH TO MAKE A PERSON MAD."

The air was loaded with the aroma of smoke and charred wood. There was a bitterness to it that irritated the lungs. All who were standing about felt it — patrons and workers who had fled the establishment, as well as the curious and alarmed drawn forth from neighboring houses, some of which stood in danger now of the fire's spread. Where, where were Mr. Mainwaring and his men? Surely someone had run to the fire office to alert the brigade; notwithstanding which the fire itself, shining like a signal beacon on Highgate Hill, ought to have been visible for many miles.

Another explosion was heard, and another. A corner of the roof, and several gables with their fine ornamental tracery, came crashing down. Steady volumes of smoke issued from every window. The fire had eaten its way through much of the building now, so thoroughly and completely, that in the opinion of most onlookers there was little either the firemen or anyone else could do.

At last the brigade arrived — the men in their somber uniform jackets with scarf at the neck, gray trousers and knee-boots, and black leather helmets — mounted atop a gleaming pump-engine drawn by four spirited horses. Alongside raced the parish fire dog, a large bull-terrier with his tongue hanging from the side of his mouth. He was panting excitedly from his sprint up the hill, and seemed as eager as the firemen to be about the business.

"All safe?" called out Mr. Mainwaring, as he leaped from the engine to take stock — and saw at once that the situation as regards the Duck itself was near-hopeless.

Assured that all persons within the house had escaped, the firemen began deploying the equipment with their customary precision. The segments of leather hose were coupled up; a canvas dam was erected about the wooden plug in the deep-water main over the way; the plug itself was then knocked out, and the frozen ice beneath it battered with pickaxes until liquid water began to flow; the water and ice rushing into the dam was collected by a suction hose, through which it sped to the pump-engine and so into the brazen hand-squirts held by several of the men. The pumps creaked, the pumpers roared, the fire hissed, the crowd cheered, and fountains of water were propelled into the air. All to little effect for the Duck, of course — old companion! — which was long past saving, but fortunate for the householders, as it appeared the fire would be extinguished before it reached any of the structures beyond the yard.

About this time there happened along in the carriage-road, attracted by the spectacle, a young gentleman on a coal-black mare. He was a slight youth, trimly built, with faint pencil mustaches and tight little eyes. His attention was wholly absorbed by the drama of the fire, until an excursive glance among the assembled humanity lighted upon the figure of Samson Icks, who as we have seen had removed his hat. As a consequence of his recent exertion the false beard had become partially detached from his face. The tight little eyes narrowed at the recognition of Samson and his smoked lenses, and of the grizzled veteran standing beside him. Reflexly the young gentleman grasped the hilt of his rapier. For a moment he considered dismounting from his horse, but being cognizant of the great numbers of people milling about, elected to pass the opportunity by. So he rode on, gazing over his shoulder at the efforts of the fire-office men, and at the illuminated forms of Samson Icks and Cast-iron Billy, both of whom remained unconscious of his presence. Trotting off into the night, he was content for now with the intelligence that had so fortuitously been placed before him.

The end of it was that the Cutting Duck was burned to the ground. The fire had eaten out its heart, leaving nothing but the scorched remnants of its hardy brick walls to mark the spot where once a venerable old building had stood. It was an accident, or so claimed the cooks in the subsequent buzz of investigation; but nothing was ever proved, and so it remains a mystery to this day.

As for the landlord of the Cutting Duck, he became thereafter a different man. Never again was he heard to raise his voice to anyone, under any circumstance. His demeanor assumed a calm and reflective aspect; some even called it meditative. For weeks after the fire he could be observed picking through the cinders and rubble of what had once been the Duck, searching for anything familiar that he might extract as a remembrance. It was during this period that the householders and others in the neighborhood first noticed his alteration of character — how thoughtful he had become, how respecting of those who happened by, how cheerful, how glad to see them, how kind; no longer swaggering or bullying in his manner, neither cursing nor challenging anyone. In all things, as I have said, he was changed.

And while there have been many reports in town and country of sane persons driven mad, by whatever mechanism, the singular case of Mr. Balliol of Salthead endures as a curiosity — Mr. Gervaise Balliol, the first madman ever known to have been driven *sane*.

CHAPTER IX

Past and Present

THERE was talk in Friday Street of going to the frost fair. Professor Titus Vespasianus Tiggs, with sprightly magnanimity, had polled the members of the household and found not a tittle of opposition to this proposal, which had been mooted by none other than Fiona. It seemed that one of her small friends in the neighborhood had told her of the wonders of ice on the river — which wonders, quite naturally, she had determined she must now see for herself. So she had importuned her governess, and beseeched Mrs. Minidew, and appealed to old Tom Spike, and implored her uncle, who had put it to a vote. And as Mr. Harry Banister was yet in town, Fiona — who had taken a liking to the handsome master of Eaton Wafers — further begged her Uncle Tiggs to please, please, invite him along. So it was that one morning the Professor and Dr. Dampe, together with Mr. Kibble and his unfashionable green spectacles, went into Salthead to discuss with Harry this particular issue, and others as well.

They had chosen to convene at a coffee-house in Snowfields — that very same coffee-house where, on another occasion, three of them had waited in vain for Mr. Hilltop and Dr. Dampe to put in appearances (the doctor's absence, at the least, having been admirably justified by his attendance on Miss Nina Jacks). The coffee-house was a desirable spot, for it was not far from Mr. Banister's club, where he was lodging; moreover, there existed always the possibility, however faint, that the elusive Mr. Jack Hilltop might walk in at the door. It was agreed on almost at once that Harry should accompany them to the fair the very next day. With this important matter settled, some talk of their plan of action as regards Mr. John Hunter and the tablets was tossed about — talk that proved ultimately less successful than that concerning the frost fair, for it generated little in the way of material progress.

It was while Mr. Banister was gazing through one of the windows of the coffee-house, into the courtyards of Snowfields which lay beyond, that he very suddenly lowered his cup to exclaim —

"Hallo — upon my word!"

"What is it?" asked Dr. Dampe.

The master of Eaton Wafers rose and hastened to the door. Striding forth, he raised a hand and called to someone over the way. You should know, there is in Snowfields a rather haphazard arrangement to its buildings of timber and plaster-work, in the old style, which are flanked by sheltering arcades and courtyards closed to horse traffic. It was in one of these arcades that Harry had glimpsed the individual who fired his interest. As it happened, though, he was too late, for the person addressed had rounded a corner into a neighboring boulevard, and so was lost among the human traffic that bustled there.

"Who was it?" inquired the professor, no less intrigued than his physician colleague. For his part Mr. Kibble asked no questions, for he had seen the fellow Harry had seen, and he too had recognized him. An image of Miss Laura Dale formed in his mind, but he did not rejoice; how could he, with his spirits trampled into the ground by the memory of a certain scene on Whistle Hill?

"It was Dick Scribbler," replied Harry, sitting down again to his coffee, with the imprint of the wild-haired clerk still fresh in his eyes. "The poor fellow."

"How do you mean? Ah, yes, of course, I see — his speech, or rather the lack of it. Yes, it is sad. Very unfortunate for him, too. Despite his outward appearance Mr. Scribbler is quite a personable young chap. He is as well a friend to my young niece, though I don't believe our governess is so very fond of him. As I think of it now, we have not seen him in Friday Street for some time."

The response of Mr. Banister to this was a look compounded of equal parts confusion and disbelief.

"My word — don't you know?" said he. "Hallo! Perhaps you don't."

"What is it I don't know?"

"Your governess, sir — that is, I meant to say Fiona's governess, naturally — Miss Laura Dale."

"Yes?"

"To be sure, I did not think it news to you. Dick Scribbler is Laura's brother."

"My goodness — you're not serious!" exclaimed Dr. Dampe, in open-mouthed surprise, as if some insolent person had just pulled his beard. "Positively ghastly, if it's true."

"I'm afraid it is the truth, Doctor. There's no mistake. To be entirely accurate, though, he is in point of fact her stepbrother. The same mother, but different fathers. Dick is several years Laura's elder. They both were raised near us at Fridley, in Broadshire. Yes, yes, I remember now your mentioning, Professor, that you had no knowledge of either a brother or a sister — that you had thought Laura an only child. It puzzled me at the time."

"Quite correct. From all she told us of her family — which has been, on reflection, exceedingly little — it was a reasonable supposition," the professor explained.

"It may be that she allowed you to reach this conclusion, sir, by selectively omitting certain facts of her history. It may be she did not want you to know them."

"Extraordinary!" cried the doctor. "The charming Miss Dale. Wouldn't have believed it, actually — though I was certain there was a mystery there somewhere. We physicians, we're trained to ferret out mysteries when dealing with our patients. And I do not refer merely to the mysteries of the body. For a patient, you see, can be a devious thing, and often one must dig for the relevant facts in order to arrive at a diagnosis. At times, I fear, it's not very pretty. Well, I could go on, actually."

Mr. Kibble's spirits, which had lain crushed upon the ground, now sprang up and began to frolic round his chair. They lightened his heart, and suffused his being with the unfamiliar glow of hope and delight. Dick Scribbler her brother! No rival now in such a fellow as that. Shining vistas of contentment opened up before the eyes of Mr. Kibble. Then just as quickly his joy cooled and his spirits fell back to earth, as there remained the very considerable obstruction of Mr. Harry Banister, sitting across the table.

"So she has never spoken to you of her brother Richard?" asked Harry, quite as interested now as the others. "He has called at your home, and yet their relationship never was made known to you?"

"Never," replied Professor Tiggs. "He has been a visitor in Friday Street many times, though as I say, not so often now as before. At the very least, Miss Dale's attitude towards him has seemed to me rather indifferent. However, Fiona is quite another matter entirely — he's rather a favorite of hers, you see. No, I'm afraid Miss Dale has never confided in us with regard to her family concerns. She is a most competent and gracious young woman, and has fulfilled her duties with unstinting devotion. She is an absolute treasure. Nonetheless there is at times a curious austerity or reticence of manner, and a propensity to self-criticism, which seem out of character for such a young person. It's very odd."

"From this I gather she has said nothing to you of her great sorrow?"

"What sorrow would that be?" asked Dr. Dampe, intrigued by the prospect of a further revelation.

"Doubtless you've observed the horrid scars upon her neck and arm, Doctor. She affects concealment of them with her hair and clothing, as I've noticed, but even so she cannot hide them completely. Haven't you wondered about them? A terrible scene, let me tell you. It was seven years ago now. The poor girl nearly died! Her brother Dick was there as well."

"Come, come — you simply must apprise us of the details, Harry. You'll not hold us off with a stick if you try."

Frowning, the master of Eaton Wafers hesitated and rubbed his handsome chin in thought.

"I'm not entirely certain, Doctor, that I ought to speak of this matter, if Miss Dale has not seen fit to tell you all herself. It could be considered a breach of her privacy."

"You know, I never for one moment would have associated Miss Dale's physical condition, or her episodes of seeming detachment, with Mr. Scribbler," said the professor. "I've known young Dick for some while now. A poor unfortunate fellow — unable to utter a word, as you know. He'd once applied for a post as my secretary, the very same one which Mr. Kibble now holds. Considering his absence of speech, an appointment simply wasn't on, of course; though he is an amusing fellow, and his penmanship and shorthand are both first-rate. All in all he has many fine points to recommend him. Despite my inability to offer him the vacancy, we became friends of a sort. Through a colleague of mine at Swinford he eventually found a situation — with a firm of attorneys in the city, I believe; I know little more of it than that. During this period he'd visited on one or two occasions in Friday Street, and it required very little time for Fiona to become enchanted with him and his peculiarities. Even after assuming his new duties in the law, he has continued to make periodic appearances, chiefly for Fiona's benefit. And of course, as with everyone who calls in Friday Street, he has become inordinately fond of Mrs. Minidew's cooking."

The doctor cleared his voice, while Mr. Kibble sighed and drank some coffee — the two gentlemen coyly trading glances, having both recognized themselves as members of this same culinary society. The doctor then pressed ahead with his insistence that Harry simply must tell them everything he knew; for perhaps there was something that could be done to relieve Miss Dale of any affliction, nervous or otherwise, that had been visited upon her as a consequence of her great sorrow (whatever that sorrow might be). In this the doctor was nothing if not sincere. Although eager to discover the secret at the heart of any mystery, he was genuinely concerned for the well-being of the charming Miss Laura Dale, and would have done anything in his power to assist her.

Mr. Banister maintained his silence for upwards of a minute while he weighed the doctor's arguments. His brow wrinkled; his lively eyes stood arrested in thought. Bestowing a glance of concession on his old tutor, Professor Tiggs, he replied —

"I suppose I shan't do harm recounting for you the events of that day. Perhaps, as you suggest, Doctor, it may even do some good. There are more scars than the physical involved, to be sure. As I've mentioned, it was seven years ago. I was at Eaton Wafers on a visit to my aunt, and was riding my horse in the high wood when I came upon a most dreadful scene. Miss Dale and her mother had come to see Laura's grandmother, who as you'll recall was in service to my aunt, but who was by then an invalid. Laura and her mother were out for a walk, together with Laura's younger sister — her name was Juliet — little Juliet, such a beautiful child! — and Dick Scribbler, who still resided in Fridley at the time. It was just before he removed himself to Salthead; indeed, the events of that day were the precipitating factor.

"As I reached a large opening in the wood, I came upon them — the four of them standing there together, across the clearing, utterly motionless in the sunlight. It was a curious circumstance, and eerie too. They spoke not a word to one another. All round was a deathly hush — not a breath of air stirring in the trees. What to think, you may wonder, as did I. At first I was quite baffled; until I saw it, at the farther edge of the clearing — what was stalking them, that is — a huge saber-cat."

A snarling face in a coach-window plunged toward Dr. Dampe; to the doctor's relief, it was nothing more than an unpleasant memory lodged in his mind's eye. The journey to Eaton Wafers, the chase, the creature clinging to the side of the vehicle, the upset, the attack upon Mr. Hilltop — the doctor knew there were good reasons not to be fond of cats, particularly those of the larger variety.

"It was a yellow female with glistening sabers. Cats, you know, are rather rare in our part of the county; certainly it was unusual to have encountered one in the middle of the day! As you might imagine it froze me to the spot, as it had the four others. There was only Dick there to defend them. I watched as he slowly and quietly drew his cutlass — the sole obstacle standing between the cat and his mother and sisters. The creature began to pace hungrily to and fro, to and fro, in that evil manner so common to their breed. But, of course — I needn't relate such a detail to you, as the late unfortunate events on the coach-road are, I fear, uncomfortably fresh upon your minds.

"I saw Dick step forward and take it on himself to challenge the cat — not with any surety of success, you understand, but simply to draw off the beast for a time so the others might contrive an escape. He called to it, mocked it, cursed it, leaped up and down, swung his cutlass round his head, all in an attempt to frighten it into retreating. It did little good. Even from a distance one could hear the quaver in his voice, which was timid and shrill and hardly threatening. Dick was never one for excitement of any kind — always a bookish, retiring, anxious sort of chap, and scarcely knew how to wield that sword! The cat crept nearer, swaying its haunches and flicking its tail about, preparing to spring. Its malevolent eyes were fastened on Dick. He began to tremble violently, and so I suppose a kind of panic must have seized him. Without another word he threw down the cutlass and fled into the woods, thereby surrendering his family to certain death.

"Well, it wasn't long in coming, I can tell you, for all I have related thus far consumed no more than a few ticks of the clock. At first the cat seemed intent on pursuing Dick — under most conditions, it's unwise to run from a saber-cat — but then its brain must have registered the fact that three very vulnerable humans remained in the clearing, not ten paces away; so it promptly dismissed Dick and turned its attention to them. I had by this time succeeded in urging my reluctant mare forward, but before the ground could be gained the cat had pounced upon the mother, quickly dispatching her, and next was stalking little Juliet. Miss Dale — the valiant, incomparable Laura, still almost a child then herself — retrieved the cutlass from the ground — sirs, I remind you, she could scarcely lift it — and in a flood of wild emotion struck out at the cat, to hold it off her sister. All in all, gentlemen, it was the most splendid, the most heroic, the most valorous, the most selfless act I ever have been privileged to witness — and as well the most foolhardy. It was ineffectual, of course; I still can hear in my ears the mad cries of rage and sorrow that issued from Laura's lips, as she saw the cat fall upon little Juliet.

"It was at that moment that my mare, jibbing and dancing and snorting, at last brought me to the scene. Her antics on approach alarmed the cat, which enabled me to land several clean hits from the saddle with my blade. It drove the monster into a fury. It went first for my horse, then for me, and poor Laura became entangled in the midst of it all. That is when the claws of the cat inflicted their horrific wounds. They caught in her hair, you see, which she

432

kept always very long, and trapped her; in less than an instant the damage was done. The sight of it enraged and sickened me. Somehow — here it is seven years on, and I remain unsure exactly how — I managed to strike a few more blows — rather severe ones these — upon the creature's skull and neck, slicing off one of its ears in the process. The beast howled and leaped for me. I was prepared then for what assuredly would have been my final encounter in this life, when the animal unexpectedly turned and bounded off, in a direction opposite to that in which Dick Scribbler had gone.

"Laura's mother was quite dead. Even more sadly, the beautiful little Juliet died shortly thereafter, despite the finest of care provided to her by Dr. Reynolds, my aunt's personal physician. She was simply beyond saving. Laura herself suffered much, and lay gravely ill from her wounds for many months. At length she recovered, and returned to whatever was left of normality in her life. Her father, you see, already was deceased; now she'd lost both her mother and her sister, and last of all her stepbrother. She had no one left but her invalid grandmother — apart from my aunt and me, of course, but that was hardly the same thing."

"Lost her stepbrother? Dick Scribbler? How do you mean?" asked the doctor, mystified.

"Poor Dick left within a fortnight of the tragedy. He informed no one of his destination, or when or if he would return. Simply put, he disappeared — as cleanly as if he had walked off the earth. About three years passed before I learned, quite by chance, that he had found gainful work in Salthead. He was always an excellent fellow with the quill and parchment, and a quick study, and so never at a loss for such employment if he desired it. His father had been a stationer, and Dick himself articled for a time to Mr. Maule, a printer and engraver by occupation, in Fridley. So as you yourself discovered, Professor, he had already abundant experience with pen, ink, and line at the time he applied to you for a situation. Unfortunately he no longer spoke."

"Yes, please — tell us what you know of that, Harry," urged the professor.

"It appears he underwent a profound change in the aftermath of the tragedy. Perhaps you are aware of similar cases, Doctor, in your practice. I suppose it can be attributed to shock and sadness, to the inexpressible horror of the event, and perhaps remorse over his abandonment of his family. His voice was completely taken away. However it isn't that he cannot speak — for he can, apparently — it is that he *chooses not to*."

"Ah! Yes, yes, of course," nodded Dr. Dampe, sagaciously, to indicate that the symptomatology was familiar to him.

"By all accounts he grew less exacting in his personal habits and choice of companions, less particular as to dress and manners. He adopted an attitude of careless nonchalance, approaching nothing with the least gravity unless compelled to do so. He acquired few if any true friends, and demonstrated, in the main, little concern for others unless they might prove beneficial to him in some way. In point of fact, Professor, these traits I list are utterly uncharacteristic of the Richard Scribbler I knew in Broadshire. It is as though his entire personality had altered as a result of that tragic day. The single exception to this — and a major exception it is — is his close friendship with your niece, sir. The Dick Scribbler described by Fiona, it seems to me, is far closer to the Dick Scribbler of old, the Dick Scribbler of Broadshire. For whatever reason, that young child has a key to his heart. Well — there it is, then! Such are the few details I can provide for you, first-hand or otherwise. Do you know, that brief glimpse of Dick through the window is the first I've had of him in these seven years."

Mr. Banister's audience had hung on his every word with rapt amazement. The professor's compassionate nature reached out to Miss Laura Dale, and to poor Dick as well. Never again would he wonder at Laura's episodes of self-restraint, at her periodic remoteness, her inwardness, considering the dreadful memories that must occasion them. Never again would he view Mr. Richard Scribbler in quite the same light as before.

For Mr. Kibble, whose sympathies were reserved for Laura alone, awe and admiration were tempered by a deep sense of exclusion. So much in the history and character of this young woman that he had not in the least dreamed of! So much had been hidden — so much had she seen and experienced in her youthful life, as was not to be guessed at! Of her courage in the defense of her family he listened with something akin to veneration. Ironically, such knowledge only served to open a new and even more immense gulf between them, when by comparison he surveyed the gray, dull, unheroic chronicle of his own brief existence.

As for Dr. Dampe, he was his usual physicianly self, stroking his beard with confident matter-of-factness now that a thorny medical question had been resolved.

"There has been indeed that something of reserve, a certain coolness, between Miss Dale and Mr. Scribbler, during his calls in Friday Street," the professor remarked. "I simply took it for indifference on her part, as I've said, and gave it no further thought."

"If you'll grant a poor scholar the privilege of conjecture, sir," said Harry. "I believe she must hold Dick responsible for the death of her mother and sister — by means of his running off, of course, and leaving them. But they had not one iota of a chance, you see. Not a prayer! No one would have had a chance in such a predicament, whether Dick Scribbler fought or fled. A single armed individual, without the aid of a horse, to best a saber-cat? Well, that would be a stunner! Our Mr. Hilltop excepted, of course."

"And on Miss Dale's part, a tendency toward exaggerated self-criticism, arising from her failure to save them herself," theorized Dr. Dampe. "As if there were anything she could have done, as Harry has so rightly pointed out. Things of this nature are not unknown, actually. Look here — overpowering guilt can be a frightful business, particularly when it's misplaced. Oh, it's common knowledge."

"And it was the purest of good fortune, Doctor, I can assure you — those final blows I landed. By all reasonable estimation, both Miss Dale and I should have perished alongside her mother and sister. It was after all a very large, very persistent female cat. Nothing but sheer luck — I am convinced of it."

"I wonder what it is Mr. Scribbler feels," said the professor, with a frown gradually contracting his brow. "Such unspeakable horror that day in Broadshire. So unspeakable that he no longer *could* speak of it — or of anything at all."

A period of quiet followed during which the gentlemen sipped their coffee, before rummaging some more in the attic of speculation.

"In respect of Fiona, perhaps Dick sees in her an image of his poor little stepsister," said Mr. Banister. "Through his kindness to Fiona, he is, in his own mind, atoning in some measure for the loss of Juliet."

"Perhaps that speaks to Miss Dale as well?" ventured Mr. Kibble, beginning now to emerge from the cocoon in which he had imprisoned himself. Gone was his lowness of spirits, gone his selfish pity for his own trifling misfortunes — both banished from him forever. For what counted they, he saw, in a world where such uncompromising heroism, such devotion, such selflessness as that of Laura Dale were possible?

Professor Tiggs found himself contemplating the memory of his own dead sister. How fond he was of tracing those dear remembered features, as they stood mirrored in the face of her daughter! It occurred to him just how marvelous and how wonderful it was, how wistful, how surprising, and how strange, too, that both he and Miss Dale, and the odd Dick Scribbler — how the three of them could have fashioned such similar imaginings from the face of one innocent child.

Late that evening in Friday Street, while passing through the hall, the professor very nearly broached a certain subject with Laura. As he came to the arch by the staircase, he found her sitting with her book in the old-fashioned drawing-room. She wore her customary blue holland dress, very plain, with her golden-brown hair falling about her shoulders. When he appeared she rose to her feet, a look of inquiry in her soft gray eyes.

"Sir?"

"Ah! There is perhaps, Miss Dale, a matter of some — ah — interest that I should like to — "

Even as he spoke he thought better of it.

"Sir?"

Changing his mind on the fly he replied, after a pause, and in his kindliest manner —

"Ah — good night, my dear. I — ah — I do hope your sleep is a most pleasant one."

Miss Dale, thinking this not a little peculiar, wished him a good night in return. She resumed her studies until her eyelids began to fail her, at which point she closed her book and mounted the stairs to her room. There, despite her drowsiness and the professor's genial good wish, she found herself tossing beneath the covers, unaccountably agitated, while awaiting her longed-for voyage to the land of Nod. When midnight came and no sleep, she rose and opened the casement for a look at the winter moon. It lay just above the horizon — a very large moon, like a big creamy coin wedged between opposing pillows of cloud. An imprint of its image remained upon her shut lids long after she had returned to bed. When sleep did come at last, it was at best fitful and disturbed.

Into this sleep slowly wound a dream. In it the moon had dropped from view, when she found herself awakened by the faintest of noises. At first she could not identify it either as to source or location. A rhythmic, ticking, clicking sound, like billiard-balls repeatedly colliding. But there was no billiard-table in the professor's house. A kind of clock, then? No, there was no clock in the vicinity of her room that made such a noise.

So she was forced from her bed to see what it was had broken her sleep. It was utterly dark now that the moon was down. She prepared a taper and ventured forth into the passage, where nothing seemed remarkable apart from the insistent clicking, which was louder there. It grew louder still as she stole to the end of the passage and went round the corner. To her great surprise, where previously there had been a dead wall, representing one side of the house, she found now an open door leading into another room.

A great yawning cold, of a depth and character she had never before experienced, oozed from the room. The clicking sound came from the room as well, together with a cloud of gloomy forebodings — a suspicion that something terrible lay in that room, or was about to occur there. Though fearful she did not shrink from it. Her eyes looked straight before her, as holding her candle aloft she stepped through the door.

On entering she found nothing in the room but a long wooden seat like a church pew, very rudely made. In an upright position on it, facing her, was a child's ragged doll. A very unusual ragged doll, this one, for its face was the face of Fiona. The rhythmic clicking sound, very loud now, came from the doll. As she approached, Laura saw that it was the wide dark eyes of the doll that were clicking — swinging in unison from side to side with clock-like regularity. *Click, click, click*. Time rattling on, the minutes passing, counting down, counting down — to what?

The room dissolved in a haze of darkness and confusion, as Laura awoke to find herself similarly disposed, though solidly in her bed. While asleep she had rolled onto her belly, and so buried her face in a pillow. Her heart was pounding so violently she could hear the roar of it in her ears, and feel the rebound of the beats upon the mattress, with something like the rhythm in the eyes of the doll.

Bit by bit her thoughts came into focus. She darted up; hurriedly she threw on her dressing-gown and sped to Fiona's room, rushing to the child's side only to find her asleep. Nonetheless she fell upon the tiny form and gathered it to her, intent on protecting her charge from any and all dangers that might threaten.

It was a most dreary-eyed Fiona who was thus roused from her slumber, in the nestling arms of her governess.

"Oh — what — is it — Miss Dale?" she cried, only half-awake. "What is it — ?"

For reply her governess rocked her gently, and hugged her, and squeezed her, and kissed her several times over.

"You are well!" whispered Laura. "Praise God — you are well!"

She brushed the tangled strands of Fiona's hair and looked expressively into the child's face, with moisture streaming from her eyes.

437

"What is it, Miss Dale?" Fiona asked again, alarmed now by the sight of Laura's tears. "Oh, what has happened? What? Is it my Uncle Tiggs? Tell me, Miss Dale!"

"Nothing has happened," murmured Laura, sniffling. "Nothing, dear."

There came a mewing from the bed and an orange tabby cat, as sleepy-faced as little Fiona, peeped out from among the bedclothes.

"Oh, Mr. Pie," giggled the child, reaching out to touch him. "Now you are up, too! He's ever so playful in the morning, Miss Dale, and likes to jump on my head to awaken me. Oh, yes, it's very true! Old Sledge called it bad manners, but I believe it's simply cat manners. Poor Mr. Pie — perhaps we should give him something to eat?"

For the briefest second Laura hesitated. "Come here, Pie," she said. The cat, alerted to the possibility of a morning treat, bounced into Laura's lap, purring mightily. Alas, it was not be; he received no food, none whatsoever, only a few pats on the head and a rub about the ears.

"Will you stay with me for a while, Miss Dale?" begged Fiona. "There is something in the air that frightens me."

"Of course, dear."

So Laura slipped beneath the warm and comfortable blankets, where she lay with Fiona snuggled against her. Mr. Pie spent some few minutes kneading the coverlet with his paws, and purring, and turning this way and that a hundred times, and purring, until he had constructed for himself another cozy nest. It appeared there would be no morning treat, but he would at the very least still have company.

Although Laura's dream had faded, the presentiment of doom it had planted in her remained sharply alive. She slept a little now, with Fiona at her side — slept better, perhaps, than she otherwise might have in her own bed — but upon rising was no less pale and restless, and infested yet with the dread of a sinister, unknown *something* waiting to happen.

Even after the sun had tracked his daily course through the heavens, it still was there.

CHAPTER X

Going...

ON the same morning that saw Professor Titus Tiggs and his companions
gathered at the coffee-house in Snowfields, a discussion of quite another kind
took place in chambers, within an ancient pile of red brick standing in Cobb's
Court; in chambers, more particularly in the outer office of that distinguished
firm of solicitors known as Badger and Winch. And — however incredibly —
this discussion too had something to do with the frost fair.

The filthy door, its surface garnished with the insignia of the distinguished
firm, was thrust open, and a wide figure of a gentleman in a plum-colored suit
came bounding through it, his gold watch-chain a-jingle at his very
considerable waist. The gentleman took his hat from his bald head and
coughed, screwed up his neck, cleared his voice, coughed again, and barked
out loudly —

"Scribbler!"

The spirits of the dozing clerk at first resisted animation; for taking into
account the earliness of the hour, he had scarcely had time enough to arrive,
unfasten the filthy door, charge the wax-lights adrift among the soaring
volcanoes of legal writ, prepare a sumptuous coal-fire in the attorney's inner
sanctum (and a miserable poor one in the outer office for himself), mount his
high seat, arrange his armamentarium on the writing-table before him, fold his
arms on that table and so plunge his head downward upon them, from
exhaustion at his labors. Under ordinary circumstances Mr. Richard Scribbler
would have had a further quarter of an hour to himself, for rest and
recuperation, before being disturbed by the surviving partner of the firm. But
his employer was himself early this morning, and the expression on his face a
trifle more ominous than usual.

"Scribbler! Wool-gathering again, I see. Lazy do-nothing. Ahem!"

This cheery hallo caused the scribe to lift head from arms and direct a
glance toward the foot of his high seat. His lips curled into a drowsy smile,
which quickly was replaced by a frown of consternation. It had been several
days since Mr. Jasper Winch had appeared in chambers, having been kept at
home by an unspecified ailment, and so Mr. Scribbler had been obliged to toil
in isolation; he had, however, been forewarned the day previous as to his

employer's imminent return. Recognizing now that employer in the fat figure standing below, the clerk bolted up on his stool, stuffed a few quills into his hair, inspected his pen-knife and blotting-paper with a business-like interest, and started in to polish the inkstand with his coat-sleeve, looking for all the world as if he were engaged in meaningful activity.

"Scribbler," said Mr. Winch, laying his hat aside. "Your attention, please, for a moment. Scribbler — ahem — this cannot go forward any longer."

Mr. Scribbler raised his eyebrows, quizzically.

"It has indeed gone forward for far too long as it is — ahem — by which I refer of course to your situation with the firm. There's simply no tolerating it. You're an idler and a scatterbrain — admit it. Ahem. Let me illustrate the point with a relevant case, if I might. Do you by chance recall, Scribbler, the name of Puddleby senior? Or Newmarsh? Or the matter — ahem — of the Puddleby quarter-sheets? Are these at all familiar to you?"

Mr. Scribbler tucked his chin between a thumb and forefinger and raised his eyes to the ceiling, in an attitude of intense mental exertion; at the conclusion of which he shrugged and tossed up his hands.

"Excellent. I thought not. Ahem. Simply capital. Allow me to freshen your memory. Ahem. You may recollect, Scribbler, that Puddleby senior arrived in these chambers by coach from Newmarsh, some few weeks ago, in the full expectation — ahem — of reviewing with me the accounts and receivables as pertain to his extensive holdings in this city, which are overseen by the firm. Ahem. When the gentleman appeared and the papers did not, do you recall his response, Scribbler? Ahem. Offhand, now, does this mean anything to you? Ahem. Think clearly. I put it to you again — the Puddleby quarter-sheets — Puddleby senior — ahem — coming up from Newmarsh, all that distance, expressly to review the quarter-sheets. Ahem!"

Mr. Scribber shook his head, then abruptly unshook it, as though his head were a gong and it had just been rung. His eyes blew up and his lips rounded themselves into an "O." He lifted a forefinger in the air, smiling and nodding as recollection took hold.

"Ah! Capital. I see you remember, then. Ahem. It was only by the most assiduous and painful of efforts, Scribbler, employing the — ahem — the humblest accents of persuasion, that I was able to preserve Puddleby senior as a client of this firm. The explanations on offer, Scribbler, were quite extraordinary. Ahem."

Here Mr. Scribbler began to chew nervously on the aforementioned thumb and forefinger.

"I offer this example, unfortunately, as but one of many. Ahem. Puddleby senior. Stiffkin. Yorridge and Chase. Harewood. Ribblesdale. Ahem! You do recall the affair of *young* Ribblesdale, do you not? That youth who precipitated himself from the cliff-face — upon the rocks, at low tide — ahem — after being advised by this firm of the insignificant amount settled on him by his late father, *old* Ribblesdale? Of course — ahem — young Ribblesdale had been left a very considerable sum by that gentleman — ahem — an estate which, clear of land-tax, would have brought him an easy ten thousand a-year. Ahem! But as the *incorrect documents* had been retrieved and *imperfectly copied* by a *certain clerk* of this firm — you do recall this, don't you, Scribbler? — ahem — so it was that in the confusion young Ribblesdale was apprised of the legacy by me, trusting in this same clerk's diligence — ahem — and exactitude — ahem — apprised of a minor legacy deriving not from old Ribblesdale but from *uncle* Ribblesdale — a gentleman not yet deceased. Ahem."

A sheepish look betrayed Mr. Scribbler's recollection of the incident.

"Have you any notion of the scene that was there, Scribbler — ahem — the scene, sir — when it became necessary for me to explain to the family — ahem — what it was had induced that promising young heir to put a period to his existence? Have you any notion whatsoever? Ahem. I thought not. Are you then similarly intent on seeing this firm put a period to its own existence? Ahem. I thought so. Just what is it you do here, Scribbler, apart from drawing your salary?"

With this speech Lawyer Winch had worked himself into a frenzy of excitation. His hat was swept to the floor; his watch popped out and was dangling from its chain; his head had been briskly wiped, and his neck screwed up further and further until it was in danger of unwinding at a considerable velocity.

Mr. Scribbler apparently had few answers for his employer. To one question he would energetically nod and smile, to the next he would shrug. He picked up another quill and stuck it in his hair, to join the odd assortment already nesting there. He chewed his fingers, crossed his arms, scratched his head, looking like a species of exotic bird perched in a tree above the volcanoes and wax-lights.

"Therefore, Scribbler," pursued the attorney, "it can go forward no longer. I have come to a decision and it is not a pretty one for you, though capital for the firm. It is irrevocable. Ahem. I'll put it to you very simply. In a word — good-bye." And he waved a fat hand toward the filthy door.

441

Mr. Scribbler knitted his brows, looking to the door and back as though he did not understand the remark.

"Well? Well? Ahem. How much plainer must I make it?" said Mr. Winch, impatiently. "Good-bye."

The import of the attorney's words struck all in a moment. The eyebrows of Mr. Scribbler flew up; he swallowed, his lips trembled, the color drained from his cheeks, and he began to look frightened. He tapped his waistcoat a time or two, to verify the identity of the clerk in question.

Lawyer Winch wiped his head and replied in the affirmative. He waved a fat sheaf of documents toward the door, in the event Mr. Scribbler had not seen the fat hand.

"Good-bye, Scribbler," he smiled, rocking back and forth on his heels in a flush of satisfaction. "The matter is no longer *sub judice*. You see — ahem — there are going to be changes here. The firm of Badger and Winch, solicitors, of Cobb's Court, must be restored to the former high regard it once commanded in every quarter of this city. It is absolutely imperative. Ahem. It is the least that can be done toward the memory of Mr. Ephraim Badger" — here he could not help but shiver a little — "the founding partner of the firm. Ahem. Changes will ensue. The people of Salthead must be made once again to pause in sign of respect at the name of Badger. Ahem. It is my obligation as surviving partner to see it done, and I shall see it done — ahem — and so that obligation commences with you. Good-bye, Scribbler."

With great sadness of heart Mr. Scribbler plucked the writing implements from his hair — slowly, carefully, one by one — and laid them on the writing-table. His eyes swept the room — swept the dusty bookcases, the soaring mounds of ledger, writ and folio, the blackened ceiling, the seedy light, the dark recesses, the tallow smoke, indeed all of the vast, imposing kingdom of the law that had been his to survey from his high seat. No more, no more! Resignedly he gathered up the few belongings of his that lay about, and with a melancholy countenance descended to earth.

"Good-bye, Scribbler," said Mr. Winch, in that odd way of speaking without actually looking in the face of the person addressed. With his head aside he groped about in his coat-pocket for a few coins. These he handed to the clerk.

"Here you go. Ahem. These will serve to conclude the matter — with Mr. Badger's respects. Well — ahem — good-bye. You've drawn your lot so you'd best get used to it. Go — make haste and enjoy yourself, Scribbler. Think of it! Ahem. Not one hour more to be wasted here in these dreary chambers. How lucky for you! Ahem. Not one more tiresome day spent dozing at your parchments, or swishing at flies with your ruler, or consorting with pretty charwomen. Whatever will you do with your time? Ahem. Well, I've got the very thing — you must attend the frost fair! Take advantage of it while you may, Scribbler. Ahem. An absolute necessity. Magnificent panorama — flourishing activity — ahem — skaters — jugglers — hawkers — tinkers — ginger-cake sellers — antic coachmen — mountebanks — jackpuddings. Ahem. Well, I'm very much deceived if there are not specimens aplenty like yourself assembled there. Ahem. And so good-bye, Scribbler."

With shoulders a-droop and eyes thrown upon the floor, Mr. Richard Scribbler quitted forever those dreary chambers. Having seen him depart, the attorney revolved on his heel and clapped hands together in jubilation, exclaiming —

"Capital!"

He had been settled for a little while in his inner sanctum, eyeglass to eye, applying himself to the many briefs, bills, affidavits, writs and other legal paraphernalia clamoring for his attention, when the door of the outer office opened to admit a youthful figure.

"You're for Badger and Winch, sir?" called out Lawyer Winch, from his comfortable easy-chair.

"That's it," replied the figure. "Specifically Winch."

"That is specifically I," acknowledged the attorney. He stepped into the outer room and bowed. As he did so his eyeglass tumbled out and dropped the length of its black ribbon, clicking against his waistcoat buttons. "Is there a service the firm can perform for you, Mr. — ?"

"Rooke," answered the youthful figure. "Joe Rooke."

"Ahem. And how may the firm be of service to you, Mr. Rooke? A personal matter, sir, or commercial?"

"Maybe," returned Mr. Rooke, his face clouded with suspicion. He stopped to peer behind several nearby articles of furniture, to assure himself that no one was there.

"Will you walk into my confidential chambers, sir?" invited the attorney, with an ingratiating smile. "No need to worry — ahem — we will be quite private there."

"This enterprise ain't got no prying clerks about?"

"Of course not, sir."

His concern somewhat assuaged, Mr. Rooke wordlessly followed the lawyer into the inner sanctum.

"Ahem," coughed Mr. Winch, returning to his comfortable easy-chair. "And so — ahem — what is it you require, sir? How can we be of service to you?"

"It ain't what I require," replied Mr. Rooke, mysteriously, "it's what you require."

The attorney folded his hands and leaned his head aside, to examine better the unpleasant features of his visitor. Dropping his gaze to somewhere about the chest region, he smiled and said —

"Why don't you simply tell me why it is you're here, Mr. Rooke? It will save time. Ahem. This is, after all, a busy firm, sir." To demonstrate which he passed a fat hand over the pile of law-papers at his desk, as if diffusing a benediction over them.

Mr. Rooke glanced round the inner sanctum (no one there but the attorney and he), and once over his shoulder toward the vast outer chamber (no one there at all). He shrugged.

"I can see how it is you're busy here. What I've got won't occupy too much o' your precious time."

"What have you got?"

"What I've got," said Mr. Rooke — leaning forward, with his fists clenched and his tight little eyes full of meaning — "is Icks."

The attorney's own eyes — small, dark, long-cut — swelled for an instant, as the sleepy glitter stirred in them. The edges of his eyelids quivered. He wiped his head, his greasy mouth, his hands.

"Icks?" he inquired, playing with his eyeglass-ribbon.

"Icks."

"What about Icks?"

"He's here."

"What! Icks — in Salthead — ahem?" exclaimed Mr. Winch, thinking he had misunderstood.

"Icks is in Salthead. I'm telling you — I saw him the other night, at the great fire that took the Cutting Duck. It was him and his fellows — that scarecrow Pilcher, and that — that — that Cast-iron Billy." (Fierce mutterings and imprecations under his breath). "I hate the lot of 'em, I do. I saw 'em there, but not a one of 'em saw Joe Rooke. Afterwards I dogged Icks, quietly, which is how I know where he's got to. You'll know as there's a warrant issued for him for theft o' the beasts. Stinking, disgusting creatures — I hate 'em! They've gone missing, and it's Icks as pinched 'em, o' course. Spirited 'em away into the mountains, with a mind to sell 'em off and pocket the coin for himself — a mind to cut you and that Tusk clean out o' the business. Now Icks is in Salthead and it's Joe Rooke can tell you how to find him."

Mr. Winch paused for a bout of head-wiping. Icks in Salthead! Could it possibly be? He cleared his voice.

"And you know where Icks is?"

"I do."

"You — ahem — you are sure of this, sir? Quite sure?"

"There ain't nothing surer in this life," smiled the youth, confidently. "It's Icks as you require, and Icks as I can deliver."

The attorney paused again, this time to allow reason rather than calculation to come to the fore. It gave him an opportunity to reflect on the new purpose to his existence, on the lofty ideals and objectives that had been chalked out by — he shuddered again at the memory — the senior partner, for the rehabilitation of the firm.

"Icks would be an idiot to return now," he said. His face grew suddenly dark. "How do we know you are speaking truth, sir? Ahem. Answer me that. There's the truth, after all, and then there's pleasant talk."

"I hate pleasant talk," returned Mr. Rooke, contemptuously. "It's the truth, it is. How do I know it? Because I was one o' the party on the ride to Crow's-end. Did my job better than any cove alive ever could, but they resented it, the lot of 'em — most particularly that Cast-iron Billy." (Mutterings again). "Then I quarreled with 'em, and told Icks as I'd take no part in his scheme. I quit him, on the spot, and rode back to the city. Sacrificed my coin, I did, on account o' conscience."

Mr. Winch, who had dealt with many consciences — though not his own — in the course of his lawyering, speculated upon the quality of conscience that might inhabit the brain of the hostile youth before him. How much of this story to believe? How much of it truth, how much absolute rubbish? Perhaps a sounding-out was in order.

"And so what is your request *vis-à-vis* the firm, sir?" he inquired, twisting his eyeglass-ribbon round a fat finger.

"It ain't much — Joe Rooke ain't a greedy sort. Just something as will replace his lost coin. A bit o' the reward as your friend Tusk is due to cut you in for, when you hand Icks over to him."

Which statement caused the attorney to burst into laughter.

"Reward? You're very much mistaken, sir. Ahem. Mr. Josiah Tusk — a captain of industry — a venerable philanthropist — to offer remuneration for the capture of a common miscreant? No, sir. Ahem. Absolutely out of the question. I'm afraid you don't know the gentleman. No, no. Ahem."

This answer appeared to unsettle Mr. Rooke. Angrily he threw himself back in his chair. Here was one wrinkle he hadn't foreseen — the possibility that there wouldn't be money! He fingered his pencil mustaches, his tight little eyes radiating sour looks in every direction.

"There ain't no coin?"

"None," replied the attorney, crisply. He sniffed and made a little motion of twirling his eyeglass round the black ribbon. He was pleased; the sounding-out was going well.

"Never was a cove driven harder to the wall than Joe Rooke," muttered the youth, with sullen ferocity. "Never!"

"I'm afraid there's no hope for it, sir. Ahem. There really is very little the firm can do to assist you."

His design for the replenishment of his purse having failed, Mr. Rooke's hatred of Samson Icks and his men was sufficiently keen as to override so common a consideration as money — which but served to demonstrate the depths to which the glowering youth had fallen.

"Suppose," he said — he hardly was able to form the words, from self-reproach — "suppose there ain't no coin necessary. No brass. Not one ducat. Suppose — suppose I tell you where Icks is, free and clear? For as I'm thinking now, to see Icks in irons ought to be reward enough for Joe Rooke."

Again Mr. Winch heard the new purpose to his existence calling; a loftier purpose, a more dignified purpose, as had been bequeathed to him by the disembodied torso of Mr. Ephraim Badger. He rose to his feet — his was a rather imposing torso itself — and directed a single full glare upon the visitor.

"I must remind you, sir — ahem — that the apprehension of a criminal, pursuant to a magistrate's order, is the responsibility of the sheriff."

"What's this?" cried Mr. Rooke, rising too, but in dismay over the reception his overtures had been accorded. One hand closed upon the hilt of his rapier.

"This is Badger and Winch, sir," said the attorney, affecting great umbrage. "We are solicitors, Mr. Rooke. We are defenders of the law and officers of the court. We are a respectable firm, sir. Ahem."

"You're Badger and Winch, dissemblers o' the law and a rascally firm. All of Salthead knows that!"

"Ahem. I repeat, sir, we are a respectable firm. Probity is our partner. We do not deal in rewards or bounties in these chambers. If you have pertinent intelligence — ahem — you should by all means communicate it to the sheriff and his officers in Bridge Street."

"To them catchpoles? I hate 'em!"

"Ahem. I'm afraid there's nothing for you here, Mr. Rooke. This is, I say again, a reputable firm — ahem — and we strongly disavow any and all representations to the contrary. Ahem."

"You're a damned hypocrite — "

"And if you continue to get up my nose, sir, I shall call for the senior partner of the firm, Mr. Ephraim Badger, who will put you in your place," retorted Mr. Winch, in what could only be described as the rashest of gambles.

"Old Badger's a corpse," laughed Mr. Rooke, his tight little eyes reduced to tight little slits. "All of Salthead knows that, too!"

Gamble lost, in spectacular fashion. Lawyer Winch was in need of some fast thinking now to recover his ground. His eyelids twitched, he wiped his head — and so elected to gamble again.

"I refer naturally to Mr. Ephraim Badger — *the younger*," he replied, with great condescension. "A formidable opponent when it comes to cutlery, sir. Ahem. I believe he's called out several young gentlemen such as yourself, sir, for far lesser offenses, and has yet to sustain an injury. As to the fate of the gentlemen — ahem — well, it's best perhaps not to dwell on it. Ahem. Mr. Badger will, I'm certain, be most distressed to hear of your unkind remarks. Ahem. Shall I call for him, sir?"

Mr. Rooke drew his breath hard while considering his next action. He didn't see anyone else about the place, and he didn't know whether or not there really was a Mr. Badger the younger, but one thing he did know — there was indeed nothing for him here. Certainly nothing worth fighting over. Lifting the hand from his rapier he shot the attorney a ferocious parting glance, and so removed his disdainful self from the premises.

Mr. Winch heard the door of the outer chamber shut with a bang. Something like regret slipped into his face — regret at the escape of Samson Icks, no doubt — but was quickly expunged by his newfound strength of purpose.

"With Mr. Badger's respects," he called after the departed visitor. And rubbing his hands he sat down again to his desk, to his task of restoring the polish to that much maligned enterprise of which he was, for good or bad, the surviving partner.

It was a clearly frustrated Mr. Rooke who jogged his horse through the snow alongside the river, his tight little eyes hurling cross and contrary glances upon the amusements of the frost fair. Everywhere around him Mr. Rooke saw people enjoying themselves, and it made him sneer. Mr. Joseph Rooke was a not unpleasant young gentleman when he wished to be and it fitted his purposes; his brain and his tight little eyes could be used just as well in the service of conviviality as of contempt. But it was in contempt that Mr. Rooke was something of a specialist. It was not that he was arrogant or disdainful by nature, so he would tell you, but that circumstances had made him so. People had so thoroughly mistreated him, so taken advantage of him, had used him unjustly and refused to acknowledge his talents, so as to make the outcome all but inevitable. *They* had taken everything; he had gotten nothing. *They* had laughed at him, belittled him, called him a cur, a pup, or worse. *They* were the cause of all that had gone awry in the life of Joe Rooke. Was there no end to their depredations! Young Mr. Rooke had however reached a critical juncture of sorts, having vowed to himself now that there *would* be an end to it. It would happen no more; *they* would have power over him no more; those who had taunted him, dishonored him, vilified him, called him a pup or worse, would rule him no more.

He squandered the better part of the day in a host of public houses in the city. He knew, as a result of his researches, that another rendezvous was planned; and though he had of course received no invitation of any kind, he was determined to be there. He was determined that no longer should this matter chew him up from the inside.

The night drew on — a sharp, cold night, though not so withering as the few before it. After a time the moon floated up and showered the landscape with a mournful radiance. Everywhere, silver on the snow. Silver on the lofty crags and wild soaring pinnacles, silver on the steeples and roof-tops of the old university town, silver on the noble clumps of spruce and pine, on the wintry skeletons of oak and chestnut, silver on the chain bridge, silver on the icy reaches of the river; everywhere silver and shadow beneath a liquid moonlit sky.

Mr. Rooke crossed the chain bridge and guided his mare along a narrow track beside the river. To his right he could see the outlines of the booths and other appurtenances of the frost fair, strewn about the ice. By this hour most were shuttered and dark, apart from the occasional glow, here and there, where a few hardy revelers were left to sample the wares of the wine-merchants. He followed the river into the east, in the direction of the high ground and the soaring crags. At a little distance from the fair he came to another bridge, a much smaller and a much older bridge, built of rough ragstone. The river hereabouts was narrowed down, and frozen over rather thickly round the arches and the deeply embayed cut-waters of the bridge.

Mr. Rooke paused for a space under the great clumber pine that stood beside the bridge entrance. There was no traffic, not even an occasional passer-by, and so the night was quiet, until a jingle of harness reached his ear. He came at once to attention. A figure on horseback could be seen approaching the bridge from the opposite bank. The stranger rode cautiously forward and drew bridle at the midpoint of the span, where he remained in an attitude of watchful waiting.

Mr. Rooke saw his chance. He trotted his horse a short distance onto the bridge, to attract the attention of the other; then dropped from the saddle and called out —

"Draw your blade!"

At the same instant the rapier of Mr. Rooke came flying from its sheath, in deadly preparation.

The rider sat smoking at the mouth from cold. He seemed to be in no hurry to answer the challenge, and was peering in the direction of the brazen youth in an effort to identify him. His face lay heavily shadowed beneath his hat; nonetheless Mr. Rooke knew very well whose face it was.

Seeing at last who had called him out, the horseman voiced a laugh and appeared more than ready to oblige. He dismounted and trod resolutely through the muck of the bridge surface, until no more than five paces separated challenger from challenged. The two stared at one another for a long cold moment.

"You've always had it in for me," growled Mr. Rooke. The point of his rapier swished the air softly at his feet. "Well, I'm telling you — it's all got to stop between you and me, here and now, it does. Joe Rooke don't take water from the likes o' nobody. Now's the time — you ain't got none o' your mates here to protect you."

The stranger offered no reply apart from the slow extraction of his cutlass. It was clear, however, that the gentleman was smiling. As the two men started in to circle one another, warily, the silver light of the moon drifted into the face of the newcomer, illuminating his eyes like steel and his grizzled jaw like stone.

"I never done nothing to you," declared Mr. Rooke.

"Never!" was the sure response of Cast-iron Billy.

"Not a damned thing. And yet you ain't had nothing but hate for me."

"Nothing!"

"So it's all on you — is that how it stands?"

"That's how it stands!" nodded Billy.

They continued to circle but their conversation for the moment was over. It seemed they would keep going round and round forever under the moonlit sky, until Mr. Rooke lost all patience and made a full lunge.

It was a stroke that Billy easily parried. He countered with a lunge of his own, which very nearly sent Mr. Rooke over the balustrade in his haste to avoid it. The youth was resolved upon his course of action; was resolved he would not be beaten, or die in the attempt. But his movements, nimble though they might be, were those of a relative amateur when compared to the calm, assured thrust and parry of the grizzled veteran, who though he fought more slowly, fought more wisely.

Billy uttered no sound during the contest, whereas the headstrong Mr. Rooke was all grunts and heaves, all gasps and howls, as he strove with every engagement of his rapier to quench the horrible fire burning within him. Feinting and parrying, lunging and retiring, the combatants roamed the length of the ragstone bridge, neither having yet landed a hit.

"I want to know why!" demanded Mr. Rooke, with a fearsome sincerity. "Why you've had it in for me!"

"Because you're a rash brand with a foul temper. Because you're young and you're stupid, and an ingrate, and you'd never understand," was the rather generous reply from Billy.

"But why, damn you? Why?"

"Because," said Billy, slowly and deliberately — "*you ain't got no heart*."

This answer only served to enrage the youngster more, like a poker stirring up the flames of his indignation.

"No heart! No heart! Well, if Joe Rooke has got no heart — then you won't neither!" he cried, and made a sudden thrust square at the breastbone of Billy. The direction of his stroke at the last moment he altered, very cunningly, so that Billy's parrying motion went askew. In the next instant the rapier was driven home.

A wild look of surprise grabbed hold of Billy's face. His eyelids fluttered; he coughed, he retched, he tried to swallow. Mr. Rooke jerked his weapon free, and a dark fluid came rushing from the wound. Reflexly Billy clamped hands to breast to staunch the flow. The cutlass slid from his grasp. He stared in dismay at the blood on his fingers — groaned — cursed — swayed like a new-delivered foal — staggered — cursed again — slipped — fell backward into the snowy muck, cursing as he went, and lay still.

Over him his youthful opponent stood puffing and gasping, and trying to make sense of his accomplishment. He, Joseph Rooke, had vanquished the great bearded fool! Joe Rooke, who had taken all the punches and given his all, had now given all with a single punch! Never more would he be taunted or his honor disparaged by this hunk of clay. He made a study of the fluid staining his blade, to assure himself of the reality of the situation. Blood! So it was ended, ended — ended at last! Still, he found the achievement of it nearly beyond belief.

"You'll never give Joe Rooke the go-by again," he growled, delivering a merciless kick to the body. "Time to clear off — *old idiot!*"

But though it may have ended, it was far from over. Raising his head the youth saw another horseman ride onto the bridge from the opposite bank. His thoughts immediately scattered in a dozen directions. Had this newcomer witnessed the murder of Billy? And if so, what to do? Should he flee, or dispatch a second victim to prevent him from giving testimony?

The horseman was coming at a good lick. On approach Mr. Rooke observed that the horse was a shock-headed hunter with a single white stocking, and that the rider was bundled up all in black, with a huge curly beard, and a hat drawn low across his brow. Mr. Rooke recognized both horse and horseman, but before he had time to act they were upon him.

"Stand aside, Joseph!" called Samson Icks.

"I won't!" cried the youth, not about to be checked in the midst of victory.

"Stand aside, will ye."

"There! See there!" said Mr. Rooke, extending the bloodied rapier toward Mr. Icks for his inspection. "This blood'll serve you. This blood'll serve the both of you! You've always had it in for me. It was you he rode here to meet, that I knew. I knew it all, I did! Well, you ain't going to meet him again ever on this earth, because Joe Rooke has settled his hash. The old fool is dead! Good riddance to him, I say. Good riddance to the lot o' you!"

High in the saddle, Mr. Icks was oddly unmoved by the sight of his colleague lying dead in the moonlight.

"Ain't that dainty. Never a kind word atwixt the two of ye, that's sure. But as to the settling of his hash, friend Joseph — I'd not be so sure o' that."

"How do you mean?" returned Mr. Rooke, suspiciously.

"Just as I said — I'd not be so sure. Aye! Ye never can know what to expect, or what may be a-lyin' in wait for ye *on this earth*, as ye say, this day or the next. Observation, Joseph, is a wery important trick o' the trade. There's many things in life what ain't as they appear to be — which is a truth ye ought to have learned by now."

Mr. Rooke appeared to take great offense at these remarks. Again he was being lectured to, taken down, patronized. Again he was the young pup with no brain, a git, a zero. And this with the corpse of his victim lying fresh upon the ground!

"What's your point?" he demanded.

"*This!*"

The voice was that of Cast-iron Billy. A well-placed kick from the supposed corpse's boot sent Mr. Rooke tumbling toward the stone balustrade. He spun round, and as he fell the nape of his neck struck the rail, knocking his hat off. He slid to earth with his head lodged between two sturdy balusters.

The veteran rose stiffly, guarding his breast with a blood-soaked hand. A sly look of triumph crept into his face. With his free hand he gathered up his cutlass where it lay on the snow, and stood awhile to catch his breath, blowing steam, with his shoulders hunched and the cutlass planted on the ground for a crutch.

"And so there's a smack for you, in exchange — *young* idiot!" he cried, these words flung in the direction of the dazed youngster. "Stupid-head!"

"How is it with ye, William?" inquired Mr. Icks, peering through his smoked lenses.

"I suppose — I suppose I'll have need for a doctor now," replied his colleague, hoarsely. It was clear that the surprise blow struck against Mr. Rooke had drained Billy of much of his remaining strength. "Ain't that a rarity. But it'll mend, Samson, it'll mend. It can't be serious — can it? *Hoo!*" (This last thrown out in a derisive snort toward Mr. Rooke, who was stirring). "Go on, you fool — weak as water — get up — get up!"

Mr. Rooke stumbled to his feet, groggy and confused. His one wish at the moment was for the world to stop swimming before his tight little eyes. He felt his neck, tenderly, where it had collided with the balustrade, and rattled his head to free it of debris. He managed somehow to retrieve his hat and rapier, saying nothing to his erstwhile associates — ignoring their very existence, in fact — and went next to catch his horse.

"Hoo! Look at him go," smiled Billy, leaning on his sword. "Like a whipped puppy!"

They were unfortunate words at an unfortunate moment. They were words calculated to strike at the very heart and spirit of the miserable Mr. Rooke.

And so they did. The youth made a move toward Billy, but broke it off; instead he closed his eyes, threw back his head, and launched into the air a searing cry of anguish — expressive no doubt of all the accumulated rage and bitterness that gave meaning to the life of Mr. Joseph Rooke.

This outburst alarmed the shock-headed hunter of Mr. Icks, which had been standing a little apart. The horse started, flattened its ears, and leaped for the moon — once — twice — thrice — each time crashing down hard on its forefeet. The gentleman in black fought bravely for control of the horse, just as the horse fought bravely for control of the gentleman in black. The nag shied, rolled its wild eyes, recoiled on its haunches, and spun violently round with its heels in the air. The force of this last maneuver caused Mr. Icks to be loosed from the saddle. Amid an eerie silence he disappeared over the side of the bridge.

"*Samson!*" cried Billy, and staggered to the balustrade.

An ugly sound was heard on the ice below. Though the sound itself was muffled on the winter air, its implications were plain.

Mr. Rooke waited to see or hear nothing more; he pounced on his mare and galloped hard away. Cast-iron Billy, with little thought to his own condition, managed somehow to cross the bridge and struggle down the embankment to the river.

The dark form of Samson Icks lay where it had fallen. The arms were outspread on either side, and it was clear from the disposition of the clothing that the body had struck face-downwards. Curiously, however, the head had gotten itself turned completely around and so was facing up. The false beard was still partly attached, but the smoked lenses had been knocked free and were lying a short distance away. The mysterious, unseen eyes of Mr. Icks were wide and staring, and frozen in place like the ice on the river.

Billy fell at the side of his colleague. There was an ache in his breast where the rapier had struck, but an even sharper pain now in his heart. He doffed his hat out of respect for Samson, looking in silence on the body with its head wrung backwards in ironic caricature of Lawyer Winch. But he did not touch the body. A veteran like Billy knew better than to search for life in a body like that.

After a time he returned to his horse. It was standing beside the shock-headed hunter, which had now all the appearance of tranquillity and with a bright eye was awaiting the return of its master. It whinnied softly at Billy's approach. He touched the strap at the head and stroked the horse's muzzle. The bright eye observed him, all uncomprehending; and in the same moment

Billy cursed himself for a *prodigious damned fool*. He didn't know exactly what to do now, but his first impulse was to ride for Lew Pilcher; his second impulse was to search for a doctor, for himself; whichever he ultimately chose, he rode off at a considerable clip.

Not many minutes later a gawking figure crept from the shadow of the clumber pine. The figure belonged to a gentleman who, not very long before, had been trudging through the lane hard by the ragstone bridge, when his reverie had been cut short by the noises of confrontation. As feared by Mr. Rooke, someone had indeed witnessed what had transpired on the bridge. That someone had seen the fall and resurrection of Billy, seen the hunter rear up, seen the body of a gentleman in black thrown high in the air. It had shocked and terrified him. Now that Billy had ridden off, however, the curiosity of this night rambler found itself aroused.

He approached the object on the ice slowly, cautiously, with fear and reverence. He dreaded looking on the dead body — any dead body — but in the same breath found himself inescapably drawn to it. In that eternal stillness, what a mystery there was! By way of compromise he positioned himself a little off to the side, which allowed him to peep at the body over one shoulder. He peeped, and quailed in horror at what he saw. It was not so much the physical state of the corpse that horrified him, as the recognition of just whose corpse it was.

Despite the wide, staring eyes, there was an unexpected calm in the face of Mr. Icks. The line of his mouth had relaxed into something of that old brittle smile, so familiar, and his brow was unruffled; though the hardy red bricks of his complexion were turned a ghastly blue in the moonlight. The appearance of the beard provided the usual dash of comedy amid catastrophe. There was calm all about, too — not a sound anywhere; nothing but the corpse, and the ice, and the bridge, and the pitiless moon to bear Mr. Richard Scribbler company.

The clerk fumbled for his purse and drew forth two coins — not the money given him that morning by Lawyer Winch, but the remnants of the commission awarded him by Mr. Icks for the delivery of a letter to Shadwinkle Old House. Mr. Scribbler understood now that there would never be more such coins. Never more, he knew, would the dry chuckle of Samson Icks be heard in the world; never more would the dapper little fellow with the smoked lenses, the wiry gentleman with his hands in the pockets of his pinstripes, be seen in the world. For Mr. Scribbler, two coins were all that would remain of Samson Icks.

He shall see stars! Such had been the words of that conscientious philanthropist, Mr. Josiah Tusk. And so it had come to pass that Mr. Icks was indeed looking at stars, on a melancholy cold night; or at the very least, his eyes were directed toward the stars; but whether he actually saw them, as Josiah had prophesied, is a question better left to philosophers.

CHAPTER XI

Still Going...

MR. Richard Scribbler did not return to Whistle Hill that melancholy cold night. Like Mr. Icks, something of him had gone from the world. His breezy and careless chambers saw him not; his grimy acquaintances in Furnival Buildings heard him not. His wind-blown garret stood dark and empty, and quiet save for the occasional piping squeak of air through the sash-boards. Mr. Scribbler did not return to his chambers that night because there was nothing for him there. There was nothing for him, it seemed, anywhere.

The brain of Mr. Scribbler was still lurching from its many collisions with recent events — the interview with Laura and the cessation of his visits to Friday Street, the horrid nightmare of Mr. Ham Pickering, his hairbreadth escape from self-destruction at his window, the loss of his situation at Badger and Winch, the dreadful scene beneath the ragstone bridge. The cruel season of ice and snow lay full upon the land now, and full upon Mr. Richard Scribbler too.

When Mr. Scribbler left the vicinity of the ragstone bridge it was on fleeing feet. He found the nearby lane in which he had been trudging, and retraced his steps along the river toward town — past the frost fair, over the chain bridge, and so into the maze of steep narrow streets and shadowy back-alleys of old Salthead. He roamed about for an hour or more, shivering and afraid, until he came to a snug public house at the foot of Timber Street, whose windows showed a light and whose landlady very kindly offered him lodging in her stable-loft. There he was treated to the snores of the ostler, all the night long, which proved hostile to sleep; though Mr. Scribbler would have slept very poorly in any case, his imagination haunted as it was by a picture of Samson Icks and his frozen eyes watching the sky. Several times he bolted up in the dark and the cold, thinking it was Mr. Icks who had awakened him; but always it was the snoring ostler.

Come morning and no purpose to his life in view, Mr. Scribbler wandered off toward the river in search of the frost fair. There at least he could find company and diversion to fill his idle hours, just as Lawyer Winch had suggested. He was determined to spend the entire day on the ice. As for what he would do the day after, or the day after that, or Thursday next, or a twelvemonth from now — who knew?

Was there neither motive nor meaning to this sorry existence of his? Were all the varied twists and turns of his life something that had been designed, toward some ultimate purpose, or were they indeed just as they appeared to be — terrifyingly random and aimless and absurd? Was there no one in charge of it all? Was there no plan, no object? Was there not some reason for the placing on earth of the individual known as Richard Scribbler, other than his own self-aggrandizement? Was there nothing more to life than this endless parasitism of others? Who would set up such a thing? What sort of a God is it, he thought angrily, would create a world where His creatures must feed on one another to survive?

Thoughts of feeding brought Mr. Scribbler's mind round to his stomach, which had of late lain vacant more often than usual. Suiting the action to the thought, he quickly lost himself among the stalls and booths of the fair. These hastily prepared cubicles stood in three irregular rows, which spanned the river in a direction parallel to the chain bridge, and were separated by cleared avenues like streets for the accomodation of foot traffic (of which there was much). The stalls themselves were remarkably colorful for the time of year, with curtained frontages and bright cloth banners proclaiming the wares on offer. So there it was Mr. Scribbler found himself among fishmongers and costermongers, booksellers and bootmakers, mountebanks, puppet-players, tailors and cigar merchants, medicinal chemists, ox-butchers, chandlers and cheesemen, pastry cooks and fruit-pie makers, milliners, oyster women, brewers and wine merchants, confectioners, vendors of hot teas and coffees, and the like. Certain of the wares he sampled — the hot teas, in particular this morning, with scones and gingerbread — and so satisfied himself a little as to hunger and thirst, before searching for a new amusement to divert him. He was not long in finding one.

"Watch it! Watch it!"

These words were flung at his ear by a small boy on skates, into whose path Mr. Scribbler had strayed while attempting to cross the avenue. The rush of air generated by this sportsman had hardly quieted before another skater, a little girl with a fashionable bonnet and fur round her boots, came speeding in his wake.

"Mind your feet!" exclaimed this damsel, petulantly.

"Just watch it, you ruddy ass!" called the small boy over his shoulder, as a warning against future transgressions.

Mr. Scribbler stared after these examples of youthful high spirits in open-mouthed astonishment. He knitted his brows and made a face, tugged at his gloves, scratched his head, made another face, straightened his muffler, made a third face, put his hands into the pockets of his old brown coat, and so resumed his exploration of the fair.

The transparent skies of dawn gave way to a gradual misting and thickening of the atmosphere. By afternoon the city was overspread with a gray blanket of cloud, which blocked whatever faint particles of warmth might otherwise have been deposited by a cold sun, and blocked its cheerfulness as well. To make matters worse an icy wind came sliding in from the north. Mr. Scribbler wiped his lips from sampling the wares of the fruit-pie maker, and found he did not care for this change in the weather. He suspected it might portend something unpleasant; or perhaps his anxiety was nothing more than fatigue from a restless night in the stable-loft.

Having quenched his appetite the clerk settled himself at the far end of the avenue, at a point where he could observe some of the activities on the ice without danger of personal involvement. There were skaters aplenty exercising themselves in the area, and a few sledders drawn by horses, and some small groups of footballers kicking and slipping at the ball like drunken fellows. Certain of the skaters were obvious masters of their craft, skimming over the ice at considerable speed while describing circles and figures of eight, and performing other even more brilliant feats of fancy-sliding. One skillful gentleman with frosty whiskers was performing that slide called by name "knocking at the cobbler's door," which in the days of my story was a rather fashionable exercise, but like Mr. Richard Scribbler is all but forgotten now.

"Ticket, sir?"

Mr. Scribbler turned to see a head protruding from the curtains of a nearby stall. The head belonged to an older gentleman of a jovial disposition, who was in command of a printing-press.

"Token o' the frost fair, sir?"

Mr. Scribbler, thinking he was for once being offered something gratis, nodded gaily.

"Name, sir?"

The clerk wrote out the answer in full — so that there would be no mistaking which Richard Scribbler was meant — and gave it over to the printer.

Shortly then he was presented with a small card, a souvenir item, apparently, upon which was inscribed the following —

RICHARD JOHN TIPTREE SCRIBBLER, *Gent.*
****

Salthead: Printed by *R. JINKIN* on the ICE, on
the frozen River of *Salt*, at FROST-FAIRE.

"Twopence, if you please, sir," smiled the printer, extending an inky hand.

Mr. Scribbler waited for the money; but upon discovering that it was he who was expected to surrender the coin, in exchange for the souvenir item, his expression soured. Grudgingly he squared the account.

"Thankee, sir," said Printer Jinkin, throwing up a forefinger to his hat-brim. "Penny in pocket's a merry companion, sir."

Mr. Scribbler was inclined to agree, for he was twopence the poorer now and not nearly so merry.

On the opposite bank of the river, just off the ice, was an amusement calculated to divert the mind of Mr. Scribbler from such things as extortionate printers and infants on skates. Two shaggy red mastodons — thunder-beasts, a bull and a cow — were standing there on the snow amid a halo of interested onlookers. Both creatures were in full harness with passenger cabs mounted at their shoulders. The cabs themselves were packed out with admiring children, whose mamas and papas figured substantially in the assembled crowd below. The children in the one cab were overseen by a goofish fellow with a gaping mouth and an enormous wide-awake hat; in the other by an antic figure with a head of fleecy hair like a sheep — both of which gentlemen appeared to be enjoying themselves at least as much as their tiny charges.

At the feet of the beasts stood a short sturdy man in greenish drab trousers and a checked waistcoat, with a wrinkled cap atop his round gray head. It was clear even from a distance that this gentleman was the master of the spectacle, the proprietor of the thunder-beasts, and it was in this role that he was engaged in animated conversation with his audience.

Intrigued, Mr. Scribbler stepped from the printer's booth — at the last minute dancing out of the way of a sliding mass of footballers — and strode the length of the avenue. The size of the beasts grew with each succeeding footstep; it was not until he was but a short distance from them that a true appreciation of their enormity was possible. The destination of Mr. Scribbler was the last stall on the left, which happened to be a brewer's — a place where

459

the clerk could easily observe the activities of Mr. Hoakum and his associates and refresh himself at the same time.

Matters were proceeding splendidly as to both observation and refreshment, when the eyes of Mr. Scribbler found themselves drawn to a party of spectators passing by in the avenue. A party of spectators otherwise unremarkable, were it not for the fact that Mr. Scribbler recognized among them the sprightly figure of Professor Titus Tiggs and other members of the Friday Street household. The clerk drew a startled breath and nearly swallowed his tongue. His gaze brushed the pretty brow of Miss Laura Dale, the bright face of little Fiona. The child was proclaiming to her uncle and Laura, to old Tom Spike, to Mrs. Minidew, to anyone who would listen, that she very, very, very much wished to ride upon a thunder-beast.

Also in the party were the professor's secretary, Mr. Kibble, and a handsome young gentleman with an athletic frame and an engaging spring in his step, a gentleman whom Mr. Scribbler remembered from his days in the country. There too was the professor's physician colleague, Dr. Dampe, in the company of Miss Mona Jacks, and beside them Miss Nina Jacks on the arm of a young curate. The group was soon joined by the starchy figure of Miss Honeywood, attended by certain of her minions from the Pelican, and by the kindly rector of St. Barnacle's parish.

Who am I — a mawkish, maundering old fool — to imagine the flood of emotion that must have washed over Mr. Scribbler as he observed this happy band? Was there not in his heart a desire to fling aside the past and go to them, to be among them, to be *one* of them — all the time knowing such a thing to be impossible? Who can know what tortures of sorrow he must have endured while watching from the brewer's stall, seeing that happiness lay not twenty paces from him and there was nothing he could do to reach it?

It seemed that Fiona had at last won the approval of her uncle for her adventure. Once the current batch of children had been assisted down the cord-ladders by Mr. Hoakum, the next group, this one to include Fiona, was led up. The brown eye of Betty, the mastodon cow, watched over the little ones as they ascended at her shoulder; Fiona thought the eye very tender and glossy, like an immense chocolate pie. Once assembled in the cab the children were urged by an enthusiastic Mr. Charles Earhart to look about them and observe the wonders of Salthead in the snow. Fiona caught sight of her uncle and Miss Dale and the others far below, all peering anxiously upward. Wonders of old Salthead there most certainly were on offer, from such a perspective; but even more so Fiona and her companions were enthralled by the enormity of the creature beneath them, by the play of her muscles each time the head of Betty shifted a little, this way or that, or her body swayed, or at Mr. Hoakum's urging she lifted her trunk and exercised her mighty voice.

As all such enjoyments must have their end, so this one did as well. Her adventure over, Fiona scampered down the cord-ladder to be received into the arms of her family with kisses and congratulations, then hurried off to join others of the children who were playing at snow-games or watching the skaters. And so a wonderful time was had by all that long-ago day on the frozen river of Salt, under a leaden sky, with the thunder-beasts towering over the frost fair just as the wild soaring pinnacles towered over Salthead town.

A wonderful time was had by all, apart from a certain dispirited clerk sitting slouched at a brewer's counter.

"Another pint, sir?"

Mr. Scribbler declined the offer; he had had enough drink and cheer for now. Unable to compose himself any longer, he broke free of the avenue of booths and made his way carefully to the riverside, to the very edge of the crowd gathered round Betty and the Kingmaker. There he stood anxiously by, folding his arms across and across and repeatedly nodding to himself, in an effort to recover something of that old attitude of breezy nonchalance.

Sensing a measure of this agitation, Miss Laura Dale turned her pretty head and so their eyes touched. The clerk lifted his hat from his sunburst of hair and offered her an apologetic smile, so as not to provoke her too severely by the horror of his presence.

They looked at one another for a long moment — it seemed very long to Mr. Scribbler, uncertain as he was of her response — until Laura dropped her eyes and glanced away. There was no doubt she was much affected by the sight of him. The temporary distraction of it caused her to lose track of Fiona, who had left the other children now and gone off to play on her own.

"Fiona! Where are you, dear? Come away, then. Fiona!"

"Here I am!" said the child, running up.

"Fiona! Where have you been? What were you doing, dear?"

"I've been playing with Mr. Blue Face."

"Who?"

"Whose face would that be, dear?" inquired her uncle, with a sprightly interest.

"Mr. Blue Face, my new friend in the ice — just over there," Fiona answered, pointing. "He's ever so fascinating, you know, though not very sociable. Of course, I suppose one can't be too sociable under the ice. It must be very difficult to breathe there."

"In heaven's name, how can anyone live under the ice?" asked Mrs. Minidew.

"Not likely!" drawled Tom Spike, with a long shake of his head.

"Where did you see this face?" asked Miss Honeywood.

"Yes, where did you meet this unsociable fellow?" chimed in Dr. Dampe, endeavoring to look very sagacious. "Hallo! — why don't you come along then and point him out for me? I'm positively ablaze with curiosity."

The doctor gave Fiona his hand and so was led away, with a twinkle in his eye and his hat cocked at a jaunty angle. The child took him round and behind a drift of snow, to a smallish patch of ice lying out of view of her uncle and the others. No one else was there; the size and seclusion of the area apparently had attracted few admirers. Here Fiona paused, cradling her chin in her tiny fist, and searched the ice with her eyes until she found what she was looking for. Very boldly she hopped onto the slippery surface, pulling the doctor after her. Together they walked and tottered and crept and slid and so finally arrived at the place of interest, which Fiona indicated by a tap of her boot.

"Here it is! This is where I saw him. This is where he lives. Do you suppose he is a kind of bear and is hibernating here?"

"And who is it who lives here?"

"Mr. Blue Face, of course! Didn't you hear, Dr. Dampe? It's ever so simple. I've named him Mr. Blue Face — for he doesn't speak, you see, being under the ice, and so can't tell me what he calls himself."

The doctor was by turns amused and puzzled, and so retired a few paces behind to take stock. "So just what did you see, exactly?" he asked, scattering a host of glances about the area.

"It was Mr. Blue Face. It was a man's face, or a bear's face — but it was blue, and there was a monstrous nose in it and he was smiling at me," explained Fiona, very patiently. (There was no convincing grown-ups of anything, it seemed). "Perhaps he's a merry-andrew or a jackpudding, then, and not a bear — for I've seen jackpuddings before, though not with such a blue face as his. But how should a jackpudding come to be under the ice? It's very cold there."

"Look here," said Dr. Dampe, with that confident matter-of-factness of the physician. "I simply can't see anything out of the ordinary. Pity, but your Mr. Blue Face seems to have gone for a ramble."

Having said this the doctor whistled through his beard and stared very hard at a spot just at Fiona's feet, the very spot she had tapped with her boot. The ice was unusually clear there — dangerously clear, he realized now, almost transparent — and for just an instant he thought he saw something move underneath it. Perhaps a fish, darting through the frigid water.

"Step back, Fiona, at once! The ice there is far too thin."

The child obeyed, while the doctor bent down to examine the thing further, his eyes filled with a mounting curiosity. He rubbed at the clear spot with his glove.

"Hallo! There's something very odd here, actually — I wonder what it is?"

"Have you found him?" asked Fiona, looking over his shoulder. "Is he there? I do hope he is; I should like very much for you to see him. He's ever so interesting."

"One thing at a time, dear," said the doctor, wholly absorbed now in his investigation. He uttered a few unintelligible syllables; the motion of his gloved hand upon the ice abruptly ceased.

"It must be Mr. Blue Face!" exclaimed Fiona.

The doctor peered deeply into the clear spot, and to his very great surprise beheld another face looking up at him — the blue, bearded face of a man, or a bear, or some other creature, with a monstrous nose or beak, just as Fiona had described. He shut his eyes and opened them to banish the image, but it refused to go. An hallucination, he thought, until he saw the eyelids blink and a wicked grin split the lips.

"Extraordinary!" he gasped.

In a single movement he was on his feet and casting about for Fiona, but his boots slid out from under him and he went crashing down. With the help of the child he regained his footing.

"Come along, Fiona," he cried. "Quickly, now, quickly! We must leave this place. We must get to your uncle and the others. Quickly, now! Titus! *Titus!*"

He had only just turned his back when sinister noises of a cracking and splitting nature filled his ear. The doctor looked round and to his consternation saw the clear spot in the ice break apart as something large, blue, and leathery came shooting through it. He called loudly to Fiona, for amid the confusion he realized that her hand was no longer in his. Somewhere he could hear her small voice crying out in terror —

"Uncle Tiggs! Help me, Uncle Tiggs!"

The doctor slipped and tumbled off the ice and into the snowbank, just as his collegiate colleague and the others appeared, gazing with stricken looks into the sky.

"Fiona!" cried Laura.

"My niece!" cried the professor.

"Tuchulcha!" exclaimed Harry Banister.

"Good Lord!" exclaimed Dr. Dampe, raising his eyes.

Suspended in the air above them was an awful apparition — the keeper of the gates of Achrum, with his blue wings lazily beating and little Fiona imprisoned in his great muscular arms. Waves of vipers rippled in his hair. His vulture's beak discharged a noisy, jeering laughter, full of arrogance and mockery. The serpent coiling round his arm raised its head and hissed; a bolt of fire shot from its mouth and exploded on the snow, at a point not very far from the doctor and his companions.

Panic struck the frost fair. The nearby stalls and avenues quickly emptied of humanity. Hordes of people retreated toward the chain bridge; some fled down the river; a few hid among the sleds and coaches remaining on the ice; others crouched here and there behind drifts of snow, overcome by sight of the demon floating high overhead. Great trumpeting roars erupted, children screamed, mamas and papas screamed even more, as Mr. Hoakum and Blaster sought to calm the startled thunder-beasts.

"We must get Fiona down at once!" cried Harry Banister. "If he has a mind to fly off we'll not be able to follow. You remember Ned Vickery's account!"

"No, no!" Laura protested, with sudden vehemence. The dream of the doll and the ticking eyes remained fresh in her mind. "The height! Pray consider the height, sir! She'll be thrown to the ground and surely die!"

"What's plain is plain, Miss Dale. I fear Mr. Banister is correct. We must make the creature release her double-quick!" urged Miss Honeywood.

"But how are we to d-do that?" stammered out Mr. Kibble.

The answer to his question came in the form of a small white object, of a generally spherical appearance, which was seen streaking through the air. It collided with a shoulder of the demon Tuchulcha and there splashed itself into oblivion. Before the onlookers had an opportunity to react, another snowball went flying at the target.

"La! It's Mr. Scribbler!" exclaimed Bridget Leek, whose heart I venture must have leaped at the recognition of him.

Laura glanced round; there indeed, standing in a drift not so very far from his target, was her stepbrother, who even then was preparing to launch another missile.

"Richard!" she cried out. "Pray God, Richard — Richard — stop! *Stop!* What are you doing?"

"He's trying to save her, Laura," explained Mr. Banister, smiling in admiration of the simple remedy the clerk had devised. Hastily he began to gather up quantities of snow and form it in his hands, while urging others to do the same. "Here — here — make more of these — just so. Then shy them at the monster! I'll get beneath him, and when he releases his hold on Fiona I'll catch her in my arms."

But Mr. Banister was not nearly fast enough, and moreover he had underestimated the skill of his troops. A lucky toss from the doctor caught the demon square in the face. With a shake of his ugly head Tuchulcha swung about, raising both fists in defiance; in so doing the tiny form of the child slipped from his arms and went hurtling toward the earth.

Terrified cries went up on every side. In desperation did Harry Banister strive to reach her, but he knew he had no chance. There was not the time! His feet were too heavy and too sluggish, the velocity of her fall too great. He watched as any hope of saving her evaporated before his eyes.

Not so! For there went another figure racing across the snow, considerably in advance of him. It was Richard Scribbler, with his arms outstretched and his eyes locked on Fiona. The clerk had planned his assault on Tuchulcha well; it had been his object all along to snatch Fiona from the air. He arrived at the spot where she would have struck the earth, but where instead she came to a flying stop now in his arms. The force of it dropped him to his knees.

For the first and what would be the only time in her life, Fiona heard the voice of Mr. Scribbler.

"Run!" he implored her, in a breathless whisper. "Run, dear — as fast as you can!"

He cast her from him like so much soiled laundry. Fiona, too frightened to protest, and seeing her uncle and her governess a short distance off, scurried in their direction.

Mr. Blue Face recovered almost at once from the doctor's lucky hit. His dark eyes tracked the fleeing child across the ground below. He drifted lower and stretched out an arm towards her, the one with the serpent coiled round it. The reptile lifted its head, spread its jaws —

Then it was that the injunction of Ham Pickering flashed through the mind of Mr. Scribbler.

Do something remarkable with your life!

There was no questioning what it was, for he saw it at once. He dashed off after Fiona, whistling through his teeth and waving his hands over his head in a frantic bid to draw the attention of Tuchulcha. The dark eyes shifted from the child to the clerk; the serpent hesitated; the leathery wings of the demon swished the air as his body swiveled round.

Mr. Scribbler came to a dead stop and pounded his chest repeatedly with a shut hand, thereby transmitting his unspoken challenge to the monster.

Here I am, he said. *Strike me if you dare.*

The delay allowed Fiona time to gain the safety of her family. Mr. Blue Face in his turn reacted with angry words for Mr. Scribbler, delivered in a language the clerk did not understand. In the same instant a young gentleman in a bottle-green coat came hurrying from the avenue of booths.

"See there, Miss! If it ain't that fancy cove — that Mr. Hunter!" exclaimed Mary Clinch.

"Mr. Hunter — indeed, I thought as much," replied Miss Honeywood.

"So that's the fellow," murmured Dr. Dampe, with narrowed eyes.

"Clear off!" the fancy cove shouted, in the direction of Richard Scribbler. "You there! Clear off! Hide yourself while you've still the chance! Don't you see, sir? He means to transform you!"

"Hear what he says!" cried Miss Honeywood to Dick, adding her very considerable authority to that of Mr. Hunter.

Their warnings came too late. The demon trimmed his wings to steady himself, and lifted an arm towards Mr. Scribbler. The head of the serpent rolled up — the mouth gaped — the tongue flashed — a bolt of yellow flame went shooting at the clerk.

As the smoke and fire cleared, the innumerable tiny fragments of what had been Mr. Richard John Tiptree Scribbler could be seen condensing into a grim, featureless mass, which gradually expanded in size several times over, shuddered, pulsed, squirmed, reorganized itself, changed from black to brown to tawny yellow, gaining strength and distinctness of outline as it solidified, and so became once more alive.

Mr. Scribbler no longer, but in his place a glowering saber-cat — at the irony of which the demon Tuchulcha laughed very heartily.

CHAPTER XII

Gone!

"HURRY! Hurry! Hurry, my child! Come down from there at once!" were the cries from the host of anxious parents clustered round Betty and the Kingmaker and Mr. Hatch Hoakum.

"I b'lieve they're a world o' gladness safer there in the cabs — considering the cat, arter all," was the response of the gentleman in the checked waistcoat. His firm voice and steady hand had succeeded in quieting the mastodons, at least for the moment, and so it was his task now to quiet the worried couples who, unlike most of the other visitors to the frost fair, had not bolted for cover. The thunder-beasts meanwhile stood warily by, eyeing both the demon Tuchulcha and the saber-cat, the latter for its part appearing content to watch and pace, watch and pace, rather than attack. Having survived the initial terror in better condition than their parents, the children up in the cabs were awaiting with interest whatever might happen next.

Mr. Hoakum thought it wise to drive Betty and the Kingmaker a little farther up the bank, toward a screen of fir-trees and away from the icy river. He instructed everyone to follow closely along, and once the beasts had come to a stop to gather round them for protection. The children loved it — the bump and sway of the cabs as the animals plodded up the embankment. It was clear the mastodons were frightened of the demon, and might have run off; but their innate courage and the reassuring presence of the sturdy little man in the checked waistcoat served to fortify them.

"I've dealt with the beasts all my life," smiled Mr. Hoakum, responding to the concerns of a particularly skittish young lady. "You're as safe here as in the rector's own drawing-room, and that's flat. My nephew Blaster and I — we trust 'em with our lives. The beasts won't trample you. They're gentle as lambs with folk and know what they're about."

The mastodons indeed knew what they were about, for while there was little they could do with respect to Tuchulcha they had managed for now to hold off the saber-cat, by interposing the very considerable bulk of their bodies between the cat and their human companions. Unusual for such creatures the saber-cat did not roar, did not growl, did not utter a sound in fact, but continued to pace to and fro with its strangely mournful eyes watching all that transpired.

"We must be brave, my good people," intoned the rector, raising a hand to gain the attention of the others. His clergyman's fervor had been excited by the rush of events; or perhaps he thought Mr. Hoakum had called for his aid by mentioning his drawing-room. "Courage! Fortitude! This is after all a test of our faith, a time of trial, and as such should be viewed as a gift from the Almighty."

To the great consternation of Mr. Hoakum and most everyone else, the rector stepped away from the shelter of the group, intending it appeared to address the demon Tuchulcha, who had been hurling upon them a stream of indecipherable taunts as he floated overhead.

"You, fellow!" called out Mr. Nash, in his finest pulpit accents. "You! Foul Fiend from Hell! Yes, I am speaking to you! You'll not be laughing long, sir. I command you as a servant of the Lord, the Prince of Peace. I command you in the name of Our Savior, the Lord Jesus Christ, to cease your — "

Yellow flame poured from the serpent's mouth and exploded on the riverbank just below the reverend gentleman, carving out a sizable crater in the snow. Dazed, the rector barely escaped falling forward into the hole. He was rescued by Dr. Dampe and the young curate, who hastened to his side and returned him to the comparative safety of the thunder-beasts.

"I expect your incantations will be of little use today, Rector," advised the learned physician. "You'd best spare your voice — before he transforms you into something worse than a saber-cat!"

"There ain't anything worse than the cats," declared Mr. Hoakum.

"What — what is it?" mumbled the rector, staring through groggy eyes at Tuchulcha.

"It is the demon of death," said Professor Tiggs.

"From the gates of Achrum, actually," the doctor added.

"The same ugly devil who dropped upon my roof at Eaton Wafers — a real stunner!" Mr. Banister chimed in.

"Summoned to earth through the auspices of Apollo by an Etruscan immortal called Vel Saties — that gentleman in the green coat standing just over there," explained the professor. "It is they who are responsible for the ghostly apparitions in Salthead, for the black ship in the harbor, and now for the loss of poor Dick Scribbler."

The rector glanced from one speaker to the other, trying to digest all he heard and reconcile it with his picture of the universe, but somehow the pieces refused to fit.

The demon gathered his wings together and flew straight off toward the chain bridge, in pursuit of the terrified citizens who were making their escape into the city. He performed a series of threatening maneuvers in the air above their heads, lunging and plunging, darting and swooping, with balled fists and flashing talons and vipers squirming in his hair and arrogant laughter flowing from his vulture's beak; while the citizens pleaded for mercy and hid their faces, horses reared and carriages tumbled over, and everyone and everything that could do so dashed for safety.

In the passenger cab atop Betty an inquisitive child had managed somehow to unfasten the door, which swung open now without warning. As he hurried to keep that same child and others from tumbling out, the Sheephead with his quaking limbs inadvertently dislodged a worn leather satchel hidden at the rear of the cab. The satchel went sailing through the door, bounced from the shoulder of Betty, and flew open. Something wrapped in a shawl came out and together with the empty satchel fell toward the ground. Both objects narrowly missed the skittish young lady whom Mr. Hoakum had lately reassured as to the complete safety of her situation. The object in the shawl collided instead with my own boot; for you see, I was there among the crowd gathered round the mastodons that day. Everything I tell you of that afternoon on the frozen river, so many long winters ago, is thus the literal truth, for I myself witnessed it with these two eyes.

The object as I have said struck me on the foot, and as I stooped to retrieve it the shawl came undone and I held in these very hands a mysterious, gleaming treasure.

"The tablets!" cried Harry Banister, utterly dumfounded. "The tablets of electrum!"

"Hallo!" said the doctor.

"Magnificent!" exclaimed Mr. Kibble.

"However did they get here?" asked Miss Mona Jacks.

Agitation and alarm gripped the face of Mr. Charles Earhart. He lurched and stumbled his way down the cord-ladder to Mr. Hoakum, and in a quivering voice, with his lips and tongue poking in and out of his dingy beard, related a not-too-comprehensible explanation of how he had found the glowing tablets — omitting, of necessity, certain delicate particulars, such as his having stolen them from the miser of Salthead — and how he had hidden them in the satchel until he might present them to Mr. Hoakum on Saturday next, which he knew to be that sturdy gentleman's birthday. He explained further in his halting way how it was the least he could do to compensate Mr. Hoakum and Blaster for their unceasing benevolence on his behalf.

No sooner had Mr. Hoakum accepted the treasure into his hands, bestowing upon it many looks of honest surprise and amazement, than Mr. John Hunter rushed in from the avenue. But his passage was barred by someone in the crowd — a gentleman wrapped up like a mummy in a great-coat, hat, and muffler, which disguise left few of his features visible. Mr. Hunter drew a startled breath and arrested his step. In such fashion did the two gentlemen confront one another, silent and unmoving, and with all eyes upon them, including those of the restless saber-cat.

"Don't you touch 'em," said the mummy to Mr. Hunter, with a gloved hand raised in warning. "I'm advising you, sir. I'm advising the blessed lot of you, gentlemen and ladies! You'll not allow this man near those tablets, don't you see." At which point the mummy removed his hat and muffler, and disclosed his spotted face to the onlookers. "The electrum — sirs and ladies — the electrum. You know what it is he means to do with it!" he said, in direct appeal to Professor Tiggs and his companions.

"Jack Hilltop, I see you there," murmured Miss Honeywood, peering sharply through her spectacle lenses.

Mr. Banister and the doctor immediately placed their hands on Mr. Hunter, to prevent his gaining access to the tablets.

"Are you mad?" cried the fashionable young gentleman, struggling against his human shackles. "Do not allow that man near the electrum! You utter fools — you don't know his purpose! Do not give him the tablets, I warn you. You've no idea what you're playing with here!"

"He's a liar!" Mr. Hilltop countered angrily. "It's self-evident, don't you see. Ask that fellow what he calls himself! Mr. John Hunter, is it? He lies! Mr. Oliver Blackwood? He lies! Mr. James Gallivan? Mr. Frederick Chandos? All lies! He's none o' those. He is Vel Saties, lucumo of Velca. Does he deny it, gentlemen and ladies? O' course not! He's Vel Saties, don't you see, and his object here is to break open the gates of Achrum, the kingdom of the ancient dead. He means to change this living world of yours forever — beyond your recognition, don't you see — by flooding it with the souls of his powerful friends, and so at last bring every blessed city under the rule of the Rasna. Surely you'll not allow him the attainment of his desire! Or belike it's what the lot of you want, is it?"

"Give no countenance to his lying words!" cried Mr. Hunter. "Ask that man his name. Mr. Jack Hilltop, is it? A lie! A lifetime of lies! It is *he* —

Avle Matunas, lucumo of Cisra, and a deceitful dog — who threatens you. What stories has he told you of me? What lies has he spread? I tell you, you're being gulled by Avle Matunas — can't you see that? It's perfectly clear!"

Those who knew something of the matter knew not whom to believe, and so kept shifting their allegiance from one gentleman to the other with each round of accusations. The remainder of the onlookers, who knew nothing whatever of glowing tablets or exploding statues or immortal lucumones, were left to watch and wonder.

"What exactly is your purpose here, Mr. Hunter?" asked Professor Tiggs, with a deep frown creasing the space between his eyebrows. "You yourself are the one who invoked the demon using the tablets of electrum, which you saw fit to remove from Mr. Banister's house without so much as a `by your leave.' As a result of this you have brought fear and sorrow to a great many innocent people. Do you deny it, sir? Why are you here and what do you seek from Tuchulcha?"

"I do not deny it. I seek nothing but relief from the torment of this endless earthly existence — this curse of life," replied Mr. Hunter. The doctor and Harry Banister loosened their hold upon him, as he had ceased his struggling. "I have petitioned the demon Tuchulcha to intercede with mighty Aplu and revoke this sentence of immortality that was delivered upon my head. I wish only to rejoin the beloved friends and family who have gone before me. This life of wandering, this eternal roaming from place to place, the loss always of those dearest to me, the whole sorry lot of it endlessly repeated, over and over and over again — I tell you, I want no more of it!"

"Was that not Mr. Hilltop's motive for his own actions?" said Miss Mona in an undertone to Mr. Kibble.

"It was," nodded the secretary.

"You see then how none of this has occurred by chance, for it all is decreed by the higher powers," continued Mr. Hunter. "You Christian folk — you believe yourselves and your actions to be free. But beware! Your freedom is an illusion. You are no more free to settle your own destinies than I am free to rid myself of this plague of unending life. All of us in this lower world are subject to the whims and fancies of the shrouded gods. We do here only as they desire us to do. If they wish for us to live, we live; if they wish for us to die, we die. It is their story we are playing out with our lives. As to the powers and purposes of these shrouded ones, they lie beyond our understanding. All that is left for us is to pray and to offer sacrifice, in the hope that the desires of the shrouded gods may come to coincide with our own. I am obliged to admit that as of now my own petition has gone unanswered. But he — Avle Matunas, who was once my friend," he said, with growing ferocity, "it is he, not I, who means to recall powerful allies from the city of the dead. You — Avle Matunas — betrayer of your sacred vows!"

"Now, you'll not be taken in by this fellow's ravings, gentlemen and ladies," protested Mr. Hilltop, with a dismissive wave of his hand. "For it's all a packet o' lies, don't you see."

"I don't know which packet of lies to believe at the moment," said the professor, none too pleased by this impasse. "However our own purpose now must be to remove ourselves from a most precarious situation. The matter of the tablets may be settled later. Mr. Hoakum, if you could see your way clear to..."

"There is no knowing which one speaks the truth," said Miss Mona. "It is all so very confusing."

"It's Mr. Hunter, I'm sure of it!" replied Mr. Kibble, more earnestly and loudly than he had intended. "For you see, Miss Jacks, I have doubted Mr. Hilltop's story from the very first we heard it, in the home of Professor Greenshields and his wife."

"Belike you've the gift of divination then yourself, young sir?" said Mr. Hilltop, in a voice that contained more than a hint of sarcasm. "That's it, is it? But I ask, what would a young university fellow such as yourself know of black lies and liars?" He tossed his head in the direction of Mr. Hunter. "There! There, sir! There's a liar for you, don't you see. A bad egg all around. Can't you smell it?"

"I suggest it is you who are the bad egg here, Jack," interposed Miss Honeywood, all starch and frost. The pale eyes behind the spectacle lenses fixed him with a piercing look. "I too have had my suspicions of you for some time. A most inquisitive person you are, Jack. Every call at the Pelican filled with questions and more questions! Always searching, always interrogating, always seeking intelligence from the honest souls patronizing our good house. I thought little of it at first; I thought more of it after your attempt to make off with poor Sally Sprinkle's locket. Shame upon you! It's either black or white with me, Jack; you know there's no gray in it in my book. You had glimpsed the two portraits in the locket. You suspected one to be that of Mr. Hunter, and so thought that the locket might somehow lead you to him. Then came the foggy night when young Mr. Rime was brought in from the dock-road by Henry Duff and by you, Mr. Hunter. That is why you left in such haste, is it not? Because as you walked into the Pelican that evening you saw Jack was there. He was on the watch for you but you did not wish to be found. Well? What do you say to this?"

Mr. Hunter responded in the affirmative.

"Both of them were searching for the tablets of electrum," said Professor Tiggs. "But it was you, Mr. Hunter, who had come upon them, quite by chance, during a visit to Eaton Wafers."

"Chance had nothing to do with it, sir," Mr. Hunter reminded him.

"You did not want Mr. Hilltop to discover your place of residence. You feared he would confront you there and wrest the tablets from you, once the apparition of the dancing sailor and those that followed became known. For it was the apparitions themselves that would persuade Mr. Hilltop you had at last found the electrum; he recognized they could be the work of no one but Tuchulcha. You hurried off when you spied Mr. Hilltop at the Pelican to prevent him from following you. No one there knew who you were and so you could not be traced in that way. As for how the tablets came to be in the possession of Mr. Earhart — "

"The financier, Josiah Tusk, had the tablets," said Mr. Hunter. "His man Nightingale took them from my house. Subsequently they were stolen from Tusk — to his very considerable displeasure, as I was present when he discovered it."

Here everyone looked suspiciously at Sheephead Charley, who squirmed and quivered and rolled his tiny, nut-like eyes, but offered nothing more enlightening than a shrug of his rags.

"But this man Hunter himself is a thief. He forcibly removed the tablets from my study," argued Mr. Banister. It seemed to Harry he could feel again that ringing blow to the chin that had felled him. "This man was entered as a guest of our household and subsequently returned the courtesy by robbing me. Are these the actions of an honorable man, sir? A man whose word deserves to be believed?"

"Perhaps not an absolutely honorable man, but a desperate one," replied the professor. "What was once considered a blessing may become an intolerable burden. You evidently felt that desperate measures were called for, Mr. Hunter, and that is understandable to me. I'll believe you for now — chiefly because the activities of Mr. Hilltop here concern me more."

"And how might that be, sir?" inquired that gentleman, with swiveling eyes and the makings of an odd smile.

"Consider this, Mr. Hilltop. You too have deceived us, by concealing your identity while you availed yourself of the confidences of Mr. Banister and Professor Greenshields. You admitted as much when you disclosed your true self and your alleged motives to us. I am curious to know why you should have done that. Why were you not content to remain silent? You had by then the desired intelligence regarding Mr. Hunter — not only the name he had taken while in Salthead but his place of residence as well. Why did you not simply act on it?"

"Yes, why not, actually?" asked Dr. Dampe, smoothing his beard.

"But he did act upon it," spoke up Mr. Hunter. "He accosted me one evening at the door of my house. He refused to believe the tablets had been stolen. Of course, I did not tell him I had discovered the identity of the low fellow responsible, through information provided by Miss Honeywood there."

"Is it true what he says of you, Miss Honeywood?" asked the professor.

Miss Moll affirmed that it was so.

"My servant can attest to the events in Raven Lane," said Mr. Hunter. "I allowed Avle Matunas to search the entire building and grounds — from the coal-cellar to the garret rooms and the kitchen-garden — to satisfy himself. He found nothing, and naturally accused me of concealing the tablets elsewhere."

"It was all to prevent a great catastrophe, don't you see," smiled Mr. Hilltop, laying one hand flat upon his breast.

"Yes, that is what you told us on an earlier occasion," said the professor. "Very noble of you, Mr. Hilltop, but surely a person such as yourself should not have required our assistance? As you made clear to us, Tyrrhenian electrum is of no practical value to mortal beings. Only an immortal — either you or Mr. Hunter — could draw on its power. Why then did you seek our help?"

"To assist in the capture of Vel Saties, o' course!" was the crisp retort.

"Ah! Exactly my point. The capture of Mr. Hunter — not the tablets. I propose that you deceived us a second time, Mr. Hilltop, by relating a story which, though largely factual, nonetheless allowed you to claim Mr. Hunter's motives as your own. There was no good reason for you to have revealed any of it except to throw unwarranted suspicion on Mr. Hunter, so that my colleagues and I then would direct our efforts at collaring him in town. By that time you fully expected to have the tablets in your possession. Our real purpose, all unknown to us, was to divert and detain Mr. Hunter sufficiently for you and the electrum to vanish — so thoroughly and completely as to make it all but impossible for Mr. Hunter or anyone else to follow you."

"So there is the cause for Mr. Hilltop's failing to appear at the coffee-house — for the words of supposed explanation in his letter — all of them a monstrous humbug, to be sure!" exclaimed Mr. Banister.

"You'll recollect Mr. Hilltop's suggestion that we carry on our pursuit of Mr. Hunter independently, employing our own methods. His expectation was that he himself would shortly have the tablets in hand. Our efforts were intended to keep Mr. Hunter at bay while Mr. Hilltop effected his disappearance. What he could not have anticipated, of course, was that the tablets had been stolen from Mr. Hunter's house."

"Look here, perhaps there's something more as well," ventured Dr. Dampe. He and Mr. Banister had been edging themselves closer to Mr. Hilltop until they stood now on opposite sides of that gentleman, like two rooks at chess preparing to check the king. "A bit of boasting, a little *rodomontade*. Yes, yes, classic response, actually. Mr. Hilltop couldn't resist a little crowing over his designs, while very safely attributing them to Mr. Hunter. But it's all rather transparent once you look at it analytically, and resolved the complex patterns into their simpler elements. We physicians, we're trained to look at things analytically. It's part of the job."

"And so I conclude — analytically — that we are being deceived yet a third time today," said the professor, moving closer himself to Spotted Face. "But it won't stand. You are the one, sir — not Mr. Hunter — who must be stopped."

Silence.

"Well? What do you say to all this, Jack?" asked Miss Honeywood, folding her angular arms slowly and deliberately.

Still silence.

"He'll tell you nothing further now," Mr. Hunter predicted. "It is the way of Avle Matunas!"

"Leave off!" growled an abruptly unsociable Mr. Hilltop. Seeing the tide of opinion going out and not likely to return, he made a calculated lunge toward Mr. Hoakum in an effort to relieve him of the tablets. He did not succeed; instead the king found himself in checkmate — held fast by Harry Banister and the doctor, in much the same manner as Mr. Hunter only moments before.

"*See where he comes again!*" cried Mr. Kibble, pointing into the sky.

It was the flying man. Weary of hectoring the good people of Salthead fleeing over the chain bridge, he had chosen now to return to the much smaller party trapped beside the river. He rolled over onto one side and executed a series of tight muscular circles in the air overhead, with much laughing and a host of threatening gestures directed toward the mortal insects cowering below.

The Kingmaker bellowed — Betty roared — the children in the cabs exclaimed — the suffering parents wrung hands and shuddered. Fiona hid behind her governess, the both of them crouched beside the immense form of the Kingmaker.

"I'm so frightened, Miss Dale!" whimpered the child, clutching at Laura's arm. Her pretty face was stained with tears, like a dirty window. "Please — please, Miss Dale — keep him away — I don't wish to fall again!"

"You are safe here, dear, he won't harm you."

"Where is my Uncle Tiggs?"

"Your uncle is just over there, with Dr. Dampe and Mr. Banister and the others."

Poor Laura! What a confusion of emotions was there. She had heard little of what passed with regard to Mr. Hilltop and Mr. Hunter, for her eyes and thoughts had been chained to the saber-cat, partly out of fear, partly out of despair and self-reproach. Horrific memories of a day in Broadshire, seven years past, went running through her mind. The loss of her brother that day, the loss of her brother again this day! Absently her hand crept to her face, to her neck, and so to the frightful scars lurking beneath her hair.

"Forgive *me*, Richard?" she murmured, fervently, while the cat watched and paced.

Huddling beside her and Fiona was Bridget Leek, herself afflicted with a very private sorrow. She turned on hearing Laura's odd request but found the governess deaf to all inquiries.

Miss Honeywood, who for much of the time had seemed to be contending with herself as regards some undisclosed course of action, debating its pros and cons and the possible consequences therefrom, now came to a decision.

"Give them to me, please, Mr. Hoakum," said she, drawing herself up to her full height.

The gentleman in the checked waistcoat responded with a puzzled stare.

"Why — what do you know of Tyrrhenian electrum, Miss Honeywood?" asked Mr. Kibble, fully as mystified as Mr. Hoakum. Many were the looks of confusion and surprise directed at Miss Moll that moment.

Miss Honeywood raised angular hands to spectacles and leveled her lenses — that familiar eccentricity of hers, displayed whenever the mistress of the Pelican was uncommonly vexed or otherwise out of humor, and which was meant to convey the notion that at any instant bolts of yellow flame might come shooting from her eyeballs. Mr. Hoakum had of course seen it before and was not overly unnerved, until he looked into her face and saw that an awful yellow light was indeed glowing behind her eyes.

"Give me the tablets, Mr. Hoakum — double-quick!" commanded Miss Moll, extending a starchy palm.

The authority in her voice and figure was unassailable. Bewildered, Mr. Hoakum gave up the treasure.

It was Mr. John Hunter who was the first to understand, followed almost at once by Mr. Hilltop. They could do nothing but marvel at Miss Honeywood; neither needed to see the awful yellow light to know now who and what she was.

With the tablets of electrum held open before her, she proceeded down the embankment toward the ice and the smirking Tuchulcha, who had abandoned his antics for now and was observing her craftily from above. She could feel the rush of air in her face from his beating wings as she walked. At a point just off the ice she stopped, and raised her eyes.

"*Thui!*" she called aloud, in the starchiest of accents. "*Tuchulcha! Thui! Thui! Mi Ramtha Seianti Hanunia, lauchum Clevsins!*"

There was more than this, too, all of which no one could make out; no one, that is, but the demon himself and the immortal lucumones who stood and listened. What could be made out was the head of Tuchulcha recoiling, as a startled look dislodged the smirk from his ugly face.

Dropping her eyes to the tablets, Miss Honeywood spoke again in that same ancient unfathomable tongue, taking special care to enunciate each word as clearly and precisely as possible. What a wonder! In concert with her voice, the electrum began to glow brighter, and brighter, and brighter still. A low, throbbing hum could be heard emanating from it.

"Oh, the Miss! Whoever heard such talk from her lips? She ain't daft, I know that, and she ain't in liquor. It's wickedness, then — it's the work o' that Foul Fiend!" exclaimed Mary Clinch, on the verge of swallowing her fingers.

"What is it she says?" asked Bridget.

"She is reading from the tablets," said Mr. Banister. "She means to call the demon down upon us!"

Here Mr. Hunter put his hands into his pockets and chuckled softly to himself. He was seeing his dream of ages slip away before him, and that, together with his fateful religion, made him laugh. Now it was he who was laughing and not Tuchulcha.

"What is it, Mr. Hunter?" inquired Mr. Kibble. "Is it true? Is she reading from the inscription?"

"She is indeed," replied Mr. Hunter, with that strange sardonic gladness. "She is reciting it, sir, and very beautifully too."

"But to what purpose?"

"We shall discover soon enough. You see, she is reading it all *backwards*."

"Murder!" cried Mr. Hilltop, struggling to free himself. "She'll murder every blessed one of us, don't you see! Gentlemen and ladies — "

"Help us restrain this man!" cried Dr. Dampe, which appeal brought immediate aid to keep Spotted Face from charging upon Miss Honeywood.

"But she has no power," protested Mr. Kibble. "The words have power only when spoken by one of three immortal lucumones — that is what Mr. Hilltop told us. Unless that too was a lie?"

"No lie!" said Mr. Hunter.

Calmly, serenely almost, with a slow, steady intonation and hardly any modulation of voice, the proprietor of the Pelican — starchy mistress of her kingdom and all she surveyed, and the mightiest lucumo of all — read out the sacred words. Three times over she read them, each time in exact reverse order. At each recital the features of Tuchulcha grew darker, the beating of his wings slower, the breath in his body fainter. There was nothing he could do to prevent it; the sacred words of Aplu written on the tablets had willed it.

When she came to the last of those words Miss Honeywood folded the tablets quietly upon themselves and raised her eyes, to observe the effect of her actions.

"End of conversation," she said, motioning to all behind her to remain where they were. So everyone waited and watched, but for what no one quite knew.

They watched the serpent curl itself round the demon's arm and lay still. They watched the blue wings fold across the head and body of Tuchulcha like a shroud, leaving nothing else visible but the talons of the bird-like feet. They watched the demon stiffen like the ice over which he was suspended, but rather than turning into ice he turned into stone — returned to that volcanic tufa in which for so many years he had lain imprisoned in a chapel vault in remotest Broadshire.

Suddenly the block of stone fell; straight down it plummeted, crashed through the ice and disappeared into the frigid dark waters beneath.

"Keep away, keep away!" cried Mr. Hoakum, with a flourish of his cap. "That ice there is breaking up!"

Miss Honeywood appeared not to hear him, for she took several steps forward; and therewith occurred a most remarkable event. If I had not myself been there that day to witness it, I would not have believed it possible.

The saber-cat had left off its pacing, and now strode up to Miss Moll and offered her its gaping fangs. No sound came from its throat. The mistress of the Pelican, in another sort of unspoken communication, offered in exchange the tablets of electrum. These the animal took into its mouth, locking them firmly in place behind its gleaming sabers.

For an instant the eyes of the cat fastened on two people standing together in the crowd. Something of a mysterious intensity shone out from those eyes — something just short of recognition but beyond mere curiosity, something compounded of equal parts yearning and regret; something growing fainter and farther away now, and ever to grow more and more distant.

"Good-bye, Mr. Scribbler," whispered Fiona, her own eyes overflowing with tears. "Run as fast as you can!"

The lips of Laura trembled so, she dared not speak.

Full sad and silent stood the cat. Then it turned and bounded off across the ice, moving upriver toward the wild soaring pinnacles and the high ground at the back of the city, and was quickly lost to sight in the gathering gloom.

SO there it is, then — my story, my true story, some of which I had from the testimony of others and some from the testimony of mine own eyes. There is little left to do now but to thank you for your indulgence in remaining until this late hour, and to furnish some few biographical words as to the participants in this history.

No sooner had the demon Tuchulcha been turned to stone and plunged into his watery coffin, than the black ship in the harbor began to take on water and so it too sank from view. The mysterious disturbances that had plagued the city were truly at an end. No more was Mr. Ham Pickering observed dancing about the streets. No more was a little red-haired boy with a green face observed floating about the Blue Pelican. No more were hated teratorns observed prowling the gray skies of Salthead. No more was anything of any kind observed anywhere, and the people rejoiced.

Miss Moll Honeywood returned quietly to the Pelican and secreted herself in her quarters for two full days of careful thought. Emerging on the second night when all in the house were asleep, she left the inn, walked into the city and then walked clear out of it, never more to be seen there. Documents lodged with her attorney transferred ownership of the Pelican to Mr. George Gosling, industrious pot-boy, and Miss Mary Clinch, head chambermaid, who thereafter managed the affairs of that good house while caring for Miss Sally Sprinkle in the twilight of her days. Miss Lucy Ankers and blue-eyed Bridget Leek continued in their employ to the general satisfaction of all. Mary Clinch became engaged to Mr. Frederick Brittlebank, the facetious clerk of Timson's coach-office, who joined her and George at the Pelican as unofficial host and *raconteur*. So jovial and diverting a presence was he at the great oak bar every evening, for so very long a time, that the Pelican came to be known informally as *Brittlebank's*; and such is the name by which it is called by some to this day.

In later conversations bearing on the events related here, Professor Greenshields described in more detail the especial place accorded the female sex in Etruscan society — a precocious attitude to be sure, considering the mores of the Greeks and others of the ancient Mediterranean world — and made reference to certain authors who held that, on occasion, a powerful woman could conceivably have become a lucumo, either by succeeding her husband or through her own unmistakable merits. No contemporary account exists, however, for the literature of Etruria has not come down to us. Whatever the case as regards Miss Moll Honeywood, it is evident that the judgment of her ancient peers was impeccable. It also was evident that the words of Mr. Hunter had particularly affected her, for they could have come from her own lips; and so made her final decision, I believe, an easier one.

Mr. John Hunter quitted the melancholy, stoop-shouldered house in Raven Lane, and with his belongings and his sullen servant was observed driving south on the road to Crow's-end. Having failed in his best effort at reversing his fortunes, he abandoned all subsequent attempts and resigned himself to the fate that mighty Aplu and the shrouded gods had prescribed for Vel Saties. I understand there was a glimpse of him some years ago in faraway Nantle, where he was preparing to undertake a voyage to the southern islands. There were those who thought Mr. Hunter a fortunate man and would gladly have exchanged places with him, holding the gift of eternal life a treasure beyond price; but the value of a gift, it seems to me, always is best judged by the one who has been given it.

Mr. Jack Hilltop and a party of skilled trackers, which included Mr. Joseph Rooke, ventured several times into the mountains in pursuit of the saber-cat and the tablets of electrum. It is reported that they found neither. In the spring, however, they did find a short-faced bear newly emerged from sleep, who promptly made short work of the face of Mr. Rooke; and so ended that disdainful young gentleman's illustrious career. Eventually Mr. Hilltop gave up the chase. Of his later whereabouts nothing more could be ascertained, and so he passes from this history.

Cast-iron Billy recovered from his wound and together with Mr. Pilcher and Busket settled into new headquarters at the Flying Horse in Tower Street, where they carried on their jolly fellowship for several years more almost as they had in the past. Closer observation, however, reveals that there was always at their table a single empty chair, in which *no one* was permitted to sit; which chair being reserved for a certain dapper gentleman in pinstripes and smoked lenses, should his wandering spirit ever have a mind to join them.

Mr. Hatch Hoakum and Blaster, along with Sheephead Charley, were a success at their new venture in freightage, and established themselves in a rich grazing district just beyond the limits of the city. This they shared with above a dozen thunder-beasts — for you see, after the mastodon train had scattered on the journey to Crow's-end, the animals from habit returned one by one to the old camp, where Mr. Hoakum and his companions happened upon them.

When opposition from a particularly tall and nasty quarter in the city was raised, it was found that no sure identification of the beasts could be made; that Samson Icks, in his wisdom, had left no clue by which the individual animals might properly be identified; and so for once the thrusts of Tusk & Co. were parried.

As for Mr. Josiah Tusk himself, that conscientious philanthropist flourished mightily — as all such conscientious gentlemen are wont to do — and was little touched by the events recorded here. Though he never fully understood how the glowing tablets had come to be removed from the press, suspicion fell heavily on his servant who had fled. Soon after this the great mastiff was found hanging by the neck from a tree, and suspicion fell heavily again. To assuage his grief Josiah immediately obtained another dog — a very much larger and nastier brute than before, and so one even more like his own self.

As regards the miser's minion, Mr. Nightingale, the cup dropped from his nose the instant the demon Tuchulcha was returned to stone; unfortunately the nose came with it — a most painful injury, and an ugly one too. I recall that that slippery rascal was discovered upon the rocks several months later, beneath the soaring crags, but whether he had perished by his own hand or another's was never clear. Mrs. Nightingale and her terrible brood mourned for above half an hour at the least, before returning to more urgent concerns.

Mr. Jasper Winch persevered in his rehabilitation of the firm in Cobb's Court, to Mr. Badger's evident approval, as that gentleman never bothered to visit him more. Rehabilitation, yes — prosperity, no. Gone are the row upon row of dusty bookcases, gone the miniature lighthouses, gone the soaring volcanoes of legal writ, all delivered into the hands of the receivers. Today the junior partner in Badger and Winch lies moldering in the same dark churchyard in the same secluded corner of town as the eminent solicitor who preceded him, while the former home office is occupied by a charity school.

Dr. Dampe married Miss Mona Jacks and promptly retired into the country. To celebrate his nuptials he purchased a shiny new dog-cart with hickory shafts and semi-elliptical springs, with which to make his country rounds. But he practiced only fitfully and in the end gave up medicine to devote himself to pursuits of a wholly philosophical nature. He survived to a great age owing to his love of morning constitutionals, which he took always in the company of Mrs. Dampe. His sister-in-law, Miss Nina, married the young curate and spent her life in the accomplishment of good works; both are greatly missed by those who knew them.

Mr. Harry Banister wed a young woman from a prominent Broadshire family, and in the fullness of time was presented with a brace of delightful daughters. Miss Laura Dale, her tutoring of little Fiona complete, left Salthead to take up a situation as governess to these daughters, which responsibility she discharged with her customary ability and grace. But there remained always in the heart of Laura a gnawing sorrow that never could be eased. It came upon her most forcefully at the close of day, when she would look out from her window to the soaring mountains rising black against the sky. Then would she feel it in every beat of her pulse, in her every breath, in her every thought — the dismal ache of remorse, which no amount of happiness in her everyday existence could diminish.

Mr. Austin Kibble, disappointed in love with respect to Miss Dale — who though she liked him well enough was not disposed to marry him, and in fact never married anyone — became a wealthy man, owing to an unanticipated legacy from a distant relation. With it he set about acquiring rare books from every corner of the land, on all manner of arcane subjects that fired his interest — particularly as dealt with the mysterious inhabitants of Etruria — and so assembled one of the finest private collections in Salthead. These volumes he eventually bequeathed to the library of Salthead University.

Professor Titus Vespasianus Tiggs enjoyed a lengthy and fruitful career as professor of metaphysics in that university, and retired with the highest distinction. He spent much of his later years traveling to and from the doctor's home in the country, where he was ever welcome and where the conversation round the fire always lingered well into the night. His housekeeper, the widow Minidew, married old Tom Spike, and both of them passed the remainder of their days in the professor's service. Sadly, his young friend Mr. Rime, having failed to heed the admonition of Ham Pickering, did nothing the least remarkable with his life, and so lived and died a cat's-meat man.

Miss Fiona Littlefield grew into a beautiful young woman. Her features were perfect, her English was perfect, her French was perfect, and she bore in nearly every respect a perfect resemblance to her long-dead mother. She made the acquaintance of a young gentleman in the legal profession with whom she has been content for a lifetime. As she grew older she put aside all childish things and thought no more of them, occupying herself instead with the obligations and responsibilities of maturity. Slowly then, little by little, all remembrance of Mr. Richard Scribbler faded from her con-sciousness. In after years it was only with difficulty that she could call up a picture of his face or recollect what he was like, or what he once had meant to her. She had been so very young, and as the years retreated so did her memory of him.

The legend of a voiceless saber-cat haunting the mountain meadows above Salthead persists to this day. Every now and again a coach party crossing the mountains into Broadshire or Chestershire will report the sighting of such a creature. Witnesses commonly describe the animal standing at the edge of the road, partly in the brush, and observing the passage of the coach through mournful eyes. The jaws then open and present their gleaming sabers to view, but no sound emerges; after which the cat hurries away into the trees and is seen no more. Though the lifespan of these monsters is uncertain, it seems to me that such accounts could well be true. At the very least it is not for me to deny them, for I am an old man and recognize how little I know of anything in this world.

As for cats of a humbler variety, *viz.* Mr. Pumpkin Pie, I am happy to relate that that young gentleman was for long after a cherished member of the household in Friday Street, pursuing hordes of field mice as well as his own tail, dining lavishly upon fish and fowl, and enduring many a lazy afternoon before the kitchen fire. There was nothing the inhabitants of the house would not do to please him. Despite his forays into polite society, however, he remained every inch a cat — or as the professor was fond of phrasing it, a very independent young man who always got along exceptionally well, thank you.

THE END